MARIEL
The Beginning
A.J. Frazier

For my **first readers**—

Thank you for believing in this world before it had a cover; for when it was a hidden story in the large world of Wattpad; when it was a story with horrible formatting issues.

To **Jerome Frazier**—I'm glad we were able to connect before you passed on. It feels surreal that I named my character "Jerome" sixteen years **before** meeting you. Rest in peace, and thank you for believing in this story. I wish you could have read it.

For **Ruth**, **Demi**, and **Sal**—y'all survived Wattpad. Respect.

To **Lisa**—for being my friend and giving my book such praise. It's a high honor with your background.

To **Stephanie**— my first non-bot TikTok supporter... you're the real MVP. Thank you.

To **Amanda**—thank you for the laughs and for reviewing the manuscript to make sure I didn't embarrass myself with errors. Eh?

To the **cryptic person** in my life (you know who you are), thank you for helping me get this out into the world... even though it caused a ripple in the government lol.

To **everyone else**—thank you for lining up to support a story you didn't even know if you'd like.

And for my favorite, **my galaxy eyes**—

I'm so lucky I get my own brown-haired, galaxy-eyed girl.

I love you.

This one's for you:

"They're called breasts, Michael."

AUTHOR'S NOTE
STOP. FIRST THING'S FIRST.

I'm not going to edit this because what comes out now is raw and real, and if I edit it, I might be nicer, and I don't want to be nicer.

So.

If you are a reader who believes that em dashes (—) are signs that a book was written by AI, then I don't want you to read this book. Because I love em dashes.

And there are a lot.

If you are a reader who wants to feed my words into a machine to see if it was written by AI, then I don't want you to read this book.

And if you're a reader who does all of that, and can't handle cussing, you might want to stop reading now. Because I am about to cuss.

A lot.

Because here's the deal—I didn't fucking pour my heart, soul, and body into this series for 17 years to have it torn apart, cancelled, and judged by people who have nothing more to do with their lives than hunt people down and point fingers. I didn't suffer the nightmares and pull the darkest memories of my mind to surface and figure out a healthy way to heal... for this to be attributed to a computer system that flags the word "fuck" as a violation to their system's policy because it's not "nice" enough.

Fuck that.

So... if that's what you do, and that's what your intention is with this book, here are my words to you.

No, not fuck off.

I hope you stop. Because you're hurting authors who have finally built up the courage to put their art into the world and say, quietly, "This is mine."

But if you are a reader who is here for the hurt, the pain, the humor, and grit, and the trauma of Mariel, then I welcome you.

The story isn't pretty. It's raw, it's real. There's emotional abuse, physical abuse, self-destruction, sexual abuse, pain, violence, grief, and desperation. It's not meant to be pretty. Because life isn't always pretty. But there's also hope, love, bonding, accountability, determination, and strength, and that's gorgeous.

Because when you shine a light on the ugliness that exists in the world and within ourselves, and we make those little decisions to face our pain, forgive ourselves, do better, and grow as human beings, life can be beautiful.

And I'm proud to say - there is a lot in this book that isn't pretty... but webbed together? It's beautiful.

Welcome to the Prophecy, Prophets.

This is just the beginning.

A.J. FRAZIER

PROLOGUE

"FOR THE REVELATION AWAITS AN APPOINTED TIME; IT SPEAKS OF THE END AND WILL NOT PROVE FALSE. THOUGH IT LINGER, WAIT FOR IT; IT WILL CERTAINLY COME AND WILL NOT DELAY."
HABAKKUK 2:3

Moscow, Russia

January 1st, 1998

I n the heavy darkness of the city, a train roared down the railroad tracks.

And a young woman stood in its path.

She, a police officer, waited amidst the snow flurries in full uniform. The train was still a distance away, but the white headlight grew larger.

Blonde strands of hair waved across her face, loosened from the normally strict bun beneath her uniform's winter hat. Staring at the oncoming light with wet, hazel eyes, she let out a deep, wavering sigh. Tears trickled, and the cold wind whipped them away.

The railroad tracks rattled.

Perhaps she was a coward, but she did not know what else to do. She couldn't live with the memory anymore—the moment on July 13th, 1996, when they ripped her screaming newborn away from her.

"It's not yours!" the skinny nurse sneered as she poked and prodded the infant like it was the result of a science project and not... human.

Her human. Her baby. Her little angel.

The train screamed.

The officer let out a desperate sob.

She'd sold her soul to the devil. In Aleksey Petrov's government, it was easy to do so, and she couldn't forgive herself.

"Please!" she screamed at the nurse. "For a goddamn minute, let me touch her!"

Two years ago, she hadn't possessed the funds to cover her partner's mounting medical bills. After a census, city officials approached her with a solution: participate in *Project Savior*, and her medical debt would disappear. It sounded innocent enough—donate eggs, sperm, or surrogacy. Create new generations, and a better future for your country.

The pitch was promising. *"War will come again. Your children will be warriors; protectors and heroes of our country."*

The kids would have a purpose greater than one could imagine. With enhanced genetics to create nearly indestructible human beings, the future warriors would execute the promise of a safer Russia.

And a safer world.

Desperate to alleviate the chaotic financial needs of her household—one that was not even deemed legitimate in Russian legislation—the young woman agreed to donate her eggs for experimentation and carry a genetically enhanced child. She signed the paperwork, ignoring the terms and conditions that clawed at her heart.

"You are agreeing that the fetus belongs to the Russian government during pregnancy, and upon birth. Sign here."

The earth began to vibrate.

Was it another earthquake? The oncoming train?

Judgment?

Weeping, the woman's body shook.

"For God's sake, just let me cuddle my baby for one fucking second!" Her scream pierced the hospital room, but the nurse rubbed the baby down as if she were forced to clean a stray dog.

"You signed the papers. Project 4 does not belong to you. She belongs to the government." Roughly, the nurse pinched the baby's toes and looked at the sobbing mother. "There is no nurturing allowed. Be grateful Project 4 will receive the necessary training to accomplish what needs to be done instead of wallowing in self-pity like you."

The new mother screamed as the nurse stormed from the room with—

—*Project 4*—

—the child held far from her body.

"I'm so sorry," she wailed, and her body shivered from emotion and the cold. "I should have found a way out for you. I should have run away."

Where was the baby now? Did she smile? Was she allowed to smile, to be happy? Would Project 4 ever experience the warmth of an embrace, or the beautiful words—*I love you?*

"My little angel," she whispered shakily, her eyes fixed on the train that tore down the tracks. "I love you."

The radio crackled. Dispatch called a unit number.

"Into Your hands, oh Lord, I commend my spirit and body." The officer closed her eyes, and the tears numbed her cheeks.

"Dispatch to Unit 02-05... reports of an infant taken from a hospital by a priest. Possibly driving a black sedan. We see you're in the area."

Her eyes snapped open.

Dispatch was calling *her* unit number.

Gasping, she braced herself.

The train approached with impending fury. Its white light cutting through the swirling snow.

Then—squealing tires.

Her head jerked right. A black sedan swiveled down the icy road, readjusted, and then accelerated towards the tracks.

The train screamed, and the police officer knew she had to make a choice.

"I copy," she said, still unable to move, listening to the impending train and the oncoming car. She didn't *want* to live anymore, but—

"Caller advised they believe the sedan is en route to the Kremlin; unknown reason," the woman over the radio continued.

As the train thundered forward, and the earth shook beneath her feet, the police officer made a decision. With a cry, she flung herself away from death.

The train roared by, creating a moving wall between her body and the black sedan. Tires skidded. Metal shrieked and scraped as the vehicle crashed.

As she staggered backwards with widening eyes, she heard the muted sound of a screaming infant.

"I've got the suspect on the other side of the train with an infant. Send backup," the officer barked over the radio, and retreated from the tracks. She drew her firearm; her eyes darted back and forth.

The train continued on, and she glimpsed the sedan between the spaces of the blurry cars. Then movement—

A man emerged from the vehicle.

"Sofiya!" A male officer's footsteps pounded up behind her. "What do you see?"

Sofiya didn't speak. Instead, she tilted her head towards the passing train. No words were necessary.

A black-haired man, clad in a black suit and a white collar, stood on the other side of the railroad tracks. In his arms, he held a crying baby.

"She's not yours!" the nurse snapped, yanking away Project 4.

"Get on your knees!" Sofiya shouted, and her heartstrings tore.

The priest stared at the officers. He spoke in English, his voice hoarse, almost a growl. "He needs to get to the Kremlin."

Together, the officers advanced.

Heart racing, Sofiya holstered her weapon and snatched the swaddled infant from the priest's arms. "Handcuff him," she commanded, and she pulled the baby against her body. She began to rock him.

"Take him to the Kremlin," the priest mumbled again, compliant as he watched her with icy blue eyes.

"What's your name? Who's telling you to take this child to the Kremlin?" the officer snapped, comforting the baby, holding him close just like she'd wanted to do with her own.

The priest snaked a tongue over his lips. "My name is Father Paul," he said, "and I follow the instructions of someone far more powerful than I am."

The officer thought of Aleksey Petrov. Who else, other than God, would be more powerful than him? She clutched the baby closer and bared her teeth. "I'm glad I stopped you." Sofiya looked down at the infant resting in her arms. "Because this baby deserves a chance to be loved."

"That baby—" the priest spat, as the other officer led him towards the cruiser, "—is a catalyst for the end! He belongs at the Kremlin!" The madman's roar haunted the night as the cruiser's door slammed. His voice became muffled.

Ignoring the priest, Sofiya gazed at the infant. "Thank you for the second chance," she whispered, and walked away from the railroad towards the flashing police lights. Her boots left deep footprints in the snow; imprints that led away from a self-destructive choice... one that could have left the world with no glimpse of hope in the final years of its life.

PART 1

CHAPTER 1: VERSE 1
~START WRITING~

September 16th, 1998

Chicago, Illinois

Last night, Jerome Nadier dreamt a series of nightmares. It was not the first time, and he knew it would not be the last.

It was 8:30 A.M. The silver crucifix that hung around his neck clattered against the marble counter while he scrubbed his teeth. As the middle-aged man with greying hair struggled to forget the images, he spat the last of the foamy toothpaste into the running faucet, returned the toothbrush to the cabinet, and then rubbed his eyes.

Why did he have to dream such horrible things on this beautiful, exciting day?

"Calm my mind, Lord," he prayed, but thought of the images anyway.

In the nightmares, the sky turned red. A screen that said "*JUSTICE FOR AHDAM*" stood above a field of burning corpses. He didn't know who Ahdam was, or why he needed justice. Subsequently, he dreamt of an earthquake. The earth crumbled and fell apart. After the earthquake, humans leapt from the sky, fell like hail, and smashed against the earth.

"Save us from tribulation!" the people screamed as they plummeted.

Jerome shivered. He splashed water on his face and looked at himself in the bathroom mirror. He allowed himself a slow, quivering smile. Today was supposed to be a life-changing morning, but his skin looked pale, and his eyes were red from restless sleep.

"Please, God... don't let them think I'm high." Jerome reached for the green hand towel on the wall and wiped his face. The prayer sounded ridiculous, but he couldn't stop worrying. In less than two hours, he would meet someone very special, and he was convinced he would ruin it for himself. He was accustomed to the anxiety. It wasn't new. Even at fifty-three, Jerome accepted reality: anxiety and nightmares were burdens he was destined to carry. Yes, he'd contemplated medication, but the last time he attempted such a thing (a couple of years ago) he experienced a panic attack that left him in the hospital for hours.

By coincidence, it was how he first met Todd Caravan, a young police officer who arrived on scene prior to the ambulance. Now, even more coincidentally, Todd and his wife Mary (who was pregnant with a daughter) lived three houses down from him and planned to attend St. Michael's—an Eastern Orthodox Church approximately fifteen minutes away from the suburb.

St. Michael's was special, particularly because Jerome prepared to hold the title of "Father" in just a few weeks and assume the role of the church's lead priest.

But today, the priest-to-be would become a father in a different manner. In downtown Chicago, at the Grand Hotel, a baby boy from Russia awaited his arrival.

"You'll be a great dad, you'll be a great dad," Jerome repeated ten times. He checked the time and left the restroom. The floors creaked as he blundered about his humble two-bedroom, one-bath home. He circled the living room. Then he went up and down the hall, desperate to find his special New Balance shoes he'd purchased for the occasion as a proper "dad joke."

"*There*," he exclaimed, and grabbed the shoes from the mantle above the fireplace. He wasn't sure why he'd placed them there. Quickly, Jerome sat on the couch and began to lace up his shoes. Outside, he heard a distant siren.

And the nightmares returned with a vengeance.

"JUSTICE FOR AHDAM!" the screen said as sirens broke across the bleak atmosphere.

Jerome rubbed his forehead and stood. For a moment, he blinked, as if fluttering his eyelids would make the terrifying images go away. He was frustrated with himself. He'd always had these dreams. In fact, he used to journal about them because he loved to write.

But he hadn't written for years.

Jerome blamed it on lack of time. Considering he had worked as a University of Chicago theology professor for fifteen years, it was an easy thing to blame. However, he knew time wasn't the primary reason he struggled to pick up a journal.

"Writing journals is for nancies," his father had told him when he discovered little Jerome scribbling away in the attic.

It wasn't the last time Charles Nadier would berate him about being a "nancy" simply because Jerome loved to express his thoughts and feelings through words. Unfortunately, Charles had labeled his son's soft-spoken, empathetic, and nurturing tendencies "nancy behavior" as well. So when Jerome came out as a gay man years later, the old man was not shocked.

"Makes sense," Charles scoffed, and flicked his cigar. "There are cures for that, you know. Well-researched and all. You like research. Maybe make that your next project to study."

Jerome grabbed his wallet from the coffee table. His mouth felt dry. His head pounded. Why was the anxiety *worse* today?

"Probably because you're about to be a new dad," he convinced himself, and he slipped his hands in the pockets of his jeans to locate his keys. The metal scraped his right hand, and he pulled the keys from his pocket. "Relax," he said, looking at the keys as if they were the culprit of his anxiety. "Let's go get our son."

Jerome reversed the white Buick from his driveway and drove past the other suburban homes. He felt blessed with a comfortable, safe place to live. He directed his appreciation to God, as well as the income from his former job as a professor. Now he was excited about his new calling as a priest.

For a temporary time, Jerome had left his home to attend seminary in New York, but his journey to priesthood had not been without extensive questioning.

"Is it your desire to marry before entering the priesthood?"

Jerome, after hesitating, replied, "No."

"Any reason why?"

Jerome shifted his eyes away from the Bishops speaking to him.

"Jerome. You can talk to us."

Easier said than done. It was uncomplicated to say he simply had no desire for marriage. But to admit that his only interest in companionship was in—

"Males," he uttered the word with no prior comment, staring at his trembling hands upon his lap. "I experience same-sex attraction."

It sounded so dirty. So wrong, and he hated the fear and shame that shook his heart when he spoke the words.

"Jerome, you do wish to follow the guidelines of the Church, correct?"

Jerome nodded, recognizing that he would soon be held to a vow that eliminated all chances of a relationship.

In the weeks to follow, he'd endured more questioning, but he explained to them that he was not tempted to act upon it. He had no desire for a relationship except that with the Church. It'd always been that way for him. He didn't believe it was fair to keep other couples from attending, but that was something he hoped and prayed he could change within the church.

It took Jerome thirty minutes to reach his destination. Hoisting the black backpack over his shoulder, and gripping the empty baby carrier, he approached the hotel. His head fell backwards. The red brick building stood fifteen stories high. An American flag flapped tautly in the wind on the overhang of the entrance.

Trying to slow his racing heart, Jerome gritted his teeth as he walked towards the spinning doorway. With a forceful push, he entered the glass enclosure and then stepped into the lobby. His eyes darted around the room.

Heels clicked on the marble floor, phones rang, and voices mingled as people passed each other in the lobby. Water rushed from within an enclosed fountain in the center of the room. Nearby sat a self-playing piano. It played a soft, classical tone that otherwise might have been soothing had it been any other day for Jerome Nadier.

Clutching the baby carrier, he walked towards the fountain. He'd forgotten the name of the woman he was supposed to meet.

Angela. That was it. Now—where was she? Was he too early? She said she would wait for him by the fountain.

Scanning the area, he noticed many people mulling about the fountain. Talking. Eating.

He felt nauseous as he began to question the location; the person the agency said he would meet; the time; if he had made some kind of mistake.

Stop it. Jerome closed his eyes, took a breath, and opened them again. Immediately, he met the eyes of a heavyset woman waving him down by the fountain. She wore a grey skirt, jacket, and kitten heels. Eagerly, he returned her wave and moved forward.

It was almost time, and he wanted to do a jig.

"Mr. Nadier? I'm Angela." She extended a hand. Clipped in a bun, her brown hair contained many strands of grey, and the pearl necklace around her neck glistened in the overhead lights.

Jerome lowered the carrier and grasped her hand. "Jerome. Pleasure to meet you. I'm very excited." Puzzled, he gulped. "Where—?"

"Oh relax, Mr. Nadier," Angela laughed. "He's down the hall in a conference room. We wanted you to meet him in a quieter room." She turned halfway and looked at him again. "Are you ready?"

Was he?

No going back now.

Jerome nodded. "Very."

"Follow me, then."

Jerome nearly stumbled over his own feet as he followed her past the seating area, the elevators, the gym, and down a long, carpeted hall. The scent of the chlorinated pool filled his nostrils.

Angela glanced at him. "He was a bit of a crank about an hour ago, but hopefully he's calmed down since. Either way, don't take it personally. He's just tired." She approached a door to their right and grasped the handle.

When the door opened, Jerome felt his heart roar within his ears. It did not take long for him to lay eyes upon his new son.

The conference room had very bright lights. In the center was a long wooden table with multiple chairs. On the other side of the table, a young woman with a long ponytail sat bouncing a child of nine months on her lap. She leaned into him, bumping her forehead against his, babbling nonsense.

He giggled.

And it was beautiful.

Beaming, the woman looked at Jerome and stood up with the baby. "Look," she said softly. "Your daddy's here. Wanna meet him?"

The baby, who had a full head of black hair, giggled again and then looked at his father with wide, blue eyes.

Jerome stopped breathing.

"Hi, Buddy," he croaked. Were his feet frozen to the floor?

Hoisting Mariel on her hip, the young woman came around the table. "Mr. Nadier, I'm Anna. Come say hello to your new son."

The older man approached her. His hands shook. "Um."

"Don't be shy! He won't bite, I promise."

His slow, trembling hands reached forward. He lifted the boy from her arms and hoisted him onto his arm. "Hi, Mariel," he said softly. "I'm your dad."

Mariel grabbed Jerome's forefinger.

For several seconds, man and boy assessed each other with awe and curiosity.

"Mariel Christian Nadier... you're beautiful," Jerome said, and tears stung his eyes when he realized he must have found extraordinary favor with God. "You're so perfect."

Mariel cooed.

"Are you ready to complete the remaining paperwork and take him home?" Angela asked.

Jerome nodded, and he kissed the child's forehead. "Let's do it."

Half an hour later, the adoption finalities were complete, and Mariel was ready to go home. The two women escorted Jerome to the lobby.

"Thanks so much," Jerome said, securing Mariel within the baby carrier, straightening up, and extending his hand to Anna and Angela. "You have no idea what this day means to me."

Angela took his hand in a firm grasp. "My pleasure, Mr. Nadier. I love seeing that look on new parents' faces. Good luck." She glanced at Anna. "I'm heading to the restroom, and then we can grab dinner."

Anna nodded and smiled. "Good luck, Jerome. You will be an amazing father." Her tone turned serious. "Remember that when he is grown."

It seemed like an odd statement, but Jerome shook it off. It was still encouraging. "Thanks. I will. Have a good flight back."

Anna smiled. "As long as I don't get nauseous again, I will. Oh, and Father Jerome?" She came forward a little and slapped him playfully on the side of his arm. "Start writing, okay?" Anna whirled and walked away.

Jerome stared at her. Had she read all of his files? How did she know to call him *Father* Jerome? And secondly—

"How did you know I write?" the confused man called across the busy lobby, but Anna did not respond. She lifted a hand and disappeared into the women's restroom.

Perhaps he'd misunderstood her. After all, he *was* getting old.

When he left, the air felt thicker with humidity, and the warm wind seemed far more aggressive.

He looked up at the sky. The hot sun illuminated the city, but storm clouds approached from a distance.

"Wanna see your new home before the weather gets bad, hmm?" Jerome spoke in a hushed tone to Mariel, whose eyelids drooped.

As Jerome looked in the rearview mirror at his sleeping child, his heart burst with emotion. Love. Excitement. Peace. Nervousness. Fatherhood was a desire that had maintained top priority throughout the years.

Once he felt ready, he'd started researching. Then he enrolled in foster care and adoption classes. Jerome originally believed he would adopt a child within the States but, when the agency matched him with an infant from Russia, he knew he wanted him.

It *felt* right.

The agency had not divulged much about the boy's past, but they'd explained he'd been orphaned soon after birth.

"You are the beginning to my world, Son," Jerome murmured, looking in the rearview mirror again. "Your happiness is my happiness."

* * *

The sky had further darkened over the neighborhood when Jerome returned home.

As he drove towards the Caravan family's house, he saw Todd, a stocky, brown-haired man with a goatee, wave him down with ecstatic vigor. In his yard stood another familiar face—a skinny, young man with red hair that could only belong to one person.

Philip Jameson.

As Phil turned and raised an eyebrow, Jerome grimaced and forced a smile. He knew Todd wanted to meet his new baby, but he didn't want to stop the car and interact with Jameson.

For only being in his low twenties, the young man certainly had a lot of opinions about the world around him.

Jerome wasn't prepared to deal with Phil's itinerary of judgments for the day.

He didn't *hate* Phil—but the man who'd berated Jerome in theology class for the entire Fall semester of 1992 did not know when to end an argument. It didn't matter what you said—even if you agreed with Phil, the red-headed beanpole found fault in it.

Phil had *never* respected Jerome as a professor. And now—since Phil also attended St. Michael's—he probably wouldn't respect Jerome as the priest either.

"Hi!" Todd darted towards the car as Jerome rolled down his window. "Did you get the stinker?"

"I did. He's sleeping." Jerome rolled down the back window. The breeze picked up and rustled the nearby trees. "Isn't he great?"

Todd peered into the window. "Congratulations. Makes me excited for my kiddo." He beamed.

"Did you pick a name?"

"Esther Marie. Mary's great-great-grandmother's name was Esther. I didn't want to name her after anyone in my family because, well—heh." Todd stopped and rubbed his jaw.

"History there?"

"You can call it that," Todd chuckled. "When your alcoholic father accidentally drowns your baby brother you just—don't want anything to do with any of that, I guess."

"Oh, jeez." Jerome's eyes bulged. He hadn't expected that much of a history. "How horrible. I'm sorry. I can't imagine."

Todd shrugged a shoulder. "I was a kid." His eyes were distant, but his voice held a dismissive tone as if he wanted to move on from the conversation.

Jerome took the hint. "Speaking of your parents, how's your mom doing?" His eyes shifted to Phil, who steadily approached the car with a tight-lipped look on his face. The remaining sunlight reflected against his round glasses.

"She's great. We're headed out this evening to go see her."

Jerome looked at the sky. The tree branches waved, and birds flocked into the sky and away from the oncoming storm. "There are severe thunderstorm alerts all evening, just be careful." He looked at Phil, who now stood by the rear passenger window to scowl at the sleeping baby. "Hi, Philip. How's life?"

Philip let out a very loud sigh, as if there could only be one answer to that question—bad. When he responded, he didn't break his stare from Mariel. "Absolutely *tremendous*," he said, but Jerome didn't believe him.

In fact, Jerome was pretty sure the sigh was supposed to encourage him to ask Phil what was wrong, but the older man did not want to engage in such a game. "That's great. Well, I should—"

"—but it'd be *better* if I'd not been *rejected* from seminary." Phil finally broke his unwavering stare towards the baby and turned cold hazel eyes to Jerome.

Jerome stared back. His face grew warm. "Phil. You know that wasn't my fault."

"You could have written the recommendation letter."

"Philip." Jerome's hands tightened around the steering wheel. "You told me you thought my ideologies belonged to that of a sinful liberal. All I'd said was that motherhood was not a calling for *every woman*."

Phil looked up at the sky and spoke through his teeth. "It's fine. It's between you and the Lord if you'd rather hold a grudge. Finishing law school is my higher calling, anyway."

He stared at the clouds, as if he expected the Lord to agree with him that very instant. "Goodness. It looks like the heavens are about to release a torrent of sinners from the sky."

"Save us from tribulation!" the people screamed.

Jerome shuddered.

Todd cleared his throat. "Did you tell Jerome the news?"

Phil shrugged. "What news? *Oh.*" He looked at the baby again. "Carolyn and I are expecting our first child."

Jerome smiled. Despite his distaste for his future congregation member, he still felt happy for him. "That's phenomenal, Phil. Tell Carolyn congratulations."

Or maybe he felt happy for *Carolyn.* There was something about Phil raising children... something that scared him. He wasn't sure what it was, but—

"I shall. You know—" Phil scanned his eyes from the baby to Jerome. "Mothers are a gift from God. Good ones, that is." His facial expression changed, as if he were counting in his head and discovered there were only a select few that were good.

Jerome gritted his teeth and closed his eyes.

"I don't believe in single-parent adoption," Phil might as well have said.

Sighing, Jerome opened his eyes and tapped the steering wheel. "Well. I need to get my son settled. Have a safe trip, Todd. I'll see you two at church this weekend."

The two men stepped back from the car.

While trying to calm his racing heart, Jerome drove onwards as the impending storm blotted the sun and cast a dark shadow over the neighborhood.

*   *   *

Thunder crashed, lightning illuminated the living room, and Jerome paced back and forth with the screaming baby in his arms. "Please," he whispered. "Tell me how to help you."

He wanted to cry too.

It was 1 A.M.

Mariel hadn't stopped crying for two hours. Jerome's heart broke with each scream, but on sudden thought he realized what might be the issue.

"You haven't pooped, buddy." Jerome chastised himself, primarily because Mariel's medical history suggested constipation, and he hadn't prepared for an event like this.

Running his fingers along Mariel's bloated belly, Jerome gave the baby a decisive nod and started searching for his keys. The store would need to deal with a tired father in pajama pants.

"Let's get you something to feel better, my love," Jerome cooed, hastening to find his flip-flops now that he'd located his keys.

The streetlights blurred amidst the pouring rain. The windshield wipers, squeaking with quick intensity against the glass, barely assisted Jerome in clearing enough rain to see properly. Still, despite the chaotic storm outside, Jerome managed to get to the store without issue.

Humming a tune he remembered from seminary, Jerome prepped his umbrella as the rain poured. His flip-flops squelched as he leaned into the car to grab his crying son.

"We'll get you something, hang in there," Jerome soothed, and he started towards the store named *Marty's*. It was *"Arty's"* though, because the *"M"* flickered on and off.

He was exhausted. He wanted sleep, but this was parenting.

He'd wanted this.

Marty's was a large store with many standard departments such as groceries, home, and kitchen. Soft music from the eighties played as a few employees wandered about with disinterest. They stocked shelves. A young clerk with a frizzy ponytail whispered to her *Tamagotchi* keychain pet.

After walking in the wrong direction, Jerome muttered to himself and then turned to walk the opposite way. He passed the entrance doors, apologizing to Mariel who, naturally, now cried with far less intensity.

The entrance doors opened.

Jerome caught sight of a white man. He entered the store in a grey hoodie and grimy jeans. Lightning lit up the rainy parking lot. The drenched man stopped and scanned the store in dazed confusion. His body reeked of cigarettes. Beneath the hood, the man's bloodshot eyes caught those of Jerome. Something stained his stubbled neck. Red paint? Blood?

With a quick nod, Jerome looked away and hurried towards the children's medication aisle. As he scanned the shelves, he couldn't help but wonder if he would get the wrong medication. What if he did? What if he read the label wrong? What if he gave his new baby the *wrong* dosage and—

"You look stressed."

Jerome looked up, his eyebrows raised.

Mariel blubbered and shrieked.

A light-haired woman scanned the shelves, reached for a package, and handed it to him. "For gas pain in infants. Is that what you're looking for?"

Smiling, Jerome nodded. "Thank you so much. I think at this rate I trust you more than myself."

The woman smiled and tilted her head towards Mariel. "Parenting is rough. Make sure you take care of yourself too." She walked past him, went towards the registers. "And start writing, please."

Jerome blinked. Was he losing his mind? What was going on? Why was she the second person to tell him to *start writing?*

"God?" He looked up at the ceiling, as if God might be perched in the rafters. Instead, thunder rumbled outside and vibrated the metal. "Huh. Let's check out and go home, baby boy."

Once he purchased the medication, Jerome hustled against the wind and rain to return to his sedan. The wind howled and nearly tugged the umbrella from his grip while he struggled to unlock the driver's side door and keep the baby carrier beneath the shelter. He didn't feel a click when he turned the key and realized he'd left the doors unlocked.

"I'm not thinking normally," Jerome grumbled as he flung open the back passenger door. After closing the umbrella and adjusting Mariel in the car, he dashed for the driver's seat, entered the car, and shut the door.

But the car had a strong stench... like cigarettes.

Jerome didn't smoke.

Had he entered the wrong vehicle? It was his first thought until he realized that everything in the vehicle belonged to him. The crucifix dangling from the rearview mirror. The baby carrier.

Jerome *wished* he'd entered the wrong vehicle, because the alternative was far worse.

There was a shadow in the passenger seat.

But it *wasn't* a shadow. It was a hooded man.

Mariel started crying, and the man raised a gun towards Jerome's head.

"Give me the keys," he said, his voice hoarse and deep. "And get out of the car."

Jerome's hands shook. The lightning forked across the sky, brightening the interior of the car, and watery shadows from the rain-spattered windshield slithered across the dashboard. Thunder crashed.

"Please," Jerome gasped. "Let me grab my son."

A low snarl rumbled from the hooded man's chest. "I *said*," he drawled, quieter than Jerome expected, "give me *the keys*, and *get out* of the car."

Many thoughts dashed through Jerome's mind. In fact, it was the fastest his mind had ever worked, and he struggled to keep up. Some of the thoughts didn't even pertain to his current situation, and that frustrated him because he needed to get to his son.

Mariel shrieked. Thunder vibrated the car.

"I am going to get my son, and then I will give you the keys." Jerome stared straight ahead at the windshield. The outline of his body looked distorted in the rain. Like a monster. But he wasn't the monster.

"I will fucking shoot you if you don't give me the goddamn keys and *get out the fucking car!*" the man roared, and slipped his finger to the trigger. His voice shook, like he wanted to cry.

Tears stung Jerome's eyes. His heart smashed against his chest. He opened his mouth to speak, but nothing came out.

He needed to make a decision.

If he gave the keys to this man, he might never see Mariel again. Or perhaps the man would grant him mercy and allow him to take the baby. After all, if he was getting carjacked, why would the criminal want to take a screaming child with him?

But could this man think logically? If he was deranged, Jerome's decisions might quickly become a game of Russian roulette, and the new father wasn't sure he wanted to take that risk. So as Mariel Nadier screamed in the car, Jerome took action, and he begged God that it was the right move.

It was the fastest he'd ever moved.

Jerome grabbed the nose of the gun and pushed. As he slammed the man's wrist against the radio, he punched, and his fist cracked against the criminal's jaw.

The man grunted. Wrestled back.

Jerome wasn't strong; he never had been. Athleticism was not his strength. As the storm raged outside the car, he felt weak, but something about the innocent life in the back seat created a surge of power he never realized he had.

The vehicle shook.

The man punched him.

His teeth rattled. Time blurred. His ears rang. He thought of Mariel, listened to his shrieks. For his son Jerome fought harder, but he couldn't keep track of the violence. He bit, punched, wrestled, pushed. Blood filled his mouth; the scent of iron, old cigarettes, and stale sweat filled his nostrils.

Jerome never believed he would have to kill someone. After all, *nancies* didn't have a violent bone in their bodies. *Nancies* wrote journals and talked about their feelings.

Until they became parents. This *nancy* was a dad now, and he'd do anything to protect his child.

Wind howled.

"I'm going to kill you." The man's yellow teeth bared in Jerome's face. He wasn't even out of breath. Was he smiling? Or crying?

Jerome gripped the man's wrist. The gun tilted towards his head.

The man's finger crawled towards the trigger guard.

Gasping, Jerome grasped the nose with both hands and pushed towards the windshield.

The gun went off. With a flash of light similar to the lightning, the bullet pierced the windshield. *Maybe* someone would come to help. Maybe that gunshot would save his life and Mariel's, but Jerome steadily weakened.

The man struck him in the kidney.

Tears blurred his eyes, and his fingers loosened. A finger jabbed his eye. Limbs twisted; he wasn't sure whose, but he could feel the momentum shift. The arm that held the gun tilted the opposite direction.

Towards Mariel.

"You realize people like you can't ever have kids when you're—that way, right?" That woman with the pink, pointy glasses from his college years had said.

Please, God! Jerome wasn't certain if he spoke the words or thought them. As he attempted to fight through the pain, he shifted upwards. Frantic, he tried to push the pistol's aim away from his baby.

Too late.

The man fired.

Jerome screamed.

White light flashed again, and time slowed.

Was it the cruelty of the harsh world that brought him here? Or something else? Jerome didn't know.

How was it that he saw the bullet move through the air, tormenting him as it approached his son without mercy? What sin had he committed that subjected him to this judgment... watching his brand new son die in violent, slow motion?

Mariel's crying ceased.

But Jerome's face went from horror to shock. The baby's small arm came up. He closed his fist around the oncoming bullet.

The child's eyes—wide, blue, and round—appeared to be in awe of his own miracle.

Mariel cooed a little. Dropped the bullet. It thumped against the seat.

For a brief moment, the two men forgot they were enemies. They were human beings—souls attempting to process the *impossible*.

Humans could not catch bullets.

No one could.

In shock, both men stared.

The gunman muttered something... something about blood. He shoved the nose of the gun into his mouth and pulled the trigger for the third time that night.

Blood and flesh sprayed across the passenger window.

Jerome and Mariel Nadier were alone once more.

As thunder crashed and rain poured, Jerome sobbed. He reached for his son. He unbuckled him, grabbed the child, and stumbled out of the car and into the rain.

The wind screamed. A tornado siren wailed across the town as he fumbled for his phone to call 911. The call taker answered the line, and the future priest fled through the weather. He stumbled towards the store in desperate hopes to get away from the dead man in his car—

And the inexplicable event he'd just witnessed.

Humans could not catch bullets.

But Mariel Christian Nadier... did.

VERSE 2

~ YOU, HANDSOME, YOU ~

September 16th, 1998
Chicago, Illinois

T odd Caravan struck the knob to the radio.

As the rain pounded the windshield, he wet his lips and glanced over at his wife. Mary's seat reclined backwards. Tousled brown hair fell over her shoulders as she slept. She rested her right palm over her belly. It was a subconscious action now—she'd started doing that as soon as her pregnancy with Esther was confirmed.

It was cute. *She* was cute. Hell, even with her small frame, at five months pregnant she didn't show that much. It'd been a miracle they'd found out she was pregnant at all. The plethora of health issues she'd had (uterine cysts; a cancer scare) had led them to the doctor. After requesting a pregnancy test, the result shocked them both.

"You're four months pregnant," the doctor had told them.

And their lives had changed.

Todd squinted through the rain. He needed new windshield wipers. It was dark, and he could barely see the road. Despite this, he felt confident. He hadn't been the best driver in the police academy for nothing.

His flip-phone vibrated against his thigh. Mouth dry, his heart rate increased a little. Shame tingled like prickly heat, stinging his neck and face with hot electricity as he fought the urge to pick up the phone. His fingers twitched.

He knew who it was.

Todd looked at his sleeping wife, and then reached into his pocket to grab his phone. Clearing his throat a little, he lit up the phone to look at the contact number. Indeed, it was a message from her... that cute brunette who worked the midnight shift with him. Her name was Ginny, and she liked talking to Todd.

A lot.

He felt special. He'd never been "the most attractive" guy on the block, so when women noticed him, it was hard not to feel validated.

Things were *fine* with Mary... and he told himself the playful banter with Ginny was innocent enough. Mary didn't banter with him anymore. He didn't blame her. With the recent life stressors and health issues, it wasn't her fault. But he missed that aspect of their relationship.

Thunder crashed. Ahead of him, red brake lights lit up, and traffic slowed again.

Todd looked at Mary again, and then he flipped open his phone.

"What are you up to today?" Ginny asked.

Flicking his eyes back and forth from the road to his phone, Todd typed with his thumb. *"Boring stuff. Headed to see my mom. You?"*

Lightning flickered. The rain increased. Todd kept the phone in his hand, and he drove with his left arm.

"Oh... just on break... missing my work husband ;)."

Mary shifted in her sleep.

He watched her. Guilt warmed his stomach as he responded. *"And who's that?"*

Red and white lights flashed as an ambulance passed on the southbound interstate. Wetting his lips again, Todd watched the lights fade in his rearview mirror, and then he returned his gaze to his phone. He shouldn't be texting in this weather. What was wrong with him?

Was that a tornado siren?

"You, handsome. You. :)"

His heart raced. The tornado siren didn't help, and he was stepping into dangerous territory. He shouldn't respond. Should he? Maybe he was overthinking this.

Without warning, a car stopped ahead of Todd.

Gasping, he slammed on the brakes and grabbed the wheel with both hands. His phone clattered across the center console and thumped to the floor near Mary's feet.

The car skidded to a stop just inches away from the sedan. Relieved, he sighed and turned to look at Mary again. Damn, she could sleep... which was good, because his phone fell at her feet with that text message available for her to see if she picked it up.

He needed to grab it and take the situation as a warning sign.

Pressing the brake, Todd bit his lip and leaned down. He could hear his breath hissing from his teeth as he strained. Rain spattered the car, and the windshield wipers squeaked. The tornado siren seemed louder.

His fingertips brushed the phone.

It slid.

Cursing in his thoughts, Todd leaned further down. His foot slipped against the pedal.

A deep horn screamed behind him.

Startled, he shot up and grasped the wheel. Traffic had moved on; he hadn't.

As Todd drove forward, Mary adjusted in her seat. Her eyes fluttered open, and she groaned a little. "How much further?" she whispered.

Todd's eyes darted towards the open phone on the floor by her feet. "A little while longer, Sweetie, go back to sleep."

"You, handsome, you." Ginny's text message mocked him with the knowledge that it was right there... within Mary's grasp if she wanted it. And she was not unfamiliar with looking at his phone for mundane reasons.

Was *this* how his dad felt before his wife found out about the other woman?

No. Ginny wasn't an "other woman," and Todd was *nothing* like his drunken, Armageddon-obsessed, conspiracy-theorist of a father. He was overreacting, but *Mary* wouldn't agree if she saw the message.

"Is there a tornado?" Mary asked, and she shifted her legs. Her toes brushed the phone.

Todd's blood pressure spiked. "I don't know, Baby. Maybe." He pressed on the gas.

Traffic moved at 50 M.P.H now. Trees rocked, and lightning zigzagged across the black sky.

Mary groaned. "What time is it?"

"It's almost 2 A.M."

"We should have stopped at a hotel, the weather is terrible. How can you see?"

"Mary." Todd held up a hand. "Please just let me focus, okay?"

"I'm *sorry*." Mary sighed, and she moved her feet again. "Is that your phone by my feet?"

He couldn't breathe. Had the windshield wipers increased their speed, or was it his imagination? "Yeah, it dropped earlier."

"We should probably call your mom and let her know where we are." Mary brushed her hair back and leaned forward.

"You, handsome, you."

The truck swerved a little. Todd wasn't sure if the wind caused it or his nerves. He clenched his teeth. "Just—don't worry about it, I don't want you to hurt yourself."

Mary laughed a little. It was an attractive laugh, one he would miss if she found that message and blamed him, just like he'd blamed Will that night for tripping him when Todd had stumbled over his own feet.

"You're silly. You act like me bending down is going to hurt our baby. Relax." She reached for the phone.

That thunder... it roared now, like God's voice within his eardrums. Mary's fingertips grasped the phone, and his pulse rose. "Mary—"

She sat up and screamed.

It made him look up.

Brake lights pierced the interior of the truck, and the vehicle hurtled towards a stopped van.

Todd whipped the wheel to the right. Thunder crashed, headlights flashed, and the bed of his truck fishtailed in the rain. Like a pendulum, the vehicle swiveled back and forth.

"*Todd!*"

"*I've got this!*" Todd roared, but he did not believe himself. The truck had too much sway, and his blood pressure was far too high.

The storm raged. The sky lit up. For a brief moment, he saw the reflection of his own terrified expression in the wet windshield.

Grinding his teeth, Todd over-corrected the wheel. The car skidded, spun, and came to a horizontal stop on the interstate.

Oncoming white headlights illuminated Mary's tear-stained face. She looked at her husband with desperate eyes. A horn roared, tires squealed, and her hands went to protect her belly.

Todd screamed. "*Ma—!*"

Glass shattered. Vision blackened. Chemicals seared his face. His body flopped, snapped, jolted. Was the truck rolling?

Mary. *She'd been struck first.*

His thoughts suffocated, much like his face within the airbag. Things, both in car and body, smashed, cracked, shattered, and ripped. Something spattered on his face.

Mary's blood?

No.

It was water.

"Mary..." he mumbled, and he realized his head was upside down. The entire truck had flipped. Outside, the storm carried on, and raindrops struck his face.

"Baby," he muttered, and tasted blood in his mouth. "Hang on."

With labored breaths, Todd attempted to find the seatbelt.

Footsteps pounded towards the car.

"Help!" Todd cried, and his throat stung. "My wife is pregnant. *Get her out!*"

Horns blared, and boots shuffled on the roadway. People shouted, asked questions, tugged at the doors.

"She's pregnant," he wailed, and tears slipped from his eyes. He couldn't lose his wife and his little girl—his squirt.

Ginny didn't matter. That phone didn't matter.

His wife did. His unborn daughter, Esther Marie Caravan, mattered. But as emergency sirens broke through the chaotic storm on the interstate, Todd Caravan realized something dire.

Mary hadn't made a sound.

Red, blue, and white lights flashed through the storm. Time was strange. On one hand, during the crash, Todd felt as though he'd been watching chaos in slow motion. Now, like a blender, time accelerated and put his processing abilities in such a state of turmoil he couldn't keep up.

He wasn't sure if he was hurt. He could only think of Mary. After a firefighter freed him from the vehicle, while he stumbled backwards towards the voice of a beckoning police officer, he could only see the pleading look on Mary's face as the white lights exploded and struck with violence he'd never forget.

It was his fault.

Karma.

And if she was dead, he would never—

"She's conscious and breathing. Not alert." A man's voice, a paramedic, cut through the commotion.

The rain soaked Todd as the police officer questioned him, asked him about injuries, and shined his flashlight on the glass-torn skin on Todd's body. The officer looked at Todd's eyes too... protocol, to see if he'd been drinking.

"*Sir.* Life EMS is trying to confirm the hospital with you. I see you're from Illinois, do you know where you are right now?"

Dazed, Todd nodded. "We're near Traverse City, I think. I don't care. Nearest hospital. Can I ride with her?"

"How many months pregnant again?" A paramedic whipped her head towards Todd as she pushed the stretcher towards the ambulance.

Tears and rain wet Todd's cheeks. "Five months."

"Okay, we've got another ambulance coming. Ride with them to the hospital, and they'll assess your injuries too. We gotta go."

The wind rocked Todd back onto his toes as first responder lights swarmed the stormy area. The tornado siren had stopped, but the other incoming sirens were eerie and loud as Todd processed the entire scene around him.

Upside-down truck. A sedan in the ditch. That tanker at the side of the road with its hazards on.

"You, handsome, you."

"Let's get you on your way to your wife," the officer said, and gestured towards another ambulance. "I'll have another officer meet you there for a full statement."

*   *   *

"Todd."

His eyes opened. Pain throbbed. His neck and head were stiff from whiplash. Cuts burned, and his heart hurt. That familiar voice though... Patricia. His mom. Thank *God*.

"Mom?" Todd struggled to sit upright in the surgical waiting room chair.

His mother stood before him, short in stature with thick, greying dark hair. She wore a black raincoat tightened with a sash. Tears welled in her eyes, and she reached for him.

Todd went to her and cried. Crying was one thing he'd never felt shame about. Had his mother not divorced Jacob Caravan, however, his father's upbringing might have swayed his ability to express the emotions Patricia had always encouraged him to embrace.

Todd wanted to tell her about the text; he wanted her to tell him this wasn't his fault, and that he *wasn't* like his dad.

The last person he wanted to resemble was his father, Jacob Caravan. Jacob cheated on Todd's mother, resulting in his half-brother, Will Caravan—a little boy who had deserved so much more than death at the age of three.

"*Karma*," Jacob Caravan had always said.

He blamed Will's death on karma. But even at age five, Todd recognized that Jacob had never treated Will fairly. Todd knew he was the favorite, and he always wondered if he'd not blamed his little brother for tripping him if—

"What's the news, Sweetie?" Patricia sat down next to him.

Todd wiped his eyes. "She went in about ninety minutes ago. They're trying to stop the internal bleeding and monitor Esther." He rubbed his head. "They said if the baby is in distress, they'd have to do a C-section."

"Oh, Honey."

"Mom, I'm scared." Todd's face went into his hands. His body hurt, and he wanted to vomit.

This was his fucking fault.

"Honey, listen. The medical field is astounding... okay? They know what they're doing. Mary and your baby will be fine." Patricia rubbed his shoulders.

"You don't *know* that."

Patricia hugged him. "I've been around doom and gloom my entire life, Sweetie. I've got a pretty good sense of intuition. Pray. Trust God."

His mother was right about one thing. She'd always been a strong soul, even throughout his parents' divorce and the mental abuse Jacob put her through. Patricia never allowed him to see or hear the fights between them.

But he didn't want to think about God. In fact, God probably hated him right now, and Todd couldn't find blame in that.

After several more minutes of conversation, the surgeon came to tell them that the surgery was going well, but that a cesarean would need to take place due to the fetus being in distress. Todd asked countless questions, desperate to know that both Mary and his child would be okay.

"We're doing the best we can," the surgeon said, attempting a smile on his solemn face. "I don't see any reason that your baby won't survive this. I'll be back with updates as soon as I have them."

Todd dozed again. In his dreams, he heard squealing tires, screams, and sirens.

Patricia awakened him when she left her seat to go to the restroom.

With heavy eyelids, he sat up and looked at the time. It was almost 6 A.M. Had he missed updates?

"Mr. Caravan. Can we talk?"

Todd straightened in his chair. His eyes met those of the dark-haired surgeon who stood in the waiting room. With a racing heart, Todd rose from his chair and approached him. "Please tell me good news."

The surgeon's face didn't change from its solemn state, and Todd wondered if the man's expression ever changed. "It's good news. Your wife's in recovery... so is your daughter. She's in neonatal care right now, but she's stable."

God didn't hate him. "Thank *God. Fuck.* I'm sorry." Todd didn't want to lose complete calm in front of the expressionless surgeon.

"It's ok. Would you like to see her and then your wife?"

Todd nodded. He glanced back towards the restroom, where he saw Patricia emerging. "Can my mom come?"

"We'd rather immediate family for now. There's some paperwork and consent to treatment forms we need you to sign too."

Patricia gestured for him to leave. "I heard. Go see your family, Honey. I'll be here."

Past the double doors, a young nurse, a stout woman with large blue eyes, instructed Todd to wash his hands. The smell of antiseptic lingered in the air as Todd stepped out of the private bathroom and took the cap and gown offered to him. He opted to wear a mask too. There was nothing he wouldn't do right now to ensure his daughter's health and safety.

Those feelings intensified when he laid eyes on her for the first time.

In the dimly lit room, Esther Marie Caravan lay in the incubator on her back, her legs curled and her tiny hands fisted. Todd saw tubes and pads all over her tiny body. It wasn't how he'd imagined seeing his child for the first time, but gratitude overwhelmed him.

He wouldn't fuck up again.

Jacob Caravan had killed Todd's brother out of drunken negligence.

Todd had almost killed his daughter over a flirtatious text message he'd wanted to hide from Mary.

"Hi, Squirt," Todd murmured, and he smiled through the mask. "I'm your daddy, and I love you so much. Just wait until you meet Mommy and Grandma. They love you very much too."

The machines beeped. Esther's little belly quickly moved in and out.

"Are you able to sign some consent to treatment paperwork for us, Mr. Caravan?" the nurse called.

"Yes. Whatever you need." Todd looked at Esther again. He wanted to hold her close to his heart. "I'll see you soon, Squirt."

In the hallway, as Todd attempted to scan the paperwork, the lines blurred. He was exhausted. The adrenaline crash left him feeling dizzy and sick. Once he reached the last page, his signature wasn't even on the line... but he did notice something interesting he'd never seen on medical documentation before.

"I acknowledge that my child's genetic information may be analyzed and used for research by the Kaseem-Sovonov Institution for Medical Advancement and its affiliate: Project Savior. This analysis is intended to advance medical knowledge, care, and potentially provide enhanced patient care."

"Hey, what's this?" Todd waved down the nurse and pointed to the paragraph. "I'm tired so I don't understand half of what I'm reading."

The nurse scanned it. *"Oh.* People question that one a lot. The best example I have is this—sometimes after surgeries where breast tissue, for instance, is removed, they ask the patient if they consent to having their tissue studied for medical knowledge and advancements. This is similar, only it's been making waves because advancements have been actually happening."

Intriguing. "Like what?"

"Well, there was someone who gave birth to a baby with a rare genetic disease that would have killed it eventually, but the infant wasn't showing symptoms. With the DNA analysis, they were able to diagnose the disease early and use the kid's own DNA to provide treatment."

"Really?" Todd looked at the paper. "Would it hurt her? My daughter?"

"Nope. Just a quick blood sample with the other standard blood work."

He pondered, and he envisioned his tiny Esther in the incubator. "Any potential benefit to a preemie like her? I just don't want to sign something weird that could potentially hurt her, you know."

The nurse smiled. "Totally get it. And it's up to you. But yes, there's a possibility that this could be a benefit to her in the long run. Worst case scenario? Nothing comes from it. Except maybe some research that turns out to be useless. *And...* you can withdraw consent at any time too."

"Oh." Todd stumbled again, desperate for sleep. "Okay. I just want her to have the best chance she can get." He looked at the signature he'd scribbled already, far above its intended line. "I'm good with it. I'm suing you if something happens though." He handed the papers to the nurse and smiled.

She laughed. "Well, I don't have much. You'll get my cat, that's about it."

"Ha."

"Now. Are you ready to see your wife?"

Reassurance, hope, and a small sense of dread that she would be angry with him sprouted in his chest. "Yes," he said. "I need to tell her how incredible our little girl is."

VERSE 3

~ JOURNAL ~

September 20th, 1998

Chicago, Illinois

It was Sunday morning at 7 A.M, and Jerome still hadn't figured out if he was a madman.

The clock ticked above the mantle in the living room. Its rhythmic sound broke the silence.

He stared across the table. His son sat in a high chair, and his fingers glistened from saliva as he stuffed Cheerios in his mouth.

Jerome looked at his own bowl of Cheerios. He took one between his fingers, and then he raised his eyes to Mariel again.

Don't do it, he thought, rolling the cereal in between his thumb and forefinger. But he was curious... because he wanted to see if it was just bullets Mariel caught, or other things too.

How else was he to deal with this? He didn't know how to navigate life as a *father* yet. How on earth was he expected to un-layer the supernatural event that took place the other night? Not to mention the added bonus of processing a near death experience, investigator questioning, etc.

He sighed. His ordainment, fast approaching, seemed far more intimidating now. The idea of leading and guiding a flock of people who'd be oblivious to his... *insanity* scared him.

Mariel stuffed another Cheerio in his mouth. The child appeared oblivious to everything. Was he? Could children that age comprehend the strange and the unusual? Did they even *notice?*

Or perhaps Jerome was a madman. It was more probable than a baby catching a bullet.

Jerome rubbed his forehead. Maybe his former seminary mentor might listen to the absurdity and give him some guidance. He hadn't contacted the priest in a while, anyway.

Gnawing his lip, Jerome lifted the Cheerio. *This is silly.*

Mariel babbled.

Closing one eye, Jerome chucked the cereal. It plopped against the baby's forehead. Mariel tilted his head and giggled.

Jerome chuckled and picked up another Cheerio. Mariel's innocent laugh warmed his heart. Grinning, he threw it. It bopped Mariel on the nose, and the baby laughed again.

"Think this is funny, huh?" Jerome laughed, and he threw another one.

For several moments, he giggled with his son. The sounds of laughter, from man and boy, cut the morning silence. Briefly, Jerome forgot the *strange* and the *unusual*. Instead, he lived in a moment he'd remember forever—the first time he heard his child laugh; the first of many laughs together.

He didn't want to think about his bad dreams. He didn't want to think about the blood-stained car window, the dead man, the police lights, and the victim statements.

But Jerome knew he could not ignore it forever. He needed to process it. It was what he would tell *anyone* else.

Just like his mentor had always told him.

Jerome stood and reached for the landline. It'd be an expensive call, but he dialed anyway. He had to. He *needed* to talk to someone, and he hardly trusted anyone enough to share this information... not with the level of social anxiety he carried.

It rang three times, but Jerome was not expecting a woman's voice.

"This is Ruby."

He didn't know who Ruby was, but she sounded tired.

Jerome stammered. "Um, sorry. I might have called the wrong number. I'm looking to speak with Father Paul Rinaldi."

The woman sighed, a loud, breathy sigh that dripped with annoyance and exasperation. "I'm his sister. Seems like everyone is trying to contact him these days. Who are you?"

"My name's Jerome. He was my mentor in the seminary. Is he okay?"

Ruby muttered something and then spoke louder. "To be frank, no, and I'll talk to *you* because I've heard about you and that you're good people. He's had deteriorating mental health for the last couple years. He pleaded insanity for abduction and now he's in mandatory psych treatment."

Mariel swept the cereal from his high chair tray.

Jerome stared at the refrigerator in the kitchen, eyes wide, mouth agape. "What? *Abduction?*"

That didn't sound at all like his mentor. Fr. Paul had been beloved amongst many. Cheerful. Wise. *Stable.*

What happened?

"I don't know everything. He was caught trying to kidnap an infant... kept going on and on about how this '*Mariel*' baby was a 'catalyst for the end times' and 'needed to get to the Kremlin'. But they dropped the criminal charges and..."

Her voice faded, distant to Jerome as he turned frightened eyes to his baby in the high chair. His hand shook, and his ear was sweaty against the phone.

Mariel. *He'd* chosen that name. *He'd* gone through the paperwork process to do *all of that.*

Jerome did not often curse. Still, he couldn't help but wonder—what the *hell* was going on?

"Jerome? You there?"

"Yes. I'm here. I'm just... astounded."

"I bet. So was I."

Jerome thought about the bullet... when Mariel had captured it with his hand. He thought about Fr. Paul's statement—

"The catalyst for the end times."

As his body went cold, he closed his eyes. "Did he say anything else?"

"Nope. I can get you the psych hospital information if you'd like to contact them. I'm sure he'd love to hear from you." Ruby yawned, as if she'd had this conversation many times before.

Jerome opened his eyes. "I'd like that. Thank you." Perhaps he could find some answers. As he scrambled for pen and paper, he was certain his heart would burst from his chest.

Ruby told him the contact information and then advised him he could call her at any time. She told him she would be in Russia for a little longer to help sell her brother's house.

After Jerome hung up, he turned to look at his son. "What's going on, little one?" he murmured. His legs wobbled, and he sat down hard.

Birds tweeted outside. Somewhere in the neighborhood, an engine started.

"We'll need to get ready for church, baby boy," Jerome said in a quiet, shaky tone. "I could use God's wisdom and calm."

The future priest readied Mariel and prepared for church. As he buttoned his shirt, Jerome looked in the tall mirror on his bedroom door. Bags hung beneath his eyes. His skin was so pale he looked sickly.

Jerome knew he couldn't delay his mind's natural need to process. He'd called Fr. Paul (or rather, his sister) in hopes to talk it out with a mentor he'd respected so much. Right now, he couldn't, and a therapist might send Jerome to a psychiatric hospital too.

He might not uncover all of the answers. But he needed to ensure the stability of his mind—not only for his son, but for the congregation he would lead very soon.

There was only one option right now... something he'd always done to settle his fears, calm his mind, and sort his feelings.

"Start writing," that woman had said at the hotel, and so had the other woman at the pharmacy.

Jerome set his teeth. He walked towards the cherry-colored nightstand by his bed and opened the drawer. Inside, he located his leather-bound journal. One that hadn't been touched for years. It was empty because he'd purchased it *just in case* he wanted to pick up writing again.

Now was the time.

"You're a nancy," Charles Nadier had always said with a chuckle that held no humor.

"Oh well, Dad," Jerome said to the air, as if Charles was there. He reached for his journal. "To be human is to feel, and it's okay to feel. That's what I intend to teach your grandson." He shut the drawer.

And long after church ended, the sun faded. Mariel went to bed, and Jerome Nadier took his favorite pen, sat in front of his fireplace, opened his journal, and began to write.

* * *

09/20/1998

Dear Diary, it's been awhile, so please excuse my awkwardness. A lot has changed. I'll be ordained as a priest next week and, furthermore, I adopted a son from Russia.

Hopefully no one reads these. If they do, you're in for a ride. A few strange things happened to me that cannot easily be explained. One, I was attacked and almost shot. Two, the gun went off towards Mariel, but the child caught the bullet. Three, I attempted to contact my mentor, Fr. Paul, to discuss this, and his sister told me he was in a psych hospital due to kidnapping an infant named... Mariel.

I'm about to be a priest. Naturally I believe in supernatural things. I guess I never thought I'd experience them from another human being in my backseat. What does it mean? I don't know. I'm not sure I'll ever know. I'm not sure I'm even sane. That's why I'm writing again—to work through this. I need to work through it or I WILL go mad.

I will attempt to call Fr. Paul at the hospital, and hopefully, he will talk to me. Perhaps he experienced the strange and the unusual too. Maybe that's why he's getting psychiatric help.

That scares me.

Talk soon,

Jerome

09/28/1998

I'm officially ordained! My heart is filled with so much joy. I had several pictures taken in my vestments while holding Mariel. That moment was one where two dreams combined. I almost cried. Well, I did cry, let's be honest. I will say, though, that Phil Jameson scowled throughout the whole service. I wish he'd understand that it wasn't my intention to dash his dreams of becoming a priest. I didn't write the letter because I genuinely don't believe he's in the headspace to take that journey. He seems... very angry. Perhaps I was wrong.

I heard from Todd Caravan too. Mary and little Esther are recovering quite well. That makes me happy. They're a wonderful family, and I would have been devastated if something far worse had happened. Praise God, it didn't. I can't wait to meet Esther!

FYI, I did attempt to contact Fr. Paul. They said he wasn't available and to try again. So, that's my goal... hopefully with success this time.

I need to go feed my little rascal.

Blessings,

FATHER Jerome

10/15/1998

Still no word from Fr. Paul. I'm becoming disheartened. Nothing strange has happened since then though, and I will continue to write. Writing is definitely helping. I'm just struggling to find the motivation and discipline to do it.

12/03/1998

I'm sorry. It's been a while. I've given up on contacting Fr. Paul. The last time I did, they said he had no wish to speak to me. I was very upset. What did I do?

On the bright side, Mariel is doing well. He eats so much... and poops a lot. TOO MUCH. I love him though.

03/25/1999

Mariel went to the doctor today. He had a high fever. He's doing a lot better now. I know it was just a fever, but it made me anxious. I hate seeing my boy suffer. Also, the amount of paperwork you have to sign at the doctor's office—phew. Too much. I put my signature on everything. Except DNA analysis. I'd rather not sign away my kid's DNA. Who knows where that's going!

Other than excessive paperwork, there's nothing much to discuss. Phil Jameson is teaching Sunday School now, and one of the children told me he was 'scary'. I'm concerned I'll have to look into that, because the child never told me WHY Phil was scary.

09/16/1999

Yes, I know I haven't been consistent with my writing. Don't lecture me. Anyway, it's Esther's 1st birthday! She's a cutie. She babbles a lot... makes my heart happy. I think she'll be able to talk her way out of a lot of trouble when she grows up.

I can't write for long though; we're headed to her birthday party. Please understand this though—I'm going to keep writing. It may not be as much, but it's definitely helped me relax and focus, and process through the things that were bothering me. I've accepted two possibilities referencing the night we were attacked. One, I was under a lot of stress. I hadn't slept. There's a good chance I'm not remembering things the way they actually happened. Or two, it happened, and God has a significant plan in my life and the event was meaningful in some way. I refuse to think of it negatively. I have my dream job and a wonderful son. I am blessed, and I will continue to give my anxieties to God.

Be blessed,

Fr. Jerome

CHAPTER 2: VERSE 1

~ PROJECT 4 ~

September 20th, 2000

Moscow, Russia

"Your lungs will feel like they are exploding balloons. Do you understand?"

She nodded and swallowed hard. The little blonde girl shifted her green eyes to the murky water in front of her. The humidity's thickness in the pool room created beads of sweat on her skin. Her body felt sticky; she inhaled a thick scent of chlorine and something rotten. The odor sat heavy in her nostrils and throat. She wanted to vomit and simultaneously rip the skin from her bones so she that could rid herself of the sticky sensation.

"*Project 4!*" the man roared, and his voice bounced against the stained tile walls. "Fix your form. *Eyes on me!*"

With a gasp, four-year-old Project 4 snapped her hands to her sides. Her eyes widened in response to the roar of her name, and she looked at the tall dark-haired man who stood on the other side of the pool.

Trainer Sergei. He screamed a lot; slapped her, held her head below water. He was scary, but if she didn't pay attention to his instructions, he would summon Papa.

And Papa was far more terrifying.

"Your brain will want to go to sleep as your lungs feel like bursting. We will not help you until necessary. You must fight sleep as long as you can. Do you understand, Project 4?"

With a thunderous heart, Project 4 nodded, and she briefly wondered what her real name was. Papa said that if she passed this test, she could learn her real name. But that wasn't important now. The test was important.

That's what all the big people said, anyway.

And there were a lot of daily tests. This one frightened her the most. She *hated* dirty water. Hated the unknown and the unseen. However, when she'd told *Papa* she hated dirty water, there'd been a sudden requirement to complete this objective.

"You've acknowledged your understanding. It's time to proceed." Trainer Sergei snapped his fingers. "On my whistle."

Project 4 looked down at the water. She stood at the edge, and nausea swirled in her gut. She didn't want to do this; she wanted to play with Hamster.

The whistle screeched. Her heart lurched. Project 4 froze, and terror shot goosebumps onto her skin.

"*Project 4!*" Trainer Sergei screamed. "*On my fucking whistle!*"

The piercing whistle reverberated against the walls and rippled through her eardrums. Tears blurred her eyesight. She tried to move, but she couldn't. Her sticky, trembling body would not budge. A sob tore through her throat.

She hated dirty water. She *hated* the slimy, gooey sensation on her skin. Didn't Papa understand?

Trainer Sergei snarled. "I will report to your father if you do not follow my instructions. Do you understand me?"

Behind her, hinges creaked as a door opened.

"Too late." A deep, cold voice echoed in the room.

The little girl stiffened. She stopped her sob and regained composure. She could not cry right now.

The door slammed.

Papa was here.

"Stand properly, Project 4." The man's voice behind her was so calm, but that did not make it less terrifying.

Her hands snapped to her sides again, and she raised her chin.

Shoes clicked. Then stopped. Papa's breathing sounded displeased and loud... she could tell he'd stopped right behind her.

"What's this about not following instructions, little girl?"

There was an area in the water where some of the muck had cleared. In it, Project 4 could see her own wide-eyed expression in the water, and Papa's tall figure loomed over her. He was in the same fancy suit he wore last night... the one with the red tie. She liked the color red, but he'd slapped her hands away from the tie when she'd tried to touch it.

"Alright," Papa sighed.

Her pulse skyrocketed. When Papa sighed, he was either annoyed, or something bad was about to happen. Project 4 never knew which, and he sighed a lot.

"You have two options," he continued, his tone quiet. "You can either complete the task..."

Project 4 saw the reflection of his arm raise something over her head. It looked like a crate.

"... or you can watch Hamster drown."

She gasped. Whirling, she broke her stance and looked up at the man that towered above her.

Papa's eyes met hers, and he dangled the crate over the water. "Your choice," he whispered.

To the little girl, that whisper sounded like a roar.

Taking quick breaths, Project 4 turned away from Papa and faced the pool again. Even Trainer Sergei stood at attention. He looked scared too.

That was normal though. Many people looked at Papa with fear. The others looked at him with admiration. At the big dinner last night, all of the men who dressed in suits admired him with awestruck eyes and very big smiles. Women flocked to him.

Project 4 took a wavering step towards the pool. She didn't want to think about the next step, so she thought about the nice women from the dinner last night.

Whenever a pretty woman approached Papa, he picked up Project 4 and held her on his hip. Sometimes he planted a kiss on her cheek, rubbed her back, and flashed her the biggest smile. The women swooned over his smiles, and they gushed over Project 4.

"Such gorgeous wavy hair! Look at those beautiful eyes. Oh, she's such a little princess."

Project 4 closed her eyes, inhaled, and dove from the ledge.

"Well, of course she's perfect," Papa responded to his beautiful friends. "I adopted her."

The warm, brown-colored water swarmed her body. It was riddled with insects that moved as if they were alive. Bubbles tickled her skin. Loosened from its ponytail, strands of her hair—

—Such gorgeous wavy hair!—

—brushed her eyelids. Amidst the plunge, Project 4 set her sights upon the two dumbbells on the pool's floor. How long would it take for her lungs to feel like balloons?

She couldn't think about that. She needed to complete the task and protect Hamster.

Project 4 swam to the bottom and gripped the dumbbells. Weird particles floated about the water. Dead insects did too. In front of her, something long and thin wiggled like a worm.

Must save Hamster.

Ignoring all of these distractions, Project 4 planted her feet on the floor and lifted the weights until she stood upright. She raised her head and saw the bright light through the rippling water. The surface looked so far up.

Her pulse thundered within her head. Her lungs began to burn. Project 4 needed to focus and complete the task before the sleep took over. If the sleep took over, Hamster might die.

With cautious, steady steps, Project 4 carried the dumbbells across the pool's floor. She needed to reach the end of the pool. That was her task. Trainer Sergei said they were testing her lungs to see if they were better than everyone else's.

Did other kids train like this? She wasn't sure, but if Papa said she was perfect, how *could* someone else be *better*?

She wanted to be the best.

Project 4 stumbled a little. Her lungs felt like balloons now, and she couldn't see the other end of the pool. Her arms ached, and she wanted to inhale, but Project 4 set her teeth and moved forward.

If she passed this test, she would learn her real name. Hamster would live. Papa would be proud... wouldn't he?

The cement floor scraped her toes. As she gripped the weights, she imagined balloons bursting. She'd seen them burst at political events for Papa. Project 4 hoped the sleep would come before *that* happened... and it might. Because her lungs couldn't handle much more, and the cloudy water gave her no hope that she was approaching the end.

Pressure squeezed her lungs. The light over the pool beckoned her, luring her with the promise of air. It'd be easy... simply drop the weights and ascend. Perhaps Papa would have mercy.

Panic consumed her mind. The inflamed sensations tore at her body. Were her lungs *shredding*?

Papa wouldn't have mercy.

He'd drown Hamster, and then she would lose her only comfort. She'd miss the way his whiskers nuzzled her cheek, the way the warmth of his body lulled her to sleep.

That thought alone drove her forward until she crashed against the tile wall. Black spots filled her sight. The weights slipped from her small hands.

The sleep was coming.

She needed to ascend, but her eyelids fluttered shut.

Rough hands grabbed her waist. She opened her mouth, and muddy, chlorinated water surged against her tongue. Abruptly pushed from the watery depths, air swarmed her face. She gasped, spluttered, and vomited water. Finally, oxygen shot into her lungs. Her gasps sounded like screams echoing in the confines of the pool room.

When she blinked, her sight cleared. Trainer Sergei stood outside of the pool.

But if Trainer Sergei wasn't the one holding her, then—

"Breathe, little girl." Papa's voice sounded gentle.

Floating behind her, he held her close, and his palm rested against her forehead.

Leaning against his chest, she struggled to catch her breath. He confused her so much. His thumb's soft caress against her forehead disoriented her. It was comforting. Papa was not a comforting person. Why was Papa so mean and then so nice?

Against the sturdiness of his chest, Project 4 felt both comforted and terrified.

"You completed the task," he said, "but not to my desired expectations."

The taste of dirty water lingered in her mouth. Her heart sank. She hadn't made Papa proud. Which meant—

"*Hamster.*" She spluttered a sob.

Papa's hands tightened on her. It was an intimidating grip. "Do *not* cry. You are a product of Russia. You were created for the purpose of being a warrior to protect your country. Warriors don't cry."

She couldn't help it, though. It seemed so natural, something her body *needed*.

"*Project 4.* I will *drown Hamster* if you do not *stop.*"

Sniffling, the little girl wiped her eyes and set her teeth. Clenching her jaw and grinding her teeth always helped her stop the tears. She wondered if it worked for other kids. Once, she bit her tongue so hard it bled.

"There." Papa loosened his grip. He swam forward and guided her towards the exterior surface, where he placed her hands. "Hold on and kick your feet while I prepare you for your last task."

One more task. What could it be? She wanted to sleep and cuddle Hamster, but she knew that wouldn't be it.

"Sergei. Hand me your firearm."

Trainer Sergei disarmed himself and strode towards the pool. Stooping, he leaned towards Papa with it.

"Don't give it to me. Give it to Project 4," he sighed.

There was that sigh again. She wasn't cold, but Project 4 began to shiver.

Trainer Sergei handed the butt of the pistol to Project 4. It wasn't the first time she'd held a firearm, but the pool room seemed like a strange environment to hold something that "killed things", as the big people said.

"Hold it with both hands," Papa said. "Keep your fingers away from the trigger until I tell you to put them there."

Project 4's tiny hands could barely grip the butt of the firearm. As Papa supported her body against the side of the pool, and the cold force of the jets vibrated her legs, she grew more confused. What was Papa *planning*?

"Little girl, do you know what empathy is?" Papa supported her hands between his and steadied the gun as it pointed towards the wall. His large hands covered hers.

She'd heard the term before in training, but she still could not quite grasp it. Project 4 shook her head.

The water swished around them. "Empathy ruins your motivation to complete your assigned tasks."

Project 4 wished he wouldn't use big words all of the time. She did not like the inability to understand certain things, so she asked the only question she could in hopes to further comprehend.

"Why?"

Papa leaned his cheek against hers. "Because then you show mercy when ordinarily you should not. You act nice to people who do not deserve it; you trust people who should not have trust." He kissed her cheek. This confused her because there were no pretty women in the pool room. "These things can get you killed, or cause you to fail your duty. I am concerned that your empathy levels are on the rise. Do you *want* to fail your duty?"

Blinking water droplets from her eyelashes, Project 4 shook her head. She wanted to vomit again. She didn't know why she had to do any of this, or what her duty *was*, but she did not want to fail.

"Do you want to be the best?"

Did she have a choice?

His voice sounded very sweet. It chilled her.

The stubble on his cheek burned against her skin. "Do you want to know your true name? The name your homeland will one day chant for you like they chant for Papa?"

"Petrov! Petrov! Petrov!"

Project 4 remembered the crowd's chants as Papa stood tall on a platform, his hand gripping hers while she stood by his side with a dark wig to hide her natural hair. She didn't understand why he did that, why he made her look different when she was in public, but she understood one thing.

Papa was terrifying, and he was also very important.

Her breath shook. *She* wanted to be important too. *She* wanted to be the best, and she wanted to know her *name*. So Project 4 nodded and said—

"Yes. Be the best."

Papa tightened his grip, his voice a loud whisper in her ear. "Then you need to place your finger on the trigger, and you need to kill Hamster."

"No!" She tried to drop the gun, but Papa gripped her hands even tighter. She kicked, and the water churned about her legs. A life without Hamster would leave her cold and lonely. She *wouldn't kill Hamster!*

"Sergei." Papa spoke firmly. "Bring me the crate."

Trainer Sergei's boots thudded and squeaked against the wet tile floor as he stomped towards the crate.

Project 4 felt her chest burn with desperation as she tried to form the necessary words to protest. A lump formed in her throat. It choked her. Tears blurred her eyesight.

If she couldn't cry, could she use big words to convince Papa that she would not complete this task? Could she flash a big smile, like he did to the pretty women, to get him to change his mind?

Trainer Sergei set the crate a short distance away from the pool. He stood next to it and straightened up.

Hamster moved around the surface and sniffed. He was hungry. Project 4 *knew* her pet; she knew when he wanted food.

"Project 4," Papa murmured. "This is your last chance. Complete this task or I will have you watch Trainer Sergei complete it for you."

She had no words. She couldn't process his demands with clarity, like she normally could. As her heart tore through her chest, and she twisted within Papa's arms, Project 4 turned pleading eyes to Trainer Sergei. It was her last desperate attempt to reason with *someone* who might listen.

But Trainer Sergei's eyes were void of emotion.

"Sergei," Papa said, and his voice chilled the humid air. It was cold, commanding, and loud. "Project 4 has failed. She has made it clear she cannot complete her duty, or protect her assets. Use whatever method necessary to destroy the animal."

Sergei nodded. He withdrew a switchblade from his pocket and reached down to unlock the little gate.

Project 4 screamed. Her wet hair whipped back and forth across her face as she thrashed in Papa's arms.

"It's sad, isn't it?" Papa's voice was soft now, almost soothing. "Watching something you love get destroyed because you could not do your job?" He spoke through his teeth now.

Trainer Sergei rattled the lock, struggling to manipulate it. He located a series of zip ties and muttered under his breath.

This is why she'd added zip ties to Hamster's crate every day... to protect Hamster from people like Papa and Trainer.

Grunting, Papa shoved Project 4 harder against the pool wall to still her movements. He murmured in her ear. "Just like our country... it will be destroyed if we have weak warriors like you. So if Hamster is so important..." his voice dropped to a whisper, "... then why aren't you protecting him?"

With a flick of his wrist, Trainer Sergei opened the switchblade and sliced through the zip ties. He unlocked the gate and stooped to snatch Hamster from the crate.

Project 4 replayed the memories of Hamster's fur against her cheek. She remembered the sensation of a smile—a rare one that crept across her face whenever she laid eyes on him.

As she watched the trainer grab Hamster by the scruff, Project 4 realized something. Papa had released her hands.

His fingers still hovered near hers, but she gripped the firearm by herself. It shook.

Trainer Sergei did not notice the gun turning towards him. He was too busy retrieving Hamster to recognize that he was about to die at the hands of a four-year-old girl.

"I've got you," Papa reassured, a hot whisper against her ear. "Protect your asset. Pull the trigger."

Project 4 aligned the sights, just like Trainer Sergei demonstrated on the range. The lump in her throat threatened to burst like those balloons as she placed her finger on the trigger.

Trainer Sergei raised Hamster in the air and eyed the animal, as if speculating on how he wanted to use the knife.

In the dim pool room, a gunshot roared.

It vibrated against the walls; the floors; the metal ceiling.

The trainer's body jolted. Still clinging to Hamster, he turned horrified eyes to Project 4. He fell to his glutes.

Hamster scurried away.

Blood dribbled from Trainer Sergei's chest. He began to stammer. "What the...?"

Relief, horror, and nausea wrecked her body.

"He taught you to shoot better than that, Project 4," Papa cooed.

Hamster was still alive... but so was the threat. She needed to do better.

It was her duty to protect Hamster.

Trainer Sergei raised a hand, the one with the knife. "No, please—"

The muzzle flashed again. Metal rang. Project 4's body jerked, and a single teardrop dribbled over her cheek. Her lips trembled as the bullet made its landing in the center of Trainer Sergei's head. He collapsed, and his head slammed against the floor.

Project 4 found herself clinging to the gun. Her mouth, dry with astonishing severity, almost craved the dirty pool water she'd choked on not long ago. Her senses came alive, and she was disoriented by the ringing in her ears.

Trainer Sergei had always made her put soft things in her ears on firearm day. Now she understood why.

"Was that difficult?" Papa asked and reached to guide the firearm from her fingers. Gently, he rested it on the ground. Placing his hands on her waist, he lifted her out of the pool and turned her to face him.

Hamster scampered around the pool room, trying to find a place to hide from the gunshots. As Project 4 faced her father, she heard her pet's little feet skittering across the ground. She clung to that sound, finding comfort in it.

"Yes," she responded.

Papa's eyes, a beautiful blue-grey, searched hers. His dark hair, normally styled and perfected, lay wet and matted against his head from the dive. It was strange seeing him like this, because he kept himself so pristine at all times. He'd discarded his jacket from earlier, now submerged in the water with his button-down and red tie she hadn't been able to touch.

"It won't be difficult one day," he said, and brushed the soaked hair from her eyes.

Project 4 closed them, her mind in turmoil. She wasn't sure if he would continue the gentle caress or shift his approach and slap her.

"Why not?" She wondered if she would be punished for questioning Papa.

He cupped her face between his hands. "Because you will be a *Petrov*... daughter of *President* Aleksey Petrov. Would you like to know what's most impressive?"

Project 4 nodded, contemplating, wondering what it would mean to be a Petrov.

"When I adopted you, I had every intention of making you perfect. I don't accept less than perfect. You *will* be the best weapon in the world... as *Agent* 4." He leaned his forehead against hers. "Young and old will beg for your approval and your expertise. They will seek you like Hamster seeks your hand for food. Agents will hate you and *love* you because they cannot *be* you."

Love. Her mind paused on that word. She'd heard it before. Once, she'd been in the presence of another child, the daughter of a server at the Kremlin. The child, to her mother, said–

"I love you."

Was it normal to tell a parent you loved them?

"I love you, Papa," she whispered, feeling the warmth of his hands against her face.

That warmth transitioned to pain.

He cracked his palm across her cheek.

The impact stung, and the sound reverberated within the room. Project 4 recoiled. She covered her cheek with her hand, closed her eyes to hide the tears.

His fingertips continued their caress, and his tone remained sweet.

"Understand something, little girl. Enhanced... agents... can't... love."

"Why?" she pressed, her hand still against her cheek.

"Only subhumans are capable of that. Sergei was a subhuman. Look at him now."

She didn't want to.

"Look at him!" Papa roared, and it was more startling than the gunshots.

Project 4 turned her head to look at the dead man behind her. Red pools of blood darkened the floor beneath his body. Her breath caught, and she shifted her eyes to Hamster, who had managed to crawl back into his crate.

If she could not love, then what was it she felt for Hamster?

"Look at Papa," he commanded. "Repeat what I just told you about love, and our duties will be complete for the morning."

Project 4 tried to remember exactly what he said. Closing her eyes again, she heaved in a breath. Her mind and body were so tired now. She felt weak, and being weak was bad. Perhaps it was because she cared for Hamster.

"Say the words."

She gritted her teeth, opened her eyes. "Enhanced... agents... don't... love."

A smile broke across Papa's face. His eyes brightened. "Well done."

He reached for her.

She recoiled again.

Papa embraced her and nestled his cheek against hers. "Tira," he murmured. "It's okay. You've done well today."

Goosebumps crawled like bugs across her skin.

Teer-ra? Was that her name? She liked the sound. Simple. Pretty. Sharp.

Tears that she refused to shed filled her eyes again. She *couldn't* cry... she hadn't gotten this far to regress.

"Teer-ra?" she whispered, sounding it out as she sat limp in his arms.

"Yes." His arms tightened. "Your name is Tira."

VERSE 2

~ MARIEL ~

Sunday, July 11th, 2004
Chicago, Illinois

Fr. Jerome's head shot up. He stood near the altar, wiping down the chalice to prepare for the first service of the morning. Seconds ago, it had been quiet. The sunlight cast a soft, welcoming glow against the empty wooden pews.

Now, the priest heard angry footsteps. They stomped down the hallway towards the sanctuary. His heart rate shot up, and he closed his eyes. Those footsteps belonged to one person.

Philip Jameson.

"Guide my words, Lord, he's upset again," Fr. Jerome whispered and then opened his eyes. His head hurt due to the nightmare-plagued sleep he'd had. The same nightmares, in fact, and *new* ones too.

The footsteps echoed against the hard flooring before becoming muffled. Phil had made it to the carpeting, which meant he was just outside of the sanctuary.

In preparation, Fr. Jerome set the chalice on the altar and turned to face the sanctuary entrance. He crossed his hands in front of his hips.

"Ow, ow!"

Fr. Jerome frowned. That was a child's voice. And if he hadn't misheard, it sounded like—

"Your son!" Phil stormed into the church, his face red, and he had his arm hooked beneath six-year-old Mariel's armpit. The red-haired lawyer yanked him, and the young boy's feet dragged across the floor as his long, black hair fell tousled over his eyes.

Fr. Jerome's teeth grinded together. Heat boiled within his skin, and he strode forward and went down the steps towards the center aisle. *"Phil!"* His voice shook. "Why are you *dragging* my son?"

With a shove, Phil released Mariel. "Your son," he snarled, "put a *roach* in my drawer in Sunday school."

Mariel shook his head. "Gabe did it!"

Fr. Jerome looked to Mariel and then back at Phil Jameson. "Phil, we'll address that, but that's no reason to put your hands on a—"

"*I hate roaches!*" Phil screamed, and his voice reverberated throughout the dome. His eyes bugged from his pale face. He looked like a praying mantis.

With far more screaming than prayer.

Behind Phil, a few congregation members entered the sanctuary for the early morning Orthros service. Fr. Jerome sent them a welcoming nod and smile and then darted his eyes back to the situation before him.

"Can we please talk in private?" Fr. Jerome said softly. He wanted to smack Phil's eyeballs back into his head.

Phil huffed. "In the hallway."

Fr. Jerome turned a warning glance towards Mariel. "Sit in the pews and do not move, understood?"

"But Dad, I didn't—"

"*Mariel.*" Firm.

The boy scowled and stormed to the nearest pew. He sat, folded his arms, and glared at the altar.

With gracious intent that did not echo his internal feelings, Fr. Jerome bowed his head, gestured towards the sanctuary exit.

Phil walked quickly, storming towards the coatroom without care as congregation members passed him.

Once both men entered the coat room, Phil whirled to face Fr. Jerome. "Your son is disrespectful," he flared. "I *know* he put the roach in my drawer."

Fr. Jerome bit his tongue, trying to remember his position as a priest. "Phil," he said. "How do you know?"

"Of course you'll defend him."

"Philip!" Fr. Jerome raised his voice. "Be reasonable. I'd ask the same question *in any other situation.*"

"You've always been biased," Phil continued, as if he hadn't heard any of Fr. Jerome's prior words. He pointed a finger. "But what he did was not acceptable."

Fr. Jerome sighed. "How am I supposed to address this with him if I don't even know the details of the situation?"

Phil blinked, as if caught by surprise at the logic. He ran a tongue over his lips. "Well, he was the first in the classroom. He's always there first. And he had this smile on his face like he'd *done* something." He ended his statement with a nod, as if the gesture would solidify the truth.

The priest struggled to maintain composure. Why wasn't Phil even giving him the *opportunity* to consider Mariel's innocence or guilt? It was clear the lawyer had made up his mind—Mariel was guilty.

"Phil, we don't have much time before service and I'd rather not argue." Fr. Jerome laced his fingers together and twisted them. His palms were sweaty. "One, I will talk to Mariel and get his side. He's normally honest with me. If he is dishonest, and I find out, there will be repercussions."

Phil opened his mouth to speak but Fr. Jerome continued. "Two, who is in the classroom with the other children right now?"

Someone laughed with another person in the hallway. Phil cleared his throat. "I—er, Mary Caravan."

Someone far more appropriate for the classroom, Fr. Jerome thought, but he nodded. "Good. Now, three. I understand frustration, and I am a supporter of discipline. But—" the priest's voice shook, "—unless my child is at risk of harming himself or someone else, you do *not* put your hands on him. Do you understand me?"

Phil's Adam's apple bobbed in his skinny throat as he swallowed. He narrowed his eyes. "Are you threatening me?"

Was he? Fr. Jerome thought back to the attacker in his car. A real threat.

He didn't want a member of his congregation to feel threatened. That wasn't his intent. However, it was necessary to set boundaries with Phil because it was clear the man had no respect for the Nadiers.

"I don't think I can convince you that a boundary is not a threat," Fr. Jerome said quietly. "I'm simply hoping that you'll respect my child's personal space. That goes for all the children here at church. Those kids in your classroom are five and six years old. There's no reason to treat them that way."

Phil worked the muscles in his jaw, and his eyes looked darker. "You always thought you were better, didn't you?"

"Phil—"

"—With your perfect little appearance, and your 'Dad of the year' inclinations." Phil lifted his fingers to quote himself. "I see right past you and your narcissistic 'leadership'."

Fr. Jerome could not comprehend what Phil was trying to say. The attack did not make sense, but the priest was fast losing his patience. "Phil, what are you *talking* about? What is it about me that you feel the need to constantly fight me? Was it the recommendation letter?"

"The *lack* thereof, you mean?" Phil hissed. "No. I merely hold you and *everyone else* accountable to their sin."

"My sin? You've lost me, Philip."

"You're not infallible."

"I never said I was?" His head hurt.

"I can read between the lines... the day you put that poorly graded essay on my desk and told me that my arguments had the potential to hurt 'minority groups'!" Phil's voice rose to a screech.

Fr. Jerome tightened his lips. He remembered that day. The essay, while well written in terms of punctuation and grammar, had argued the economical benefits of slavery and female servitude.

"Ah," he said. "I remember that."

Phil nodded again, once more to drive his point home.

Fr. Jerome rubbed his forehead. "Phil, I'm sorry if I said anything that made you feel like I was putting you down. That truly wasn't my intent. You're very talented, but your content was concerning." He held up a finger when Phil attempted to interrupt. "And you may never like me—but it's not fair for you to involve my son because we can't get along. Can we agree on that at least?"

Phil came closer. His eyes bugged out again, and he lifted a finger. "Talk to your son," he snarled. "And watch your pride. It will dethrone you one day." He stormed from the coat room.

Tears burned Fr. Jerome's eyes. He wasn't sad. He was angry. If Phil Jameson hated him so much, why did the man come to St. Michael's?

Why make everyone else's life miserable?

"Father Jerome?" A little girl's voice broke the priest's reflection.

He turned towards the entrance, looked down. There stood a little brown-haired girl in a sunflower dress staring up at him with wide, strange, blue-brown eyes.

A smile broke across his face. "Hi, Esther. What are you doing out of class?"

Esther hopped one time on both feet. "Had to go potty. And mommy's boring. And I don't like Mr. Jameson. He's scary. Are you sad, Father Jerome?"

Shoot, was his face that telling?

The priest knelt before Esther Caravan. He cupped her face between his hands. "Miss Caravan," he said. "I just had a tough conversation, but I will be just fine."

"Okay." Esther smiled.

Children were often simpler than adults. "Now head back to class, okay?"

Esther frowned. "I don't like Mr. Jameson, though."

Neither do I, Fr. Jerome thought, and then he chastised himself. "I think maybe Mr. Jameson just needs someone to cheer him up. I think you're great at cheering people up, because it worked on me." The priest booped Esther's nose.

Esther giggled. "Okay." She flounced towards the exit, and then she stopped. "I've got a question."

"Of course, kiddo."

Esther tapped her foot. "Will I go to Hell if I did something bad?"

Fr. Jerome tilted his head. "Why are you having those thoughts, Esther? You're human. Humans sometimes make bad choices, right? You shouldn't have any fears about Hell. Okay?"

Esther pondered. She nodded. "Okay. In class, Mr. Jameson said we might go to Hell if we do bad things. And I did a bad thing."

At this point, Fr. Jerome was experiencing bad thoughts, particularly about punching Philip Jameson again and again, but he did not voice that. "I'll talk to Mr. Jameson about that. What did you do that you feel is bad, kiddo?"

Esther sighed and played with her hair. "I put a roach in Mr. Jameson's drawer," she confessed in a whisper, and the she ran away. The sundress flounced with her retreating footsteps.

A snort blurted from Fr. Jerome's throat. That girl would be big trouble as she grew up. And he was certain she was acting out for attention. She hadn't been very happy about the April birth of her baby brother—Jason Caravan. Esther had claimed she would lock herself in her room and starve herself until they got rid of him.

It was a miracle, really... Jason's birth. Fr. Jerome had baptized the child. During coffee hour, Mary had told the priest that, with her health issues, she hadn't expected another pregnancy. Her face had been flushed with excitement and pride. Jason was wanted. Both children were precious in their eyes.

But despite the hilarity of Esther's statement, the confession solidified the fact that Phil Jameson had targeted Mariel.

"Time for service," he said. "I need the Lord before I lose my temper." With a sigh, Fr. Jerome exited the room and prayed for a heart of forgiveness.

He asked God to bring Phil Jameson peace, but he had a dark suspicion that the lawyer would continue to walk down a path of pride, anger, and revenge.

*   *   *

7/11/2004

I wasn't sure if I should write in my journal today due to my outrage with Phil Jameson. I don't want to write negative things about people... but I also have no other outlet. I will keep it brief.

Phil Jameson is a narcissistic, pompous, prideful man. He could curdle milk by looking at it. Even his poor wife, Carolyn, always looks as though she might cry. He had the audacity of putting his hands on my son today. If it happens again, so will the consequences.

I spoke with Mariel on the way home. I asked what has been taught in Sunday School. Mariel said that Phil read a scripture from the Bible. Revelations 3:10– "Since you have kept my command to endure patiently, I will also keep you from the hour of trial that is going to come on the whole world to test the inhabitants of the earth."

Phil is talking to little kids about the rapture... an event that is not fully understood and has multiple interpretations. I'm not happy.

Mariel said the conversation scared him. I told him he has nothing to fear, but then he said something that concerns me. He said... "I'm just scared because I'm the one who will start it all."

I thought about Fr. Paul's wild statement about Mariel, that he's a "catalyst", and then I asked why he thinks he will start it all. Mariel said—"Because the nice shadow and the mean shadow both told me I would."

Shadows? He's seeing shadows? Oh, this chills me to the bone. Is my son dealing with hallucinations?

Or is something else going on?

Regardless, I think I need to get Mariel psychiatric help. Just in case. I might need it too. I'm not doing well right now. I'm anxious. The nightmares are frequent. Last night I experienced two new ones.

I dreamed about a little crying girl with bloody shins, and I dreamt of a dead man in an alley–his face beaten in. A bloody brick lay beside him.

I don't want to dream anymore.

Blessings,

Fr. Jerome

12/15/2005

It's been a very long time, I know. I'm okay, though. I've been living my best life as a priest and a dad. I'm very busy, so I've not even thought about writing. This is just an update, though not the most encouraging. Mariel has been with a therapist for a little bit. The therapist dropped him... she never said why. I guess I'll keep trying. Maybe I am overreacting. Mariel seems like a happy kid. I'm just concerned about a few things, like his statements about the shadows he sees. I suppose it's a little silly of me to be concerned about that considering I thought I witnessed him catch a bullet... but I don't want him to be scared about anything. Whenever he talks about "the mean one" he seems scared. God bless him.

Fr. Jerome

9/3/2008

Good evening. I've neglected my journal, I'm sorry. My heart hurts. Mariel told me he wished I had never adopted him. I get that he's ten, and he probably questions a lot about his life. It still hurts me. I love him so much. I thought we were close. I told him I was sorry, and I left the room. When he's angry, something switches inside of him, and his typically sweet demeanor changes into something... unsettling. One time, he told me that his anger was righteous, and to feel was to be human. That's true, but it's as if he's been told there is no wrong way of handling anger. His anger episodes have increased since I last wrote. I have attempted many therapists in hopes that he might find a connection with someone who might be able to help him. The last therapist's office called me today and said that she wanted to transfer him (again) because she "just could not help him". I talked to him today and asked him what I could do to help. I sounded more frustrated than I should have. Mariel told me no one understood him, and that I didn't either, or else I wouldn't be asking him about these things. It turned into an argument, and then he told me he wished I had never adopted him. Giving it to God today.

Love,

Fr. Jerome

12/25/2008

Merry Christmas! I bought Mariel a video game system today. It was a little outside the budget, but I wanted to get him something nice for once. He was so excited. I love his smile. He said, "I will care for you one day too, Dad." My heart.

5/4/2010

Wow, this book is dusty. Mariel is twelve now. He is quite the good-looking kid. He insists upon keeping his hair long. I only protested because I have always been jealous of his hair.

Mariel has not had many angry episodes lately. His friends keep him occupied. Gabe Donovan is his closest buddy, alongside Esther Caravan. The three are inseparable. If there is a weekend where they are not here playing video games, I start questioning my life. What is my weekend without providing Dad's Greatest Snacks to three hungry tween-agers?

Good night. Good to write again.

6/25/2010

I found pornography websites on Mariel's laptop today. He isn't home right now, and I need to figure out how to address this when he gets home. I understand he is a young boy, but what I found was unsettling. I didn't watch all of it. A man beat a distressed woman and then used her sexually until she cried and bled. The video was bookmarked. He's home now. Lord help me.

6/26/2010

Yesterday was rough. I talked to Mariel about the porn on the computer, and he said it was none of my business. I made him sit down, and I told him that it was my business. I said I'd gone through the same teenage boy phase (minus the Internet, of course), and that he could talk to me. He didn't talk. I became frustrated and asked why he had bookmarked the video. Mariel looked at me and said, "The mean one told me to do it." Now, Mariel has not spoken of "the mean one" for many years. I hoped it'd been a phase as a young child. After he made that comment, I stared at him, and I told him that he was not allowed to use the laptop unless I was home, and it was in the same room. He stared back at me, squinted a little, and then said, "Dad, just because you don't like pussy doesn't mean I can't appreciate it." He left the room. That stung. I didn't even call him back. In fact, I didn't talk to him the rest of the night. What right did he have to use that against me? I am still angry at him, and I pray to God that the anger diminishes. I can't hold on to this bitterness. I am the parent. He is the child. But I feel sick.

9/16/2012

Sorry, it's been a while. I left on a negative note, and with the trauma surrounding my dad's comments about writing my feelings in a journal, sometimes it's hard for me to pick back up again. I wish there was

9/17/2012

Sorry for stopping the journal entry so abruptly. Mariel attempted suicide last night. I received a phone call from Todd saying Mariel found his pistol and, in front of Gabe and Esther, put it in his mouth, and pulled the trigger. The pistol malfunctioned and did not fire, but the terrifying reality, according to Todd, is that it should have. Todd said until Mariel resolves his issues he cannot see Esther. I am at a loss. No clue what to do. He is better now, but today, when I asked him why he wanted to die, he said— "Because I don't want to hurt you, Gabe, or Esther, Dad."

He's fourteen now. Full of so much life, and I wish he was happy. My heart hurts so much, I love him... and I am genuinely terrified for my child.

Guide me, Lord.

Fr. Jerome

Verse 3

~ Esther ~

Sunday, September 30th, 2012
Chicago, Illinois

"Your dad's gonna kill us if he finds out."

Esther looked at Mariel and smirked. She raised the chocolate ice cream cone to her lips. "Not *us*. Just you."

"Ha," Gabriel Donovan said, and shuffled ahead. "Let's go to the track so I can piss."

Fourteen-year-old Esther Caravan, accompanied by Mariel Nadier and Gabriel Donovan, walked slowly through the suburb. It was still warm outside, but the trees rustled with the hint of autumn in the wind. Dogs barked. Vehicles rumbled. The rhythmic sound of a basketball thudded in the neighborhood. It was just after 4 P.M. The day was overcast; the sun peeked through the clouds on occasion.

"Yeah," Mariel deadpanned to Esther's jab. "Me."

Esther licked her ice cream, appreciated the cool chocolate taste, and snuck a glance at her crush. The wind tugged his shoulder-length wavy hair, and she struggled to keep up with his long strides as she looked at his lanky body. He wasn't the *most* attractive boy she knew, and a lot of boys talked to her, but his quiet demeanor enhanced his cuteness.

When he attempted suicide with her Dad's gun, though?

Not cute. Not cute at all.

"He just doesn't get it," Esther said, and stared at her ice cream cone. "He doesn't get you were just joking."

"Right." He shoved his fists into his sweatpants' pockets.

Esther thought back to the moment when Mariel placed the gun in his mouth; when he pulled the trigger.

"Two things," he'd said, raising the gun to his lips. *"If this magic trick works, then I'll be a god amongst my peers. But if it doesn't... well. At least, I'll fucking die."*

Esther caught her breath. As they approached the gated track and soccer field, she turned her eyes to him again. "You—you *were* joking, right?"

Mariel tossed his head back. Laughed. "Why would I want to die?" He stopped outside the entrance of the open gate, and he looked at Esther with her favorite blue-eyed gaze. "I'd miss seeing your face. A lot." His voice cracked. Puberty. It was hilarious to watch with boys.

"Yeah?" Esther's heart thudded harder, but for a different reason. Despite the acne on his face, and the strange behavior he exhibited sometimes, she thought he was charming. Hot. Not as hot as the shirtless actor poster she'd hidden in her closet, but definitely a close fourth or fifth.

Mariel stepped closer. His eyes fell to her lips, and then the cleavage peeking from her black tank top. "Esther—"

"Hurry the fuck up, you goons, I gotta pee." Gabe stopped a distance away and flopped his hands at his sides. His short blond hair looked ridiculous with two wild strands that, on random, stuck up at the center of his head.

Face hot, Esther returned her attention to the ice cream. Had Mariel been about to kiss her? If he was, he'd been looking at the wrong location. "Do you need help peeing or something, Gabe?"

"No, I'm more talking to Mariel. I wanna tell him a guy thing."

Mariel sighed and treaded forward. "That's never good, and it's normally always gross."

Esther scoffed, entering the track as ice cream dribbled down her fingers. "Don't hide your guy things from me. I can appreciate guy humor."

"Nah. You wouldn't get it."

Mariel nodded his forehead towards the other side of the track. Two tall subjects leaned against the wall beneath the bleachers. On the track, a runner sprinted the one hundred meter length. "I'm going to guess you're just looking for moral support."

"For what?" Gabe scratched his jaw.

"To hit on that girl who's running."

Gabe laughed and then stopped. "Well..."

Esther watched the runner. She couldn't see the individual very well, but she looked fucking fast.

Mariel spoke again. "Go piss. I'm gonna walk with Esther. We'll meet you over there."

Gabe let out a large sigh and then jogged towards the restrooms.

"He's so predictable," Esther said, as if she'd known the whole time what the "guy thing" would be.

Mariel snorted. "Yeah."

Though... it did bug her when the boys left her out. She could participate in *any* conversation they did—even about women.

Esther loved women.

However, *that* was something she didn't dare reveal to her dad. He had a thing about girls liking girls and boys liking boys.

"Marriage is between one man and one woman," Todd liked to say whenever a news segment about gay marriage came on. *"These people just don't get it."*

Those comments bothered her, made her heart hurt. She loved her dad, and she'd always been close to him. It sucked to think she might never be able to share her true self with him.

"How's your Mom doing?" Mariel inquired. He shuffled his feet, and the tennis shoes made a harsh scraping sound against the track.

To distract herself from the oncoming emotional pain, Esther tasted her ice cream again. Tears filled her eyes. The topic of her mom brought anxiety to her otherwise simple world.

"She's struggling," Esther murmured. Her fingers went to the necklace she wore—a dancing girl pendant her mom had given her for her birthday. Esther loved to dance.

A whistle sounded. The runner, a female with blonde hair, sprinted again.

As they walked across the soccer field, Esther's mind snapped back to the hospital stench; the beeping monitors; the sight of her mother's thin, pale face turning towards Esther while she sat upright in the hospital gown. The woman's smile held beauty, tenderness, and love.

"I'll be okay, baby girl," Mary had said last night, brushing her fingertips through Esther's brown hair. *"I always am."*

Esther adored her mom. She couldn't relate to many of her friends, the ones who found every opportunity to escape their mothers. However, she *wished* she could experience her teenage years the same way they did: worry less about illness and more about how "annoying" a mother could be.

"Is Jason still being a brat about everything?" Mariel asked.

"He's eight. Of course he's a brat." Esther took another bite. Her fingers were sticky from melted ice cream. "If he's not screaming about what's being served for dinner, he's obsessively reading health book shit. Or reading about hawks."

"Hawks?"

"Yeah, Mom started calling him Hawk."

"Ah. I didn't know eight-year-olds could read advanced stuff like that."

Esther sighed and played with the dancing pendant on her neck. "He can. All he does is read and talk about how he's going to heal mom one day. It gets annoying. Like, you're eight. You barely poop on the potty, shut the fuck up."

Mariel grinned. "I feel like he's toilet trained now."

"Yes, well, he smells like a poopy brat, so I forget he's eight. How's your dad?"

He shrugged. "Good. Boring."

"Stop. Fr. Jerome is amazing. He's like a bonus dad."

"More like a bonus grandpa," Mariel snickered.

Esther glared at him. She hated when he mocked Fr. Jerome because she *loved* the priest. Yeah, he was old, but at least he was authentic, wise, and empathetic–almost to a fault. "Be nice. He has to deal with you. He *chooses* to deal with you."

"Yeah, yeah."

Esther looked at the brick building ahead of them. The empty concession stands looked grim without lines of people. "I think Gabe got lost in the toilet."

Mariel rolled his eyes and trotted away. "I'll check. I need to pee now, anyway."

The sun peeked out from the clouds. It warmed the top of her head as Esther wandered onto the track. She still wondered if Mariel had planned to kiss her. It'd be her first kiss.

Had *he* kissed anyone before?

A dark SUV pulled into a parking space in the lot past the gate. Esther stared at it and licked her ice cream. The SUV looked like it was staring back.

Goosebumps prickled her skin. Why did she feel unsettled—like someone *was* watching her?

It wasn't an unfamiliar feeling either. Since a young age, she'd always experienced this indescribable *feeling* of being *watched*.

It was probably her dad's fault. He was a cop. He believed everyone was out to get his family.

Licking her hand, Esther took another step forward. She couldn't wait until her father quit law enforcement and just worked at the family bookstore: *Caravan's Books.* It'd be much safer and—

Why were footsteps thundering in her direction?

Esther turned her head. Shrieked.

She'd stepped into the lane of the oncoming sprinter.

"Mmph!" Bone cracked against bone. A human body darkened her vision and blotted the sun. An elbow smashed her jaw. Her teeth rattled. Shins collided. Legs tangled with hers. Were they airborne?

They were.

"Hoomph!" Esther's body smacked against the track. So did her head. It bounced, and the runner's torso collapsed against her face and flattened her nose. The remaining oxygen hissed from her smothered nostrils as she realized three very unimportant things.

One—the runner was definitely female; two—she didn't know someone *so* sweaty could smell *so good*; and three—Gabe would be very jealous that *she*, Esther Marie Caravan, currently had a girl's breasts smashed against her face.

It didn't last long. Daylight re-appeared. Spluttering what sounded like expletives, the runner scrambled away and lunged to her feet.

Esther groaned and rubbed her shins. She caught sight of black tennis shoes, black spandex, and slender, toned, *smooth* legs that carried a golden hint of sun exposure. Esther noticed deep scars on the girl's shins, but that didn't distract from how *good* her legs looked.

But the pretty-legged sprinter was fucking pissed, because she wouldn't take a breath between the words she hurtled towards Esther. Words that sounded *nothing* like English and more like...

Russian?

With tousled brown hair that tickled her face, Esther sat up and nearly gasped.

The runner, blonde and maybe slightly older than Esther, was achingly beautiful. Her angry countenance did nothing to change that. In fact, it enhanced her features. The rage widened her sharp, green eyes. Every time she spoke, dimples appeared very briefly, as if to hide from her temper. Her moving mouth brought Esther's attention to her soft-looking lips.

Distracted, Esther wondered if *those* lips had ever been kissed. Maybe the runner needed it. Maybe it would calm her down a little?

"You're beautiful," Esther said, and then covered her mouth.

Fuck... *fuck!* Had she seriously just said that? *Aloud?*

The runner stopped mid-sentence. Or perhaps it was the end of the sentence. Esther didn't know—because it wasn't fucking English.

"What?" the runner spat. Her hair, tightened in a pristine bun, glowed in the re-emerging sun.

Self-awareness snapped her back to reality. Covered in ice cream, Esther sat on the track, embarrassed; hot; self-conscious. Why would she eat *ice cream* on a *track?*

"I—I—" she stammered. "I'm sorry, I don't understand your language."

The runner rolled her eyes. "My *language* is Russian."

"Oh." Esther gazed. This girl was ten times better than the poster in her room. In fact, she would have offered a lot of money to replace her hot guy poster with this goddess that stood before her.

Suddenly, the excitement of a possible kiss from Mariel faded into the desire to know this runner.

"You messed up my record time," the runner snarled. "I *almost had my best time!*"

"I'm sorry!" Esther cried. She'd never argued with a stranger before. She hadn't expected to feel this comfortable doing so. "But maybe watch where you're going next time?"

The girl's face reddened. "Watch for *what?* Little girls with ice cream? Please."

"Hey." Esther raised her chin. "I'm *fourteen.*"

The runner laughed, and even though it oozed with mockery, it brought chills over Esther's body... and the chills felt good. But—

"You're very rude," Esther snipped. "A fucking apology would be nice."

"I do *not* apologize to—"

"Hey!" One of the men beneath the bleachers—a very tall burly man with a five o'clock shadow—stormed towards them.

The girl flinched at the man's voice. Then she straightened up taller and turned to face him. The man towered over her.

"Help the leetle girl get up," he said to the runner, his accent thick. "So we can move on with our day."

Her face burned. Why did everyone think she was *little?*

"I'm fine." Esther rose to her knees. She was getting mad. The abrasions on her legs burned. "Don't let me inconvenience you guys."

The man clapped his palm against the runner's back and gave her an abrupt push. "Gather your things and meet us at the car." He turned dark eyes to Esther and scanned her. "Maybe next time you don't... eat ice cream on track. Eh?"

Esther wobbled to her feet. Her nose flared. Who *were* these people?

It didn't matter. They were rude as fuck, and she didn't want a poster of *any* of them on her wall anymore.

The pretty runner scanned Esther again. Her facial expression softened a little before she turned and followed the man.

"What was that about?" Behind her, Mariel's voice brought Esther back to earth.

"Oh man, you got to talk to *her*? Look at the ass in that spandex." Gabe.

Esther didn't like the runner... but she *did* have a nice butt. It was very perky, and there were no rules against checking people out even if you hated them.

"That girl just ran me over," Esther admitted, still watching the runner, feeling a sudden ache in her chest.

"I'll kick her ass," Mariel hissed.

"I don't think you could," Esther said so quickly it surprised even her.

"I would be willing to try," Gabe swooned.

Wait. The girl stopped walking. Turned.

And started back.

Esther walked forward. It was as if her body moved in response to the Russian blonde's silent command.

"Where you going?" Mariel demanded and tagged along.

"I think she wants to talk to me."

"But you said she's rude."

"Maybe she wants to apologize." Esther doubted it.

The runner held something in her fist. It glistened in the sunlight. Her emerald eyes found Esther's, but they also scanned the area with a level of hypervigilance that Esther hadn't even seen from her dad or his cop friends.

As they drew closer, Esther saw what was dangling in the runner's fist. To confirm, she reached up to touch her neck as her eyes locked onto the approaching girl.

"Is this yours?" the runner asked, her voice still cool but much calmer now.

Now that they were closer, Esther noticed light bruising on her face. Her throat felt tight. Was she being abused by those men?

"It was tangled in my watch." The runner stopped a short distance from Esther and held out her hand. There it was–the dancing girl pendant.

"Yes," Esther said. "My mom gave that to me. It's important." Reaching out, she took it and smiled a little. "I appreciate you."

The girl's face reddened. "Mmph." But she didn't look away.

Neither did Esther.

Was there a hint of warmth in her eyes?

Mariel cleared his throat. "Yeah. Thanks."

The runner's eyes snapped to Mariel. Indifferent, she scanned *him* now, and whatever warmth might have been in her eyes turned to ice. "I should go."

Esther was disappointed.

The girl waved a nonchalant hand towards Esther. Her toned shoulder flexed. "You have ice cream in your hair."

Esther's fingers darted to her hair. She fluffed it a little. "Oh," she laughed, and her hand shook.

"We should go." Mariel's voice was gruff.

The runner ignored him. Looking at Esther, she backed away. "One last thing."

Esther's attention belonged to the runner, and she disregarded Mariel's loud sigh. "Hmm?"

Faint dimples emerged again. "You're annoying..."

Her ears went hot. Esther opened her mouth to protest.

"... but you're not so bad looking yourself." The runner bowed her head a little and departed, jogging towards the two men she'd accompanied.

Esther couldn't sort the range of confusing thoughts in her mind. As her body trembled and burned, she realized she didn't want the runner as a single poster on the wall.

Because that girl could be *wallpaper*.

"What the fuck is she on?" Mariel snapped. "Why'd she say that?"

"She's beautiful," Esther said again, and she watched the sunlight glow against the blonde's hair. "Isn't she?"

"She's not *that* pretty." Mariel kicked a pebble across the track.

Esther disagreed, and she hoped the girl was new to the neighborhood. She wanted to see her again.

"Esther!" Gabe wheezed as he ran towards her. "Your dad's on the phone. You forgot yours at home. He needs to talk to you."

Nausea swarmed within her belly. Breathing hard, she turned to look at him.

This wasn't good.

Her mind ran rampant. For a moment, she wondered if she was in trouble for finding the running girl attractive. Then her palms went clammy when she remembered she wasn't supposed to be hanging out with Mariel.

"What's wrong?" she croaked, but she knew the answer.

At least she thought she did.

Gabe's response was far worse.

"He says you need to come home now," Gabe said, and his voice trembled. His face was pale. "Your mom's not doing well."

Something in his voice curdled her stomach. Light-headed, her knees almost gave out. "Okay," she whispered, and remembered her mother's thin face turning towards her. *"I'll be okay, baby girl."*

Mariel put a gentle hand on her back. "Let's go. You'll be okay." His demeanor reminded her of Fr. Jerome's kindness, and she remembered why she liked him.

But as night fell, despair struck the Caravan household.

Esther Caravan said her last goodbye to her mother, Mary, before she passed away.

Screaming against her father's chest, Esther's heart bled. It was the first time she'd ever felt her heart ripped to shreds.

It wouldn't be the last.

Verse 4

~ Tools and Three Tires ~

Sunday, September 30th, 2012
Chicago, Illinois
11:36 PM

In the dark motel, sixteen-year-old Tira Petrov stared at the ceiling.

If she looked at her bloody hands, she'd panic.

Enhanced agents weren't supposed to panic. As she sat on the foot of the bed, her heart collided against her chest. Each labored breath hurt her lungs, worse than her sprints today. Enhanced agents slowed their breathing, but hers came fast. Enhanced agents calculated many actions with multiple different outcomes, but her thoughts migrated to one common denominator.

Papa.

He'd kill her.

Tira gasped and clenched her sticky hands.

No, think logically! She blinked at the ceiling. With frantic repetition, her feet thumped against the carpeted floor. The movements shook the mattress, and Tira envisioned the dead man face down on the bed, his body wobbling behind her.

That image brought her to her feet. She whirled to make sure he was still on the mattress. She should *never* turn her back to a dead man.

They weren't always dead.

She remembered learning that at five-years-old from the trainer with the scar across his lips. He'd replaced Trainer Sergei.

With trembling hands, the girl brushed disheveled hair away from her eyes. Then she regretted doing that, because now she'd have blood in her hair, and it'd be *evidence*. Had she learned *nothing*?

But the man was dead. He'd bled out near the center of the bed. The moonlight broke through the curtains; it glowed with impending judgment against the large bloodstains on the sheets.

As Tira processed one problem, she backed up and stumbled over the other two problems: Trainers Artyom and Boris.

They were dead too.

"Fuck," she whispered, and she struggled to breathe. Glancing down, she looked at their large bodies, still in athletic wear, strewn across each other with fresh bullet holes. Trainer Artyom had one through the forehead; Trainer Boris had another through the left eye. Their blood pooled and merged on the floor.

Her meticulous shots might have been something of pride if her trainers had been professionally assigned targets. Instead, the gore was a stark reminder that—

"Papa will kill me." Her hoarse whisper broke the silence, and then her mind moved faster as she contemplated the common denominator again.

Or Papa might be proud.

"I'm always concerned about your empathy levels," Papa said after he caught her scratching a dog's ears. "Could you kill this dog?"

Tira didn't understand him. Animals were different. She'd proven she had no issue taking another human life. Wasn't humanity its own biggest threat?

"Why are you training me?" she responded, urging the dog onwards before Papa got any ideas.

"I've told you. To become Russia's greatest weapon and her best assassin. You know this," he scoffed.

She took a risk. "So do you plan for me to assassinate a dog?" Tira braced for his strike, but it never came.

In fact, he smiled at her. "I will give you that one, little girl. Just this once."

Loud laughter brought her back to the present. Her pulse rose. Outside, footsteps galloped down the outdoor stairs that led to the parking lot. Tira's room sat on the second floor... which wasn't a concern when she'd arrived with her trainers.

Now she had to get three bodies downstairs.

What had she done?

She should have complied. *It* would be done by now, and there'd be no risk to her lifelong dedication... her future as Tira Petrov, a name her homeland would *chant* like they chanted for Papa.

Aleksey Petrov: Russia's greatest leader.

Tira Petrov: Russia's greatest weapon.

A car rumbled outside in the parking lot. Tires whirred, then squealed. The world was moving faster than she. People were making decisions; strangers raced several steps ahead.

Tira had been created to outpace the world, not vice versa.

It was her duty to assess, re-analyze, adjust to the situation, and act in accordance to her training. If she wanted to be the best, she needed to act now.

Tira spun. Her shadow danced across the wall as she moved to the bathroom and turned on the faucet. The water gurgled and then hissed from the spout. Wetting her lips, she scrubbed her hands. Blood reddened the water and trickled down the sink. When the water turned clear again, she looked in the mirror and met her own gaze. Her emerald eyes, wide with shock, caught sight of her untamed hair.

You're beautiful. A soft voice echoed in Tira's memory from earlier. It almost soothed her.

Did Americans always flirt so aggressively, or was that ice cream girl just weird?

A horn blared. Her pulse peaked again.

Now wasn't the time to think of the annoying girl at the track—the one with the brown, wavy hair and gorgeous eyes. She'd had ice cream in her hair.

Tira had blood in hers.

Papa would say she looked embarrassing—like shit.

"Fix your hair," he'd say, and force his fingers through her long, blonde waves until her scalp stung. *"What the fuck have you done to yourself? You look like—"*

"Shit," she whispered, and turned her attention to someone banging on the door.

Was it the cops? Had they heard the man in the bed scream? When she shot Artyom and Boris, had the silencer not done its job?

The fist pounded again. Tira remained very still. Against her will, her soft breath grew louder.

She didn't want to kill the cops. She would, if necessary, but she didn't *want* to. Papa would laugh at her for that thought.

"I see no reason to disturb natural order without logical purpose," Tira had said when they continued their conversation about the dog.

"I think this is the wrong room," a drunk man slurred outside the door, and a woman's giggle followed before footsteps staggered away.

Tira let out a steady breath. Drunks. She hated them. They were useless in society. Definitely a logical reason to "disturb the natural order", but too loud to dispatch without proper preparation. Luckily, they were gone, and Tira exited the restroom and wiped her wet hands on her black sweatpants.

She went to her bag. First, she needed gloves. The moonlight faded as Tira pulled black surgical gloves over her hands and reached for the pistol laying on the floor.

"One, two, three, four..." As she untwisted the silencer and stowed the weapon in the case, she counted in conscious effort to keep track of the time. Her whisper hissed through the room.

"Five... six... seven... eight..." Tira stepped across the entirety of the floor, memorizing the areas it creaked.

Once complete, she scurried to Trainer Boris, who lay face down with his head near Artyom's. The blood looked black in the darkness of the room.

Both men were huge. She didn't believe in a supernatural deity, but she prayed that there was no one beneath her room. It'd be a bitch trying to explain the dragging noises across the floor. And she couldn't forget the third body on the bed.

Fuck! Tira screamed inwardly. This situation wasn't ideal. There was still a flight to catch tomorrow, and it was her *trainers* who had the necessary documents to get her back to Russia.

A siren wailed and then faded. Blue, red, and white lights flickered past the window.

She couldn't panic now... but reality became much more dire when the sixteen-year-old attempted to move Boris to the bathroom tub. He was heavy. Blood smeared. His hand thumped against the floor.

A dog barked outside. Not aggressive. Just curious.

Tira straightened up, closed her eyes, and focused on each breath. She'd trained on this. It was overwhelming, yes, but her brain stored the necessary information.

Tira opened her eyes and observed the dead man near her feet. Then she scanned the entire hotel room, where one man bled through the bed, and the other two soaked the carpet.

Her mind went frantic again. She had no tools to cut the bodies apart. No bleach; no purchasing abilities. She needed transportation for herself and the bodies.

And *where* would she go?

She had less than eleven hours to solve these problems with perfection. There was no room for error, but here she was... standing in the midst of the chaos she'd created for herself.

Tira couldn't do this alone.

With a frustrated snarl, she kicked Boris in the stomach. His body wobbled a little. This was their fucking fault... for putting her in this situation. They deserved to die, but now she had to atone for her actions.

She could flee. Burn down the hotel, possibly?

Tira sank to her knees. Her belly swirled with nauseating fear.

No. Burning down the hotel would cause a much bigger investigation. And why would she flee? Papa was a horrible man—but he was her only key to success; a place among gods and goddesses.

An identity.

And Papa would never stop hunting until he found her.

Tira let out a spluttering breath and flicked her hand so that her wristwatch lit up. She hovered her lips over the screen.

"Imərjənsē..." she whispered, "... Project 4."

Severe consequences would come from this. But at least she had no hamster for Papa to threaten.

Or kill.

A man's voice crackled in Russian through the watch. "Someone's en route, Project 4. Standby. Are you injured?"

More sirens outside.

"I am not injured," Tira responded. "My car has broken down. I need tools and—" she looked at the three men, "—and three tires."

The voice crackled. "Understood. Assistance will arrive at your location shortly."

Now it was time to be patient and wait; to observe; to not make a further mess of things.

Project 4 stood up and returned to the edge of the bed. She sat, and she swallowed hard, hoping it would remove the violent pulse in her throat.

Shortly. How long was that? An hour or a day? Who would come to assist her, and would this person try to sell her too?

What if help didn't come before the police?

Or housekeeping?

Her body shook. It ached from earlier training and the struggle on the bed. For a moment, she wondered what it might be like if her only concern was ice cream in her hair.

Her eyelids fluttered. In response, she straightened her back. Fatigue had no place here, not after what she'd done. So, she stood, retrieved the pistol from her case again, twisted on the silencer, and waited. She couldn't make assumptions.

The next person to knock on her door might need to die too.

The knock came sooner than she expected. A voice murmured through the door.

"I am here for your car," he said in English. "I have tools and three tires."

The weapon went up. Tira crept towards the side of the door, removing herself from potential gunfire. "Who called for you?"

Without hesitation, the man responded with a scoff. "Technically, the owner of the LLC."

The password.

Tira went to the peephole. A man with a black hood stood outside the door with his back to it.

Biting her lip, she unlocked the door and stepped to the side with her firearm held in position. "Come in." She tried to sound firm, but her voice was hoarse.

The man slipped inside the room and closed the door. He wore a black mask over his face and kept an athletic bag strapped across his body. He was rather short. Stocky.

Tira could not tell how old he was. Young, maybe.

"First, put that thing down," he said in a quieter tone than she'd expected. "I don't like working while someone hovers... even if she *is* the daughter of my boss."

Something in his voice made her listen. Tira gritted her teeth and stowed the weapon.

"Second," he said, analyzing the gore, "we have a lot of work to do. Have you changed tires before?"

"Only in training," Tira muttered.

The man set the bag on the floor. "Well, pay attention," he said firmly. "This is a goddamn issue."

Tira suddenly realized how thirsty she was.

With soft footsteps, the man assessed the creaking on the floor and moved towards the bed to look at the man laying on it. He tilted his head a little and analyzed the dead man's pants that were crumpled at his ankles. "I see what happened here."

Tira wanted to vomit.

The masked agent said something she didn't expect. "I'm sorry to ask this. Any semen?"

It was almost like he cared, and that was very *strange*. No one in Petrov's organization *cared*.

Hastily, she shook her head. "It didn't get that far."

"Good," he said, and he peered at the man's face. "But we have a problem."

Weren't there enough problems?

"What?" Tira asked, and she prepared for the worst. She rubbed her clammy palms against her sweatpants.

The hooded agent straightened up and crept towards his bag. "I will do my best to fix this—" he unzipped the bag, "—but we might be fucked."

"Why?" Tira didn't want to know.

The agent held up a finger, scribbled words on a pad, and tossed it to her. "Give that back to me when you're done reading it."

Tira knelt and retrieved it.

The words she read turned her body cold. For the first time, she hoped a supernatural deity existed, and hoped she'd be granted mercy.

But... *Papa* was the only god she served, and he was not merciful. So she bit her tongue until she tasted blood in her mouth and read the words again.

"We need to ensure everything we do now is perfect... because you just killed a Senator of the United States."

VERSE 5
~ THE WRITINGS OF FR. JEROME ~

11/2/2012

I'm writing to tell you how heartbroken I am for the Caravan family. At the end of September, Mary Caravan passed away from cancer. It sounds like it developed very fast and there wasn't much they could do. Esther, Jason, and Todd haven't been to church since the funeral. Todd talks to me on the phone once in a while, but he's so depressed. I'm worried for him. They moved about twenty minutes away several years ago; otherwise, I'd be over to their house every day to make sure they're okay. It's so sad. I'll keep praying for healthy grief and peace.

Speaking of tragedy, the same week of Mary's death, controversy and media coverage exploded because Senator Thompson, the senator of Illinois, vanished. They're saying they haven't found a trace of him—at least, that's what the media says. There is a lot of speculation—you know, the usual. Senator Thompson leaves behind a wife and a teenage son. I'm not big on political discussion, but I'm bringing this up because Gabe Donovan's father, James Donovan, was close friends with the Thompson. James Donovan is a well-respected judge and, as I've mentioned before, his family attends St. Michael's. Sounds like James may take a swing at politics and run in the special elections to take Thompson's place.

1/1/2013

Happy New Year! Things have calmed a little. Todd and his kids returned to church. They're still grieving naturally. Esther has come to me in tears multiple times. I feel horrible for them. I'm glad they're back in a community that cares for them though.

Christmas was good. Today's a special day, because it's Mariel's 15th birthday! He is almost 6 feet. For his birthday, I took him snowboarding for the first time. Gabe came with us. I didn't attempt to snowboard. I am too old for that crap. Despite the fun he had today, Mariel was disappointed Esther could not come. Since the gun incident, Todd has been hesitant in letting her be with Mariel. I don't blame him, but I can tell it hurts Mariel. Todd is not as strict as he was at the beginning. I think he knows Esther finds joy with her friends, so they still spend time together, but only if Todd is there. Mariel respects that decision as well. In fact, since that decision, he has calmed down significantly. He has so much respect for me and the people around him. Mariel is consistently seeing a therapist (thank the Lord), and it is going well. This makes me very happy. I want Mariel to be happy, no matter what he thinks about his future (whatever that may be, but may it be blessed).

Talk soon.

5/23/2013

I need to write more often. I think Mariel and Gabe may both have a little crush on Esther. They both look at her when she isn't looking. I'm not sure if she's oblivious. She's definitely a beautiful girl, full of life and eagerness. She's constantly dancing. In fact, she's on the dance team at her school. When she talks, both boys listen. If Mariel talks to her, Gabe tries to get her attention. If Gabe talks to her, Mariel stares longingly but does not try to interrupt. I taught him well. I think Todd has a completely different situation to worry about now, however.

Side note: Still no trace of Senator Thompson. They presume he is deceased. Mayor Kaemon Spears has spoken on it because he was also a good friend of his. He believes it is likely foul play. Federal law enforcement suggests the same. What a sad situation.

Update: James Donovan is now the Senator of Illinois. I was a little concerned about a Thompson vs. Donovan feud, but so far, so good. Our mayor has, however, offered disdain at James for taking Thompson's seat, suggesting James didn't respect his friend's death. They can argue all they want—my concern is Gabe Donovan. He's in good spirits, but all this political mayhem with his father is definitely affecting the boy. He seems sad.

May God grant these politicians wisdom, and the ability to discern right from wrong.

10/3/2013

I am going to say this once and one time only. I wish Phil Jameson was not part of my congregation. He comes to church with something to complain about all the time. It isn't clean enough, it's too hot, it's too cold, the women dress inappropriately, the congregation is too liberal, etc. etc. I have had patience for YEARS with that man, but I nearly lost my patience the other day when he commented on Mariel's hair because it was long and "men should not have long hair". I asked him why.

"Because it is effeminate," he said. "Do you want people to perceive your son as a homosexual?"

I nearly lost my temper, but I remained calm. I said, "I might remind you to take a look at the icons of Christ. He is depicted as having long hair. Are you calling Jesus Christ a homosexual?"

It was the most satisfying thing I have said in a while. It left him red-faced and unable to respond. He left, and I smiled. Lord, forgive me for using your name to humiliate Phil.

12/25/2013

I had a series of nightmares again. My head hurts. I wanted to enjoy Christmas Day without a headache. The nightmares used to happen a couple times a year. Now they happen every few months. A rally attack; Justice for Ahdam; the people falling from the sky; a man with his face bashed in. It's horrible.

Merry Christmas. I hope my next entry is more positive.

P.S. Still no sign of Senator Thompson... and no suspects. So odd.

—Fr. Jerome

2/12/2015

"For God so loved the world, He gave His only Son, that whoever believes in him shall not perish but have eternal life."—John 3:16

I wrote this in hopes I might have something profound to say, but I feel nothing inspiring today. I have had this journal since 2004 and don't have many entries. Shows how much I commit to my writing!

The years have been good. Mariel is 17 and six-foot-four. He is such a good gentleman. His hair is still long (surprised?), and he is in his first year of college. I'm very proud of him. He wants to pursue a career in forensics. I have high hopes for him.

I am concerned, though. He's had no interest in women other than Esther. I've asked him if he wants to date her. He insists that he isn't interested in dating anyone. But I see the way he looks at her, and on that note, I see the way she looks at him too. Gabe is in hot pursuit of her, and Todd seems to like him more than my son. I see why... he is outgoing and bold. Mariel is quiet and some may consider him depressed, but he truly has so much love to give. He's had his moments, but don't we all? He's still seeing his therapist, and that seems to help. I truly hope he can find someone eventually. I don't want him to be lonely like me.

Blessings.

3/3/2015

Mariel was in a car accident last week. The entire car was destroyed. Mariel was pinned in. Everyone on scene said the car was filled with blood. When they got him out, he was bleeding from his femoral artery. They were astounded... because he should have been dead. I'm so happy Mariel is okay... but I haven't had a break from anxiety or nightmares since then. I am trying to be calm. I can't stop thinking about the bullet incident, and Fr. Paul. Why am I so afraid? Why can't I just be happy that my son is alive?

As my dad said, "Give your anxieties to God." He also called me a "nancy" soon after that, but that's beside the point.

11/4/2015

Been busy. Mariel got Employee of the Month for July! So proud of him.

01/13/2016

Looks like Mayor Kaemon Spears will be the next governor of Illinois. Following his success as a young mayor of Chicago and transitioning to governor has been interesting. He has introduced a lot of good policies for the city of Chicago, so I am hoping he will do the same for the state. He seems to be a solid character, which is probably best because Mariel told me the other day he would be President. Mariel was correct the last time he said Spears would win the election as Mayor.

I still don't understand my son. I have had him for close to 18 years and I still don't feel like I know him. Is that normal?

Update: Senator Thompson, while still missing, was declared legally dead. There's outrage now. Hopefully his family finds peace.

Fr. Jerome

5/1/2016

I'm tired. I am also disappointed that I could never provide a more fulfilling life for Mariel. Priests don't get rich. It's a depressing journal entry, but I am feeling old and not very worthy at the moment. I have to stop helping Mariel with college for a little bit because I mismanaged my money in my younger years and am paying the price for it now. I think Mariel has a sense of how I have been feeling because he keeps telling me that he will take care of me one day. I don't want him to think like that...mainly because I feel like my days are numbered. I am healthy, I have no health concerns at this point, but the reality is I am 71 years old. I won't live forever. No one will.

I need to write an entry that is less depressing. I'll talk the next time I have something positive to share.

9/23/2016

Happy birthday to me! Mariel surprised me today by taking me to an apple orchard. We spent the day picking apples, drinking cider and eating donuts. Mariel ate seven. I don't know how he can keep as fit as he does with the amount he eats. I had the opportunity to spread the gospel as well today! We started talking to a couple with four adopted children and a fifth in process. What a great couple! They were looking for a church to attend as they are new to the area, and I suggested my church. They had said they had been attending Protestant denominations and were looking for something different. I hope to see them this Sunday! I am 72, don't judge my excitement for the little things.

Time for bed. I am glad I could make a positive journal entry today. Good night, and God bless.

10/2/2016

I found an old letter from Fr. Paul today. It brought me flashbacks to the day I talked to his sister, and she told me about his crime in Russia. I still wonder to this day what led him to do such a thing. Part of me wants to dismiss him as a crazy person that had an amazing ability hiding his true self. The other part of me wants to give him credit and believe there was a reason. It has been eating at me lately. I never tried contacting him again. I was afraid of what I might find out. It's been haunting me lately though. I never told Mariel that history... does that make me a horrible dad? Mariel has never asked me much about his past either. He genuinely doesn't seem curious. I don't know if that is a good thing or a bad thing.

He is doing very well in college. Still hasn't dated anyone; still seems all eyes for Esther. I asked him about this recently and told him that it wasn't healthy if she was the reason he wasn't dating. He tried to dismiss me. He even got angry. Finally, he broke, and he admitted he liked her—but did not want to pursue a relationship due to "personal issues". I refrained from telling him that Todd probably would not approve of the relationship anyway and merely nodded my head. I was, and am, a little hurt that he referred to his reasons as "personal". I guess I thought at this point in years he would feel more comfortable telling me certain things. I will let it rest though. He will tell me if and when he is ready.

Time for bed. Blessings.

1/1/2017

Happy birthday, Mariel. 19 years old. Goodness, time flies. Unfortunately, he received some sad news today. A friend he was attending college with was killed in gun violence. It hurts my heart. Kids so young have so much promise and instead are exposed to horrors they should never experience within communities that should be their safe haven. That aside, we held a birthday celebration at the church today for him. Most of the congregation got him a card or stayed to celebrate with us. He was glowing. I could tell he appreciated the love. Happy New Year, and may it be a great 2017.

CHAPTER 3: VERSE 1
~ COFFEE. MARIEL. BOOKSTORE ~

Saturday, January 12th, 2019
Chicago, Illinois

The buzzing sound wouldn't stop. Neither did the dull, nauseating throb in her head. Her eyelids opened. With blurred sight, Esther saw a black vertical fan. It rotated back and forth. Cool air tickled her face. It was a nice fan. Sleek.

But she didn't have a fan.

The vibrations stopped, and she closed her eyes. Then it started once more. That fucking buzzing. Her eyes opened again, a little wider this time, and she regretted it. Sunlight stung her vision. Groaning, she crawled her fingers across the nightstand and grasped her purple-cased phone. She lifted it and read the caller identification.

"DAD".

Fuck.

Adrenaline worsened the pain in her head. Her stomach gurgled. As she swiped her thumb against the screen and brought the phone to her ear, another surge of panic went straight to her bowels. She didn't own *Chicago Cubs* blankets, posters, and the other collectibles on the walls. Her bedroom had no lounge chair. It was also not this organized.

"Hello?" Esther inquired, as if she had no clue who occupied the other line.

"Where the *hell* are you? It's almost 10:30!" Todd's roar vibrated her ear.

Wincing, she pulled the phone away from her ear and rolled. Something solid stopped her from completing the movement. It was warm. Soft. Hairy. Like a *man's* goddamn arm.

Her panic rose.

"Esther! Did you hear me?" Todd's voice cracked. It often did when he reached a certain level of rage. Normally, it was funny listening to a middle-aged man's voice crack like that of a pubescent boy.

Not today.

"Dad, sorry, I was really tired." Her voice cracked too.

None of this was good. The pain in her head felt intense, but the dull, painful ache between her legs eliminated all other reality of pain.

Could she not remember what happened last night?

Or did she not want to?

"Esther," Todd hounded, "we had people outside the store waiting for it to open. If it weren't for Mariel seeing the damn line from the diner and calling me, I never would have known. Where the hell are you?"

Esther gasped. The arm against her back moved.

Mariel. Now she needed to shit. Not only had she failed to open the Caravan bookstore (whatever—maybe her dad should open more often), but she had missed her coffee date with Mariel.

"Dad..." Esther didn't know what to say. How to lie. How to keep herself from vomiting bile. "I—"

"Get to the bookstore *now*." The phone call ended.

Esther sat up. The sheets fell from her bare torso. She wrapped her arms around her breasts, and, gritting her teeth, she turned her head to look at her bedmate. She stared at the muscular chest of a blond young man with a close-cropped cut. A snore gurgled from his mouth. Drool plopped against the white pillow.

"Holy *hell*." Esther scrambled from the bed, dragging the sheets with her. She stumbled backward, gasping like she hadn't had an inkling who occupied the bed with her. "Gabe, wake up!"

Shivering, she stood in the middle of the room. Her brown hair cascaded past her shoulders. It tickled her back, and the sunlight blasted her eyes from the large, city-view window.

People usually woke up on the wrong *side* of the bed.

She'd woken up in the *wrong* bed.

This was not going to be a good day.

"Gabe!"

"Huh?" The man flopped onto his back. He rubbed his head. "What? God, it's early—stop screaming."

Incredulously, Esther stared at him. "Are you kidding me? What the *fuck* happened last night? Why am I in your *fucking bedroom?*" Her knuckles whitened as she clutched the sheets against her body.

Gabe raised himself onto his elbows and squinted. His muscles flexed. "First of all, calm down."

"Don't fucking tell me to calm down."

"Second of all, we were at Ashley's birthday party last night. Remember?" He wiped the drool from his mouth. "You wouldn't stop drinking. I had to switch your vodka with water and tell you it was booze." He frowned, contemplating. "And somehow you believed me."

Shaking her head with horror, Esther began a wild search for her clothes. Black panties by the lounge chair. Push-up bra by the doorway. Jeans in the hall.

Shit.

"Esther, relax. It was one time."

Furious, she stomped toward him. "I don't *remember* much, *you fuck!*"

Gabe shrunk back. His face paled. "Dude. Don't. It was something we *both* wanted, I promise. Please sit down and talk to me for a second? I can make coffee, and we can clear this up."

Coffee. Mariel. Bookstore.

Esther wanted to scream. Instead, she snatched her undergarments from the floor. "I don't want coffee with you, Gabe, I was supposed to have coffee with *Mariel!*" Her head spun. The nausea intensified.

Gabe blinked. "*That's* what this is about? Get over him, Esther, he doesn't like you like that."

Struggling to cover herself with the sheet, Esther attempted to slip into her black panties and nearly fell. "You don't know *shit* about our relationship."

Gabe snorted. "Welp, by the looks of it, you fucked me last night and not him, now *didn't you?*"

With wide eyes, Esther straightened up. Rage activated her legs. She stumbled toward him, determined to commit some act of violence. Then it came. The puke. Alcoholic bile, mixed with disgust and shame, spurted from her mouth onto the white carpet.

"Oh *God*, really, Esther?"

As if vengeful, her abdominals strained again. She spluttered, coughed, and spat what was left in her esophagus. When she finally caught her breath, she turned her eyes to him. "Fuck you."

Gabe sat up. "What do you want from me? I was just as fucking drunk. It's not like I planned this."

"I was a *virgin*."

"I just said I didn't plan this. I'm sorry."

She'd lost her virginity to a childhood friend, the *wrong* friend. If there was *any* chance of Mariel having feelings for her, it wouldn't be for long. He would never respect her after this.

"Esther? What can I do? *I'm sorry.*"

"Yeah, I'm sorry too." Esther zipped and buttoned her jeans. It took extraordinary willpower not to beat the shit out of Gabe right now. She'd end up on the news for stomping the senator's son, and then she'd *have* to tell Mariel why she beat up his best friend.

"Am I *really* that bad?" Gabe reached for his phone and slid towards the edge of the bed. His mouth flopped open.

Esther scrambled around the room, dizzied as she searched for her shirt. "Why's your mouth open like a fucking fish?" she snapped, dropping to the floor to look under the bed.

"My dad... he just texted me."

"Big whoop. So glad you didn't have to wake up next to him."

Gabe disregarded her comment and stood up. His hairy legs wobbled next to her as she searched under the bed. "No, this is legit news. He's going to run in the Republican primaries for president next year."

Unable to locate her shirt beneath the bed, Esther crawled back to her feet. She didn't give a shit about Gabe's dad. How could her childhood friend act like *nothing* was wrong?

"Where's my shirt?" Esther barked, huffing towards the hallway.

"Somewhere in the living room, I think. I don't know."

This was a nightmare.

"Esther, come on," Gabe persisted. The floor creaked. He was following her.

"Don't talk to me." Esther stormed about the apartment kitchen. Now searching without a logical method, she opened cupboard doors and slammed them.

Gabe's voice held a hint of desperation. "Please don't let this ruin our friendship. I'll do anything."

Esther stopped moving and glowered at him. He stood there, hands up, and the sun cast a ray on his limp penis. Right now, she couldn't even think beyond this horrific morning. The thought of spending any further time with him made her feel even sicker. But he offered to do *anything* so—

"Say nothing. Don't say *anything* to *anyone* about this." Esther pointed a large kitchen knife in his direction.

Unbothered by the knife, Gabe nodded once. "I promise."

"I mean it, Gabe. This never fucking happened. I was never here." The knife bobbed in rhythm to her words.

"I promise."

"And don't call me. Don't come sniffing for more. Don't ask me on a date. *Nothing* happened between us." Esther caught sight of a green sleeve dangling from the top of the refrigerator. "Why the fuck is my shirt on top the fridge?"

"You—"

"You know what, don't answer that." With a snap, Esther brought the green, long-sleeved shirt down from the refrigerator. A box of *Mini Wheats* followed the shirt, bounced off the counter, and fell to the floor. Cereal clattered.

"Do you have to leave my apartment a complete disaster?"

Yes. In fact, she was tempted to burn it.

Esther pulled on the shirt, yanked up the scoop neck to cover her cleavage, and exited the kitchen towards the door where she found her small black purse and zip-up knee-length heeled boots. "I'm sure '*the First Lady*' will clean it for you, Gabe."

Gabe groaned. "Would you *stop*?"

She zipped the last boot and straightened up. Her eyes fell to his crotch. It looked like a little tumor between his legs. "Put your small dick away." Esther jabbed her middle finger into the air, exited the apartment, and then slammed the door.

The wind was so cold it hurt. As her hair blew across her face, Esther slipped and stumbled through the snow on the sidewalk. She hugged herself as the long-strapped purse flapped against her hip.

Her car was home. She needed to call a ride service. Was there still alcohol on her breath?

Why was she a fucking idiot?

"Whatever choices you make in life," her mom always said, *"make sure they're wise ones, my angel."*

The tears came. A sob spluttered from her throat, and so did a burp. It was gross, and she could definitely smell alcohol on her breath.

As mucus threatened to dribble from her nose, Esther reached for her phone.

Three missed calls from *"Hawk the Turd"*. When had her brother called, and what the fuck did he want?

He could wait.

Blinking the tears away, she swiped across the screen with numbed fingers and opened the ride-service app. As she worked her fingers across the screen, the prior night's events came back in brief flashes.

Dancing. Laughing. Bass-driven music and the warmth of booze.

Esther licked her numbing lips and almost slipped in the snow as she pulled up her contact for Ashley Morris. As her breath swirled in the frigid air, she typed—

"My dad can't know about the party last night. No one can. He will kill me."

Dramatic, yes, because Todd wouldn't kill her. After her mom died, he hadn't even managed to figure out what discipline looked like.

"You're grounded for two weeks," he'd say, and then leave them to figure out what exactly they'd been grounded from doing.

This embarrassed Esther. She was twenty. She was in college, and she wasn't a child. Her friends reminded her of this. They laughed at her because—

"Who the fuck gets grounded at twenty, Esther?" Then they would giggle. And she'd have to giggle too, because what else was she supposed to fucking do? She couldn't explain her household dynamic to her self-sufficient group of friends because she barely even understood it herself.

She wanted to put her foot down and remind Todd that she was an adult now, but mixed feelings always halted her: trepidation to lose the security she had under her dad's roof, and guilt that he might feel abandoned. The man didn't date, and he rarely spent time with friends. Esther, Hawk, and Mary's bookstore defined his life.

Moving out was tempting, though. Countless times, Esther had considered it to experience college and get a break from Todd's constant hovering. She adored her father, and she understood his protectiveness after Mary's death, but she needed a moment to figure out her own fucking identity.

Hell, she still hadn't told him the truth about her sexual orientation. In his eyes, Esther was a young, Christian woman destined to find a good husband with a stable career before engaging in any sexual relations. What he didn't know was that she *was* a young, Christian woman... one who'd sucked dick and kissed a couple of girls in high school.

The horror.

Regardless, Esther hadn't intended to lose her virginity yet. She'd wanted to save that for someone special. Gabe Donovan was not it.

As she awaited the ride, Esther shivered in the snow and opened the other text messages from Mariel Nadier. Her heart beat with dread.

7:55 A.M. *"Hey. Just got here. See you soon."*

8:13 A.M. *"Are you okay? You usually aren't this late, lol."*

8:51 A.M. *"I need to clock in. Hope you're okay. Let me know."*

"Fuck," she hissed.

How was she supposed to respond? *Sorry, Mars, I got slammed last night and then fucked our best friend, haha.*

Yeah, no. He could never find out about this.

Chewing her lip, Esther typed. *"Hey, Mars, I am so, so sorry. Long night, I was passed out. Are you stopping by the bookstore when you get out?"* She waited.

Ping. *"No, I need to get to the church and help Dad do some stuff. Have a good day, sorry I couldn't see you."* Even when he was mad, he was a gentleman. The hangover was horrible, but the disappointment and shame felt worse.

Last night, after losing the hip-hop dance competition for University of Chicago, the team and other friends went to Ashley's apartment to celebrate her birthday. Esther, both dancer and choreographer, had wanted nothing more than this win. She'd worked her ass off for first place, not second place. So she went to the party with Gabe and she drank. A lot.

Esther should have known it'd be an issue. She knew drinking made her needy, emotional, and horny. First, she and Gabe cuddled on the couch. It was fine—a comforting touch belonging to a childhood friend who cared. Then, several drinks down, the hand on her thigh had no gender, nor was it attached to the kid she grew up with. It was a hand attached to a human being who could take care of business and help her forget her failures.

Esther didn't remember who asked to go to his house. Together, they took an Uber to Gabe's apartment. With an ill feeling in her gut, she remembered how they'd barely been in the door before they exchanged awkward, drunken kisses. Clothes came off. They were on the bed. She remembered flashes—Gabe's aggressive thrusting and grunting. It hurt. There'd been no warm-up, and she definitely hadn't experienced an orgasm.

In the icy roadway, a sedan sped past her. With panic, Esther tried to figure out if Gabe had put on a condom. Her thumbs flew over the screen again. *"Tell me you wore a condom."*

Ping. *"Okay. I wore a condom."*

That fucking monster. *"You didn't wear a condom, did you?"*

Ping. *"I don't think so..."*

Esther wanted to scream. It rose from her throat, and she bit her tongue. Now she'd have to consider other resources, and if her dad found that out, he would definitely kill her. Bending her head, Esther covered her face with her hands.

As she stood there, she heard an engine. Tires crunched against the snow and the vehicle came to a stop in front of her. Embarrassed, she looked up, shocked that her ride arrived so fast.

It wasn't her ride service.

Inside of a familiar, blue sedan sat Fr. Jerome. The window came down, and he bent over the steering wheel. That comforting smile she adored played across his lips. "Little cold to be going for a leisurely walk, don'tcha think?"

With wet eyes and a numb nose, she nodded.

"Can I take you somewhere?"

Without hesitation, she rushed towards the car and opened the passenger door. The heater's warmth surrounded her like a hug.

Fr. Jerome looked at her with concern and curiosity. His veiny hand shook a little over the steering wheel.

It bothered her—how old he was getting. She never wanted to lose him.

"First of all, are you alright? Second, where am I taking you?"

Esther rubbed her arms. She stared out at the city through the windshield for a brief second before responding. Her mind felt numb too. Then, squeezing her hands together, she looked at the old priest and flashed a quick smile. "I'm okay. Just feeling a little sick. I need to get to the bookstore for work though, can you take me there?"

Fr. Jerome pressed the gas. "Absolutely. Do you have a cold? And why don't you have a coat?"

Esther lifted her hands to the heater. Her palms tingled. "I don't know," she answered, and she realized she'd provided one answer to two questions. Her thoughts were scattered, directed towards Mariel and last night's screw up; Gabe's lack of a condom, what to tell her dad.

Sitting here with Fr. Jerome made her realize how easy it would be to spill her chaos to the kind priest, a man she loved like another father. Still, she feared condemnation. Growing up with her dad's stance against premarital sex didn't help her social anxiety around religious figures, even ones she trusted. Yes, Todd's conservatism had always driven her to rebel a little, but not by means of fucking a friend she had no romantic interest in. Rebellion meant underage drinking; sneaking a joint, and spending time with Mariel against her dad's wishes... which was stupid, by the way.

Ever since the "suicide" attempt, Todd hadn't allowed much leniency for Mariel. It drove her mad, because while it hadn't been the most virtuous of humor, it'd been a joke.

At least, that's how Mariel explained it.

But Todd's compliments towards Gabe never faltered, and that also pissed her off. Gabe was a douchebag. Mariel? A gentleman. Gabe was the type to not wear a fucking condom on a one-night stand. Mariel was the type to keep his eyes in respectful places (usually), despite her multiple attempts to wear clothing she hoped might spike his interest. It didn't seem to work. He'd made no effort in validating her flirtations.

Gabe's animalistic thrusting popped back into her memory. She smelled his alcoholic breath, and she felt the saliva that sprayed her face each time he grunted. Disgust boiled in her gut. Was she a *whore*?

"Esther. Your face is white. Are you sure you're okay?" Fr. Jerome's voice held deeper concern now.

Nope. Not okay.

"I'm fine, I promise. I just need to get to work." She tried to smile again and pulled out her phone to cancel the ride service. "I really, really appreciate the ride. Thank you."

Fr. Jerome glanced at her and smiled a little. His brows curved up, something she noticed he did whenever he felt concern for someone he cared about. "Anytime, Esther. You know I think the world of you."

"I feel the same." Esther reached for his hand, squeezed it, and then returned her attention to the oncoming city. She hoped she would never disappoint Fr. Jerome.

They arrived in the heart of downtown Chicago. It was quieter than normal for a mid-morning Saturday. People, clad in their winter garments, walked briskly down the sidewalks.

Fr. Jerome pulled to the right side of the street where an ice cream shop (*CLOSED UNTIL SPRING*), a few clothing stores, and *Caravan's Books* all connected in side-by-side suites. But Esther's eyes clung to the other side of the street where the diner (*Pete's*) was located.

"Mariel works today," Fr. Jerome spoke quietly, as if he knew her thoughts.

Esther lowered her eyes, hoping it'd block his insight into her mind. "I know." She moved her hand to the door handle. "Are you going to see him now?"

"Not for long, just grabbing a coffee to go and heading to the church for a little bit."

Esther opened the door and turned to him, keeping one leg out of the car. "Will you tell him to come see me when he gets off of his shift? I missed coffee with him this morning and I'd like to apologize."

Fr. Jerome smiled. "Of course. I'm sure he will understand. He'd better. I raised the doof."

"Thank you, Father. I'll see you at church tomorrow." She exited the car, darted one last glance at *Pete's Diner*, and then entered the bookstore.

* * *

Esther loved the smell of the bookstore. Her mom always described it as "sweet, musty comfort", something Esther couldn't explain to people who didn't ever hold a book to their nose.

The mid-sized bookstore contained multiple couches, lounge chairs, and coffee tables. It was a welcoming environment. The lights weren't overwhelming, and it rarely got so crowded that the environment became overstimulating.

Not far from the entrance, a few people stood in line as Todd Caravan accepted their purchases behind the counter. Todd handed a bag to a patron before his eyes found Esther. With an abrupt cock of his head, he gestured for her to come to him. Hastily, Esther scurried forward.

When the last customer left the store, Todd turned to his daughter and leaned against the counter. He folded his arms over his small beer gut and stared at her.

Mouth dry, Esther stared back.

"You wanna tell me where you were? Your car was home. We thought you were in your room all night until this morning when, you know, your car was *still* home when you were supposed to be *here*." He directed his forefinger down.

Esther tried to control her body's involuntary trembling. "I spent the night at Ashley's last night."

"Why didn't you take your car?"

"I didn't feel like driving in the snow, Dad."

"Okay, well, is there any reason you didn't want to send a text and just let me know?"

Because I'm fucking old enough to do what I want, Dad.

An angry horn blared outside. Esther jumped. "I was depressed that we lost the competition last night. I should've let you know." She took a risk. "Call Ashley. She will tell you the same thing."

Todd turned and gathered receipts strewn about the counter. "I'm going to let you have this one. But if I find out any differently, you won't have any privileges." He faced her again. "*None.*"

"I'm sorry, Dad. It won't happen again." It probably would.

Todd gathered the rest of the receipts and exited the workspace. "Are you good to stay here then so I can go home and get some work done? Your grandma will be here soon."

"Yes, Dad."

"Lose the attitude, Squirt." Todd walked towards the exit. "Let me know if you need anything. You know the drill. I'll come pick you up at six. Oh—" he stopped at the door. "Call your brother. He's pretty upset with you."

Esther frowned. "*Why?*"

Todd stared. "Apparently you promised him breakfast this morning. Now *I* have to listen to his 'special project' talk all day. Which would be fine, except that it's always when he's forgotten deodorant, and he gets all animated and waves his arms and then I smell armpit all day. So, thanks." He shook his head, smiled a little bit, lifted a hand to wave, and then pushed open the door.

Puzzled, Esther watched him leave. *When* had she promised Hawk breakfast? She didn't remember ever agreeing to such a—

Oh.

"Goddamn it," Esther groaned and leaned against the counter with a sigh. She remembered now.

Two days ago, she had finally responded to her little brother's plea: let him tell her about this "world-changing science project" of his. Esther hoped that might shut him up. Then, one day later, she forgot the promise and scheduled coffee with Mariel.

Oops.

Now, of course, Hawk would throw a bitch fit like he always did when he didn't get attention or get whatever he wanted.

She would deal with that later.

Esther reached for a spray bottle and a rag to get to work.

She didn't mind working here. In fact, she enjoyed it, but work would be daunting today. Esther began her hourly upkeep of the store as she listened to the murmur of the television. In the corner, it hung suspended over the enclosed counter space where Esther and Todd worked the registers. It was only there because Esther begged for it, but now her dad used it more than she did. He watched two channels—sports and conservative news. Sometimes, to fuck with him, she changed it to liberal news.

"Illinois Governor Kaemon Spears has discussed running in the 2020 Republican primaries next year. He spoke on Project Savior and the opportunities it has given healthcare in the United States. Can you tell us what you think about—"

"Who the fuck cares?" Esther grumbled and flipped the second copy of *War and Peace* right side up on the bookshelf.

Her phone vibrated. Hopeful that it was Mariel, Esther retrieved it and moaned with frustration.

"Hawk the Turd".

Why was her little brother calling now? It was too late for breakfast. The deed was done. She'd failed; she didn't need a reminder right now. But... the increasing guilt drove her finger to swipe and answer the call.

"I'm sorry, Hawk."

Her brother's pubescent voice cracked over the phone. "What the *fuck!* Why are you so fucking selfish?"

Esther's face went hot. She dropped the rag. "I'm not in the mood, Hawk, don't come at me." The guilt wouldn't go away though.

"Dad doesn't have time, *you* don't *make* time. You promised me breakfast like two months ago, too!" he screamed.

Esther closed her eyes against the throbbing pain in her head. Why did he have to be so loud?

"Hawk, stop screaming. I'll make it up to you."

Was he crying? Esther didn't know, but she heard a sniffle right before the call ended.

"Fuck!" she cried, and she pounded the heel of her hand against her forehead. Inhaling sharply, Esther tossed the cleaning supplies on the couch and approached the bookstore exit.

A male guest spoke on the television. *"Project Savior is like Roe V. Wade. You're gonna have the protesters, and you're gonna have the supporters. You're gonna have the truth, and you're gonna have the conspiracy theories."*

Esther flipped the *Open* sign to the *Closed* side. It clattered against the cold glass. Hesitant, she looked across the street. What if Mariel didn't want to see her?

"What conspiracies?" the female news anchor asked.

Esther thought of her brother too. She would call him back after she saw Mariel.

The man on the television laughed. *"For years, people have thought Project Savior and anything affiliated is a means to an end, you know? A few rumors have people thinking Project Savior is producing, I don't know, DNA anomalies. Superhumans. It's hogwash. This is America. We'd have to stop eating fast food!"*

Esther braced herself and pushed open the door. The freezing wind made it difficult. It tugged at her hair, sending it flying about her face.

As the Open/Closed sign on *Caravan's Books* swung back and forth, she checked for traffic, and then she stepped from the curb. Snow swirled in the air, and Esther Caravan began her short journey towards *Pete's Diner.*

She needed to make amends... a lot of them.

Mariel Nadier would be the first.

VERSE 2
~ AGENT 4 ~

Saturday, January 12th, 2019
Moscow, Russia

The dim lights in the spacious bedroom cast shadows. Tira Petrov leaned closer to the mirror. Her cheekbone was swollen, but the makeup covered the bruise—hopefully enough for Petrov's satisfaction.

It wouldn't do to piss off the President of Russia before attending this formal dinner.

"Meet me at the ballroom doors at eight," Papa had instructed. *"Cover the bruises. I don't want you to look like shit."*

Atop her desk, the bulbs lining the vanity mirror illuminated Tira's cold green eyes. She analyzed her appearance. Her red evening gown looked like a river of blood against the dark atmosphere.

One hour. In sixty minutes, she would link arms with Papa and step into her role as an agent. Not a project.

Was this what joy felt like? She didn't know. Perhaps it was something else. Something *better*.

Accomplishment.

Fools felt joy for trivialities such as relationships, material items. True accomplishment—fulfilling a duty with which *she* was entrusted—was far superior.

From the stool, Tira reached for the lipstick. Behind her, a woman's whisper stopped her.

"Wait."

In the mirror's reflection, a young woman approached. Raven hair cascaded over her bare shoulders, and the naked woman slipped her fingers onto Tira's shoulders.

"Let me kiss you first," she murmured.

Tira turned in the stool and met the woman's blue eyes with hers. She stood up, taller than her lover, and bent her head for a kiss. The kiss was slow, tender, a culmination of their earlier satiated desire.

As the young woman's fingertips crept within Tira's, the agent wondered if she would ever experience such a nurturing touch again. This beauty, Olivia, had introduced Tira to the concept of nurturing. She'd also taught her the ability to reciprocate the tenderness.

Running the tip of her tongue across Olivia's bottom lip, Tira pulled back. "I need to finish getting ready," she whispered.

Olivia protruded her lip.

"Do not pout. You need to get ready, too." Tira raised an eyebrow.

"I don't want to serve Petrov's friends." Olivia reached for the lipstick on the table and twisted open the cap. "I want to serve you."

Tira's face, warm, relaxed a little, but she did not respond.

Olivia raised the lipstick. "May I?"

Hesitant, Tira studied the woman before her. "Olivia—"

"I won't mess up," Olivia said, quickly. "I promise." She stepped closer. "Trust me."

Tira did not trust anyone. She couldn't. However, she glanced at the time. "I cannot be late to meet Petrov. Do not mess up." Her voice sounded harsher than she wished, but it didn't deter Olivia. It used to, but the Kremlin server had grown accustomed to the *tone*.

Olivia smiled and gestured to the stool. "Sit down, please." Hovering, she ran the red lipstick across Tira's bottom lip. "You're beautiful."

Tira stiffened. She thought of the racetrack in Chicago, how that ice cream girl had told her the same thing. But the memory of the ice cream girl didn't make her heart race.

The aftermath did.

That bloody, *bloody* aftermath in the hotel room later that night.

"You know what you are?" Papa had asked. *"A cunt. A fucking dumb one, too. We wouldn't be in this situation had you just—"*

"Tira?" Olivia's fingers touched her chin. "You're trembling."

Tira slapped her hand away and stood. "I'm not."

"I'm not finished," Olivia protested.

"Yes, you are." Tira took the lipstick from Olivia and leaned towards the mirror to complete the task... but her hand *was* trembling. She could see it in the mirror. With a quick sigh, she lowered her arm.

"Olivia, I shouldn't have slapped your hand." It was difficult... admitting fault. But Olivia hadn't deserved such treatment. It wasn't her fault Tira had been an inexperienced sixteen-year-old with the mindset of a fool.

Olivia rubbed her arms. "I should get ready."

Tira watched her retreat towards the bed and then returned her gaze to the mirror. She adjusted the pin in her hair, assessed the thick blonde bun on her head, and then slipped her feet into the red stilettos near the dresser.

"Will you come later tonight?" Tira approached the long mirror in the corner of the room. The evening gown fell to her left ankle. It slit at her right knee and exposed a smooth, muscular leg that threatened to cramp from yesterday's final training session. The dress embraced her curves, but it still allowed the option to move with ease.

One always had to be prepared.

"You don't think you made me come enough this afternoon?" Olivia teased.

"You know what I mean." Tira wanted to jest in return, but she was exhausted. Unlike yesterday, the day hadn't been physical. It'd been mental. Final exams; tests that not only challenged her intelligence, but her psyche. After that, something akin to graduation—a meeting in Petrov's office when he withdrew the final results, stared at the paperwork, and then said—

"Congratulations. Not only did you pass, but your results are the highest."

She, standing at attention, hadn't blinked. *"In my class?"*

Petrov hadn't blinked either. *"In... Russia."*

His voice, despite its stoic tone, had almost sounded—*shocked.* Like he hadn't *expected* her to succeed.

Then, Petrov had produced a black case from beneath his desk. *"Ready for your reward?"*

Movement snapped Tira from her memory.

Buttoning her white shirt, Oliva came to stand beside Tira and looked at her in the mirror. "I can't get enough of you. I'll be here."

"Good." Tira stood in a militant manner before the mirror and forced herself to relax. Training, for now, was over. "I've got a lot of pent-up frustration."

"I'll take care of that for you." Olivia tucked her shirt into her black skirt. She left a button open just above her cleavage. "Shall I leave it like this?"

Tira eyed her. "You may do as you like."

"But I like when you tell me what to do."

Tira smoothed her dress, turned to Olivia, and cupped her chin. "You are not mine. Do as you *like*." She kissed her once and then withdrew, ignoring the look of disappointment that crossed Olivia's face. "I need to finish preparing alone. I'll see you in less than an hour."

With a sigh, Olivia slipped on her shoes and then walked towards the door. "One of these days, I'll get you to admit it."

"Admit what?"

"That you're capable of love." Olivia smiled, but her eyes lowered, as if she didn't believe her own words.

Tira scoffed and left the mirror. "I am a biological result of *Project Savior*, Olivia. Even if I *could* experience such a thing, I don't want to."

Olivia rested her hand on the doorknob. Her smile left. "Why not?"

"Because I wouldn't accomplish what I truly want," Tira deadpanned. She despised explaining something so obvious.

"Truly want?"

"I want to be the best product that has ever come from *Project Savior*." Tira tilted her head. Her eyes darted to the small bruise on her wrist.

"Ready for your reward?" Petrov clicked open the case. Inside of it contained a device: a microchip remover. "Congratulations again. You're your own agent, Tira. Take this and remove the tether."

Tira raised her eyes. "I want to be the best in the world."

In silence, Olivia searched her face. Then, she acknowledged Tira with a nod and unlatched the lock on the door. "Then you will be. I'll see you soon."

*   *   *

Classical music swelled in the hallway, and Tira's heels clicked against the polished floor. Though she'd walked the Kremlin halls throughout her childhood, she remained vigilant. Familiarity didn't mean safety.

Her eyes captured each movement, her ears each sound. Tira's nose flared. The combined scents of male cologne, cigar smoke, and a well-seasoned meal thickened the air.

Her heels echoed. It was strange to hear such a sharp sound. It contrasted against the rhythmic drills in the *Project Savior* task force and the military, where boots stomped in synchronized cadence against unyielding cement.

The lights radiated the hallway, and the music in the ballroom vibrated the floor. Armed guards lined the walls. They straightened their stance in response to Tira's approach.

And outside of the Grand Ballroom's doors, President Aleksey Petrov awaited her.

"Hello, my sweet," Petrov called, and reached out his hand. Within a dimpled smile, his white teeth competed against the blazing lights. "You look *stunning*."

Tira resisted the urge to roll her eyes. Instead, she bowed her head a little. "I wouldn't want to embarrass you, Papa. Obviously."

He raised an eyebrow and offered his arm. A smirk played across his lips. "And yet, you've managed to do so countless times."

"Perhaps you're easily embarrassed."

Petrov's arm tightened against hers. The music swelled behind the double doors. "You're not free to be a brat simply because you've completed training," he murmured, and his eyes met hers. "Watch yourself."

Goosebumps tickled Tira's skin. Facing the doors, she responded with a curt nod.

"Do you know what is about to happen in this room, Tira?"

It seemed like a trick question. She had many different answers, but she chose the only one that would appease him. "Anything that you wish to happen, Papa."

The guards on both sides of the doors looked like statues. The music grew louder, and Petrov smiled. "Only with your help."

Tira looked at him. She assessed the strong jaw and his wavy black hair. Last week, she noticed grey hair. Now it was gone. He must have dyed it. On sudden thought, she realized why he never grew a beard. It always came in more grey than black. Papa feared aging. For the first time, Tira realized this powerful man had a weakness.

"Inside of this room, there are very important people with a lot to lose," Petrov continued. "And I have a lot to gain." He met Tira's gaze and gestured at the guards. "Do not fucking fail me."

Tira frowned. "How will I—"

The music quelled her voice as the guards opened the double doors. Her mouth moved, finishing the question, but the president's focus had shifted.

The groaning doors exposed a huge, dark room with searing white, blue, and red lights. Showcasing the colors of the Russian flag, the lights circulated, knifing through the ballroom and illuminating the seated occupants like a concert. The center aisle led to a sprawling stage where a man stood before a wooden podium.

"Ladies and gentlemen..." he said, "... the President of Russia, Aleksey Petrov!"

The audience rose to their feet and applauded. As a white light shone upon his face, Aleksey's face broke into a radiant smile, a smile that had always melted people's hearts.

The Russian Anthem played across the surrounding speakers, converging with the audience's applause.

Tira's eyes shifted. Her teeth hurt; she grinded them together as if the tension of her jaw might save her from the evening. She hated these events, and she despised crowds. In these settings, Petrov flourished. For Tira, it worsened her vigilance. Preparing to battle other agents, military members, or assassins did not intimidate her. There was something far more dangerous about a mob of politicians, international arms dealers, and military leaders. As Petrov's daughter, she understood one single decision involving powerful leaders could change the temperament of the world.

That bloody hotel room had been her contribution.

Continuing down the walkway, Tira passed a table where Olivia stood serving a tray of cocktails. The server adjusted the towel over her shoulder and winked.

Blushing, Tira looked away and set her eyes on the round table near the stage.

Participating in the applause, nine well-dressed individuals stood around the table. Eight were male, one was female. They were all graduating agents of *Project Savior's* task force. Most were her age, and she had trained with them for years. She'd always wondered if, in certain circumstances, these recruits would ever reveal her true identity as Petrov's daughter to an enemy.

Sweat moistened her skin.

He'd always kept her from the media—from prying eyes that could harm her status as a developing agent. As a little girl, she'd worn a wig and eyeglasses to his political events until he'd ended her appearances long before puberty. After the hotel incident, he'd placed her in the military.

Petrov had wanted her to disappear for a while.

Now, just over six years later, her face was set to re-emerge before international leaders... the greedy ones. The ones with their noses deep in Petrov's assets.

Like the gentleman he was, the president pulled a chair out for Tira so that she could join her colleagues. He strode to the stage, stopped and waved, and then climbed the short stairway to approach the podium.

"Thank you, please be seated," he drawled. Subtitles flashed on the large screen above the stage.

Chairs squeaked and scraped against the floor as everyone took their seats.

Tira's eyes did not stop scanning the room. Upon observation, she noticed the other agents at her table were doing the same thing. They appeared as uncomfortable as she did. Tira's hand crept to her thigh where she kept the small handgun holstered on her leg. After Olivia's departure, Tira had completed her standard preparation—holstering the only items she trusted. Her weapons.

Aleksey's voice dominated the room. "I want to thank everyone for accepting my invitation to this event. I believe all of you will leave here enlightened, knowledgeable, and *excited*. Who is *excited*?"

More applause. Tira clapped three times and then returned her hand to her thigh.

"As you all know, my colleagues and I have always put the safety of the Russian people first in many things. We love our country. Our country is great. But we acknowledge our allies. Russia would not be where she is today without their help."

The crowd roared. The applause was deafening. Petrov gripped the podium and scanned the ballroom. When the noise faded, he continued.

"For that reason, we desire to provide our allies the help and protection they also deserve. Many years ago, I began a project that may sound familiar. Can you all take a guess?" The president held a hand to his ear and leaned.

"*Project Savior!*" the crowd chanted.

The roar was chilling. Tira tilted her head, watching Aleksey's smile. It was interesting... the program's popularity amongst international leaders gave her both a sense of pride *and* concern.

"Yes," Petrov said. "*Project Savior*. It took years to gain approval. But after Russia's best scientists came together and advocated for the cause, it was finally approved. We began the creation of genetically enhanced human embryos for the purpose of weaponry, intelligence, and espionage."

Tira lifted her eyes to the ceiling. Her lips parted; the hairs prickled on her skin. When had a metal cage been installed above the stage?

A glass of red wine appeared before her. A woman's familiar whisper brought her temporary respite from the strange atmosphere. "For the sexiest person in this room," Olivia hummed in her ear, and then she departed.

A small smile played across Tira's lips. She reached for the wine and tasted it, the first drink of alcohol she'd consumed in over a year.

"I watched this program become successful. Firsthand. By age four, this little warrior surpassed all expectations, both in physicality and intelligence. *She* outran the fittest children in Russia. Her shooting skills? Unsurpassable."

Tira's hand twitched against her thigh. There wasn't enough wine for this. That man, who'd labeled her a "dumb cunt", was *bragging* about her to his international friends.

Petrov stood straighter. "This little child solved equations that I didn't know existed."

"One plus one isn't that difficult, Papa," Tira murmured. She wouldn't dare say it any louder, but the agent next to her snorted his wine.

"Ladies and gentlemen," Petrov gestured towards the overhead screen. "Please watch this video we prepared to show you the capability of *Project Savior*."

Tira shifted in her seat and raised her eyes.

The bass vibrated the room.

"How are they shielding this from the public?" the young man beside her whispered. He was careful not to touch her as he leaned close.

Tira's eyes shifted to the cage suspended from the ceiling. "Infrared rays with encoded data. It disables the cameras."

Frowning, the agent nodded.

"And probably the threat of an *early* retirement for these old cunts." Tira straightened back up.

The agent grabbed his wine.

The video was uncomfortable to watch. It displayed her childhood as she sprinted, lifted weights, manipulated weapons, and engaged in hand-to-hand combat. It showcased her solving equations and puzzles. She wondered if the room knew the truth—that some of the equations she solved would have detonated had she not completed the task.

Minutes later, the video ended, and the crowd clapped again.

The president looked at Tira and called her over the applause. "Please continue to give a hand for my beautiful and talented daughter—born as Project 4 and now? *Agent 4*. Come on stage, my sweet."

Wildly, her heart pounded. She felt hot. A prickly kind of heat. She arose, and the rest of the crowd stood with her, clapping with an urgency that almost looked violent. Tira's face warmed, and she approached the stairs and lifted her gown as she ascended.

"Smile, my sweet, don't snarl!" Petrov laughed. The crowd laughed with him.

Tira hadn't realized she was snarling.

Aleksey directed her to the center of the stage. Trying to slow her breathing, Tira walked across the stage and stood to face the crowd. The white overhead lights illuminated her body, and her red dress shimmered.

She stared at the EXIT sign. Silence fell. Did her breath echo, or was it her imagination? Probably, but that wasn't what heightened her concern.

It was the cage.

Aleksey Petrov had placed her directly beneath it.

"Agent 4 just graduated top of her class in *Project Savior*. She has served four years in our military. She ranked junior sergeant in her last year, and she was promoted to sergeant in her final year."

Tira's eyes darted across the room, catching the gaze of the older male audience. Many of them nodded in admiration. Some licked their lips.

Just like the senator.

Tira's fingertips tingled. She wanted to ensure her knife was still secure, but the fidgeting would alert someone to the location of her weapons. That was one mistake she'd never repeat. On her hip, Tira's skin still bore the training scar from that mishap.

The microphone squealed. Petrov grimaced. "Agent 4 dedicated her life to *Project Savior* even during her military service to this country. She's fluent in countless languages, including sign language."

This was embarrassing. Why was he publicizing her? Was she for sale? Because Petrov for sure wasn't *this* fucking proud.

"Agent 4... do that impressive thing that you do, please." Aleksey turned to her and winked.

Tira narrowed her eyes at him but complied. She proceeded to speak a paragraph, changing the language for each sentence, and utilizing each country's sign language while she spoke. Once finished, she returned her attention to the EXIT. The crowd applauded. Someone whistled. The sign glowed red, and she desperately wanted to follow its summons.

"Isn't she impressive?" Aleksey beamed.

The roar was thunderous.

"Now," Petrov leaned into the microphone. "I admit I am a little biased... which is why I would like to recognize nine other agents who have also proven to be the best from Russia's extraordinary. The *best* from the many we created within *Project Savior*. Agents, will you please stand and join your colleague on stage?"

An old man in a tuxedo, wobbly on his feet, struggled to stand up. The rest followed and cheered again.

Tira's eyes shifted back and forth from agent to agent, from table to table, to Aleksey, and to the ceiling where the cage hung. Her skin prickled... a phenomenon that always happened every time she felt something was... *wrong*.

The agents climbed the steps. Smiles lit their faces. She felt sorry for them. Did they know Petrov like she did? Did they *know* that Aleksey Petrov never just *bragged*?

Petrov's voice grew louder. "These agents have worked hard. It would be nearly impossible for regular human beings to get this far."

Did the cage creak above her? No. It was a chair in the audience.

Aleksey leaned into the microphone and lowered his voice. "They rose above all odds to succeed. But... there is only one who can withstand the *final* test."

What?

Tira whipped her head towards her father. Her heart raced. *Now* her hand went numb.

She wanted to draw her firearm.

The crowd leaned in.

Aleksey smirked. "Tonight, I have something incredible for you. I would like to provide you with a live example of what my genetically enhanced agents can do."

His voice echoed in the ballroom, and Tira could no longer contain her snarl. Next to her, the other agents stood in stiff anxiety, but Tira Petrov stared down her father.

Petrov didn't care. He kept talking, and his voice shook with excitement. "The winner of this test will receive an *outstanding* monetary award for succeeding as *the* top agent. He or she will obtain *the* top assignment."

"What's the top assignment, President?" a drunken man called from the crowd. Laughter followed his question.

Tira's teeth screeched. A low growl rumbled from her throat. *She* had finished at the top. *She* was the best in Russia. Why was there always *one more test*?

"The top assignment is none of your concern, General," Petrov chuckled. "But you'll thank me in the future if you're still alive by then."

The crowd roared with laughter. Wine sloshed. The drunken fools salivated and slammed the tables in jest with their palms.

Tira watched with nauseated disgust... but the top assignment sounded *intriguing*.

"Agents." The lights shadowed his face as he angled himself to look at them. "You've done your country a great service." He paused, and the remnants of his voice faded into the sudden silence. "Now, please disarm yourselves."

Tira cleared her throat.

Petrov looked at her. A grin touched his lips, and he gestured towards her with his head. "You too, little girl."

She wanted to withdraw her firearm and kill him. Instead, Tira bit her lip and lifted her dress to un-holster the weapon. Snarling, she placed her firearm in a basket provided by a suited guard. The other agents did the same.

"Tira," Aleksey sighed, and her blood pumped harder. "Let's be honest and fair. Remove the other weapons."

Honest and *fair* for *what*?

She bit her tongue to refrain from protesting. Whatever was coming—he'd make it worse for her if he wanted to.

So she raised her dress further to un-holster the switchblade she kept on her person. The knife she'd used against the Senator.

It was special.

Tira tossed it into the basket and sneered at the guard. "If you lose that," she hissed, "I will kill you."

The guard nodded, glanced upwards, and then scurried off the stage.

"Now," Petrov deepened his voice. "Our most important event of the night." He smiled, and then he addressed an unseen man. "Andrei. Please adjust the lights and flip the switch."

The room went black. The crowd gasped.

Tira's hand slapped against the empty holster.

Fuck.

Something groaned above her head. A machine. A metallic rattling. It descended upon them. For a brief moment, Tira considered fleeing, but she remained grounded. Petrov wouldn't allow her such an easy solution.

Inhale. Exhale. Breathe.

Her hands relaxed. Then her limbs. Flexibility won. Tension did not.

Metal crashed against the floor. It vibrated. Stage lights snapped on, and a collective murmur rose from the crowd.

The cage surrounded the agents. Its metal wiring glinted beneath the white lights. Spacious in circumference, it allowed plenty of room for movement.

For fighting.

"What the fuck?" Tira whispered, her voice more annoyed than shocked.

Petrov turned towards the cage. His hand rested on the podium. "Agents of *Project Savior*—with you all, in that cage, is one weapon."

The agents swiveled their heads. As they looked up, down, and around, Tira took a step backwards and focused on her breathing. With searching eyes, she kept the agents in her line of vision as she assessed the cage.

"The rules are simple," Aleksey said, and raised his palms. His blue eyes glinted in the lights. "Find the weapon and survive."

Seats creaked; murmurs erupted amongst the crowd. Glass shattered to the floor.

Olivia, near a table by the exit doors, had dropped a wine tray.

Tira looked at her. As sweat beaded on her forehead, the young agent tightened her lips in an attempt to smile.

"Can't we all just tell him no?" an agent whispered beside her.

"There's a higher chance of surviving *this*." Tira spoke through her teeth. It was true. Insubordination had always been Petrov's worst trigger.

"You're his daughter. Can't you *convince* him?" His face moved closer to hers.

Tira could smell the wine on his desperate breath. If he came any closer, she would kill him then, but she turned her face to his.

She wanted to chastise him, to tell him he must be a subhuman to make that suggestion. Agent 4 refused to pump the brakes now. Twenty-three years with *him* would not be a fucking waste.

But as the boisterous crowd rose to their feet, and a twenty-second countdown timer slammed against the overhead screen, Tira spoke a different truth. It tumbled from her lips as her mind prepared for combat.

"Agent," she said, and her voice sounded quiet against the chaotic atmosphere. "Your breath smells like shit. If you do not get out of my face, I will start by killing you first."

His sweaty face paled. With widening blood-shot eyes, he retreated.

"Twelve, eleven, ten—!" Counting down with the screen, the crowd grew more aggressive as the timer struck ten.

Tira slipped her feet out of her heels.

"Wait, please!" One of the male agents sprinted to the end of the cage and grabbed onto the wires. Vomit projected from his mouth and dripped from the cage.

"Seven, six, five—"

Tira gripped the stilettos and watched the other agents scramble to the cage. They grabbed the wires and shook it until it rattled.

"We *won't do this!*"

Tira didn't know who screamed those words. It didn't matter. The person was wrong. It was human nature to resort to violence in desperate times. Ensuring you were the last one standing? That's what mattered. Not because death was something to fear—quite the opposite. Life without purpose and success—*that* was something to fear.

As the agents panicked, Tira remained calm. If she died, it'd be deserved. If she survived, it'd be earned.

She looked at the top of the cage and allowed her shoes to swing in her hands.

Within seconds, chaos would erupt.

Overthinking kills, Tira reminded herself, narrowing her eyes. She'd watched a colleague's head get blown off after hesitating.

"Three, two—!"

Don't overthink.

"One—!"

Just do.

The buzzer screamed.

VERSE 3

~ SEPARATE THE PACK ~

The buzzer activated Tira's body.

Agent 4 tossed one of the heels. As it flipped in the air, its deep red sheen glinted in the overhead lights. With a clatter, it caught the cage's top wires and hung. For a brief instant, silence filled the arena. In the corner of the cage, Tira positioned herself in a defensive stance.

The silence broke. Agents shoved and stumbled. Shoes squeaked and thudded against the stage. As chaos ensued and bodies blurred, Tira assigned herself the first task.

Slow it *down.*

Her eyes darted. In theory, within a group of ten, six traits might exist—the leaders; aggressors; cautious observers; the diplomats; the followers; and the frightened. As she zoned in, she initiated the second task.

Separate the pack.

Three agents crawled up the cage. The metal rattled. Their gasps came fast and in rhythm with their exertion. They scrambled towards the top where the shoe dangled.

On the stage, bodies collided. Agents tumbled, punched, kicked, and choked each other. Tira watched, waited, and braced herself as a man with a large frame stormed towards her.

She crouched. So did he. It became a dance of wit, speed, and reflexes. Breathing with slow rhythm, Tira kept her back against the cage so she could observe the agents in front of her.

"What chaos!" Petrov roared, and the crowd cheered.

The man reached for her but leapt back when she responded to his movement. Tira watched him. Right now, he was an aggressor; she, an observer. She followed his feet, his hands, the angling of his body. In training, they'd done this before, again and again. She knew his weaknesses. He knew hers.

At the center, a man screamed and plummeted from the top of the cage. His body struck the stage. With a sickening crack, the front of his skull broke against the surface. Blood pooled.

Tira's opponent flinched. She attacked. With a sweeping arc, her shin smashed against his ankles. His legs flew out from beneath him, and his eyes widened with realization that he was living his last seconds.

As he struck the floor, and the cage rattled around her, Tira delivered a powerful strike to his throat. Eyes bulging, he gurgled, and Agent 4's elbow cracked against his temple before she straightened and backed against the cage again.

From the top, another agent plummeted. His ankles snapped, and he screamed. As others stumbled over his body, he tried to crawl to safety. Collapsed. If no one else took care of him, Tira would later.

"Kill *Agent 4!*" a shrill voice shrieked from above.

Tira looked up, but only long enough to note the female agent clinging to the top of the cage with Tira's shoe. Agent 7—Katarina Popov. In training, she'd often been a follower. Now, she exhibited aggression and diplomacy.

The other agents didn't respond to Agent 7's call, but Tira did. Snarling, the president's daughter leapt onto the cage and pulled herself towards the woman with incredible speed.

"Look at my daughter *climb!*" Aleksey boomed.

The crowd laughed. Howled like another pack of beasts.

Ignoring the noise, Tira approached the top of the cage. The metal creaked as Agent 7 crawled towards her like a spider.

"Why don't you save your strength?" Tira clung to the wiring, positioned at the top like a cat prowling a ceiling. "Let the others die, and then fight me."

Agent 7 continued her approach. "You're afraid."

As sweat trickled over her skin, Tira smiled through her teeth. "No. I just don't want the only other cunt in this group to look weak."

Agent 7's dark eyes glinted with menace. Letting go of the cage, she dangled with one arm and swung the shoe with the other.

The red shoe blurred. Tira cocked her head. The stiletto heel nipped her chest and blurred again.

One, two, three. She memorized the rhythm, predicted her opponent's strikes. Tira shifted, protecting her vitals. The shoe cut her arm. She twisted to face Agent 7 and dropped her legs to hang suspended by her hands. She gripped her other stiletto.

Someone screamed below, but she kept her eyes focused on the opponent dangling from the cage. Tira was patient. Each attempted strike lessened in power, because Agent 7 was weakening.

"Last chance," Tira deadpanned, whipping her head to the side. Her arms, legs, and abdomen burned. Sweat stung her eyes. *Three, two, one—*

Agent 7 attacked. With impressive flexibility, she raised her hips before propelling her feet towards Tira's face.

Anticipating the move, Tira rocked her head backwards. Her reflexes prevented full impact, and the woman's heels tapped against Tira's chin and clattered her teeth.

"Look at that cat fight at the top!" Petrov roared through the microphone. Laughter filled the ballroom, merging with the sounds of men coughing and spluttering on their wine.

Every sound and touch heightened Tira's senses. Her loosening hair tickled her face. As Agent 7's legs came down, Agent 4's came up. With a hiss, she gripped the metal wiring and extended her legs. The evening gown coiled up. Overhead lights beamed upon her scarred shins and muscular thighs as Tira locked her legs around Katarina Popov's neck and arm.

The woman's eyes met those of Tira, and her dark orbs filled with tears, panic, and despair.

Tira gripped the cage. Like a snake, she tightened her legs and trapped the agent. "I warned you," Agent 4 hissed, and she squeezed. As Popov's head drooped in sleep seconds later, Tira watched her with calm intent. A feeling of satisfaction swirled with the rage she'd experienced towards Aleksey Petrov.

If he wanted to force her to complete *one more test*, to put her on stage for world leaders to see, she was determined to imprint a memory.

A deadly one.

Popov's body relaxed, and Tira released her. Limp, she dropped from the cage, her arms relaxed as her dress fluttered in a breeze created from the fall. Her skull hit the stage. Cracked.

Aleksey's voice echoed. "Well, she's dead. How many do we have left? *Who* will come out on top?"

The crowd chanted.

"Four! Four! Four!"

Tira swung her legs and grasped the cage with both hands. For so long, she'd desired to hear her name chanted. It was happening, and the thrill made her lips quiver.

As the crowd boomed, the men below her stopped fighting. Tira clung onto the top wires as they looked up at her with torn suits and bloodied faces.

They were coming for her.

"Shit," she whispered.

The men rushed the cage walls. The cage rattled, groaned, and creaked. The roaring crowd pierced her ears. Gasping, Tira scrambled to the center of the cage ceiling. There was no time to over-analyze. Her actions needed to be quick, effective, and violent. The agents would attempt to surround her.

"Four! Four!"

Tira crawled to meet the first agent at the top.

He grabbed at her. With a kick, Agent 4 drove him back against the side. She targeted his widening eyes. Exhaling, she slammed the sharp heel of her remaining shoe deep into his eye. The wet, squishing sound rendered Tira no empathy as she drove it towards his brain. The shoe's vibration felt familiar, and she fought to keep her thoughts from returning to that night at the hotel—the night she'd killed the United States senator with her *special* knife.

"It feels like bursting balloons, doesn't it?" Tira growled, stabbing the senator again, and—

Blood drained. The young man collapsed from the wires.

Retreating back to the center, Tira moved fast. Her stomach churned, and the bright lights dizzied her. Still, as her red dress coiled around her thighs, and her hair fell from the pins she'd adjusted with meticulous care, Tira swiveled her head to avoid an ambush.

Like children on monkey bars, the other bloodied agents approached. The closest one, the man who'd begged her to use her status as Petrov's daughter, swung towards her with bared, bloody teeth. Behind her, two others clambered for a kill.

"Four! Four! Four!"

Tira leapt.

Her hands left the wire. This risk could kill her. But wasn't that the reality of their training? To participate in high-risk duties while minimizing the chance of death as best as they could?

Her body glided through the air, and her arms encircled his waist. She clung to him as he tried to kick free and maintain his grip.

"Kill them both!" one of the other agents screamed.

Tira squeezed tighter as the agent thrashed. Her arms slipped a little, and her mind summarized the outcome of the fall. If it didn't kill her, something in her body would break. What then? How could she use lethal force against multiple men if her arms or legs snapped?

"If you want to live, do as I say," she commanded.

"Fuck you!"

"Let go and grab hold of the agent you are facing. Do you understand me?"

He did not respond.

"It's your only chance, or else we both fall."

"Four! Four! Four!"

Without second consideration, the remaining agents tore at the unlucky fingers clinging to the metal above Tira. Any moment now, and they'd fall.

Would her career end as a spectacle to Petrov's political fans?

Above Tira, the man fought for his life. Her arms burned, and her body swung around like bait in water. Sensing a shift in his balance, Tira used her momentum to yank his legs and pull him from the wire. Gravity did the rest.

They fell.

Grunting, Tira twisted and maneuvered her agile body in efforts to redistribute the impact and force the man beneath her. His hands came up. His scream cut short as they hit the ground with a bone-jarring thud.

Tira landed on top. Sharp pain rattled her, dizzied her. Had anything broken?

Groaning, she crawled from the man's body and staggered to her feet.

The crowd vibrated the floor. They stomped and clapped in rhythm to her name.

"Petrov. Petrov. Petrov."

Tira wobbled amongst the bodies at her feet and gasped for air. The air held a stench of iron, sweat, and fecal matter. The smells triggered images that swarmed like buzzards in her mind. She stood with shaky, bloodied hands in the hotel room again.

Two dead trainers. One dead senator.

Her heart pulsed in her ears, and Petrov's voice brought her back to focus.

"Will this be the end, or the beginning, of my daughter?" Petrov laughed. "What a performance!"

Tira ground her teeth and gripped her shoe. She was tired. The thrill was gone. It was time to end this.

The men came for her. Tira's body moved, but her brain felt numb. She didn't analyze her movements... she just moved. Strikes. Kicks. Jabs. Knees. Flips. Body slams and crunching bones.

Using her shoe, Tira stabbed. Blood spurted from an agent's neck. It spattered her face. She tasted it on her teeth, and she snarled like the lab-created animal Petrov trained her to be.

An arm broke. A man screamed, and Tira stabbed again. She whirled, searching for the last agent with wide eyes.

"Petrov! Petrov!"

The last agent, the man who'd snickered at her joke during the dinner, crawled towards the remaining shoe. Blood covered his left eye and spattered his sweaty black hair. He'd always been the kindest of the bunch.

Standing tall amidst the carnage, Tira eyed him. The torn suit and the slow, steady movement reminded her of the senator. The politician had crawled like that too, before the bed sheets went red.

The memory gave her renewed energy. Tira staggered forward, stumbling over someone's foot, and kicked the man in the face with her scarred shin. The impact flopped him onto his back.

"Kill him! Kill him!"

Tira raised her shoe.

"Come here, pretty little lady," the senator had taunted.

Her arm blurred as she struck the agent below her. Warm and slick, blood spattered against her face. Her heart raced. Any remaining pain dissipated from the rage that overwhelmed her senses. The agent's body went limp.

But she couldn't stop beating him.

Her breath came in ragged gasps as the sneering senator's face leered in her thoughts.

Fuck him. Fuck the senator. And fuck Petrov.

Tira withdrew and spat blood from her mouth. The thunderous crowd rose to their feet. Their bodies shielded Tira's quick glimpse of Olivia, who stood in the far right corner of the ballroom. Her blue eyes peered through splayed fingers that she'd placed over her face in horror.

Exhausted, Tira almost fell, but she didn't allow herself the luxury. Everyone in the cage *appeared* deceased, but she couldn't lose vigilance now.

Especially with Papa behind the microphone.

Tira blinked sweat from her eyes and squinted. Her body whirled; her eyes scanned. The lights seemed brighter. The bodies, scattered, lay broken and strewn in pools of blood. Had one of them moved?

Had Tira *won?*

"Friends and allies of Russia," Petrov said, commanding the attention of the audience. "What did you think of my weapon?"

A cacophony of male voices filled the room and echoed.

The shoe slipped from Tira's hand. With a squeak, the cage lifted and freed her from the prison.

Aleksey adjusted his tie, looked at Tira, and said, "Those agents were not genetically enhanced. They were a placebo group. Can you imagine having thousands of—" he pointed aggressively at Tira, "—*her* to protect your countries?"

Another standing ovation.

With hot cheeks and a headache that formed like a storm within her head, Tira remained on stage. She felt ill. As she shifted her feet, she realized they were sticky. Blood, probably.

"Congratulations, Agent 4." Petrov tilted his head a little and murmured into the microphone. "You've completed your final test... and Papa is very proud."

Her eyes widened. This was the first time Petrov had spoken such words since the incident with the senator. Did he even mean the words?

Was she *truly* finished?

As politicians, military leaders, and other high-status individuals talked amongst themselves and shouted questions towards Aleksey, Tira narrowed her eyes and retrieved the other stiletto that lay in a pool of blood. She sucked in a breath, puffed out her cheeks, and then walked towards the stairs.

"Leaving us so soon, my sweet? Have some wine. Let us celebrate you!"

Barefoot, Tira strode past him and stormed down the steps. "Good night."

As Tira walked down the aisle, men outstretched their hands, but they were wise enough not to make contact with her skin. With hot cheeks, she approached the double doors, and the guards stepped aside and opened them. The hallway lights flooded into her vision, and the sound of the screaming crowd faded as the doors closed with a thunderous slam.

Verse 4

~ Phil ~

Friday, January 11th, 2019
Chicago, Illinois

"Tomorrow morning, I'll be skiing with Governor Kaemon Spears." Phil Jameson took his fork and prodded at his meatloaf. It was over-cooked, and he could see a sliver of oatmeal in the center. "I expect you to get groceries while I'm gone since you didn't today." He stopped moving his fork and scowled at his wife. "What were you *doing* all day, anyway?"

The bumblebee clock ticked. It hung on the dining room wall, next to a large wooden cross and a painting of *The Last Supper*. In the painting, Judas had darker skin than the others.

On the other side of the table, Carolyn Jameson lowered her eyes and took a bite of roasted broccoli. Shoved in a clip and intertwined with grey, her black hair looked lopsided and unkempt. "I spent some time catching up on chores."

Phil scoffed. He flicked the piece of oatmeal from the meat. "Well, you didn't do a very good job."

Dishes still lingered in the sink, and the living room hadn't been vacuumed.

"Dear—"

Phil smashed his palm against the dining table. The dishes rattled, and Carolyn flinched. "I didn't leave my mother's pigsty to return to one," he snapped.

Carolyn slouched and kept her eyes low.

"You must *think* we live in one. This food belongs in the mouths of pigs." Phil shoved his plate away. His belly roared with hunger, but he couldn't eat this filth.

Had she made *any* effort cooking? The food tasted bad, and that was unusual. Phil did not often take issue with Carolyn's meatloaf. She'd made it for him since the start of their twenty-seven-year marriage.

What had distracted her today?

"What did you do today? Where did you go?" Phil regretted purchasing the 2005 minivan for her. It was unwise to give a housewife too much freedom. Females were immature and, left unchecked, it often led to one thing—sin.

Carolyn set down the fork. "Nowhere."

"Don't lie to me." Phil leaned forward. He pointed the butter knife at her. "One last time. Where did you go?"

Her lips trembled, and she reached for a napkin. "Um—"

"Go on, spit it out."

"I..."

"Have you been sinning with another man, Carolyn?" Philip sneered. The knife clattered against the table.

Carolyn let out a squeal. She made that sound whenever the tears were en route. "No, I would never!" She shook her head.

"Then *what* were you *doing?*" Phil came up halfway from his seat and pointed a finger.

"I went to *see Fr. Jerome!*" Carolyn screeched, and her head shot up with tearful eyes.

His chest felt heavy. Phil remained where he was, his butt inches from the chair, his finger in the air. His teeth cracked together. *"Why?"*

"Because I'm trying to save our marriage," Carolyn sobbed. "I needed advice!"

Phil took his plate and dashed it against the wall. With a crash, thick shards exploded. Food rained in the air.

Carolyn shrunk into her chair.

"How *dare you?*" This was *worse.* He might have been gentler had she admitted to cheating. Instead of trusting his own spiritual lead as her husband, she sought advice from *Fr. Faggot* himself.

And *marriage advice?* For *what?*

"What in Lucifer's name were you thinking?" Phil stomped around the table. He wanted to vomit her horrible meatloaf on her face.

Carolyn covered her face with her arms. "I—I just want—"

Phil slapped her. It struck her elbow. His palm hurt from its contact with the bone. He leaned close and screamed at her. "You go to a man who *ensured* I didn't make it to seminary? A heretic who thinks he's spiritually *above* me?" His spittle misted the air between them.

Carolyn hugged herself and bent her head. Her shoulders shook. "Phil—"

"And on *top of that,* about our *marriage?*" Phil's throat burned. He gripped her arms and squeezed. *"There is nothing wrong with our marriage!"*

Carolyn screamed. "Stop hurting me!"

Phil hissed and covered her mouth with his palm. Her voice muffled, and her teeth stabbed his hand as she protested. "Shut up," he sneered. "Do you want the police here? Do you *want* them to arrest your husband?"

As a defender of the public, Phil had seen it many times. The police, often misguided, would arrest a man who simply wanted to ensure the well-being of his wife's soul.

Wheezing, Carolyn shook her head and looked up with imploring eyes. It pleased him to see the submission return, but he wasn't finished with her.

God wasn't finished with her.

"Our daughters deserve a father and mother who are united under Christ." Phil took a handful of her hair and yanked her from her seat. "What did you think you'd achieve going to that homosexual man? What advice did you think he'd give you?"

Carolyn stammered. "I'm human, I have doubts!"

Sweat trickled down his back. He gripped her hair and roared in her face. "You gave those doubts to God when you said your vows! What did Jerome say?"

"Please—"

Phil shoved her. Floundering, her frail body crashed against the wall.

He wanted to scream, to beat her until she understood the pain she'd bestowed upon him. "Tell me what Jerome *said.*"

Carolyn sank down to the floor and embraced her knees. "He suggested divorce."

Phil heard a low growl. His own. As he stood over his wife, he clenched his fists. His thoughts turned to Jerome, how much hatred he felt for the priest.

But he'd deal with Jerome later.

With a strange, animalistic cry, Phil slapped her. Multiple times. The sharp sounds echoed in the kitchen. Then he stopped, gasping for air, and stepped back. "Go repent, you filth."

Carolyn's hair covered her face. She kept her head bowed in submission. A droplet of blood reddened her white blouse.

Phil stared at the bloodstain. "Don't make me repeat myself." He raised a shaky finger and pointed to the living room. "Crawl to the repentance corner. *Move!*"

Carolyn jumped. Shaking, she crawled towards the living room. Blood from her nose trailed behind her.

Phil walked behind her, wrinkling his nose. "You're dirtying the floor behind you. You'll clean that up when you're done repenting."

The floor creaked as her knees thumped against the surface.

"I am the best thing that has ever happened to you," he said, nudging her more gently now with the toe of his dress shoe. "You will thank God for me, and you will never consider leaving me again. Now get to the corner and repent. God will forgive you."

Gasping, Carolyn managed to bring herself up to her knees and shuffle past the brick fireplace in the living room. In the corner, several icons depicting Jesus on the cross hung neatly on the wall. She stopped and looked up at the icons.

"*Prostrate*!" Phil screamed and slapped the back of her head.

Carolyn placed her forehead against the floor. Her fingers twitched.

"Let me hear you."

With a timid voice, she prayed. "O Lord my God, I confess that I have sinned against You in thought, word and deed. I have also omitted to do what Your holy law requires of me. But now with repentance and contrition I turn again to Your love and mercy. I entreat You—"

"Louder!" Phil wasn't convinced.

"... to forgive me *all* my transgressions and to cleanse me from all my sins! Lord, fill my heart with the light of Your truth. Strengthen my will by Your grace. Teach me both to desire and to do only what pleases You. Amen."

Sudden silence replaced Carolyn's tremoring voice. Cars rumbled through the suburb, and Phil closed his eyes and wobbled a little. "I can feel it."

Carolyn stirred at his feet and whispered. "What can you feel?"

Phil's eyes moved back and forth beneath his lids. A strange warmth tingled from his fingertips and into his arms. "God's forgiveness," he murmured. Opening his eyes, he knelt beside his wife. "Let me see you, my little flowerpot."

A loud sob screamed from her throat. Carolyn lay against the floor, scraping her nails on the carpet as blood and tears pooled onto the surface.

"Come here." Phil gathered her into his arms and cradled her. "Ssh." He watched as her eyes squeezed shut, spilling more tears that mixed with the blood on her nose. He watched a red line trickle over her lip. He'd split her skin. Perhaps he'd been too harsh. One slap, or two, might have sufficed.

"God's forgiveness will heal you," Phil said, and laid his palm over her face.

He didn't expect the subsequent event. Phil jolted, and his fingers curled into Carolyn's skin. She let out a muffled plea and, with a gasp, he released her.

Carolyn opened her eyes. "Phil?" Her inquisitive voice still shook.

The blood was gone. The cuts on her nose and upper lip were gone.

Was this the work of Satan?

Or a miracle of God?

"You... er." Phil looked at his palm. No blood; no sign of injury. He grasped her cheeks and scanned her face. He stuttered. "Does your face hurt?"

With confused eyes, Carolyn stared. "Why are you asking me this? Please don't hurt me again."

Phil's hands shook against her face. "*Carolyn*. I—I think something miraculous just happened."

What if he'd gone mad? He *was* related to Beatrice Jameson, and that woman was an *ungodly* example of insanity.

"What are you *talking* about?" Her voice sounded muffled as her lips moved like a fish.

No. He wasn't insane, and Satan wouldn't give him such a gift. This was pure. This was holy.

But *what if he'd gone mad*?

Phil bent and placed his lips on her forehead. Beneath him, she whimpered. He loved that sound—the sound of a woman retreating back to her place. "Carolyn," he whispered. "I will show you."

He needed to confirm it for himself. Just to make sure.

Phil scrambled to his feet and raced to the kitchen.

"Phil!" Distraught, frightened.

As he stormed into the kitchen, he thought about Fr. Jerome. A small, nervous smile quivered across his lips. If this *thing* wasn't a signal of madness, then he had a far greater edge over Fr. Jerome than the priest would ever comprehend.

Phil approached the island and reached for a steak knife in the knife block. His teeth chattered with excitement as he rushed back to the living room.

Carolyn still sat on the floor, wide-eyed and horrified.

He approached her with the knife. "Watch this."

Carolyn shrunk back. "No, *please*, I—"

Phil sliced the blade across his left arm. Hot pain seared his skin where it split and pooled blood. Hissing, he dropped the knife.

Depicted in the icons, Christ appeared to stare at Phil while blood trickled down the lawyer's arm. Shuddering, Phil raised his arm and looked at Carolyn.

She held her hand over her chest. With rapid speed, her lips moved as if in prayer.

Nausea stirred in his gut. Wetting his lips, Phil brought his palm to the cut on his arm. He closed his eyes. Inhaled and held it.

What if he was mad?

He opened them, moved his hand, and then exhaled with a smile.

Carolyn screamed.

*   *   *

Saturday, January 12th, 2019
Wilmot, WI
12:30 P.M.

Phil Jameson's mother, Beatrice, would have rolled in her grave if she had known he went skiing with a black man.

That is, if she was *dead*.

He'd murdered and buried her so many times in his mind she might as well be. Regardless, she'd be appalled.

In Wilmot, Wisconsin, approximately sixty-five miles from Chicago, Phil sat next to the black man on a ski lift that glided through the air. The man was not just *any* black man. He didn't grab his crotch and ogle white women. He was a professional. The governor of Illinois.

Kaemon Spears.

"It's a cold one today, isn't it?" Spears adjusted his ski mask and chuckled. He had a deep voice. Soothing. It captured the intrigue of many voters, but his medium-brown skin, runner's physique, and light brown eyes attracted more than voter interest.

Phil looked down at the skiers that darted over the snowy hills. Shivering, he adjusted his coat and nodded. "A tad."

They'd met years ago through Senator James Donovan, a man Phil greatly admired. If James trusted Kaemon Spears, so did Phil.

"Have you processed my proposal yet? Or is your brain still thawing?" Spears asked and patted Phil on the knee.

Phil recoiled. Peering at the black man through his oversized ski mask, he leaned as far away from Spears as he could. "Give me a moment, for Pete's sake."

Wind whistled and snowflakes swirled. A hint of sun peeked over the snowy horizon.

"It's an opportunity you wouldn't regret," Spears continued, ignoring Phil's protest. With a veiny hand, he adjusted his ski mask again.

"I have a job, though." Phil thought about the firm. He made great money. He'd shared the word of God with many criminals. In fact, he'd often provide a Bible to them alongside his services.

"But this would give you more status and money. More independence. On top of that—" Spears wiped his nose, "—you'd have endless access to what KS Industries and *Project Savior* provides."

"Hmm."

"That means innovative and evolving healthcare for you and your family. For free."

Phil frowned. "I don't believe in science. It's witchcraft." He thought about the prior night—healing Carolyn. He remembered the knife wound closing on his arm.

The governor laughed. "Philip, you're ridiculous. Your mere existence is science."

Phil clenched his gloved hands. "Don't call me ridiculous."

"But am I wrong? Science exists, just like you do. Are you telling me that God did not create science?" Spears cocked his head.

Phil shifted his eyes. He didn't have much of an argument in response to that, and it bothered him. So he avoided the question. "Why are you offering me this job anyway?"

Kaemon took a brief glance over the lift. Wind whistled through the cables as the lift climbed upwards. When the howling ceased, he spoke. "I'm not going to bullshit around the bush with you."

"Watch your language."

"Nigger?" A glint darkened Spears' eyes. The corner of his mouth curved upwards, and he tilted his head a little.

"I did *not* say that."

"Then watch your tone with me, Mr. Jameson."

It felt much colder now. Shivering, Phil gripped the handlebar before him and gritted his teeth. The vast snowy space below him suddenly seemed far more threatening. "I..."

His teeth rattled. He didn't want to apologize, but he also didn't want to be chucked from the ski lift.

Kaemon Spears seemed like the sort of man that would make an issue disappear.

Phil didn't want to be the issue.

"I regret my tone," he said and hugged himself. He was too skinny for this weather.

The ski lift creaked. Spears cleared his throat. "On to my point. KS Industries, its affiliates, and *Project Savior* have been internationally integrated into society with minimal setbacks."

The ski lift began to drop. Skiers raced down the snow-topped hills. Governor Spears continued. "But global tensions have risen since Senator Thompson's disappearance."

"Memory eternal to his soul. He was Senator Donovan's best friend, did you know that?" Phil completed the sign of the cross over his chest.

Amused, Spears eyed him. "I did. I'm sure that's why Donovan rushed to fill the empty seat for Illinois."

Phil glared. "If you're implying that *my friend*, a faithful member of *my* church, took *advantage* of Senator Thompson's tragedy—!"

"Phil, shut up. We're off topic, and the lift will land any moment now. This is not meant for public ears, so let me finish."

Phil huffed. "Fine."

"Senator Thompson's disappearance and potential death caused tensions for several reasons. One, because the case hasn't been solved." Kaemon lifted a gloved thumb to count. "Two, everyone likes to point fingers at each other for foul play."

"What does this have to do with KS Industries, *Project Savior*, and *me*?" Phil was getting bored. He wanted to test his healing powers again. Maybe that would teach the governor some respect.

"Thompson was heavily involved in KS Industries. He left a large money trail. His name was attached to almost everything *Project Savior* produced and researched out of KS. Which leads me to my third point regarding global tensions."

"And what's that?" Phil sighed.

Spears unzipped his coat as if he was hot. "There is a potential rumor that Thompson, as well as others affiliated with KS, were involved in certain activities that, if brought to light, could drive KS Industries into the ground. And KS is the father of Project Savior. That would mean all health research, DNA tracking, etc, might come to an end if this rumor gets out."

Phil frowned. "Why does that cause global tension?"

"To some countries, *Project Savior* is a binding contract for peace. Think of the world as an intricate domino display, with *Project Savior* at the forefront. What happens if you tip the first domino?"

"It collapses." Phil sighed. He wasn't convinced getting involved in any of this was a productive idea. He shot a curious glance at the governor. "Wait a minute. Is KS at risk of collapse? Does that mean *war* is coming?"

Phil imagined the chaos. He envisioned the healings, and the people who would bring their wounded to him.

To *him*.

Not Fr. Jerome.

"Your services are preventative methods." Governor Spears zipped his coat again. "Election year is coming. People like to stir things up. Your job would be to keep any and all rumors to stay *rumors*. Make sense?"

Phil closed his eyes and took a deep breath. The ski lift's descent flipped his stomach. He processed the prior night's events: Carolyn's sins against—

—him—

—God, and the healing miracle he'd performed. That miracle was a sign that he was God's elected. He wasn't sure for what role, but it was for *something*. It was a reward. If he went off course now, he was concerned he'd lose God's favor.

His phone buzzed. With frozen fingers, he reached for it in his coat pocket. "While I appreciate your offer," Phil said, "I need to decline. I'm very happy with my current life."

Spears sighed and nodded once. "It would have been a phenomenal opportunity for you."

Phil tapped his phone to look at the message. "*God* gives me my opportunities."

Why on *Earth* was Carolyn messaging him now?

The blistering snow increased in its intensity. The ski lift creaked as it glided towards the landing point. Awaiting their ride, skiers milled about the resort.

"Well. The offer still stands if—what's wrong?"

Phil's grip tightened around his phone. His teeth squeaked as he grinded them and, despite the cold, his body went hot as he read Carolyn's message.

"I need to leave," Phil croaked, and he turned wide eyes to the governor. "I need to get home now."

VERSE 5

~ TIME TO CHANGE THE WORLD ~

Saturday, January 12th, 2019
Chicago, Illinois
12:00 P.M.

Fourteen-year-old Jason "Hawk" Caravan hated winter, but today he hated his sister more.

How dare she?

Cold air stung his lips and ears as the teenage boy peddled with vengeance. The bicycle spokes churned, and the mountain bike tires crunched the snow. The back of the bike went over a lump of snow and thudded against even ground. The impact jolted Hawk's butt into the air, slammed him back down, and the force rattled his tailbone.

Esther was a selfish bitch. Always had been. He hated her.

Hawk sped through a stop sign. His teeth chattered.

He didn't understand why his father, Todd, treated her like the favorite. Esther wasn't smart, and she didn't do anything worthwhile in her life. What did she have to offer the world? A love of dance? That wouldn't change the world.

But he would.

Most of the sidewalks were cleared from snow, save for patches of ice. This did not discourage his speed. He loved to bike fast, and he experienced an electric thrill when the tires slipped on ice and nearly tipped the bicycle.

Unlike the other boys at school, biking was the only sport he liked. Hawk preferred to spend his time studying technology and science. He'd often earned the role as "assigned group leader" for class projects because he could solve problems and observe patterns with calmness and speed. His mind never stopped working. Because of this, Hawk knew he had the potential to be great. He realized he could create something that would change the world.

And he had.

Hawk blinked away tears that he blamed on the wind. He'd been so excited to have breakfast with Esther and share his blueprints. He wanted her to be proud. For months, she'd promised to take him to breakfast and let him brag about his project, but it never happened. Something else always changed the plans.

"Fuck you!" Hawk cried, and he wheeled around a corner.

As he approached the next block, cars rumbled past him. Snowblowers roared, and people scraped shovels against icy cement. Kids rolled in the snow and shrieked.

Hawk scoffed. These people wasted time. There was so much to be done in the world, and folks busied themselves building snowmen. Snow-people. Whatever the politically correct term was.

But if people focused on what was important, the world would be far more successful. What was success?

Curing disease. Feeding the hungry.

Things greedy people like Esther would never understand.

Fucking bitch.

He pedaled faster, and his legs burned as he turned his bicycle towards the city. The massive buildings grew closer.

Hawk approached an alley near a ministry center and made an abrupt turn between two old brick buildings. The tires skidded and almost flung him from the bike, but he adjusted and held on.

As he entered the alley, Hawk saw an old man in a stained winter coat leaning against the wall of the ministry building. Cigarette smoke coiled into the air. He rested one hand in his coat pocket, and his beady eyes shifted towards Hawk as the boy dismounted.

"Hey, Rob. How's your day?" Hawk kicked the support stand for the bicycle and walked towards the man.

Rob nodded and exhaled smoke from the cigarette. "Same as usual, kid. What are you doing out here right now?"

Hawk's eyes drifted to the billboard at the end of the alley. It pictured a lanky black man in a suit with a radiant smile and perfectly aligned teeth.

GOVERNOR KAEMON SPEARS: SERVING YOUR COMMUNITY WITH KINDNESS AND LOGIC.

"I needed to get out of my room for a while. My sister pissed me off. Are you hungry?"

Rob chuckled. "Always."

Hawk reached into his coat pocket. "I have six dollars. It's yours."

"Hell yeah, thanks, kid." He reached out.

Hawk placed the money in Rob's grimy hands. "Just wanna make the world a better place."

Unlike his useless sister.

Rob stuffed the cash in his coat. "You will. You won't end up out here like me. You have a pretty big future in store for you."

"Do you really think that?"

The man tossed the cigarette and crushed it with the heel of his boot. "Yeah. People like you actually care, y'know? Too many greedy people. Y'know what pisses me off?"

Hawk shook his head.

"People who sit around on their asses, let the government feed them, and still complain. Look at me. The government don't give a fuck about me. Where's my free food? My medicine?"

A horn blared in the distance.

Hawk thought about his mother. No one had helped her. "I'm sorry. I want to do something about that. My mom died because the medical staff fucking gave up and let her." Tears blurred his sight.

Rob eyed the boy. "There's a little something forming in your head, ain't there, kid?"

"What do you mean?"

"I mean, you have an idea that's going to make a difference. A good difference. I can tell."

Wiping his eyes, Hawk smiled. "You're wise for—"

For being homeless. He'd been so close to saying that. "You're wise."

Rob stretched. His large, hairy belly peeked from under the coat. "Well, if you start something, just commit to it. Don't be a disappointment like the rest of these shitheads walking around the country." He walked past Hawk to leave the alley. "Going to get some food. Thanks again, kid."

Hawk's numb lips broke apart into a smile. After taking one last look at the billboard for Kaemon Spears, he hastened to his bike.

Hawk needed to meet with Spears and get his idea to the research center.

KS Industries.

Hawk smiled and mounted the bike.

Phil Jameson knew everyone, so he would be the first point of contact.

What had he been upset about again? Ah, yes. His sister. How dumb. There were better things to concern himself with.

Hawk pedaled back towards his neighborhood. The wind whistled past his ears as a to-do list formed in his head.

Organize the blueprints. Contact Phil Jameson. Meet Kaemon Spears. Get into the research center.

Change the world.

His legs moved faster, and his chest heaved up and down.

A car horn screamed as he cut into traffic. He bounced over a curb, onto the next block, and ignored the angry protests behind him. Snowy trees and mailboxes blurred past him as he rode.

If Esther wouldn't make time for him, he wouldn't make time for her. He had better things to do, anyway.

He approached the next intersection.

A snowman smiled.

No.

A snowperson.

Time to change the world.

"For you, Mom," he whispered, excited for the future, and he whipped into the next intersection.

Tires squealed. A blunt force struck his body. Bones snapped. Glass cracked. Pain electrocuted his nerves. Hawk realized he was airborne and confused but—

Time to change the world.

His body smacked against the icy ground.

VERSE 6

~ CAROLYN ~

Saturday, January 12th, 2019
Chicago, Illinois
12:00 P.M.

*D*ear Diary,

I, unfortunately, had a disturbing dream last night, and I'm feeling very unsettled. It felt so real. When I woke up, I thought it'd actually happened. It was horrible. Here is what took place.

I stood before the icon of Christ at my church. I was trying to pray, but I kept hearing this odd pounding against the sanctuary doors. Finally, I approached the doors and opened them. Phil's wife, Carolyn, stood outside the doors with a bloodied face. Her skull looked split, and I got the sense that she'd pounded her head against the doors in an attempt to break her face.

"I can't do this anymore!" she cried.

I reached for her, and she fled. I chased her, calling for her to come back and let me help her. Sobbing, Carolyn continued to flee. She screamed that she would go to hell for speaking to me. I ran after her, but you know how dreams are. Everything is slowed. You can only run so fast.

I told her she would not go to hell. I told her to speak to me and let me know what was bothering her. Carolyn kept running. We ran outside, down the snowy roadways and sidewalks. Then she disappeared around a building. I followed. I could hear her scream, and it will haunt me forever. When I turned the corner, I saw no one.

But I did see blood. It was splattered all over the road and the building walls. I suspected she committed suicide. Her voice, still desperate, echoed in my mind as I stood in horror.

"You can't tell me what to do anymore!"

I woke up. I could not go back to sleep. I am at the church now, trying to find some peace of mind, but I can't. Did I ever do anything to imply to Carolyn that she is going to hell?

Did I, as her priest, ever tell her to do something that brought her harm? I would like to call her soon and see if she is okay. Maybe my dream was just that... a dream.

But it felt so real. Every nightmare I have feels real, and I want it to end. I've continued to have the same nightmares. The night before my dream of Carolyn, I dreamt of a date. February 15th, 2020. I heard screams, explosions, and gunshots. I woke up. Before that, I dreamt of a boy who could move the earth and control the weather. As the earth quaked, and rain poured from the sky, I saw the young Arab boy with his arms in the air. He screamed. He seemed heartbroken, and I sobbed for him. Somehow, I knew his name. It was on my lips.

"Ahdam!" I screamed, and I woke up.

Before that, I dreamt of people falling from the sky. I hate that one. It's horrifying.

"Save us from tribulation!" they scream and pummel the earth.

But despite these horrific dreams, there is one nightmare I still cannot comprehend. I still don't know if it was a dream or reality.

I still don't know if Mariel caught that bullet or not.

Guide me, Lord.

Love, Fr. Jerome.

Fr. Jerome closed the journal and placed it on his desk. He sighed and rubbed his fingers in circles against his temples. Though common after his nightmares, the headaches still felt dreadful. Over the counter medication took the edge off, but nothing like he hoped they would.

He just wanted the nightmares to stop.

The old man leaned back in his chair and thought about the morning. He was worried about Esther. Despite her attempt to convince him that she was fine, he knew her better than that. She wasn't fine. In fact, he didn't suspect she'd been *fine* since her mother's death. Certainly, she'd grieved, but he wasn't sure that she'd found the best coping mechanisms.

Esther was like a daughter to him. He wanted to make sure she was okay.

When Fr. Jerome stopped by the diner to speak to Mariel, he noticed his son also looked dour.

"I'm just tired," Mariel had stated.

Fr. Jerome suspected otherwise... especially because he'd noticed the young man's eyes darting towards *Caravan's Books*.

Had something happened between Mariel and Esther?

He wanted to know, but he also knew asking Mariel about Esther might cause him to shut down. It always had. So, he held his tongue.

Sometimes, Fr. Jerome felt he was too passive about situations. But after years of strange phenomena, what more could he do? The questions had always been there; the answers hadn't. He'd go far more insane if he continued to question things he'd receive no answer to.

Like the fact that *humans couldn't catch bullets.*

But Mariel *was* human. The young man lived, breathed, experienced, and felt just as everyone else did. That horrible night hadn't made sense. Would it ever?

Fr. Jerome jumped in his chair as the shrill tone of his cell phone broke the silence. Breathing heavily, the priest grabbed the phone, swiped the screen, and brought it to his ear. "This is Jerome."

"I can't do this anymore!" A woman's voice slurred into his ear.

Goosebumps rose on his skin. He began to tremble. "I'm sorry?"

"I can't," the woman sobbed, and her voice sounded muffled. A horn screamed on the other side of the phone, and Fr. Jerome realized she was driving.

"Carolyn?" he murmured, and his voice shook too.

Tires screeched.

"Why is there Hell when we live it every day?" Carolyn sobbed, and her words slowed. She sounded drunk.

"Carolyn, are you okay? Where are you?" Fr. Jerome stood up and darted towards the office exit.

"I'm drunk," the woman screeched. "And I think I hit someone."

"Tell me where you are." Fr. Jerome yanked his keys that dangled from the hook on the wall. The hook tore from the wall as he exited the office. His body moved as if it knew exactly what it wanted to do, but his brain did not.

What *could* he do?

"I'm going to hell because I drank, and I hit someone, aren't I?" Carolyn moaned, and her voice broke. A door slammed. Wind whistled. "I wish I was strong."

"Carolyn!" Fr. Jerome fled from the church. It was the fastest he'd moved since the night Mariel had caught the bullet. He was chasing her.

Just like in the nightmare.

"What is it, Father Jerome?" she asked, as if she'd been having a normal phone conversation with him.

"Where are you?" The priest slipped on the ice but fell against his car in an effort to catch himself. He needed to get her help, but he didn't want to end the call.

"I'm going to catch a train," she responded, and the sudden calm in her voice drove the situation's urgency even higher.

"Where?" Fr. Jerome buckled his seatbelt. His chest felt tight. He couldn't help but wonder if he was overdue for a heart attack. His family *did* have a history of cardiac disease.

"I don't know," she wailed through the phone, her voice rising in emotion again. "It doesn't matter."

The call ended.

"Lord, have mercy." Fr. Jerome looked at Carolyn's name flashing on the screen. The phone almost slipped from his shaking fingers as he dialed 911.

Would she follow through on suicide plans? Was that even her plan, or was something else going on?

"911, what's the location of your emergency?" a young, male voice asked.

Fr. Jerome trembled. Why was he in his car? He couldn't *do* anything. As he struggled to breathe, snow flurries fluttered through the air. He recognized that he was speaking, but the numbness in his brain made it difficult to comprehend what was coming out of his mouth.

"Do you have your friend's number? We can possibly ping the location."

Fr. Jerome withdrew the phone from his ear and looked up Carolyn's phone number. As he spoke into the phone, his pulse pounded in his head. He tried to remember his nightmare in hopes that it would reveal a location. Did that make him a narcissist for thinking he'd had a vision? There'd been no scientific evidence that one could experience prophetic dreams. But *biblically...*

He caught his breath. In his dream, Carolyn had disappeared behind a brick building with distinct red graffiti. What had it said? *Pe...pea...peace of mind.* That's what it said, and there was one building in the city where he'd seen that lettering. It was outside the *Ayre Community,* a gated business community that was amongst the richest in the city. He'd taken Mariel to a barbecue place a few miles from the rich community. People called it the *"bad"* area, but he'd never had any issues.

Fr. Jerome pulled out of the parking lot. It was a fifteen-minute drive from his location... *if* she hadn't crashed her vehicle some place.

Fr. Jerome placed his phone in the cupholder and raced down the icy road. His lips were chapped.

This was insane. Was he chasing reality? Or a nightmare?

"You should stop and let first responders do their work," he said to himself.

A traffic signal turned yellow. He came to a halt, and it transitioned to red.

He couldn't forget the sound of disappointment in her voice, like *he* had failed her as her priest. Was he responding to help her because he cared, or because of *pride*?

This was not about him.

But she was a sheep amongst his flock, despite her marriage to the man who hated him the most: Phil Jameson.

Fr. Jerome's eyes widened. Had *Phil* driven her to do this?

"You can't tell me what to do anymore," Carolyn had said in the nightmare.

And Phil *always* told her what to do. He was horrible to the woman. He condescended her, rebuked her, laughed at her when she stated an opinion. Granted, Phil was horrible to everyone... but if he was such a monster in public, how was he behind closed doors?

As his stomach churned with nausea, Fr. Jerome wondered if intervention might have prevented this. When she came to him to discuss her marital problems, she'd been so closed off. Perhaps he should have prodded her more.

The sun peeked from the clouds and illuminated the snow. The city stirred with traffic from vehicles and pedestrians. Traffic signals blinked, buses hissed, and Fr. Jerome bit his lip as he drove through it all. A siren wailed. Was it for Carolyn?

His knuckles paled as he gripped the steering wheel.

The minutes passed. The area grew quieter. The buildings deteriorated. Graffiti grew more prominent. He was close to the railroad, and terror increased his pulse.

He didn't want the nightmare to be right.

"Lord," he prayed, "guide me."

Two emo teenagers crossed the road with laced fingers. They swung their hands back and forth.

Then... Fr. Jerome saw the building with the red graffiti.

Peace of mind. It flashed like a neon sign, taunting him.

He slowed to a stop at a stop sign. Breathing hard, he waited. When he turned right, he would see the railroad tracks. As if in warning, the sign screamed at him.

STOP.

Should he?

"Maybe you're wrong," the priest muttered and turned right.

There it was. The railroad. The red lights flashed, the bell chimed, and the arms dropped. In the center of the track stood a figure, and despite blurred vision, Fr. Jerome knew who it was.

"No!" the priest screamed. He put the car in park and scrambled from the vehicle.

Carolyn stood with her fists clenched. She faced the oncoming train with a defiance the priest had never yet seen from her. Despite the odds, she looked powerful. Confident.

Like she'd made her decision.

For a moment, Fr. Jerome wondered if his presence would disturb her. He'd never seen her like this before.

The cold air bit his skin. The screaming train brought him back to reality.

"Carolyn, I love you! Don't do this!" The priest slipped on the ice and almost fell, but he stumbled on. He wondered when she'd last been hugged, when she'd last felt safe. He should have embraced her at their last meeting.

Carolyn didn't look at him. She swayed on the tracks and reached towards the train as if it was the only embrace she needed.

"You can't tell me what to do anymore!" she screamed, and she flung her hands into the air.

"Carolyn!"

In a blur, the train roared across the railroad where she'd been standing seconds ago.

A bystander screamed. The priest did, too. Lost his balance. Slipped on the ice again. As tears whipped from his face, he tried to grasp something, anything, to hold him up, but his hands only found air.

The priest fell, and his head bounced against the icy cement.

Chapter 4: Verse 1

~ Normal ~

Saturday, January 12th, 2019

Chicago, Illinois

That Saturday morning felt like Christmas Day to Mariel Nadier. It was cold, snowy, and, just like a child awaiting gifts, he'd had something—

—someone—

—to look forward to before work.

That is... until she failed to show.

Earlier, Mariel had waited at the diner. He'd sat at a corner table in black slacks and a white button-down, reaching back and adjusting his ponytail again and again. There he'd waited, his eyes shifting from his phone to the snowy streets of Chicago.

Disappointment, and a touch of anger, had rattled him after he told Esther he had to clock in to work. Then he'd started to worry. Usually, she alerted him if anything changed. He'd almost called her, but fear that she'd think him annoying overcame the desire. Despite their friendship that had lasted years, Mariel was very shy around Esther Caravan.

He wished he had the boldness of Gabe, who he *knew* was attracted to Esther. Gabe made it evident based on comments and his excessive ogling. Mariel feared their personality differences would give Gabe the upper hand if he ever asked Esther to date him. This fear induced jealousy whenever she and Gabe spent time together, and he often wondered if there *was* a romance occurring of which he was unaware.

The idea made him anxious.

Mad.

When his dad stopped by the diner to visit him, he tried to hide the sullen look, but the priest noticed it immediately. His dad always did.

"Are you alright?" he'd asked. "I just dropped Esther off at the bookstore."

Mariel wanted to ask where Fr. Jerome picked her up, but instead he asked: "Is she okay?"

"I think so. She wasn't acting like her usual, energizer bunny self. Stop by if you can. I'll see you later at the church."

After their embrace, Fr. Jerome left with his steaming coffee.

As Mariel wondered about Esther's circumstances, he refilled an old couple's coffee.

"Can you bring us our check, please?" An old man asked feebly. He stared up at Mariel's tall frame with beady eyes surrounded by drooping skin folds. They were shadowed by the lid of a discolored white baseball cap.

"Of course, Sir. Anything else?" Mariel's eyes darted to the bookstore across the street.

"No. Just the check, please."

With a brief smile, he nodded and retreated to the back of the diner where the register was located. Servers bustled; chefs clattered dishes and yelled out completed orders. As Mariel returned to the table with the bill, his eyes drifted outside.

A bus with a *Project Savior* logo sped past the window. Then, he saw Esther step from the bookstore.

His heart pounded hard. Was she coming to the diner?

She glanced back and forth before she crossed the street. As her brown hair blew about her face, the young man watched with awe.

Shivering, arms folded, Esther Caravan walked towards the diner. She *never* had a coat with her.

"Sir!"

He started a little. "Sorry, Sir, here's your check. No rush."

"Just take my card now. Don't walk away. You'll never come back," the old man grumbled.

Mariel hung his head and took the card with the receipt. "I'll be right back."

Working fast, Mariel glanced towards Esther as she approached the diner. He looked at his watch. Maybe Jeff would let him take a quick break.

With long strides, he returned to the table. "Thank you, both, I hope you have a wonderful weekend." He raised his eyes as the diner door opened, and Esther stepped inside. Her eyes met his.

She smiled.

His heart slammed against his chest. Raising his forefinger, clad with a silver ring that contained a cross in its center (his father's gift), Mariel rushed past coworkers and customers to ask his supervisor if he could take a break.

"Did you clear the other tables?" the short, bald man with a red goatee asked and stared up at his tall employee.

"Yes, Sir."

"Then, go ahead. Keep it short. *Short.*"

Nearly colliding with another server, Mariel fled from the kitchen.

Hands in her back pockets, Esther stood waiting for him at the entrance. She smiled again. "Hey, Mars."

He looked down at her, lost himself in her eyes, and then shifted his gaze away. "Hey."

The possibility that his eyes might show her what he felt terrified him. And she was so beautiful that it hurt his chest to admire her. It hurt because he couldn't have her.

He *shouldn't.*

There were several reasons.

Esther deserved someone who came at least a little close to her level of vigor. Most of the people he knew loved to be in her presence; adults and children alike. They craved her attention. Mariel was introverted; sullen. Esther would get bored.

Also, he respected Todd Caravan. The man made it clear he wanted Esther's time with him limited. Fr. Jerome raised him to respect boundaries. It sucked, but Mariel understood why.

Mariel remembered closing his mouth over the pistol in hopes that he would pull the trigger and the voices would go away. When it malfunctioned, the evil voice laughed at him... even as Todd had wrestled him to the ground.

That was the number one reason he *shouldn't* have Esther. Throughout his life, Mariel had *tried* praying the voices away. Medication hadn't helped. Therapy hadn't helped.

Esther couldn't find out. She'd view him differently if she knew about those *things* that followed him and often told him that he wasn't... normal.

The mystery enraged him. One of the voices told him to embrace the rage, because to *feel* was to *be* human.

And man, did he *feel.* He felt for Esther, but she deserved someone without his level of baggage. Someone normal.

Like Gabe.

Mariel winced.

No! Fuck that guy.

"Are you okay?" Esther stepped closer.

A flowery scent, mixed with a hint of booze, drifted into his nostrils. Despite the other smell, her perfume scent almost drew him closer. "Yeah, I'm fine. I have a fifteen-minute break. Do you want some coffee?"

Esther shook her head. She did not break her gaze. "I just want to talk with you. I'm so sorry about this morning."

Mariel scratched his head. Then, feeling bold, he reached down to take her hand. He walked towards a table in the corner. "Let's sit."

To his joy, as Esther followed him, her fingers responded and entwined with his.

He pulled out a chair for her and then seated himself across the table. Heart racing, he folded his hands on the table like he was preparing for an intervention. "Are you okay? I was worried about you."

Esther ran her fingers through her hair and brushed it to the opposite side again. "I was depressed about coming in second at the dance competition last night. I spent the night at Ashley's and woke up late."

"Ah."

"I appreciate you calling my dad. He wasn't frustrated with you, was he?"

Mariel shook his head and stared at his hands. "No. He appreciated me calling him. He was worried too, you know."

"I know." She played with several strands of her hair.

Both were quiet. Then Mariel looked at her and said, "I'm really happy you're my friend."

What the heck? What was the point of even *saying* that?

Esther looked at him. Mariel noticed her expression... she looked *sad*. But the expression was brief, and she flashed a smile as she continued to play with her hair. "You're a blessing to everyone, Mars, including me."

"No, I'm not."

"When are you going to start liking yourself?"

As he stared at the table, Mariel shrugged. The corners of his mouth twitched to create the potential of a smile. "I like myself enough."

"Mars."

"What?"

"Why can't you ever look at me?"

Because it hurts.

But he raised his eyes and met her gaze again. "I don't know."

"Do you do that with other people?" she persisted. "Or just me?"

"I struggle with eye contact."

Esther leaned forward and kept her arms underneath the table. Her hair fell over her right shoulder, and the green shirt dipped low enough to expose soft cleavage.

Mariel's face went hot, and he twiddled his thumbs.

"Mars... you'll never get a girlfriend if you don't look at a girl." Her voice was soft, teasing, and he was certain she could hear his heart thumping.

"I don't need a girlfriend. Or want one."

"Hmm. Phil Jameson was right then. That long hair?" Her eyes twinkled. "I *knew* you were gay."

He gritted his teeth. "Don't say that." Was she teasing? Or did she view him like that?

"Well." Esther leaned back into her chair, scanning Mariel's face with mischief and enjoyment. "Prove it."

He wanted to. So badly.

Mariel allowed himself to look at her, to notice her curves; the swell of her breasts, the skin of her throat, her soft, inviting lips. It was as if he'd noticed her for the first time again. Then, quickly, he lowered his eyes.

Lord Jesus Christ, Son of God, have mercy upon me and save me, a sinner. Lord Jesus Christ, Son of God, have mercy—

"*Mariel*. Stop muttering to yourself, I was just teasing."

Shit, had he been whispering? Without a doubt, if she hadn't thought him strange before, she would now.

"Mars? Hey. It's okay, I'm sorry. I wasn't trying to be cruel. Just a joke."

He felt her fingers touch his. Stammering, he said, "N-no. It's not you, I'm just—" He stopped and allowed his thumb to brush across the side of her hand. Had it been his imagination... or had she shuddered?

"Esther, I just think you're really—"

His phone buzzed in his pocket. Thank *God*, something to stop the train from derailing. He stopped talking to reach into his pocket.

"Oh come on, *tell* me, Mars."

"Sorry, I need to take this." He put the phone to his ear. "Hello?"

He heard sirens and a man's voice. "Is this Mariel Nadier?"

"Yes?"

"Your dad had an accident. He's on his way to the emergency room at the Savior Center, are you okay to drive here?"

Was he breathing? He couldn't tell.

The siren screamed in the phone, and Mariel began to stutter. "Is he *okay*? I'll be there." Aggressively, he stood, tripped, and knocked the chair backwards.

Restaurant patrons turned their heads.

"Mariel, what's *wrong*?" Eyes wide, Esther stood up too.

Mariel held the phone hard against his ear. "What happened? He's okay, right?" His voice grew more ragged, tearful.

The man spoke fast. "He slipped on ice, struck his head on cement. He's unresponsive. If you can get here safely, we will have more information for you when you get here, okay?"

"O-okay. I'm on my way."

When Mariel ended the call, he caught Esther's eyes.

Something else was wrong.

She stood across from him, hand across her mouth, tears and terror in her eyes. Body frozen, she lowered her own phone from her ear.

"Mars... someone struck my brother on his bike. He's on his way to the Savior Center in critical condition."

What the *fuck?*

Gritting his teeth, Mariel rushed around the table. "I'm getting my keys, and we'll go. My dad injured his head, and he's being taken there too."

With his heart in his throat, Mariel alerted his supervisor, grabbed his coat, and ran towards the front. Stumbling past the servers and patrons, he jogged back to Esther and extended his hand with the black jacket in its grip. "Take my coat. Let's go."

Gusts of freezing wind blew into the diner. With hands locked together, Mariel Nadier and Esther Caravan rushed from the building.

VERSE 2

~ OLIVIA ~

Sunday, January 13th, 2019
Moscow, Russia
1:03 A.M.

Each time she shifted, her body ached. So, in the darkness of her room, Agent 4 lay flat on her back and stared at the ceiling.

"The world wants you, Agent 4!"

Papa's voice rang louder in her mind than the screams of her dying colleagues.

She loved it. Not his voice, but his *words*. They had purpose. The words reminded her that everything she'd accomplished had purpose... and *that* would be revealed tomorrow morning when she received her first assignment.

Tira Petrov blinked. Her eyelids hurt too, and she snorted at the absurdity. As she closed and opened her fists beneath the sheets, she analyzed the violent night.

Nine agents... agents she'd known and trained with since childhood. Of course, she had no emotional attachments to them. If necessary, she would repeat the violence again. But despite her elevated state of pride and sense of validation, Tira decided the whole ordeal had been wasteful. Though *subhuman*, the other agents had performed well in their years and could have been utilized for positions within their abilities.

Aleksey Petrov's lust for entertainment confused and, to some extent, disturbed her if she thought too hard about it. If things had been up to her, she wouldn't have wasted her agents' talents against each other. She would have found enemies or, even better, traitors of the country and used them as test subjects.

But, alas, she was not Aleksey Petrov, and she had no interest in being him. Right now, tonight, she bore the name *Agent 4*—the only name she'd ever wanted. And unless she aspired further, the only name that would ever matter.

In the darkness, her phone lit up. Groaning, Tira stretched an arm toward her nightstand and grabbed the phone.

"Are you resting, my sweet?"

With a brief snarl, Tira typed. *"What do you think?"*

"You deserve it, my sweet, little girl."

Tira made a retching noise. *"So was I an advertisement or an agent?"*

"Well... both."

Agent 4 rolled her eyes. She didn't understand how the president of Russia could demand such respect and yet simultaneously let on like an idiot.

The phone lit up again. *"We will speak tomorrow about your assignment. Get some rest."*

Tira set the phone aside and closed her eyes to imagine her placement as an agent. She'd travelled the world, and she'd trained and studied throughout the United States, Europe, Asia, and the Middle East. She had a penchant for problem solving and violence. As the young woman lay still on her bed, she imagined her duties as *Agent 4*—every mission's thrill, every assassination, battle, and opportunity to decode complex problems. Perhaps she'd be stationed within different countries for a brief period of time. That'd be ideal.

Arrival. Task completion. Relocate.

The agent smiled.

A soft knock broke her from her trance. Her eyes opened, and she turned her head to the door.

The knock came again, a coded rhythm she knew well.

Hissing through her teeth, Tira sat up and winced. Her ribs felt as though they'd been stomped, and her joints ached with each movement.

Was this how a *subhuman* felt after an easy jog?

But Tira made it to the door. With an eager sigh, she opened it.

Familiar perfume filled her nostrils.

Olivia, the raven-haired beauty, came forward into Tira's arms.

The door clicked shut. An automatic whirring noise broke the silence as it locked.

"Are you okay?" Tira held the woman close, staring at the door behind them as Olivia trembled in her arms. That's what one was *supposed* to ask, wasn't it? *Are you okay?*

What Olivia saw that evening wasn't normal... at least, not for a subhuman whose only concern was ensuring the gluttonous politicians were fed.

"I was scared," Olivia whispered, her breath warm against Tira's neck.

"Of me?" Agent 4 asked, voice flat.

"No," Olivia murmured. "I was scared *for* you."

"Oh."

Silence.

"Are *you* okay?" Olivia asked, and her fingers traced lazy circles over Tira's tank top.

"Of course I am okay. I had a good night."

"A good night?"

Tira frowned. Perhaps it'd been a poor choice of words. "A *productive* night."

"Tira—"

"What do you want me to say, Olivia?" Agent 4 stepped backward, stiffening. "I completed a task, and that task brought me toward my next goal. If you are looking for an emotional response referencing tonight's event, you should find someone else."

Olivia took a step forward and outstretched a hand. "I'm sorry. Touch me? Please?"

The agent's eyes dropped to Olivia's outstretched hand. It was then that she noticed what the young woman was wearing... a silk, purple slip, one that Tira had purchased for her a few weeks ago. Its straps fell just below her shoulders, and the neckline drooped low. It exposed her cleavage, soft fair breasts that made Tira's mouth water with anticipation.

"Come here," the agent whispered and grasped Olivia's hand.

Their lips met. Then their tongues, and Tira snaked her fingers through Olivia's hair before pulling her to the bed.

As they collapsed against each other, Olivia returned her kisses with equal intensity, and Tira Petrov came undone. As she crawled on top of Olivia, her palms roamed the server's body, reaching beneath the slip and finding the softness of her breasts.

"I lied," Olivia moaned, arching her back. "I *am* afraid of you."

Tira hovered over her and pushed her hand higher up her thigh. "Are you?"

In response, Olivia's legs came apart. "I'm afraid of what you do to me, how you make me fee—"

Tira interrupted her with a rough kiss and pushed her harder against the bed.

Agent 4 had warned Olivia, told her those statements and feelings were unwise. She'd been fond enough of Olivia to give that advice early in their relationship.

"Protect your heart," Tira had told her. *"Because I will not."*

"Get on top of me," Agent 4 ordered and rolled onto her back.

As the straps fell from her shoulders, Olivia followed and straddled the agent's lap. "Do what you want with me," she whispered shakily.

It'd been a summary of their relationship from the beginning.

A year ago, Tira had first noticed Olivia as a new hire in the Kremlin. The twenty-four-year-old server had encouraged her approach through flirtatious glances until brief conversations hinted towards a strong, mutual attraction.

Tira slipped her hand between Olivia's legs. Breathing hard, she slid her fingers up the soft skin of her thigh until she felt the wet warmth she was searching for.

Olivia gasped, and her fingernails dug into Tira's shoulders. "Inside me."

"What do you say?"

"Please."

With an abrupt jerk of her arm, Tira entered Olivia with two fingers and tightened her fist around the woman's black hair. With a cry, Olivia's hips responded and rocked with slow, rhythmic thrusts against Tira's hand.

Tira gazed up at her. The woman's black hair cascaded over her shoulders and tickled Agent 4's arms. Would she *miss* Olivia or miss *this*?

They'd bonded, and Tira recognized that she *did* appreciate the nurturing she'd received from Olivia.

When Olivia noticed Tira taking peanut butter and carrots from the kitchen, their relationship began. Olivia, who'd proven she wanted every opportunity to speak to Tira, offered to bring the snack to the agent's room. At the time, Tira didn't trust anyone in her room, but agreed to meet at a private study. It became a tradition, and Tira soon lost her virginity to the black-haired server on the couch in the study. Eventually, Agent 4 allowed her to come to her room where they consummated their relationship as frequently as Tira's schedule allowed. It became a *routine exchange* for Tira, but for Olivia...

"I have to tell you something. Something you may not like," Tira spoke sharply, curling her fingers into her lover.

Olivia's eyes opened dreamily. "You're... you're—*fuck*—telling me something bad *now*?" Olivia's voice shook as she took small gasps of air with each movement. Her fingernails dug deeper into Tira's skin, and her hips moved faster.

Tira released Olivia's hair and brought her other hand down to grab her hip. Her own hips arched, but her words came without emotion. "Petrov is giving me my first assignment tomorrow." She raised her thumb against Olivia's clitoris and rubbed. It brought short, abrupt cries from the server.

"Isn't that—*mmm*—isn't that a good thing?" Olivia bent down and clasped Tira's lips with hers, catching the agent's bottom lip with her teeth.

Both women lay tangled in each other, their skin glistening with sweat. Olivia began to thrust against Tira with a sense of urgency that nearly destroyed the agent's calm demeanor.

"Yes." Tira broke the kiss to speak. "But I will be leaving Russia." She bit her lip and arched her hips again. The movement thrust her fingers deeper, sending Olivia into a series of cries and intense trembling.

And if Olivia had heard Tira, she could not tell. The Kremlin Palace server was in another world of orgasmic intensity and pleasure. With high-pitched cries and heavy gasps, Olivia sat upright, and her head fell back, granting Tira the view of her exposed throat. Agent 4 watched her with hungry eyes until Olivia collapsed, trembling and exhausted, next to her.

In silence, they both lay for several moments.

Olivia turned to Tira and placed her lips against the agent's ear. "Let me do something for you," she whispered, tracing her fingers towards the agent's breasts.

Tira grasped her wrist and held it. "It's okay. I'm satisfied through you tonight." She wanted the pleasure, but thoughts of her future distracted her. Every nerve in her body hummed, but not with pleasure. She wouldn't be able to orgasm, and it'd piss her off.

Olivia propped herself on her elbow. "So... what were you telling me? About your mission?"

Tira stared at the ceiling. "I said that I may be leaving the country. I will find out tomorrow."

Olivia's voice shook. "Let me come with you."

Tira turned her head towards the server. "You know who I am. You know *what* I am. I explained that from the beginning, and I have no interest in a long-term relationship. Do you understand that?"

"Please," Olivia whispered. "Don't."

"Olivia." Tira's voice carried a warning.

Hastily, the woman wiped her eyes with the back of her hand and sat up. "I'm sorry."

"There is no need to apologize. I cannot control how you feel, but consider it a relief. You will not be hurt due to unrealistic expectations of our bond." Tira raised a hand to her forehead and rubbed it. She wanted to sleep.

Olivia looked at her, her head low. "Promise me you'll tell me what he says tomorrow? You won't leave without saying goodbye?"

Tira dropped her hand and brushed her fingers against Olivia's cheek. "I cannot promise anything with how unpredictable my life is, but I will do my best."

Olivia shivered. "May I sleep with you tonight?"

Tira rubbed her thumb over a teardrop that had slipped over Olivia's cheek. "Okay."

As Olivia faded to sleep in Tira's arms, the young agent breathed in her scent and closed her eyes.

Where would she go? What would life look like with a new level of independence? Despite Tira Petrov's desire to sleep, she remained awake the majority of the night as she contemplated the next step of her fate as President Petrov's Agent 4.

* * *

Sunday, January 13th, 2019

"A *what?*" Tira shrieked.

Cigar smoke filled the office, and Aleksey Petrov rolled the cigar in his fingers. His white teeth almost glinted as he grinned at her. "Calm down."

Eyes wide, Tira glanced around the office as if expecting another person to emerge. "*Papa!* Explain what's going on."

Petrov leaned back in his seat and eyed her. "Since when do you make demands of *me?*"

Tira growled and struggled to breathe. She needed to calm herself... overreaction would earn her a reprimand, and a *reprimand* from Petrov was not an easy challenge to overcome. "Please tell me why I am going to be a *street* cop in Chicago, Illinois, Papa."

"You aren't considering the bigger picture, my sweet."

"You haven't given me much of a picture to consider," Tira retorted.

"Well, perhaps if you *listen...* you will see it?" Petrov dragged on the cigar. Smoke coiled.

Tira glared. "I am listening," she snapped.

The president drummed his fingers against the desk. "You are intelligent enough to know that global tensions are on the rise. They have been since—" he gestured towards her, "—since your little stunt the last time you were in Chicago. You know... the senator?"

Tira's palms felt sweaty as she gripped her seat. "I'm aware."

"Mmhmm. Anyway, for that reason, there have been international negotiations between different countries, including but not limited to an increase of security, federal law enforcement, military, etc."

"Okay?"

"No need to concern yourself over the details on that," Petrov gestured again, and the cigar journeyed with his hand. "Here's where you're concerned. One of the negotiations grants you asylum in the United States in return for *our* aid."

Tira scowled. "Please explain."

"In a nutshell, you impressed someone very important last night. And they want to offer you an opportunity to train a new, covert sect of federal agents in Chicago."

Tira eyed the large desk, tempted to flip it in hopes that it would crush him. "You aren't serious? I did *not* train to the level I *am* to *babysit* federal agents of *the fucking United States!*" She stood up.

"Sit *down,* Tira." Petrov bared his teeth at her, and his voice held a threat.

She snarled back but plopped down like an angry child.

"Are you done? Or shall I remove your status of top agent and gift it to someone else?" Petrov raised an eyebrow.

Seething, Agent 4 gripped the armrests. "I am done."

"Excellent... because your asylum in Chicago is simply a cover." Petrov set aside the cigar, entered a code into his desk drawer, and pulled it open.

Enraged, but curious, Tira watched.

Petrov slapped a folder in front of her. "While you're training the federal agents, as well as participating as a *street* cop, *this* will be your assignment from me. Open it."

CONFIDENTIAL.

Narrowing her eyes, Tira reached for the manila folder. With sudden eagerness and relief that her role hadn't been simply reduced to aiding the United States, she flipped it open.

MEMORANDUM:

This description of the assignment and its attached contents are highly confidential. It is a federal crime to share the contents of this memorandum, and such conduct will be prosecuted—

Bla, bla, bla. That was the first page. Tira scanned the document, and then she turned the memorandum to reveal the second page.

Déjà vu. That was what society called a strong sense of familiarity... and it was what Tira Petrov experienced so abruptly that it startled her.

The assignment was a photo, stamped in Russian with another *CONFIDENTIAL* warning. A young woman with wavy brown hair and a graduate cap stood leaning over a city bridge at dusk. Blurred lights glowed in the background, and her eyes—a strange combination of light brown and blue—gazed in soft concentration at the camera-holder. Her lips, glazed with light lipstick, were parted.

"Um... is this *it*?" Tira questioned, but did not look away from the photo.

"Her name is Esther Marie Caravan. She is twenty, and she was born on September the sixteenth of 1998. Her birth location was in Michigan, but she's been an Illinois resident her entire life. And yes," Petrov picked up the cigar again, "*that* is your assignment."

A low growl rumbled from Tira's throat. Her hands shook. "Please tell me that my assignment is to assassinate her? And then I move on to my next assignment, hmm?"

"*No!*" Petrov roared. His face contorted and grew red. "You are testing me, my *sweet*."

Heart racing, Tira sat back in the chair and drew a breath.

Inhale. Exhale. Breathe.

She let it out. "I overstepped. My apologies."

"Fucking yes, you overstepped, you presumptuous cunt. I will knock your fucking teeth out if you make one more snide remark. Do you understand me?" Petrov wheezed. The cigar smoke continued coiling through the air. The ashes glowed.

"I understand."

"No harm comes to her. Your role is to monitor her and ensure her safety at all times."

Babysitting, Tira thought. "May I ask a question?"

"You may."

"What is her importance?"

Petrov put out the cigar. "She's carrying a microchip that will give you the ability to monitor her location and activities at all times."

He hadn't answered Tira's question. In fact, he'd *avoided* her question by diversion.

"So *she* isn't important," Tira added. "The chip is."

"Tira," Petrov's voice deepened, and he leaned forward. "Let's ensure we are on the same page on this. Her importance is above your pay grade right now. Understood?"

"...Yes." Her mind went mad with countless questions she couldn't control.

And she despised losing control of her thoughts.

"Repeat after me then," Petrov ordered.

Tira ground her teeth. Her face was hot now. "Her importance is above my pay grade right now."

"Excellent, your hearing abilities are still there."

Tira ignored the quip. "Do I make contact with this girl? Is she a subhuman?"

"She's a subhuman, yes." Petrov kicked his feet up onto the desk. His polished shoes glinted in the light. "There's no need to make contact with her unless necessary. If you do, I'd advise that you do it under quick necessity, or as a friend."

Tira snorted. "I'd rather—" she stopped and folded her hands in her lap to ensure the *snide* remark didn't exit her lips. "Is there a specific goal to this process? Do I have further instructions that go beyond monitoring her?"

"Not until I issue them." Peering into the small mirror on his desk, the president grabbed a toothpick and picked at his gums. "I will ensure you receive step by step instructions on your role in Chicago. You'll be replacing an agent who's been stationed there. Michael. He will be your first contact once you arrive. Is there anything in my teeth?"

Glowering, Tira spoke through her own teeth. "Yes."

"Where?" Petrov brought the mirror to his face.

"I am joking. Your teeth are impeccable as usual."

The president looked past the mirror at his daughter. "You're cute."

Tira shrugged.

"Any further questions?"

"No."

"Pack lightly. Your closet is already filled with clothes you wear and clothes you like."

Tira raised her eyebrow again. "How do you know what clothes I wear?"

Petrov smirked. "You say that like I don't own every panty you've purchased."

The clock ticked.

Tira snarled.

Petrov tossed the toothpick into the trash. "You're leaving in a few days."

"This subject—Esther—does she know anything?"

"Nope, and she shouldn't." The president met her eyes. "Don't look so sullen. Once you've received your first paycheck—from the States, *and especially* from me—you'll cheer right up."

Tira twiddled her thumbs. Money was wonderful, but *purpose* was better.

This babysitting job did not seem *purposeful.*

It was another cage, even worse than Petrov's world. At least in Petrov's empire there came an unexpected thrill, a *demand* to achieve more, and more, and—

"Tira," Aleksey said, coming around the desk to lean against it. "Listen to me. This assignment may not seem critical, but it is. *You earned* top status as an agent, and I would never give this assignment to someone beneath that level. This girl is important. *You* are important. Don't take that for granted, and I promise you that your reward will be great."

Tira raised her eyes. "My reward?"

Petrov smiled. "Think about what you really want... and it shall be yours."

Her head hurt. What more *could* she want outside of being the top agent? She'd worked her entire life to attain this status. It seemed impossible to want anything more. But—

"Okay," she said. "Are we finished?"

Petrov nodded and extended his hand. "Congratulations, Agent 4. You're free."

VERSE 3

~ AIRPLANE BANNER ~

Saturday, January 12th, 2019

Chicago, Illinois

When Hawk was born, Esther had been less than enthused. In the hospital, she'd looked at him, scrunched her face, and screamed that she wasn't *fucking* pleased. Verbatim.

Her father had gasped, and nurses had giggled. But her mother, Mary, had smiled with grace and love, pulling her close to say—

"You're going to be a phenomenal big sister. I can feel it."

But she'd tried to lock herself in her room. Scattered Legos around the floor in hopes that it'd prevent her parents from entering. Unfortunately for Esther, they took away her Legos after warning her multiple times to pick them up. After realizing that it took too much energy to protest, she decided she'd try to like her little brother.

Soon, she grew to love him and begged to babysit him.

That thrilled her mother.

And as Esther watched him grow into an extraordinary little boy, she realized just how nice it might actually *be* to have a child one day.

Not this year though, and definitely not Gabe's.

Now, Esther stood before her brother's hospital bed, just as she'd stood before her mother's on the day she died.

Room 237. She remembered that room number with a clarity she wished she could forget.

Right now, though, guilt burned her throat like the bile she'd puked earlier after waking up in Gabe's goddamn apartment. She felt *guilt* because, for a moment, she almost wished she could trade her brother for the return of her mother.

How *horrible* was that? God, she was pathetic. Why would she even think such a fucked up thing?

Granted, she wasn't *particularly* close with Hawk, partially because he had the tendency to treat her like she was trashy. He gave her so many mixed signals.

"Hang out with me. No wait, you're not smart, don't bother. Let me show you this project I'm working on. You're a dancer? Well, that's a waste of time."

And Esther *knew* she was "the adult". He wasn't, so she wasn't sure why his childish behavior *bothered* her so much.

"Take your pompous, nerdy ass and go fuck yourself," she'd told him over a week ago, when he'd mocked her for daring to express the fear of losing her dance competition.

And he'd deserved that response, but now Esther was terrified. He'd actually gone and fucked himself, clearly, since he was wrapped up in a hospital bed, and she didn't want that for him.

She didn't want that at all.

Esther *wanted* him to succeed at whatever the hell he was so focused on. She wanted him to come to her and share his new ideas and aspirations, *even* if they seemed a bit grandiose for his age. She wanted the opportunity to support him all of the ways she'd wanted her mother there to support *her*.

But now?

That chance might be gone.

Tears spilled. Splashed over her chin and plopped against the bed railing. The hospital smelled. She *hated* the smell of the hospital. And it was cold.

"Hawk," she whimpered, coming closer. "Listen. I promised to take you to breakfast, and I didn't. That's not reason to get hit by a fucking car for attention. So... wake up and heal. Okay? Dad can't take another loss. *I*—" her voice broke, "—can't take another loss. Mom is the *last* Caravan that dies until Dad goes from natural causes."

The machine beeped in response. She hated hospital noises too.

God, she needed a drink.

"Okay," Esther said, wiping the back of her hand across her nose. "I'm going to step out for a while. I'll be back. I love you."

And with a racing heart and scattered mind, Esther Caravan left the room to find solace in the only way she knew how.

* * *

"It was just a one-night stand, you'll be fine," Ashley laughed, and she tipped the wineglass to her lips. Her face looked flushed in the dining room light, and her dark hair framed her face as if she'd put effort into doing it. According to her, she hadn't. "Did you do a Plan B?"

Esther finished the last of her glass and reached for the unopened *Chardonnay*. She wasn't tipsy enough for this conversation yet. She didn't know why the fuck she'd started it. "No," she said and grabbed the corkscrew. "I didn't exactly have enough time considering I was late to the bookstore. If I'd been any later, my dad would have killed me."

Ashley leaned back in her chair. The wooden high-level table in her apartment dining room was simple, but nice. Nice *enough* for a college student who'd purchased it herself. "That sucks. Did you get to see your guy?"

The cork popped. The wine hissed and bubbled—Esther's favorite sound in the world. Wetting her lips, she tipped the bottle and filled her glass. It misted from the cold liquid. "He's not *my guy*. He's my best friend who doesn't seem to have much interest in me. I don't know. I'm getting mixed signals."

Was it wrong to talk about this while her brother was still unconscious? It seemed like it should be. But what else was she supposed to do? Pray all night? Cry?

No. That'd be unbearable.

"He's playing hard to get," Ashley said, and ran her forefinger over the rim of her glass. "Trust me, he *wants* you. Also, isn't he, like, super religious or something? That might be part of his hesitation."

Esther thought about his fervent prayers, the way he mumbled to himself even in the presence of friends. It didn't even seem like a call for attention. It was almost as if he couldn't help himself. "Maybe. It's frustrating. I've thrown myself at him for years and all I get is mixed signals. And now that I've fucked up, I'll never get him. If he finds out I slept with Gabe, it'll probably be game over."

"Girl, you're confusing me. You don't think he likes you, but you think he'll freak if he finds out about Gabe?" Ashley reached for the bottle. "That tells me there's something there and you know it."

Shrugging, Esther swirled wine in her mouth before swallowing it. "Maybe I'm delusional. Who knows."

"Well," Ashley winked. "When in doubt?"

"Drink wine," Esther finished, and clinked her glass against her friend's. "Maybe it'll kill whatever's in me, and I won't need to do a Plan B."

That was a bit harsh, too far for her even. She winced from the statement, but it was out there already, darting through the air like those airplanes that dragged banners behind them.

YOU'RE A SHITTY HUMAN BEING LLC! the banner said, rippling through the clouds.

"Maybe you'll meet another guy," Ashley said, looking up at the ceiling, as if Esther hadn't said anything strange.

As her eyesight blurred from booze, or maybe tears, Esther chugged the rest of her glass. "Or a woman."

Ashley frowned, confused, and then brought her eyes down from the ceiling. Perhaps she'd been looking at Esther's airplane banner too. "Wait. Really? You're into girls?"

"Yes. I've never hidden that I'm bi." Esther tilted her head, her speech slurring. "Or have I? Shit. I don't *know*."

"Everyone I've ever seen you lock lips with has been a guy. That's drunk Esther though, so..." Ashley giggled.

Esther giggled too, but she didn't know why. None of this was really funny. She'd never *intended* to hide that she was bisexual, and she'd expressed it in the right company, but her father had such a strict, conservative view on anything LGBTQ-related that she just kept her mouth shut most of the time.

Fuck. Esther rocked her in her chair a little and scowled. She *really* needed to be more out and proud then.

"I've made out with several girls," Esther said, pointing a finger towards her friend. "Haven't we kissed?"

Ashley threw her reddening face back and laughed. "No, I'd remember that."

A slow smirk spread across Esther's lips. No doubt, the alcohol *consistently* made her want some lip-locking action. She set the glass down, and it wobbled and tipped over. "You wanna?"

No! You idiot... this is how you ended up fucking Gabe.

Ashley touched her finger to her chin. "Hmm. I'm intrigued. How much tongue do you use? I'm not a big *tongue* fan."

Esther sighed with loud exasperation. "You have *no* issue when you're slobbering over a dick in your mouth, but the mention of a tongue? Oh *no*."

Ashley roared in laughter and stumbled from her chair, coming around the table. "Okay...whew, I'm dizzy. Okay, let's try this. Come here."

Esther tipped forward, her eyesight blurring again, and she swung her feet from the chair and opened her arms to welcome Ashley. "Yeah, you're never gonna go back to a guy again." She grasped her friend's wrist and pulled the laughing girl towards her. "It's not romantic if you're laughing, shut the fuck up!"

Ashley rocked forward and landed a loud smack on Esther's lips. "Mwah!"

Esther's head went back, laughing, and tears streamed down the sides of her face and into her ears. As her eyes landed on the smooth white ceiling, she realized they weren't tears of laughter. But she continued to laugh.

"Okay, now I can say I kissed a girl," Ashley said, stumbling backwards towards her seat. Her eyes widened. "Wait. Does that make *me* bisexual?"

Esther stared at the ceiling, let out one last giggle, and then lowered her head. "No," she murmured and leaned against the table. "It doesn't."

Suddenly, she wanted to go home.

"Good," Ashley said, smiling and grabbing the wine bottle again. "I don't need *that* reputation on top of everything else."

Wow. What the *hell* was that supposed to mean?

"You know," Esther said, trying to move past the comment. She leaned her jaw into her palm. "When I was fourteen, I met a fucking *gorgeous* girl. And, not gonna lie, she wanted to murder me for interrupting her run time."

Ashley was drinking from the bottle now. "Oh? And?" She didn't sound like she cared much.

Esther closed her eyes and thought of the runner with the electric green eyes. Eyes that seemed so fiery, and yet so filled with pain. "I think if you'd said something like that in front of her, she would have broken your neck," she said matter-of-factly. To be honest, she didn't really *know why* she said it. Was it a defensive response? A random thought? She didn't know.

"Weird," Ashley said, and burped. "Good thing she isn't here then." Her head thumped against the table. "I should sleep soon."

Esther's phone buzzed. Adrenaline surged. She grasped for the phone in her right pocket and then realized it was in the left.

"Grandma".

Because, of course, why would her father call? He zoned the fuck out every time there was a family emergency.

"Hey, Grandma." She tried to sound sober.

"Hey, Baby. Where are you?" There was a tone to Patricia's voice, one that she'd heard before.

Oh God, no, no, *no*. Not Hawk, not—

"At Ashley's, why?"

"Honey, your brother is stable, but did your dad tell you the bad news?" Her grandmother's voice shook, as if she were holding back tears.

No. *No*, he hadn't. She hadn't even seen him much, and when she did, he had that same dazed look in his eyes like he'd had the day her mother died.

"What didn't he tell me?" Esther whispered, and she turned her eyes to the ceiling again, as if the airplane banner might appear and tell her the bad news, and that maybe it was even her fault.

"He's not going to walk again, Honey. I can explain better in person, but the spinal damage was too severe. Can you come back to the hospital?"

"What's wrong?" Ashley asked, behind her.

Esther covered her mouth, her eyes shifting in confusion. She wasn't even sure why she was confused—bad karma ran strong in the Caravan family. Her father always spoke of it.

Running her fingers through her long hair, Esther spoke in quiet humiliation. "I'll be there soon."

"Esther, you're *drunk*," Ashley protested, and tapped her wildly on the shoulder. "Get an Uber, please?"

She lowered the phone. "I'm fine."

"Um. No. I swear to God, Esther. I will call the cops. *Get an Uber.*"

Esther let out a tearful sigh. Nodding, she slowly reached for her phone again and then stopped. "Can you get one for me? I can't deal with my phone right now."

Ashley tightened her lips and brushed a tear from her friend's face. "I got you."

As Esther waited, and the alcohol continued to dilute her thoughts, she wondered what life might look like in the near future.

She thought of Hawk, and she wondered if her *father* would survive this news.

She thought of Fr. Jerome Nadier. She loved him, and she *needed* him to pull through.

But what if he didn't?

With that lingering question, Esther thought of Mariel, and she wondered if he, once again, might put a pistol in his mouth and pull the trigger like he had many years ago in the darkness of her bedroom.

Verse 4

~ The Humanoid ~

Saturday, January 12th, 2019
Chicago, Illinois

Mariel almost forgot to contact the deacons of the church to alert them of his dad's situation.

"Please, please keep us updated," Deacon Williams had pleaded. *"The church members will want to know."*

It was true. The members of St. Michael's *adored* Fr. Jerome. With good reason. He, too, adored his dad, which is why he couldn't get his heart to stop racing in panic, even though the medical staff had stabilized the priest after his emergency surgery.

But finally he drifted to sleep next to Fr. Jerome's bed in the uncomfortable chair by the window.

Mariel dreamt that his father opened his eyes, smiled, and said—

"Sorry about the scare, Son. I'm ready to go home now."

But the dream transitioned from a hopeful desire to a gory nightmare.

As Fr. Jerome exited the hospital room, a dark, blurry figure blocked the doorway and raised a shotgun. The figure fired the gun and then racked it, and a sea of flesh and blood rained into the air where his father's head had been.

It didn't awaken him with a jolt like other nightmares. Instead, Mariel's eyes opened slowly in the darkness.

Nauseated, he turned his head to look at the hospital bed. It was strange to be relieved at the sight of Fr. Jerome's body in its current state, but it was far better than seeing his headless torso on the ground.

Scratching his cheek, Mariel rose to his feet. Shadows moved outside the closed door, cutting through the bright lights as medical staff passed the room.

He looked at the clock. Almost midnight.

How was Esther's brother? How was *Esther?*

What a clusterfuck of a day. It'd begun with a dream of coffee with the girl he adored, and it had ended in tragedy for both of them.

It almost seemed like karma.

Like a *sign* that he wasn't meant to have what he wanted.

Mariel looked at his father. That man always fought for what he wanted, and he seemed to get it. His drive, motivation, and *faith* had always brought him joy, and Mariel didn't understand why he couldn't amount to the beautiful example of a man that was his dad.

But Fr. Jerome wasn't young. If he survived this, it'd be a wonderful thing, but how much longer would he live after the fact? Would he even *want* to live? The priest had never been shy in expressing his desire to, as he said, *find theosis* (unity) with God and join Him in the Kingdom of Heaven.

Was it horrible to wish such peace for his father?

Or was Mariel, perhaps, jealous that he *couldn't* find that peace.

That he couldn't *die.*

Blowing out air and tipping back his head, Mariel reached for his dad's limp hand. "It should be me," he mumbled, and he wasn't sure if he was talking to God or to himself. Did it matter? No one ever answered except—

"You wish it'd be you," that voice said, that cackling, disgusting voice that'd haunted him for as long as he forged memories.

The humanoid.

The figure that had blown off his father's head in the nightmare.

"Leave me alone," Mariel whispered.

"Why don't you like to talk to me? We're family. I've been with *you* since you were *conceived*," it giggled.

Mariel began to sweat. He turned.

There sat the dark, grainy humanoid. He reclined in the chair, his legs crossed, his arm casually draped across the armrest; and even though he had no eyes, Mariel knew he was watching him.

"What do you want from me?" Mariel snarled.

The head cocked to the side. "I like fucking with you. I'm stuck with you until further notice."

Mariel's lip quivered. "What does that mean?"

The head cocked to the opposite side again. "Never you mind *that* just yet. But while I'm here, we should be friends. Yes?" Ecstatic, it clapped its hands together.

"Lord Jesus Christ, Son of God—"

"*Don't!*" In an aggressive flash, the humanoid lunged from the chair. In less than a second, his body towered above Mariel, and the humanoid's face dropped close to the frightened man. "So help me, I will kill your dad." The voice deepened to a sinister growl. Back and forth, the humanoid cocked his head again and again until he'd retreated back to Mariel's chair.

"Now," he said cheerily. "We don't want that, do we? Wouldn't look good, your dad's *brains* all over you and the hospital bed." The humanoid burst into shrill laughter, stopped abruptly, and then crossed his legs and cocked his head again.

Mariel stared at the humanoid with a combination of terror and disgust. "Who are you? Why won't you tell me?"

"Listen," the figure cooed. "I'm just here because the boss told me I needed to be. PTO is running thin these days, especially as we approach the end of the world. Now, shut the fuck up and let's watch your dad die. Never did like him much. Do you like popcorn?"

"*Get out!*" Mariel screamed, lunging towards the chair. "Fuck you, get out, get out, *get out!*" He reached for the chair and grasped the sides, lifting it over his head. Mariel slammed it to the ground, and it bounced.

The footsteps outside the room scurried in madness. Multiple nurses burst into the room, and the light exploded into his eyes.

Great, now he was fucked.

"Get security," a middle-aged woman called, glancing at Fr. Jerome and then coming towards Mariel. "Sir. You need to step out of the room. I know you're upset, but—"

"*To feel is to be human, though!*" the humanoid cackled in his head.

Mariel grabbed his hair, squeezing his eyes shut as tears threatened to pour. "I'm not leaving my dad," he wheezed, breathing hard. Pacing. Doing all of the things *crazy* people did when they lost their shit.

"Then what can I do to help? You can't be doing this here." Her voice was firm, but genuine.

Mariel stopped and faced her and the other nurses, thrusting his arm towards his comatose father. "Wake him up!"

The nurse stepped back a little. "Sir, I know you are upset. Do you have anyone you can call or be with right now?"

Yes. *Yes.* He wanted to be with Esther, but she had her own tragedy. Why would she want to see him like this anyway?

"No," he said quietly, staring at the floor. "I just need you guys to help my dad. He's all I have."

Two security guards approached the room, but the nurse gestured them away. "I promise you, we will do everything we can. But we need you to stay calm here. If you need to leave, get some air, do whatever, do it. But you need to stay calm in this room and on this floor. Okay?"

Mariel nodded, then he hung his head. This was embarrassing. "Sorry. I think I'll step outside and clear my head. Did I break the chair?"

The nurse laughed and walked towards the door. "We'll bill your insurance if you did." She winked.

Mariel ventured to the cafeteria where he purchased a small box of *Fruit Loops* and a boxed container of milk. While eating, he realized it had been the first time he had eaten anything since early afternoon, and he devoured the cereal within a minute.

He prayed, and he dozed off in his chair before awakening to a text from Gabe Donovan.

"Bro. I got laid last night."

"What the actual fuck, bro?" Mariel sneered at his phone.

That was the *last* thing he cared about. Did Gabe know his dad was in the hospital? He hadn't *told* him yet, but he figured the grapevine might reach his best friend's ears.

To give him the benefit of the doubt, Mariel returned his text.

"Dude, I have zero interest in your sex life. Never have, never will. My dad's in a coma."

The phone rang. Gabe.

"Dude! You okay? What the hell happened?"

Silverware rattled, and trays slammed in the background as people wandered in and out of the cafeteria, gathering items and condiments for their food. Mariel tried to block out the noise. "I'm fine. I'm honestly not sure of the details, but it sounds like Dad hit his head on the cement by some railroad tracks. They think he was trying to help someone who got hit by a train. Did you hear about Hawk?" Mariel covered the other ear with his hand.

"Wait, what? No?"

"Esther's brother was riding his bike, and someone hit him. He's currently at the same hospital."

Gabe's voice sounded frantic. "Is Esther okay? What the fuck? Why did no one tell me about this sooner, and when did it happen?"

Why was he so annoyed at Gabe's tone when he asked about Esther? The man had an equal right to be concerned about Esther's wellbeing.

"She's fine," he said, his tone curt, and then he realized that perhaps she was not fine. "I mean, I don't know. She seemed okay when I saw her, but she's probably not."

How pathetic of him not to have even checked up on her. Now Gabe would, and fuck—that shouldn't make him angry, but it did. He didn't want it to... but it *did*.

"Should I come to the hospital? Man, this sucks, I'm so sorry. You doing okay?"

"No. I'm not. I'll be fine though."

"Bro, I'll come see you. You can't deal with something like this on your own."

Mariel leaned his head into his free hand. "I don't need anyone. I'm fine. I'll be okay. Just pray. Please."

"I got you, man. I love you, brother, please call if you need anything."

When the phone call ended, Mariel leaned back into the chair and closed his eyes.

"Bro, I got laid last night." Like, what the shit?

Mariel opened them again and caught his breath.

The humanoid had returned.

He sat by Mariel.

With a wavering breath, Mariel looked away from the figure. "You will never leave me alone, will you?"

"Nope!" the humanoid replied gleefully.

Tired, Mariel closed his eyes again. "You're evil."

"Oh, that's *rude*. No way to talk to family."

"You're not my family," Mariel whispered, grinding his teeth and keeping his eyes closed.

"Heeheehee!" The voice sounded closer. "Yes—I—am. Oh, *look*. Your girlfriend."

Mariel's eyelids flew open.

Esther stood at the front of the cafeteria near the refrigerated sandwiches. With her arms folded, she stared at them.

"Don't look at her," he mumbled.

"You talking to me, or yourself? I'd personally like to look at her sweet piece of ass. I know you think God will end you if you look at it, but do you *see* it?"

He wanted to lose it again. Rip this cafeteria to shambles. *Just ignore it.*

"Ignore me? Well, that's rude too. Listen, I've got an extended stay here. We can be friends, or we can annoy each other the whole time, your choice."

Mariel stared at Esther. Abruptly, he stood, ignoring the humanoid and walking towards her with his hands in his pockets. He stopped beside her to stare at the sandwiches as well. "Hey."

She looked at him. Her eyes were red, wet with tears, and an odor of alcohol drifted into his nose. "Hi."

"What's going on? You okay?"

Esther shook her head. "No. I'm not okay. Hawk's never going to walk again, and I can't fucking decide if I want a tuna sandwich or chicken salad." The tears came, and they rolled down her cheeks and over her quivering lips.

He couldn't stand this.

Awkwardly, Mariel stared at the sandwiches and clicked his tongue.

Then, he straightened his shoulders and held out his hand. "We're getting out of here for a few. You deserve a sandwich from the heavens, not hospital crap."

She looked up at him. "I can't leave my family."

"Esther. I just lost my shit in my dad's room. Yeeted a chair. The nurses sent security in, and they almost kicked me out." The corners of his mouth moved to suggest a smile. "I need a break, and you need a break. Before you smash a chair, of course. Come with me?"

Catching a sob, Esther nodded. "Where?"

Mariel took her hand. "I know a place." He ignored the humanoid that sat cocking his head back and forth on the checkout counter.

*   *   *

That *place* was *Pete's Diner*.

Confused, Esther looked at Mariel as he parked. "They're closed."

Mariel took the keys out of the ignition and held them up. He grinned. "I've got a key... and the ingredients for the best sandwich you've ever eaten."

Esther angled her body, leaning back against the car door and searching his face with raised eyebrows. "This seems unusually *bold* of you. Are you allowed to do this?"

Mariel opened the car door. "Would you tattle on me if I wasn't?" He got out.

"No. I'm too hungry."

Mariel unlocked the back door, and they entered through the kitchen. He gestured to the front of the diner where the bar was located. "Go sit. I'll have food out for you in a second. Leave the lights off though."

The small diner was silent, almost eerie with its lack of clattering dishes and talkative patrons.

Esther lingered, a small smile on her face.

"What?" Mariel's face warmed. His heart raced just looking at her.

"This is adorable. Can't I stay and watch you?"

"No. Go sit." He turned away and walked towards the large refrigerator.

Disappointed, Esther left the kitchen, calling, "the more meat the bigger the tip!"

"That's what she said," Mariel called back, and retrieved the sandwich ingredients from the cooler.

Esther laughed as she left the room. "You have humor, Mariel, I never knew!"

Mariel prepared her a chicken salad sandwich with cranberries, grapes, pecans, and bacon on warmed, seeded rye bread. He added chips to the side of the plate and brought it to the bar with a cold glass of foaming root beer.

Esther's eyes lit up. "This looks pretty damn incredible, Mars, thank you. Didn't you make yourself anything?"

He shrugged. "I had fruit loops."

"Oh, that's filling." She lifted the sandwich to her lips and took a bite. In reaction, her eyes fluttered to the back of her head, and she melted into her chair with a contented moan. "So much better than hospital sandwiches."

Pleased with himself, he watched her. "Good."

Esther took a sip of her root beer and patted the bar stool next to her. "Come sit by me?"

He was afraid of being that close to her, but he obliged. In silence, they sat beside each other in the dim light. Esther's feet swung just above the floor as she ate. Mariel bent his head, his heart beating loudly in the silence. He wanted to tell her how he felt, and the words almost left his mouth, but he thought of the humanoid, the voice that never stopped haunting him. He thought of the *other* figure, the quiet one, the one that looked upon him with judgmental silence.

"You're just a vessel," both voices had told him multiple times.

Just a vessel. Nothing more than that? Not human? Not Mariel Nadier, the son of the wonderful priest? Not *Mars*, Esther's best friend with *feelings*, true human *feelings*, for her?

There was a light touch of fingers against his hair. Shivering, he looked up, and Esther's blue-brown eyes locked with his.

"Your dad will be okay," she whispered. "I know he is your closest friend, the rock and joy of your life. I believe that he knows that too. You aren't ready to have him leave, and he isn't ready to leave you."

Mariel looked at her, noticed her eyes filled with tears yet again. The light of the kitchen shone softly on her brown hair, and he felt something turn in his stomach.

He stood; he reached out for her and pulled her into his arms until her head rested against his chest. They stood in the darkness, their breaths an echo in the diner.

Esther's arms encircled his waist. Her embrace was firm. "I can hear your heart," she whispered. "It's beating hard."

Shit, now he was scared. He was scared he'd do what he wanted to do—lift up her face and kiss her tempting lips, maybe let his hands roam and find skin that he'd wanted to touch for so long.

Mariel's face felt hot as he held her with his eyes closed. "Stress," he said softly.

Esther's body pressed against him, harder, and he could hear her breath quickening as well.

She didn't believe him.

"To feel is to be human."

The humanoid wasn't *wrong*, was he?

Mariel inhaled the scent of her hair and felt the curves of her body align with his.

She let out a breath.

"Stay away from her."

His eyes snapped open. He'd heard a male voice, one different from the humanoid, and it'd almost sounded like his *father*.

Shaking, he stepped away and avoided eye contact. He stammered. "Thank you. I—I needed that. Feeling a little shook up."

With parted lips and wide eyes, Esther's face was flushed.

God, he wanted her. Everything about her drove him mad, and he wanted nothing more than to pull her back to him and experience the first kiss that everyone but he had experienced. He'd had opportunities, but he'd saved himself for *her*, even though he fought against it for a reason he didn't understand.

Esther returned to her seat on the bar stool. "You're welcome. I needed that too." She stared at her empty plate. "I should get back though. So should you."

Was she angry? Fuck, he didn't know.

Mariel cleaned the dishes while Esther wiped the counter. Once finished, they journeyed back to the hospital in awkward silence.

During their embrace, Mariel felt as if a wall crumbled between them.

Now, when they bid each other good night, the barrier returned.

He knew it was his fault.

Because Mariel couldn't shake the cold, lonely feeling that Esther Caravan would be much safer if that barrier between them stood strong.

VERSE 5

~ HOME ~

Monday, January 14th, 2019
Moscow, Russia
4:30 A.M.

"Tira?" A soft plea in the darkness.

"Hmm?" The agent's hair shielded the woman's face like a curtain as she molded her body against hers beneath the sheets. Her lips parted above Olivia's, and she awaited the server's response.

"Tell me you love me."

Annoyance. She didn't want to feel annoyed. It wasn't Olivia's fault she was a sub-human with feelings. It wasn't Olivia's fault she'd fallen for an enhanced agent, one who couldn't, nor desired, to love in that way.

Tira bent down and brushed her lips against Olivia's nose. "Ssh."

"Tell me you won't be with anyone else," Olivia moaned, almost wailed, and her breath tickled Tira's lips.

Tira almost laughed, but that would have been cruel. She wasn't sure what to say. Here she was, lying atop a naked woman who was begging her for a commitment she *could not* and *would* not give. What *could* she say?

"Olivia," she said, and she rolled from her. "I can't do this. I can't have this conversation with you, and I don't want to have this conversation with you. I'm leaving in a few hours... we can either enjoy each other, or end it now."

Was that too harsh?

It didn't matter. It wasn't her fault the server didn't read social cues.

But the sudden silence made her uncomfortable. Lying there, staring at the ceiling, made her realize just how much she wanted to get up and leave. *Do* something else that didn't waste her time with this useless drama.

"Why do you have to be so cruel?" Olivia sniffled, and she sat up and covered herself with the blankets.

Cruel? She'd been anything *but* cruel.

Petrov was cruel. The trainers throughout her life? Cruel. *Necessary*, she supposed, but definitely crueler by definition than her blunt statement to Olivia.

"I'm not trying to hurt you," Tira snapped and sat up too. She wasn't naked. She didn't like going to bed naked. "There's nothing malicious in my intent. If anything, I'm releasing you to do what, and *whom*, you please."

Olivia flung off the blankets. With a strangled sob, she searched for her clothing. "Fuck you."

Confused, Tira watched her. "What? Olivia, stop!"

The server found yoga pants and pulled them on. Her breasts jiggled as she snatched her shirt from the nightstand. "Good-bye, Tira. So nice to know that all of this has meant *nothing* to you."

Tira lunged from the bed, grasping at Olivia's arm. "Olivia, please. I wasn't trying to hurt you, I—"

Olivia ripped her arm away. "Too late." She stumbled towards the door. "You're right," she said, pulling open the door. "Enhanced agents can't fall in love. And if they did? I'd feel sorry for the victim."

The door slammed shut.

Olivia was gone.

Tira rubbed her forehead. Her head hurt, and her body felt hot. She didn't like that Olivia had left in such a way, but there wasn't much she could really do about it now, was there?

So she began her morning, ignored the aching sensation in her heart, and tried to erase the image of Olivia tearing her arm from Tira's grasp.

Right now, she needed to focus on the mission at hand—preparing to leave her home for a city she despised.

Not just because she'd been tasked to babysit—but because the last time she'd been there, a senator had paid her trainers so that he could—

"Get on the bed," he ordered.

Tira clenched the switchblade in her pocket and snarled.

Chicago was a dirty, ugly memory, and she wasn't looking forward to the return.

But she'd been given orders, and it was her duty to follow them. It had always been that way.

And it always would be.

*   *   *

Coffee brewed from the Keurig as the plane tipped over the Atlantic Ocean. It spluttered and splashed into the white cup.

Tira Petrov gazed out of the window in an attempt to process... well, everything.

"Good-bye, my sweet," Papa said, *yanking her into his arms so that he could lay his lips upon her forehead. "This isn't forever. I look forward to seeing you back home."*

She'd wanted to puke against his suit; the expensive one he always wore when he was *excited* about something. Some new policy; a new, innovative idea.

Or a new weapon.

Tira stood up, brushing her hands over her grey joggers to smooth the wrinkles that didn't exist.

How could one feel simultaneously unsettled *and* relieved?

Tira didn't understand it.

She didn't *want* to go to Chicago.

But she certainly wouldn't complain about the distance it was from Petrov.

The private plane descended a little, just enough to send an odd sensation through her stomach. The agent took her coffee from the machine and searched for flavoring. A little hazelnut wouldn't be bad for her, right? Just a dash of syrup within the black coffee?

Yes, a little celebration for earning the status of top agent—even though the assignment reward was stupid and hadn't been worth years of training, bloodshed, and near-rape experiences.

"Fuck you, Petrov," she said, raising the coffee to her lips, smirking at herself for calling him by his name rather than *Papa*.

Once the coffee touched her tongue, and she burned her mouth, she set it aside and unlocked her tablet. After entering in the security codes, Tira opened the subject's file and eyed the photo in disdain.

Why did she look so fucking familiar?

"Because she's like any other female college dumbass," she scoffed to herself and flicked her forefinger to re-analyze the file.

Subject: Esther Marie Caravan.

Age: 20

Height: 5'6".

Weight: 143 lbs.

Eyes: Blue and brown

Hair: Brown

The subject listed above attends the University of Chicago and works part-time at Caravan's Books, owned by Todd Wyatt Caravan (please reference his separate file). She is an avid dancer, and she performs and choreographs for the hip-hop dance team at the college. She drives a white Jeep Cherokee, owns primarily Apple products, and orders pizza from Juliano's at least twice a month. She is not currently dating anyone, but does appear to have a strong interest in Mariel Christian Nadier (son of their parish priest, Jerome Nadier). She spends time with Mariel and her other friend, Gabriel James Donovan, who is the son of James Donovan (Senator of Illinois, who replaced the open seat after Senator Thompson's disappearance). Esther Caravan lives with her father, her brother (Jason "Hawk" Caravan), and her grandmother (Patricia Elisabeth Caravan). She owns no pets, and her favorite—

"*Jesus fucking* Christ, this is boring," Tira exclaimed, and she slammed the laptop shut. Growling, she beat the back of her head against the seat and let out an exasperated sigh that she knew was over-dramatic.

Later. She'd do this later.

So Tira Petrov—well, Tira *Arcelin* to everyone else now—placed headphones over her ears, tapped her phone, and hit *play*. She was free now, separated from her father, her trainers, and their goddamn judgment. She could listen to one of her favorite bands in peace, without fear of interruption or scoffs. And yes, she was a little embarrassed to find pleasure in this band (even though she held an intense appreciation for most music), but she couldn't help it.

So, as *Lay All Your Love On Me* from *ABBA* burst into her headphones, Tira Arcelin leaned her head back, closed her eyes, and allowed herself a smile.

When the plane landed, she awoke with drool crusted on her cheek. Embarrassed, she took a napkin, dipped it in her water, and madly scrubbed as the plane rumbled against the runway.

Tira glanced out of the window, gathering her items and scanning her surroundings. It was icy, and a thin blanket of snow covered the earth. She wasn't quite sure what else she expected to see, but there wasn't much to analyze.

Where she'd landed was a small, private helipad that Petrov (and the U.S. powers that sucked his cock) arranged for their use. It was boring—much like she expected from her new life in Chicago.

"Agent Rostova will meet you there. His cover name is Michael Bradley. He's been the agent overseeing Project Caravan since the beginning," Petrov had said.

Tira had wanted to scoff at the name. *Project Caravan*—as if it needed an official term to seem more important than it was.

When the plane came to a stop, Tira stood ready to exit with the few items she had. It was 10:03 in the morning, and the agent wasn't sure if she was hungry, tired, sick, or just confused.

The door lifted. Cold air whistled and chilled her face. It blew the thick blonde strands of hair that hung free from her loose ponytail, which she suspected wasn't much of a ponytail anymore. In fact, she didn't feel very presentable right now, and she hoped this agent wouldn't tattle to her Papa.

She could hear him now.

"Agent Rostova reported to me. I was informed that, upon your arrival, you looked like absolute shit."

Tira snarled, and it was then that she noticed the black truck parked outside of the long security gate. That must be him.

Tira gulped. Suddenly, she needed to shit.

"Are you going to leave the plane?" Behind her, in Russian, an annoyed pilot spoke. "I would like to stretch my legs."

A low growl rumbled in her chest.

Get blood clots for all I care, Tira thought. She almost said it, too. And if she turned around, she'd yank the man's nose from his face. As much as she despised this situation, she had no desire to return to Petrov. So, Tira closed her eyes and sank her teeth into her tongue.

A horn blared.

Her eyes opened.

It was the truck outside of the opening gate. Impatient, too.

What was *with* these people?

Tira Arcelin grasped her luggage and stormed down the ramp. Her athletic shoes slammed against the metal, vibrating the surface like a volcano about to erupt.

Whoever this Michael Rostova was—well, she didn't care. He could get blood clots too.

But Tira was nervous to meet him, because as the rest of her hair blew from the ponytail holder, she suspected she actually *did* look like shit. Now, as Petrov's top agent, she'd meet a suited agent with years of experience looking like—

"—*absolute shit,*" Petrov liked to say.

But Agent Rostova (rather, Bradley) wasn't the man that exited the truck. Someone else did, because she'd seen the agent's photo identification. Clean-shaven. Lean. Attractive with black eyes that'd looked almost nightmarish with their intensity.

Tira's eyes widened, and she froze.

Had Petrov sent an *Uber* driver as a method to *mock* her?

He *would* do that.

Because country music blared from that vehicle. A middle-aged, stocky man with thick black hair and a trimmed beard leapt from the truck. He wasn't tall, perhaps five-seven, and he certainly wasn't in a suit. He wore dark jeans, a zip-up hoodie, and a grey baseball cap that sat backwards on his head. He was muscular, but his sweatshirt did not hide the roundness of his hard beer gut.

"Agent Tira Arcelin." The man spoke with a thick, midwestern accent and came forward with a hand extended. "Let me grab your things."

She clung to her luggage. "I am meeting someone else."

The man dropped his hand to his side. "You're meeting Michael Bradley, right?"

"Yes."

"Kid, that's me. Throw your luggage in the truck. I haven't eaten breakfast yet, and I'm hungry."

What?

"Do you need some identification?" Michael said, reaching into his back pocket to withdraw a worn, brown wallet that had far too much shit crammed into it. He flapped it open and, sure enough, the identification verified his statement.

"Er," Tira stammered, and she cleared her throat. "Thank you. Is it alright to throw my items in the backseat?"

"Go right ahead."

During the ride, as her ears twitched from the obnoxious country music, Tira found herself staring at his gut. She tried to be inconspicuous, but her gaze kept shifting back to him.

In reality, she'd never in her life seen a Petrov agent with a *beer* gut. Did Petrov know that *this* was the man tasked with protecting Esther?

"You know," Michael said, snapping her out of her wide-eyed daze. "Is there something on my stomach? Because I'm getting a little self-conscious with you looking at me like that."

"You have a gut," Tira said simply.

"You're definitely Petrov's kid. Straight to the point. Yes, I have a beer gut, and you have drool on your cheek. So?"

"Where?" Tira pulled down the sun visor and scratched at the white, dried saliva on her cheek. "Shit."

"Just use the napkins from my console. I'm not judging." He shot her a humored look. "Unlike you."

Perhaps she'd been a tad too forthcoming, but she was fucking *confused*.

"I'm just... trying to get adjusted to my situation," she said, spitting on the napkin and rubbing her cheek until it was red.

"Well, might I make a suggestion?"

"You seem like someone who will even if I say no."

"Fine, I won't." Michael turned his gaze to the road.

"No, please," Tira sighed, slapping the visor back up. She sulked, staring at the distant but impending city buildings that stood outlined against the overcast sky.

A smile formed at the corner of his lips. "Maybe start with *not* saying the first thing that's on your mind. You're going to stick out like a sore thumb."

"What is a sore thumb?"

"It's a saying. Like—hold on, I've never had to explain this before. Like your status as a Petrov agent is going to really show if you aren't careful."

Tira let out a sigh and fought to control her annoyance. "You are very audacious. You're making it seem like I don't know how to adapt."

"Do you?" Michael turned his eyes to her and tilted his head a little.

She wanted to kill him. A subhuman, one who looked like he'd stepped out of a goddamn farmer convention, had the audacity to challenge her ability to adapt?

"You have *no* right to—"

"There. *Right* there," Michael said, and pointed his finger towards the windshield. "You made my point."

"What are you *talking* about?" Tira cried. She hated this man.

"You can't just *talk* to people like you're a *Petrov* agent. Nonchalant threats, statements of entitlement, etc. That don't fly here."

Tira's face was hot. She opened her mouth to address his poor use of grammar and then caught herself.

Inside thought.

But despite her desire to bash Michael's face against the steering wheel, there was truth to his statement. Tira *knew* she'd need to adapt, and she realized that some of her behavior was due to—

"Disappointment," she admitted quietly. "Disappointment is a big reason I'm going to struggle for a while. I'm used to the empire. I've learned how to *maneuver* the empire. And I'm disappointed because I expected to be in a role that didn't involve *needing* to *adapt* to a domestic, Americanized lifestyle."

As the truck rumbled to a stop sign, Michael nodded and looked at her with a solemn expression that gave her a glimpse of the hardened Russian agent she'd seen in his portfolio. But there was something else in his eyes that she hadn't seen in the photo.

Patience. Kindness. Oddly, it gave her a sense of familiarity that she couldn't quite place.

"You'll get used to it," he said, and smiled a little. "You will."

After Michael insisted that he stop for an egg McMuffin and a coffee at *McDonald's*, they finally arrived at the gated condo that Tira would call home.

After Michael entered the code, they waited in awkward silence as the black gate opened sideways. It was slow. Very slow.

"Sucks waiting for this shit when you have to pee, not gonna lie," Michael chuckled, tapping the steering wheel. The gate beeped in a loud rhythm.

"How many neighbors will I have?" Tira asked, frowning. "I don't see how it's wise to be this close to people."

"Trust me, it's quiet. And everyone keeps to themselves. You're about ten minutes away from the bookstore and fifteen minutes away from the subject."

"The subject?"

"Yes," he said, driving into the private lot. "Esther Caravan."

"How long have you been here?" Tira asked, grasping the luggage from the backseat after he'd parked in the assigned garage.

Michael shut the back door. "A long ass time. Twenty years."

Devastation and horror dropped her jaw. "*Why?* For the *subject?*"

Grimly, Michael smiled. "Yup."

"I... don't feel well. Please tell me I'm not expected to—"

"Arcelin." Michael said sharply and paused at the edge of the garage. "Enough. I wouldn't run your mouth, and I wouldn't bitch, and I wouldn't *question anything* about this if you value your status and your goddamn life." His eyes had that deadly look, matching the eyes she'd seen in the portfolio identification.

It made her heart beat faster, and her sweaty palm almost slipped from the luggage handle. "Okay," she said, stunned. "Sure."

With a curt nod, Michael cocked his head towards the multi-story condos. "Let's get up there. I'm cold."

There was nothing lavish about the building, but it was sleek and modern. Dim, bulbed lights lined the hallway. They glowed along the winding staircase. It led to a second floor that, in reality, seemed high enough to be considered the fifth.

"There's an elevator," Michael assured her as they reached the top. "I was just curious to see if you'd ask."

"I'm the last thing you need to worry about," Tira snapped, heaving her luggage up the last couple of steps. She fought to control her breathing and hoped her face wasn't flushed.

Fighting nine agents in the cage had been less exhausting than this. What the hell was wrong with her?

Michael entered a code into the security system and the door to the condo unlatched. He stepped inside and held the door open for her. "Welcome home."

Behind her, the door shut.

The lock bolted.

And Tira Arcelin felt trapped.

But the condo was nice. Tira wanted to hate it. Yet, she couldn't.

In fact, Agent 4 rather liked it.

She liked the open-concept kitchen, the central island, and the glossy wood floors that flowed into a small dining area and the large, spacious living room. The adjacent den contained sliding glass doors that led to a balcony. The balcony overlooked the neighborhood and offered a glimpse of the city.

In the Kremlin, her room had been luxurious... but something about this place seemed far more attractive.

Maybe because it wasn't within range of her father's room.

Tira followed Michael down the hallway to the bedrooms. It housed two of them—a master and a guest—both carpeted and furnished with queen-sized beds and simple, metallic headboards. The master, slightly larger, boasted city views, a walk-in closet, and an en-suite bathroom with a shower-hot tub combo, while the guest room was nearly identical in layout.

Michael gestured to the hot tub. "This thing brought me a lot of women," he said. "Might bring you some guys."

"I do not like men. I have taste like you."

"Whoa, did you just compliment me?"

Tira arched an eyebrow. "No. I was speaking fact."

"I'm going to take it as a compliment."

"I was told my items for duty would be supplied here." Tira changed the subject. "Where are they?"

A slow grin spread across his face. "I think the better question would be... where *aren't* they?"

Above the bed, the long, abstract painting with dramatic black and silver paint strokes opened with a voice-activated code. It was operated by artificial intelligence, and Tira nearly squealed with lust at the illuminated light that flickered on over the well-stocked weaponry. Rifles. Handguns. Blades. Accessories. Oh, the *accessories*.

"There's a spare key if the system dies," Michael said, chuckling as Tira nearly scrambled onto the bed. "Is this like Christmas Day for you?"

She grabbed a handgun case, opened it, and smiled down at the scope and the associated silencer. "I've never had a Christmas Day," she murmured, tracing her fingertips over the cool surface of the gun. "But it can't be as grand as this, can it?"

Michael was quiet. Then he spoke again. "Come check out the closet. There's a whole new section you haven't explored yet."

After recovering from her joy about the weapons she was certain she'd never get to use, Tira sat at the dining room table with Michael as he opened a sturdy, black laptop and began to type. "Forget the weapons and forget the other fun toys. This," he turned the screen towards her, "is where your attention needs to be at all times."

She wanted to disagree, but she wasn't in the mood to be yelled at again.

Tira leaned in. "Is this it? The monitoring system?"

Michael double-clicked a program icon—a silver shield. A mapping system loaded immediately, and Tira's eyes followed the red dot that blinked on the screen.

Michael pointed to the dot. "That's our girl," he said. "This system shows where she is at all times." He clicked around the screen so fast that she was convinced he could do it in his sleep. "Cardiograph here." He circled the mouse hand over the red lettering on the screen.

60 B.P.M.

"She's sleeping," Michael said and unmuted the volume. "Must have ditched her classes today."

Thump-thump-thump-thump.

Tira listened with growing intrigue, as if she'd never heard a heartbeat before. In fleeting curiosity, she wondered if the subject had any remote sense of concern that she was being monitored.

"The chip is innovative. The best we have. You can hear conversations, but they're muffled. The program gets it wrong sometimes when it transcribes, but if you know what you're doing you can get the gist of what's being said. Most of her conversations are dumb though. She's drunk a lot. And *no—*" he added, catching Tira's threatening glare. "You don't need to listen to her blab twenty-four-seven."

"I didn't say anything."

"You didn't need to."

Both sat silent for a moment, and a soft, breathy sound whistled through the speaker. The subject's breathing.

It was odd to listen to someone sleep and *breathe.*

And there was nothing riveting about it.

"Her brother's in the hospital," Michael said.

"Is that my problem?"

"Well, we have to monitor her mental health too."

Tira sat back. *"Why?"*

Michael smiled. It was condescending, and it pissed her off. "Because suicide would be counterproductive to our mission to protect her."

"Who is she?" Tira blurted, leaning forward again. She looked at the screen as if it'd provide the answer. "Petrov told me minimal information."

Michael shrugged. "What you know is what I know. Nothing."

She didn't believe that. How could he have watched this person since infancy and know *nothing?*

There was something *off* about this entire situation. But so were many things that Petrov did, so it was best to keep her mouth shut and stick her head into the fucking sand.

"No need to sit in front of this screen all the time either. The program connects to a watch that I'll give you. If she's in a situation that needs to be addressed, you'll receive a distress signal alert. It's like an electrical shock to the wrist, and it vibrates like crazy. You'll know."

Tira shook her head and frowned. "So why doesn't Petrov just bring her in if she's so important? Imprison her? She could step in front of a bus, or get shot in a drive-by, or die in a burning vehicle, or—"

"You're having way too much fun imagining her death, Tira. But your concern is valid, and I've wondered that too."

None of this made sense. Her entire life had been grounded in reality and logic; fear and respect of the *seen* rather than the abstract. Petrov instilled these things in her.

"How much has he *spent* on this? Millions?"

"Think bigger," Michael murmured.

Billions?

"And wait until you see your paycheck," he added.

Aghast, Tira stared at him. Why the hell wouldn't this *multi-billion-dollar* project be kept in a well-lit, air-conditioned *prison* somewhere?

"You're going to drool again if you're not careful," Michael said as he switched programs on the laptop. He opened a file and then pointed to a photo identification of an older male with white hair and uneven stubble. "One last thing. This guy? His name's Jacob Caravan. He's not an active threat at this time, but he's been stalking around the Caravan bookstore, their neighborhood, and the college."

"I read about him. Esther's grandfather, right?"

"Yes." Michael stared at the photo. "But he's estranged, mentally ill, and very rarely is he sober. He has a history too. Countless police contacts. Was in and out of jail. Back in the seventies, he was under investigation for killing his son—William Caravan. Turns out it was just negligence, but still. Keep an eye on him, because I've no idea why he might be hovering near Esther."

Tira analyzed the photo. The man had icy blue eyes with specks of brown, similar to those of his granddaughter. "Okay."

"Any other questions?" Michael stood.

Many.

"Not right now." Tira stood, too.

"Cool. I'll take you to pick out the vehicle you want and show you around. There are some other places we need to hit. When do you meet with Chicago PD and the secret service agency?"

"In two weeks."

Michael nodded. "Let's go."

Tira Petrov, *now* Tira Arcelin, spent the rest of the day learning locations necessary to her mission, purchasing necessities, and discussing knowledge with Michael that was pertinent to her new role.

Later that night, she returned to the condo. She stepped onto the terrace and allowed the wind to comb through her loosened hair. She'd showered, eaten, and now she allowed herself a moment to breathe.

Process.

Because what else could she do? Now she had an unspecified amount of time to, apparently, *exist.*

It terrified her. So, with a desperate need to remember that she still had an important role to play within her Papa's organization, that she was still *needed*, Tira went inside and hooked up the laptop. Placed the earbuds in her ears.

And listened.

Quietly, Tira leaned back on the bed.

Thump-thump. Thump-thump. Thump-thump.

And something else. A soft, erratic sound that almost sounded like—crying.

It was.

Esther Caravan, the girl with an unexplained tether to the Petrov empire, was crying.

Tira thought of Olivia, remembered her cries as she fled the room.

"Oh, please," Tira whispered, and she turned off the volume. "I am sure your life is not that bad."

She closed her eyes, leaned her head against the headboard, and fell asleep.

And she dreamt of a hotel room, a blood-soaked bed, and a girl with ice cream in her hair.

CHAPTER 5: VERSE 1

~ RUNNER ~

Saturday, January 19th, 2019
Chicago, Illinois

"I don't want to go in there, Dad." Esther's voice broke.

They stood in the hallway just outside of the visitation room. The hallway smelled of candles, mismatched perfume, and cologne. It didn't help the nausea that plagued Esther's belly, and she found herself running her hand along her stomach as if it'd keep the vomit inside of her. She felt bloated too, which she hated because she'd worn the tighter black dress for the funeral. That wasn't even important or respectful to think about right now—but it was better than thinking about the last funeral she'd attended.

"Just go in, Honey, and you'll feel at peace," her grandmother, on Mary's side, said. *"You'll see how pretty she is."*

How *fucked* up was it to tell a fourteen-year-old to go see her mom's dead body because she was *pretty?*

"Esther." Todd's voice was firm. "We need to go in. Please don't make this a thing."

And where had *he* been when her grandmother guilted her into going inside the visitation room? Because when she'd entered, he wasn't there.

Her dad wasn't fucking there, and he was Mary's husband.

Her husband was *supposed* to be there.

"You fucking owe me," Esther hissed, straightening her dress over her hips. She hadn't meant to look slutty today. Elegant. That'd been her goal, and, as shitty as it was, she'd dressed with Mariel Nadier in mind.

Was he in the visitation room?

Fuck, she was a horrible person, especially since she pined over a man who drove her crazy with mixed signals.

"Please don't curse," Todd warned, and he shook the hand of a passerby. "Let's go in."

Why were they even doing this? It was a closed-casket funeral, for obvious reasons. There hadn't been much left of Carolyn Jameson when they'd found her on the railroad. An arm over here, a leg over there, and a hand that, according to rumor, hadn't contained her gold wedding band.

She'd *always* worn her wedding band.

Esther followed her father, keeping as close to Todd as she could and nodding to parishioners when necessary.

When they entered the dimly lit room, Esther's eyes scanned the area, searching for the man who made her heart go wild. Instead, she made eye contact with a priest she'd never seen before—a black-haired man with blue eyes, and a thick, well-trimmed beard. He smiled. It was an odd smile that she couldn't read, but she smiled back. Seeing him, though, brought pain to her heart... because he was not Fr. Jerome.

No one would *ever* be Fr. Jerome—the man who'd nurtured her from as long as she remembered. *He* belonged here. Esther assumed the other priest was at the church to do the service since Fr. Jerome was still in a coma, but she didn't like it. It only served as a reminder that Fr. Jerome could, at any moment, leave her too.

Just like her mother.

God, she hated funerals.

And Mariel wasn't here yet. That worried her. He'd texted her yesterday to ask if she was going to the funeral. He said that if she planned to go, he would join on behalf of his father. Regardless, it was none of her business if he came or not, but maybe if she could see him and talk to him in person, she could tell him how *she* felt since he seemed *incapable* of giving her a sense of direction.

Esther's eyes met Gabe Donovan's. In the corner of the room, he stood near the senator of Illinois—his father, James Donovan.

Gabe tilted his head with a sly grin that Esther was *certain* he'd given in an effort to lessen her misery.

It didn't help.

It only reminded her of the slick grin he'd had when he'd leaned in to suck her fucking tongue the other week.

Esther looked away, and she re-adjusted her bun at the nape of her neck.

She needed to talk to Gabe, to let him know she wasn't pregnant, and that he had no right to fuck around like that with drunk girls ever again.

It wasn't right.

And yes, it'd been her fault too, but... still.

She'd felt used.

"Ah, thank you for coming, yes." Phil Jameson's voice broke through her thoughts as he stood next to his daughters, Hailey and Victoria, shaking hands with parishioners. "I would like to say she's in heaven, but, well. Thank you for coming, yes."

He said the same *damn* thing again, and again, and again. When Todd approached and extended his hand, Phil grasped it.

"Thank you for coming, yes. I would like to say she's in Heaven, but, well."

Esther stared with wide eyes at the floor.

Who the *fuck* spoke like that about a dead spouse?

"Oh, *Esther*."

Shit, it was her turn.

She looked up, and her eyes scanned the red-haired, middle-aged man with eyes that looked more reddened from allergies rather than tears.

Maybe if she spoke first and darted, she could avoid his awkward statement.

"Hi, Phil, I'm really sorry about—"

"Thank you for coming, yes. I would like to say she's in Heaven, but, well." He smiled. It was a disgusting, grim smile. Not fucking genuine at all.

"You know what," Esther said, clearing her throat, coming closer to whisper in the man's ear. "She must be in Heaven... because she's not here with you."

Yanking her hand from his, Esther moved past him and ignored the gasp that escaped from his mouth.

With a warm face, Esther approached Hailey and Victoria to give sincere condolences that she knew they deserved. They stood at the other end of the casket, and Esther wasn't sure if they were embarrassed of Phil, or vice versa, but she empathized with them.

She knew what it was like to lose a mother.

She had *no* idea, however, what it was like to lose a mother to suicide.

"I'm sorry for your loss," Esther said, offering an embrace for Hailey.

Hailey was a shy, thin girl close to eighteen. She wore a denim jumper and a white polo. Her hair, clipped in the back, looked frizzy and unkempt. It'd always been that way, as if Phil Jameson didn't believe in hair products for young ladies.

Victoria Jameson, however, had *fled* that household. She, at twenty-one, was nearly finished with college and would graduate soon from UCLA.

"Hey, Victoria, I'm sorry," Esther said, reaching up to give the tall young woman a hug.

Victoria kept her dark auburn hair straight, and she wore a black dress that came to her knees, something her father was certain to consider scandalous. Her eyes, normally fierce, were dim. "Thank you, Esther. How's your brother?"

Esther let out a shaky sigh. "Grandma's with him. He's awake. Paralyzed. Barely speaking. But he's alive, and we're grateful."

* * *

"What does one say—" Phil's voice echoed through the microphone. He stood at the podium and squeezed his eyes shut. As if to capture a sob, he covered his mouth with his fist.

Esther's eyes shifted to her father, who nodded in silent encouragement as Phil Jameson mourned his wife.

At least, *Todd* probably thought he was mourning Carolyn. Hell, Phil likely believed he was mourning his own wife, but it all seemed too—how could she put it nicely?

Self-obsessed?

"*How* does one say words for his wife?" Phil repeated, and his loud sniffling hissed into the microphone. "When his own wife sins so *horribly?*"

What the fuck?

You're making her sound like a slut. Goodness. Esther stared at her hands. She couldn't look at him.

The sanctuary doors creaked behind her. Curious, she turned her head, and her heart sped up.

There he was.

Mars.

He wore his black hair tied back in a ponytail, exposing a jawline she'd love to kiss and—well, she was still in church.

But her gaze didn't care.

Mars was dressed in a suit that, to be frank, looked like it'd been thrown together from his closet. The suit jacket was a different material than the pants. But it fit his tall, muscular frame, and good *Lord* she was going to hell with Carolyn for ogling the man in church.

"How can I speak of God's mercy when the Bible speaks of Hell for those who... wait. What are you doing?"

Loud heels echoed through the sanctuary. Esther tore her eyes from Mariel and watched as Victoria Jameson stormed up the stairs towards the podium with papers in her hands.

"Go sit down," Victoria whispered, but her whisper carried through the loudspeakers in the sanctuary.

Phil's face reddened. "Young lady, you—"

"So sorry about this," Victoria said, bumping him from the podium. "My father hasn't slept and brought the wrong eulogy. Please allow me to..." her voice faded, and her head lowered. She was trying... trying *so* hard to hold it together, but the tears came.

So did Esther's.

Because she remembered that exact moment when it *struck* her like a freight train that her mother was gone.

Horrible analogy.

But she *understood.*

So when Victoria's head rose, and her eyes turned to Esther with a quiet plea, the young woman rose from the pew, smoothed her dress, and stepped from the pew.

"I got it," Esther whispered, and she felt the congregation's eyes on her as she approached the podium.

Esther Caravan walked with poise—something she didn't know she possessed. Today, she did. She moved past Phil Jameson, who still stood to the side with his own papers clenched in his hand. She didn't look at his face. There was no need.

Instead, she stepped in front of the podium, adjusted Victoria's papers, cleared her throat, and then spoke.

"My mom," Esther read, and her soul cried.

But her voice held strong.

"My mom once told me that a sunflower couldn't bloom without rain. She told me that tears were nothing to be ashamed of, because tears were rain for our growth. I was six. I'd just fallen from a swing. I told her I didn't want to be a flower." Esther bent her head a little and smiled. Tears filled her eyes. "I told her I wanted to be an airplane, and I was mad because I didn't land properly."

Rumbled laughter threaded through the congregation.

Esther continued. "My mom wasn't an airplane. She wasn't a flower. She was everything a person should aspire to be… a kind, patient human being that could see the beauty
in a person, an animal, and even insects that Hailey and I, and even our father, were
terrified of."

Softly, Phil cleared his throat.

And Esther continued.

She spoke of Carolyn's life. As she stood behind the podium, she imagined Mary
Caravan's face—her smiles, her tears, her rage, her laughter, and embarrassment.

When Esther was done, and she sat next to her father again, Todd Caravan took her
hand and squeezed it.

"I felt her," he whispered shakily, his stubble against her cheek. "I fucking felt her
with us. Thank you, Squirt. Thank you so much."

And as Todd drew away, Esther finally allowed the tears she'd held back to fall.

* * *

"Mars." Esther caught his sleeve.

Mariel turned, and he towered over her. His eyes widened with pleasure. "Oh, hey.
Sorry, I was trying to get back to my dad, not trying to ignore you."

They stood close. The breeze whistled past their bodies and nipped Esther's ears.

"You need a coat," Mariel chuckled, scanning her with a look that suggested he rather
liked the fact that she didn't have a coat.

It made her blush. "Oh? Well, maybe I was hoping you'd get me one."

The parking lot was empty. The parishioners were still in the church. They were
alone, and Esther couldn't stop looking at his lips.

"I forgot," Mariel said, and he came a little closer. "I could give you my suit coat?"

No.

No, Mars.

Esther didn't want his suit coat. She wanted *him*.

"Mars," she said, and she ran her fingers down his tie. "What's it going to take to get
you to admit you like me?"

Fuck. Shit! That wasn't supposed to come out. It was supposed to be a fucking inside
thought, and now—oh.

Oh, hell.

His hand was on her hip, and his fingertips brushed the side of her thigh where the dress fit tighter than she'd planned for a funeral. Shivering, Esther raised her eyes to his.

This seemed sacrilegious.

But just like that time at the track, when she was fourteen, he came closer and lowered his head. "Mars," she said, and her lips parted with eagerness as she brought her head up to meet him.

But he stopped.

And as Esther opened her eyes to see why, it was what she *didn't* see that concerned her.

Muttering to himself, Mariel stepped back, and his eyes looked straight through her as if she didn't fucking exist.

As if she were *translucent,* and he were staring at someone else through her body.

"I need to leave, sorry," Mariel said hoarsely, and dipped down to get into his car.

He reversed, almost striking her as his tires squealed.

Esther had to jump back, wobbling in her heels and clutching at the air to grab onto *something* so that she wouldn't fall and expose her fucking panties to the parishioners of Fr. Jerome's church. The dress was stupid. This funeral was stupid.

Mariel-fucking-Nadier was *stupid*.

And Esther was furious the rest of the evening. She was pissed during the ride back home and pissed long after Todd dropped her off.

Steadily, as the evening wore on, her heart rate settled, and she relaxed on the couch to watch television with her grandmother while Todd spent time with Hawk.

"You okay, Honey?" Patricia asked, glancing over at her with that smile that always made Esther feel safe.

"Yes, just tired."

"Funeral went okay?"

"Mmhmm." Esther chewed a pretzel stick, watching the reality show that she considered unrealistic but great background noise. "Hey, Grandma?"

"Yes, Sweetie."

"Why doesn't Dad talk about his upbringing much? Like, the time before you divorced his dad?"

Patricia blinked with slow concentration at the screen. Finally, she responded. "That was a rough time for him, Honey. I think he still carries some guilt about—did you hear that?"

Esther bit into the pretzel and shifted her eyes. "Hear what?"

Then she heard it—a soft knock on the front door. A repetitive pattern of five taps.

"You expecting anyone?" Esther asked, getting up.

"Nope, are you?"

Esther shook her head and set aside the bag of pretzels. Her slippers scuffed against the floor as she exited the living room, darted around the hall, and stopped at the front door to look through the peephole.

An old man with blue-brown eyes looked right back at her.

"Um," she said, and her heart rate suddenly rose. "Can I help you?"

The man, who looked almost as tall as Mariel, didn't blink. He had white stubble, and he wore a tan overcoat. Baggy skin drooped under his eyes.

"This the Caravan residence?" he responded, his voice deep and raspy.

"Who's asking?" Esther demanded, and she turned her head as Patricia came around the corner.

"Todd home?" the man persisted.

Patricia shooed Esther away from the door and took her place.

"We're not interested!" Esther called, leaning against the wall. "Grandma?"

Patricia's eyes were as wide as saucers. Dipping away from the door, she covered her mouth with her palm.

"Grandma, you're scaring me."

Patricia stammered. "Um... I'm sorry, Sweetie. I—just. Hold on." She rose to her tiptoes again and peered through the peephole. "Jacob! Can you hear me Jacob?"

Esther's eyes widened. Was this...?

"Patricia?" His voice was muffled. "That you? Open up."

"No. Jacob, you listen to me. Todd doesn't want to see you. *I* don't want to see you. Now, please leave us alone before I call the cops."

"I just wanna talk to Todd and see my grandchildren."

"No!" Patricia shrieked. "You lost that privilege a long time ago. Leave us alone! Go home!" She was screaming at him now like he was a dog, but her fingers grasped the doorknob as if she thought he was primed to beat down the door.

Esther imagined the moment. His long arm reaching into the house, grabbing at her face, and his body thudding like a rhythmic drum—

—*in a repetitive pattern of five thumps*—

—against the door until it burst from the hinges.

"Should I get the gun?" Esther whispered, and then remembered Patricia wasn't supposed to *know* Todd had given her access to the gun.

The same gun Mariel had tried to shoot himself with.

Also, *fuck* him.

Pale, Patricia turned her eyes to Esther and reached for her phone. "I'll just call 911 and—"

Esther held a finger to her lips.

Was he talking to someone else?

A *woman?*

"Fine, I'll leave," Jacob said suddenly, and his footsteps thumped against the sidewalk, fading away as if he had some place more important to be.

"The fuck?" Esther mouthed towards her grandmother. With a frown, she stood up on her tiptoes and peered through the peephole as Patricia gripped her arm and whispered her protests.

Someone was out there, but it wasn't Jacob. It was a runner. At least, it *looked* like a runner. By the shape of the person's *curves*, she presumed it was a woman in running gear and a balaclava mask.

The woman ran in place for a couple of seconds. Then, she jogged backwards into the street. With long strides, she took off, running down the road until she'd disappeared into the darkness.

"Is he still out there, Honey?" Patricia asked in a low whisper.

"I don't see him," Esther said, frowning, but she found herself searching for the mysterious runner, not for the old man.

"Oh, good. I should probably call the police though."

Esther didn't respond. She stared through the peephole at the darkness of the dimly lit street. "I guess, yeah," she said. "But, ironically, I think Jacob just got scared away by a soccer mom."

VERSE 2

~ WHAT'S THE FEELING? ~

Monday, January 21st, 2019
Chicago, Illinois

After leaving Esther like that, forgiving himself *and* God was not an option. Lack of forgiveness for himself? That was easy. He'd lived a lifetime of self-hatred.

But anger at God? It unsettled him—because God (thanks to his dad) had always been the only reminder that hope *could* defeat despair.

Right now, Mariel didn't feel like that was the case at all.

Fuck, she'd been stunning.

He'd wanted to kiss Esther, and for a moment he thought the humanoid would leave him alone long enough to do it.

"Mmm. Kiss her. Put that serpent tongue in her mouth and possess her like I possess you."

And he'd stopped.

Because he didn't *want* to possess her like the humanoid possessed him. That'd be unfair.

Eyeing the sign on the thick cement wall that said—

—SMALL CARS ONLY—

—Mariel sat in his car in the hospital parking garage. He drummed his fingers against the wheel. He loved sitting in his car. It was a great place to decompress, and normally, he'd listen to music, but every fucking song made him sad. Even the happy ones, because the music notes were fucking happy.

How come music notes had more purpose than he did? Music notes could create and shift emotions in human beings. Songs eventually ended. Yes, they could be *replaced,* but they still *died.*

They could still fucking die.

Mariel grabbed his backpack and left the car. The slamming door roared through the parking garage like thunder and faded with the sound of his footsteps.

His dad was still intubated, still comatose. There'd been attempts at discussions of the future—the *what ifs* that Mariel refused to discuss yet. Belief that his father would awaken was his last bit of faith... he couldn't lose that right now.

So, Mariel had gone home to grab his father's beloved journal and his favorite ball-point pen. He wanted to deliver it to him now, and maybe the old man might sense a shift, a *reason* to awaken. Fr. Jerome *loved* his journal, and Mariel knew that he'd want it as soon as he woke up.

It wouldn't hurt to try.

"Just burn the journal, it's useless, and he loves it more than *you-hoo-hoo!*"

The humanoid.

Mariel walked faster, gripping the straps of his backpack as he stormed towards the hospital entrance.

"Did you see her? Her dress all high on her thighs? Is that why you almost hit her with your car? So you could see her pretty panties?"

"*Shut up!*" Mariel cried, and his voice echoed throughout the garage. Tears stung his eyes. He didn't *want* to look at her that way, he didn't *want* to do the things to Esther like he'd seen those men do—the men in those porn videos that were only *good* because—

Because they weren't acting.

"Lord Jesus Christ, Son of God, have mercy on me and save me, a sinner," Mariel whispered, stalking past an older black man before approaching the elevator.

The humanoid wasn't there anymore. When the humanoid disappeared, it was like a drink of cold water after hours of being parched—except he was lost in a desert with his last cold drink.

Because the humanoid always returned. Always watched.

"Hi, Dad," Mariel said. He approached the bed and reached for his father's hand. He squeezed it, looked out of the window at the twinkling city lights.

Shit, he needed to just man up, ignore the humanoid, and take her on a date. That wouldn't hurt her, right? Maybe he could even tell her his struggles—not *all* of them, of course, because the violent pornography thing was embarrassing and *his* cross to bear, *and* she likely wouldn't look at him the same... but if he opened up just a little and told her his fears, maybe it'd be a hint to the humanoid to fuck off.

And he'd almost hit her with his freaking car. She deserved an apology.

And not one through text.

He glanced at his watch. 7:30 P.M. Esther would close the bookstore soon. If he left now, he could get there in time to see her.

To tell her how he felt.

To finally kiss her.

Yes. Satan fed lies and fears to those with the weakest faith. Maybe there was a reason Esther had been the only girl he'd ever wanted—maybe it meant he didn't have to *fight* himself anymore.

Mariel sucked in a breath. "Dad, I'll be back to see you."

He darted from the room. Even though he'd just gotten there, he ran from the room because he *knew* he'd change his mind if he loitered any longer.

Mariel didn't know if his dad would wake up. He couldn't control that.

But he *could* control his future with Esther Caravan.

So... Mariel Nadier darted past nurses, doctors, and patients.

What would he tell her first? An apology? Or, would she rather that he kiss her first?

Anxiety burned in his chest, and his backpack thumped against his back. Mariel turned a corner and—

Smack!

Pain shot through his teeth. He saw a flash of red hair, heard a high-pitched howl, and stumbled backwards as a bony elbow crashed into his chest. At first, he thought he'd struck a bony woman, but as the individual fell back against the wall, Mariel realized who it was.

"Phil?"

It was not a bony woman. It was Philip Jameson, and the man clutched at his chest as if he'd just been shot during a golfing match. The peach-colored button-down he wore was rumpled, and he straightened his blue suit coat and struggled to regain his dignity.

"Mariel, where are you running to? Is everything okay?" Phil demanded, and his voice suggested that he didn't actually care if everything was okay. His tone suggested he wanted a damn good reason as to why he'd almost been trampled.

Mariel didn't have time to engage. "I'm sorry, Phil, everything's fine. I just need to—"

"Your backpack zipper is undone, Sir, you dropped your homework behind you." Behind him, a female nurse interrupted his attempt to leave.

Mariel turned, and he caught a glimpse of his father's journal in her hand. Fuck, he'd forgotten to leave it with his dad.

Quickly, he grabbed it from her. "Thank you. Phil—"

Phil interrupted. "I'm here to pray with Hawk, and I was just about to see how your father was doing. Can he take visitors?"

God, Mariel really didn't have time for this. And Phil didn't even *like* his dad—why did he insist on pretending right now?

"Yes," Mariel said as he extended the journal. The brown, leather-bound journal looked small in his large hand, and its torn edges reminded him that even men of faith could be anxious, because he'd seen his dad scratch at the binding during moments of stress.

Phil looked at it.

Mariel puffed out his cheeks. His heart slammed against his chest. Why was he so desperate to get to Esther now? There was no reason to—

"—make sure my dad gets this?" Mariel heard himself speak, but didn't remember initiating the question.

With a confused frown that arched one eyebrow higher than the other, Phil looked down at the journal. "Er..."

"Please? I really need to get going, and I want him to have it when he wakes up." Mariel would never forget this moment—the moment he found himself *begging* Phil Jameson.

Phil sucked in a big breath, as if he were about to decide whether or not he *wanted* to purchase the $100,000 vehicle. Then, he let out the air.

Took the journal in his hands.

And smiled.

"Room 245," Mariel blurted, and then he patted Phil's shoulder. If he hadn't been so excited to see Esther, he might have recoiled from touching the man. "Thank you so much!"

And Mariel continued down the hallway, hastening towards the woman he wanted most, and away from the man he knew he shouldn't trust.

* * *

Mariel made it to the *Pete's Diner* parking lot five minutes before the bookstore closed. After putting the car in park and turning it off, Mariel lifted his arm to smell his armpit and almost gagged.

He needed a fucking shower.

Desperately, he opened the glove box and flung papers, gum, a baggie of *Oreos*, and—why the *fuck* were mini condoms in his car?

Gabe. That fucker thought he was funny, didn't he?

"I'll deal with you later," Mariel muttered, grabbing items and throwing them to the floor until his fist finally closed around the plastic deodorant case.

"Yes!" He unzipped his sweatshirt and rubbed it over his shirt and into his armpits. "There we go." With a grimace, he tossed the deodorant back into the glove box, slammed it shut, and then burst from the car to head towards *Caravan's Books*.

Mariel saw his reflection in the bookstore window. He could see the bright lights in the store. If they were bright, she hadn't closed yet, because she liked to close in dim lights, listen to music, and dance as she completed her store closing duties. His heart warmed, and he almost smiled until he saw the reflection behind him.

There stood the humanoid, cocking his head back and forth.

With a snarl, he ignored the reflection, walked towards the entrance to the bookstore, and flung open the door.

He caught his breath and froze.

Gabe Donovan stood leaning over the register counter, his face animated like he was frustrated. But he didn't matter.

Esther did.

And *Esther* looked flushed and upset, her hands in motion as if her words were venom.

What the *fuck* was going on?

"Uh-oh," the humanoid said, in his ear. "You better claim that bitch."

Heat crawled through his skin and prickled it. His breathing grew more labored, and words tumbled from his mouth before he could stop them.

"Am I interrupting something?"

It bothered him. It wasn't his business, and yet if he didn't find out what this was, he might burst.

And it'd be violent.

Esther's wide eyes shot towards him, and she moved away from the counter as if being that close to Gabe would electrocute her. "Mars! Hey there."

Gabe straightened up and turned, a slow grin spreading across his face. "Hey, bro! How's your dad?"

No. He didn't want to make his comatose father the center of Gabe's fucking small talk. That fucker needed to bash his head against the corner of the counter until it—

"Good, I guess," Mariel said hoarsely. "Not really sure how good you can be when you're in a coma."

"Bash his fucking head in!" The humanoid giggled.

"He'll be okay," Gabe said, and he looked at Esther.

Esther played with her ponytail and smiled at Mariel. Was the smile forced? Or genuine?

"Alright, this is awkward, so I'm just gonna go," Gabe said, tapping his hand against the counter. "See you guys."

The world paused when Gabe left the store, as if it was giving Mariel a chance to recover his thoughts. He watched Esther with a sudden ache in his chest.

"Hi," she said, softer than he'd expect from a girl he'd almost run over. She moved a little closer to the counter, and he saw that she had earbuds in her palm. "Need a book?"

Mariel's eyes darted from her lips to what she was wearing, noting the swell of her breasts in the snug, green polo, and the curve of her hips in the dark jeans she wore. Her ponytail draped over her shoulder and gleamed in the overhead light. Suddenly, he wasn't angry anymore. He was too captivated, and the anger was turning into something far worse.

Lust.

Because lust meant he couldn't get rid of *those* thoughts—the disturbing images where she'd beg him.

Not to beg him to keep going.

But where she'd beg him to *stop*.

"Earth to Mars?" Esther teased.

He needed to speak up. Now.

"Esther," he said, and he came forward with his hands deep in the pockets of his sweatshirt. "I didn't come here for a book. I—I came here to apologize for the other day."

She looked at him, and her eyes searched his face—probably to determine his intentions after all he'd put her through. "It's o—"

"It's not." Mariel stood near the counter now, his heart thumping faster than he wanted. "It's not okay. You've been patient. You've been gentle. You've been *so good* to me... and I keep fucking it up and running away from how I feel."

Her eyes widened, and her chest rose and fell at a quickening pace. "How do you feel, Mars?"

There it was—the question he needed to answer with filtered honesty.

Which didn't seem all that honest.

"Esther—" He was floundering again.

"Tell me, Mars," Esther whispered, color rising higher into her cheeks. "Please."

He could see the pulse in her throat, the heaving of her breasts, her parted lips as she searched his face. His heart exploded. Each strike against his chest felt like a hammer, and his knees felt weak.

He'd never confessed feelings to a girl before. Probably because he'd never had feelings for anyone other than *Esther*.

"Esther," he began again. "I have this feeling. I've only ever had it with you, and I want to make sense of it. Every time I'm around you, my heart goes wild." Mariel could not believe he was finally saying the words. "I can't breathe around you, and I physically *hurt* when I'm around you because you're so beautiful."

Was she closer?

Mariel was. He towered over the counter, and he found himself leaning towards her. But this time he wouldn't run away.

This time he'd kiss her.

Breathing fast, Esther's eyes darted to his lips.

"What's the feeling?" Mariel whispered, allowing his eyes to fall to her mouth as well.

The counter was the only thing that separated them.

The earbuds clattered to the floor. Esther's hand, flat against the white counter, slid over the surface towards him. Her fingers brushed his abdomen, and her eyes glued to his as her palm journeyed upwards towards his chest.

Mariel dared not move.

Esther's fingers curled around the cloth of his sweatshirt and gripped it tightly with her fist. She placed her knee on the stool behind the counter and lifted herself higher, to become more level with his height, and she leaned forward with steady intent.

Shit.

Mariel began to panic. He'd never kissed a girl before. What if his inexperience scared her away?

But his eyes darted to those soft, inviting lips that inched towards him. The blood pounded in his head. His ears *roared*. He could not pull away from the magical—

—cursed—

—hold that Esther Caravan had over him, and hazily, he leaned towards her as well. He could smell her, that soft flowery smell he adored, and he felt her breath on his lips as their heads came together.

God.

Fucking *God.*

How could a girl's lips just melt like butter against his?

How could a girl's tongue just slip into his mouth with such gentle and bold confidence?

A groan rumbled from his mouth, and the world turned upside down as her mouth opened with his, and his tongue snaked into her like a—

Serpent.

Just like the humanoid said.

A goddamn serpent. And oh, it felt so good, so fucking *good*, because the mouth against his sucked his—

—serpent—

—tongue like a delicious fucking candy, like Eve in the garden of Eden, and it triggered hot jolts of pleasure that tore from his mouth and rained down like meteors towards his pelvis.

No.

His cock.

And suddenly, his tongue was just a tease of what could be *inside* of her, forcing its way in and—

"Ahem." Behind him, someone cleared their throat. "Are you still open?"

Esther fell from him, banging her knee against the counter. She was embarrassed. He could tell, because she always got *really* clumsy when something embarrassed her. "We're closing in sixty seconds," she gasped, and her voice held a tone of contempt.

"I'll just come back tomorrow," the person said. He couldn't tell which gender.

But this was a sign that he needed to stop. He'd almost gotten carried away; had almost lost himself to the physical temptation that belonged to Esther Caravan.

Mariel turned to see who spoke. It was just an older woman with purple eyeliner and grey hair in a clip. Her thin mouth drew a straight line in judgmental silence as she assessed them both. She looked pissed.

"You know," she said, and turned to leave. "I don't appreciate seeing that disgusting shit in a public place. Grow up."

And she left.

Mariel scratched his head and turned back to Esther. "Listen, I—"

Still flustered, Esther held her phone. "I'm sorry, my dad's calling. I need to make sure Hawk's okay. One sec... hello?" Her eyes darted about as she responded, and she turned away as if she'd be able to hear better if she didn't face him.

Awkward, Mariel glanced outside the store and nearly gasped.

A tall man with a tan overcoat stood outside the glass doors, hands deep in his pockets, eyes reddened. Distant.

Just staring.

Muttering to himself as if he had a humanoid too.

"What?" Esther blurted, and it brought Mariel's attention back to her. Still turned from him, she reached behind her neck and grabbed a handful of her hair.

Mariel looked back at the entrance.

A runner in all black jogged past the window.

But the overcoat man was gone.

"I'll be there soon," Esther said, and whirled back to Mariel with wide eyes.

"What's wrong?" he asked, and his heart dropped. Hawk died. Her little brother had died, and she'd have to go through loss again.

"I need to get to the hospital," Esther murmured, dazed.

"Is Hawk okay?" Mariel demanded.

"Yes," she said. "That's the thing. He's more than okay."

Mariel tilted his head, and he wasn't sure how good news could be so chilling. "So, what's... wrong?"

Esther closed her eyes, drew in a breath, and let it out. "Every bruise on his body is gone. Every scar from surgery. And they found him standing outside the room just now." She turned her eyes to his. "My brother just fucking walked."

And then, as Mariel processed her words, it was his turn for his phone to ring. He reached for it, his stomach suddenly nauseous with fear that the hospital would say the words he most dreaded.

That the humanoid would soon revel in Fr. Jerome's death.

But they didn't speak the words he feared.

"Your dad's awake," the nurse told him, and he didn't think he'd ever forget the kindness in her voice. "He's awake. Alert. And he's asking for you."

Verse 3

~ Pandemonium ~

Monday, January 21st, 2019

Chicago, Illinois

The four stages of grief, anger (a sin), denial (a sin), bargaining (definitely a sin), and acceptance (less often a sin unless one accepted non-biblical things), did not fit Phil Jameson's itinerary after Carolyn's death. Rather, he'd thrown himself into his research of KS Industries to determine if he wanted to accept the legal position.

Despite being *black*, Kaemon Spears was well-spoken and convincing, and Phil had almost said yes to the legal counsel offer before he'd been told that his wife was dead on some railroad tracks in Chicago.

Inconvenient.

How did one grieve for a woman who'd descended into madness and chosen death over eternal life?

One didn't.

Rather, you prayed for her soul—despite the bleak reality that she was in Hell.

It was a lonely cross to bear—being the only one who knew the reality of Carolyn's situation. His daughter Hailey was far too immature and naive, and his daughter Victoria—oh, she grinded his gears. That little wench was a heretic—running away from her family to put herself through college, wearing slutty outfits, and engaging in God only knew *what* sins at her liberal, demonic college. So, naturally, Victoria wouldn't have *any* clue about the reality of her mother's hell-bound destination.

She probably encouraged the woman to jump in front of the train.

Yes, it was a lonely existence bearing this cross, so Phil's interpretation of the situation turned upside down and exploded into flames the night Mariel Nadier placed Fr. Jerome's journal into his palm like it was the most important thing in the world.

Because he *never* expected to see Carolyn's name written in there.

So, after Mariel fled from the hospital, Phil Jameson took a quick trip to the restroom where he'd been headed, anyway.

And while he didn't really want to sit on the toilet and read Fr. Jerome's journal, he didn't feel entirely comfortable enough doing that in the man's hospital room.

He was done using the bathroom, yes, but he was too intrigued by the journal entry to stand up and pull up his pants.

The journal entry with his wife's name.

Carolyn kept running. We ran outside, down the snowy roadways and sidewalks.

Phil scanned the words with wide eyes, muttering each sentence with intense focus.

But I did see blood. It was splattered all over the road and the building walls. I suspected she committed suicide. Her voice, still desperate, echoed in my mind as I stood in horror.

The automatic light clicked off.

"When was this written? He didn't *predict* this!" Phil exclaimed, sitting up on the toilet as his voice bounced against the walls. The light clicked back on, and he flipped to the previous page to find the date.

January 12th, 2019.

"Well!" Phil nodded in satisfaction. "He didn't predict this. He wrote it after her death so that he could feel good about himself and believe his own delusions. *Mmhmm.*" He felt *pleased* with himself until his error smacked him across the face like a brick.

Fr. Jerome had been found comatose at the scene. He hadn't woken up since then, and presumably, Mariel hadn't delivered the journal for him to *write in his sleep.*

Upright on the toilet, Phil shook his head. It couldn't be. A sinner like Jerome Nadier *wouldn't* be a prophet. It simply wasn't biblical.

And if Jerome was there, why didn't he *stop* Carolyn from taking her life? If the priest presumed he *knew* the future, then maybe *do* something about it!

Growling, Phil tossed the journal to the floor, wiped himself, and stood up. Yanking his pants to his waist, he zipped them and buckled the belt as he scowled at the journal.

How *dare* Jerome write about his wife without consulting him? Without letting Phil *know* that Carolyn was thinking about committing such a dreadful sin?

Now, thanks to Jerome, his wife was burning in Hell.

She was *in Hell.*

Despite that little statement from the Caravan whore. You know, the one implying that *Phil* was the problem.

"*She must be in Heaven,*" the harlot had said. "*Because she's not here with you.*"

Fuming, Phil scrubbed his hands, snatched paper towel from the dispenser, and then grabbed the journal. For a moment, he stood by the door and skimmed the rest of the journal entry.

The night before my nightmare of Carolyn, I dreamt of a date. February 15th, 2020. I heard screams, explosions, and gunshots. I woke up. Before that, I dreamt of a boy who could move the earth and control the weather. As the earth quaked, and rain poured from the sky, I saw the young Arab boy with his arms in the air. He screamed. He seemed heartbroken, and I sobbed for him. Somehow, I knew his name. It was on my lips.

"Ahdam!" I screamed, and I woke up.

Before that, I dreamt of people falling from the sky. I hate that one. It's horrifying.

"Save us from tribulation!" they scream and pummel the earth.

Phil rubbed his chin, finishing the journal entry. He paced back and forth, his palms clammy, and he paused on one of the final lines.

I still don't know if Mariel caught that bullet.

Fr. Jerome Nadier was insane. He'd gone mad. *No one* could catch a bullet, unless... Could the boy, Mariel, be a *demon?*

Phil slapped the journal shut. In Revelations, false prophets would emerge. Signs. Wonders. The antichrist. Things were starting to make *sense*—Biblically, of course.

The end was near. God would call together an army in the end times, as well as one to lead it.

This journal hadn't been placed into Phil's hands for nothing.

"Okay," Phil said, and smiled a little. "I have a lot of work to do to bring people to Christ."

* * *

Phil placed the journal on the table next to the bed. He did so with a reverence that did not coincide with the fact that he'd just taken photos of the January 12th journal entry. He'd flipped through the other pages, hoping to find more information that might grant him the foresight necessary to bring the world to Christ, but the journal was either illegible or boring.

Mariel this, Esther that. Gabe this, bla, bla, bla.

Maybe if the man spent less time whining in his journal and worshipping those sinful kids, he'd write better sermons and bring more to Christ.

Not that Jerome would bring more to Christ, anyway, considering the old man had *bragged* about giving communion to a faggot in his journal.

Phil smiled.

He'd hold on to *that* knowledge for future use, if necessary.

The room was cold and sour smelling, and the machines beeped in rhythm. With an arched brow, Phil inched forward and eyed the intubated priest on the hospital bed.

For a moment, he wondered what would happen if he pulled the intubation.

Or, even better, if he *touched* Jerome.

Oh, imagine the look on Jerome's face if he found out that Philip Jameson, the man who hadn't *earned* his recommendation letter for seminary, *healed* him. That look of humiliation and awe would bring Phil great joy, giving him the opportunity to say—

"God's grace has been extended to you by my hand, Jerome."

Wetting his lips, Phil brought his hands closer to Jerome's face. "You've really done it, haven't you?" he whispered, watching Jerome's chest rise and fall. "But this is what happened when you play God and—"

Jerome's eyes opened.

Phil gasped.

Alarms went off. Phil wasn't even sure which ones, but they were loud, judgmental, and desperate. He fell backwards, raising his hands in the air as if he'd been caught by the cops, and his eyes widened as Fr. Jerome Nadier reached over the bed and grabbed for his journal. Pages tore as he caught it, and medical staff raced into the room and shoved Phil aside as if he didn't matter.

Because, right now, he didn't.

But he would.

Pandemonium filled the room, and Phil wondered if it even *was* pandemonium, or if his mind had intensified the scene before him.

"We're getting the tube out, Hon!"

"Support his head!"

"There we go!"

A splattering cough burst from Fr. Jerome's mouth, and Phil stood frozen in terror with what happened next. The priest's eyes met his in dazed confusion, his chapped lips opened, and words spat from his mouth like angry bullets.

"Stay away from Esther, my son, or you will undo us all!"

"Huh?" Phil said, suddenly feeling targeted, and he inched his way towards the door. He didn't *ever* seek out that *whore*. If anything, *she* should stay away from *him*.

And everyone, for that matter, before she got herself smacked for that smart mouth she had.

But that wasn't the point, and Phil Jameson no longer wanted to stay in this hellhole of a room, so he raised a quick hand to bid goodbye and left.

Mind-frenzied, Phil stormed to his next destination. As he moved through the hospital, he replayed his actions. He hadn't *touched* Fr. Jerome, so had God given him the ability to heal on mere presence?

What if he didn't *want* to heal someone he didn't like? Did he have a choice in the matter?

There was only one way to find out.

Phil knocked on the door.

A moment later, it opened, and Todd's bloodshot, weary face appeared. "Oh hey, Phil, thanks so much for coming. Come on in. Hawk is sleeping."

"And you should be too," Phil said, smiling and stepping into the room. "Tell you what, you go get some sleep and I'll stay here with my favorite Caravan. Sound good?"

Todd rubbed his eyes. "You sure?"

Phil thought for a brief moment, considered the consequences, considered the reward, and remembered that God hadn't appointed him for no reason. So—

"Yes," he said, and nodded with finality. "I'm absolutely sure."

Verse 4

~ Vessel ~

Friday, January 25th, 2019
Chicago, Illinois

When his dad was cleared to go home, Mariel couldn't stop the tears from rolling. The staff kept him until the end of the week to ensure no other brain hemorrhaging took place, and then they said the words Mariel Nadier had been praying for.

"You ready to go home, Sir?"

Looking bright and incredibly youthful in the hospital bed, Fr. Jerome nodded with an eagerness that resembled that of a child by a Christmas tree. "I sure am."

But even though Mariel's joy overwhelmed his thoughts, he still couldn't shake the unsettling events that had happened. Hawk's mysterious healing. Fr. Jerome's immediate recovery.

He didn't even know *why* these events were unsettling, especially since *he* himself could not fucking die. Especially since he couldn't go one day without seeing the humanoid or the *other* figure, following him and reminding him that he was *just a vessel*.

And Esther? He hadn't heard from her—probably because she was *wrecked* from the oddity of Hawk's situation. Still, his mind spiraled in all sorts of directions. Had he gone too far the other night? Did she like *Gabe?*

There were so many unanswered questions, and Mariel wanted to bury them all and enjoy the fact that his father was fine.

He was *fine*. He'd *prayed* for his father to be fine, and he'd delivered the journal to Phil Jameson's hands in hopes that his father would be *fine*.

Yet here he was, second-guessing it all.

"You okay, Bud?"

Mariel's eyes snapped towards Fr. Jerome, who sat across the table from him at their favorite twenty-four-hour coffee shop. The priest's tea sat before him in a white, porcelain teacup, and steam drifted hazily into the air.

Gently, Fr. Jerome smiled. "You haven't rested much, have you?"

Shrugging, Mariel laughed a little. "About as much as I normally do, Dad." He wondered if that sounded harsh, if it implied that his dad's hospitalization hadn't concerned him.

Fr. Jerome appeared unaffected. "So you partied all night like you normally do, huh?" He winked.

"Yes, definitely. Had a rave in the house. Got a few girls pregnant."

"How long until they're due?" Fr. Jerome sipped his tea. "And do my grandchildren have an Amazon wish list?"

Mariel laughed, and the endorphins flooded his senses. It felt good. "I didn't ask, I didn't want to have to pay child support on *Pete's Diner* salary." He brought his coffee to his lips.

"Well, you did it wrong," Fr. Jerome said, and he lifted his tea. "That's why you knock up the rich girls."

Mariel spat out his coffee. It sprayed. Coffee-house patrons looked up from their conversations as the young man coiled over in laughter.

"What? Just because I'm gay doesn't mean I never had straight guy friends," Jerome said calmly, as if he hadn't just been sprayed with coffee.

"Dad! Stop!" Mariel sat back in his chair and wiped his mouth. "Fuck, it's good to have you back."

Fr. Jerome reached across the table and squeezed his son's hand. "I missed you."

"You were unconscious," Mariel chuckled.

"I still felt you there, Son. I missed you." The priest sat back and smiled again. "Now. I know you've had a rough time, because you're not really saying much. Did anything happen that you feel comfortable talking to me about?"

No. Not at all. He wasn't inclined to delve into his intrusive thoughts about Esther.

"No, I'm fine," he said, while playing with his napkin.

Fr. Jerome raised his eyebrows, opened his mouth to speak, and then closed it again as if he decided he'd let it go.

For now.

"The funeral was great," Mariel said, and then realized how awkward he sounded. "I mean, not *great*, but it was nice to see how supportive people were for Carolyn."

Fr. Jerome's eyes lowered, and he placed his tea on the table. His lower lip trembled. "I loved her. It hurts my soul that she's gone. And it hurts even more that she felt she had no other choice."

Dishes clinked. A coffee grinder whirred.

Mariel nodded. "I'm sorry, Dad. I know it's hard for you to see anyone from your congregation hurt."

Fr. Jerome wiped his eyes. "I don't like placing blame on her husband. I don't. I feel like a horrible, judgmental person. But Phil didn't help, and it bothers me that there wasn't anything I could—"

"Dad." Mariel grabbed his hand. "Stop. Don't start the guilt thing. You'll give yourself another brain bleed."

"But—"

"Nope. I don't need that from you right now, I need some hope. You asked what happened while you were in a coma? Despair." Mariel's voice shook. "I lose faith so fast when you're not there to lift me up."

Was it selfish of him to rely solely on his dad to help him maintain faith? It didn't seem fair that Fr. Jerome had to take responsibility for *everyone's* trials.

"I'm sorry, Mariel."

"No, *stop* apologizing, Dad. You're too fucking nice. It's how you got tangled up in Carolyn's bullshit anyway," Mariel snapped in a low whisper.

Fr. Jerome sighed. "Oh, my boy. Fine. But I'm allowed to have feelings on the matter." He finished his tea. "Now, how is Esth—" He stopped, and his face paled. Blankly, he stared past Mariel as if he'd seen a monster from his past.

"What?" Mariel said, suddenly terrified that his father was having a stroke.

"She's going to shoot me," Fr. Jerome mumbled, and his fingers twitched on the table.

Frowning, Mariel leaned in. "Dad? *Who? No* one is going to *shoot* you, who are—"

"Her," the priest said, a little louder. "The woman with the green eyes."

Mariel turned in his chair. A line of people stood awaiting their coffee. A large-bellied man in a tailored suit. College-aged girls in yoga pants and coats. A middle-aged man with a *Carhardt* coat. A blonde woman with a tall athletic build, wearing a cap, joggers, and a hoodie.

"Um," Mariel turned back to look at his father. "I'm so confused, Dad."

"Why?" Fr. Jerome said as he relaxed.

"Dad. You literally just said some chick with green eyes was gonna shoot you. Are you sure you're okay?"

Fr. Jerome frowned. "When did I say that?"

"Just *now*. What the heck?" Mariel said, and he looked past his shoulder again. The line hadn't moved. The blonde was on her phone, and his eyes flickered to her ass.

Fuck.

That was disrespectful to Esther.

Fr. Jerome cleared his throat. "Maybe I'm still high from narcotics. Not impossible."

Mariel pushed his chair back. "I'm taking that as a sign we need to get you home. Come on."

Fr. Jerome didn't protest. He insisted upon delivering his teacup to the front counter, and Mariel tossed the keys back and forth while he waited.

It was then that the blonde took her coffee, turned, and their eyes met briefly.

She had striking green eyes.

But she moved on quickly, looking at Mariel as if he were a mosquito in her ear, and she dipped her head and brought the to-go cup to her lips as she exited the coffee shop.

"Alright, naptime," Fr. Jerome said, patting his son on the back. "And I think you may need one too."

* * *

Monday, January 28th, 2019

"Hey, Esther. How are you? I hope you're doing okay."

Mariel typed beneath the desk. He couldn't pay attention to the forensic pathology professor, who always kept his dark hair combed with immaculate perfection and smiled like he'd just gotten laid.

In reality, he couldn't pay attention to much of anything right now, because he hadn't been able to stop thinking about Esther Caravan and that addicting kiss—the one that'd been interrupted by the—

—*bitch*—

—customer.

Now that his father was doing better, Mariel's thoughts and worries turned to everything else he'd buried.

Like that conversation between Gabe and Esther.

It shouldn't matter, and it *didn't*. But it gnawed at him when Esther was quiet, or secretive. Yes—he, Esther, *and* Gabe had always been an inseparable trio, but Esther had always chosen *him* first. Confided in *him* fucking *first*.

What had changed?

What the *fuck* had—

—*that bitch*—

—Esther been whispering to Gabe Donovan in the bookstore?

"Stop it," he growled through his teeth before realizing he'd spoken too loudly. His classmate, a young woman with dirty blonde hair who'd always made a point to sit next to him in class, glanced at him and smiled a little.

Distracted with momentary curiosity, Mariel's eyes flickered to her blouse. She was a larger girl, and the feminine clothes she wore did nothing to hide the fact that she had large breasts—

—*tits*—

—that, if Mariel weren't so devoted to Esther, he might consider playing with.

If she let him, of course.

Great, he'd caught her gaze now, and his face went hot. Looking away, Mariel turned his eyes back to the professor in an attempt to calm his mind.

It didn't.

He wanted Esther. He wanted her to text him back. He wanted to take her on a date and have a normal goddamn relationship with a girl without having to worry about the humanoid.

He wanted someone to love him with as much passion as *he* loved. But more importantly, Mariel wanted to find a way to love himself too.

Maybe then he could rid himself of the humanoid.

"Mariel."

"Hmm?" He looked up.

"Are you paying attention?"

His eyes landed on the professor, and he stiffened when he realized the professor was staring right at him. "Er, I'm sorry. Yes."

College wasn't high school. Why the hell was the professor asking him if he was paying attention?

And why was the room so quiet now?

"Are you paying attention?" the professor asked again.

"*Yes!*" Mariel exclaimed.

"Then you need to stay away from Esther, let her go, and turn your attention to your greater purpose." The professor's dark eyes glimmered in the light. His face, normally bright with his love of teaching, had a look that reminded Mariel of a secret service agent that was two years past his retirement.

Mariel glanced around the room.

Like frozen stone, students sat in their original positions. They did not move, and they did not breathe.

"Excuse me?" Mariel murmured, afraid that if he spoke louder, he'd embarrass himself. He glanced at the clock near the classroom entrance.

Had the battery died?

Or had time stopped?

The professor looked at the clock and clicked his tongue. "What questions do you have?"

What the hell?

"About *forensics?*" Mariel wondered if he'd taken his father's narcotics.

"No, Mariel," the professor sighed. "About me. About your purpose in the last days."

His heart stopped. At least, it felt like it did. "What?"

The professor began to pace. His dress shoes clicked against the floor, and he shoved his hands into his grey dress pants. "You can't die because you have a specific purpose in the last days, Mariel. You're a vessel."

There. He knew that phrase. But the humanoid phrased it just a tad differently.

"*You're just a vessel,*" it said, his entire fucking life. *Just...* as if that was all he'd ever be. Just.

"You're the other follower." Mariel sat with his palms flat against the desk. His lips trembled. "Aren't you?"

The professor just stared at him, as if the thing inside of him didn't know what to do with a human body.

"Why haven't you ever talked to me?" Mariel asked, and the rage that warmed his body alerted him to the reality that he'd been *freezing*.

"I disagree. I talk to you all the time."

"The *fuck* you do!"

"Mariel." The professor stood briefly onto his toes and then dropped back down again. "Whether you hear my voice or not... I always have."

"I would know if I heard you," Mariel protested, half-wondering if this was a dream, and he hoped he'd wake up soon to a response from Esther.

The professor resumed pacing, and his pointed dress shoes gleamed in the light. "Would you agree that you've made a series of decisions, based on what you believed to be good, proper, and of God?"

Mariel hesitated. "I guess?"

The man's strides lengthened. "Who do you think proposed some of them to you?" He stopped walking. "Not to take credit for your entire moral compass, but who was that whisper in your head, telling you to care for your father? To treat everyone with respect, compassion, and kindness? Telling you to be diligent in your prayers and your duties in the church?"

Mariel tilted his head. "I can't take credit for any of that? I don't even get to take credit for my own ability to *think* like a good human being? Who the *hell* are you?"

The professor came forward a little. The light reflected against the gold belt buckle he wore below the grey tuxedo vest. His eyes were dark. "Are you taking credit for the whisper that tells you to *stay away* from Esther?"

Those words stung. Its claws clamped against his heart and crushed it. Tears stung his eyes, emotions collided, and he fought to keep himself controlled.

For a moment—if *time* even existed anymore—Mariel sat with his hands folded tightly on the desk, his knuckles white, surrounded by the immobile students.

"Please," he said, his voice shaking. "I love her."

The professor's expression did not change. In fact, he stood unhindered by Mariel's emotion. "I am not here to guide you away from her. That is not my role. But I do know that every human on this planet receives a fair chance to make certain choices. You deserve to have that chance as well."

"No!" Mariel screamed. "I don't want to be offered a fucking chance. I don't want a divine purpose! I want to exist without *you,* and without *him,* and be trusted to make my own decisions without the threat of some *fucking* judgment, because that's why you're here, isn't it? To tell me I don't get what I want, but I should be *blessed* because *God Himself* appointed *me* for some *holy,* divine, *fucking* role? Oh, *goodie!*" Tears flooded over his cheeks. His scream echoed in the still room.

The professor didn't blink. In fact, he hadn't blinked at all. "One day," he said quietly, "you will face the final hour, and you will be reminded of the words your father will have written. Someday, you will know who you are, and it will be too late." He looked up with raised eyebrows. "Leave her alone, Mariel, that's all I can tell you. Please, appreciate what humanity you have left, because if you continue this obsessive path, you will lose yourself very soon."

Mariel wheezed, raised his fists into the air to scream and then—

"Mariel? Are you good?"

The whisper in his ear flipped his reality upside down. Gasping, Mariel whipped his head towards the whisper and saw that the hot blonde had leaned towards him.

Sweat trickled into his eyes. "I'm...*good*," he croaked, and then he vomited.

* * *

"I'm going to head to the coffee shop to do some journaling. You wanna meet me, Son?"

In the darkness, soft snowflakes fell, almost with the consistency of rain.

Mariel sat in his car. His chest heaved. Up. Down. Up. Down.

The windshield wipers squeaked.

Up. Down. Up. Down.

"I'll be home soon, Dad, I've got some studying to do. You enjoy your journaling."

Fr. Jerome chuckled on the phone. "Look at you being responsible. Okay. Sounds good. Are you sure you're okay?"

Mariel looked out of the window, where his eyes settled on the white Jeep outside of the bookstore. He swallowed hard, and he struggled to keep his voice steady. "I'm fine. Just tired."

"Are you sure, Bud? I want to be there for you. I'm scared that you're going to—"

"Spiral again?" Mariel finished. "I'm not. And I'm not gonna hurt myself. Even if I tried, I can't die. So..." His voice faded.

Silence on the other end of the line.

"Son, this is not about if you can or can't die. It hurts my soul that you'd *want* to. I love you so much, Mariel. I'd do anything for you, to make sure you're okay."

Mariel knew that. Fuck, he *knew* that with every ounce of his being. His dad deserved a better son. A happier son. One who smiled more, one who hugged him more, one who—

"I love you, Dad. I'm fine, I promise. Go write." Mariel forced a smile onto his lips and he watched as someone's shadow crossed the bookstore's dim lighting. His heart beat faster.

She'd texted him back.

She'd asked for him.

Told him to come to the bookstore after closing time.

Because to her? He wasn't *just a vessel.*

He was Mars.

"See you later, Son, I love you."

The call ended. Mariel cleared his throat, opened the car door, and stepped out of the car.

Each step he took brought him closer to the bookstore, closer to Esther, and further away from the nightmare in his head. He didn't care about the humanoid he saw to his left, and he didn't care about the dark figure he saw to his right.

Esther was real. She was *human.*

She wasn't a figment of his fucking imagination. Even if the professor's words rang true, that he had a *purpose* in the last days, then he deserved every right to live *his* last days in happiness for once.

And Esther? *She* was happiness.

Still, as he approached the door, Mariel Nadier was afraid. What if he *took* her happiness?

"Lord Jesus Christ, Son of God, have mercy on me and save me, a sinner," Mariel muttered, opened the door, and stepped inside. His body moved forward, but his thoughts scrambled.

Maybe he shouldn't.

But that willpower faded as he rounded the corner and saw her.

Between the shelves, Esther stood on a stepstool loading books onto the shelf. Her hair was in a loose bun at her neck, and her black, long-sleeved shirt rose above the button of her jeans as she reached upwards to place a book on the shelf. It exposed a hint of skin, and Mariel watched in fascination as the sinewy curves of her body moved gracefully like a curved spring of fresh water.

And he began to shake.

"Esther," he said in a low, shaky voice.

Esther placed the last book on the shelf, turning towards his voice as her forefinger slipped down the spine of the book. Her eyes were wide, and they dimmed with sudden hunger as her lips parted and almost beckoned him.

Mariel could not feel his legs. Yet he walked towards the girl that made him feel human, the girl that made him feel not only good things, but vile things. The girl that made him question his own reality whenever he looked at her.

Esther Caravan—the girl he'd reject *everything* and *everyone* for.

Her eyes pulled him, as if connected to his soul like a rope. Every protest, every voice in his mind muted as he approached her.

And, for a moment, they stood near. Silence covered the universe.

Then, reaching down, her fingers touched his face, and his arms went around her waist. He buried his head against her abdomen. Her body trembled, and her hands were in his hair, pulling the black, silky waves on his head, drawing him closer to her warm body. Mariel breathed her scent, and he lifted her from the stepstool.

When her feet touched the floor, Esther stepped onto his toes, her fingers still laced within his hair, and raised her lips hungrily to his.

Time stopped, everything warmed, and the beat of his heart pulsed into his head.

Their lips met roughly at first. Then, the kiss softened, as if their lips needed time to get to know each other. Mariel's breath grew steadily more ragged with each kiss. So did hers. Had the store lights flickered? He wasn't sure, because their breaths came with harsher intensity, their kisses more ravenous.

Esther pushed him against the bookshelf. Her body pressed into his as her mouth opened, and an urgent moan escaped her throat.

"Stay away from Esther."

Those damning words in the back of his mind left him reeling.

How could he?

His body roared with desire for her as he felt her breasts against his chest, the vibrations of her hips against his groin, and the heated gasps escaping her mouth as it devoured his. His hand crept to her throat, and Mariel turned her body until it was Esther pressed against the bookshelf. Her tongue slid into his mouth, soft and wet, and she caressed his lips with it. Shaking, he allowed his tongue to meet hers, and they flicked against each other, again and again, fighting for an entrance to each other's mouths, and he groaned as he felt himself lose control of his body.

"Stay away from Esther."

But his cock hardened against her.

And in response, she raised herself higher in an effort to rock her hips against his, teasing him, tempting him to rip down her jeans and—

The store door opened.

Gasping, their heads came apart.

Mariel leaned his forehead against the bookshelf, his breaths coming in gasps, his hand moving down to adjust himself in his underwear.

"My God, Mars," Esther panted, her hands curling into his collar. "Don't... go anywhere. I'll be right back." Her whisper was more of an urgent demand than a request.

"Hello? Can I get some help?" A man's voice.

She slipped from under his arm, her face flushed. Adjusting her hair, Esther walked unsteadily towards the bookstore counter.

Mariel brushed his hair back. It was hot. He hesitated for a moment, listening to the conversation just outside of the bookshelves.

"Sir, the store is closed. I just forgot to lock it."

"I need a book. Just one." a man whined. "Can't I go grab it real quick?"

Esther's voice held defeat and exhaustion. "Okay, quickly please."

Mariel wandered to the back of the store. Still sweating, he rolled his sleeves to his elbows. Now that he had time to think, his mind fought his body.

What if the professor had been right? What if, for a moment, he stopped to think about what he was actually doing and stopped the fucking spiral before it was too late?

Humans couldn't catch bullets. Humans *died.*

Mariel *didn't.*

None of that seemed safe for Esther at all, and yet here he was, tonguing her like a fucking teenage boy who'd never gotten laid before. Which... he hadn't, but that wasn't the point. He needed to calm the fuck down and think through this.

But Mariel couldn't calm down, because now he wanted her more than ever.

"Just leave," he whispered to himself, staring at the exit to the back alley. "Do it."

He didn't move.

"Leave," he whispered again, trying to move. "Leave!"

Stay.

"He's gone." Esther came around the corner towards him. "Thank goodness. Weirdo."

Mariel watched her as she approached him. "Esther," he said, trying to stop her before she took hold of him again. "Um—"

Ignoring him, she took his tie in her fingers and looked at his lips. "The sign says *closed* now," Esther whispered. "And this time... the doors are locked." With sudden aggression, she shoved him, and he fell into the couch. "Now," she said, biting her lip and straddling his lap. "Where were we?"

"Esther, we—"

Her mouth fell over his again as her fingers worked their way into his hair.

Shit.

With a groan, Mariel lost himself in her again, and his hands found her hips and traveled beneath her shirt.

If the professor was right, wouldn't that leave him *no choice*? Wasn't it more of a *threat*? Telling him he'd lose himself if he didn't stay away from her?

That didn't seem fair.

Esther groaned into his mouth.

His fingers found her smooth skin, gently rubbing the length of her abdomen, up and down, his thumbs caressing the skin just beneath the wire of her bra.

"Fucking hell," Esther whispered, trailing kisses over his ear and down his neck as her fingers tugged and pulled desperately to undo the tie at his neck.

What if the professor and the humanoid weren't real?

What if he could *actually* die, and he'd built an illusion around himself that he couldn't?

Mariel's breaths came hard, and he lifted his hands higher until his thumbs brushed against her hard nipples over the cloth of the bra.

Maybe he'd built an entire world for himself.

Or maybe none of this was real.

Esther caught her breath, and his touch prompted her to work more quickly. She stared into his eyes with fiery intent as she whipped the tie from his neck and unbuttoned his shirt with shaking fingers.

His eyes closed, feeling the hot warmth of her groin move against his. But when her cool fingers touched the skin of his chest, and her hot tongue slipped across his neck, his eyes opened.

"Stay away from Esther, my son, or you will undo us all!"

But he didn't see the professor.

Mariel saw his dad in the hospital bed, and blood poured in torrents from the man's mouth, as if he'd lost his tongue.

Suddenly, the urgency to stop overcame the urgency to continue.

With a throaty whimper, he pushed her away and lunged from the couch. "Stop," he gasped, his eyes wide. The half-buttoned shirt hung loosely out of his pants.

Struggling to keep herself upright on the couch, Esther looked up at him, her face distorting with anxiety. She stood up. "Mars, what's wrong?"

He paced back and forth. The humanoid paced with him. "We can't."

Her eyes followed him. "I said I was sorry, Mariel, what more—?"

"I mean, us." He could not look at her, and he continued to pace. His chest hurt. "Esther, I'm sorry, I lied to you."

Her voice shook. "What do you mean?" She started towards him. "Please, Mariel, talk to me. *I love you!*"

The words echoed in the bookstore.

No.

No, God couldn't do this to him. If Esther *loved* him, if she said those fucking words, he'd never stand a chance against himself.

Mariel stepped back from her. "Don't," he said, shaking his head.

All of this hurt too much.

The incessant throbbing between his legs.

And the things he was about to say.

"Mars, whatever it is you feel, tell me," she protested, and she reached for him.

Mariel pulled his arm away. He buttoned his shirt while she watched him with confusion. "I lied. I feel really bad about it. Dad taught me to be better than this." His voice shook. So did his hands. His shirt was lopsided now, one button in the wrong location.

"When I came in here the other day—" he retrieved his tie from the couch and twisted it, "—I told you I had feelings for you because I wanted to see if you'd fuck me. That's all."

The humanoid giggled.

"You're lying to me," she said softly. "There is something about yourself that you are either afraid to tell me, or don't want to tell me. Frankly, I don't care." Esther came towards him again with impassioned eyes. "I've waited years for you to tell me you cared about me, Mariel Nadier, and you seem to forget that I've known your ins and outs..." She stepped even closer. "Your ups and downs..." She stood close again, and her eyes searched his. "...Your lies and your truths. Mariel... I *know* you're lying to me."

Mariel's heart beat wildly. Her face was close again, and it took everything in his soul not to reach for her again.

The humanoid sighed. "Just fuck her, Mariel, this is so goddamn *boring*."

Mariel chuckled. "You're one naive, horny bitch, aren't you? Do you really think that I'd drag you along for this long if I *really* wanted you? I woulda fucked you by now."

He watched as her face paled, as she believed his lie, and he stepped backwards. "But my dad taught me better. I just figured I'd make a bet with myself and a few of my buddies."

Esther's lips quivered, and the tears that'd been glistening in her blue-brown eyes spilled to her cheeks. "You're still lying. Aren't you?"

"What's going on here? Mariel? What are you doing here?" Todd's deep voice behind him sent chills down Mariel's spine, but he turned with sharp finality.

Here, he could end it.

"Hello, Mr. Caravan," he said, stepping towards the couch and holding up his tie. "I'm leaving. Your daughter almost fucked me, but I had a realization at Carolyn Jameson's funeral." He laughed and staggered towards the door. "Esther wouldn't look as good on her knees as Victoria would."

Too far.

Too far.

He heard footsteps thundering behind him. It was like the night in 2012, in Esther's room, when he'd put that gun in his mouth and pulled the trigger.

"Daddy, *no!*" Esther screamed.

Mariel wished the gun had worked.

"You *fucking* piece of *shit!*" Todd roared.

He wished he'd died.

Todd grabbed the back of Mariel's collar and yanked.

Mariel lost his footing and fell backwards against the coffee table. The legs snapped beneath his weight, and the table collapsed with a crash, sending magazines and books sliding to the floor.

Wailing, Esther grabbed her father's waist, her face wet with tears as she pleaded for him to stop.

"Get the fuck out of my store before I beat the goddamn *shit out of you!*" Todd screamed, his face red. Spittle filled the air. The veins pulsed in his forehead and neck.

Mariel stood and brushed his pants. "I'm leaving."

He caught a glimpse of Esther's face.

Distraught, her tearful eyes pleaded with him, begging for answers.

Mariel needed to vomit again.

Tearfully, he flung open the door.

As Mariel walked into the howling wind and biting sleet, he thought of Todd's explosive rage, and that chilling cry from Esther.

He cursed his existence.

He cursed the humanoid.

And, for the first time in his life, Mariel Nadier cursed God.

Chapter 6: Verse 1

~ Confession ~

Monday, January 28th, 2019

Chicago, Illinois

Hawk could walk... he could walk again. In fact, he maneuvered through life now as if he hadn't been struck at all.

As if he'd been given a complete physical reset.

Yes, Hawk could walk again, and Esther was sobbing about a fucking boy. Not a man. A boy, because what man would treat a human being how Mariel Nadier just treated her?

If he wasn't interested, fine. She could move on from that. If he had struggles that he needed to express, she could provide a listening ear. But what Mariel just did to her suggested he had no trust in her at all—that he'd rather make her feel like the stupidest, most disgusting cum-dump on earth rather than tell her what was really going on.

It fucking hurt.

A stack of books collapsed from the end of the shelf as she grabbed them in a desperate attempt to organize. Her breathing quickened, and she tried to pull herself together as Todd Caravan paced back and forth in the aisle.

"I'm going to bash his fucking teeth in!" Todd said, stomping down the aisle.

Or he could fucking help her clean the bookstore so there wasn't a mess to clean up in the morning. "Dad, please just stop," she sniffled, stooping to pick up the largest book that'd fallen on her toe.

War and Peace. It was a hardcover—massive enough to bash Mariel across the face.

"I don't want you near him anymore," Todd snapped, stopping mid-aisle with flared nostrils. "Esther? Did you hear me?"

"I'm a *fucking* adult, Dad!" Esther cried, slamming the Russian novel on the shelf. She didn't want to cry again, and she hated that she cried when she was angry. Why couldn't she just *be angry*?

"I'm just trying to protect you!"

"Oh, *now* you want to protect me?" Esther whirled, her eyes now streaming with tears. "Where were you to protect me when Grandma Jocelyn forced me into the visitation room to see Mom? Where were you to protect me when I *clearly* set a boundary the other week and *told* you I didn't want to go into the visitation room with Carolyn, and you pushed me to do it anyway?"

Todd blinked. "Squirt, I didn't know—"

"You're right, you didn't know. You *don't* know. You're in your own little world all the fucking time." Esther stooped to pick up another book, floundered, and it dropped again. "*Goddamn it!*"

The bell to the store rang as the front door opened.

"*We're closed!*" Todd and Esther screamed at the same time.

The door shut again.

"Why didn't you lock it?" Esther demanded.

"Well, I was a little distracted with the fact that a shit-headed piss-stain was being a prick to my daughter," Todd fumed.

"Don't call him that." Esther slammed another book onto the shelf.

"That's what he is."

"He's *hurting*," Esther exclaimed, and she grabbed the feather duster on the floor. "He didn't mean any of that."

Todd shook his head. "He's always been a prick. Always obsessed over you and put you in unsafe situations."

Esther laughed. It was bitter. "You seem *way* more concerned about Mars than you did about your deranged father on our fucking doorstep the other week."

Todd scowled. "What was I supposed to do? Or say? He hasn't come back! Okay?"

"Grandma was freaking out! I've never seen her so scared in my life, and you won't even tell me *why!*"

"He's just got some mental problems, is all. Drank too much, might have hit her a few times! He's not a murderer or anything like that."

"Oh, might've hit her a few times, okay," Esther mocked, flinging the feather duster around. "Whatever. He's creepy, and you're missing the point."

Silence filled the space.

Esther dusted the same spot over and over, hoping her father would just go away and leave her to be pissed in peace. She loved him, so damn much, but *fuck...* he was an inconvenient nuisance at the wrong time.

"I'm sorry, Squirt," Todd said quietly. "I'll drop the Mariel thing for now. I just don't trust him, not since he put that gun in his mouth in front of you. And to be honest, it makes me feel like I failed as a dad because it was my fault. He never would have gotten his hands on that gun had I locked it."

Esther lowered the feather duster and turned her head to look at him. "You always locked it. It was a one-time mistake."

Todd shook his head. "I was stressed about your mom because she was dying. I was depressed. I was suicidal." He cleared his throat. "You deserve to know the truth. I had it out one night because I was thinking about suicide. Forgot to lock it up. That's how Mariel got a hold of it. Not his fault."

Esther lowered her eyes and stared at her dad's white tennis shoes, and they weren't very white anymore because he'd tracked through mud. "I'm sorry, Dad. I hope you know you can talk to me if you are struggling with anything. Right?"

"Yes." Todd nodded and gestured for her. "Come here, please. I need a hug, I don't like when you yell at me." He smiled.

Esther went to him and buried her face into his chest. More tears came, and this time they spilled from sadness. And when she was done, she raised her head and looked up at her dad. "I need some time by myself. Would you mind finishing here?"

Todd patted her head. "Yep."

"And, Dad?" Esther asked after gathering her items and hesitating by the back door. "Can we talk about what happened with Hawk soon? There's something—*not right* about what happened."

Todd nodded. "Sure. But hold on to your faith, Honey. Sometimes miracles can be scary when you're not close to God."

Wow. Okay. *Great* discussion up until that point.

"Mmkay," Esther said, offended, and left the bookstore as a headache brewed within her mind like a storm.

*　　*　　*

First of all, who the hell even came up with those lame things to say to a girl?

"You horny, little bitch," Mariel had said, as if his fucking dick hadn't been standing at attention sixty seconds earlier.

Fuck him.

She would have, too. She would have fucked the shit out of him on that couch, but he'd lost his chance, and he'd never get it again.

"Bitch," Esther spat, her car hitting the curb as she tried to parallel park. There weren't even any cars along the sidewalk. Why was it so hard to parallel park when she had all the space in the world?

Finally, Esther stopped the car, got out, slammed the door, and looked at her hand-iwork.

The Jeep's front was halfway in the street.

"Whatever, no one's here," Esther said, and she slipped a few coins into the parking meter.

Pulling the hood to her coat over her head, Esther stormed down the sidewalk towards the gated entrance to the park. The cement glistened in the streetlights, and the breeze whipped across her face and numbed her lips.

Maybe if she tried hard enough, she could numb her heart just as much as her face.

The neighborhood was quiet. Across the street, a long brick building with several closed businesses shielded her from the rest of the neighborhood. This area had a few old businesses and homes. According to her father, it was considered the "ghetto" part of town. He'd kill her if he knew she was out here, but she didn't care. She'd always loved this park—few people used it, but it was still kept up nice, because the residents *cared*. They *wanted* their children to have a nice place to play. And if they cared about their children like that? Then it wasn't a ghetto.

It was a home.

"Brr," she whispered, and she noticed a black, sporty motorcycle parked at the edge of the building across the street. A figure in black gear and a darked-out helmet stood straddling the motorcycle. Phone in hand, the figure bobbed his head up and down to soft playing music. The person's left boot, slim, black, and tactical, tapped against the cement in a lazy rhythm.

Esther smiled, and she wasn't sure why, because the motorcyclist didn't even look at her. But maybe she should say something to him, give *him* her number and let *him* fuck her into oblivion if Mariel was so determined to be a goddamned prick.

No. God, no. She was better than that. What the hell was wrong with her for thinking that? It wasn't that casual sex was *bad*, but she refused to whore herself out for vengeance.

Esther played with the small bottles of Fireball whiskey in her coat pockets.

That's what drinking was for.

The black gated door squeaked as she unlatched and pushed it. It swung open, faster than she expected, and it clashed against the fence and made her jump. Embarrassed, she glanced over her shoulder to see if the motorcyclist was judging her.

He was gone, but the motorcycle was still there.

Esther's shoes squelched against the melting snow, and she trudged to a bench near a large tree on the other side of the park. There she plopped down, opened the whiskey, and started to drink. The warm liquid burned her mouth, her throat, and soothed her esophagus before its effects quietly drifted to her head.

Now she could process in peace.

The last couple of weeks had been beyond chaotic. Hawk. Fr. Jerome. Carolyn. Hell, she'd almost forgotten that she'd slept with Gabe.

Her eyes widened.

Had Gabe *told* Mariel? Maybe Mariel found out and wanted to hurt her. Would he *do* that? Play with her feelings just because he was angry?

It seemed unlikely. But she didn't understand why they'd had so many precious moments together—the coffee shop, the hospital, the sandwich diner, and the bookstore—if he was that angry at her.

None of this made sense.

Neither did Hawk's healing.

Esther chugged the other bottle.

How the *fuck* could a smashed-up boy, with irreparable spinal injuries, just get up and walk? What divine, or perhaps *evil*, miracle had taken place for every bruise, scar, and internal trauma to just... disappear?

"I need to talk to Fr. Jerome," she whispered, trembling as the wind picked up. "Maybe I'm losing it."

"Oh, I'm losing it too. I get it." A man's voice chuckled.

Esther's head snapped to the left. Trees. The right. The street.

"Behind you," the man said, and Esther whirled.

Her eyesight blurred a little. But with growing dread, she recognized him as he towered over her like a wider version of the slender man.

The overcoat man. Jacob.

Her grandfather.

"Mind if I sit?"

Yes, she minded, so why was she so frozen in her damn seat?

So, as if taking her silence as permission, Jacob Caravan sat next to her and crossed his legs.

"Little cold to be out here, huh?" He stared straight ahead.

Run! Esther thought, but her tipsy body mirrored his, and she crossed her legs and stared across the park too. *Okay, this is why white people get their limbs sawed up in the movies.*

Jacob reached into his pocket and pulled out a flask. He twisted the cap, brought it to his lips, and then drank. With a contented sigh, he lowered the flask. "My whiskey's better'n your whiskey."

"What do you want?" Esther said, and she gripped her whiskey tighter, as if it'd protect her.

"I'll tell you what I *don't* want. I don't want you to be so afraid of your own grandfather," Jacob slurred, and he tilted his head in her direction.

"I don't know you. You're a stranger to me, not family." Esther brought the bottle to her mouth and drank the rest. Might as well. Gabe told her once that sometimes bodybuilders (or power lifters?) took a shot of whiskey before their heavy lift. So maybe it would give her the energy she needed to bolt?

"I miss your dad, Kiddo," Jacob said, and his voice had an edge of regret. "I miss my boy." He took another drink. "I'm not here to hurt you, but—you have to understand some things."

But? What did he *mean* by *"but"?* No *but* should come after a statement of assurance. It kind of turned the assurance into a threat.

"I need to get home." Esther twisted the cap onto the Fireball, stood up, and then realized how fucked she was because she couldn't *drive* like this.

"Do you believe in karma?" Jacob stood up too. A stench of alcohol wafted in the air between them like the mist of their breaths in the chill air. His large frame blocked the street from her vision, and she wondered how the hell Jacob could be so tall when her dad was so short. "Because I need to confess something to you."

That *word.* Karma. Her dad used it on repeat, especially when he did something he considered wrong.

"Break the cycle, Squirt," Todd had told her many times. Sometimes with a chuckle. Sometimes without. *"I want you to break the Caravan curse so karma doesn't haunt us like it always has. That was the one thing my dad got right—he knew karma was a threat to this family. He was almost like a darn prophet."*

"I need to leave, I'm sorry," Esther said, and she attempted to step past him.

His hand clapped against her bicep.

She gasped.

"I'm not going to live much longer," Jacob said. His eyes had a distant look—almost identical to her father's whenever he checked out of life. It was both frightening and devastating. "I want to come clean about a few things before the Lord takes me. I've lived with myself and this guilt for so many years... I have to tell *someone*."

"Tell them *what?*" Esther's eyes shifted to her car. It was so far away. "Let go of me!"

The flask dropped to the ground. Jacob lifted his free hand and looked at it with wide eyes. His fingers trembled. "Your Uncle Will didn't drown by accident."

Oh, God. Oh, fuck.

"I killed him, Kiddo. I killed my own son."

Esther searched for an escape, even more aware of how tall Jacob Caravan stood and how wide his frame was. He was old. He didn't look healthy.

But he still looked strong.

Thanks to her love of dance, Esther was athletic. She ran fast. But as she stood frozen and terrified in the falling snow, she began to question her abilities.

Especially with booze in her system.

Jacob looked at her with wild eyes, and she realized they looked like hers too. "The angel told me to," he whispered. "I didn't want to. Esther." He pulled her closer. "I didn't *want* to. I *had* to."

"Stay away from me," she shouted, and she ripped herself from his grasp. "You're *fucking* nuts, crackhead. Leave me, *leave us*, alone!"

Jacob lunged. "Esther, listen to—"

Esther backhanded him across the mouth, forced her numb legs to move, and sprinted for her car. She'd drive drunk a couple of blocks. Run him over. She didn't care. Now was not the time to obsess over morality.

Now was the time to flee.

"*Esther!* Wait!"

And as her chest and lungs burned, she understood why her father never spoke of him.

She understood why her grandmother had looked fucking *terrified*.

"*Esther! Karma will find you too!*"

Esther heard his long strides behind her, felt his footsteps against the ground.

"Help me!" She lost her footing. With a yelp, she slammed against the cold, wet earth. Her mouth cracked against something hard, and she tasted blood on her tongue.

"Esther!" A clammy hand grabbed her ankle. "Let me *help* you! The Lord can save you if—"

Spitting blood from her mouth, Esther rolled onto her back and smashed her foot into his face. "Get *off me!*"

His nose crunched. Grunting, Jacob released her ankle.

Without hesitation, Esther leapt to her feet, hurtling herself towards the open gate.

"Esther!"

She fumbled for her keys. The car was less than one hundred feet away, but he was hot on her heels again.

"Esther, Will was *evil!*"

"Help!" Esther screamed, and she turned the corner to race towards her car. The wind whipped tears from her eyes.

Behind her, a different sound echoed in the night air. An engine roared to life, a deep, whining scream that ripped through the neighborhood like an apex predator made of steel. It issued a warning.

It was coming.

But was it coming after her?

Or Jacob?

As Esther tripped towards her car, Jacob grabbed her by the arms and screamed inaudible nonsense into her ear. His arms encircled her, and his palm planted against her belly as he growled—

"It's gonna come out of you, like Will came outta his *harlot mother!*"

The engine cut through the street. Tires squealed.

Esther flailed, and Jacob lifted her until her feet dangled over the icy cement. Screaming, she kicked her foot into his groin. He released her, and as she landed on her knees—

—but *not as* good looking as Victoria would be, according to Mariel Nadier—

—Esther saw a police car at least a half-mile down the road racing in her direction with flashing lights.

Rather than stopping at her car, she fled towards the cop. When she looked back, she saw Jacob Caravan rise to his feet. Behind him, a wall of light illuminated his body like he'd just stepped from Heaven.

But it wasn't Heaven behind him.

It was a motorcycle.

And it slammed into him.

With a guttural grunt, Jacob's body went airborne, and his lower leg flopped at an abnormal angle as his large, flailing body crashed against the cement.

The motorcyclist tipped sideways, revved the engine, and then whipped around Esther's vehicle as if it were an obstacle course. Esther's eyes landed on the darkened helmet, staring through its blackened visor as if she'd met the rider's unseen gaze. As the street came alive with white and blue lights, the mysterious motorcyclist raced away from Esther and the responding police until its red taillight faded into the city.

"Ma'am!"

Esther snapped out of her trance. She hadn't realized she'd collapsed to the road, and that she'd been staring at the motorcycle, which was now long gone.

Had she even *seen* a motorcyclist?

Next to her car, Jacob wailed, and his left foot looked completely turned around.

Yep. She'd seen a motorcyclist.

Moments later, the Chicago police placed Jacob Caravan under arrest for multiple felony warrants and assault. Two ambulances arrived—one to transport Jacob to the hospital, and the other to evaluate Esther. As Jacob's stretcher rose into the ambulance, she heard him scream one last thing before the doors shut.

"Tell your father that Will had to go! The boy could do *supernatural things!*" The doors slammed shut.

"I'm Sergeant Eric Carter," a young black man approached the ambulance and pulled out his notepad. "I'm sorry you're having a rough night. Can you tell me in more detail about what happened?"

Wiping sweat from her eyes, Esther let out a shaky breath. "Well, where do I start?" Her lip stung. "I can tell you one thing for sure—there's something very, *very* wrong with my family, and I'd like to divorce them, please."

After getting medically cleared by the ambulance and dumping the alcohol in front of the sergeant, who assured her that he wouldn't tell her father about the underage drinking, Esther Caravan went home with her father and went straight to bed.

Putting Mariel Nadier from her mind, Esther slept harder than she'd slept in weeks.

Her brother was home.

Jacob Caravan was gone... at least for now.

But her dreams faded into a nightmarish reality the next morning, on January 29th, 2019, when she sat down to eat the first full breakfast she'd had in a long time. Two eggs, a banana nut muffin, and a glass of milk.

Esther Caravan received a call—one that would haunt her for months to come, and alter not only her life trajectory, but that of the world itself.

VERSE 2
~ MOTORCYCLE ~

Monday, January 28th, 2019
Chicago, Illinois

On Tuesday, January 22nd, Tira Arcelin almost made a dire mistake—simply because she was bored.

Well, it'd be a dire mistake to *her*... not necessarily to anyone else.

She almost purchased a ferret.

Unsure of what to do with her life since arriving in Chicago, Tira learned the city. Of course, this led her to wander malls and hot spots for shopping closest to the subject's residence, and one store just happened to be a pet store. So, as she looked at the larger-than-life signage that depicted dogs, cats, parrots, and snakes, Tira stepped inside to take a look.

...Not for the animals, of course, but to see if any suspicious individuals worked there.

There were no suspicious individuals.

But there *was* a ferret named Peter. He was brown with a splotch of white on his chest. According to the sign, Peter was one year, in need of a family, and "fun loving".

Tira couldn't help but stop outside of his cage. She lingered, and as other patrons wandered past her, she glanced around to make sure no one was watching before kneeling in front of the cage.

Curled in a circle, Peter looked like he'd just awoken, and he peeked open his little eyes.

"Hi," Tira whispered, and she poked a finger into his cage. "Naptime, hmm? Lazy little thing." Her voice was smooth, and she cooed at the little ferret. "Time to wake up and be productive, don't you think?"

Peter didn't really care, but he appreciated her finger in the cage. With his nose in the air, he sniffed her as she patted his head.

And that led to her decision to take him from the cage and cuddle him against her shoulder. No one was really watching. In fact, many people didn't even seem to care that she was cuddling a ferret because they were concerning themselves with other matters—like petting dogs, cats, and rabbits. To be honest, they were all very abnormal activities for her to behold, because most animals she'd seen in her environment were tortured or killed.

It'd always destroyed her, and she'd been mocked many times when she wouldn't partake in such things. People, yes... as long as it was purposeful.

But animals? Absolutely not.

At thirteen, Tira Arcelin observed a boy, an agent in training, torture a cat. So, as justice might demand, Tira built a small explosive and placed it in his right boot. It blew his entire leg apart, all the way up to his hip. He was no longer an option as a Kremlin recruit.

Tira had expected her Papa to punish her with severe consequences. He didn't. Instead, he slapped the gory photo in front of her and drilled her with questions.

"You've floundered with explosives training. You've shown no interest in development. How did you manage to gather the materials and do this on your own?"

To which Tira had replied—

"I don't like to watch other people do it. Give me an objective, and I will do it myself." She'd gestured to the photos of the recruit's splattered leg. *"He was an objective worth the focus."*

As Tira allowed her cheek to rest upon Peter's head, she noticed a little girl. The girl had golden hair, much similar to hers, and the child held a cage in her arms. Inside of the cage was a hamster.

Suddenly, Tira no longer felt at peace.

Her heart rate increased, her body warmed, and her breathing quickened as if the atmosphere demanded more oxygen.

As she stood by herself in the pet store, Tira couldn't stop the memories.

Hamster's screech. Dr. Sovonov's laugh. Papa's smug, condescending face that said—

"You did this, little girl."

"Ma'am!"

Clinging to the ferret, Tira gasped and snapped her head up.

A disgruntled female employee with spiky hair and a red vest scowled down at her. "You can't hold the ferreths without permithon." Her lisp didn't lessen the frustration in her voice.

Clearing her throat, Tira placed Peter back into the cage and stood up. "Well," she snapped. "Maybe put up a sign that *says* that."

With a fed up gesture, the employee stuck her hands out towards a large, neon-orange sign.

PLEASE DO NOT OPEN THE CAGE WITHOUT EMPLOYEE ASSISTANCE.

Face burning, Tira scoffed. "I didn't need assistance opening the cage. I opened it just fine."

"Ma'am, you need to athk—"

"Don't bother speaking anymore, I am leaving," Tira interrupted and snapped her thumb and fingers together like a clamped mouth in hopes the girl would shut up.

It worked.

Tira took one last look at Peter, who eagerly stuck his mouth over the tube in the crate. "It's fine," she said quietly now, and Hamster's screech wouldn't leave her alone. "You'll be safer with someone else."

And so, with that, Tira left the store and did not purchase Peter. It hurt her heart, and she despised the pain she felt in her chest. So, in effort to forget the emptiness and boredom she felt as she navigated her new life in Chicago, Tira purchased something else instead.

A motorcycle.

It was sleek, black, and sporty. Efficient, she told herself. A good backup vehicle to have due to the unexpected nature of her ridiculous *Caravan* assignment. The roads had been clear the day she made the purchase, so she did not hesitate taking it for a 4 A.M. spin outside of the city and through the rural roads. That being said, she was very surprised and furious when she received a paper ticket in the mail one week later, on Monday, January 28th, for speeding.

"I saw no cops! I was *not* stopped!" Tira screamed at Michael over the phone as she waved the ticket in the air.

Michael sighed. "Illinois has cameras that take photos of plates. They issue tickets if you go over the speed limit."

"I am not paying it."

"You need to, otherwise you'll have a warrant out for your arrest, Tira."

"Petrov will make it go away."

"*Tira*. Use your brain. You're supposed to *blend in*, not stick out like a fucking sore thumb."

"It's an invasion of people's rights." Tira crumpled the ticket.

"Did you just crumple the ticket?"

"No." Tira smoothed it out and spoke through her teeth. "Fine. I'll pay it. But Chicago will burn for this."

"Tira—"

She ended the call.

With a snarl, Tira stomped to the coffeemaker, filled her black mug, and slapped her hand against the hazelnut syrup spout. It trickled out, and she stared at the black coffee.

Chicago was *fucking* ridiculous. Americans were ridiculous. She didn't understand how Michael had Americanized himself so well, considering how shitty the government treated their people.

"You can't hold the ferreths without permithon," Tira mocked, and she stormed to the refrigerator. She opened it, stared at the unopened hazelnut creamer, and then grabbed it. She could afford the extra 140 calories today.

With a towel on her head, and wearing a comfortable white robe, Agent 4 slurped her coffee and looked out of the window at the sunlit city.

It was 8:30 in the morning. Workout—complete. Breakfast—complete. Coffee—en route to her mouth.

In two hours, she'd be on her way to *Kaseem-Sovonov Industries* to meet with the executives that bought her talent from Petrov. She'd arrive at the designated parking garage and then receive an escort to the secured facility.

KS Industries wasn't unfamiliar to Tira. Its tendrils were vast, reaching deep within most health, economic, military, and political organizations. Project Savior, the international program, was its first-born child, but thanks to embedding Dr. Sovonov into the start of the organization, Petrov managed to obtain the blueprint and create his own weaponized recipe of Project Savior.

That's where Tira came in.

Sipping her coffee, the agent tapped her watch, entered her code, and pulled up the GPS system. Very slowly, a little red dot moved on the map. The subject, Esther Caravan, appeared to be en route to the college.

Slipping an earpiece into her right ear, Tira turned on the sound and listened to the rhythmic pulse.

Thump-thump. Thump-thump.

Esther's muffled voice bled through the earpiece. It was difficult to hear what she was saying, and her words faded in and out, but Tira heard enough to raise an eyebrow.

"...*Brother—just magically—walk again. I know, right?*"

Boring.

Tira turned off the sound.

She hadn't paid much attention to the events of the subject's personal life, as she found it all incredibly dull. Esther's life appeared to be a chaotic web of booze, boys, and family crises. If she wasn't a sniveling, sobbing mess, she was bitching about *something*—be it work or school.

And God—Mariel Nadier.

Tira wished Esther would just fuck him and get it over with. It was very difficult to listen to her pine over the weirdo in her drunken ramblings to her friend Ashley.

As for Mariel? He needed to man up—find some courage, kick the booze from her hand, and fuck her so she would shut the hell up.

Tira had never seen reality television before, but she'd watched twenty-five seconds of it in absolute horror since coming to the States. Monitoring Esther Caravan's dumpster fire of a life was the equivalent of watching reality television, and it humiliated Tira.

Jacob Caravan was an interesting character, however. The man was definitely unhinged, but didn't appear to be a threat to Esther's life. Still, Tira did her job and monitored his location. Whenever his red dot navigated closer to Esther's location, which had been twice in the last couple of weeks, Tira responded to the area, put on her running gear, and went for a jog.

Jacob Caravan had noticed her for the first time—when he'd gone to Esther's home.

Tira had jogged to the area, and, very flatly, told him two words.

"Move along."

There'd been no need to raise her voice. Then she'd been disappointed, because the man had looked at her, given her a quick nod, and left without protest. A successful mission? Yes. But she was bored.

Fucking bored.

And so she'd hoped to have the opportunity to assassinate him in the suburbs, or at *least* kick his ass.

With a drawn out sigh, Agent 4 finished her coffee and went to her room to get ready.

As metal-dubstep music pulsed through the Bluetooth speaker, she applied light mascara and eyeliner, and it enhanced the sharpness of her emerald eyes as she leaned into the mirror to make sure she'd perfected the application.

After straightening her hair and tying it into a strict bun, Tira dressed—a crisp, white button-down shirt, black dress pants that hugged her strong thighs, and a black blazer. She slipped on heeled boots, loaded her weapon, clicked it into the holster beneath the blazer, and then left her room with one, snarling statement in Russian that lingered in the air.

"This had better be worth my fucking time."

* * *

"Make sure you give them my best!" Petrov sounded gleeful.

With the phone to her ear, and her eyes rolled into her head, Tira stepped out of her new, black GMC Yukon and waited in the parking garage as Petrov spoke in her ear. "I am not going to exchange pleasantries on behalf of you."

"Respond in English, you need to adapt to the United States," Petrov snapped. "You will stick out like a sore thumb."

Tira closed her eyes and then opened them. The cool air chilled her ears. "Why does everyone use that analogy? It makes no logical sense. What is a sore thumb? My brain is sore, I know that, because I have to be here."

Petrov's voice lowered to a growl. "Do you want to go back into the military? I *will strip* you of your status and make sure you serve the men their lunch. Is that what you want?"

Possibly. Might be more exciting than listening to a blubbering Caravan. But—

"No," Tira said, and she softened the tone of her voice. There was a line with Petrov, and she knew not to cross it. "I'm joking, Papa. I will not embarrass you."

A white man in an American military uniform entered the garage and approached her. "Are you Tira Arcelin?"

"I need to go," Tira said.

"Let me know how it goes."

"Alright. Goodbye." Agent 4 ended the call, withdrew her identification, and responded in controlled Americanized English. "Yes. I am Tira Arcelin."

The man, who had a soft jaw and hazel eyes, scanned her identification and then looked at her. "Good. You might need a coat."

Moments later, wind burned across her face as the motorboat sped across Lake Michigan.

"Sorry, the nice interior boats are under maintenance today!" the soldier screamed over the motor, looking back at Tira. "Wish you had a coat now?" His eyes sparkled as he looked at her, as he gave her that *look* she'd seen on Senator Thompson's face and countless other males.

"Where I've trained," Tira yelled back, clinging to the side of the boat as it bounced over the waves, "this would be considered summer weather!"

The man laughed and winked. "I ain't complaining!"

In Russia, she would have killed him. Dumped his pompous ass over the boat and let the motor shred his disgusting face to ribbons. Fish food. And she would have laughed and moved on with her hot summer day.

But here? She had a noose around her neck. She had to be *nice* to the Americans. So, with a deep breath, she looked at him and said the only nice thing she could.

"At least you *have* something good to look at! I do not!" Tira shouted, and she turned her eyes to the rocky waves of Lake Michigan.

Despite her statement, she did appreciate the view of the lake. As water sprayed in the air, she looked at the shore and noted to herself that she'd have to consider a morning jog on the shoreline.

"How much further is the facility?" Tira demanded, as if she hadn't just called her escort ugly.

"Just up ahead! See that tower?"

Agent 4 followed his pointer finger and located an impending pier and what looked to be a lighthouse. She'd been advised that the facility was underwater, but she hadn't managed to obtain coordinates to its precise location because she, admittedly, had been too busy trying to navigate the *Caravan Family Reality Show!*

Still, Tira was disappointed in herself for not rising to the level of discipline she strove for.

Was *that* what subhumans meant when they said they were "*overwhelmed*"?

The boat slowed to a rumbling stop next to the dock, where security guards and military personnel lined the pier with rifles slung over their necks. Male and female; tall and short, black, white—the facility was well guarded and did not discriminate.

"Yo, Matt!"

A tall white security guard in black tactical pants and a winter jacket turned his head. A gust of wind blew his dusty blond hair away from his forehead. "Yeah?"

"Take Ms. Arcelin to the registration center, please. She has a meeting in thirty minutes."

The young man nodded and stepped out of his line. "Sorry, Ma'am, I need to do a weapons check."

Tira's heart rate shot up. "I have clearance."

"It's protocol, Ma'am."

What could she say?

"Do you know who I am?"

"I'm the daughter of the most powerful man in the world?"

"I am a weapon. I could disarm you and eliminate your comrades in a matter of seconds?"

"Will I get my service weapon returned?" Tira said, her voice steady. She assessed the man—the boyish face, the blue eyes that looked oddly familiar, and his physique. Muscular, but with a higher body fat percentage.

"I will radio down and see what—"

"Jesus Christ, Matthew, she's obviously a federal agent." A pretty, dark-haired young woman in a military uniform glanced their way. Her eyes settled on Tira, who was considering the idea of commandeering the boat and leaving the United States. "Just radio down and let them know she's here to see the execs, and they'll let her through."

"Miels, shut up, just let me do my job."

"Ooh, did you just tell your girl to shut up?" the boat escort laughed.

"Enough!" Tira exclaimed and stepped onto the pier. "I'm armed with a Glock. I will hand it over, but I'll need to reach for it first. Will that be a problem?"

"No, it won't be," Miels said loudly. "Matthew's just mad because he couldn't do the boat escorts today. Aren't you, Babe?"

Matthew rolled his eyes and watched as Tira unloaded her weapon. "I appreciate your cooperation."

"Please just take me to my destination," Tira snapped, passing him her firearm.

The walk to the lighthouse took less than a minute, but it wasn't really a lighthouse. It was an elevator and a staircase to the depths of KS Industries.

Down they went, and they did not speak.

Thirty minutes later, Tira Arcelin found herself in a conference with elite officials, the types she'd seen her whole life with her Papa, in the Kremlin, on the news...

And in that Chicago hotel room.

As Tira sat centered at the cherry-top table that gleamed beneath the fluorescent lights, she analyzed the suited executives before her.

Ben Wilder. A large dark-haired man with a beard and eyes far kinder than she expected in this room. Status: Chicago Chief of Police.

Jeff Divets. Thin. Grey-haired. Hazel eyes and a smirk that made Tira's stomach turn. Status: Federal Liaison for the Department of Homeland Security.

James Donovan. Middle-aged. Blond. Attractive. The build of a linebacker. Status: Senator of Illinois, CEO of KS Industries, a rumored potential 2020 presidential candidate and, as mentioned in the *Project Caravan* file, the father of Esther's best friend—Gabe.

But the meeting could not start yet. Someone was missing. Not only the *face* of KS Industries, but the charming smile of Chicago.

But as Tira sipped her small glass of ice water in a continuous attempt to avoid small talk, the double doors opened. A tall, lighter-skinned, hooded black man bounded into the conference room with a thick folder in his hand. He wore a *Nike* sweatshirt and joggers, and his face glistened with sweat.

"Sorry," he said, and his white teeth illuminated the room. "My doctor says I need to get my steps in because being a politician with pre-disposed high blood pressure isn't healthy."

Tira blinked.

He extended a hand, and his smile grew brighter. "Miss Arcelin?"

Tira stood up and took his hand. "Yes."

"My name's Kaemon Spears. I'm the governor of Chicago. Did they treat you well coming in?"

"Er..."

"Glad to hear it," Spears said, and he took a seat at the head of the table. He slapped open his manila folder. "Alright, Agent Arcelin." He tossed off the hood. "Let's begin."

* * *

"They were a strange group of people, to say the least," Tira said, typing her password into the laptop on her kitchen island.

"Welcome to the American side of KS Industries," Michael responded on speaker phone.

A small flash drive sat next to the laptop. It had pertinent files referencing the task force she'd been assigned to manage—recruit backgrounds, training locations, expectations, etc. She'd look at that later. Right now, she needed to pay the speeding ticket.

"Did you send the link?" Tira demanded, pulling open the web browser.

"Yes, I texted it."

"Ridiculous," she hissed, pulling up the site and withdrawing her wallet from her black, reinforced riding pants. She had every intention to ride her motorcycle tonight and find the spots without a camera system.

"You'll live," Michael chuckled. "When do you start the task force program?"

Tira pulled out her credit card. "August. I'm going through an accelerated academy for Illinois state law, then one for federal. Meanwhile, they want me to review their current program and make adjustments based on my experience and training."

"Ah, be sure to refrain from adding your stance on deadly force. Deadly force doesn't apply in every situation here."

Tira clicked with an annoyed scowl. "Why do you think I am a serial killer? I haven't killed anyone since January 12th. And I was stuck in a cage, there wasn't much I could do to prevent—"

"I was joking," Michael sighed. "Do you ever laugh?"

What kind of question was that? Of course, she laughed. She laughed when the bomb blew off that monster's leg, and she laughed recently when she observed Petrov slip on the ice in front of live cameras. "Yes, when—"

"Rhetorical."

Tira let out a grumble and then clicked on the surveillance program.

"What'd you think of the facility?" Michael asked. A televised crowd roared in the background. Basketball, maybe.

"It was fine," Tira said as she logged into the program. The GPS system flashed up, and Esther's red dot blinked in the same location she'd been in for the last several hours. The bookstore.

"You getting more comfortable with Chicago?"

"Why are you interrogating me?" Agent 4 cried and pulled up the location for Jacob Caravan. He was home.

"Damn, woman. My apologies, I just figured you might want some conversation since I know the job is lonely sometimes. Jesus."

"I am not lonely," Tira said, dropping her forehead down onto her arm. "I am bored. How did you do this? I can't drive fast. I can't keep my weapon on my person at secured facilities. Did you know that the police department requires use of force reports for each use of force?"

Michael laughed. "That's actually quite normal."

Thump-thump-thump-thump-thump.

Esther's heart rate skyrocketed through the speaker system.

So did Tira's, and her head shot up. The red dot was still at the bookstore, but the agent couldn't hear anything more than Esther's heart rate.

"Everything good?" Michael asked, crunching on something now. Chips, maybe.

"Ssh." Tira waved her hand as if he were in the room with her.

Thumpthumpthumpthumpthump.

It was even faster now, and Tira clicked her tongue as she connected the speaker to her earbuds and put them in her ears. Was Michael talking? Maybe. If he was, she couldn't hear him anymore.

Just Esther.

Tira slipped from the barstool and grabbed her items. Then, as she checked her weapon, she heard something else through the earbuds.

A moan?

Was that a goddamn *moan?*

Oh God, another one. A male.

Esther Caravan wasn't in danger.

Tira pulled out the earbuds, her face warming faster than she could handle.

"Hello?" Michael was still on the phone. "Are you ignoring me, or did you leave? I'm just gonna hang up now."

"Okay, goodbye," Tira said hoarsely, and pressed her palm to her face to cool herself down. She didn't want this job anymore. It was disgusting, and Esther was never in any real danger.

Why the *fuck* did Petrov find her such an important asset?

Tira straightened the flash drive, the laptop, and her water bottle until they were lined neatly on the countertop, as if the objects had become her troops. She didn't know what else to do with her hands.

Was it Mariel Nadier? Or someone else? It didn't matter. Unless it did. *Did* it matter to Petrov? Did Esther have any boyfriends that could be considered a threat?

She didn't know how to do this job. At what point did she need to *act* in these situations?

"Time for a ride," Tira growled, and she placed her phone in her pocket. In flustered confusion, the agent slammed the laptop shut, grabbed her jacket and blacked-out helmet, and left her new apartment.

But the night turned out to be far less simple, far less *boring* than she had complained. As Tira darted through the night on her new motorcycle, and the wind whistled past her helmet, a programmed alert came through her watch.

Esther was moving to a different location. *That* was to be expected, because it was past closing time for *Caravan's Books*. She'd be heading home.

But Esther wasn't heading home. In fact, that red dot was headed the opposite direction—right towards Jacob Caravan's neighborhood.

And that wasn't good.

That wasn't good at all.

So Tira Arcelin changed her course of direction and raced towards the most neutral place she could. The park. Because why else would Esther Caravan head that direction? There was nothing significant in that neighborhood, especially to a young, white woman like Esther. Tira's best guess was that she was heading there to "*clear her head*" or "*find herself*".

Whatever it was these *Instagram* women thought they needed to do to live a fulfilling life.

So that's where Tira went, and she worked against the Chicago camera system to get there before the subject, Esther Caravan, did.

* * *

Tira arrived moments before Esther did, and she turned off the motorcycle, planted her boots on the cement, and turned on dubstep music.

It blasted.

It vibrated through the block.

With a frantic gasp, Tira turned down the volume to a low level and tried to calm her breathing.

In Russia, she would have never made this tactical mistake. Here? She'd lost discipline already, even though she felt like she was working harder to maintain her rigid routine. Perhaps it was because she'd allowed herself a little freedom—coffee creamer, later morning workouts, and hazelnut lattes from that twenty-four-hour café she was drawn to.

The café where she'd noticed Fr. Jerome Nadier and his son, Mariel Nadier. That'd been entirely coincidental—she hadn't been tracking them. She'd gotten her treat for the week (the latte), and there they were. Their presence hadn't concerned her, until the priest turned his eyes to hers and then froze as if he'd seen someone he'd recognized.

And feared.

Tira had tried not to think much of it, because he'd just been released from the hospital. But something in his eyes had given her chills, and she couldn't explain *why*.

Perhaps it was because he'd looked at her like he'd known her for his entire life.

And Tira Arcelin, the world's best-kept secret in plain sight, didn't like that.

A door slammed and echoed in the block. Glancing at her watch, Tira saw the alert—Esther had parked. She was here.

Sleet fell.

Without looking up, Tira tapped random icons on her phone. Moments later, she heard oncoming footsteps and frustrated sighs.

Tira bobbed her head to the music, her body warming as the footsteps stomped closer on the other side of the street.

How long would this girl *be* here? At what point could she just go home and let Esther *find herself* in peace?

Then, Tira heard it. A meow, like a cry of distress. It was somewhere around the corner, further away from the park. It cried again, and Tira's heart went mad.

"Fuck," she hissed, turning a sideways glance towards the approaching subject. "Okay. She's fine right now."

And with that, as Esther Caravan approached the gate to the park and turned her back, Tira Arcelin dismounted the motorcycle and crept around the building to look for the distressed cat down the block.

She looked at her watch and swiped. Jacob Caravan was close, *very* close, but he hadn't shown any signs of violence in the past.

She'd just have to keep the situation well-monitored.

Her boots thudded against the cement, and her eyes darted to the left as she heard random laughter, a barking dog, and a few cars further up the street. Graffiti lined the business walls, and broken glass crunched beneath her feet. Streetlights flickered.

This was a bad idea, walking away from the subject while Jacob lurked, but her body wouldn't stop. It wouldn't turn.

Each time she heard the cat cry, Tira saw that boy torturing the Calico cat, and she heard Hamster's screech in the dark, shadowy dungeon of her mind—the same place where Senator Thompson crawled towards her in the hotel bed, the same place where Petrov looked at her many times throughout her life with that look that said—

"You did this, little girl."

So yes. Esther Caravan and her little reality show could wait, because—

Wait a fucking minute.

Straight ahead of her, in a yard across the street—were those two boys pulling on a cat's tail?

Michael had told her she just couldn't kill, or even maim, people anymore. But he didn't say *shit* about scaring them.

So Tira stomped forward, reminding herself of the state laws she couldn't break, yet trying to formulate a plan that would serve to upend these cum-stains' entire existence.

"Hey!"

The boys weren't too old, maybe ten, but she didn't care. With widening eyes, they released the cat, and it fled down the block as Tira stormed upon the two kids, grasped them by their jackets, and lifted them into the air.

And Agent 4 cursed them. Not in English, nor in Russian.

In an effort to protect her cover, Tira Arcelin spat at them in Mandarin.

Their lips moved in silent protest as she rambled curses upon their families and their futures.

Then, she spoke to them in English.

"Where I am from," Tira said through her teeth, maintaining a Chinese accent. "I break the law to protect animals. If I ever catch you, or your friends, or your family hurting an animal again, I *will* break the law."

It was at that moment that she felt it for the first time—an electrical current from her watch. It zapped her skin and shot up her arm like static tendrils. Not for anxiety, Michael had told her, and not for workouts.

"Like real threats," he said.

And the *real* threat was, in all likelihood, Esther's grandfather—Jacob Caravan.

In the night air, the boys kicked their legs. Tears streamed down their cheeks.

Tira tilted her head.

And the watch buzzed like an angry hornet.

Ah yes, the distress signal for Esther Marie Caravan. This was no longer a reality show—it *was* reality, and the subject needed help.

"You're free to go," Tira snapped, and she dropped the kids from the air. They fell in a tumbled pile, and as the agent turned to race down the block towards the park, she heard the children scream in the distance.

"Mom! *A Chinese assassin just threatened us!"*

Perhaps in a different situation, she might have laughed—the laugh that Michael expected. But right now, she couldn't, because the watch wouldn't stop buzzing. On one hand, it was good news, because it meant Esther was still alive. But on the other hand, it was a reminder that the threat was still there, and that her life could end in a matter of seconds.

So Tira sprinted. Her breath fogged the mask. Her own adrenaline spiked. Endorphins, dopamine, *everything* she'd craved exploded through her body like a surging wave. But she didn't feel excited—she felt frightened—terrified that she'd just failed her test as Petrov's top agent because she'd sought out a distressed cat.

But as she sprinted towards the corner of the building, she realized she'd never regret her actions.

Because she'd failed to act at eight-years-old when she'd watched Petrov kill the only thing she'd ever cared for.

And because no one had come for her in that hotel room while the senator grabbed her hand and—

"Help me!" Tira had wanted to yell in that room, but she hadn't. She'd taken care of the threats herself. Right now, her brain recognized the cry of distress, heard the cry that never escaped her mouth—and then, as she hurtled towards the end of the block, she realized something.

She hadn't imagined that scream for help.

The scream belonged to Esther Caravan.

Her blood boiled.

As Tira came to the corner, she saw Esther tear out of the park and sprint towards her Jeep.

Jacob Caravan was hot on her heels. Reaching for her. Screaming.

"Esther, Will *was evil!*"

Much farther down the road, police lights lit up the night. Briefly, Tira wondered if they were coming for Esther, or for the Chinese assassin.

"Help!" Esther screamed, and something in her voice lit a storm within the agent's body.

So, Tira took a breath. Analyzed every possible option. Just like she'd done in the cage on January 12th—the day she'd last killed someone.

Option one—let the cops respond. Potential risk—they were still a distance away. Jacob Caravan could snap the asset's neck in that timeframe.

Next option—she could attack on foot. By then, the cops might reach her. She'd be forced to give a statement.

That left the third option.

So, as the police lights grew closer, Tira lunged for her motorcycle, mounted it, and slammed her gloved fingers against the starter button. The engine rumbled and then shrieked, a loud, metallic scream that ripped through the once quiet night. The white headlight burst through the darkness. Tira pressed the gas, lifted her boots, and turned the motorcycle towards the violent chaos on the sidewalk down the road.

Esther's scream danced with the shriek of the wind. It whistled past Agent 4's helmet as she guided the motorcycle onto the sidewalk, dipped her torso, and hurtled forward. Parking meters blurred. The headlight expanded and illuminated Jacob Caravan's body as if he were a target.

Oh, wait. Yes.

He was.

But he was on his knees. Esther Caravan, the reality TV star herself, had *hurt* him.

Three...

Now, Esther was fleeing down the road towards the police.

Two...

Jacob rose to his feet.

And Tira bared her teeth, tilted the bike, braced for impact, and—

One.

—struck.

The collision rattled her teeth. It almost sent her flying. A grotesque sound cracked into the air, and Jacob Caravan's breath left his body as the tire snapped against his right leg and buckled it.

Tira could have killed him. She *wanted* to kill him. If the cops weren't there, she might have. So she settled with breaking him, and she heard his body slap against the cement as the bike raced by.

Farther ahead, Esther slipped on the ice. She fell on her butt. The white light radiated her pale face as she turned her head towards the oncoming noise and looked directly at the helmet-shielded biker.

And as Tira guided the bike around the corner, and gravity tilted her closer towards the earth, the agent looked at her too.

And noticed Esther's blue-brown eyes.

How pretty they were.

And how *familiar*.

"You're beautiful," the cute, brown-haired, ice cream girl had said, blinking up at her from the ground that day on the track.

The day she'd killed her trainers and the senator.

With a quick gasp of realization, Tira re-aligned the bike, set her eyes forward, and raced away from the ice cream girl—from Esther Caravan—as fast as she could.

The night swallowed her. The adrenaline plummeted. She dipped around a corner and sat in a secluded area to listen—to ensure the subject was truly safe.

Agent 4 listened to Esther Caravan's statement through the earbuds. Soon, the red dot traveled towards the Caravan home.

Tira went home, too. When she arrived, she stripped herself of the gear, stepped into the shower, and shivered as the shock of the evening chilled her muscles. She'd been in far more adrenaline-spiking situations. Why was today's situation so much worse?

"Th-the la-la-lattes," Tira blubbered as warm water splattered against her face.

Exhausted, the young agent crawled into bed. She placed the earbuds into her ears. For a moment, as the sleet grew heavier, the rhythms of Tira and Esther's heartbeats merged as one.

Tira slept well. In fact, she slept in. Past nine in the morning. When she awakened, she looked at the red dot to make sure Esther Caravan was still safe.

She was.

But the young woman was crying. Sobbing. *Screaming*. Not in pain, or fear, or anger.

Sorrow.

And Tira flinched. Something turned in her stomach.

So, to avoid the drama of it all, the agent took out the earbuds and went to work.

As Tira sipped her coffee, she reviewed the flash drive for the task force. She started with the history of Amelia Travis, and Tira realized she'd been the pretty soldier on the pier—the girlfriend of that annoying security guard. Matthew.

She wondered if he was one of the recruits, how annoying he'd be to train.

He was.

He looked just as much of a brat in his photo as he did on the pier.

But when her eyes settled on his name, a twinge of nausea threatened to worsen in her belly.

"Just a coincidence," Tira whispered, but her eyes fell to his brief biography on the screen.

The nausea worsened, and the coffee burned through her esophagus and threatened to spew all over the laptop. Her breathing came fast—

—like real threats—

—and Tira's hand knocked the coffee mug from the island as she reached up to grab her hair and squeeze it. It crashed, and coffee splattered over the floor.

Matthew Thompson—24. I would like to work for the federal government to protect the United States from foreign terrorism—terrorism that I believe had a hand in my father's disappearance, and in all likelihood, death. My father was Senator Thompson, a well-respected man, and I hope to one day hold those who took my dad from me accountable.

Suddenly, once again, she was in the hotel room, feeling the bed shift as the senator crawled towards her with a predatory leer. Blood dribbled over her hands again. It was smeared around the hotel room.

She was a child, by herself. And as Tira Arcelin sat alone in her kitchen, she realized what Michael had meant when he asked if she was lonely.

Was that what it meant? Because she'd felt it then.

And she felt it now.

So, as the coffee pooled across the counter, Tira reached for the phone, dialed, and hit send.

"Hello?"

"Michael," Tira said hoarsely, and humiliation burned her skin. "Can you come over?"

"Sure. What's wrong?"

"Nothing," Tira said hastily, and then lied. "I am bored. And you are entertaining."

VERSE 3

~ RED PEN ~

Wednesday, October 14th, 1992
Chicago, Illinois

"*5*0%. *Excellent writing prose, grammar, and punctuation. Please come talk to me after class referencing the grade. Prof. Nadier.*"

The red ink had a face of its own—one that seethed at him; mocked and spat at him in a venomous manner that reminded him of his pig bitch mother, Beatrice Jameson.

Eighteen-year-old Philip Jameson snarled at the graded essay. It blurred on his desk, and his fingernails scraped against the wood as he bared his teeth.

Professor Jerome Nadier paced the front of the classroom, his hands gesturing with excitement while he spoke his—

—*venom*—

—lecture to the class.

Phil looked to the right, finding his classmate's graded essay on display for the world to see.

For *Phil* to see.

95%.

Phil let out a small sound—one of devastation.

This wasn't right. It wasn't *fair*.

So, he clenched his fists, raised his eyes, inhaled deeply, and then said— "Professor Nadier." His voice sounded meek, and he *hated it*.

And he'd have to try again, because with a beaming face, the professor kept talking, his eyes darting to everyone *but* Phil.

Or so it seemed.

So, as rage crept through his veins like a bomb nearing detonation, Phil cleared his throat, heaved in his chest, and tried again.

"*Professor Nadier!*"

His voice erupted in a boom this time, and the classroom fell silent.

Mid-sentence, Jerome Nadier finally looked at him. Despite the confused look on his face, the professor still looked *kind*—and it *pissed* off the skinny, red-haired young man.

Why *pretend* to be kind when he judged and *hated* his own student?

"Yes, Mr. Jameson?" Jerome asked, and he smiled. His tan cardigan sweater hung loosely from his body, and his styled silver-blond hair radiated beneath the light. He almost looked like an angel.

A sinful one.

A homosexual man who had no business lecturing *him* on morality when Jerome *claimed* to follow God but also lusted for men.

"Care to explain," Phil started slowly, "why you feel the need to speak to me after class? Why can't you explain the reason you gave me a *fifty percent* on my paper in front of the class, rather than within the shadows of your office?" His voice bounced off of the walls, and he raised his chin.

Jerome winced a little, adjusted his cardigan, and smiled a little. "I was trying to respect your privacy, Mr. Jameson. That's all."

"I'd like to discuss it now," Phil demanded, leaned back into his chair, and adjusted his blue tie. Surrounded by pajama pants and hoodies, he was the only one in a suit.

Jerome sighed a little, scratched the back of his head, and glanced around the classroom. "We need to complete class. Let's wait until—"

"No, we want to see what Phil's going on about now," Randy, the classmate next to him, said. He was a light-haired young man with an uneven beard.

Phil shot him a glare, but he noticed the rest of the class nodding in unison. He wasn't sure if he should be offended or feel a sense of pride.

Even if it was negative, he'd gotten the classroom's attention. That was the first beautiful step to bringing salvation and the knowledge of Christ to the world.

First, they had to listen.

Professor Nadier closed his eyes for a moment, as if he were saying a quick prayer, and then he opened them. "How about we open the room for questions on the essay topic, then? Sound good, everyone?"

"Yes, Sir," the majority said.

Phil let out an impatient sigh.

"Now. I encouraged you all to write about a topic of your own choosing, so long as it used our themes of ethics, morality, and theology's role within these ideas." Jerome looked at Phil. "How about you tell us about your essay, Mr. Jameson?"

Phil cleared his throat. Sweat trickled down his back. This was his moment to prove himself worthy of an A, not an F.

So why was it so difficult to speak now?

"I, er," Phil stammered, and he sounded *meek* again, a word that'd been weaponized by his mother.

"You think you're gonna to preach to a congregation like Jesus, with that meek-ass bitch voice?" Beatrice had laughed, slapping her knee when she discovered him, as a boy, teaching his stuffed animals about the Word of God. *"You realize Jesus was a man, right?"*

"My paper addresses something we are all too fearful to discuss with objectivity in today's world," Phil said, and straightened in his chair. He turned his eyes to the young, black-haired woman near the door, several rows to the right from his desk. She was *looking* at him and smiling.

Smiling.

His face went hot, but it fueled his speech. "The Bible, as it is written, does not speak exclusively against slavery, and it certainly encourages the role of the woman as a homemaker."

Groans echoed through the classroom. Protests. And Phil played with his tie and shifted in his seat.

The Pharisees fought against Jesus too.

Jerome nodded, rubbing his chin, but he did not flinch. "There are definitely a lot of things in the Bible that could be considered morally grey, I'd agree. What was the biggest point in your paper that you wanted to bring home?"

Goodness, why was the man quizzing him? The essay had been clear in its message. God did not always view—

"...*morally grey* things as inherently *evil*," Phil said. "And one might argue that some, in today's terms, 'necessary evils' for the greater good are just that—necessary."

"What the hell, dude?" A young guy yelled from the back of the classroom. "What are you saying?"

Jerome raised a gentle hand and acknowledged Phil. "Such as?"

"As written in my essay—government mandated work for those who are criminals or are not productive in society. It'd save countless funds that could then be used to actually *help* those who genuinely need it."

"Government *mandated work?*" A girl laughed across the room. "You mean slavery?"

Phil scratched his nails across the desk. "I *never said*—"

"Oh, I heard what you said."

Phil twitched. That bitch. That vile blonde bitch always showed up to class in low-cut shirts, about as low as his mother wore hers, and thought she had something to say. Looked at him like he was beneath her because he wasn't the largest, most muscular male in the room.

That bitch had no idea what an *alpha* looked like. One day, he'd show her. He'd show all of them. But right now? Bad start. He needed to speak with more eloquence and clarity so they wouldn't associate him with the trailer trash environment he'd been raised in, where the only education Beatrice Jameson had consisted in was a GED and dick.

Phil turned his eyes to the dark-haired girl across the room, the one who smiled at him. He couldn't remember her name, but he'd seen her before in a different class. Sheryl, maybe?

Wetting his lips, he looked at Jerome again.

"How do you think this all ties into theology, Phil?" Jerome nudged him with quiet patience.

How could it not? Did the man not read the Bible? Did he not even *read* the essay, where Phil had clearly stated how the themes threaded together with both logic and faith?

"*Ephesians 6:5,*" Phil stated, and his voice cracked a little. He hated that it still cracked, because he was eighteen-years-old, for goodness' sake. "It says, 'Slaves, obey your earthly masters with respect and fear, and with sincerity of heart, just as you would obey Christ'. It's stewardship." He folded his clammy hands in front of him. "The Bible gave clear instructions on how to handle these things. If the United States integrated productive labor amongst those wasting resources, the economy would *blossom.* The cost of living? Lower. Wages for those who've earned it? Higher." His voice stopped cracking, and he felt a boost of confidence. "It's the *liberal* dream, minus their inability to problem solve. We could lower taxes on the working class, and the environmentalists would shut the hell up. Why?"

People were listening now. The room felt still.

Phil continued. "Because not only would an increase in federal funds assist the scientific organizations that study methods in reducing the negative effects of their so-called '*climate change*', but we'd have *mandated workers* to complete certain tasks rather than constantly relying on fuel and power sources."

"Oh, my God." Another male student in the back almost yelled. The black one. "Hypothetically, say this was a thing. *Hypothetically*, mind you. Guess who they'd pluck off of the streets and outta their homes first? Black people."

"And Hispanics," the blonde girl argued. "Undocumented Hispanics are already kind of doing this, anyway. It's disgusting."

Phil spoke through his teeth. These idiots always made everything about race. "It has nothing to do with skin color. The government would mandate *all unproductive* members of society—black, white, purple. It doesn't matter."

"Sorry, Grandma, I know you're retired but you gotta go pick cotton," the black man laughed, but he didn't sound happy.

Ignoring the rest of the classroom, Phil turned his eyes to Jerome. "I wasn't trying to *say* we needed to bring back slavery of the past with whips and chains. I was simply saying that it'd logically serve an economic *and* theological purpose."

Jerome closed his eyes for a second and then opened them. "I don't want to assume to be in your head, or know what you're thinking, Mr. Jameson. But I will say this—ideas that *work*, ideas that are even *brilliant*... are not always *good* ideas. They're not always ethical, or moral, and while I understand that we will exist in a morally grey society until the end of time, it's important not to encourage ideologies that may cause harm to less privileged groups. *That's* why I graded your paper the way I did."

Condescending. Always so *condescending.*

Like his mother. And now this wannabe theologian, who claimed to understand morality but did not hide the fact that he was a homosexual.

"I'll talk to you in private later," Phil said, and he sat back in his chair. His upper lip curled, and he flipped the essay over so that he didn't have to look at the red ink.

Jerome gave him a brief nod and then, with a brighter smile, addressed the rest of the class. "Let's go back to our original agenda, I don't want to hop too far away from the outline."

Phil sulked in his chair, and when class ended, he stormed from the room before giving Professor Nadier a chance to speak with him.

The day was ruined. He'd presented a phenomenal argument, one that economically appealed to both sides of the aisle, only to have the liberal professor humiliate him in front of the class by throwing out a few terms about *morality*.

Now he had to go back home to that disgusting trailer and listen to his mother chastise him too. *Everything* was his fault. That's what she thought.

It was *his* fault Beatrice didn't know who his father was, *his* fault he'd been born, *his* fault he was ugly, and *his* fault he'd never amount to anything all that great.

That pig bitch was in for a violent beating. And today might have been the day—had a soft hand not caught his arm in the university hallway near the water fountain that never worked.

Gasping, he whirled.

There stood that small-framed, dark-haired girl, the one whose name he could never remember. The shy one who smiled at him and wore a black sweatshirt with a smiling bumblebee.

"Hi," she said softly, and looked up at him with wide eyes that sparkled in the hallway lights. "I've never had the pleasure of introducing myself. But I was very honored to hear you speak today in class."

His face warmed. "Really?"

She nodded. "Yes. I thought you made sense, and I don't think you're a bad person. Not at all. You're very intelligent, you're very well-spoken, and your commitment to God is profound."

Was she joking with him? *Mocking* him?

"Er, thank you, I think," he croaked, and he thrust out a hand. It wasn't sinful to shake a woman's hand, was it? "My name is Philip. Philip Jameson."

The young woman nodded, smiled, and took his hand. It was small and frail within his. "Nice to meet you, Philip. My name is Carolyn... Carolyn Sharpe."

*   *   *

Monday, January 28th, 2019
Chicago, Illinois

"What do you find so necessary to talk to me about?"

Next to Hailey Jameson, Phil sat at the dining room table with his phone propped up. Victoria, his other daughter, filled the phone screen with her angry, bratty face.

"Why do you need to be rude to me?" Phil demanded. "I'm a grieving widower. You're a grieving daughter. Why can't we be kind?"

"I don't know, hmm," Victoria placed a finger on her chin. "Maybe it's because you weren't *fucking kind to mom!*" Her scream vibrated the voice.

Phil narrowed his eyes. "Don't use language like that, not in front of your little sister."

"She's a grown ass woman, Dad."

Hailey blinked and bent her head. "I don't like to hear that language either, Victoria."

Victoria's eyes widened with incredulous rage. "Are you kidding me? Hailey, you weren't afraid to be a spitfire with me a couple years ago." Her voice rose, and her eyes shifted to Phil as if they were daggers. "Are you abusing her too?"

"Stop *saying that!*" Phil roared, slammed his fists on the table, and then scrambled to keep the phone from falling over as Hailey gasped and covered her ears.

Victoria sat tight-lipped with a flushed face. "You're all about logic and facts, Dad, aren't you proud you created a child who states the facts?"

Phil wanted to slap that smug look off of her face. But he couldn't do that, because she was already back in California at that liberalized college she insisted on attending. "I am not abusing *anyone*. Your sister has a mind of her own."

"She does. Yes. But she's also shy and autistic and doesn't know how to stand up for herself because you've spent your whole life gaslighting all of us."

Phil rolled his eyes. He looked at Hailey and patted her head. "Don't listen to her. Autism is a man-made lie." He cleared his throat and looked at the phone again. "I'm not here to argue. I wanted to give you some *hope*."

"There is no hope. Mom's dead and I'm stuck with you."

Phil closed his eyes and counted to three. "I'd really appreciate it if you treated me with a *little respect!*"

"I want to be *very* clear when I say this," Victoria leaned closer to the screen. Her eyes glistened. "I will *never* fucking respect you, and I think—

"I can get her back!" Phil's roar bounced from the walls.

Hailey shrieked, and then the room fell silent. Carolyn's favorite bumblebee clock ticked loudly in the kitchen.

Victoria's chin trembled. Tears trickled over her cheeks.

Phil watched her, and he wanted to *feel* for his own child, but he couldn't. He *couldn't*. He'd never been able to *feel* for her when she cried as an infant. He couldn't *feel* for her when she stubbed her toe, or screamed from a nightmare, and he couldn't *feel* for her now as she cried.

But he *wanted to.*

"I can bring her back," he said simply, as if that would take away her tears. Was he certain he could bring her back? No.

But Phil had touched a boy who couldn't walk, one who'd just been doomed to paralysis for the rest of his life.

And he *now walked.*

Jason Caravan walked.

Nothing was guaranteed, but one thing was certain. It was worth trying. Saving Carolyn's soul—giving her a second chance to repent for the dreadful sin of suicide was worth the attempt.

"How dare you?" Victoria said, and her voice was low, deep, like a monster riding from the depths of a pit. "How *dare* you?"

What had he done?

"Victoria, I—"

"Hailey, get out while you can," Victoria spat. "Fuck you, Phil." Her hand whipped towards the camera, leaving nothing but a black screen and blinking words.

VIDEO CALL ENDED.

And then—

"How would you rate your call?"

A window with five stars popped up, waiting for his blessing before the phone blackened due to inactivity.

Then, the rage tingled from his fingertips to his arms, and it spread as a physical sensation through the rest of his body until his skin moistened with sweat.

"Don't listen to her," Phil snarled, and he wasn't sure if he was talking to himself or to Hailey, who sat with her face in her hands. "She's a jezebel, just like her grandmother. She'd spit in the face of Christ."

The clock ticked. Phil straightened his tie.

And his phone lit up again.

"K. Spears."

"Go in your room," Phil ordered his daughter and brought the phone to his ear while Hailey scurried away. "This is Philip."

"Phil, it's Kaemon. Sorry I missed your call, had several meetings today. What's up?"

Phil closed his eyes. "I'll take the job."

"What? You will?"

"If the offer still stands, yes."

Silence. Then—

"You know the job's pretty big, right? We've got a lot of rumors we need to put to rest, Phil." Kaemon's voice darkened. "They need to rest *for good*."

"I can handle it," Phil said, and he opened his eyes. "But I'll need to know what's been said, and I'll need to know *what* and *whom* I'm up against."

"It's ugly, Phil. Real ugly."

"I need to know," he demanded.

Kaemon sighed on the other line. "There are internal allegations that names involved with KS Industries have been associated with a human trafficking ring. Senator Thompson was on that list."

Phil blinked. That was *absurd*. Senator Thompson had been an outstanding man of God. "Oh?"

"Yes. I need a squeaky-clean record. You understand? Can you do—"

"It's handled." Phil ran his fingers through his wavy hair. His mouth was now pasty. "Now. Another thing."

Kaemon wouldn't believe him. He wouldn't, and he'd fire Phil before he even started the job.

"Go ahead," Spears said, yawning.

"Has KS ever studied seemingly supernatural events? Healings, foresight, etc?" Phil *knew* these events were of God, but when speaking to pagans, one had to speak *their language*.

"I mean, yes. There's a kid overseas who can control the weather and move the earth. Earthquakes. We've got KS operatives over there to monitor him until further notice. Why? You seeing or experiencing weird things, Phil?" The governor laughed.

"It's not funny. I can—*do things* too," Phil said, and his voice cracked.

Forty-three years old, and it *cracked*.

"What things, Phil?"

Wait a minute.

Kaemon just said something important about a boy who could *control* the weather and *move the earth*. And not just important.

Familiar.

"Phil?" Kaemon persisted. "What things?"

"When I touch, I heal." Phil's eyes slammed shut, as if closing them would prevent him from hearing Kaemon's response. "There was a boy with a spinal injury beyond repair—I prayed over him, and then I touched him, and he walked moments later."

"Oh." Kaemon sounded disinterested. "Like I said, there's a boy overseas who can control the weather. Rain, sunshine. That's all that's been noted, of course, but—"

Phil didn't hear the rest of Kaemon's words. He moved his phone from his ear, clicked open the photo gallery, and zoomed in to one of Fr. Jerome's journal entries. Mouth moving, he skimmed.

Before that, I dreamt of a boy who could move the earth and control the weather... "Ahdam!" I screamed, and I woke up.

Another coincidence... *correct?*

"...so, if you'd like to have your DNA studied at KS Industries," Kaemon was saying, "I can make sure—"

"The boy," Phil interrupted. "Is his name Ahdam?"

Kaemon went silent.

The bumblebee clock ticked.

And Phil gulped.

"Listen to me very carefully," Kaemon Spears said, and his voice turned from its normal, cheerful tone to a deep, guttural bass. "You need to be honest with me. I am not playing here."

Phil began to sweat. What had he done *now?*

"There is no reason for you to know that name. The only people who know this kid's name are KS officials and that operative. So tell me, Mr. Jameson—how do *you* know the boy's name?"

"I—I—I—" Phil licked his dry lips and pulled his hair. What the heck was he supposed to say now? He felt as though an interrogation had light just switched on over his head. Answer wrong? Death by firing squad.

"*Speak, Philip Jameson!*" Kaemon Spears screamed.

Phil jumped in his chair and whimpered. He covered his other ear with his hand, just like Hailey. "*I can see the future too!*"

More silence.

Silence that crushed him. Silence that raped him while whispering in his ear, telling him—

"You're funny. Fr. Jerome can see the future... not you."

A sob caught in his throat.

"People will flock to the man who humiliated you time and time again.
In class.
When he didn't send the recommendation letter to the seminary.
And when he encouraged your fucking wife to divorce you."

"Philip. I'm not joking. I need to know you're telling the truth, because this isn't just a boy who creates rain and sunshine like some goddamn Native American lore. This is a boy who could potentially—"

"—move the Earth," Phil whispered. "I know."

"We need to meet." It was an order, not an option.

"Kaemon," Phil said. "Another thing."

"What now, Philip? My fitness watch is telling me that my stress level is too fucking high. That's your fault."

"And what if there was a watch that *did something* about that?" Phil closed his eyes again and pictured his interaction with Hawk Caravan, the smile on the boy's face when he'd agreed to bring up his *idea* to Kaemon Spears—for an exchange.

"I can heal you," Phil had said. *"I want you to walk again. I will talk to Spears about your idea if you let me heal you... on camera."*

"What the hell are you talking about, Jameson?" Kaemon sighed.

"I'm talking about a *genius*, a boy who may have the answer to lowering insurance costs, increasing longevity, developing cures, ensuring less call-ins. *Your* boy can control the weather. *Mine* can control molecular biology." Phil opened his ears. A tad dramatic, and if it fell through—well, he wouldn't think about that.

It'd be humiliating, to say the least.

"If you waste my time, I'm going to tear out your tongue," Kaemon said, annoyed, but still believable.

"I won't waste your time. When can you meet?"

"I will send you a zoom invite after my run tonight. Is there anything else you need before I hang up?"

Phil listened to the bumblebee clock. It ticked seven times before he responded.

"I do need something," he said. Cleared his throat. Straightened his tie. "It's going to sound insane."

"Nothing you ever say gives me the impression you're sane."

Phil ignored the insult. "I need access to a grave."

"Not gonna lie, this seems like something I should say no to."

"I need access to my wife's body," he added desperately, and he let out a shaky breath. "If you allow me this opportunity... I guarantee you will reap political rewards from it."

"Still seems like something I should say no to."

"But you haven't yet," Phil persisted, leveling his voice. "You haven't."

The bumblebee clock.

Tick. Tick. Tick.

"Alright. Here's the deal. Prove yourself at KS, and we'll talk. I'm not so convinced you're not unhinged. But you're wickedly smart as a lawyer, and I expect you'll do a great job if, for no other reason, you're allowed to chase your unhinged beliefs. Good-night."

Phil lowered the phone.

Straightened his tie again.

And smiled a little.

But it was a nervous smile, because he wasn't quite sure what had just happened, and he certainly wasn't sure how he was supposed to *feel*.

But Phil had proven himself before. When Beatrice told him he'd never get to college, he did. When she told him he'd never succeed as a lawyer—he did.

He wasn't worried. No one believed in him now, but they would.

Kaemon Spears, with his self-obsessed arrogance.

Victoria, with her radical feminism.

And Fr. Jerome... with his satanic red pen.

They would all believe.

And they would all believe soon.

VERSE 4

~ THE BEGINNING OF MY WORLD ~

Sunday, September 16th, 2012
Chicago, Illinois

"I didn't want to get the cops involved. I figured you'd want to talk to him first," Todd said quietly. "And... it sucks saying this, but... I think, for now, I'd rather him stay away from Esther." He lowered his head.

It was dark. Humid. It'd been a hot September. Fr. Jerome Nadier didn't mind, because he enjoyed windy, seventy-degree walks in the Fall. Sixties were good too, but anything below that became a bit too chilly for him.

Tonight, as he stood outside of Todd Caravan's doorway, despite the warm air, Fr. Jerome shivered. He'd cried on the way to the Caravan house, and the wind had whipped the remaining tears from his eyes while approaching Todd's house.

"I understand," the weary priest said, and he lowered his own head to find Todd's downcast eyes. "Is Esther okay?"

"Yeah. Just freaked out."

"And Gabe?"

Todd nodded. "Yes. Making jokes, per usual."

Fr. Jerome noted Todd's demeanor—baggy skin under his eyes, down-turned lips, slumped shoulders. "Are *you* okay, Todd?"

"Yes," Todd said too quickly.

The wind whistled.

"Please give Mary my best when you see her. I'd like to come pray with her in the hospital if she's open to it." He needed to help somewhere, and he hated feeling guilty for his son's actions tonight. It was all a mess. A horrible mess. What could a man responsible for his flock *do* when he felt completely helpless?

"She'd like that," Todd said and stepped backwards into his house. "I hope Mariel's okay. I really do. I appreciate that. I hope so too."

The conversation was over, he could feel it.

"Goodnight, Father Jerome.

"Goodnight, and thanks again for contacting me."

Fr. Jerome wiped the corners of his eyes and walked back to the sedan.

Fourteen-year-old Mariel sat in the front passenger seat, his head leaned back against the headrest, and when the priest entered the car, the rain came.

No one spoke—not for several minutes, at least. Fr. Jerome wasn't sure how long it was before he said the first word. He kept both hands on the wheel, cleared his throat, and then spoke.

"Are you okay?"

"I'm fine." Abrupt. Almost disinterested.

He'd heard it time and time again. Mariel was always "fine." It made it difficult to help the boy when he wasn't.

"Then why?" Fr. Jerome gripped the steering wheel.

"It was a joke."

"A *joke* doesn't *terrify* your best friend! A *joke* doesn't terrify your dad!" He didn't *want* to be angry.

"Well, clearly a joke does," Mariel said, eyes still closed.

Jerome fought to calm himself, tried to remember that Mariel was hurting in some way, that of course he'd respond like a—

"—brat!" Jerome realized he'd lost the fight against rage. Words spewed so fast he wasn't even sure what he'd shouted.

"I'm not acting like a brat, Dad. Please just relax." Mariel opened his eyes. Streetlights flashed over his face, and raindrop shadows freckled his skin.

"It's very hard to relax when you're told your son took a gun, put it in his mouth, and pulled the trigger." Fr. Jerome's chest hurt. Was this what a heart attack felt like?

"It was a joke, let it go. You've never done stupid shit?"

"Mariel!" Fr. Jerome roared, and his foot slammed on the brake as they hurtled towards a stop sign. "Please! *Talk* to me!"

Mariel's body came alive. "You wouldn't *fucking* get it! You've brought me to therapist after therapist after motherfucking therapist, and you've never *once* taken the lead on figuring out what the *hell* is wrong with me!"

Fr. Jerome pulled to the side of the road and put the car in park. He couldn't breathe well. "What do you mean?"

"I *mean* I'm tired of you thinking that a therapist is going to make those voices go away! I'm not fucking schizo, Dad, I'm a kid who can't seem to—" His voice trailed off.

"Seem to what?"

Mariel shook his head. "Get it together."

"That's not what you were going to say."

"I keep trying to commit suicide, and I can't *fucking die!*" Mariel screamed, his eyes bulging. "Something goes wrong! The trigger malfunctions, the bullet doesn't come out, the truck spirals before hitting me!"

Horror ripped through his chest like a hot serrated knife. *"What? What truck, Mariel?"*

Mariel's eyes slammed shut. "I don't want to *fucking be here* anymore! Don't you understand? Every Sunday I sit and listen to your sermons about hope and faith, and I *see* the hope and peace in other people surrounding me, but I don't *feel it. I can't feel hope.* Do you have any idea what that's like? *Wanting* peace and never getting it?" The boy was sobbing now.

Fr. Jerome reached for him, and tears poured from his own eyes. His son's words sat like a steel wall on his chest, crushing him, but not in one blow. Each word felt like a steady pressure that worsened with each breath. "I'm so sorry, Mariel." His fingers gripped the teen's hoodie.

Mariel shrunk back. "I don't want your sorrow, Dad, I want the voices to go away. I want them to stop saying I'm nothing more than a vessel!"

"Then don't listen to them!" the priest cried, and he felt like a lost sheep, and he wished, for once, he could turn to a Shepherd.

And for a moment he wanted to curse God, because why would God let a *child* suffer like this?

"I can't stop them," Mariel wailed, and his hands went into his long hair. "They're always there, telling me I'm a vessel, I'm a catalyst, I'm the *end of the fucking world!*"

The shriek pierced the air. Thunder crashed like judgment from the heavens, and Jerome choked on his own sobs. Should he tell Mariel? Tell the boy that he'd seen him catch a bullet? Or was this conversation a reminder of his own madness?

Humans couldn't catch bullets! Nor could they survive oncoming trucks, and a gun that should have gone off?

Perhaps the therapy in Jerome's youth hadn't helped him. Perhaps he should have ended up in a mental health institution—just like his father.

And just like his mentor, Fr. Paul—the man who'd kidnapped Mariel as a baby, racing across the city of Moscow, screaming—

"That baby belongs at the Kremlin! He's a catalyst for the end!"

Yes. Just like him.

"You're the beginning to my world," Fr. Jerome said as tears dribbled over his cheeks. "You were the beginning to my world the moment I saw you, the moment I held you." His voice rose with emotion. "You're the beginning to my world each day I see you, each day I get those stupid little eggplant emojis whenever you think I say something 'gay', whenever you drink out of the milk gallon despite my OCD, whenever you hug me and assure me that there's no need for anxiety because *God has me.*"

Mariel's shoulders shook, and he buried his face in his hands.

"You're the beginning of my world when I see you despair, because it tells me you exist in my world, that you're alive, that you're *my son*, and I think of every little decision I could have possibly made to *get* you." Fr. Jerome reached for him again, but he didn't touch him. As lightning flickered, his hand shook in the dimly lit car. "Please, *please* know that I love you. I want you to be happy, and it's not fair that I make this about me, but please, Mariel—" His voice cracked. "Please don't try to end your life. Because if you do, you'll be the end of *my* world."

"Dad." Mariel grabbed for him and put his forehead against the priest's hand. "I need help. Please help me."

Fr. Jerome reached his other hand across and placed it on Mariel's head. "I promise I'll listen more, but you *have* to talk to me. We can battle this together."

Mariel nodded, sniffling, and his body trembled. "Can we—can we have a movie night? Watch something funny?"

Fr. Jerome let out a shaky breath and closed his eyes. He thanked God, thanked Him for allowing him to be there for his son. "Of course, son. Let's go home."

* * *

Monday, January 28th, 2019
Chicago, Illinois

Dear friends,

I don't think I can put into words how good I feel. How young. How light. It's almost frightening, because I am not young, and I was released from the hospital not that long ago from a traumatic brain injury. Yet—I feel as though I've had a reset. I see people, strangers, with more clarity, and not in a manner you think—I see their sorrows, their joys, their anger. I've always been an empath, but something feels different. I don't know what it is. Maybe I shouldn't question it, especially since it's God's healing that brought me back to health.

I am blessed to see my boy again. Goodness, I adore him. He was the beginning of my world, and he always will be. Whenever I say that, he sends an eggplant emoji because apparently that's a 'gay' thing to say. I don't care.

I've been told that Mariel stayed by my side the majority of the time. He helped with the church whenever they needed him. I raised him well. I am proud of him, and I wish I could express my gratitude. I'd probably get an eggplant emoji if I did, though. :)

But despite all of this, there are some things that happened that I wish I could understand. First of all, I am devastated. I remember the moment Carolyn was struck by the train, and I wish I could remove that memory from my mind. It was horrible, and I don't do well with suicide—not since the day Mariel attempted to take his own life. That day still haunts me, and he wasn't even successful. There is something devastating about hearing your child, from the depths of his soul, scream for death.

But back to Carolyn. I need to contact Phil and give him my condolences. I don't know if he will listen to me, but it's worth a try. I wish I could reach him too, and understand his mind. I feel for him. He must be lonely, especially now. Lord have mercy.

I did reach out to Todd. I found out Hawk was struck by Carolyn, who was drunk, and that the boy had severe spinal and internal injuries. But oddly, one day they found Hawk outside of his bed. He could walk, and he wasn't supposed to walk. I try not to read too much into these things, but it's hard not to when I've been surrounded by seemingly supernatural events my entire life.

That's not the only odd thing that's happened either. The other day, when we stopped at the coffee shop (where I currently am), I saw a young woman with blonde hair standing in line. Athletic pants. Beautiful hair in a ponytail. Perfect stance, like she was military or something. Not odd at all. Just a young, athletic woman. But then? She turned, and I locked eyes with her.

I knew those eyes. I'd seen them before. But something unexplainable happened. My head began to pulse, as if time froze, and I saw that young woman point a gun at me, tell me she was sorry, and then pull the trigger.

Then I remembered. I'd seen her in my nightmares. She shoots me every time. Just like those people fall from the sky, and the earth splits apart, and people scream that there needs to be justice for Ahdam, that young woman shoots me in the head.

Mariel told me I'd zoned out in the coffee shop, repeating over and over again that 'she was going to shoot me'. Now, it took me all day to even realize I'd had this 'vision', but it finally clicked when I went to bed.

I wish I could explain these things. I wish Fr. Paul would contact me, because he was always such a joy and a comfort when he mentored me. I'd always wished I had his level of confidence and ability to speak to people without feeling anxious. But, something clearly shifted in his mind... just like sometimes I'm afraid something shifted in mine.

Maybe I'll never have answers. But, until then, I shall keep writing, just like that woman told me on the day I picked Mariel up from the hotel.

I need to make some phone calls. Phil. Esther. The other clergymen.

Talk soon, and God bless.

Fr. Jerome.

The priest raised his mug to his lips before realizing he'd finished his coffee. He hated when the coffee was gone, because it meant he'd have to decide if consuming another one was worth being up late.

Scratching his jaw, Fr. Jerome looked outside as he sat in the red fabric booth. Sleet spattered the windows.

The coffee shop, set up like an old fashioned diner, wasn't crowded tonight. Soft, jazzy piano trickled through the speakers, and the dim lighting might have lulled him to sleep had he not just finished a large coffee.

Fr. Jerome adored the local shop, owned by an old, lesbian couple from Israel. It'd been around for close to ten years.

"Hi, Father Jerome!" A young barista called from behind the counter. Her red-haired ponytail bounced as she moved. The sides of her skull were shaved, and skull tattoos covered the skin. "I haven't seen you in a while. I missed out on my scripture of the week." She pouted and reached behind her waist to tie her apron.

The priest smiled. "I had an accident. I'm okay now, but I was in the hospital for a bit. I owe you a couple of scriptures, Abbi."

"I think I'm ready for a full book now. Any suggestions?" Abbi had just been released from prison on a felony drunk driving charge that'd caused death, and she'd noticed his priest collar the first day she'd met him. She requested a scripture from him each week, one that would aid her in finding hope and encouragement.

"Yes," Fr. Jerome beamed. "The Book of St. John. God's love through Jesus is abundant there."

Abbi tilted her head. "Isn't that the book where God talks about sacrificing Jesus for the world, or whatever?"

"Mmhmm. Good job. John 3:16."

Abbi snapped her fingers into guns. "Knew it. I'm retaining information. How's that scripture go again?"

Radiant headlights brightened the coffee shop as a vehicle parked near the doorway. A door slammed shut.

Fr. Jerome glanced towards the noise and then back at Abbi. He spun the pen in his hands. *"For God so loved the world, that He gave His only—"*

Bells jingled on the glass door. It crashed open. Wind howled into the shop, snapping everyone's attention to the man standing in the doorway.

Not just any man.

A priest.

And something about him was *very* familiar. *Too* familiar. As if he was—

"... were you saying? You stopped talking." Abbi's voice.

Catching his breath, Fr. Jerome tore his eyes away from the entrance as a young couple entered the shop and wandered towards the register. His heart raced, and sweat formed on his brow.

Was he *high? Seeing* shadows like Mariel?

"Sorry," Fr. Jerome stammered. He rubbed his head and tried to smile. "Caffeine rush, I think."

Was that a hint to go home? Mariel had sounded sad on the phone, anyway. Maybe he should just go home and get some rest.

"You've always overdone the coffee, Jerome." *That voice.*

Whipping his head to the side, the priest gasped. His eyes caught sight of black pants, a black button-down, and a white collar that sat on the neck of a man he never thought he'd see again.

His seminary mentor—Fr. Paul Rinaldi.

Fr. Jerome's mouth fell open.

The wavy-haired priest, an Italian man with olive skin tone, smiled down at Jerome. His stubbled jaw had no signs of grey. In fact, he didn't look like he'd aged a day. His hair was still pitch black.

It'd been *over twenty years* since Jerome had seen the man. How could a man in his sixties look just as he had in his *forties?*

"Jerome. *Sir.*" Fr. Paul dipped down a little. "You're drooling."

"I—" Fr. Jerome stuttered and sat up in his seat. His head fell back, looking with awe at the man who'd mentored him, who'd been locked in a mental institution after *kidnapping an infant* and—

"May I sit, please?" Fr. Paul's blue eyes were gentle. "I know this is a lot to process, and I'm sorry I started out with a joke. Let's start over."

"You owe me an explanation." Fr. Jerome's lips trembled, and he placed his palms on the table as if he needed to prove he had no weapons.

Fr. Paul raised his eyebrows, shifted his glance, and then sat across from Fr. Jerome. The light glinted against his eyes, and his face grew serious. "You're right. I do."

"Start talking." Jerome loosened his collar.

"About? Where do I start?" Fr. Paul blew out a breath. "I've been in a mental institution for a long time, so bear with me."

"I've tried contacting you for *years*, Paul. *Years.* To get answers. To find *hope*. And then your sister tells me that you—" Fr. Jerome lowered his voice and leaned forward. "*Kidnapped* a boy. Sound familiar? Tell me that isn't true!"

Fr. Paul didn't flinch. The sleet clattered against the window like icy nails. The jazz piano rolled through the speakers.

"It's true. I kidnapped a boy," he said quietly. "A boy named Mariel."

The air left his body. At least, that's how it felt, because Fr. Jerome's hand crept to his chest, and he clenched his sweater.

Now was a moment of truth. Would this conversation end like a brief nighttime terror?

Or would it finally give him answers to everything he'd been desperate to know for the last twenty years?

"Why?" Fr. Jerome asked, digging his nails into his chest. "*Why,* Paul?"

Fr. Paul chewed his lip and then leaned forward. A wavy strand of hair dangled over his eyebrow. "Alright. Soon after I mentored you in seminary, I obtained dual citizenship in the U.S. and in Russia. I pastored a large Orthodox church in Moscow. Hundreds of members. At that time, the government was going through a transition of power, and there were rumors of potential persecution of the Christian Church. It was suggested that infants of Christian parents were being taken at birth for genetic testing and enhancement research under a program called *Project Savior*. Sound familiar?"

"Like the *Project Savior* program here in the States?"

"Yes and no. Darker. More intentional. This one specifically researched the potential for enhanced DNA and weaponizing of human beings."

Fr. Jerome shivered. He thought of Mariel's little hand as it reached to catch the bullet.

What if he was *one of them?*

"How would this horror not come to the attention of the people? Protests? *Anything?*"

"Under that regime, people are either persuaded or silenced."

Fr. Jerome dared ask the next question. "And what does this have to do with my son?"

"I met Mariel's mother through all of this. Natasha struggled with drug abuse, and she started rehab through our program at the church. She wanted to get clean because she was pregnant, and she claimed it was the child of someone who offered her drug money in exchange for sex. Eventually, she turned to the church and attempted to leave the relationship, but he threatened that if she left him he would kill her and the baby."

"Do you know who the father is? *Was?*" Fr. Jerome cried.

Fr. Paul tapped his thumbs together. "No. She never said." He reached for a spare napkin and tore at the corner. "Natasha begged me to be with her during the birth and to make sure the baby would be okay."

"What happened?"

"She hemorrhaged." Fr. Paul lowered his eyes. "The staff pronounced her dead soon after Mariel's birth." His voice grew more panicked. "Jerome, I had to act fast. And, I'll admit, I was high on adrenaline. I let my fears and my desire to be a hero overcome my senses. So—I took him."

"And?"

Fr. Paul swallowed more of his coffee. "I tried to flee, and I didn't get far. So, to avoid prison, I feigned insanity. I *know* I was wrong. They took the baby... but I never knew he'd end up with you, Jerome. I thought he'd end up at the Kremlin with—with Aleksey Petrov's organization."

Oh, the little decisions that had to be made in order for you to be mine, my boy...

Fr. Jerome took a deep breath. "Was Mariel part of this—this enhanced DNA program?"

"Jerome, I'm sorry, I truly don't know. Given the circumstances, it'd make sense. But I can't be sure. Have you noticed anything about him that could suggest—*unusual* abilities?"

"I keep trying to commit suicide," Mariel screamed. "And I can't fucking die!"

Suddenly, reality felt much too terrifying to discuss. Not right now.

And not with him.

"How did you find me?" Fr. Jerome asked.

Fr. Paul smiled a little. "I called your church. They told me about your injury, and about your parishioner's wife. So, I came to St. Michael's to help where I could. I'm proud of you, Jerome. For putting that collar on. For pastoring that beautiful church." The priest rested a hand over Jerome's. "For loving and raising a good man."

Fr. Jerome felt tears brim into his eyes. "I'm scared."

"Of what?"

"Of what you're not telling me."

A coffee grinder shrieked.

Fr. Jerome locked eyes with the priest across the table from him, and suddenly, he wondered if he was dreaming.

Fr. Paul nodded. "Do you trust me?"

"I don't trust *myself*."

It was true. Jerome's head pounded, as if he'd struck it on the cement again. He didn't trust any of his thoughts, and he didn't trust the man in front of him. Not yet, at least.

"That baby belongs at the Kremlin! He's a catalyst for the end!" Fr. Paul had been quoted.

No, Jerome didn't trust him yet.

Because why did this priest, feigning insanity, say a phrase so very similar to Mariel's cry of desperation seven years ago?

"I'm a catalyst, I'm the end of the fucking world!"

The coffee grinder screamed again, and Abbi glanced at the two priests with a mix of curiosity and concern.

Fr. Paul did not flinch. "I know you have a lot of questions, and I'm here for you when you do. I won't disappear again. This situation was far too coincidental, which leads me to believe Mariel is a part of something far bigger than two priests in a coffee shop."

Those words cut deep, because if it were true, he knew it'd be the last thing Mariel wanted.

"My son wants normalcy," Fr. Jerome murmured. "Nothing more."

"Well, I'm afraid *He*—" Fr. Paul pushed his finger towards the ceiling, "—can't always offer that."

"Sometimes it just starts with a movie night," Jerome said, before clicking open his pen and extending it towards his former mentor. "Write your number on a napkin."

Fr. Paul's eyes flickered to the journal that lay at the edge of the table. He took the pen, pulled a napkin from the rack, and scribbled. "Still journaling?"

"Yes."

"Good." Fr. Paul closed the pen with a click and shoved the items back to Fr. Jerome. "Journaling helped me work through my own madness."

Fr. Jerome wasn't particularly encouraged by his statement, but he couldn't mentally process anything further. He stood up. "I'm going home to see my son. I'd appreciate it if you didn't speak to him about any of this for now."

Fr. Paul nodded and smiled a little. "As you wish. I'm sorry it took me so long to get back to you. But I'm glad to see you, Jerome, I really am."

Fr. Jerome could only muster a nod as he grabbed his journal from under Fr. Paul's curious gaze and walked speedily from the coffee shop. He managed a brief wave to Abbi before he darted into the sleet.

Driving home, he called Mariel's phone, but it went straight to voicemail. He'd sounded tired earlier, sad even.

"Hey son, on my way home. Thinking a movie night might cheer us both up. I love you." Fr. Jerome hesitated. "You're the beginning to my world."

When he arrived, Mariel's car was in the driveway. The priest scurried to the door, unlocked it, and entered. "Mariel, I'm home." The wind howled as he shut and bolted the door.

The living room lamp was on, just like Fr. Jerome always requested. Once, years ago, the priest had tripped over himself because the boy had turned all lights off. So, that night, Fr. Jerome had created a new rule.

The rest of the house was dark. The priest hung the keys on the wall hook and, sleepily, walked towards the dark hallway to his room. Muffled electronic music pulsed through the wall. Beneath the door, the bathroom light emitted a soft glow against the darkness. Shower water spattered against the tub.

Fr. Jerome knocked. "Mariel, I'm home. I need to get some pain killers, my head hurts. May I come in? I don't want to see your eggplant."

The music vibrated against the door in response as the bass dropped.

"Ugh," the priest groaned, grabbed the door handle, and turned the knob. "I'm coming in!" He walked in.

Steam swirled. The humidity was overwhelming. Shower water rained. The music crashed.

And time halted.

First, he saw the blood spatter. It was on the shower wall. Then he saw Mariel.

He wasn't sure how long he stood there with his hands at his sides, his eyes wide, his mouth open.

Water cascaded over Mariel's naked body. It lay lifeless, large and muscular, sprawled within the bathtub with one leg idly resting on the outside. A trail of brain matter and blood smeared against the wall where he'd slipped downwards. A black pistol lay in the tub. But—

Humans can't catch bullets.

This was the worst vision he'd ever experienced. The rest he could handle. This one went too far.

"Mariel?"

His knuckles cracked as his hands opened and closed.

"I need to wake up from this."

The blood didn't disappear. The shower water continued its rain. The song kept playing.

And Mariel's body did not move.

Maybe if *Fr. Jerome* moved, he'd wake up from the vision.

So, the priest angled his head a little bit, and his eyes settled on an envelope resting atop the sink faucet.

"Dad".

"No, no, no," Fr. Jerome snatched it, shaking, terrified that he'd be stuck in this loop of insanity, *praying* that God would save him from this horrible dream. Despite the flap being open, his fingers tore into the envelope. As time sped up, the old man unfolded the paper and read the words he'd never forget.

"Dad,

I'm sorry. I should have warned you, but you would've tried to stop me. This isn't your fault, and don't you dare shut down, but you need to understand why I did this.

For my entire life, I've been followed by two figures—a humanoid, the one who whispers evil, and another—one who guides and encourages every good decision I make. But it's been exhausting trying to dissect what they tell me, and why. It's been exhausting trying to understand why I can't physically die. I know I can't—based on my personal experiences, and based on your very first journal entries. I'm sorry, I know I shouldn't have looked in your journal while you were in a coma, but I'd always wondered if you knew anything that I didn't. You did.

It broke me. So, I tried to find comfort in Esther Caravan because she's the only one who has given me a sense of purpose. I panicked. Then, emotionally, I hurt her. So I made a decision. I prayed.

The Good Follower came to me, and he told me that I would be allowed to do this. One time.

I know you are confused, and you probably think what you're seeing is unreal, but I need you to be brave as you've always been. Please don't be afraid. I'm safe, I'm in the Kingdom of Heaven, and I am certain I will return with the guidance I need and the answers we both desire. I love you, Dad, and I'll be with you again soon.

—Mariel."

His world collapsed, the letter dropped, and Fr. Jerome Nadier let out an animalistic scream. Time sped up, and he stumbled forward, falling, crawling towards the bathtub to reach his son. His screams tore through the music. Lifting Mariel's shoulders, he rocked him back and forth, rocked him like he'd done when Mariel was little, when the boy wouldn't stop screaming from pain in his stomach, or terror from his nightmares. The water beat upon the priest as he cried and clutched the young man's head to his chest.

But soon, the priest came to understand that it was not a vision, and he would not wake up.

Soon, first responders arrived, and the old man kissed Mariel on the forehead one last time before he let him go.

Then, it was morning, and, as everyone else's world continued, Fr. Jerome picked up the phone, dialed Esther Caravan's number, and held the phone to his ear.

The young woman wailed in his ear, and the priest sat alone on his couch, staring at the floor as Esther wept. And after she'd screamed, she choked over the phone and reminded him that he *wasn't* alone—that she'd pull herself together.

"I'm not going to let you be alone," she cried. "I'm coming over, and we can be together. I love you."

Esther Caravan held up on her word.

And, in the days that followed, Fr. Jerome did something he never thought he'd have to do, something he thought impossible, something no parent could ever fathom.

He laid his son, Mariel Nadier, to rest.

PART 2

"For I do not do the good that I want, but the evil I do not want is what I keep doing."

Romans 7:19

Chapter 7: Verse 1

~ Father Paul ~

October 17th, 1996

Moscow, Russia

"Did you hear about the people that died? Horrible thing yesterday."

"Hmm?" Fr. Paul looked up from his notebook. His eyes drew focus again, and he realized he'd been lost in the task of writing his sermon. "Oh. Hi, Jakob." Fr. Paul responded in Russian. "Yes, please refill that coffee for me. Sorry, what else was it that you said?"

Jakob leaned forward. The black coffee splashed into the ivory-colored mug. "I was commenting on that incident in Guatemala. Before the soccer match."

Fr. Paul poured cream into his coffee. "Ah yes, the stampede. Killed over eighty people, I think. Horrifying."

That's what one was *supposed* to say, right?

He looked out of the window. Rain glistened against the streets of Moscow. Hour five of constant rain. "Who willingly tramples another human being for a soccer game?"

Jakob placed the check near the priest. "I don't know. No rush, by the way."

The forty-year-old priest with handsome, youthful features smiled. "Thank you. I'll have the booth free soon."

He looked at the notebook, scanning the text. The sermon discussed fear and finding the ability to use it in service for God.

Fr. Paul was not unfamiliar with *fear*. The humanoid's harassment had gotten worse, more consistent. It'd first been in his nightmares, but now it appeared just before he fell asleep, cackling, taunting, saying—

"Remember your past, you dirty, little priest? Wasn't your life more fun? Less lonely?"

Usually, prayer scared it away, but not lately.

Not lately at all.

"Ma'am. No pay, no food. We've been over this."

Fr. Paul raised his eyes.

Jakob stood near the entrance. But past the waiter was a young woman with black hair that clung to her face from the rain. She wore blue jeans, a dark coat, and she carried a backpack on her back. She held the hand of a black-haired child, a little girl who looked no more than three, or four, years of age. Soaked, both of them shivered.

"Please," the woman said. "Just a meal. Just one. My child is starving."

"I'm sure there's a shelter near here who will help you. The boss doesn't like panhandlers."

The woman turned her eyes to Fr. Paul. Their eyes met, and the pleading desperation in her wide, blue eyes sent icy chills to his chest.

"Jakob."

The young waiter turned.

Fr. Paul raised his hand and gestured for them. "I'll buy them some food."

The woman grasped the child's hand and approached Fr. Paul's booth. She smiled, and rain glistened on her skin. Despite being bedraggled, the woman was pretty.

Fr. Paul stood and extended his hand. "Hello," he said, smiling. "My name's Fr. Paul. Please, have a seat. What's your name?"

"Natasha." Once seated, the woman brushed wet, black hair behind the little girl's ear. "And this is my daughter. Olivia."

The priest smiled at the little girl. "Hi, Olivia. My name's Fr. Paul. Would you do something for me?"

Olivia nodded.

"Great. I need you to take a look at this menu and tell me what you'd like to eat, okay? Anything you want." He turned his gaze to Natasha. "You as well," he said softly.

Natasha took a menu from the end of the table and opened it. Rubbing her arms, she shivered. "I can't tell you how much I appreciate this." She raised her eyes to his. "Thank you."

"Of course."

After the food order, Natasha looked at the notebook Fr. Paul had swept to the side. "What are you writing?"

"This week's sermon."

"I see. Anything in particular that you're discussing?" Her eyes were inquisitive, but their steady gaze seemed more interested in the priest than what he had written in the notebook.

Fr. Paul raised the mug to his lips. "I'm discussing the topic of fear."

"Yeah?" Natasha leaned forward. "And what are you afraid of?"

The priest turned his eyes to the rainy streets outside the window. "A lot of things," he murmured.

"Oh, you're afraid to become your father, but you're already there, my friend," the humanoid had whispered in his ear last night.

And he saw a familiar image, a bloody, *bloody* image, of a corpse on a bed, while his father knelt over it and—

"—sermon is also about finding God's hope, even in the midst of that fear." Fr. Paul raised the mug to his lips again. There were coffee grounds in this cup.

Natasha shifted in her seat and rested her elbows onto the table. "I'm afraid of a lot of things too. Being homeless with a child doesn't help."

"Tell me your story."

Natasha played with the corner of her silverware napkin. "I was living with an abusive boyfriend. I left. I've been going from shelter to shelter." She lifted tear-filled eyes to Fr. Paul. "You're the first person who's bought food for us." Natasha kissed her daughter's head.

The little girl stared at Fr. Paul. Then, she smiled.

Fr. Paul winked at her. "No family?"

"Either in prison or dead."

"I'm sorry."

A smile played on the corner of her lips. "Don't be. Misfortune has always been in my family line."

Fr. Paul considered her words. A misfortunate family line. *That* was putting it lightly. "I can relate." He looked at his watch. "Do you have a place to stay tonight?"

"No, we don't." Natasha looked at her daughter, as if driving the point home that a child's life should determine his next decision.

It did. Somewhat. It helped that she was cute, but he shouldn't—*couldn't*—go down that road. Maybe he shouldn't offer to—

"Come stay with me. You and Olivia can take my room."

"I can't do that."

As if she hadn't *planned* on manipulating him into this.

Body language didn't lie.

Fr. Paul reached across the table and grasped her hand. "Please. At least for tonight. I will get in contact with the leaders in my church and see if we can find a place for you."

Always trying to prove how good you are, aren't you? he thought.

But tears welled in her eyes. "Thank you so much," she said. "God bless you."

It grew darker outside. Fr. Paul paid for their meals, and they left. The drive to his apartment was quiet, but as they stopped at a redlight, Natasha grabbed his free hand.

Startled, Fr. Paul looked towards her and smiled nervously. "What is it?"

Natasha smiled. A large, genuine smile. Or perhaps she'd gotten good at masking her true emotions. "Thank you. I'll say it again... there *has* to be a way I can repay you."

Fr. Paul squeezed her hand, and when she made no effort to move it, he brought his hand back to the steering wheel and cleared his throat. "I wouldn't do this from my heart if I expected anything in return."

The apartment was small, containing a living room with a couch, television stand, and a tall lamp. It had a modest-sized kitchen, and a bedroom with a full bath. The lights were off, and Fr. Paul flipped the switch to the living room as they entered. He set aside his keys.

"The bedroom is all yours," he said, gesturing towards the small hallway. "The kitchen is yours, the shower is yours, the television." He smiled. "If there's anything I can get you, let me know."

Natasha took Olivia's hand. "Are you sure? I can sleep on the floor. Olivia can take the couch."

"That's not even a question. You have my room, Natasha." Fr. Paul winked. "Sleep tight. I'll be in the living room if you need anything."

Moments later, Fr. Paul heard the shower running. He turned off the lamp and undressed, watching the television flicker. His shoulders, large and well-defined, rippled in the white t-shirt he wore as he took off his belt and settled onto the couch. He kept his black pants on. No sleeping just in boxers tonight.

The shower water ran for a half hour and then shut off. Fr. Paul dozed. As it grew late, he heard Natasha's murmur in the other room as she soothed Olivia to sleep. His eyes blinked open and then closed, repeatedly, as his body begged for sleep. The hypervigilance wouldn't allow him.

Because the priest *knew* it was in the living room, in the shadows, and he could not sleep when he felt its presence in the room.

And that presence felt like icy needles jutting from his skin.

Fr. Paul tried to ignore the sounds it made, but his eyelids fluttered open again. And he saw it.

The humanoid.

It crouched beside the television.

"Horrible thing yesterday. Those people that died," the humanoid mocked, cocking his head to the side.

Fr. Paul closed his eyes again, and they shifted back and forth beneath his eyelids.

"Lord Jesus Christ..."

It was closer.

"Son of God..."

Breathing in his ear now. Hoarse. Raspy.

Ignore it, he pleaded to himself.

"Father?"

His eyes flew open.

Drying her hair with a white towel, Natasha stood near the couch in one of his bathrobes.

God, she was pretty.

He swallowed. Hard. "Hi, Natasha. Need something?"

Natasha tossed the towel aside and knelt before him. "I just wanted to talk to someone. I'm sorry, did I wake you?"

"No."

The television lights danced on her face, casting a flickering glow on her full lips.

Fr. Paul studied her face, then looked at her throat. From her throat, his eyes trailed down to the hint of cleavage where the robe parted and revealed skin.

He averted his gaze. He could not go back to this, back to the lust he'd struggled with in the past, the sin that'd almost ended him while he was in seminary. All it'd taken was a night out, a waitress, and a few suggestive comments. He'd almost ended his journey to become a priest.

"I can't sleep. Will you tell me more about yourself?" Natasha asked, scooting closer.

Fr. Paul sat up and swung his feet to the floor. He scratched his cheek, and his body warmed with pleasure at the question. "There's not much to know about me."

She searched his face. "What was the hardest thing about becoming a priest?"

He leaned forward, scratching another itchy spot on his nose. "I don't know. I think the loneliness. As an Orthodox priest, you can get married before becoming a priest... but I never met anyone before I took the vow."

Natasha smiled a little. "I find that hard to believe."

"What?"

"That you never met anyone." Her blue eyes wandered over his face, his shoulders, his chest, and then rose up to settle on his lips for a moment. "You're sweet. How old are you?"

"I'm forty."

"Well," she slid a little closer. "You wear forty very well."

This was getting dangerous.

Fr. Paul leaned back against the couch to create some distance. His hands quivered. "I appreciate that. I think eating healthy and committing to the gym helps."

This girl wouldn't try anything with a priest, right? She'd *understand* the boundary... right?

"I can tell it helps." Natasha closed the space between them again, this time rising to her knees and resting her hands on the couch near his knees, on either side. "Father..."

With a cough, Fr. Paul shot out of his seat, and the blanket dropped to the floor as Natasha moved backwards to avoid getting struck. "I've forgotten. I have something for you." He hastened to the kitchen and searched for his wallet as sweat formed on his skin.

This was ridiculous. He was running away from a woman fifteen years younger in his own home.

"There it is." Fr. Paul snatched the wallet from the mail-covered counter and returned to the edge of the living room.

He shouldn't do this either. In fact, he'd probably regret this in the morning because—

"I'd like you to have this," he said, retrieving a wad of cash from his wallet. "It'll get you by until we figure something out."

It wasn't his. It belonged to the church. It'd been donations—a repair fund for the damage done to the church during the riots two weeks ago.

Fr. Paul closed his eyes and then opened them, trying to erase the guilt from his mind. If he didn't help this young woman, she'd be trafficked.

He'd pay this money back to the church.

The television hummed.

Outside, a car door slammed. A horn beeped twice.

Natasha shook her head. "You'd do this?"

"Of course. And don't argue about it." He set the money on the dining room table and cleared his throat.

It was time for bed. How could he relay this message without being rude?

"May I make a confession, Father?" Still on her knees, Natasha rested her palms against her thighs.

Awkwardly, Fr. Paul stood there, his pants sagging onto his hips, threatening to drop without a belt. "Of... course."

"No one trusts me with money, because I'm a recovering drug addict." Natasha stood up. "I'm clean now. I just wanted you to know how much I appreciate you."

Fr. Paul shrugged. "I'm not here to judge. Or to decide what you do with it. I'm here to help." He stepped towards the couch, but she made no effort to move as he came close.

And suddenly he realized just *how* close she was, and he smelled the shampoo on her hair. His heart pulsed in his throat as he looked at her, realizing that she stood just a bit taller than him.

"Excuse me," he whispered shakily, "I should get some rest."

Natasha's eyes locked with his, and her lips parted. "It was hard for me," she whispered, lightly brushing his cheek with her fingers.

He shivered. "What was hard for you?"

"Stopping the drugs." She played her finger across his cheek, rubbing the pad of her forefinger gently against the stubble on his jaw. "I'm sure you understand, Father."

It sounded rather gross, the sound of his Adam's apple bobbing in his throat as he swallowed. And breathing? Far more difficult now.

This woman knew she was tempting him, didn't she?

What on earth did she have to *gain* from it?

"What does it *matter?*" the humanoid said, resting his palm atop the television. "Stealing from the church is far worse, anyway."

Fr. Paul exhaled loudly. "I'm sorry. I don't understand what you've experienced. I've never done drugs."

Natasha bit the corner of her lip, bringing her finger across his cheek and down his neck. "You've never desired something... *craved* something so much that you would do *anything* to get it?"

Yes. Oh, *yes. This* right here.

And worse.

Fr. Paul shivered.

Natasha's finger had a mind of its own. It pushed his collar down and nestled itself within the small, black hairs on the top of his chest.

"Please, Natasha," the priest said, breathing hard. "You need to stop."

"Do I? Well." With a gentle smirk, Natasha loosened the strap on the robe, and it fell open. "That's disappointing."

Fr. Paul stood motionless, eyes wide, his chest heaving up and down as he took in the first woman's naked body he'd seen for years. She wore black panties, but no bra. The robe covered her nipples, and he could see the soft swell of her breasts peeking from the edges of the cloth. "Natasha—"

She pressed against him.

Wrapped her arms around his neck.

And brought her lips to his ear.

"I think God will forgive you for treating yourself just this once."

Fr. Paul raised his hands to push her away. He grasped her shoulders and pushed her from his ear, stumbling away from her embrace. "Natasha. I can't. I'm flattered, but we can't do this, and you know why."

But *God,* he wanted to.

Fr. Paul stepped past her and sat on the couch. "Please go be with your daughter." He was shaking. His groin pulsed.

"Father Paul."

"What?"

"Look at me."

"Yeah, you nerd, look at her," the humanoid cackled.

He squeezed his eyes shut, clenched his fists. "I can't," he gasped. "*Please.* Don't tempt me, Natasha."

What happened next went quick—so fast that he did not have time to raise a defensive wall.

Natasha pushed him backwards, upright, against the couch and crawled onto his lap. He felt her breath on his lips, and then her mouth. His body burned as her soft lips melted with his, and memories of this former pleasure flooded his mind.

It's just a kiss, he thought, but his words were not his own. *Just... a kiss.*

Fr. Paul had almost forgotten how wonderful this felt—the feel of her lips against his own, her tongue in and out of his mouth, and her magical gasps of pleasure. It all sent ripples of satisfaction humming through his nerves.

"It feels good," she whispered, catching his bottom lip in her teeth, "to have that *fix*, doesn't it, Father?" Her hands grabbed the bottom of his shirt and lifted it, allowing her palms to press upwards against his hairy abdomen. Then, she pulled the shirt over his head, and Fr. Paul raised his arms to allow her.

"Don't go any further," he panted, reaching for her lips again. "Just a kiss. Nothing more."

But their lips met again, and she unzipped his pants. It would be too late if he did not stop her now.

Yet suddenly, Fr. Paul Rinaldi no longer cared.

Groaning, he gave his mind to the control of his body, and he pushed the robe from her shoulders and ran his hands against her skin. It felt so good, to feel a woman again, to get that *fix*. His hands moved everywhere, taking her in, feeling her breasts, her buttocks, everything for which he had longed after taking his vow as a priest. It was everything he'd craved when he saw men walking hand in hand with their wives, their girlfriends, kissing them, embracing them.

And online? Fucking them.

Fucking them while making them bleed.

Fr. Paul turned her over and slammed her against the back of the couch. Roughly, his hand grasped the underside of her knee, and he raised her leg as she pulled down his pants. Their breaths came quickly as he tore at her underwear, ripping them down, lifting her leg again. He was prepared to enter her, but he hesitated, staring at her flushed face and inviting eyes.

There was still time... time to stop and perhaps even save his life as a priest.

"I can't thank you enough for helping me follow my dream," Jerome Nadier said, proudly gripping the seminary books he'd received from Fr. Paul.

Fr. Paul had changed lives. He'd guided other young men and *older* men like Jerome Nadier to the vows of priesthood. He'd seen men *ecstatic* to give themselves to God. He'd watched men *weep* with devastation when they did not fulfill the calling.

And yet here he was, drowning in the musk of a desperate woman who'd managed to capture his pity and turn it into lust.

Please, just stop, he begged himself, as his hand gripped her thigh, and he stared into her eyes. But he couldn't resist the wet warmth between her legs, the soft swell of her breasts against his bare chest.

I'm so sorry, God, he prayed, with a thundering heart.

Natasha bit her lip and dug her nails into his bare hip. "Fuck me," she whispered. "Do it."

Fr. Paul closed his eyes. *I'm so sorry. I'm not strong enough.*

"Do it," she repeated, urgently. "Fuck me, Father."

"Yes, Father, fuck her. It's what you've always wanted, isn't it? If you could choose between the priesthood and your desires, you would choose 'fuck me, father' over 'bless me, father'. So do it. Fuck her. Fuck the devil out of her." The humanoid was relentless. "Did you hear about the people that died? So many poor people. Oh the images... gives you a big erection, doesn't it, Father?"

No, he wasn't like that anymore. Not since his vows. But—

Gasping, his lips took hers with furious lust. For the first time in years, he entered a woman, and his hips responded with that knowledge. His breaths came in quick pants, and Natasha's body swallowed his cock like a serpent's pit as he thrust into her with harsh urgency.

"Come on," she whispered into his ear, meeting his hips with her own, raking her nails over his back. "Get that fix, Father. How long has it been?"

"Too long," Fr. Paul gasped.

Pleasure. Shame. Disgust. Fear.

He felt it all.

The light of the television flashed in the background. An image settled on the screen—a bloody body, a man shot by the government during the riots.

It surged more blood to his cock.

"Harder then." Natasha's lips fell against his ear. She tightened her grasp on his hip and matched his rhythm with her own. "*Harder.*"

"Harder, Father. What are you afraid of, Father? Didn't you write your sermon about fear? What is it you said? Find God's hope within that fear?" the humanoid giggled.

"*Shit!*" Too loud.

He remembered the child in the next room.

That poor child.

He needed to be quiet.

And he needed to pull out.

Oh *God*, he needed to pull out.

But the man lost himself within the serpent's lair, and electrical spasms struck him with ferocious rage. It slammed into his body, an intense reminder that he'd maintained celibacy for a long time. With a yell, Fr. Paul's body stiffened, the veins stood out on his neck, and his seed spilled into her body.

Moist from sweat, he collapsed against her.

Softly, Natasha kissed his cheek, and she leaned back a little. "How did that feel?"

Shameful. Wonderful. Disgusting. Addictive.

Fr. Paul pulled himself from her. "I need you to go to your room. Please."

"A bit too late for that, eh, Paulie?" The humanoid.

Calmly, he stood and pulled his pants back to his hips. His hands shook as he zipped and buttoned his fly.

Natasha closed the robe and slipped from the couch. "Good night," she said softly, and left him to think about what he had done.

And he did.

Good Heavens, he did.

Fr. Paul wept until morning.

And the humanoid remained in his presence until the sun rose.

*   *   *

In the following days, Fr. Paul offered her more money.

Then, she'd give him her body.

Soon, Natasha and her daughter did not leave his home, and Fr. Paul found himself forced to remain diligent in keeping it unknown to his church.

His sermons were dry. Weak. Fr. Paul knew his heart no longer belonged to the Church, but to the homeless woman's body in his home.

The more he paid, the more she'd give.

He knew how the woman used his funding. One day, he found a syringe in the cushions of his couch.

But his guilt rose higher each day.

Fr. Paul soon wept before the altar and begged for forgiveness for all that he had done. He wanted the cycle to end; he felt trapped, ashamed, and alone.

At first, the sex had been thrilling. Now, months later, he could not reconcile his behavior any longer. It was time for a fresh beginning.

"Please, God," he prayed, sobbing as he knelt at the altar. "Forgive me and tell me how to fix this. Help me find a way out. I'm losing this war, and I can't go on without You."

In the quiet sanctuary, as if caught by a draft, pages fluttered at the top of the altar.

Frowning, he stood and approached the altar where the Bible lay open. Wiping his eyes, he bent to read the text on the pages.

The Book of Proverbs.

To his disbelief, the priest watched as a small black line formed beneath Proverbs 11:3.

"The integrity of the upright guides them, but the unfaithful are destroyed by their duplicity."

Fr. Paul glanced around the sanctuary, as if expecting to see the appearance of an angel.

He didn't.

But as he returned his gaze to the Bible, the pages turned. He watched with amazement. As if controlled by an invisible hand, the pages fluttered quickly until they stopped in the book of Revelations.

"What on Earth?" Fr. Paul whispered.

Another black line formed beneath Revelations 3:3.

"Consider how far you have fallen! Repent and do the things you did at first. If you do not repent, I will come to you and remove your lampstand from its place."

"Lord, I *repented!*" Fr. Paul screamed, staggering back from the altar and pulling his hair. "I *repented*. Just hear my prayer... I'll get rid of her. I won't do it again." The tears streamed over his face. His shoulders shook.

The pages fluttered again. Stumbling forward, he almost tripped as he rushed to the altar. There it was again, that little black line that bled beneath the verse.

Romans 2:5: *"But because of your stubbornness and your unrepentant heart, you are storing up wrath against yourself for the day of God's wrath, when His righteous judgment will be revealed."*

With a roar, Fr. Paul swept the Bible from the altar. It crashed to the floor. Crying, the priest buried his head in his hands. He knew what God wanted from him... but he could not accept it. His career in the priesthood would end, and the shame of his actions would follow him for the rest of his life. He had already mentored many promising seminarians, in the States and in Russia, and he was certain his sins would follow him there as well. They would scorn him, mock him, judge him.

No.

Perhaps he'd misinterpreted the scriptures.

Because God would not do this to him. God would not shame him.

But the humanoid would.

Gritting his teeth, he gathered the Bible from the floor and returned it to its original location on the altar. He commenced the sign of the cross over himself, straightened his shoulders, and left the church to remove Natasha and Olivia from his home.

She screamed at him, struck him, spat on him, and destroyed his home. Natasha wasn't beautiful now—her face was sweaty, her pupils were dilated. It made his decision easier.

Nevertheless, it hurt him to see Olivia emerge from his bedroom, clinging to the stuffed bear he'd purchased for her as she watched her crazed mother throw a drug induced tantrum in the kitchen.

"I'm sorry," he mouthed to the little girl, who watched with wide eyes.

Eventually, Fr. Paul alerted the police. On that beautiful spring afternoon, mid-April of 1997, they forcefully removed Natasha and Olivia from his home.

But it was not the last time he would see them.

*   *   *

On a hot day in July of 1997, after his three-mile run, Fr. Paul received a letter from an unknown address. It was written on notebook paper, and the handwriting was nearly impossible to read, but he managed.

And it wasn't good.

"You don't deserve the name of Father, so I am going to call you Paul. I lost custody of my daughter. You're a piece of shit, and I hate you. All you had to do was give me a place to stay. We didn't even have to fuck anymore, if you were that guilty about it. But I have some news for you. I'm pregnant.

I expect help. Believe it or not, I want this baby, especially since you tore Olivia from me. I'll be in contact, Paul, because this isn't negotiable. I will fucking tell your church what you've done. Natasha."

Palm to his mouth, Fr. Paul read it over and over again, hoping the words would change.

They did not.

God's wrath was forthcoming, and he *would* be punished.

He was on his knees again, begging and cursing God, attempting negotiations. No answer came this time. Fr. Paul looked like a crazed man as he drew out every Bible he owned, every sheet of paper in his home, to see if he would receive an answer from Heaven.

It did not come.

Surrounded by his own mess, Fr. Paul sat down on the couch.

Pregnant. *Now* what?

In reality, the whore *could* have been impregnated by another poor, unsuspecting fool who'd merely wanted to help a woman and her daughter.

"Shit," he whispered, clenching his fists under his tearful eyes.

The television flickered in his peripherals. It'd been turned off.

Quickly, Fr. Paul turned his head. The screen went white, and a grey, blurred figure, similar to the shape of the humanoid, appeared on the screen.

"Paul." A deep voice. Commanding.

He blinked.

"Why have you been avoiding God, Paul?"

Had he gone mad? Or had his madness *worsened?*

"I'm *not,*" he cried. "God abandoned *me.* What do you want from me? Who are you?"

The grey figure remained stationary on the screen. "You aren't doing as God has requested."

The priest kicked the coffee table, and its contents fell to the floor. "I made a mistake. I repented, and I removed her from my home." Snarling, he pointed at the television. "I see another figure *just like you.* I don't fucking trust you."

"Paul."

"It's *Father Paul!*" he screamed.

"In Heaven's eyes," the figure said, "you are not."

Fr. Paul fell to his knees. "Then tell me what I have to do."

"You know what you need to do. This is your final warning."

Tears streamed down his face. "Is there any other way? Anything else I can do? Is God going to kill me if I sin again?"

"Paul. You are already at the edge of a cliff. One wrong step, and it'll be over. Your pride is your downfall, and you know it." The figure loomed on the television. "You *know* what haunts your lineage, Paul. You're its prime candidate. God's given you multiple chances in the past, and you've ignored His warnings. Please, listen to Him, or you'll merely be a vessel for what's about to strike this Earth."

"I don't know what you're—"

"*Satan*, Paul, *Satan!*" the figure roared into the television, and its blurred face came closer again.

The priest sobbed on the floor.

Mucus and tears tickled his face and trickled into the facial hair he hadn't trimmed. "I can't do this. This is too much." His eyes shifted to the kitchen knife on the counter.

"Suicide won't save you."

"*Fuck you!*" The priest slammed his fists on the carpet. "Just *make this end!*"

"Right now, you have a choice. Tell the clergy what you've done, and you'll have another chance. You're making this harder on yourself."

"Will the humanoid go away?" Fr. Paul wailed, and he could hear it cackle with glee.

"The demon of Cain is attached to your lineage, Paul. It will never go away, not until Jesus returns."

The priest wiped his eyes and heaved in a breath. "So it will always haunt me, no matter what I do."

Momentarily, the figure didn't respond. Then—

"It is prophesied that it will pass on to your son."

Fr. Paul stared up at the ceiling fan. It spun slowly and cast shadows on the floor. He wished he could hang from it.

"My son?"

The figure didn't respond.

"I'm going to have a son?"

His heart beat within his ears. Never, in his life, had he even considered what it'd be like to hear those words.

Nor did he expect to feel the level of apathy that he did.

But he wanted the humanoid, this *Demon of Cain*, to leave him alone so that he could move on with his life without the disgusting little whispers in his ears. So, with a heavy sigh, Fr. Paul made a decision.

"Okay," he whispered. "I will tell them."

* * *

When Fr. Paul returned to confession, he was asked to speak of his sins. When questioned, he admitted that he'd had sex with a woman. With nausea in his belly, he spoke the words he believed might undo him.

"For months," he whispered. "I slept with her for months."

But he did not mention the child growing in Natasha's womb.

He did not mention the cash he had distributed to her.

And he did not bring up the night she'd told him—

"No!" Natasha screamed. "Get off of me!"

The humanoid did not disappear. The messenger did not reappear. On the brink of insanity, Fr. Paul attempted to talk to his television at least once a day. He demanded the screen to speak to him, to explain to him why the humanoid hadn't left yet, hadn't attached itself to the child in Natasha's womb.

Fr. Paul's life continued as normal—blessing the sick, mentoring new converts, leading services, and giving the sacrament—until December 31st, 1997, around 10 P.M. He awoke to someone pounding on his front door.

"It's Natasha. Open the *fucking door so we can talk!*"

Fr. Paul stood listening to the drumming of her fists. His teeth bared, and his eyes darted to the kitchen knife on the counter—the one he'd wanted to use to cut his own throat.

"We need to *talk*, Paul! Open the door."

Natasha pounded against the door, and Fr. Paul stared at the knife. He cocked his head.

How easy it'd be to open that door, yank her inside, and then drive the knife into her belly again, and again, and again, and—

"*Paul!* I'm having contractions, I need to get to the hospital!"

How convenient. *Now* she was having contractions.

"Don't you open that door," he whispered, and his fingers twitched.

It was cold outside. Snowy. Likely a full-term pregnancy. There was a good chance she was lying, but there was an even better chance that she wasn't.

Which was more sinful? Interacting with the whore? Or doing nothing at all?

"Please..." she was crying now.

"Fuck!" Fr. Paul grabbed his keys, his coat, and flung open the door.

Though reluctant, Fr. Paul drove the screaming woman he'd, *allegedly*, impregnated to the nearest hospital. At first, he screamed back at her, telling her to shut up, telling her it was—

"—your *fucking* fault you're in this much pain!" he roared, reaching into the back seat and planting a hand over her mouth. "*Shut the hell up!*"

The humanoid reclined in the front passenger seat. "Shut the hell up!" it mocked.

"It'll be okay," he said, listening to her cries in the back of the car. He said it, not because he wanted to comfort her, but because he needed comfort himself.

On January 1st, 1998, at 1:05 A.M, the nurse alerted Fr. Paul that the child had been born, and that Natasha was doing well. The priest had fallen asleep in the family waiting room. When the nurse touched his shoulder, he sat up.

"It's a boy," the nurse said. "Congratulations."

"I'm not the father," Fr. Paul said. "Just a helping hand. She's homeless."

Natasha was awake. The infant lay in her arms. Fr. Paul approached the bed and peered down at the swaddled infant on her chest.

Natasha looked up at him, and her hand moved to rest on the infant's head. As if to protect him from Fr. Paul.

That stung.

"Hi," he said, frowning a little.

What had he gotten himself into?

He considered leaving, running away from this drug addict who'd only served him to get her fix, just as he'd served her to get his.

This swaddled infant was a stark reminder to him that he'd only confessed partial truth to the clergy. After discussion amongst the higher clergy, they'd settled on a decision—a warning.

The church members, however, were not aware, and he intended to keep it that way. After all, how could he lead his flock if they did not respect him?

Despite his initial desire to flee, he fell asleep on the cot near the window where the moonlight gleamed against the hospital floor. He was tired, and he wanted to come to an understanding with Natasha before he left her to live her life.

Her life.

Not his.

Something hissed.

Fr. Paul sat up on the cot, and his eyes shifted to the corner of the room. To his disbelief, he saw the humanoid bent over the infant's bassinet. Blood pulsed to his head.

The humanoid straightened up and turned its dark head in the direction of Fr. Paul. "We're a family. We're family, Fr. Paul. What a cute little boy." The humanoid giggled and cocked its head.

Fr. Paul closed his eyes and opened them again, hoping it would go away. It did not. '*Lord Jesus Christ...*'

"—Son of God?" the humanoid giggled again. "There's no point. He left. You didn't do His, um... His bidding! Yes, His bidding. You didn't do it!" The humanoid clapped his shadowy hands.

"God didn't leave," Fr. Paul said, rising to his feet.

The humanoid did a jig. "I know it must have been hard for you... telling the clergy about the dirty stuff you did with Nataaa-shaa."

"I did what He asked of me, I shouldn't have to explain *anything* to you."

"So you confessed to the clergy that you used her? Like a prostitute? That you took church relief funds to wet your dick?"

"I *didn't!*" Rage boiled.

"The more she did, the more you'd pay!" the humanoid sang in a high-pitched voice, clapping his paws again. Suddenly, he stopped and cocked his head. "You know she knew that, right? That the more she did, the more you'd pay? The more drugs she could get in her system?" He tilted his head again. "Coercion, stealing church funds. Isn't that all... illegal? Dreadfully immoral?"

With his fists raised, Fr. Paul's feet thumped against the floor. He swung, but he knew he couldn't harm this demon. He'd tried. His father had tried before him. Before his father, Fr. Paul's grandfather had tried.

The Demon of Cain could not be touched... not with how weak his family was.

"Father," the humanoid said in a raspy voice, slowly cocking his head. "The Boss just wants me to tell you... he'll be here soon."

"Who are you talking to?" Natasha murmured, rubbing her eyes.

Fr. Paul wiped the sweat from his face. "No one. Go back to sleep."

Natasha sat up a little and glanced at the sleeping infant beside her bed. "We should talk."

"About?" But he knew.

If it wasn't the humanoid harassing him, it was this fucking bitch.

"About the note I sent. About the help I need. We can either go through the court system or you can—"

"Let's get this fucking clear." Angry blood roared through his body. He lurched forward, his finger aimed towards her pale face like a dagger. It was time for the fucking understanding. "You're not in charge. I'm going to leave this hospital, and you're going to leave me the fuck alone. Understand?"

Natasha shook her head. "He is *your* child."

"No one will believe a drugged-up prostitute," he sneered, cocking his head as spittle flew from his mouth.

Natasha bared her teeth at him. "Don't test me. I've been in survival mode for *years*. I know how to—"

"I'm *leaving*," he growled. "You can shove your threats where I put my dick the last time we fucked."

He hated this bitch. He hated her child. Suddenly, Fr. Paul knew exactly how his father had felt. He understood *how* his father could have snapped and—

"If you do not give me financial support, I will go to your church." she said slowly. "I will let your church members know *everything* that we did, and that you paid me for it."

"They already know what we did, you manipulative bitch." His knuckles were white from the grip he held on the hospital bed railing. He didn't even recognize himself anymore.

When had he turned into a monster?

When had he become his father?

Natasha was relentless. "Oh? They know you paid me, and they know you have a child?"

"Yes," he lied. "You can't blackmail me."

Tears trickled from her eyes. "Do they know about the night I said no?"

No. He'd never do that. That'd be too far. Wouldn't it? There was no way he had done such a thing.

She'd consented with every interaction. She'd consented when she entered his home. She'd consented when she opened her robe. She'd consented when she took the cash, placed her child in front of the television, and brought him to the room and locked the door.

Yes, he remembered the night she said no, but he'd paid her. It was the most money he'd ever given her, because the donations to the church had grown fatter from the riots. So did his wallet.

"It was a transaction," Fr. Paul whispered, and his eyelids twitched.

"A *transaction I said no to!*" Natasha cried. "You made me bleed, and you *kept going!*"

The blood, yes. He'd struck her mouth and nose until she bled, and then he'd entered her mouth, watching the blood dribble onto his cock like red tears, because it wasn't just her mouth that made him hard.

It was the blood.

"I didn't do anything wrong," he stammered. "I paid you."

"I don't think the church will like *any* of your actions. How will you live that down, Father?" Natasha's voice broke.

Fr. Paul couldn't breathe. He was losing himself again—this time to that rage he hadn't felt in years.

"Do you hear me?" Natasha screamed. "You, a man of *God, raped* me!"

"Ssh! Stop!" Fr. Paul brought a finger to his lips, sweating, his eyes darting to the door in fear someone would enter.

God, or the messenger—*someone* from Heaven needed to step in to save him and tell her she was wrong.

Natasha had placed him on trial in the hospital room, where she'd birthed a son he did not want, and now blackmailed him for money he did not want to give her.

Someone laughed outside the hospital door.

His mind raced. What could go wrong? What could go right? He *wanted* to believe the church would take his side, rather than the side of a filthy drug-addict.

"Shut up," he whispered. "Shut up before someone hears you."

Natasha leaned forward. Hatred twisted her face in reply to his own disgusted leer. The beautiful temptress was now a snake, an ugly serpent who'd taken advantage of a poor priest's help.

"Money," she hissed.

The humanoid sat on the bed next to her, his head resting on his palm. As Natasha extended a hand towards him with greedy expectation, the humanoid cocked his head and did the same.

Yes. He knew how his father felt.

Fr. Paul wanted to kill her.

He closed his eyes, losing the fight to his rage.

"You'll have to fight a lot harder to hide who you actually are, boy," his father said, when he was thirteen. "You and I, we aren't different. We both have the same demons. You'll be tempted differently, I'm sure, but you gotta watch what you do. I know you want to be good. I wanted to be good too. Yet, ya see what I've done?"

With a cigarette between his fingers, Paul's father gestured to his mother, who lay sprawled on the bed with the kitchen knife through her neck.

Paul looked at her with curiosity, fascination, and remorse. He looked at the knife jutting from her flesh—the knife she'd just used to cut the roast for dinner.

Now, after a screaming moment of rage with his father, the woman was dead.

"I don't wanna be like you, Dad," the boy responded. Yet looking at the dead body fueled something inside of him... an urge he had experienced like no other. His fascination turned swiftly—from cars and sports... to death.

"You have no choice, Son. I can't explain it, but this thing that haunts us goes way back. The humanoid I see. The Demon of Cain. You'll meet him." His father flicked ashes onto his wife's body. "Goes back near the beginning of time, probably. Tempted Cain to murder Abel. I guess its reappearance means we're getting closer to that time."

Paul watched the blood drain from his mother's neck. "Closer to what time, Dad?"

The man cocked his head. "The Revelations of St. John. Armageddon." He sighed. "Come on. Help me with this body. We never speak of this again, understood?"

After starting the fire in his home, Paul's father drove him outside of Montana state lines with one last statement on his lips before the murderer never spoke of it again.

"I guess it finally got to my head."

The hospital room grew colder. Was Natasha speaking? Or the humanoid?

"You *think* you are virtuous but you're not."

Natasha. Fuck her. *Fuck* that whore. He was better than this, better than *her*, better than the bastard child she'd just birthed for her own financial gain.

"Excuse me," he said calmly, and left the hospital room. The humanoid followed him. His mind blurred, but he knew what he was doing.

Fr. Paul approached the hospital desk and gestured for the nurses.

"Do me a favor. Please don't disturb us for about an hour. She finally got to sleep." He smiled.

The nurse smiled. "We'll do our best. She needs medication in about half an hour. Congratulations, by the way!"

"I'm not the father," Fr. Paul said coldly, and turned to walk away.

He entered the hospital room, shut the door, and approached the bed.

Natasha watched him. "What did you do?"

He lifted the sleeping infant from the bassinet, rocked him a few times as the humanoid watched, and placed him beside Natasha. "I arranged for you two to take a nap undisturbed." He pulled the sheets higher.

"I shouldn't sleep with the baby. What are you doing?" Panic rose in her voice.

Fr. Paul strode to the other side of the bed and grabbed a pillow from the cot. He came back; a cold grimace masked as an attempted smile. "You'll be fine."

"I can't thank you enough for helping me follow my dream," Jerome Nadier said, beaming like a child on Christmas Day.

Natasha's blue eyes widened. Her mouth opened, and her body jolted to protect herself and the infant. *"Paul—!"*

"It's *Father* Paul," he spat, and slammed the pillow over both the faces of mother and child.

VERSE 2

~AHDAM~

Saturday, January 4th, 2020

Jerusalem Governorate of West Bank

When the boy felt the vibrations, he knew the monsters were in town. He lived less than half-a-mile north of the tiny Palestinian village of Khan Al-Ahmar, and he could often hear the terrifying roars.

His name was Ahdam Kaseem. He was eleven-years-old and mute. His parents, as well as the villagers he knew, did not know why he couldn't speak. Many times, he'd tried, but all that came from his mouth was a little raspy croak. It didn't bother him much, because he was used to it. No one mocked him. In fact, he was the most respected person in the little village. He knew why.

But he could not explain *how*.

Ahdam had an unexplainable gift, but he'd learned to use it for the benefit of the villagers. Near the pen where his father kept the goat, a medium-sized tent stood behind his family's lopsided, wooden shack. Within the tent, Ahdam's father planted seeds for different vegetables, and then Ahdam encouraged the seeds to blossom. It did not matter the time of year, for Ahdam could control the temperature within the necessary area, and the crops grew due to the gradual change in the atmosphere. Once the crop was complete, the other villagers humbly offered what they could in exchange for food.

It made him proud. It made his father, Haleef Kaseem, even prouder.

Most of the villager men worked for a minimum wage in Jerusalem. Their wives traveled a shorter distance to the nearest village in the West Bank to shop at the market. Many were forced to journey on foot for hours. The families did not own vehicles. This was all too familiar for the Kaseem family.

Ahdam's father worked construction in Jerusalem. The boy rarely saw him but, when he did, he never heard him complain. Ahdam could tell that Haleef missed his family, and that the long days of walking to Israeli Checkpoint 300 drained his energy, but Ahdam only ever heard words of praise for Allah and gratitude from his lips.

To Ahdam, Haleef seemed fearless... until the monsters arrived at their village. Only then did the boy see fear in Haleef's eyes, and when Haleef murmured about the monsters to his wife in the flickering lamp fire at night.

On the morning of January 4th, 2020, the vibrations rumbled through Ahdam's cot and woke him up.

He opened his brown eyes, scanned the shack, and noticed the empty cots where his parents slept. He was alone. The morning, grey and dim, peeked through the splintered, wooden shack.

Quietly, he sat up and kicked his thin, lanky legs from the blankets. His black joggers were a size too large, as was his white t-shirt. His body was thin and sturdy, with signs of fast approaching puberty.

Ahdam's tan feet struck the cool, brown earth; he stood up and pulled his arms upwards to a full stretch. Usually, his mother was here at this time to provide him breakfast, but it was Saturday, which meant she'd gone to the market. Ahdam enjoyed those days. Sometimes she'd bring him a flavorful treat. He adored his mother.

So did his father. Ahdam often listened to the words Haleef would whisper to his wife.

"I would move the earth for you, my love."

It was nauseating, those sweet words, but sometimes he couldn't help but grin.

Ahdam moved aside the bolt on the door. He always wondered why their door contained such a strong bolt. The other villagers did not have one.

The wooden door creaked as he stepped outside. The sky was grey, almost white, and the sun hid behind thick clouds. Ahdam cocked his head towards the goat pen and saw his father.

Yawning, the boy's feet padded softly towards the pen where Haleef stood feeding the goat. The man turned as soon as Ahdam approached the wooden enclosure.

"Good morning, Ahdam," Haleef said, and a smile spread across his brown face. His dark, curly beard almost touched the top of his chest. "Did you sleep well?"

Ahdam nodded, but he hadn't forgotten about the vibrations. He gestured his hand in the direction of the town and raised his eyebrows.

Haleef followed his eyes. The smile faded. "Yes. They came back." He leaned against the wooden fence and folded his burly arms, which bulged from the dirty blue shirt he wore. "I pray to Allah that He will deliver us from this madness."

Ahdam looked up at the sky and squinted a little. He returned his gaze to his father, and then to the crops.

Haleef spoke gently. "We will hold our ground as long as we can." He turned his eyes to the walled Israeli settlement almost a mile from where they stood. Atop the hill, its new and modernized housing only brought them the bitter reminder that their little village might be next.

That was why Ahdam feared the sounds and vibrations of the metal monsters. He loved his home—he couldn't fathom its destruction.

Haleef stood up straight and looked at his son. "Would you like to go to the village and take a stand for our neighbors?"

His pulse quickened. With rigor, he nodded.

Haleef climbed over the fence and bent down. There was a look of urgency in his eyes. "Remember what I told you, Ahdam. You do not ever use your gift to harm others. We are not savages, and we will not act as savages. Allah is a God of peace. We do not want to put our family in danger of death, and our country at risk for war. Do you understand?"

Ahdam nodded, but he was confused. He wasn't certain *how* he'd manage any form of attack. He'd only ever produced rain and warmth for the crops, and that by itself exhausted him.

What *more* could he do to harm anyone?

"I mean it. Whatever you see today, you must control yourself. You *must*."

The boy raised his hand, and Haleef touched his palm against his son's. They both nodded in agreement.

It was time to face the monsters, and the warm air turned chilly as they left the area of their home.

* * *

Only fifteen families lived in Khan Al-Ahmar. The town had an oval pattern, and shacks stood side by side.

Ahdam could hear multiple men yelling as he and his father grew closer to the village.

One of the homeowners stood outside of his shack with his wife and two daughters. He was a skinny man with a long beard, and he stood tall, his bony chest jutted out, facing the monster and its driver before him.

Ahdam had heard his father call this monster a "bulldozer", driven by evil men who wanted to tear down people's homes.

With mockery, the construction worker inside of it revved the engine.

"You have no right to be here," the homeowner yelled, angrily raising his fists. "I will not let you take our home!" The man sounded angry, but his face was pale.

Ahdam wondered if the man was sick, or afraid. Both, perhaps.

The loud disturbance brought out the other neighbors. Ahdam followed his father as he walked towards the angry man and the Israeli construction worker.

"You've been given the opportunity to leave," the worker said. "I am here to do my job. Gather your necessities and leave, or everything you own will be destroyed." The engine roared again, and Ahdam shook with fear as the earth vibrated under his bare feet from the monster's scream.

Raising his hand, Haleef strode forward. His large frame, usually intimidating, looked small compared to the orange bulldozer in front of him. "What you are doing is wrong." He gestured to the Israeli settlement in the distance. "Please, I'm begging you—do not destroy our homes on our land. We only want to live here in peace."

The worker leaned forward. His yellow teeth looked too large for his skinny face. "This is not up to me. I earn a paycheck. I have a family to feed too. You've all had multiple opportunities to leave and start life in the land that the government offered to provide for you. What happens now is your consequence."

Ahdam ran his fingers over his short-cropped hair as he watched his father square his shoulders. He admired Haleef, and he hoped he'd grow to have the same courage of his father.

"We won't let you do this," Haleef said, and his fists opened and closed.

Some of the other male neighbors were approaching. Ahdam's eyes scanned the area, searching for an army he knew did not exist.

The construction worker laughed and revved the engine again. With an aggressive thrust of his arm, the worker flipped the bulldozer switch from park to drive. "Move," he said, and he drove forward.

Upon instinct, Haleef and the homeowners staggered away from the bulldozer.

The machine roared to life like a rabid beast, and dust billowed into the air.

With aching horror, Ahdam watched as the monster smashed into the village home. In an attempt to block the high-pitched, blood-curdling screams from the homeowner's wife and daughters, he covered his ears.

He wanted to fight.

Why would his father *bring* him here if he could not fight?

Ahdam's body trembled, and he closed his eyes, but he heard wood splinter beneath the machine, heard the weak pillars collapse.

Perhaps he'd wake up from the nightmare if he opened his eyes.

So he did.

Haleef had his arms wrapped around the villager's body, holding the man back as he kicked, flailed, and shouted.

Ahdam's eyes narrowed. His heart slammed against his chest. Fists clenched, he stood in the middle of the dusty road.

The place erupted in chaos. Several villagers gathered handfuls of small stones and pitched them at the driver, who only reversed the bulldozer before driving it further into the shack.

Haleef, still holding the man, looked at Ahdam. Tears dribbled from his eyes, and it hurt the boy's heart.

It was the first time he'd seen Haleef Kaseem cry.

Something caught his eye—a cloud of dust in the distance—and Ahdam looked ahead. A grey, square-shaped SUV sped towards the village, and sharp, anxious pain tore through his stomach.

The Israeli police.

The police never took their side.

In fact, they escalated things.

His teeth bared, and he growled like a dog.

The government had stolen their crops, their lands, their people, their homes. Ahdam watched as his father clung to the homeowner and mourned with him, and he fought tears as the other neighbors retreated back into their homes.

Ahdam did not blame their retreat, because the police often beat villagers if they took a stand against them.

And yet... did pride not exist anymore?

This was *their* land.

Ahdam feared the monsters. The Israelis did not *fear* peace.

And it was time for them to fear something.

An icy sensation spread over his skin. Cold rage chattered his teeth. He set his eyes upon the approaching vehicle and took short, labored breaths.

The SUV hurtled forward. Dust filled the air.

And then ice.

The vehicle jolted as if it'd struck a wall. Dust particles froze and then suspended in the air like diamonds in space.

And Ahdam couldn't stop it.

He wasn't even sure how he was doing it.

Frost formed on the tires, turning them white, and then thickened to ice and spread over the car. The grey vehicle quickly turned white, and Ahdam's eyes met those of the two horrified police officers inside of the vehicle as the frosty ice spread over the windshield and cracked across the glass until—

"*Ahdam!*"

He went airborne, his body jerked backwards. A large hand covered his eyes. His father's arms surrounded him, and Ahdam's body flopped as Haleef flung him over his shoulder. Ahdam's lanky frame flopped unevenly against his father while Haleef fled the area.

"*Forgive him, Allah!*"

Upside down, the boy opened his eyes. The dusty earth jostled up and down with each monstrous step Haleef took.

And, one last time, Ahdam recognized the monster's roar as it destroyed the remainder of the shack.

Haleef ran the entire way home. When they arrived, he approached the pen and flung Ahdam into the enclosure. The boy's body hit the ground, and he covered his face as he rolled onto his back. He looked up and saw Haleef's looming figure over him.

"You *promised*, Ahdam!" The man cried, glancing to and from the boy as if guarding himself against a possible attack from the police. "Why would you break your promise?"

Tears filled Ahdam's eyes. Sniffling, the boy looked up at his father. Why *bring* him to take a stand if he could not *fight*?

Shaking his head, Haleef pointed to the shack. "You must pray. Pray for forgiveness and swear never to do this again. You could have killed them! What did I tell you?"

Ahdam scrambled to his feet. With shame, he bent his head. How could he tell his father that he hadn't been able to control it?

That it'd just *happened?*

"Never use your gift to harm others, or else it isn't a gift!" Haleef dropped his hands to his sides. His face was sad. "Go pray, Ahdam."

Ahdam followed his father's bidding, but he didn't understand Haleef's panic. Allah, praise be to Him, hadn't done *anything* to help the villagers. Why was he so terrified of using a gift in defense?

And what damage could Ahdam do if he *could* control it?

But Ahdam prayed until his mother, Dina, returned from the market moments later. The boy heard Haleef talking to his mother outside the shack, and he stopped his prayers and prostrations to listen to what they discussed. They spoke in low voices, and he could only hear certain words, but not enough to piece together what they were discussing. When the voices stopped and the wooden door creaked, he quickly returned his forehead to the ground.

"We must talk, Ahdam."

Frightened, he sat up in response to his father's quiet voice. Why did his father sound so grim?

Haleef and Dina stepped into the shack and knelt beside him.

Ahdam scanned their faces. The black hijab covered his mother's silky black hair that he loved to see when she was safe in their home.

But... had she been crying?

He'd betrayed both of them, hadn't he?

"We don't know what is going to happen," Haleef said, his eyes low. "I *pray* it does not come to this, but we may have to take some desperate measures to protect you, Ahdam. You are very special—to Allah, to *us*, but also to the wrong people if they discover what you can do. Do you understand?"

Ahdam nodded. He reached for his mother's hand. The woman looked up, and her dark eyes, normally bright with love and joy, held something else.

Terror.

He squeezed her hand.

Haleef continued, and his voice broke. "I am sorry. I shouldn't have brought you to town. This is my fault, and if the police return, you may need to leave."

Ahdam gasped. He shook his head.

"At least until it is *safe*. Haleef grasped Dina's other hand, but she withdrew it from him and looked away.

Ahdam had *never* seen her do that.

"For today, stay inside. Do not go outside. Understood?" Haleef leaned closer.

The fear sat like a monster on his chest, but Ahdam nodded again. He *knew* he'd gone against Allah's will, as well as his father's, but he'd only wanted to help the other villagers, to avenge the oppressed people within the West Bank.

Haleef had told him to take a stand. The military used their own resources. Why couldn't the villagers use theirs?

How could they take a stand without using their resources? Ahdam knew the system because he *listened*. Recently, villagers discussed the rumor of a recent Palestinian bomber in East Jerusalem, how the man had blown himself to pieces at an Israeli checkpoint. One soldier died, and several others were injured. The village men seemed happy about it.

Ahdam's father had never spoken in such a way. Haleef didn't believe that innocent men should die.

But to Ahdam?

The Israeli government wasn't innocent.

Still, Ahdam dared not go against Allah, or his father, again. He stayed inside for the rest of the day, studied the Quran, and prayed in intervals with his mother.

Haleef worked outside and, on occasion, spoke with other village men in a tone too low for Ahdam to understand. But he heard one thing that made him pause his readings.

The police had left—but they'd promised to return.

His lips trembled, and he clung to the Quran.

Allah was angry.

It was dusk when the Kaseem family had begun to eat their dinner, when Ahdam heard the roar of an approaching engine.

Ahdam's eyes widened.

Haleef lunged to his feet and rushed to the door. He peeked through the crack between the door and wall, and then he turned to his wife and son. As headlights sliced through the cracks of their home, Ahdam caught a glimpse of his father's face.

Pale. It was pale like the homeowner in the village.

It'd never been pale before.

"They're here," Haleef said urgently. "The police are here."

Ahdam felt a lump in his throat. His mother scrambled to her feet. Eyes wide, he lunged up, too. Quickly, Haleef looked through the cracks again as more headlights flashed inside of their home.

"Okay," he said, turning. "Ahdam—"

The door shook as a fist pounded five times against the wood. A man outside yelled in Hebrew. "Police! Open the door!"

Haleef rushed towards Ahdam and grasped his shoulders. "Ahdam," he whispered. "If I tell you to run, you *must run*. Break the back window and go through it. Run as fast as you can. You know the house of Ali Saddam? I talked to him, he knows what to do. You understand?"

The officer slammed his body against the door again. It rattled, and suddenly Ahdam understood why his father had worked so hard to maintain a sturdy home with bolts that none of the other villagers had. *"Police! Open the door!"*

Shaking, Ahdam nodded.

Dina grasped her son's shoulders and pulled him close as Haleef strode towards the door, unlatched the bolt, and opened it.

Ahdam couldn't see the officers, because Haleef's large body blocked the door. The lamp flickered and danced in the shack as his father stepped outside and spoke to the soldiers in a language Ahdam did not understand.

Dina clutched him, and he heard her whisper brush his skin. "I love you, Ahdam, and whatever happens? None of it is your fault."

He wanted to tell her that nothing would happen, that she needn't be worried about anything, but when his father lurched forward with a roar, Ahdam knew something was wrong. Very wrong.

Because his father was not violent. His father only spoke of peace.

Orange flames erupted outside of the shack. Ahdam gasped.

They'd set the tent with the crops on fire.

Dina screamed.

Ahdam froze. Was it time to run yet? Because he couldn't move. He couldn't feel his legs. Where was his father?

"You need to run!" Dina cried, shoving him towards the back window.

Two officers barreled into the shack.

"Ahdam, *now!*" Dina shrieked and flung herself towards the men.

An unexpected gust of wind howled into the shack. The door slammed open and cracked against the wall.

Ahdam grabbed a pot and cracked it against the window. It splintered, but it did not break. With a grunt, he tried again, and the window shattered. Wind screamed into his home, and Ahdam leapt up and flung himself over the windowsill. Glass shards tore his legs as he tumbled to the other side.

Rat-tat-tat-tat-tat-tat! Sharp, popping sounds ripped through the air. Had someone screamed? Or was it the wind?

Overwhelmed with the abundance of sounds, Ahdam landed on his knees. He heard footsteps thudding around the shack. Gasping for air, the boy looked behind his shoulder and scrambled to his feet as an Israeli officer sprinted towards him.

Ahdam grasped a handful of dirt. Flung it towards the officer. It filled the man's face with dust, and he stumbled a little before Haleef tore around the corner towards the Israeli.

"Ahdam!" His father's voice. *"Go!"*

Ahdam ran.

But he looked back.

Haleef landed on his back, and the police officer went down with him. His legs wrapped around the man's neck and tightened like a snake. The officer's legs kicked and flailed, just like the limbs of the villager when Haleef kept him from attacking the construction worker. But that time had been different—he'd been protecting the homeowner.

This time?

His intentions were deadly.

Ahdam scrambled forward. Howling winds knocked him backwards, and he fought to remain on his feet as he sprinted away. Eyes watering, he looked up.

The heavens blackened.

Allah was angry.

Shelf clouds moved fast. *Odd* weather for the climate. Rapid lightning forked across the sky. Again. And again.

And again.

Wheezing, Ahdam looked backwards once more.

His mother's scream tore across the field, but he couldn't see his parents anymore. He only saw police lights and flames that soared through the crops he'd worked so hard to grow.

Ahdam opened his mouth to scream. A strange, gurgling moan came out instead.

It began to hail.

He wanted to run back, figure out a way to save his parents.

But his beloved family had instructed him to run.

So he ran.

His bare feet pounded against the earth, and his chest hurt. The earth blurred and shook as he sprinted across open land, away from his home.

Behind him, doors slammed. Engines roared.

They were coming for him.

Ahdam could run fast, but he would not win against the vehicles.

He prayed to Allah. Thunder responded. Hail spattered the ground, bounced against the surface, and bopped him on the head.

When he looked back, he squinted against the bouncing, oncoming lights from the four vehicles that chased him.

Far above the earth, the angry storm filled the sky. Clouds swirled, and lightning flashed.

Legs burning, the boy tripped and caught himself with the palm of his hand. Gasping, he looked across the open land and realized he was at the mercy of the oncoming vehicles.

Do not look behind you! Ahdam told himself, but he didn't listen.

He looked. And his eyes widened.

Aligned side by side, the vehicles swerved. Above them, three ashen clouds thickened and swirled like pillars of judgment. The cyclones plunged towards the earth.

Ahdam couldn't look away, and he nearly fell.

Debris rocketed through the air. The winds shrieked, as if his mother's screams had combined into bloodcurdling chaos. Lightning surged in jagged lines and reached across the sky like monstrous claws. The ground vibrated beneath Ahdam's feet, and as heat rushed through his body, and his heart rate reached a speed he would have never believed possible, the tornadoes struck.

Allah was angry.

The powerful storm swallowed the atmosphere. Dirt and brush spun into the air.

The boy ran for his life across the broadening West Bank land.

The tornadoes came upon the Israeli police. One by one, the violent, spiraling clouds devoured the trucks. It seized them into the air, and the vehicles spun and flipped before the cyclones spat them out like poison.

Glass shattered.

An officer crashed through a windshield, and the tornadoes sucked him screaming into the whirlwinds.

Ahdam gasped and covered his head.

The vehicles plummeted. They smashed against the earth.

Rolled.

Flipped.

And exploded into fiery rage.

Unsure if he would ever see his family again, Ahdam ran from—

—*his own*—

—Allah's wrath.

And Ahdam Kaseem did not look back until he had reached the home of Ali Saddam.

VERSE 3

~ RECRUIT THOMPSON ~

Monday, January 6th, 2020
Chicago, Illinois

"Are you comprehending my words, Miss Arcelin?"

Tira's eyes snapped back to the man speaking. Her eyes settled on the pristine, red tie beneath his collar, and she imagined the pleasure she'd experience if she wound it around his throat and pulled. It looked expensive, so surely it'd contain enough thread count to strangle him without snapping.

"Miss Arcelin."

"Yes." Tira brought her gaze back up to meet the frustrated blue eyes across the desk. "I'm listening."

It was six in the morning. Jeff Divets, the federal liaison for the DHS, cocked his head and pursed his lips like he didn't believe her. "Do you understand how serious this could get if you don't get your act together?"

Tira almost snorted. Ironic, coming from the man who'd buried three affairs with his secretaries, but she was in enough trouble right now.

She wasn't about to tell him she'd hacked into his personal files.

"I understand," Tira mustered through her teeth.

"Do you?"

"Why do you keep asking me the same question again and again?"

The office belonged to the former Chicago chief of police, a man who'd stepped down almost three years ago after reports of improper conduct with female cadets. It was a cold room, sizable and private, with golden-framed oil paintings on the dark tan walls.

Divets shook his head and tapped his fingers on the desk. "Because your face is telling me that you're giving me the answers I *want* to hear so you can shut me up and leave."

There are easier ways to shut you up, Tira thought, and then smiled briefly. It'd taken a year to be mindful of what Michael called—

"—inside thoughts versus outside thoughts," Michael said, shaking his head. *"A lot of your thoughts need to stay inside. Like in the basement somewhere."*

"I'm sorry," Tira said, and she straightened her black training polo. "I'm not feeling well. I think I consumed a bad batch of chicken."

Divets clicked his tongue. "Mmhmm."

Tira didn't like the way he looked at her. He always had that *gleam* in his eyes—the same one Senator Thompson had in the hotel room.

At least she'd put out that fucking gleam in 2012.

And fucked his son's fiancée two nights ago.

And many nights before that.

Which, unfortunately, was the reason Tira Arcelin was here.

Recruit Matthew Thompson had discovered text messages between his fiancée (Miels) and Tira, and he'd marched straight to internal affairs to tattle on the two of them.

It'd taken two months. Technically one, because the first month had been a confused scramble to determine who'd be responsible for the investigation. After determining that Thompson had marched his complaint to the wrong internal affairs (Chicago PD), the department of Homeland Security took the case and started questioning Agent 4.

"Yes," Tira responded to Divets' initial questioning. *"I fucked Amelia Travis."*

"Can we start over?" Divets said, flustered, throwing aside the pen. *"Off the record—please fucking lie. Don't be so honest. Thompson is powerful, you're necessary to the United States, and I don't need my department under a microscope right now."*

So, annoyed with her entire life, Tira Arcelin had changed her answer.

"We flirted," she said. *"It wasn't anything more than that. I regret stepping outside of my professionalism. It won't happen again."*

But it did. Five more times, to be exact. Twice in the kitchen, once in the guest bedroom, and two times in the SUV. No emotion, no strings—just chaotic sex that wasn't even the best she'd had. But it was a thrill she needed.

Violence was not an option.

And, in unhinged desperation to fill her time, when Tira had returned to the mall to look for Peter the ferret, he was gone.

Adopted. It didn't *surprise* her, because it'd been since January of 2019 that she'd seen Peter. But still—

"Am I free to leave? I have paperwork to do before training." The recruits would kick off their morning with a physical fitness session.

She was looking forward to it.

"Jesus, Arcelin, you're not being detained."

Oh, but if only that were true. She *was* detained—detained in this shithole of an American city while being expected to babysit a self-obsessed, whiny Midwestern girl who couldn't even go a week without pizza or a weekend without alcohol.

Hell, she wasn't detained. She was *in custody*, and she'd become so bored that she'd offered to work road patrol for the Chicago Police Department on weekends.

A *street cop position* offered more excitement than *her top status position under Aleksey fucking Petrov*.

Tira stood up, her tactical pants swishing in response. "I appreciate your time."

Divets didn't stand. He leaned back in his chair and looked at her with slow concentration. "Be careful, Arcelin. Pissing off a Thompson isn't good for you, or for my department. That family's powerful. Look at what happened when the senator died... almost started a World War."

Tira's fingers twitched as she tried to ignore the image of the man crawling towards her in the bed. That's right—the government didn't *care* that the man was a monster.

Nothing a quick cover-up wouldn't fix.

"I'll be careful," Tira said, nodded with curt finality, and left.

Pulling her phone from her pocket, the agent stormed down the hallway and clicked the text message she'd been afraid to read since receiving it two hours ago.

"When your day is finished, little girl, I expect you to call me. I'm not happy with you."

"Fuck," Tira growled, and she burst through the exit door and stomped down the stairs.

This wasn't good.

She'd done so well for the past year. Petrov hardly talked to her, and she liked it that way. It meant he trusted her to do her job, and it meant she didn't have to often listen to his annoying, cocky voice.

But when he called her *"little girl"*? It meant Petrov no longer trusted her to do her job, or that she'd disrespected him in some way.

Or both.

That, itself, wasn't the issue.

The punishment was.

* * *

"Sprint!" Tira screamed.

Footsteps pounded against the turf. There were twelve recruits left in the program, and they all raced across the one-hundred-yard field that stretched across the stale, hot building.

"I didn't say to fucking stop!" Agent 4 spat, pacing the edge of the turf as the recruits stumbled to a stop on the other side. *"Sprint!"*

Gasps, moans, and wails hissed in the air as the exhausted group turned and ran back towards her. Clad in black shorts and neatly tucked t-shirts, the men and women raced with agonized, distorted faces. Spittle misted the air, veins pulsed, and someone dry heaved.

Thompson.

Thompson fucking dry heaved.

"You're just over a month from graduation, and all I see is a bunch of pathetic, undisciplined, pizza-obsessed alcoholics who want nothing more than to allow a goddamn terrorist attack as long as they get their indulgences for the day!" Tira mocked, pacing faster, rage spitting from her tongue as she watched them approach. *"Sprint to the other side!"*

Recruit Eric Carter, the former Chicago PD sergeant, took the lead and raced across the field again. Matthew Thompson followed him, almost at his heels, but vomit exploded from his mouth as he hoofed it to keep on pace with the black recruit.

"Come back to the line and stand at attention!" Tira yelled, straightening her black baseball cap and waiting with stiff impatience. It was 7:59 A.M. The recruits had thirty minutes to shower before changing and meeting Tira and a few other instructors at the range for firearms.

The recruits rushed to the line, adjusted their stances, and stood at attention. Sweat glistened on their faces; their black shirts stuck to their bodies. Most looked pale. The two black recruits, Eric Carter and Annette Kennedy, had reddened cheeks.

Push-ups, sprints, bear crawls, burpees, abdominal work. All reasonable exercises, and yet these recruits acted as though they'd been exposed to torture.

They knew nothing of pain.

Hands behind her back, Tira walked past each recruit. With a subtle snarl, she assessed their faces, their clothing, and their stance. She analyzed their breathing, the way their chests heaved in a desperate attempt to increase oxygen, and she watched the sweat trickle into their eyes, the mucus from their nostrils.

"Who wants to graduate?" Tira asked, her voice quiet.

"We do, Ma'am," the recruits chorused, and their voices echoed.

"Well, I can't fucking tell." Tira stopped at Eric Carter, sized him up, and caught a small grin at the corner of his mouth. She'd deal with him later. Because they'd worked together on the police force and indulged in playful banter, he'd formed the opinion that they were *friends*.

Tira didn't *have friends*. And she never would, because she had no intention of making any.

She moved on to Amelia Travis—the woman whose hair looked and smelled like Olivia, who'd made little effort in preventing the sexual tension that'd fast risen between them. The young woman liked guns, blunt conversations, motorcycles, tattoos, and animals. She'd invited Tira over to her apartment to meet her cats, Rudolph and Reindeer—which Tira thought were ridiculous names for cats—but appreciated how soft and cute they were. That's how it'd started.

She wasn't really Tira's type. Miels had a strong body with little body fat, and her breasts were small. Her ass had been acceptable, the plumpest area of her body, and Tira appreciated her long dark hair and inviting eyes. She'd appreciated the hint of submission, especially in comparison to how Miels treated Recruit Thompson. All of that combined created a logical reason, in her mind, to pursue the brief encounter.

Miels, on the other hand? Slightly too attached. She'd get over it, but Tira owed her a conversation and a boundary.

"No more fucking," she'd tell her, and that would be that.

Without lingering too long in front of Miels, Tira moved forward, analyzing each recruit until she stopped at the very end of the line where Recruit Matthew Thompson stood at attention.

His face looked pale green. Sick. His eyes were red, as if he hadn't slept, and his lips trembled as she looked up at him. He smelled of vomit and lingering remnants of alcohol.

"Are you feeling sick today, Thompson?" Tira hated looking at him. While he had strong features of his mother, she recognized the jawline, the nose, and the eyes of his father.

Senator Thompson's face would be forever sealed in her memory.

Tira hadn't known how to respond to the news of Matthew Thompson's existence, much less that she'd have to train him in the task force program.

"I'm fine, Ma'am," Thompson said through his teeth.

Matthew Thompson had been a recruit who followed her everywhere like a lost puppy, asking her for advice, groveling, desperately trying to prove himself as the best recruit in the program.

Yes, Ma'am. No, Ma'am. Can I help you? Let me run an extra lap for you, do another pushup for you, carry your items, etc.

"*Leave me alone,*" she'd wanted to scream at him. "*Fuck off and leave me in peace.*"

But the recruit hated her now, and for good reason. She'd fucked his fiancée, his *girl*, and she didn't feel an ounce of remorse. He knew that too, and he'd hate her even more when it got out that she'd been cleared from the investigation.

"Are you sure you don't need to go home?" Tira pressed, pausing in front of him and looking up at him with a brief snarl.

She hated Thompson too. Not because he'd come from the loins of a demon (that wasn't his fault), but because he *worshiped* the demon. Swore vengeance for the demon as if he—

"—*was a good man,*" Recruit Thompson had said to Eric Carter one day during defensive tactics and ground fighting. "*My father didn't deserve the shitty investigation they did for him. He was a fucking great man. And I—*"

"—am fine," Thompson croaked, and he wet his lips with the tip of his tongue. Sweat rolled down his neck, where Tira watched his skin pulse from his heartbeat. "Remnants of food poisoning."

Ah yes, a bad batch of chicken.

"Did you consume a bad batch of Vodka?"

Silence hung in the air.

Recruit Thompson twitched, but his stance remained pristine.

"No, Ma'am."

"You're going to scrub that vomit from the turf, you fucking liar," Tira hissed in Spanish, and she stepped backwards.

Agent 4 scanned every recruit. They were all diverse. She'd started with a class of twenty. Six months later, after grueling days of training in physical fitness, defense, firearms, tech manipulation, and scenarios, twelve recruits remained.

"February 15th," Tira said in Arabic, standing with her hands behind her back. "That's the day of your final scenario. It's coming fast, and none of you are ready. So what's your next goal for the next forty days and forty nights?"

"Get ready, Ma'am!" they roared in Arabic.

"Dismissed."

Footsteps shuffled. Recruits jogged to the sidelines to guzzle water and grab their bags. All of them scrambled—except for Thompson.

He stood there, hands limp at his sides, staring at her with glossy eyes.

"What do you need, Thompson?" Tira grabbed her bag and slung it over her shoulder.

He wiped his nose with the back of his hand. "Karma sucks, you know," he said hoarsely, and his lips trembled.

What was he on about now? What an idiot.

"I'll be fine," she said, and shrugged. "And maybe if you weren't so overly sensitive, you'd be fine too."

A growl came from his throat, and his eyes glistened as if he were about to shed tears. "Fuck you," he murmured, low enough so that only she could hear him.

Your father wanted to. He bled out on my bed.

Tira wanted to say that. It'd almost slipped out. But, with a smile that was anything but gentle, she said—

"Get in line. You're not the first to want to."

And Tira walked away, shaking, to keep herself from gutting him like his father.

* * *

After a day of firearms and defensive tactics, Tira Arcelin spoke with Recruit Travis in the well-lit women's bathroom and advised her that they could not, and would not, have sex anymore.

"Is that all it was to you?" Miels asked, pouting a little and coming forward with amorous eyes. "Just sex?"

"Yes. What else would it be?"

"Friends with benefits? Sounds a bit more meaningful, at least."

"There was no meaning to it."

"But I like you."

"I do not like you," Tira deadpanned.

"And that's *exactly why* I like you," Miels giggled. "It's sexy when you tell me you don't like me, and then you fuck me. Won't you miss that?" She came closer. "Fucking me?"

Tira's face warmed. The bathroom was very hot. "Stop."

"I'll miss your tongue," Miels sighed, her bottom lip protruding.

Tira waved her off. "Your fiancé has a tongue. I know this, because he blabs too much and disrespects everyone around him."

Miels shook her head and sighed. "I don't think this marriage is going to happen. He hasn't un-proposed though."

This wasn't important to her. "Get better with your pushups," Tira said, and backed away. "They're pathetic."

It was grey and windy when she left the old KS Industries recreation center. The agent took the long way home.

Tira never took the long way home.

But Petrov awaited her call, and she didn't want to talk to him. It brought a gurgling sensation so sharp in her gut that she wondered, for a moment, if maybe she *had* consumed a bad batch of chicken.

"Shit," Tira whispered, and she stopped at a red light near *Caravan's Books*. Gripping the steering wheel, she turned her eyes towards the store.

Wearing a black, long-sleeved dress that touched her knees, Esther Caravan turned the sign from *Open* to *Closed* and exited the bookstore. With her arms folded, she approached the crosswalk and looked both ways. The wind combed through her loose hair, and Tira realized just how long and wavy it was as she walked past the agent's SUV.

Agent 4 tilted her head.

How could a girl so chaotic be so graceful?

The way she turned her head to check for traffic. The way she walked, calling attention to her hips as they swayed in that form fitting dress.

Tira tilted her head the other direction.

She wondered what Esther's hips looked like during dance practice, how her butt might look while she worked out, and, by the look of it, she'd need a significantly large bra size to contain the breasts she had if she were to do any activities that contained bouncing or—

Bwooonk!

A semi-truck horn.

The light was green.

"Go fuck a horse," Tira snapped in Russian, slamming on the gas and squealing forward.

But the agent still looked.

As the wind caught her hair and blew it across her face, Esther Caravan glanced towards the commotion.

She looked sad.

Very sad.

Tira stared in the rearview mirror and watched her subject step to the sidewalk. A young man with blond hair stood waiting for her, and Esther's fingers locked with his before the traffic shielded them from Tira's view.

Gabe Donovan.

She was dating Gabe Donovan, her best friend.

But Tira didn't think Esther had completely moved on from Mariel Nadier, because she still cried on some nights—and those were the nights Tira turned off the sound.

But Mariel's death meant she had one less person to monitor in Esther's presence.

That being said, Jacob Caravan hadn't been an issue since she'd mowed him down a year ago. Since then, he'd been in and out of jail. When he wasn't in jail, he wandered around his neighborhood or stayed at home. Even though he wasn't currently a threat, she'd considered getting rid of the old man to prevent future problems. But—

"You're chasing dopamine, kid. Don't fix what ain't broke. Jacob isn't bothering any-one," Michael said, chewing something crunchy over the phone again.

"What do you mean, 'don't fix what ain't broken'?" Tira snapped.

"What ain't 'broke'."

"But I did break him," Tira cried, confused. *"I broke his leg! I don't want to fix him, I want to kill him, Michael, are you drunk?"*

Eventually, he'd explained that it was another one of his sayings, and that he didn't think it'd be a wise idea to kill Jacob if he wasn't a threat anymore.

"Well, just say that then," Tira replied before ending the call.

When Agent 4 arrived home, she set her phone on the counter and prepared a venison steak for dinner. While it cooked on low heat, Tira shook out her hair and walked to the double doors that led to the terrace. Sighing, she pushed aside the curtains to look at the city.

And she thought of Olivia.

Tira wasn't sure *why* she thought of Olivia, but she did, and it wasn't the first time. In fact, she'd grown used to the dull ache in her chest whenever she thought about their last interaction. It still irked her, and she didn't want it to anymore. She wasn't sure how to make it stop.

Was that like *guilt?* The feeling that subhumans experienced?

Tira combed her fingers through her hair. It was normally silky and fun to play with, but it was tangled tonight. If Olivia were here, she'd offer to brush it.

Tira's eyes widened.

Did she *miss* Olivia?

Her head hurt now. She thought of the times Olivia managed to get her to crack a smile, or stuck food in her mouth, or begged Tira to spoon her in bed after having sex.

Rubbing her forehead, Tira wandered back to the kitchen to check her venison. Juices bubbled, lazily popping around the steak as the agent stood alone in the large kitchen.

Okay.

She did miss Olivia's company. In fact, sharing the venison with her would be nice, and it'd take her mind from the reminder that she still had to call—

Her phone buzzed in rhythmic vibrations, and Tira's heart lurched in her chest when she looked at her watch.

Petrov.

"Shit," she spat, and she stormed to the island where her phone lay.

Why didn't the man ever sleep in? It wasn't like he *did* anything productive anyway, despite his constant air of superiority. If anything, he was one of the laziest men she'd ever known, simply because he didn't *have* to do much anymore.

Why would he work when loyal slaves worked for him?

God, she wasn't in the mood. So, with a frustrated sigh, Tira answered the phone, put it to her ear, and exhaled. "*What*, Papa?"

Silence. And then—

"Watch your fucking mouth..." Petrov growled, "... you entitled little *cunt*."

Tira sat on the stool, closed her eyes, and tried to relax. "Yes, Papa."

It bothered her to submit.

No, it *destroyed* her. But she had to.

Because even though *"little girl"* was bad, *"little cunt"* was worse.

"Are you alone?" Petrov demanded.

"Yes." The venison would burn.

"Good," the president said, and his voice was dark. "We need to talk about your status in Chicago."

Verse 4

~ Closure ~

Monday, January 6th, 2020
Chicago, Illinois

In the city of Chicago, across from Buckingham Fountains where many tourists lingered, there was a walkway called Lakefront Trail. Alongside the tossing waters of Lake Michigan, it ran just over eighteen miles. Sometimes, in the morning before class, Esther Caravan ran three to five miles on this trail. She loved watching the sunrise.

Tonight, the sun had already set when she sat on a bench that overlooked the lake. It was warm for a January evening, and, as the wind tugged her brown hair, Esther watched Lake Michigan's choppy waters.

Her phone buzzed.

Another Facebook message.

Groaning, she turned it over, as if it'd make the message go away. Lately, she'd been bombarded with online messages that annoyed her.

"Congratulations!"

"Oh, you two are so cute together!"

Normally, she did not mind the attention, but last week was different. Being online, especially on January 1st, reminded her that she hadn't wished Mariel a happy birthday on Facebook for the first time in years.

When Esther thought about him, she felt sick. Other times—angry. Most often? Guilty.

She wasn't sure why. Logically, Esther knew it wasn't her fault he'd committed suicide. In fact, she now understood her father's protectiveness. Still, a lingering, torturous thought kept her up at night.

What if she'd said something different?

What if she'd asked him the right questions?

What if she'd not *fucking* missed breakfast with him last year when she'd awakened in Gabe Donovan's bed?

What if *that* day had been the day he'd needed her the most?

God, she could fucking handle the anger. She couldn't handle the *guilt*.

And knowing Mariel? It would *be* like him to reject her right before committing suicide. That was worse. She would have preferred him hate her so she could just fucking move on from the goddamn guilt.

The water slapped against the rocks.

Esther wiped her eyes with her palm and sniffled.

It tore her to pieces, but watching Fr. Jerome's attempt to lead a church while mourning the loss of his son was *unbearable*.

Esther still attended the service, primarily to see Fr. Jerome. It was also to keep her father from breathing down her neck, because Todd believed it was their Christian faith that had brought about Hawk's unexplained healing last year and hadn't missed one service since then.

Maybe he was right... Esther didn't know. She supposed she'd never know, because no one had bothered to talk with her about it. She'd considered talking to Fr. Jerome, but it seemed disrespectful since nothing had mysteriously healed *his* son.

So she settled on "scientific anomaly" as her answer and moved on to worry about other things.

Like her father's growing heart issues.

And the fact that she was *fucking dating Gabe*.

The phone vibrated again.

"Oh, you two are so cute together!"

Esther turned off the volume.

How the fuck had that happened? She wasn't in love with him. She *loved* him, but her heart didn't beat the way it had when she looked at Mariel. She wondered if it ever would.

Now her *dad* was happy about it. Gabe represented the nice, white American boy raised in a conservative family of faith.

Oh, and rich.

Definitely rich, considering his father—Senator James Donovan—was now an official candidate in the Republican primaries for president of the fucking United States.

But none of that was Gabe's fault. Despite still feeling a bit used from their accidental fuck last year, Esther recognized that Gabe could actually be very sweet, attentive, and warm. He'd also apologized for last year's incident, to which she'd replied—

"We promised we'd never bring this up again. So don't."

Ultimately, she was content. Being content was okay, because it meant she wasn't miserable. Misery led her to do stupid things—like drink too much and end up dating Gabe.

That was mean.

But things were fine. She'd be fine.

This was healthy for Gabe too, probably. He'd mourned with her, one of the only people in her life who genuinely understood the loss she felt. Mariel had been his *"beloved bro"*, his *"ride or die"*, his *person,* and losing him had destroyed the young man's joyful demeanor. It'd taken him a long time to recover.

During that time, they bonded.

One evening, while the two of them discussed childhood memories of Mariel, Gabe kissed her.

Esther kissed him back. She didn't know why, and she'd pulled back with an *odd* feeling that she'd just betrayed Mariel, that she'd just committed an unforgivable sin.

So, for a while, she avoided Gabe. Eventually, after weeks of phone calls and texts, she agreed to go on one date with him.

Just one.

But the dates continued. Then, last week, Gabe announced their relationship on Facebook.

Thus began the messages of support.

"Oh, you two are so cute together!"

Yes. She was content, and content meant she wasn't miserable.

"I made it, Babe!"

Esther heard shuffling footsteps behind her, and she glanced back. Gabe came around the bench with a goofy grin on his face and two hot chocolates in his hands.

"I asked for double whipped cream on yours, and they sprayed so much the fuckin' lid wouldn't close. So, I might've licked some of it off." He handed her the cup, sat beside her, and slurped from his own lid.

"Thank you."

Gabe slipped his arm around Esther's shoulders. "You okay, Babe?"

Cold, Esther shivered and leaned into him. His thumb brushed her shoulder. "Just thinking about Mars."

Slowly, Gabe nodded, and he was silent for a while. Then, softly, he spoke. "You know, I miss him too. A lot."

"I know." Tears fell again. Quickly, she brushed them away. "Sorry."

"I know how you felt about him, Hon, it's okay. I knew what I was getting into." Gabe kissed the top of her head and allowed his face to linger against her hair. "But I want to tell you something, because I need to be honest too." His voice was a murmur.

"Gabe, don't. Please."

"I love you."

Fuck.

Esther stood up. She clutched the cup in her hands and walked closer to the railing that separated them from the lake. Breathless, she focused on the waves as the wind tickled her face, and then she closed her eyes.

Damn you, Gabe.

She felt him close again, heard his voice.

"Esther, I mean it. I don't expect you to say it back."

Awesome. She felt like she was in the middle of some young adult soap opera.

After a moment, she turned to face him and leaned against the railing. "I know you don't, Gabe. I'm not ready. I'm *really* not." Esther stopped talking as an elderly couple passed them. "And now I feel guilty and pressured."

He leaned his forehead against hers. "I get that," he whispered. "I want you, Esther, I've wanted you for a long time. Having you as my girlfriend... I can't begin to express how fuckin' lucky I feel. I'm so *damn* happy you're with me, and I'm willing to wait for you to feel exactly how I do."

Something about that seemed *terrifying*, as if she'd stepped into a hole she'd never escape.

Did she even *want* to love him?

Or did she want to move on from Mariel Nadier?

The tall, quiet, dark-haired man still lingered.

He always lingered.

"May I kiss you?" Gabe asked.

"Please do."

He brushed her hair behind her ear and then bent towards her. Esther closed her eyes as his lips, sweet with cocoa, searched hers. She enjoyed the taste, and she touched his lips with her tongue to savor it. It was cruel, and she knew it, because—

"*Esther*," he whispered against her mouth. "This is excruciating for me. I don't know how much longer I can go without touching you."

She hadn't done *anything* sexual with him. The most she'd allowed was making out. *I want to wait until I'm sure*, Esther had told him on their third date.

And it wasn't because she wasn't horny. Good lord, she was horny. But it didn't feel *right*, and she couldn't just spread her legs for someone conveniently available.

And Gabe was conveniently available.

But before anything could happen with *anyone*, she wanted closure. *Something* to help her move on from Mariel.

But she couldn't *tell* Gabe that. Fuck, that'd be mean.

Gabe took her face in his hands and looked down at her. Suddenly, he grinned. "I'll even wear a condom this time." He squished her cheeks until her lips pursed like a fish.

Laughing, Esther pushed him away and stepped past him. "You're a dumbass."

Gabe sniffled and wiped his arm over his nose. "Welp." He looked at his hand and chuckled. "It's you n' me, buddy. She's gonna make you do all the work."

"Shut the fuck up, Gabe. Let's go."

* * *

Esther settled into her bed, comfortable now in her t-shirt and burgundy pajama pants. But she wasn't ready to sleep. Instead, she lay in the darkness with her hand beneath her cheek.

Then she reached for her phone on the nightstand and tapped Fr. Jerome's contact icon.

She hoped he'd not think that she was selfish.

After the fourth ring, Esther heard the old man's voice, tired but nurturing. She *loved* his voice. It was soothing, kind, and clear. In fact, she'd told him once that he should be a narrator

"Hello, Esther."

"Hi, Father Jerome. Is this a bad time?"

"Of course not. What can I do for you?"

Esther rolled onto her stomach and turned her head to stare at the wall as she held the phone to her ear. "I feel really selfish for this. I don't want to hurt you, or bring up the past." Her voice cracked.

"Esther." Fr. Jerome's voice was quiet, sincere, and gentle. "You can talk to me about Mariel. I don't mind."

It was either the sound of his voice, or his mention of Mariel, that broke the dam. Her voice shook; tears trickled.

"I'm really, *really* struggling with closure. I just need to know if, um... if Mars ever talked to you about me. I—I need to know—"

"Mariel loved you, Esther."

A sob broke through her throat.

For a moment, silence fell between them, and then the priest continued. "He has always fought... his own demons. Mariel was afraid that these demons would get in the way of your happiness. You know?" The priest's voice shook too. "The love that boy had for me, and *you*, and Gabe... enormous, Esther. It was enormous. And I miss it."

Esther could not stop crying. "I'm sorry. I'm so sorry. It was selfish of me to make you talk to me about this."

Fr. Jerome took a wavering breath. "Please don't apologize. I've had no one to talk to for a while. I needed this. You're my daughter, Esther, and Mariel has always loved you. I hope that gives you peace."

It did not give her peace. It gave her pain. *Turmoil.*

And she'd *known* it would hurt more to find out he actually cared. God, she was an idiot.

"May I make a suggestion to you, Esther?"

Sniffling, she nodded as if he could see her. "Yes."

"When I need to find peace or express my feelings in a way other than prayer, I write. Maybe write to Mariel? Tell him how you feel? Tell him goodbye."

How could that man be so composed?

Wiping the tears from her face, Esther rolled onto her back again. She'd thought about that idea, but hearing it from someone who busted at the seams with wisdom solidified it. "I think you're right. I couldn't bring myself to tell him happy birthday on his Facebook page like everyone else did, but I think a personal note would help." She closed her eyes. "Father Jerome, I *love* you, and I truly appreciate this and *everything* you do for me."

"You're welcome, Esther. Love you too, hon. Get some rest, okay?"

After she ended the call, Esther opened Facebook Messenger and searched for Mariel's name. For a moment, she stared at his profile picture and lived in the memory from two years ago.

"Hop on, Dad! Piggyback ride!" Mariel laughed in the church sanctuary. Candles from the Easter service flickered behind them. The light danced on his long black hair. "You said if I went without energy drinks for Lent, you'd do this."

Fr. Jerome let out a sigh. "I'm going to break a hip."

"Hurry up, I want to take a picture, and I need to pee," Esther said, raising the phone in the air. "Say 'Christ is risen!'"

Almost tripping on his vestments, Fr. Jerome climbed onto Mariel's back, gripped his neck, and they both exclaimed—

"Christ is risen!"

Esther snapped the photo.

"Fuck," she cried, and emotion crushed her chest.

Mariel had been so... *alive.*

After allowing herself more tears, Esther wiped her arm across her face and then began to type a message to Mariel.

"Hey Mars, I can't let you leave me like you did... not without expressing my feelings. I need closure, and remembering the last thing you said to me hurts like hell, but I think I understand why you did what you did, and said what you said. You wanted me to be happy, and you were afraid you'd ruin that. But I feel like I didn't know you at all, because you hid something from me that maybe I could have helped clarify, or worked through with you. Maybe it would have scared me away as a potential partner... but you'd be alive. You'd still be with your dad, with Gabe, and I doubt it would have been so bad that we wouldn't have maintained friendship.

But I'm angry that you didn't give me the chance to make that decision for myself. I'm angry that you thought your unhappiness would make me miserable.

Mars, I am stronger than you gave me credit. I wanted to make you happy, and you didn't allow me that chance. I wish you would have trusted me. I loved you so much, and I still do. It hurts to think about you, but I don't want it to hurt anymore. When I think of you, I want to remember your smile, your eyes, and how full of love they were. So I am leaving you with this: I hope you found peace. You deserve it, Mariel. I wish we could have been together. I wish you would have told me what you were feeling, and why you were in such pain, because I don't think it would have pushed me away. I think it only would have made me love you more. Sweetheart... I will see you again soon. Until then, I love you. Happy belated birthday, Mars. Love, Esther."

With a trembling thumb, Esther sent the message. She turned off her phone.

Soon, after tears moistened her pillow, she fell asleep. In her dreams, she stood near the railing that overlooked Lake Michigan. This time, her forehead touched Mariel's, and as he bent closer, he whispered in her ear.

"Esther," he said. *"Thank you."*

And, for that moment, she felt peace.

Verse 5

~ Fire Alarms ~

Monday, January 6th, 2020
Chicago, Illinois

"What the *hell* are you doing over there, Tira?" Aleksey Petrov roared over the phone. His voice vibrated the speaker.

The venison hissed. Juices popped. And smoke filled the air.

"I am doing my job," Tira said. "Just like you asked." The man caused her more headaches than the recruits and the *Caravan Reality Show*.

"Internal affairs? Not your job. Fucking around with a Thompson is also not your *job!*"

"Well, technically, I fucked his fiancée, Papa, not him."

The other line went silent.

A deep, smoky haze drifted through the kitchen.

Then the fire alarm went off.

Beep. Beep. Beep.

"Tira," Petrov growled. "If you don't drop your *fucking* attitude, I will bring you back to Russia where I will marry you off to Dr. Sovonov, and you can learn to *fuck* him since you like fucking so much. Then maybe you'll stop *fucking me* over since you'll be put to *better use!*"

Petrov was screaming now.

The smoke triggered the alarms in the other rooms, and Tira slid from the stool and stomped towards the stove as her ear chafed against the phone. Sinking her teeth into her lip, the agent turned off the stove, turned on the fan, and waved her hand around the smoke as if it'd stop the alarms.

"What is that god-awful noise?" Petrov snapped.

"Fire alarms."

"I *know* that, but why?"

Because some of us have to cook for ourselves, your majesty, Tira thought, opened her mouth to say it, but stopped. "I am cooking."

"Well, turn it off so I don't hear that goddamn sound while I'm trying to have a conversation with you."

Jesus Christ.

Was he menstruating? Pregnant?

The alarms faded as Tira stepped onto the terrace and closed the glass door. The cold air brushed her hair while she stood in the darkness and leaned against the railing. Her stomach hurt, and her chest felt tight as she slipped her fingers into her hair and pulled it at the top of her scalp. "I'm listening, Papa."

"Good, now listen to me *closely*. You are in a position of your dreams. If we lose asylum in the U.S. because you're playing stupid games and calling attention to yourself, you'll not only lose your status as top agent, but you'll lose your fucking life. I'll kill you myself," he hissed. "No one will remember who you are."

Tira rolled her eyes. It wasn't untrue, considering only those in close, political quarters knew of her. He'd done a good job keeping her life under the radar.

She liked it that way. It gave her a sense of agency, even if false.

"Okay," Tira said, her voice calm.

"This isn't a game. The Thompsons are a political dynasty in the U.S. The Donovans? Related by marriage. The *Ayres?* The family who owns an entire business community in Chicago? Related by marriage. These are American politicians, little girl, they breed, and breed, and breed, so that they can gain an *edge* of what I've had in the last twenty-plus years."

God, the man droned on and on.

Was he also applying eyeliner in front of the mirror while he blabbed?

"...understand what that means?" Petrov's voice faded back in.

Tira's grip tightened on her hair. She was about to scream. "Yes, I understand."

"But do you understand that *pissing them off* raises the potential of losing asylum? Putting *my* organization under the spotlight? I need someone to *fucking* watch my asset over there, Tira, and Michael can't do it forever."

"Okay," she said, grinding her teeth.

"And I've already cleaned up your 2012 mess," Petrov added. "I'm not about to clean up another."

"Understood." Tira extended her middle finger and closed her eyes. "Anything else?"

"Yes. How are things with the asset?"

Tira opened her eyes, and her gaze followed a distant car. The asset. By definition, things were *fine*. Logically, Petrov didn't care about how often the asset cried, or how often she drank, or how unhinged her dating life appeared to be. So yes. Things were—

"Fine," she said, and realized the fire alarms had turned off. "She appears to be healthy."

"Is she, or is she not?"

How the hell was she supposed to know?

"She *is healthy*," Tira sighed. "I've had no need to make contact with her other than when I ran her grandfather over with my motorcycle."

"You what?"

"Did you not read that report? I sent it to you."

Had she? She couldn't remember. Fuck.

But Petrov laughed. "When did this happen? I'm sure the report is on file, but I've had my hands tied. I don't get around to leisurely reading too often."

Tira relaxed a little at his laugh. "Almost a year ago. Jacob Caravan attacked her. I ran him over with my motorcycle, and he went to jail."

"Esther never saw your face?"

"Nope. I had a helmet on."

"Hmm. Well done. I rather miss those thrilling days from my younger years, I won't lie."

Oh, *now* he wanted to chit-chat?

What ever had she done to bask in the everlasting glory of Aleksey Petrov?

"I need to go," Petrov said. "Reports are coming in of possible protests near the Kremlin. Apparently they don't like the security and stability act I signed into law." He laughed, and then his tone darkened. "I hope I can trust you to get your shit together."

Tira almost laughed. Instead, she pulled open the glass door and entered her smoke-hazed home again.

Could he?

She wanted to tell him yes, that *of course* he could trust her, but she wasn't even sure she could trust herself.

Even a year later, Tira hated it in Chicago. Even a year later, she was still bored, chomping at the bit to find pleasure in something—*something* to remind her that she hadn't endured years of physical and psychological torture, only to be placed in this position for an *unknown length of time.*

Agent 4 certainly hadn't forgotten about Michael's years of service for *Project Caravan.*

Double. Fucking. Digits.

Double digits of domesticated life, beer, and fat-inducing boredom.

So Tira opened her mouth to say *no,* to tell the most powerful man in the world that she couldn't be trusted and that she wanted to go home. She opened her mouth to tell him that she'd serve in the military again, that she'd cook for the men, because at least *there* she'd have the *possibility* of rising in the ranks through diligence and reliability.

The military members were nothing like politicians. As a child, she'd stood before them, commanded their drills, and they'd respected her—not because she had a voice, not because she belonged to Petrov, but because she could do what they did.

Tira Arcelin had a fucking *purpose.*

Here?

She had none.

But Agent 4 didn't tell him no.

Because Tira wouldn't end up in the military. Her father would do *exactly* as he promised—strip her of her status and throw her into a room with hungry wolves.

Then... she'd kill them all.

And Petrov would kill her.

Here?

She had some agency—a false sense of freedom. So—

"Yes," Tira said, and tossed the burnt venison into the trash. She wasn't hungry anymore. "You can trust me."

VERSE 6

~ THE DUMPSTER MAN ~

Someone screamed. Something was burning.

Flames kissed his skin. The heat bit deep, but the stench was worse—thick, rancid. Rotten eggs. Fish. *Cat litter*.

Sharp objects prodded his back. His twisted legs sank into a gooey surface. Something else crinkled beneath his arm.

Nausea shot through his stomach.

Then—more screams. Squealing tires. Shouting. Wind howling through unseen cracks.

Somewhere, as if in protest, powerful voices chanted with rhythmic passion, but he couldn't open his eyes.

Couldn't move.

Why couldn't he move?

A fresh burst of fire scorched his arm. Something sizzled next to his ear.

Open your fucking eyes.

Maybe he was in Hell. It'd make sense.

After all... he'd died.

He'd died.

His breath hitched. A wheeze rattled out of his lungs. His body jolted back to life—like an engine that finally turned over.

And his eyes opened.

He screamed.

Not at the fact that he was in a dumpster.

But because a man lay beside him in flames, and his face drooped as it melted like wax.

Oh, thank *God*—it wasn't a man. Its torso was lined with angry red letters that warped in the heat.

The dumpster man didn't process this.

He rolled away from the flames.

Shit, his legs were twisted. Angled wrong. Bent against the metallic wall as if he'd been stuffed in a box too small.

Trash shifted and sank beneath him as he shrieked, clawing at the dumpster's edge. He looked up, staring at the grey sky like a drowning child at the bottom of a pool. Snowflakes fluttered, kissing his nose.

Flames and sparks burst upward.

The dumpster man reached for the edge.

And pulled himself out of the burning pit.

Blistering cold wind burned his face.

The shouting grew louder.

The dumpster man tumbled out. His back cracked against icy cement. Freezing temperatures stabbed his fingertips like needles.

Someone yelled.

Footsteps pounded past his head.

Someone trampled his chest.

He swatted at their legs, rolling back toward the dumpster. His forehead smacked metal.

Then—he heard them.

More footsteps. Rushing toward him. Storming against the cement. Angry, rhythmic roars. A language he didn't understand. He only comprehended the syllables, shouted in thunderous waves that suggested a stand against injustice.

"*Yeb-ty...*"

"*PETROV!*"

"*Yeb-ty...*"

"*PETROV!*"

The dumpster man sat up, arms raised in defense. He first saw dirty, icy cement. Shattered glass. Burning debris. And several feet away—

Someone's hand. Charred and blistered. A wedding band.

"*Yeb-ty...*"

"*PETROV!*"

Horrified, his eyes widened.

"*Yeb-ty...*"

"*PETROV!*"

Smoke billowed. Flames roared. Debris shattered. Cars burned; bottles rolled.

The dumpster man struggled to get to his knees, and glass tore through his pants. His suit pants.

He was in a *suit*.

"*Yeb-ty...*"

"*PETROV!*"

In front of him, masked people swarmed in hoards, like fire ants crawling from a disturbed nest. Fists pumping.

"*Yeb-ty...*"

"*PETROV!*"

The dumpster man wobbled to his feet and gasped. The cold air stung his lungs.

Someone swung a bat into a building door. Glass exploded.

"Help," the dumpster man groaned, rubbing his eyes, staggering towards the oncoming protesters. He didn't even mean to—his body just *moved*, and it collided against a masked man who stared not *at* him, but *through* him.

"Yeb-ty, Petrov! *Fuck you!*"

English. Thank goodness, *English*.

Fuck you, Petrov.

That's what they were chanting. But who was Petrov?

"Help me," the dumpster man cried, but the crowd knocked him forward, forcing him to move their direction. Their chants—

"*Yeb-ty...*"

"*PETROV!*"

—shuddered the earth, reverberated through their bodies, and vibrated against the dumpster man as he fought to maintain control in the surging crowd. He was taller than many, but it didn't matter.

"*Wait—!*"

Thick smoke filled the air. A protester slammed into the dumpster man, and he staggered, grabbed at someone's jacket, and then fell to his knees. Legs shuffled around him. A banner lay torn beneath the angry mob—a suited man with devil horns.

"Get up, hurry!" A voice hissed in English, and strong hands grabbed his shoulders and helped him to his feet. "Move with the crowd."

"*Yeb-ty...*"

"PETROV!"

The dumpster man glanced around. He could not find the voice. Shivering, he faced the same direction of the crowd and stumbled forward.

Then—he saw it.

Their target.

A grand building—surrounded by gates. Majestic. Tall. Almost surreal in its power.

Recognition clicked.

The Kremlin.

"Yeb-ty..."

"PETROV!"

Sirens sounded, warnings from the skies that shrieked upon the crowd like judgments.

Dogs growled.

Fuck.

Aligned in perfect formation, law enforcement officers held the line. Pants tucked in boots. Legs spread. Shields elevated. Officers held leashes; shepherd dogs lurched, growled, and snapped at their ties. Barked. Fogged the air. Foamed at the mouth.

"Yeb-ty..."

"PETROV!"

"What's happening?" The dumpster man cried, hoping the English speaker would respond. He didn't.

A dog strained on his leash.

Glass shattered again.

Bottles whirred through the air, bouncing against shields before clattering to the ground. A bundled protester pushed past the dumpster man, a bat over his shoulder—he charged the police, his feet slamming against the cement.

"No, don't—" the dumpster man cried, staggering to keep balance against the crowd's push.

The mob drowned his cry.

An officer withdrew his firearm.

The protester swung the bat.

The gunshot—it was a brief sound. It cracked above the sirens. Echoed through the chanting.

And the bullet pierced the protester's skull. He crumpled, and the bat clattered as he collapsed.

The dumpster man gasped.

Blood pooled.

The mob went still.

And then hell broke loose.

Screaming, the mob charged. Police dogs surged forward. Foam flew from their mouths; their claws pattered against the ice.

Someone screamed—a woman. Bodies slammed into him, pushed him, yanked him. Panicked, the dumpster man fought to stay alive, and suddenly he could only think about *who* he was, and *why* he was in Moscow, Russia, as if *knowing* would help him escape this hell.

Unless this *was* Hell.

An elbow slammed against his teeth. There was a growling dog nearby. Something snapped, like a bone. A blood-curdling shriek penetrated the atmosphere.

Quick, choppy sounds added to the chaos. He jerked his head up. A helicopter, as its blades spun, surfaced from behind the dome of an enormous cathedral. The chopper soared past him in the grey skies.

Who was he, and why was he here?

A large police officer lifted a man into the air and slammed him against the ice.

Petrov. Who was Petrov, and why did that name sound so familiar?

The chopper circled like a predatory hawk around its prey.

"Hey. Steady. Grab my arm and we'll find a way out."

That voice again—the one he'd heard earlier. A hand grasped his arm, but *everyone* touched him in the chaos. But this time, he responded. "What the fuck is happening?"

"A protest against a new law Aleksey Petrov signed," the male voice shouted. "Come on. We need to get out. It's about to get worse."

Something blew up, shaking the ground. Flames erupted in the midst of the crowd, and it dispersed a little.

"How can it get worse?" The dumpster man twisted and turned, knocked around. Shaking. Trying to find that *fucking voice.*

"Because the drones are coming."

The dumpster man looked down, noticing a bundled man with a balaclava mask, standing shorter and yet seemingly more unfazed by the escalating events.

Stumbling to avoid a collision between an officer and a protester, the bundled man faced the protesters and looked towards the sky. "We need to move."

The dumpster man looked up too, and a faint buzzing sound filled the air. It grew louder, like angry hornets, and then he saw them.

The drones.

Surging towards the Kremlin, dotted against the sky, countless drones glided through the air like predators on a hunt. The voice from the helicopter spoke again. The dumpster man didn't understand the language, but he recognized *tones*.

And that tone was a warning.

"*Yeb-ty, Petrov!*" someone roared, and a bottle flipped through the air in the direction of the police. It exploded. Officers scattered. A woman screamed, and the dumpster man caught a glimpse of a female officer on the ground in a pool of her own gore—where her leg was supposed to be.

"Shit," the dumpster man whispered.

Then it began. Bullets rained. The drones dipped low like birds, and bullets spat from the flying tech.

Panicked screams and thunderous footsteps filled the streets of Moscow. The crowd scattered in every direction.

It created space for the dumpster man and his new friend to flee.

The drones pounded bullets into the desperate protesters as they tripped over each other, fell over each other, trampled each other. Gun-smoke clouded the cold atmosphere. People collapsed. Blood droplets shot upwards, outwards, splattered back down, as gore exploded into the air within the chaotic crowd.

Tears spilled over the dumpster man's cheeks.

"Keep moving!" the stranger yelled, darting past bodies and slipping on blood.

The gunfire ceased. The drones lifted into the sky and darted away from the Kremlin. Still fleeing, the crowd spread out. Wounded people limped, crawled, sobbed.

They ran for countless minutes.

"Follow me!" the bundled man said, and took him down an alley.

Something fluttered from his suit coat pocket. The dumpster man stopped, gasping and clutching his chest. His ears and face burned from the cold. "Wait!"

The shorter man stopped. "Let's go!"

The dumpster man searched for the item and found it laying on the ice. A Polaroid photo. With numb fingers, he picked it up as several protesters sprinted past him down the alley.

With hope that he'd find answers, he turned it over.

His heart sank. The earlier nausea erupted from his belly into streams of vomit.

He recognized the man in the picture. He recognized the laughing priest. He recognized the church.

And he remembered the beautiful girl who'd taken the photo.

"Can you help me?" the dumpster man asked his new friend, spitting out the last of his vomit.

"I can try," the shorter man said, "but you have to come with me."

It wasn't the image that made him sick. It wasn't the memory of that day. It only reminded him what he'd been through—where he'd been, and why he was here in Moscow, Russia.

Kill.

"My name is Mar—" he rasped.

Alek.

"Mar?" the shorter man responded.

Aleksey Petrov.

He shook his head, trying to formulate his words. "Mariel."

And it was all he said, because he dared not admit why he was here. He wasn't even certain he believed it himself.

Because with his memory came a secret—a direct order from the Heavens.

From God Himself.

His name was Mariel Christian Nadier, and he'd been placed here to kill the president of Russia.

CHAPTER 8: VERSE 1
~ NEIGHBORHOOD WATCH ~

January 1st, 2020

*D**ear sweet son of mine... happy birthday. I haven't written much this past year because I've been in too much emotional pain. I'd freeze when I looked at the journal, because it makes me think of you.*

I'm better. I'm healing. But I'm still so lost. I'm angry with myself too, because I morphed my own reality by believing what happened the night I adopted you was real. I believed you caught that bullet, and I believed you couldn't die. There's nothing worse than thinking you'll never need to worry about your child's death and then—it happens.

It happened, Mariel, and I couldn't stop it. That's what I struggle to deal with. I couldn't protect you from harming yourself. Throughout my life, I've helped so many people grieve. I remind them that what-ifs aren't fair—and yet I'm doing it myself.

Perhaps pretending that self-blame doesn't exist isn't healthy. Maybe we should admit that it's there, stare it in the face, and conquer it.

I hope you're living in a dream, a reality far better than what you experienced on Earth. I miss you. I miss your ridiculous music and your offensive eggplant emojis. Now it's just Phil Jameson who's shaming me for being gay.

I love you,

Dad.

January 4th, 2020

Hello friends—I thought it was time to update you on my health.

Since the accident last year, my nightmares have gotten worse. They used to come every few days. Now? They're every night. People falling from the sky. That green-eyed woman shooting me. A sign that says "Justice for Ahdam". An earthquake.

Who is Ahdam, and why does he need justice?

The dreams mean nothing, I'm sure, but something is happening that makes me believe I need to be admitted. I keep experiencing moments where I space out and specific images pulse through my mind like visions. I saw a billboard for a February 15th Kaemon Spears rally (he's a presidential primary candidate), and I almost crashed the car. I saw "Justice for Ahdam" across a large screen, and I saw something else. A large, orange, pulsing emblem—like a symbol for innovative new tech perhaps. But the moment got worse. I physically heard screams and smelled fire and burning flesh. It was then that I snapped back and had to whip my car away from the oncoming building. It was horrifying.

I've had strange ones about Phil Jameson too. When I saw him for the first time at Mariel's funeral, he went to shake my hand, and I had a horrific image of him at a pulpit in a church, bloody hands raised in the air. That wasn't it. Carolyn's body hung suspended in the air, and she woke up.

Again, confused, I snapped back to my reality, and I almost vomited as I stood near my son's casket. Luckily, Esther caught me and made sure I was okay.

I can handle the nightmares. I can't handle hallucinations, and I'm terrified that my head injury is causing this. Should I just see someone?

I still have anxiety about therapy. My dad didn't make it a healthy discussion point when I was little. Now it's kind of ruined.

I still haven't seen or heard from Fr. Paul since the night Mariel died. I'm beginning to think that was a hallucination too.

I'll pray about it.

Fr. Jerome.

January 6th, 2020

Hello friends,

On a brighter note (I think), I see that Esther is dating Gabe Donovan. That was unexpected, because she's never seemed interested in him, but she's smiling again. Choreographing her next dance competition from the sounds of it. That'll be in March.

I worry for her family though. There's a sadness in their eyes that I wish I could make go away. It's been there for years, since Mary Caravan died. It's understandable (trust me, I get it) but I hate to see those I love in pain. They are wonderful people and deserve happiness.

Esther—I truly worry for her. She's made comments that suggest she is carrying guilt for Mariel's suicide. She shouldn't. She did absolutely nothing wrong, and if my son made her feel that way? It was wrong of him.

That's all I will say on that for now.

Love, Fr. Jerome.

* * *

Wednesday, January 8th, 2020
Chicago, Illinois

It was almost six in the evening when Fr. Jerome Nadier received a phone call from Victoria Jameson. He'd just put on a pot of tea and stooped to scratch the ears of his calico cat—Harlow.

After losing Mariel, he'd decided that while a cat wouldn't eliminate his grief, it'd soothe the pain of being alone.

He didn't realize how quiet it'd be at night, because he was so accustomed to Mariel's late night video games, television, and snacks. Especially chips. Goodness, the boy would buy the loudest, most crinkly bags, and he'd stomp through the house to get his water because he'd always, without fail, forget that chips made him thirsty. The noise used to bother the priest.

Now he missed it.

So, he adopted a cat from an animal shelter. Six years old and a ball of energetic fluff. She brought noise back into the house, and it wasn't as silent anymore.

Harlow purred against his leg as the phone rang on the counter. Humming, the priest stepped to the counter and frowned when he saw an unknown number on the screen.

"Hello?"

"Hi, Father Jerome, it's Victoria Jameson. Is this a good time?"

He smiled at the young woman's sweet voice. "Of course. What's going on?"

"This might be a strange ask, and I completely understand if you don't want to do it."

"Try me." Fr. Jerome leaned against the counter.

"As I'm sure you're aware, I haven't spoken to my dad since my mom died. I'll avoid getting into the bloody details, but it's for my own mental health and sanity. He's *not* a good man, and he abused Mom." Victoria's voice held strength, and yet despair.

Fr. Jerome rubbed his jaw. "I'm sorry, Victoria."

"It's not your fault. He's been an absolute dick to you too, and I'm the one who should apologize, because my request involves you talking to him. Does he still attend your church?"

"He does." Granted, Phil hadn't been to service as often as he used to be, which Fr. Jerome found quite odd. But when he did show up, he participated as normal and opened his mouth for communion while staring down at the spoon as if he suspected Fr. Jerome might poison him.

"Has Hailey been with him?"

"Yes. Is something wrong?" The priest's heart rate went up.

"Well, I was hoping you could stop by his house and see. Just make sure everything's okay. I don't think he'd hurt her or anything, because she's like his pride and joy, but he'd definitely brainwash her into some weird shit. Pardon the language."

"It's okay. Um, sure?" Fr. Jerome frowned. "Is Hailey not talking to you?"

"No, I've been banned from all contact ever since I, more or less, called him a piece of shit." Victoria cleared her throat, just like her father did whenever he made a point.

Isolation. Okay, that wasn't good. Unfortunate signs of narcissistic behavior. "I'll go over there," the priest said, and water hissed from the tea kettle. "I'll see if I can't talk to them."

"Thank you so much, Father Jerome. Seriously. You're amazing, and I hope you're doing okay."

Fr. Jerome rubbed Harlow's back. "I am. Have a good night."

*   *   *

If there was a house that looked like Phil Jameson, Phil Jameson owned that house.

Fr. Jerome could never understand how, of all houses in the neighborhood, a man could buy a home that *looked* like the outlier.

It was a white, boxed shape house—the enclosed sunroom looked like an open mouth, and the attached steps held the appearance of a lolling tongue. The roof was red—just like Phil's hair. The eyes, two windows side by side on the second floor, stared at Fr. Jerome in analytical judgment.

In fact, the house looked like Phil's face when the lawyer took communion.

"Give me grace, Lord," Fr. Jerome sighed, and he exited his car with the mint brownies he'd purchased from a nearby bakery. Hailey loved brownies.

It was seven in the evening. Streetlights lit up the neighborhood and reflected against the—

—NEIGHBORHOOD WATCH—

—sign. The suspicious figure on the sign eyed Fr. Jerome as he crossed the street and stepped onto Phil's property.

No turning back now.

Fr. Jerome rang the doorbell. The glass sliding door was locked. The brownie pan shook in his hands. Humming, he waited.

And waited.

He looked up.

Ah yes, a security camera. It made sense.

Clearing his throat, he raised his fingers to the doorbell again. The front door opened, and he jumped.

Disgruntled and surprised, Phil Jameson stood in the doorway, his lanky figure blocking the hallway light. His blue polo looked rumpled over his khaki pants. "Yes?" he called across the enclosed porch.

Fr. Jerome raised the brownie pan. "May I come in?"

Phil pressed a finger to his nose as if contemplating a life decision. With a curt nod, he strode onto the porch, unlatched the sliding door, and gestured for him.

With a shallow breath, Fr. Jerome ascended the steps.

"I suppose you'd like to come into the house?" Phil asked, eyeing the priest with a level of disdain similar to that of the neighborhood watch figure.

"I mean, I don't *have* to if it's an inconvenient time?" Fr. Jerome wasn't really sure how to respond. What the heck was he supposed to say to that?

"It's fine," Phil said, and he walked into his home.

Shaking his head, the priest followed him.

Moments later, the two men sat across from each other at the dining room table. A clock ticked in the silence—a bumblebee clock. Right next to the icon of *The Last Supper*. The one that portrayed Judas with darker skin.

The house was so clean it almost sparkled. No dust. Did Hailey scrub the house? A hired helper?

Surely not Phil.

He was the man of the house.

"Where's Hailey?" Fr. Jerome asked.

Phil smiled. His eyes did not. "Studying her scriptures."

"Ah." The priest wondered if *he'd* ever made anyone feel uncomfortable when mentioning the scriptures. Because right now?

He felt uncomfortable.

"What can I do for you?"

Fr. Jerome pushed the brownies to the center of the table. In response, Phil centered it and cleared his throat. Ignoring that, the priest spoke. "It's a rough month for both of us. January 12th is coming up, and I was thinking about you."

It wasn't untrue. In fact, he'd planned to send a card to the Jameson household. But being here right now hadn't been his idea, and he couldn't help but feel as though he'd just lied.

Fr. Jerome didn't hate Phil. He'd come close to losing his sanity when Phil laid hands on Mariel as a child, but he'd never crossed the threshold from passion to hate.

Phil nostrils flared. He stared past Fr. Jerome, grinding his teeth as he contemplated his next words.

And Fr. Jerome had a feeling they wouldn't be good.

"How dare you?" Phil said, his voice low. "*How* dare you?"

Fr. Jerome blinked. What had he done?

"I'm sorry, I..."

"You come into my home and offer me brownies in honor of the date *my wife* died because of you?"

"What?" Fr. Jerome's breathing quickened.

"She was *fine*," Phil sneered. "But *you* filled her head with nonsense about divorcing me. You *confused* the woman!"

"Phil, she was in *pain* before that conversation!" Fr. Jerome exclaimed, leaning forward. "She was *hurting*. You're upset because she came to me for *genuine* advice, and she wasn't happy because—"

"You've *never* wanted me to be successful, even in my own marriage!" Phil roared, and spit landed on the table like glistening speckles of foam. "You've always thought you were better than me. Well, listen here, *Father* Jerome—before you go blaming *me* for my wife's suicide, let's just remember your son wasn't too happy either now, was he?"

Well.

He *hadn't* hated Phil Jameson.

What was that saying?

Hurt people... hurt other people.

As a priest, he'd offered years of advice for people suffering through all types of pain, including hatred. The saying was very true—hurt people *did* hurt others. So, *Father* Jerome might have responded differently had he kept that in mind, but tonight?

Jerome spoke.

"God created man in his own image," Fr. Jerome said under his breath. "God doesn't make mistakes... which makes me think *something else* made *you*, Philip Jameson."

That was a *horrible* thing to say. Why didn't he feel guilty?

The clock ticked.

And there was another sound. Something *rattling* beneath the floor. Like a chain. A long chain.

His eyes darted to the basement staircase. The door was closed. Bolted.

As if to keep someone, or *something,* from getting out.

"Where's... Hailey?" Fr. Jerome asked, and his breath hitched.

Was Phil sweating? His freckled skin looked *clammy*. A vein pulsed in his forehead. "Hailey," Phil called, staring at Fr. Jerome as if he'd seen the ghost of his worst enemy. "Hailey! Fr. Jerome would like to see you."

The chain rattled again.

Fr. Jerome couldn't move. He couldn't stop looking at the basement door.

Was *Hailey* down there? Surely, Phil wouldn't—

"Yes, Dad?" A young, sweet voice.

Fr. Jerome let out a sigh of relief as Hailey's figure appeared in the hallway.

She stood next to the basement door, hands limp at her sides, hair tousled as if she'd been in the wind. Her eyes, wide and innocent, turned to Fr. Jerome.

"Hi, Father Jerome. How are you?" The poor girl sounded so scripted.

"I'm doing well, Hailey." Fr. Jerome scanned her face and arms with quick intention... no signs of bruising on her skin. "I brought you mint brownies."

Hailey gasped with glee and looked at Phil, who nodded slowly as if the young woman couldn't eat a brownie without his permission.

"Wait," Phil snapped, blocking Hailey's hand as she went for the package. "These are not marijuana brownies, correct?"

Fr. Jerome blinked one time. "No, Phil. I put cocaine in them."

Hailey's face fell.

"I'm being sarcastic," the priest said, and he stood up. He couldn't be in this house anymore. As the young kids said—

I'm out.

"Enjoy the brownies, Hailey," Fr. Jerome said, and he turned to leave.

Phil didn't get up to follow him. "I will see you at church on Sunday, Father. *Please* drive safely." His voice dripped with false joy.

Fr. Jerome left and did not glance back, but he couldn't forget the memory of the chains that rattled beneath the floor.

Truth?

Or hallucination?

"Guide me, Lord," Fr. Jerome said, and he slammed his car door shut. Shivering, he turned the key in the ignition. A static-filled radio host blared through the speakers.

"—*still active in the streets of Moscow, but rioters have kept away from the Kremlin after the government responded with deadly force. John, what do you think about what Petr—*"

Fr. Jerome turned it off. His line-in cable must have disconnected again. Bluetooth *was* an option for his car, but he hadn't succeeded in figuring out how to connect it. He'd just committed to using the old cable Mariel had purchased for him five years ago.

Lifting his phone to plug it in, Fr. Jerome felt it buzz in his palm.

UNKNOWN CALLER.

Glancing at the time, Fr. Jerome shrugged and brought it to his ear. Maybe Victoria Jameson was calling from a different—

"Dad."

Fr. Jerome dropped the phone. It thumped against the glove box and fell between the seats.

"Dad? Don't freak out."

The cable was working now, because the voice came through the vehicle speakers.

Not just any voice. Mariel's.

His son's voice.

"Don't," the old man wailed. "It's *cruel.*"

"I'm sorry, Dad, I know you're not going to believe me."

He didn't know what to believe. That his mind had slipped? That there was no hope for mental sanity?

"My son is dead," Fr. Jerome screamed, and sobs quaked his body. The car shook.

"I love you, Dad," Mariel said, and his voice was a murmur. "I am your son, I am not dead, and I'm going to be home soon."

VERSE 2

~ THE FOUR HORSEMEN EMERGE ~

Saturday, January 4th, 2020
West Bank

A hdam stopped to catch his breath. Bending down, he rested his hands on his knees. Sweat spilled into his eyes as he wheezed, and his throat burned.

Most, if not all, of the police were dead. He was certain of it. The boy wanted to cry, wanted to go back to see if Allah had had mercy on his parents, but he knew it would be a mistake. He had already possibly killed his own family through his stupidity in the village of Khan Al-Ahmar. Now, he needed to do as his father had instructed.

In the darkness, he straightened up. He stood on the outskirts of the village, and his eyes lingered on the home of Ali Saddam, his father's best friend since childhood.

Ahdam Kaseem stood several shacks down from Saddam's home. He lived alone, and he was one of three villagers who owned a vehicle, a small white truck that helped his commute to work in Jerusalem each day. Even though he worked different hours than Haleef, he would often ask Ahdam's father to ride with him to Checkpoint 300 to avoid the walk. Ahdam always thought that was a nice thing to do for his father.

He approached the back of the shack. The truck was there. From where he stood, he could see the other villagers milling about the town, talking about the "*wrath in the skies*" and the flames in the distance.

Talking about *him.*

Trembling, Ahdam crept through the darkness, walking low. He darted behind the cover of each home, listening to the villagers talk in the streets as he peeked around the corner. In the center of the street, one of the men turned his head, but the boy snapped his head back behind the shelter before he could be seen.

In the distance, just outside of the town, headlights flashed. Engines roared.

More Israeli cops.

Maybe even the military.

But as the lights approached, he recognized them as fire trucks. He'd seen one in Jerusalem. His father had snuck him across the street to an area where Palestinians were not allowed to walk so that he could touch the truck. He'd loved it.

Right now, he had to hurry.

When the man in the street turned his back to him, Ahdam sprinted to Ali Saddam's home. He approached the back window, stood on his tiptoes, and then lightly tapped on the glass. It was dark inside. No one moved.

Pulse slamming within his ears, Ahdam tapped again.

Engines grew louder on the other side of the shack. Tires screeched to a halt.

Gasping, Ahdam turned his head towards approaching footsteps. At the corner of the shack stood Ali Saddam.

He was a man of medium build, brown skin, and stubble. The breeze caught a few strands of his short hair as he put a finger to his lips.

Ahdam nodded his understanding.

Ali returned the nod and then disappeared around the corner of his home. Ahdam crouched low.

Police pounded on the front door.

Eyes wide, Ahdam waited.

His heart sounded like a clock that wanted out of his chest. Leaning closer to the house, he listened.

Voices. Multiple. But he couldn't understand what they were saying. Then Ali raised his voice.

"You have no right to search my property."

Ahdam darted away from the house. He wasn't safe *anywhere*. Gasping, he snapped his head around. Open land. Shacks. Other villagers.

The truck.

Ahdam bolted.

Flashlights cut through the darkness.

Praying to Allah, the boy scrambled beneath the truck. Oncoming footsteps crunched towards him; white light darted over the ground.

Could the officer hear him breathe?

Ahdam held his breath, grabbed the pipes on the bottom of the truck, and hoisted himself up.

May Allah have mercy.

The boots appeared. Stopped.

Ahdam closed his eyes and then opened them again. His muscles trembled.

The rusty truck creaked and shifted a little. Something shuffled in the bed, like the officer had moved a blanket.

"What's so important about this boy?" Ahdam heard Ali ask, but the man's voice was further away.

"If you don't know, then you're not privy to that knowledge." Another man responded. "Unlock your shed."

More footsteps moved past the truck. The boots near the truck shifted around to the other side.

Ahdam's arms cramped. The muscles burned. He could not hold on much longer.

The boots next to the truck pivoted, stepped away, and then stopped. Turned back.

Sweat trickled down his forehead, and he let out a soft breath. It shook. His entire body shook.

The officer crouched. His knees touched the ground, and Ahdam almost screamed.

He was trapped. The officer would crawl beneath the truck and find him. Grab his leg and drag him out.

"I'm telling you, he's *not here!*" Ali cried, his voice a distance away.

The knees shifted, and two hands planted against the ground. A face appeared—a pretty woman with a black cap and a dark ponytail that flopped over her shoulder as she looked beneath the truck.

And their eyes met.

His breath shook.

Her lips parted.

The other officers were talking, but their voices seemed so far away. Right now, Ahdam's world narrowed to the officer in front of him. It was all that mattered.

The officer searched his face. She didn't move. Her eyes fluttered shut, and she moved her lips as if talking to herself. No sound came out. She was *thinking*, which was more than Ahdam was, because his entire self *froze.*

The officer opened her eyes, bared her teeth, and then her face disappeared. So did her boots. She was gone.

"No one!" Ahdam heard her yell in Arabic. "There's no one here!"

Ahdam's muscles quivered and then betrayed him. He landed onto his back.

Footsteps faded. Ahdam heard Ali's voice and then rumbling engines. He lay motionless, thinking of his family, and awaited further instruction.

"Ahdam. Come with me." Ali's voice.

Thanks to Allah.

Once inside of the shack, Ali closed the door. It was dark.

Ahdam scrambled to the furthest corner in the room and sank to his bottom. He pulled his knees towards him and wrapped his arms around his legs.

Ali approached the boy and knelt. His black eyes glinted as headlights passed through the room. "I'm so sorry, Ahdam. I pray that your family is alright."

Ahdam's lips quivered, and he shook his head. As he rested his forehead against his knees, his shoulders trembled.

He cried.

And outside—it began to rain.

Ali pulled him close, pressing the boy's head against his chest. The center of the man's chest was hard, almost bony, against Ahdam's ear. "Ahdam, listen to me. You are not bad. You are not evil. You are safe now." He stroked the boy's head. "Now, in the middle of the night, we need to leave. We need to get to Gaza."

Ahdam looked at him and shook his head. He did not want to leave his home. Where would he *go?*

Were his parents *still alive?* Would they know where to find them?

"The Palestinian police won't hurt you. They'll be on your side. But soon... any place under Israeli control will be looking for you."

Ahdam grinded his teeth. Maybe if his father had let him use his gift to hurt more of them, to bring *war* to their country, perhaps he wouldn't be in this situation.

He thought of the Israeli woman who'd spared him.

He'd spare her.

"Get some rest," Ali said, moving across the room to prepare a cot for the boy. "I know this is hard for you, but my God will protect you. He must."

Ahdam's head shot up. He made a sound, like a moan, to ask Ali what he meant by saying that the *Christian* God would protect him.

Ali did not look at him as he shook dust from a blanket. However, he spoke as if in response to the glance Ahdam had given him. "Your father and I always had different religious views. Your family is Muslim, mine is Christian. But, in each religion—" he snapped the blanket one more time, "—the world must end." He spread the blanket and smoothed it over the cot. "In the Quran, and in the Bible, there are signs of the Great Apocalypse. Did you know that?" Ali looked towards the boy.

Ahdam nodded. Fear crawled over his skin.

Ali took a seat on the ground and pulled his knees towards him, just as Ahdam had done. More headlights cut through the darkness, and several men yelled in the distance.

"There are different signs of the end times," Ali said, clasping his knees with his hands and idly brushing his thumb across the skin of his bottom hand. "Some of these signs come in the appearances of people, strange events, or—" his face darkened as the headlights disappeared once again, "—unusual weather."

Ahdam tilted his head. He wasn't sure why Ali was telling him this.

"In my religion, the Four Horsemen emerge," he said quietly. "Death, War, Conquest, and Famine."

Did that matter? Would it bring his parents back or save him from the Israeli government?

"I don't want to scare you, or confuse you, Ahdam," Ali said. His voice sounded distant. "But always remember what you are capable of, and how that can be used for evil. Remember what your father always told you. Never use your gift for evil."

"You promised, Ahdam!" Haleef's distressed face appeared in the boy's memory.

"I believe you are a symbol of the end." Ali was silent for a moment, and then he gestured to the bed. "Get some rest, Ahdam. And don't worry about what I told you. Your father was a good man, and I believe you will be as well. Sleep, and I will wake you when it is time to leave."

Why would Ali tell him something like that before sleep? *He* was a symbol of the *end?* Was that a Christian belief? Or Muslim?

Should he be worried?

Fuming, Ahdam crawled to the cot and curled into the fetal position. As he closed his eyes, he heard Ali say his prayers, praying for an outcome in the chaos that would give glory to God.

The boy did not want to sleep. He was too angry. However, though his mind protested against his body, Ahdam could not fight the exhaustion.

He fell asleep.

Ahdam dreamt of his father. He was burning—screaming as his body caught flames. As the flames swallowed him, Haleef told his son never to use his powers again. He told Ahdam that it was his fault that he was burning.

Then, Ahdam dreamt of his mother. An Israeli officer stood over her, and he beat her face until the earth around her head was red.

He awoke with a silent scream, and Ali Saddam knelt before him with an outstretched hand and an unconcerned expression.

"Good," he said. "You are up. We need to go."

Outside, the breeze was cool. The air smelled of smoke from the previous evening, but there were no more flames. The sky was black, stroked with an occasional grey cloud. The world was finally quiet.

Saddam secured an old, stained tarp over the bed of the truck. He loaded the bed with multiple crates and blankets and instructed Ahdam to hide amongst the items in the truck.

When Ahdam prepared to enter the bed, Ali pulled a handgun from his waistband and uploaded a magazine.

Ali racked the slide and then gestured towards the boy. "Don't worry about this," he said. "It's only to protect ourselves if necessary. I have prayed that we succeed today without injury. Now get in, and if we are stopped, be silent. You understand?"

The boy nodded and then entered the bed of the truck. Behind him, Ali shut the tailgate. He couldn't help but wonder where they were going, and how the Israelis wouldn't find him hiding.

Shivering, Ahdam crawled past the crates and buried himself in the blankets. As the engine roared to a start, the truck vibrated, and Ahdam's body jostled.

Heart pounding, he closed his eyes. And he wondered.

What if he *was* evil?

Did he signify the end?

Shaking, he pulled the blankets tighter around his body. The truck sped up, and the movement rocked his body back and forth.

He decided that if he did signify an end, it would be the end of anyone who harmed his family. *He* was not Jesus Christ, and he did not believe in mercy for those who had none for him.

Ahdam fell asleep again.

But when he awoke, something had changed. Something *bad*.

Because he was no longer in Ali Saddam's truck. In fact, he had no idea where Ali Saddam had *gone*.

Ahdam was shackled in the back of a much larger vehicle, a military vehicle with camouflage print. He'd seen Israeli trucks like this in Jerusalem. But the soldiers that sat next to him were pale-skinned, and they did not wear the same flag. It was different.

Red, white, and blue.

The boy let out a wail.

VERSE 3

~HELL~

If God had *truly* loved her, she would not be in Hell. As promised in the Bible, He would have *saved* her from Hell.

But it wasn't fire and brimstone. Oh no, it was far worse than that. If able, she'd beg God for the opportunity to burn forever.

No.

It was much, much worse.

The Lord had placed her in a torture chamber.

Back with her husband—Phil Jameson.

Carolyn had no concept of time. Could one keep track of *forever?*

Piss. Shit. Vomit. All over herself.

For a while, the demon who portrayed Phil would clean it for her, shaking his head, telling her that it was not ladylike. Sometimes while she was in chains, he would make *her* clean it. He'd provide a bucket of water and soap, and she'd weakly scrub the floor until the demon was content. Then he'd pat her head, gaze at her with smug pity, and take the bucket and leave her again.

Yes, if God had *truly* loved her, she would not be in Hell. But this was her fault, wasn't it? Carolyn had indeed sinned. Perhaps if she'd submitted to her husband in her earthly life, she might not be here. Maybe if she hadn't committed the grave sin of suicide, she wouldn't be here.

In Hell.

The radio was on. She was pretty sure the radio host had just said it was Sunday, January 12th, 2020.

A loud religious leader preached about the end times—ironic, considering she was in Hell. It was Day 93—an *approximate* count since the time she woke up, and it felt very cold in the hell-basement.

On Day 89, the Demon had been courteous enough to give her a blanket before he left to *"see what Fr. Jerome wanted"*. He'd looked up at the camera in the basement, noticed the priest outside the house, and stormed up the steps while muttering to himself.

This was a strange Hell, unlike anything she would have assumed it to be.

Why, of all people, would *Fr. Jerome* be in Hell?

Ah, *yes*. Because he was a homosexual. Homosexuals did not go to Heaven—at least, that is what Phil believed when she was alive.

That poor priest. Despite the things Phil had always said about him, she'd always liked Fr. Jerome.

On Day 89, she'd considered screaming when she heard the priest's footsteps upstairs. But that was part of the Hell torture, wasn't it? Screaming and never getting help?

"The end times are inevitable!" the preacher yelled. *"We can't run from it. We can't hide from it. We can't change it! Now, what we can do is abandon all sin and pray that Jesus takes us in the rapture before the Great Tribulation."*

Her thin, bony body shook. The chains rattled. Hearing only the sound of her quick inhalation, her eyes shifted around the dark basement. She looked at the old, empty paint can by the wall, next to the stairs.

"The Best Resistance, Guaranteed!"

Carolyn remembered it from her life on Earth. A couple of weeks before she died, Phil used it to touch up the walls. She remembered *that*, because he'd slapped her before storming down the stairs. She couldn't remember why.

"If the Antichrist rises, then it's too late. You've been left behind. That means you got a whooole lotta prayin' you better catch up on."

Carolyn's eyes followed the pathway of a little bug that moved across the floor towards a droplet of water. She didn't want it to drown. Gently, she blew at it, and it scurried the other direction.

Not long ago, the Demon left her a bowl of water and a small plate of dry, canned tuna before leaving the house. He'd ripped the tape from her mouth, exposing her burning, raw skin. This treatment was a rarity. He'd normally keep the duct tape on, *and* her hands chained behind her back.

The tripod was still in front of her—the one she saw on Day 1 when she first opened her eyes and realized she was in Hell. At that time, it held a phone—aimed in her direction too. Like it was filming her.

Demons were strange.

Why *film* someone in Hell?

"*You see those riots in Moscow? That's just the beginning. That's just the beginning of the end,*" the preacher yelled.

Why did preachers always have to yell? Fr. Jerome had never yelled. He'd always had such a gentle tone.

She missed it.

Thirsty, Carolyn inched forward, and the chains rattled as her knees scraped against the unfinished floor. With ragged breaths, she bent to lift the bowl. Her hands shook. The water sloshed. She returned it to the floor.

She had no more strength. Her body looked grotesque. The muscles had atrophied, and her ribs bulged. Blue veins pulsed through the skin on her arms. It almost looked translucent.

Her teeth, however, were in fine shape.

The Demon brushed her teeth twice a day, if morning and evening existed in Hell.

He'd sit behind her, wrap his legs around her waist, and massage her teeth and gums with the brush. The Demon whispered in her ear, telling her that she had always had a healthy, beautiful smile, and that he wanted to keep her mouth at its healthiest.

Then afterwards, he'd have intercourse with her. It was not pleasurable. She hated it. But it was an accurate portrayal of Phil.

When Carolyn was alive, Phil rarely allowed her to experience pleasure. But sometimes she couldn't help it. Sometimes he'd hit a pleasurable nerve, and she'd squeal.

Earlier in their marriage, she once proclaimed God's name in vain during intercourse, and he beat her. After that, sex had only been for *him*.

"*Women should never use the Lord's name in vain for the sake of pleasure,*" he proclaimed. "*That was your last time.*"

After intercourse, Demon-Phil would *pray* with her—just like he used to do when she was alive. It was a strange hell, a hell where a demon prayed, but nevertheless... Hell.

Carolyn bent low. Hair fell over her cheeks as she brought her face to the bowl of water. She licked it with her tongue like an animal. It was no longer humiliating.

It would be like this for eternity.

The water sloshed into her nose and cooled her raw skin. It wet the tips of her hair and water droplets plunked into the bowl as she came back up for air. Sniffling, she inhaled water. Coughed a little.

Her stomach growled.

She moved towards the tuna. Carolyn took pieces of fish with her fingers and stuffed it into her mouth with desperate eagerness.

Hell could be worse, she supposed.

The preacher spoke very fast, very passionately. *"Signs of the end? I'll tell you signs of the end. Uptick in homosexuality. Women are leaving their husbands to be lesbians. Transgenderism. More and more men are dressing as women. Bestiality. Women are claiming they just need cats, not children. Segregation is back—these so called DEI, eh—inclusive whatever hires? Whites are getting excluded. What's next, slavery?"*

Her head came up.

Was that the front door upstairs?

It opened. It slammed. Then footsteps. The floor creaked in protest.

The Demon had returned.

As Carolyn swallowed the last of the tuna, she slid backwards against the wall and closed her eyes. She was prepared for the torture this time. *I can handle it now*, she thought.

The footsteps thumped over her head now. Bits of dust and ceiling tile flurried into her wide eyes as she looked at the ceiling. Wildly, she blinked to bring tears to her eyes. It fascinated her that she could still control aspects of her body in Hell.

The footsteps stopped at the basement doorway. Trembling, Carolyn waited, her eyes glued to the door at the stairway top.

The doorknob squeaked. It turned. Then it rattled.

The Demon could not enter.

Why couldn't the demon enter?

Quickly, the footsteps left the doorway and stomped above her head again. Like snow, tile flakes fluttered down again.

Carolyn breathed fast.

Drawers opened. Then slammed. Opened again. Silverware jostled. Clattered. More footsteps. This was strange. What was the Demon doing? Was he planning a new way to torture her? Some form of psychological confusion?

Perhaps he'd heard her thoughts when she said that she could handle the torture. It *would* be like a demon to change his tactics; to make things *worse*.

Tears flooded to her eyes. She never should have committed suicide.

This was *so much worse* than her life on Earth with Phil.

Swift footsteps returned to the door.

"*Repent, sayeth the Lord. Repent, and ye shall be saved!*" the preacher cried.

The knob rattled. The door creaked.

It was open.

Shaking, she closed her eyes, squeezing out tears.

Thump. Thump. Thump.

Each footstep against the stairs worsened her nausea. The wood creaked, groaned, *protested* the Demon's feet.

Funny... even buildings objected to their lives in Hell.

Then, in a matter of seconds, Hell became much, *much* worse.

"*Mom?*"

Carolyn's eyes opened. The light was on. And, standing at the bottom of the stairs, was her daughter Victoria.

Her eyes widened, and she choked, and then it became a strangled scream. The chains jangled and slapped against the floor as Carolyn crawled, on her hands and knees, towards Victoria, but her body snapped back as she pulled the chains to their full length.

She would rather her flesh melt again and again rather than face this psychological torture.

"*Mom!*" Victoria rushed forward, her face pale, her eyes wide with horror, disbelief, and confusion. She came closer and knelt. Lips trembling, she shook her head.

"*Be warned,*" the radio wailed. "*If you are left behind, it will be the worst horror you've ever witnessed in your life!*"

"I'm not crazy," Victoria whispered. "I'm not crazy, I'm *not* crazy." Her body shook.

Wheezing, Carolyn leaned forward and tried to speak. The chain rattled again as she outstretched her bony, trembling hand. She wanted to speak, to tell her daughter to *run*, but her voice came in short, muffled grunts.

Frightened, Victoria shrunk back. Then, after taking a breath, she came forward and reached for Carolyn's hand. As soon as she felt the woman's cold fingers, her face paled even more.

"I saw you," she said. "I saw the body bag. You committed suicide by *train*. Did Dad lie? Did that fucking piece of shit *lie and do this to you?*" Her eyes bulged with furious terror. "Tell me this is a nightmare, Mom, *please!*"

Carolyn coughed, and then she puked. Bile, saliva, and strands of meat projected from her mouth. Spitting on the floor, she raised her head as the chains shook behind her.

"I'm... in... *Hell*," she croaked, her voice ragged.

Face blanched, Victoria whispered to herself. "I came to check on Hailey. I remember traveling here. The plane landed. I *drove* here. How did I fall asleep?"

"Demon," Carolyn whispered.

Upstairs, the door slammed.

Victoria opened her mouth to speak and then stopped. Her brow furrowed.

"Demon," Carolyn rasped.

Rising to her feet, Victoria slapped herself across the face. Then, she dug inside of her pockets, looking for something. A phone, perhaps? The poor girl had no clue that there was no phone reception in *Hell*.

Carolyn watched her. Wanted to help her. Wanted to get her out of Hell. Had Victoria died? Would the Demon torture them together? It'd make sense because...

... Because Phil never liked his children.

The footsteps came quickly and then stopped at the doorway.

Shaking, Victoria looked at Carolyn and then looked at the stairs. The girl was frozen in place.

Carolyn didn't know what to do.

Victoria searched the basement, pacing, looking for *something*.

Again, she didn't find it.

Hair disheveled, the young woman turned desperate eyes to Carolyn, and tears spilled over her cheeks as she whispered—

"Mom, *please...* wake me up."

A shadow appeared behind her daughter.

Carolyn's eyes snapped up.

Behind Victoria, Phil Jameson crept down the stairs. Face red. Lips tight.

Victoria caught Carolyn's eyes. She whirled.

Phil held a cell phone between his fingertips. Lifting it, he raised his eyebrow. "Left your phone on the counter."

Victoria screamed.

Carolyn screamed too.

"You fucking *psycho!*" Victoria shrieked. She rushed towards the red-haired man with raised fists, her hair a mess, her teeth exposed.

Phil dropped the phone. It bounced across the floor. He grabbed the young woman at the wrists, and with an abrupt snap of his arms, flung her against the wall.

"Earthquakes, hurricanes, comets, and fire, all judgments from the sky shall come!" the radio shrieked.

Phil slapped his daughter as she screamed.

Carolyn sobbed.

"You shouldn't *have come here, Victoria!*" the lawyer roared, pulling her by the collar, slamming her against the wall again.

Carolyn yanked the chains.

This *was* worse. So much worse than what she had dealt with.

Victoria fought back. She smashed her knee into Phil's crotch.

He howled, bending over, and the veins bulged from his neck.

Victoria came after him again, pushing him, and then grabbed the paint can—

—*The Best Resistance, Guaranteed!*—

—and swung it at his head. The bottom of the can struck him against the temple.

Blood dribbled. Phil yelped, and he reached up to guard his face as she swung at him again.

"Stop it, Victoria! I can explain!"

But Victoria swung it again, this time too quickly, and it smashed against his elbow as her father staggered backwards.

What kind of torture was this?

Carolyn yelped, groaned, and tugged at the chains, trying to intervene. Not that she *could* have, because she was in Hell, and *this* was another *creative* round of torture.

"Fuck you!" Victoria raised the can again.

As blood rained down the side of his face, Phil lunged for her. He collapsed on top of her. The fight was on.

And Carolyn watched as father and daughter struggled for their lives in the depths of Hell.

Gasping, Victoria kneed him in the stomach and flung her arm backwards to reach for the cell phone that lay on the floor.

The cell phone that had no reception.

Because this was Hell, and in *Hell*, you could not call 911. Here, God would not help you, and neither would the police.

"Don't make me *sin*, Victoria!" Phil shrieked, reaching for her arms.

The young woman pushed her nails into his eyes, and he rolled from her, screaming in agony and covering his face.

Victoria grabbed the phone, scrambled to her feet, and fled upstairs.

Phil followed her.

The stairs screamed in their own agony as his feet pounded against the wood.

Carolyn could only listen now. She heard as the footsteps slipped, squeaked, and pounded against the floor above her head.

They were in the kitchen now.

Something slammed against the floor, like a body. Victoria was screaming.

Phil was screaming too—saying something about not wanting to be a murderer.

Not wanting to kill his own daughter.

Glass shattered. Furniture crashed. More screams. More slams.

Pulling her knees to her chest, Carolyn rocked back and forth and cried. The chains jingled, and it might have sounded joyous had it not been Hell.

Then, above her head, Carolyn heard a peculiar, repetitive sound—like someone's skull being smashed against the kitchen floor's surface.

Thud. Thud. Thud.

Someone grunted with exertion.

Thud. Thud. Thud.

More white pieces of ceiling tile flurried to the basement floor.

Carolyn closed her eyes again.

She never should have committed suicide. Never should have said the Lord's name in vain. Never should have rebelled against her husband.

The thudding sound stopped. One last piece of tile fell to the floor as someone shuffled on the floor. The person stood. Again, the floor creaked as footsteps approached the basement entrance.

Carolyn sniffled and looked towards the stairs. She expected to see the Demon.

And she did.

Slowly, Phil came downstairs. He was sweaty and dazed. He even looked confused—an expression that did not seem like it belonged on the face of a Demon in his own domain.

Red strands of hair fell across his forehead—hair that she used to brush away from his skin. Blood leaked from his temple and ran like a stream down his cheek and neck. He looked at his bloody, trembling hands.

"Hailey is—is at choir practice," he stammered. "She'll be done in an hour." Phil turned bloodshot eyes to his wife, as if seeking her help. "I... didn't *want* to do it," he cried. "She made me. Victoria *made me* do it."

Sliding through her own vomit, Carolyn shrunk back.

"It was self-defense," the Demon said, and he approached her with wide, glazed eyes. She shook her head. Her hair slapped her across the cheeks.

This was horrible. *She should not have killed herself.*

Phil knelt before her and touched her face. The blood on his hands smeared across her cheek.

Carolyn wailed.

Quietly, the Demon spoke to her.

"I want to bring her back to life," he said. "But I can't. If I do, she might tell someone that I'm bad... that I'm *doing something wrong* when all I've tried to do is protect you and *save your soul!*"

Carolyn whimpered.

Phil sat hard onto his buttocks and rested his arms over his knees. His body trembled. "I don't know what to do. What should I do, Carolyn?"

Why was the Demon asking for her advice? He'd just subjected her to the worst torture imaginable, and he had the audacity to *ask her advice?*

Phil ran fingers through his hair and then struggled to his feet. "I'll pray about it. God will show me what must be done."

Carolyn looked at the Demon as he turned.

"You should pray too," Phil said, and then he left her alone.

And she did. She prayed. Because something stirred in her mind, and she began to wonder... maybe she wasn't in Hell.

Maybe they'd all been wrong.

Maybe Hell only existed when one was alive.

VERSE 4

~ KINGDOM OF HEAVEN ~

January-*something*, 2019.

He remembered the drive home after making Esther cry.

That was a horrible thing.

Watching her cry. Watching her fall apart. Seeing the hatred in Todd Caravan's eyes. Todd was a merciful man, but he'd had no mercy in his eyes that day.

Mariel hadn't blamed him. He couldn't. He'd been disgusted with himself too.

So *fucking* disgusted.

"Stay away from Esther," the professor had told him.

Was that why? Because the good follower *knew* he'd commit suicide?

While driving away from the bookstore, his mental state deteriorated. So, even with the knowledge that his plan wouldn't work, he made a decision.

Three years ago, he'd purchased a gun—a secret kept from his father. From Esther.

From everyone who cared about him.

It'd been a fantasy, really. Russian Roulette wasn't quite the same when you couldn't die. In fact, it was much scarier when the gun never fired, or the bullet never landed.

Far more depressing.

Mariel wondered if it were somewhere in a dark, musty evidence room at the Chicago Police Department where dusty shelves collected other items from different cases.

At home, while Fr. Jerome was at the coffee shop, Mariel had paced the house. Eaten a handful of *Oreos*. Paced faster. *Chewed* faster. Prayed. Begged. Attempted to bargain. He asked God to kill him... to at least *let* him die.

Mariel wrote a note to his father.

He wept. Wrote texts to Esther. Deleted them. He felt unclean.

Thinking back to the vile words he'd said to Esther at the bookstore, he took the gun and went to the shower.

Mariel turned on his favorite music. Electronic.

He loaded a magazine, charged a round into the chamber, placed it on the toilet lid, and stepped into the shower.

Then he saw the messenger—a blurry, grey figure that stood in the doorway like a divine phantom.

"You may do it once to understand the life you've been given," the messenger said. *"But understand that this is your first and last chance to have your path set clear for you. It's your only chance to negotiate."*

The water pouring over his shoulders had abruptly turned cold. There'd always been a problem with the water temperature in this house.

"I understand," Mariel said, and reached for the gun.

He fixed the muzzle beneath his chin.

And pulled the trigger.

First, he felt an overwhelming sense of peace. Indescribable. It was strange... being disconnected from the human body with all its aches, pains, sensations, and emotional chaos.

Mariel felt happy.

It was the *first time* he felt *completely* happy.

White, misty fog filled the atmosphere. It revealed a golden throne. The throne wasn't adorned. In fact, it was rather plain, with three domed spikes that jutted from the top of its back. Suspended within this throne were four beautiful creatures that, on Earth, would have been a thing of nightmares.

The living creatures had the faces of a lion, an ox, a man, and an eagle. Each creature had six wings and countless eyes. Merged together, the faces looked in all directions and embodied every point of a compass.

Without communicating, Mariel instantly realized that these creatures knew *everything* about him; about his father, about *every* single soul that existed in the Universe.

Behind the creatures, within the white mist, stood an enormous golden gate that was taller than the eye could see. It looked solid, strong, and indestructible. He could not fathom what existed behind that gate.

Still... he *knew*.

And he also knew that it was not time for him to see past that wall.

With different unified voices, the faces spoke as one—almost in melody. They greeted him by name.

Immediately, Mariel prostrated. He was overwhelmed with peace *and* fear combined. He trembled before them and dared not speak. He knew they would address him as needed.

Speaking in unison, in a Holy language that Mariel had been given the ability to understand, the creatures introduced themselves as the Cherubim—the Guardians of God's throne. They welcomed Mariel to the Gates of Heaven, and explained that the gates would soon open. He'd be given the opportunity to step into the Kingdom's doorway to experience a portion of the awesome power of Heaven.

The Cherubim told him that he would also experience the horrors of Hell.

Fright. Indescribable fright. More than he experienced with the humanoid. More than he'd experienced when he thought his dad might die.

He hoped he'd never have to hear the Cherubim utter that word again.

Then, the Lion, the Ox, the Man, and the Eagle, speaking from North, the South, the East, and the West, asked: *"What is it that you would like to know?"*

He responded in the language they spoke. *"Who am I? What is my purpose?"*

In a haunting chorus, the Cherubim responded. *"And I looked, and beheld a pale horse: and his name that sat on him was Death, and Hades followed with him. And power was given unto them over the fourth part of the Earth, to kill with sword, famine, and plague, and by the wild beasts of the Earth."*

Mariel trembled. He knew the scripture of Revelations. He knew it well.

"But what is my purpose?" he had pleaded. *"If I am the Horseman of Death... aren't I evil? How can I enter the Kingdom of Heaven if I am evil?"*

Mariel feared the answer.

"There is no need to fear if you adhere to the Will of God," the voices had assured. *"You were placed with the man you call father for a reason. You have listened to him, respected him, and you have opened your heart to God. Your purpose is not easy. Your purpose is to initiate and make way for the end times—to do that, you must take one life."*

These divine creatures were asking him to kill—how could that be?

It subverted all expectations and beliefs that his father had taught, that Mariel had *believed.*

But God had killed. In the Bible, God had *allowed* divine judgment through the hands of human beings.

"What is it you are asking me to do?" Mariel had cried.

"The First Death will trigger the final events. The Demon, Ba'al, worshipped by the Israelites in the Old Testament, has entered his vessel: Aleksey Petrov, the President of Russia. Years ago, Aleksey traded his body and soul for youth, wealth, unlimited power, and the promise of life eternal. He cannot die by the hand of anyone on Earth, other than you."

It seemed unreal, this request. Yet, so final.

"Why must someone die to trigger the final events? What good can it bring to a world that is already doomed to die?" Mariel had insisted.

The Cherubim were patient with him, but they did not budge. *"Ba'al must be the First Death, Mariel, and thousands more lives will be saved before the Great Tribulation."*

Mariel remained prostrated. *"And if I make a mistake? If I can't do it?"*

"Then Petrov will not stop building his empire if he doesn't die, no matter the depravity it brings."

They explained that the Prince of Hell's death would save more lives; it would liberate more people that would no longer be doomed to the hands of a dictator. But if Mariel failed—

"But it shall come about, if you do not obey the Lord your God, to observe to do all His commandments and His statutes with which I charge you today, that all of these curses will come upon you and overtake you."

They reminded him of the Humanoid, the demon who drove Cain to murder Abel due to his jealousy. They reminded him of the struggles Mariel already had, how much worse they could become, how he might destroy the lives of those he loved if he did not do as God asked.

The Cherubim also comforted him, provided him hope. They reminded him of Fr. Jerome's love, of his guidance. They assured him that, even as the appointed Horseman of Death, he could still enter the Kingdom of God.

They asked him one more question.

"What is your greatest desire?"

Mariel did not answer with haste. So many answers called to him, beckoned him, lied to him, confused him. He even questioned the motive of the Cherubim, trying to determine if the question was meant to trap or *trick* him. When he spoke, however, they listened, but the cold feeling that shuddered his soul told him one thing—he wasn't being entirely truthful.

That he wanted Esther, not—

"My greatest desire is to attain the Kingdom of Heaven with my Dad, Father Jerome, when it is our time."

The cold feeling remained as he looked upon the four faces of the Living Creatures, the Cherubim. They responded with power. *"Go and do as God has commanded, and your desire will be granted."*

The Council of the Cherubim would not, and could not, explain anything further. The creatures told Mariel that there were unknown details within the Scroll of Seven Seals. However, this was a scroll that only God and his Son, the Lamb, were worthy of opening in the Kingdom of Heaven.

Even they, the Guardians of God's throne, were not allowed to look within the scroll. They were not allowed to look upon the events to come. The powerful Cherubim had no knowledge of the timeframe in which these events would unravel and come to pass.

As they instructed Mariel to his feet, the Gates of Heaven opened.

Now, as he opened his eyes on a stranger's couch in Russia, he could not remember what he saw past Heaven's doorway. He remembered a feeling though, one unlike anything he would ever experience on Earth.

An overpowering feeling of complete love, combined with a level of unspeakable joy and peace. Washed clean.

And made anew.

But Hell... when he stood at the gates of Hell—oh, it was opposite of everything he'd felt at Heaven's doors.

Chaotic. Void. *Horrible*. Yes. Chaotic and *void of God*.

Empty of all things good.

Like he'd been there before and would always circle back.

Then—the dumpster.

And a reality that terrified him.

He was alive again, and back within Earth's chaos.

* * *

"Good, you're awake." The cheery voice startled him awake again.

As Mariel looked around the small apartment with the eighties and nineties style furniture, he frowned as he tried to remember what had taken place since awakening in the dumpster.

At the end of the hallway, a dark-haired man smiled. His clothing looked all too familiar to Mariel.

He was a priest.

"I hope I haven't been rude! I've been trying not to wake you."

Swinging his feet to the floor, Mariel groaned and then struggled to stand. He outstretched his hand. He had a lot of questions, but a friendly introduction wouldn't hurt. "My name's Mariel Nadier. I'm an American, and by your accent, I assume you are as well?"

"Father Paul." The short priest grasped Mariel's hand. "I know who you are. I mentored your dad, Fr. Jerome. Great man."

Mariel blinked at him, and then his legs gave out. He staggered backwards and sat back down on the couch. "Sorry," he said, scratching his head. "I guess this is all very weird for me."

His head hurt.

Fr. Paul nodded towards the kitchen. "Can I get you anything? Coffee? Food? When's the last time you ate?"

Mariel raised his eyes to the priest. "You won't believe me."

"Try me."

"Nope. I'm not comfortable sharing yet."

Fr. Paul smiled—a large smile that seemed very knowledgeable—and he entered his kitchen. "I've got leftover soup. I'll heat some for you."

Mariel watched him.

Fr. Paul opened the refrigerator. "I'd be hungry too if I hadn't eaten since last January."

Mariel stopped breathing. Then he shook his head. "Excuse me?"

"I know more than you'd assume, Mariel." The priest slammed the refrigerator door with his foot and then, with a deep thud, placed a large pot onto the counter. "And I'm willing to bet you're here to kill Aleksey Petrov." His eyes latched onto Mariel.

What the fuck?

"Who are you?" Mariel demanded.

Fr. Paul opened a cabinet, retrieved a bowl, and then slapped the cabinet door. The door struck the wood. Bounced back. Struck it again. "Call me a messenger," he said, and ladled white-colored soup into the brown, wooden bowl. He slid the bowl into the microwave and then hit the start button.

Then he stopped moving, and he looked at Mariel with narrowed eyes. The cabinet's overhang cast a dark shadow over his face. For a moment, he looked like an odd creature that begged to remain hidden in darkness. "Can you trust me?"

Did he? *Could* he?

"No."

The microwave let out a long, obnoxious beep. Fr. Paul shot one more glance towards Mariel before he withdrew the soup.

"What can I do to help you reach that point?"

"I don't know. Honestly, I want to get my task done, so I can spend whatever remaining time I have on Earth with my dad and—" He thought of Esther Caravan and stopped. Was *she* part of the equation? "Yeah. My dad."

Fr. Paul set the bowl of potato and mushroom soup on the coffee table in front of Mariel. "And? Don't hold back, Mariel, you had someone else's name on your tongue."

Yes. Esther Caravan.

His true desire.

If he said her name, it'd distract him from his order. His divine order... which thinking of it in that way sounded narcissistic beyond all reason.

But reality had changed. He knew his purpose now, and he couldn't help but feel an overwhelming sense of pride.

That is, if his purpose truly came from God. And if it did? God would guide him.

So Mariel said her name.

"Esther," he said softly, as steam rose from the bowl. "She's my best friend."

Gunfire popped somewhere in the city.

Mariel raised a spoonful of soup to his lips and blew.

The priest sat cross-legged on the living room carpet. His face was grim. "We need to talk about her."

Mariel dropped the spoon. "What do *you* know about her?"

Fr. Paul smiled a little. "Relax. I'm not a threat to her. I'm here to help."

Mariel wished everyone would stop speaking in riddles. Anxiety shot through his chest. Suddenly, it sank in that he hadn't asked one very important question.

"What month and what year is it again?"

What if Esther had moved on?

"It's Tuesday, January 7th. 2020." Fr. Paul outstretched his legs.

Shit.

Esther was a gorgeous woman, of *course* she would have moved on! God, he felt sick now, imagining her with someone else.

Someone like Gabe Donovan.

"Gonna puke," Mariel said, and bent over the couch. "Sorr—!" His stomach lurched, but nothing came out.

What could come out if he hadn't eaten anything for a year?

"I'll get you some tea," Fr. Paul said, and rose to his feet. "But we still need to talk."

His sickness worsened. "What?" Mariel croaked and wiped his mouth.

Fr. Paul filled the tea kettle and slammed it on the stove. "Your *task?* Whatever it is you need to do—if you do this in a hurry, you're placing Esther in danger."

Mariel sat up again. His legs felt numb. Did this priest *know* about God's orders? He'd said he was a messenger—a messenger from *where?*

"What the fuck do you know about Esther that you're not telling me?"

"I can't tell you. It'll determine how you respond, and I'm not allowed to fuck with free will."

More gunfire. Someone screamed.

"What?" Mariel cocked his head.

Fr. Paul scratched his head as if he'd cussed for the first time in years. "Trust me or don't trust me. It's your choice. But there is a kill chip inside of Esther. If you complete this *task* without removing it, she'll die."

He couldn't breathe. What kind of joke was this? A test from God?

It wasn't fucking funny.

"You don't know that," Mariel growled.

Fr. Paul didn't flinch. Sweat beaded on his brow.

"You'd have to know what task I need to do in order to know something like that," Mariel insisted, as if he were trying to convince himself.

Because if this was true, his orders *from God* just became far more complicated.

"I've been given just enough truth to help you where I can. I know you have a task to do, and if I had to guess? It'd have to do with killing somebody."

The tea kettle went off.

Mariel jumped.

Fr. Paul turned off the burner. "When God commands you to do something, you do it," the priest said, reaching for a mug in the cupboard. "But there are ways to go about it without causing harm to others." The liquid sloshed into the mug. "After all," Fr. Paul said, and he added a tea bag to the water. "God commanded you to take one life. Not two."

Mariel couldn't stop the rage that swamped his thoughts.

This *was* a means for the Cherubim to mock him.

A way for *God* to mock Mariel as He sat upon His throne with the Scroll of the Seven *fucking* Seals that only *He* could read.

Mariel couldn't do this alone. He needed his dad, but his dad wasn't *here*.

So he took a risk, because there was no such thing as a coincidence. Not in his world.

Not as the Horseman of Death.

"Petrov," Mariel said. "I've been instructed to kill Aleksey Petrov."

Fr. Paul bit the corner of his thumb. "Okay." He closed his eyes. "*Okay*. Yes. Let's address that."

Wringing his clammy hands together, Mariel nodded.

The priest brought the cup to the coffee table and knelt on the carpet. "Okay. I'm a messenger, so I've only been given *glimpses* of the future. *Glimpses* of knowledge that I've had to sort out over time. Here's what I think is happening... I think Petrov *knows* someone is after him. Someone close to Esther. I think he found a way to buy himself time by using Esther as bait. Meaning—"

"—If I kill him, Esther dies." Mariel bit his lip. Shit. *Shit.*

Fuck. Fuck. Fuck. Fuck.

What the hell was he supposed to do? Waltz back to Esther like he hadn't *died?* Tell her that the president of Russia put a kill chip inside of her? That'd be a phenomenal way to ask her out to fucking dinner.

"You're spiraling," Fr. Paul said, and smiled a little. "One step at a time."

"Yeah, okay. That'll *fucking work!*" Mariel screamed and dug his fingers into his hair. He hated this. Hated God.

Fuck!

A question circulated in his mind.

What if your Kingdom of Heaven... was actually Hell?

Then, something occurred to him.

Since his return, he hadn't seen the humanoid. The humanoid was *gone,* as if Mariel had been washed clean.

Made anew.

Mariel opened and closed his fists. He'd solve this. He'd solve this problem in his own time.

"Can you help me get home?" Mariel asked, and his hands shook with excitement. He'd go home and figure it out with his father's help.

Mariel didn't trust Fr. Paul, but the man was right. Why *wouldn't* Aleksey Petrov try to outsmart God's judgment?

"I'll help you," Fr. Paul said. "Whatever you do, however you decide to do this, take your time to figure it out, and I'll be here to help you how I can. Ultimately, God's will be done. Correct?"

It sounded so... distasteful. He couldn't explain why. But—

"Yes." Mariel reached for the tea and sipped it. The warmth trickled through his stomach and soothed its chaos. "Now... the elephant in the room."

"What's that?"

Mariel puffed out his cheeks and then blew out air. "Any suggestions on how to get home... overseas... when you're supposed to be dead?"

VERSE 5

~ I'M THE HORSEMAN OF DEATH ~

Saturday, January 11th, 2020:

I found my son, Mariel, dead in the shower from a gunshot wound last year. Today, he is coming home.

I've spent the last several days praying, begging God not to torture me. But I've talked to Mariel multiple times on the phone since he called me a few days ago, and nothing has changed. He's consistently told me the same thing: "Dad. I know this is confusing, but I'll be home soon and I'll explain."

I don't know what more to do with this information other than wait and pray that I've not been living as a ghost in some form of purgatory... or hell. Don't think I've not considered that. Living my life as a celibate homosexual priest hasn't stopped others from listing the reasons why I'm doomed to Hell. Maybe this is it—a constant reminder that Mariel died. A glimpse of hope before it's snatched away.

Would God send me to that place? Hell? I am frightened. I'm frightened to hope that I'll see my son today and he'll be ripped from me once more.

Have I been damned? Am I living a lie?

Blessings,

Fr. Jerome.

A plane roared over the airport roof.

Fr. Jerome stopped writing. Shivering in his jacket, he looked outside of the large window in the O'Hare airport lobby. A cacophony of bustling footsteps, chatter, and rolling suitcases filled the area. The orange sun sank into the horizon and glowed into the building.

Mariel's plane would be here in ten minutes.

Ten minutes.

This felt familiar—like the day he'd adopted Mariel.

The day the boy had caught the bullet. The day reality twisted into some form of strange existence that he feared he'd never be able to explain.

But Fr. Jerome hoped and prayed that Mariel's return *was* reality—even though he'd hyper-focused on Googling how the heck the States would allow a dead man to return from Russia.

And, on that note, how a man who died in Chicago ended up in Russia in the first place.

Someone shrieked with excitement, and the priest's eyes shifted to the walkway where a middle-aged woman ran into the arms of a young man.

Fr. Jerome smiled and then turned his eyes to the television.

It was a live broadcast. Kaemon Spears. Cameras flashed. He was all smiles.

BREAKING: *New innovative health technology to be released to the public soon.*

Footsteps grew louder, and Fr. Jerome noticed a large Arab man walk past his line of vision before sitting two seats down from him. Smooth, dark skin. A black cap. A strong, clean-shaven jaw, and scarred skin on his hands. The black cargo pants seemed too small on his legs as he lifted one to cross the other.

And he looked angry.

Very angry.

Fr. Jerome followed the man's eyes, which bore into the television as Kaemon Spears spoke.

"*Yarhamhum Allah,*" the man whispered through his teeth.

And Jerome caught his breath.

Stopped breathing.

And images exploded.

"*Yarhamhum Allah,*" *the man said, turning his palms to the air as the angry mob overtook him. "And justice for—*"

"—Ahdam. Justice for Ahdam," Jerome whispered, his body frozen in his seat. "Justice for—"

A hand covered Fr. Jerome's. Squeezed very hard.

The priest gasped and turned his head to the source. It had happened again, hadn't it? That *odd* moment in another world—where reality warped into something else.

Like a vision.

Breathing hard, the priest looked at the scarred hand that covered his, and then he raised his eyes to meet those of the Arab man who sat next to him now.

"You are muttering my son's name," the man whispered, almost without sound. "You need to stop."

Embarrassed, Fr. Jerome tried to pull his hand from beneath the larger one. He didn't budge.

"I'm sorry, I don't know what I said," Fr. Jerome whispered back. "Please let go of my hand. Security is watching."

His grip tightened.

"How do you know my son's name?"

Fr. Jerome gasped a little. His eyes shot to an older man slumped sideways on a chair across from them. Was he dead? Or sleeping?

"Let me go," the priest said, a little louder.

The Arab man released him, and the slumped man let out a loud snore. Fr. Jerome breathed a sigh of relief.

"I reacted too quickly, I'm sorry," the Arab man said, moving away from Fr. Jerome and rubbing his jaw. "I'm former military. I have PTSD. I thought I heard you say my son's name."

Fr. Jerome tried to settle his racing heart. He couldn't. He had an inkling that there was something more going on with this man that had *nothing* to do with PTSD.

"Is your son okay?" Fr. Jerome turned his head towards the man.

The man stared at the television, where Governor Spears spoke. The muscles in his jaw ribboned as he clenched his teeth.

He must hate Governor Spears, Fr. Jerome mused.

"My son will be okay," the man said, and he opened and closed his fists. He closed his eyes for a breath, opened them, and then smiled at Fr. Jerome. The smile seemed genuine, far different from the threatening demeanor he'd displayed a moment ago. "I'm sorry again. What's your name?"

"Father Jerome. Well, Jerome. Sorry, my circle is normally my congregation. What's yours?"

The man hesitated. "Haleef. May I buy you water for giving you troubles? Or some food?"

"I'm fine, really. I am. Who are you waiting for?"

"My ride. He's late." He scratched his jaw again and returned his scarred hand to his thighs to tap it against his legs.

Fr. Jerome nodded and looked towards the clock. His body quivered with adrenaline, and his eyes darted to the walkway.

Mariel would be here at any moment.

"My ride is here," Haleef said, and rose to his feet. He looked at Fr. Jerome with a sudden devastation in his eyes, as if he wanted to plead for his help. "May God bless you, Father."

Sadness crept through his body. "You too, Son. Be safe."

And with that, Haleef took his luggage and left the priest to work through what had just happened.

Fr. Jerome watched him walk away, and he noticed how Haleef glanced about the area as if he suspected he'd be captured by other armed forces.

And then... he saw Mariel.

And the world stopped moving.

Standing tall above the others, dressed in sweatpants and a hoodie, Mariel looked for him, his eyes moving in desperation to find his dad.

A sob lurched from the priest's chest, and he started forward.

And Mariel's eyes met his.

Perhaps this was Hell. Maybe someone *would* rip Mariel from his arms. But if this moment was Hell, it was beautiful.

But when they collided in an embrace, and Fr. Jerome sobbed against his son's chest, no one took Mariel. The vision didn't end.

This wasn't Hell.

It was Heaven.

*　　*　　*

"Did you travel alone?" Fr. Jerome asked, stepping back to wipe his eyes. He still couldn't believe who stood before him—his son, the son he'd held in his arms after finding him in the bathroom with a bullet wound.

Mariel shook his head. His wavy hair almost bounced with life. "No, Dad. Your mentor came with me—Fr. Paul?"

Confused, Fr. Jerome stepped back a little. "He's here?"

"Right here, old friend."

Fr. Jerome recognized his voice immediately. Gasping, he snapped his head in the direction of the voice and saw him, Fr. Paul Rinaldi, standing off to the side of Mariel.

"You look good, Jerome."

Fr. Jerome wiped his eyes. He wasn't sure how to respond to the man that stood before him, the man that looked like he hadn't aged a day since his forties, the man who'd ignored his futile attempts to contact him after Mariel's death. "Paul? Did you help my son get home?" He wasn't sure why he asked, but he needed an answer, as if hearing it would build a certain trust again.

"Yes." Fr. Paul smiled. "I'm here to stay for a little bit, and I was able to get help from the Russian Orthodox Church in getting a 'poor, helpless American' back to the U.S." He chuckled a little, as if he thought the situation was funny.

Fr. Jerome didn't think it was funny, but he was happy right now. So, he laughed a little. "Thank you so much. Do you need a ride anywhere?"

Fr. Paul shook his head. "You two spend some time together. I'll be around. See you guys." He looked at Mariel. "Be strong, kid."

"Thank you, Father."

And Fr. Paul was gone.

Fr. Jerome drove straight home. At first, both men were silent. The priest wasn't sure how to initiate conversation. He wasn't certain he wanted to know the details of Mariel's situation yet, but small talk wasn't an option either.

Finally, Mariel drew a sharp breath. As he stared out of the frosty windows, he spoke. "It felt like a day."

"Oh, what? What's that?" Fr. Jerome jumped and coughed a little.

"In Heaven. It felt like a day to me. And here we are, almost a year later." Mariel ran his finger across the glass, creating a line through the mist. "It was beautiful."

The priest gripped the steering wheel. Glued his eyes to the road. Refused to look away.

No car accidents. No more *death*.

"Can you tell me about it?"

Mariel brushed his fingers across the dusty dashboard. His voice sounded distant. "It was unreal. Both frightening and beautifully glorious. I don't know how else to explain it."

Fr. Jerome's voice trembled. "What happened?" He needed to know now.

Mariel turned soft, blue eyes to his father.

Something about the way he looked at Fr. Jerome forced the old priest to briefly take his eyes from the road. The young man's eyes spoke to him like a soft, comforting breeze.

"It'll all be okay," Mariel said, reaching for his father's hand. "I'm not comfortable sharing the instructions I was given yet, but it'll all be okay."

No. Withholding information? *This* was how it all started, how he found Mariel dead in the shower.

"Mariel." Fr. Jerome's voice was gruff. "I spent the last year trying to survive on my own, trying to understand *everything*. And—and *electronic music? Really?*" He was laughing and crying. The tears blurred his eyesight. He wiped his eyes. No car accidents. No death.

"I knew you'd be mad at me for that," Mariel said, grinning. He squeezed the priest's hand. "It's okay, you can go insane if you need to. You have every right to be angry with me."

Trying to clear his eyes, Fr. Jerome blinked rapidly. "My *point* is that I've been through—*shit*. Absolute bullcrap. I think I can handle whatever it is you tell me, because I need answers too."

"Alright, Dad."

"Alright. Good. Now tell me."

Mariel brushed fingers through his dark hair. "They told me that I'm the Horseman of Death, as referenced in Revelations."

Fr. Jerome swallowed, but did not respond.

"Dad?"

"Yes."

"Did you hear me?"

"Yes, Mariel, what does that mean? I don't know what that means."

"Dad. You're a priest, I feel like I don't need to explain—"

Fr. Jerome pounded the steering wheel. "Don't *patronize me, Mariel!* Just *tell* me!"

Mariel leaned away from him a little. "I'm *sorry*. This has been stressful for me too, you know." He rubbed his forehead. "Alright, they basically told me that I need to—fight someone. Remove them from their seat of power."

"You're being vague on purpose, Mariel. If I'm *not supposed to know* something, just *tell* me that."

"I *want* to! But you won't believe me."

Fr. Jerome slapped on the blinker. "I wish you would trust me. You've never trusted me."

"That's not true, and that's not fair."

"Oh, it isn't?" Fr. Jerome tapped his fingers against the steering wheel. "Ever since you were a little boy, you kept me at arm's length. You rarely told me anything unless I begged you for information. I've always wanted to help, and be there for you, but you have to let me in, son. I need to know if I am supposed to do something with this."

"Do something with *what*?"

"*You!* The fact that you're alive, here, in my car again. The fact that you couldn't die before this. The visions I have, anything, *everything*. I need to be involved before I lose my *fucking mind, Son!*"

The silence between them was thick, with only the noise of the heater on full blast. Small bits of dust circulated from the air vents, reminding Fr. Jerome that he had forgotten to clean the interior of the car once again. Honestly, in the wintertime, it did not concern the priest as much. Today, however, it bothered him.

Again, Mariel sighed. "I didn't know you were having visions, Dad."

Visions? Or hallucinations?

"I haven't quite figured out what they are," Fr. Jerome said, clearing his throat. "I feel like I'm going mad."

Mariel nodded. "If it makes you feel any better, I've felt that way my whole life. I'm still not sure what's real, especially now."

"I'm sorry, Son."

"Can we start over? Please? I don't want to fight with you." His voice faded, and his eyes drifted elsewhere.

Fr. Jerome did not need to follow his son's gaze. Based on the familiarity of the surroundings, he knew he'd just passed *Caravan's Books*. He opened his mouth to speak, but refrained.

Because *something* in the depths of his gut told him not to bring up Esther Caravan.

"Yes," the priest said, exhausted. "Let's start over. Let's talk when you are ready." He reached over and squeezed the young man's shoulder. "I love you, and I'm sorry."

"I love you too."

"Are you hungry? Do zombies eat anything other than brains?" Fr. Jerome winked at Mariel. He decided the joke sounded dumb a few seconds after he spoke.

Mariel smiled a little, but did not respond.

Once home, Fr. Jerome warmed up leftover chili that Esther had made for him the other week. Often, there were times throughout the last year that she'd surprise him with a dish. Enchiladas. Chili. Many were very good. As he served Mariel like old times, once again, he did not mention her name.

As Mariel sat down to eat, Harlow peeked around the corner to assess the newest human being in her domain. Then she darted into the kitchen, stopped, and fled into the hallway as Mariel shifted his feet.

"Your cat hates me, Dad."

Fr. Jerome smiled. "Harlow is a one-man girl. She'll warm up to you." He sat down at the table, and both men bent their heads to pray.

As it darkened outside, Harlow wandered into the dining room and rubbed against Fr. Jerome's legs. She purred, curling her tail around his leg, but she glared with suspicion at the newest pair of legs beneath the table.

Neither brought up the resurrection. Together, they watched a movie and shared fleeting smiles.

The adrenaline crash wreaked havoc on Fr. Jerome's body, but he was hesitant to sleep. He was afraid he'd wake up, and it'd all be a dream. He was frightened he'd open his eyes and see only the memories of his son.

So the priest tried to stay up as long as he could, but exhaustion won the battle. In the living room, the television murmured as he drifted to sleep with Harlow on his lap.

And while Harlow dreamt of catnip, Fr. Jerome dreamt of a dark-skinned Leader.

The Leader had peace on his lips, but war in his eyes.

He dreamt of a frightened boy. The boy brought life to Earth, and in the same breath the boy destroyed it.

And Fr. Jerome dreamt of his son.

Mariel did not remove one man from power.

He removed ten.

And in that same dream, Esther Caravan screamed.

When the priest awoke with a gasp of despair, the time was almost midnight. A note rested on the couch.

"Going for a drive. Maybe stopping by the church. I can't sleep. See you later, and don't freak out. I'll be back."

Fr. Jerome rose to his feet, turned, and stood before the picture window in the living room with his hands clasped behind his back.

Outside, the snow fell in thick gusts. Harlow purred and sat next to his ankles.

The priest didn't need a vision, a dream, or a nightmare to tell him where Mariel went. He knew.

He had no desire to admit it to himself.

But he *knew*.

Visions, dreams, and nightmares did not match his fatherly intuition, and the intuitive pang in his gut told him one frightful thing, something he didn't understand—that Mariel's destination would change the lives of everyone Fr. Jerome held dear.

Chapter 9: Verse 1

~ Secretary ~

Friday, January 10th, 2020

Chicago, Illinois

On January 10th, 2020, approximately twenty-four hours away from a mistake she'd make that would forever change her life, Tira Arcelin met a skinny, red-haired lawyer outside of the gender-neutral restroom on the first floor of KS Industries.

It was 4:15 P.M. In fifteen minutes, she'd meet with Kaemon Spears about his upcoming political event that was set to take place in February. She was not particularly interested in this meeting—for many reasons. One, it meant she'd have to discuss the progress of the recruits, which also meant she'd have to think about Recruit Matthew Thompson. Now that she couldn't fuck his fiancée, there wasn't much more she could do to piss him off.

That nettled her.

A Thompson had no right to exist, much less exist without pain.

But alas, thanks to Petrov's threat, she now had to suffer through Thompson's existence *and* keep her mouth shut *and* keep her hands to herself.

She missed Russia.

Rules did not exist in Russia.

Well—more or less. Petrov's mood played a role in that. And he wasn't in the greatest of moods right now, considering Moscow had gone mad in recent days, and so had the headlines.

Moscow Gone Mad.

Is Petrov the next Hitler?

Multiple dead or wounded by Petrov's police state.

Liberal, right-wing, and independent media attacked Aleksey Petrov from all angles, claiming that law enforcement's use of deadly force against the rioters on January 7th had been excessive and unethical.

Tira disagreed. The rioters had threatened her home—she felt no pity for them. In fact, one had injured a K9 with an explosive, and she found that unforgivable.

As she exited the restroom, Tira smoothed her white V-neck and straightened her black dress pants. The door swung shut with a slam, and her heels echoed against the tile-floored hallway. There, she saw a man standing alone by the elevator that would take her further into Lake Michigan's depths—the third lowest floor.

Tira knew who he was. His name was Philip Jameson, and she'd seen him before, but they'd never crossed paths. In fact, she rarely saw him at the research center. In the times she had, Kaemon Spears accompanied him in an office somewhere for what she presumed to be a legal briefing.

Head of legalities, or something like that. That was his role.

It didn't matter to her, because it had nothing to do with her role in the United States.

But Philip Jameson had *everything* to do with her patience when he opened his goddamn mouth for the first time.

"Second floor?" Philip asked, stepping onto the elevator and tapping the button. His navy blue suit, brown shoes, and white shirt looked crisp, clean, and professional. His red hair, combed and styled to perfection, almost triggered Tira to reach up and smooth out her tight ponytail.

"Third floor." Tira stepped onto the elevator and stood on the other side. Her hand slipped into her pocket where she located a switchblade she'd managed to smuggle into the research center for almost a year.

"*Third* floor?" The lawyer frowned and shot her an incredulous look. "You need *clearance* for *anything* lower than the second floor." He reached into his suit coat, produced a swipe card, and wagged it in the air.

Tira, who'd refused to look in his direction, stared at the numbered buttons. "Excuse me?"

The elevator stopped at the second floor. It let out a ding, and the doors opened.

Philip gestured outwards. "The secretary offices are located on the second floor, Miss. Are you new?"

Oh. *Oh.*

If Tira were in Petrov's kingdom, she'd dump this pointy testicle hair into the toilet and flush it. But she wasn't. She resided in the United States of America—*Chicago* to be exact—where one couldn't even ride a motorcycle on the roadway without a speeding ticket.

A low snarl rumbled through her throat and vibrated her upper lip. Toying with the switchblade, her fingers had a mind of their own as she turned her head to look at him with building rage.

Unfazed, Philip stood there, his hands directed towards the open elevator.

Tira started to speak. "I—"

"*Hi*, Tira." A young woman with bouncy dark curls and a penchant for wearing knee-length skirts and low cut blouses passed the elevator and ran her tongue over her lips. "Coming to say hi to me again today?"

Tira pulled her swipe card from her left pocket. "I have a meeting."

Philip scowled at the both of them.

The young woman pouted, flounced off, and then said, "I'm jealous of the people you're meeting with. See ya."

The doors closed.

Philip straightened his tie. "How unbecoming. Women throw themselves at anything these days."

Blade in her hand now, Tira leaned past the lawyer to scan her card. It beeped. As she tapped the button for the third floor, the blade flicked and sliced the cloth behind him. "Clearly," she said, straightening up. "Your wedding band proves that."

Philip Jameson gasped and looked at his ring, as if it'd remind him that he *wasn't* a pointy testicle hair, and that what she'd said was *mean* and untrue. He was speechless. It wasn't until they reached the third floor that he opened his mouth to protest.

And Tira darted from the elevator before he could.

The research center had always fascinated her. The top floor—break rooms, a coffeehouse, and fitness facilities including a basketball court and a pool. The next floor down: more offices, conference rooms, *secretaries*. The third floor down consisted of labs, medical centers, and more offices. Many of these rooms required authorized personnel only, and Tira was not considered authorized. Not that she cared, but her boredom led her to wonder what newest research took place in those labs. She'd seen many patients, all ages, escorted in and out of those rooms, and she wondered what the medical files might say if she hacked into the system.

Tira swore to herself that, no matter how bored she got, she would not do such a thing.

But there *was* another level. A fourth floor. She hadn't been privy to that floor, and no one discussed the fourth level. So, of course, natural curiosity prodded her like a pointed fingernail, but she tossed it to the back of her mind.

Tira decided that her monthly income was far too valuable to dig deeper into things that had nothing to do with her.

But God, did she want to.

As she approached conference room 0367, her heels echoed against the floor. Armed guards stood stationary at every corner. Two males guarded an elevator that, she presumed, went down to the fourth floor with proper key card access.

"Hi, Agent Arcelin," one of the guards said, and nodded once.

"Hello." Tira kept walking.

Straight ahead, the door was closed. The handle turned. It opened, and a brown-haired teenage boy in dress pants and a white polo stepped out of the room. He looked at her.

Tira looked at him.

And she almost stopped walking.

Jason *"Hawk"* Caravan—Esther's little brother.

What was *he* doing at KS Industries, and why on Earth was he in the same conference room as Kaemon Spears?

A security guard met Hawk outside the room and walked with him down the hall, past Tira and away from room 0367.

Tira did not glance back.

But she heard the boy exclaim something she didn't expect to hear.

"Hi, Mr. Jameson!"

"Hello, Mr. Caravan." A cool, pompous voice.

Why the fuck was that pubic hair following her to the conference room?

"I won't be at church Sunday, I'm going out of town with my dad and my grandma."

"Well, I'm sure you won't miss anything considering Fr. Jerome's sermons haven't really called to the congregation as of late. Where are you guys going this..."

Tira growled, and the rest of his sentence faded as she entered the conference room.

Kaemon Spears sat with his legs on the long table, looking up at the television suspended in the air on the other side of the room. His forefinger rested on his lips as he squinted at the news coverage for—as she suspected—the Moscow riots. "Hi, Agent. Have a seat."

Tira moved past him and sat several chairs down from him.

Kaemon rubbed his chin. He had the sleeves of his black *Puma* hoodie pushed up to his elbows. His legs jittered, vibrating the table and sending ripples through the water pitcher. His chair creaked.

It drove Tira nuts.

"Just waiting on Phil," Spears said, finally looking at her.

He seemed distracted. Unsettled.

Oh, God.

That was why he'd followed her.

Seconds later, Phil Jameson walked in. Face red. Disheveled. His eyes snapped to Tira. Rage and surprise twisted his expression, but he sat down very quickly and cleared his throat. "I'm here."

Kaemon stared at him. "I see that. Why do you look like you've been caught jacking off?"

Tira coughed to cover a snort. She reached for a small glass and the water pitcher.

"There is *no need* to say such *foul* things."

"Kiss my ass, Jameson. Agent Arcelin—have you two met?" Spears gestured between the two.

Tira nodded. "Today. In the elevator."

Phil glared at her and straightened his tie. "Let's get on with the meeting."

"Oh, do you have some place more important to be, Phil?"

"Well, *no*, I just—" His face was still red.

Tira knew exactly why.

Kaemon interrupted him. "Alright. Phil, you're here to discuss any glaringly obvious legality issues we might run into with this upcoming rally pertaining to KS Industries and the new health watches I'll be discussing. Tira, we'll go over recruit placement and expectations since that's their final fieldwork test. Let's begin."

They spoke for an hour and a half. Tira briefed the governor about the recruits, and Phil discussed the legal state of KS Industries. The meeting bored Tira, but she reminded herself that the weekend was coming.

And she shuddered with the knowledge that she was *excited* to work third shift as a patrol officer in downtown Chicago.

But what else was there to be excited about?

"Hello." Spears answered the phone. His eyes shifted. "They're here? Okay. Yeah, I'll come out. Yep. Bye." He lowered the phone. "Meeting adjourned. We'll have another one soon."

"Good night." Phil stood up and did his best to angle his backside away from Kaemon and Tira.

"Philip." Kaemon eyed him.

"Yes?" Phil cleared his throat.

"Why are your boxers hanging out the back of your pants?"

Tira slurped her water.

Phil's blue boxers dangled from his backside where his dress pants split over his butt cheeks. His face turned redder, and he stammered. "I—er. Oh goodness, I'm not..." He grabbed his own backside in a desperate attempt to close his pants. "*She* did it!"

"Hmm?" Tira glanced up from the itinerary sheet in front of her. "Pardon?"

"Oh, don't you *feign innocence,* you little *blonde wench!*"

"I am not certain I understand what you're on about." Tira raised an eyebrow.

Kaemon looked back and forth at them.

And Phil pointed his finger. "Listen, little girl—"

Tira lunged from her seat. Glided over the table as if it didn't exist. Blood surged to her head.

Eyes wide, Phil backed against the wall.

Her switchblade snapped open. Spittle flew from between her teeth. "Don't *ever* call me *little girl!*"

"Agent Arcelin." Kaemon's calm, but firm, voice. "Please don't ruin your career and do something you regret."

The blade glimmered near Phil's carotid artery.

Tira hadn't realized she'd gotten to him so fast.

The blade clicked back into place. She stepped away and brushed hair from her eyes.

Phil gurgled and rubbed his neck.

A dark stain filled the front of his pants.

"Philip, go clean yourself up and change your pants," Spears sighed, rising from his chair. "Go."

Blubbering, Philip Jameson tried desperately to cover himself as he darted from the conference room. He left a small, quarter-sized wet spot on the carpet.

"Agent Arcelin." Spears turned dark eyes to her.

Was she fucked?

She was fucked, wasn't she?

"That made me laugh, thank you." Spears smiled. "Keeps that fool in his place."

"Er." Tira wasn't sure how to respond.

"Now, there's an important package arriving in five minutes." He hesitated. "Come with me. I'd like you to see it."

* * *

Tira was not sure what to expect when Kaemon Spears took her out to the hallway. She envisioned a package, one contained in a cardboard box. But she was smart enough to recognize, based on Spears' cryptic behavior, that this would not be the arrival of an *Amazon* package.

Tira expected innovative medical equipment. A weapon, perhaps.

But she did not expect what came through the elevator doors.

First: two KS security guards.

Then the United States army. Three of them.

Next: a man and a woman in lab coats.

Then the wheelchair. And in it?

A child.

Dressed in sweatpants and a hoodie, an Arab boy with close-cropped hair lay slumped and strapped in the wheelchair, his head rolling to the side. A blindfold covered his eyes.

He looked no more than ten or eleven.

"There he is," Kaemon whispered.

A young Middle Eastern woman pushed the wheelchair and followed the group down the hallway. They were headed down to the classified elevator.

The fourth floor.

Tira watched the boy's head wobble side to side as they brought him to the elevator. She could tell he wasn't sleeping.

The boy was *sedated*.

Something in the agent's gut twisted—similar to the feeling she'd experienced when she heard about the injured K9. It was a horrible, painful sensation.

"You're looking at history in the making, Agent Arcelin," Spears said, his lips quivering into a smile. "You've just been privy to seeing something that other people in your position *wished* they could."

A *child?*

What was so special about a *child?*

And *why* did she feel as though she had no right to inquire any further into it?

"Thank you," Tira replied. What else could she say?

A security guard scanned his card. The elevator opened.

"This way, Adela," the woman in the lab coat snapped, gesturing for the Middle Eastern woman to hurry up and push the wheelchair into the elevator.

The boy's head came up. A howl echoed from his lips.

"Inject him again!" a man screamed.

The floor vibrated beneath Tira's feet.

"Oh, my God," Spears said, and his face twisted with a strange level of joy.

The wheelchair disappeared into the elevator. The boy's screams abruptly stopped.

And with a loud thud, the elevator doors shut.

* * *

Just under twenty-four hours later, on Saturday, January 11th, Tira Arcelin hadn't stopped thinking about the bloodcurdling wail from that boy's mouth.

Kaemon Spears had offered her no further information. Instead, he'd gone about business as usual before sending her back up to the first floor to continue on with her day.

So, knowing that her curiosity would only grow if she kept thinking about it, she put it in the back of her mind. It wasn't her problem.

But what the hell had caused the floor to vibrate?

"Anything could have," Tira laughed at herself, prepping her meals for the weekend on road patrol. God, she was so bored she'd created dumb fiction in her own mind.

The laptop sat open on the counter. The surveillance program filled the screen.

Nothing exciting was happening in Esther Caravan's world either, not that *that* surprised Tira.

As the chicken sizzled in the pan, Agent 4 stomped towards the laptop and glared at it as if it'd committed a crime against her.

Location: *Caravan's Books.*

Vitals normal.

"Ugh!" Tira looked at her phone. No emergencies. No missions. No new messages. Well, she had *one* from the flouncy girl at the research center.

"Here's my Snapchat if you have one. Maybe I'll send a few photos you like ;)."

"Why would I have that?" Tira snarled. "What the hell is Chatsnap, and why would I want it?"

The chicken popped in the pan, and she tossed her phone aside. She was frustrated. There was nothing to *do*. She'd spent *years being* a weapon, using weapons, building weapons, deconstructing systems and reconstructing them. Now, she existed in the presence of politicians who dangled *just enough* knowledge for her to feel important, but not important enough to know the *full* truth of anything she was involved in.

In Russia, she'd felt like a weapon.

Here?

Tira existed on the second level—between the first and fourth floors. Close enough to *see* and *hear* the political rumbling, but *too far* to know *why*.

Because Tira Arcelin was the secretary.

As a lemon-odor wafted into the air, Tira leaned over the counter. The program, at the surface, appeared simple. Most of the buttons pictured their intended function.

VITALS.

SOUND.

GPS LOCATION.

EMERGENCY SIGNAL.

EMERGENCY SHUTDOWN.

Wait.

"Emergency shut down?" Tira said, squinting and leaning into the laptop screen as if it'd give her more information if her face was inside of the laptop. When had *that* button been installed?

Frowning, Tira checked for recent updates. Ah yes, the laptop had completed a full update last night in her sleep.

"Has there always been an emergency shutdown button?" Tira asked herself, clicking through the other tabs in the surveillance program. She supposed she'd never *looked* for one, because Michael had never told her that an emergency shutdown for the subject was necessary.

"Don't break what you can't fix, I suppose," Tira said, quoting that ridiculous saying he liked to say.

Or maybe it was the other way around.

Shrugging, Tira exited out of the other tabs and hovered the mouse hand over the *SOUND* button. There was nothing to watch on television, and television was a ridiculous waste of time. Listening to the subject use her customer service voice with bookstore patrons was also a ridiculous waste of time, but at least she said something once in a while that made Tira laugh.

"I'm so tired today."

"Ugh, that woman was rude."

"Oh, fuck my life." That one was Tira's favorite. It was comical listening to a spoiled American brat complain about her life as if it amounted to something that *was* fuckable.

Just because *she* was fuckable, it didn't mean the universe had any desire to involve itself in Esther's life.

Heat warmed Tira's face. *Not* that Esther Caravan was fuckable, she'd just meant that—

"Move! *Work!*" Tira roared, tapping the button again. The mouse had jammed. It didn't budge. Every time she clicked, the laptop would issue a *dinging* sound—a sound that she despised. Years ago, in class, one of her colleagues had made the *dinging* sound over and over, knowing it peeved her, and so she took the laptop and smashed it over his head.

She'd been forced to swim laps in dirty water for hours as punishment.

"Goddamn it!" Tira screamed and gave the mouse one last resounding smack with her finger before rising from the counter to storm back to the stove.

As Tira yanked the spatula from the counter, a chaotic beeping sound blasted through the kitchen like a time bomb nearing an explosion. Her watch vibrated on her wrist like a monstrous mosquito.

Eyes wide, Tira raised her watch to her face.

EMERGENCY SHUTDOWN ACTIVATED.

"Fuck-fuck-fuck-fuck-fuck! No!" Spatula flopping in her hand, Tira Arcelin raced to the computer.

A female voice aired over the speaker.

"Emergency microchip shutdown in ten, nine, eight, seven—"

"Jesus Christ, where's the code? *What's the code?"*

She should have paid attention to Michael. She should have taken this more *seriously*.

"*...six, five, four...*"

"Uh—code, code, *code!*" Tira typed the first five-digit code she could think of into the window. It'd be something stupid. Something *easy!*

12345.

"*Three... two...*"

Frantic, Tira typed. *54321.*

"*...One...zero... system deactivated.*"

The beeping stopped.

The kitchen went quiet.

Spatula in hand, Tira stared at the laptop screen that had given her complete access to Esther Caravan's life. Big red lettering mocked her as it flashed over and over again.

SYSTEM DEACTIVATED.

The chicken hissed in the pan.

Outside, a driver blew their horn.

The fire alarm went off.

And Tira Arcelin, standing in the smoky haze of her kitchen, said one Russian word in a tone so low she almost couldn't hear herself speak—a universal term that many folks from all walks of life would understand if they'd just ended potentially their own career with a click of a button.

"Blyat."

VERSE 2

~ DATE NIGHT ~

Saturday, January 11th, 2020
Chicago, Illinois

"**B**abe!" Gabe shrieked.

"*What?*"

"Don't drink from the bottle like that. We just passed a cop!"

It was early Saturday evening. Date night. Comfortable in Gabe's toasty truck, Esther lowered the liquor bottle and glanced out of the window as they crept along the city streets towards the parking garage. Indeed, a bundled police officer with a reflective traffic vest stood directing people across the street.

He directed zero interest towards them.

Esther raised the bottle to her lips and turned her eyes to Gabe with a coy smirk. "It's fine."

"I don't wanna go to jail. And you're still a minor."

Esther lowered the bottle again, capped it, and slipped it under the seat. Smiling, she brushed a finger over the young man's solid jaw.

Dear God, she loved muscular men.

And *damn...* she felt tipsy.

Maybe that's why she thought he was hot right now.

Fuck.

"You just like using the term minor with me, don't you?"

"Naw."

"Well good. Because I'm fucking twenty-one now, asshole!" She popped him on the cheek. "You don't remember my age?"

Gabe blushed. He switched on his left turn signal and gripped the steering wheel. He seemed perplexed, as if he wasn't sure if he should turn or wait for the oncoming car to pass.

"Just turn."

"Eh..."

"Do it, Gabe. Impress me. Make me horny with your driving skills."

Gabe slammed his foot on the gas and screeched towards the entrance ramp. The driver of the oncoming vehicle blared their horn, and the headlights flickered into the passenger side where Esther sat.

She opened her middle finger.

Gabe shook his head. The engine roared in the parking garage as he drove up the ramp. "Really, Esther?"

"I'm really happy your dad's important and can buy reserved parking spots," Esther said, leaning her head back. The orange-yellow garage lights flashed across her face.

Gabe stopped, reversed, and then pulled into a reserved spot. "You only like me because I'm rich, don't you?" He grinned, turned off the ignition, and looked at her. "You're beautiful."

She was, and she knew it.

Esther had finally convinced Gabe to take her swing dancing. She wore a green, V-neck, and knee-length polyester dress with snug sleeves that cut off at her elbows. She'd purchased the dress because it looked great on her curves, and it spun when she danced. Her green high heels matched the dress. She'd styled her hair into a thick braided bun at the back of her neck.

Yes. She looked good.

But her heart felt empty.

Esther looked at Gabe, who wore a three-piece grey suit without a tie. He'd left the crisp white shirt unbuttoned at the neck and chest to expose the well-built muscles he so often called "*his gains*".

"And you're hunky," she said, realizing it sounded way less sincere than his sweet comment towards her.

Gabe reached into his pocket. "I got something for you. And don't freak out, it's not an engagement ring." He lifted his hips and dug for the item before he realized it was in the other pocket and switched sides. Finally, he withdrew a black box and handed it to her.

Cautious, Esther took the velvet box and eyed him. "Gabe. What did you do?"

"Just open it."

With trembling fingers, Esther opened the box. It contained a silver necklace with a solitaire pendant—a dancing girl in white. It was beautiful, and something about the gift's perfection made her pause—made her almost tell Gabe that she was sorry she kept using him for emotional support, and that it was time to end things because—

"Do you like it?" Gabe murmured.

Quickly nodding, she lifted it from the box. "Put it on me?"

Eagerly, Gabe took it from her hands and clipped it around her neck. For a moment, his fingers lingered on her shoulders, and Esther felt his breath against the skin of her neck. Then, his lips.

She shivered. The way he worked his lips up the side of her neck, towards her earlobe, sent electric signals from her brain to her groin, and she let out a gasp. "Okay, stop," Esther whispered, pulling herself forward to evade his hands and his kisses.

"What'd I do?"

"Nothing. I'm just ready to eat and dance, and it's hard to do that when you send my brain to the gutter."

Gabe grinned and opened his door. "Whenever you are ready, Esther, my dick will be waiting."

"And yet you *always* manage to turn me off faster than you turn me on."

Gabe had placed a reservation at a steakhouse that—

"... *serves steak that would change the world of steak for you, Babe,*" he'd said, winking. "*Dad always takes my mom here for their anniversary.*"

Ah yes, Senator James Donovan—candidate in the Republican presidential primaries. Despite growing up around him, Esther hated his politics and didn't particularly care for him as a person either. He'd always looked down his nose at the middle-class.

And yet, here she was about to eat a $150 cut of meat that his son would pay for.

Probably with his father's money too.

After a big dinner and several glasses of wine, they left the restaurant to begin the highlight of Esther's night—dancing.

The streets bustled with Saturday night crowds, headlights, and cops. Cold air whipped against Esther and her beau as they walked hand in hand down the city sidewalk.

When they approached the dance club, Gabe reached into his pocket and withdrew Esther's cell phone. "Your dad's callin'," he said, passing it to her.

They paused just outside of the club. Loud, jazzy, swing music vibrated the sides of the brick building. Another young couple flung open the door, staggered outside, and laughed while lighting cigarettes.

Esther coughed a little as she answered the phone. "Hey, Dad."

"Hi, sweetheart. Doing ok?"

"Yes, Dad. I'm fine. How's your trip?" It was fucking cold, and she should have remembered a coat.

"Good. I wish you would have come. You used to love water parks and lodges and all that."

"I still do. Alone time in the house for once is great, though. I needed it. But you guys have fun, okay?"

"Thanks, Honey. Don't forget to open the store tomorrow for maintenance, and tell Gabe hello for me!"

Esther looked at Gabe, who stood waiting patiently for the call to end. "My dad says hi," she whispered, and her breath drifted into the cold air.

He grinned and jerked his fingers into the shape of a gun.

"He says hi back. Can you let me know when you are on your way home tomorrow?" Esther shivered, and in response, Gabe wrapped his arms around her.

"I will, Squirt. Be safe tonight."

Esther slipped the phone back into Gabe's pocket and then grasped his hand. "Let's go fucking dance."

The swing music went from loud to ear-splitting when they entered the illuminated dance club.

Esther's face brightened with excitement. Dancers spun, went airborne, and twirled. There was something about dance, any kind, that set her body on fire.

Trumpets screamed.

Blood rushed to her face, her cheeks tingled, and she pulled Gabe onto the dance floor. He smiled, she laughed, and their bodies came together. If there was one thing she appreciated about Gabriel Donovan: he had rhythm. He could swing and ballroom dance as if he'd been coached his entire life.

As their bodies separated, came together, and spun, Esther finally felt liberated. *Happy.*

Perhaps it was the dopamine from dancing, or the effects of the alcohol. Nonetheless, right now she *felt* like she *could* be happy with Gabe.

And *maybe* if she tried making love to him, her feelings might deepen.

As Gabe pulled her into his arms, his sweet cologne drifted into Esther's nostrils. She could feel the rhythm of his pulse, the hard muscles of his back flexed against her skin as she rested her palm against him.

He was fun, and he *loved* her. She was safe with him, and he'd matured since last year's... incident. Since sending her message of closure to Mariel, she'd experienced a new feeling of liberation and peace. In reality, she still missed him, but moving forward would *help*.

But Gabe... was he the path forward?

"Having fun?" Gabe yelled into her ear. He rested one hand on her hips and spun.

"*Yes!*" Esther shouted, spinning with him. The lights flooded her eyes. She felt warm from Gabe, from dancing, and from the effects of the liquor. Her mind buzzed. The drums pounded her ears.

Gabe released her, twirling her outwards as he held onto her fingers before drawing her back against him. His hand pressed into the small of her back, pushing her hips against his, and Esther let out a sharp breath as he gyrated his hips against her in rhythm to the music.

The song ended. Gabe pulled back from her, smiling and kissing her palm as other dancers in the building applauded the band. "You alright?" he asked, wiping sweat from his forehead.

Esther nodded and smiled, but she was frustrated with herself. *Frightened.* As the next song began, the young woman attempted to understand the war inside her mind.

During the slower melody, their bodies merged. As Esther rested her head on her boyfriend's shoulder, fear and desire collided and burst into flames of panic.

"Gabe," she said, pushing her lips against his ear. "Do you have that flask in your pocket?"

Fuck. Why am I doing this?

"Yeah, you want it? It's in my left pocket."

Heart pounding, Esther nodded. She sank her hand into his pocket, felt the metal bottle against her fingers. She slipped it between the folds of her dress.

"Be right back!" she yelled, and she navigated through the dancing couples to get to the restroom.

With only three stalls, the restroom was fairly small. Luckily, a woman exited a stall, and Esther stepped inside and opened the flask.

Isn't this what you did the last time you had sex, Esther?

Ignoring her thoughts, Esther threw her head back and allowed the warm liquor to seep into her throat. Heels clicked just outside of the door as someone entered the stall next to hers.

Is this fair to Gabe? You're literally drinking so you have the courage to fuck him.

The faucet ran. The woman in the next stall seemed to piss for a very long time. More heels clicked. Another group of young women entered the restroom, laughing; talking about another friend they'd ghosted.

If you need to drink to have sex, you shouldn't have sex.

Esther finished the flask and leaned against the wall. Next to her, the woman finally completed her twenty-seven-year piss and left the stall. The faucet ran again.

Loosening up isn't bad. Everyone loosens up.

Despite her desperate attempt to warn herself of the dangerous waters (or perhaps flames) she'd entered, Esther ignored her logic.

Logic sucked. Logic would never bring her happiness.

Risk *might*.

So, she appreciated the liquid courage as it warmed her body and blurred her mind. It heightened the pulse between her legs, and she tried to associate the physical urges with Gabe Donovan.

Gabe deserves a girl who will touch him, at the very least. I haven't been fair to him.

With her head held high in an effort to remember her dignity, Esther walked out of the restroom. But sadness and one last attempt at reason tugged at her heart.

Why are you doing this?

Searching for Gabe, she pushed through the crowd again.

Everyone looked happy. Strong, energetic bonding in platonic friendships. Love, adoration, and passion in couples.

Esther felt displaced. Even though she knew Gabe awaited her love, her mind and heart still whispered someone else's name. She didn't understand.

That message to Mariel was supposed to *help*.

Just hours ago, she'd lost herself in the evening with Gabe, and *now*—

"Hey, you good?" Gabe took her hand and smiled.

Head spinning, Esther came close, grabbed his collar, and kissed him. He let out a surprised grunt, and as she planted soft kisses against his lips, he pulled her closer and shuddered.

Pulling back, Esther leaned into his ear again. "Let's get out of here," she said, grabbing his hand.

You're trying to move on. You're using Gabe to move on.

Tugging his arm, Esther pulled the young man behind her, and they left the club. The air felt even colder now as the dance-induced sweat trickled over her skin. Her teeth chattered as they returned to the busy sidewalk.

"Where we goin'?" Gabe asked, squeezing her hand.

Esther looked up at him and smiled a little.

He persisted. "What? Why're you keepin' secrets from me?"

"It's best you don't ask questions," she said, winking at him. "Just do what I say."

Several people pushed past them. Laughter filled the air. Engines echoed in the city, sewers smoked, and horns blared.

"Well, she's having a bad day," Gabe chuckled.

Her efforts to keep up appearances and look sober were not working, and she wobbled a little in her heels as she pulled Gabe along. "Hmm? Who's having a bad day?"

"That cop back there. She was in her cruiser, looked like she was screaming at someone on her phone."

"Oh, *boohoo*. Poor po-po. Must be nice to only worry about a citizen's complaint." Esther tugged him again, giggling for no reason other than the fact that she was tipsy.

The predicted snowstorm hadn't arrived yet, but the clouds looked threatening as they journeyed through the city.

"Where are we *goin'*, Babe?" Gabe whined. "Are we about to break the law again?"

Briefly smiling at an older couple walking by, Esther bit her lip as her eyes darted over the buildings they passed.

"Babe?"

"Be quiet." Esther brought him to a quiet, dimly lit alley. Her head spun, and she needed water. It was cold too, but the public thrill encouraged her.

She *wanted* to do this.

"What are we doin'?" Gabe seemed confused.

Esther pulled him past a large burgundy dumpster. Flattening her palms against his chest, she slammed his body against the brick wall of a building. A tattoo shop, if she remembered correctly.

When Gabe reached for her, she slapped his hands down. "Don't touch me," Esther whispered, moving closer and reaching for his silver belt buckle. She was fucking cold, but she knew *this* wouldn't take long.

He was a horny bastard.

"Esther." His voice shook as he looked down at her. "What're you doing?"

Trying to move on.

"Stop talking for once," she ordered him, quickly unzipping his pants and tugging them down a little.

"Esther, it's cold and—*oh, shit*." Gabe's head fell back against the brick wall as her hands found him.

"Ssshh." Her breath was foggy in the cold air. When she found the warmth of his cock, his breathing grew labored. Esther watched his face as she worked his dick with slow, steady movements. The liquor fogged her mind, her arm moved faster, and Gabe lifted his hips.

Admittedly, Esther liked this. She liked making her partner feel good—but she knew this was her proactive method to avoid sex with him tonight.

Get him off here, in an alley. Give him a thrill, and then she could go home and dismiss the idea of him staying at her place. She wasn't ready to fuck him.

But Esther wasn't ready to let him go either.

She couldn't fucking lose anyone else.

Listening to his quick breaths, Esther spat on her hand and pumped him faster. She leaned her forehead against his chest.

You've already fucked him once already. Right?

Yes, she had, and she had been drunk. Definitely drunker than she was now, but still—

You're drunk. And disgusting. You can't do anything with Gabe unless you drink, you fucking bitch.

"Fuck!" Gabe exclaimed through clenched teeth. He slapped his palms hard against the wall; his eyes squeezed shut as his hips jerked against her hand. "Holy *shit!*"

Tears flooded into her eyes as she continued, moving faster now, and then faster.

Now she was drunk *and* unhappy. Esther no longer enjoyed this, but she didn't suspect that young man sensed that as he jerked, shuddered, and cried out from the long-awaited pleasure she was now granting him.

"Here it comes, don't stop," Gabe hissed.

Nausea burned her gut.

He ejaculated. All over her hand. Some landed on her dress.

Now she wanted to burn it.

You're disgusting, Esther thought, but she wasn't thinking about Gabe.

A flashlight guttered from the start of the alleyway. It caught her eye. Gasping, Esther released him and stumbled backwards.

"Hey!" A woman's voice, commanding. Strong. *Pissed.*

"Shit." Pulling up his pants and gripping them by the belt, Gabe bolted down the alley and laughed a little. "Come on!"

"What the *fuck, Gabe!*"

Esther ran. In her liquored haze, she couldn't recollect when she'd *started* to run.

In an abrupt torrent of knowledge and fright, Esther realized she was fleeing down an icy alleyway in high heels and a dress that flowed in the wind. Unable to keep up with her boyfriend, Esther found herself laughing, and then sobbing, and then laughing again as the wind slapped her face and whipped the tears from her eyes.

Stumbling, she glanced back.

No flashlight.

Ha. Running in *heels*, and she'd *still* smoked that pathetic cop.

But Gabe was gone. He'd smoked her.

"Gabe! Fuck you! Don't lea—"

Coming from the shadows of a side alley, a figure emerged and struck Esther.

Her arms flailed upwards. She slammed against the icy cement. It hurt—cracking her bones against the cement like that—and her heart thundered in her chest as hands gripped her arms and pressed her against the ground. Frustrated, drunk, and furious with Gabe, Esther tried to wriggle free.

"Police, do *not resist!*"

Fuck.

She hadn't smoked the cop.

Cold cuffs clicked around her wrists. The woman's knee sat against her upper back, and had she not been under arrest it might have felt good because it pressed into a muscle that was sore from dance practice the other day.

God. She was drunk.

What was the woman saying to her? Indecent exposure?

As her cheek burned against the ice, Esther inhaled and exhaled quickly as her foggy mind attempted to understand why a Chicago police officer had a *Russian* accent.

Oh, the things that mattered to her when she was drunk. The most mundane, senseless things.

The police officer spoke into her radio, told the other units that another suspect was at large. Then—

"Come on. Get up."

Commanding.

So goddamn bossy.

Tears flowed down Esther's cheeks as the police officer grasped her arm, just over the elbow, and forced her to roll onto her back.

As she felt the snow seep through her clothes, Esther looked up.

And caught her breath.

Her gaze met striking green eyes, almost abnormal in their coloring. Hovering above her was the flushed face of a woman who was certainly the most beautiful Esther had ever seen. And familiar. *So* familiar.

Like *déjà vu.*

For a brief moment, the misty breaths of both women swirled and then merged in the cold air.

Esther found herself staring in drunken awe of the woman leaning over her, noticing the loose bun of thick, blonde hair at her neck, the soft-looking lips that were parted in a look of mild surprise, the cheeks that were red from the cold.

Abruptly, Esther's quiet appraisal was interrupted. The police officer's eyes widened, as if she'd made a mortal mistake.

"Shit. *Shit!* Get up. Now. Come on." Roughly, the officer yanked Esther to her knees, and then, slipping her arms beneath her armpits and around her back, she lifted the drunk young woman to her feet.

Esther swayed. "What did I do? *Please* don't arrest—"

"Shut up." The beautiful officer reached into her uniform pocket and glanced around, wetting her lips as if she was nervous. Gripping Esther's arms, the officer spun her around to face away from her.

"Hey, cancel that backup. Wrong subjects."

What was even happening?

Why was the officer angrily muttering in Russian now?

Esther swayed again, but the officer tugged her close. She inhaled a lovely scent. Body wash? Shampoo? Perfume?

Confused, her eyesight blurred as she felt the handcuffs on her wrists manipulated and then removed.

"Alright, go. Leave. Your boyfriend is around the corner a block from here. Find him and go home. Got it?"

Frowning, Esther turned. She felt nauseated. "Am I not under arrest?"

Backing away and returning the handcuffs to the case at the front of her belt, the officer shook her head. "You need to go, or you will be."

The Russian accent irked her. She *needed* to know this woman's story. Nevertheless, Esther folded her arms and shivered. With curious eyes, she assessed the tall slim officer—from the top of her head to her perfectly shined boots—as she stepped past her to find Gabe. The young woman looked so *rigid* as she stared angrily at the brick wall instead of Esther.

Autistic and gorgeous. Lethal, Esther thought, giggling even as tears of relief leaked from her eyes.

"What is funny?" the officer snapped through her teeth, and it annoyed Esther that even her teeth were so fucking gorgeous. What did this woman do outside of her miserable life as a cop?

Model?

"... *nothing* funny about this. Or you." The officer's voice faded in and interrupted Esther's drifting thoughts.

"No need to be an asshole," Esther murmured. "But thank you. I'll be on my way. Have a good—"

"*Leave!*" the officer roared, waving her away as if she were an annoying pest.

Esther turned and almost lost her footing. She heard the officer call after her as she started down the alley.

"I mean it. *Go home!*"

The snowfall came, and she attempted to shield herself from the cold. Bruised and sore, Esther staggered down the alley and, as she came to the corner of another building, she saw Gabe in the darkness with his back against another dumpster. She stopped.

"Hi, Babe," Gabe said sheepishly.

Fury rose, higher and higher, warming her body again.

"What in the fucking hell is wrong with you?" Esther swayed, caught herself a little, and her ankle nearly gave out as she balanced herself.

Gabe came forward, his eyes wide with concern. "I'm sorry," he hissed. "Are they gone?"

"Yeah, she fucking let me go! Seriously, what the fuck?" Her voice was shrill. It echoed a little.

"Keep your voice down!" He looked around and gestured with his hands as if he'd lower her voice that way. "Are they after me?"

Esther whirled, her dress twirling with her, and she walked away. "Take me home, Gabe."

Neither spoke on the walk back to the car. They walked separately—Gabe took the lead. Esther lagged behind. As tears spilled over her numb cheeks, Gabe walked with his shoulders slouched, his head low.

Guilty, she bent her head as well. She didn't *want* to be pissed, but she could not make the rage just *go away*. But somewhere in her cloudy thoughts, she knew Gabe wasn't the issue.

She was.

In the truck, the silence carried on.

It was 9:46 P.M. The date ended earlier than planned. Gabe and Esther both glowered into the snowy evening as the truck moved through the city streets. Twenty minutes later, when they reached the suburbs, Gabe finally spoke.

"So you gonna be mad at me forever, or what?"

Oh hell no.

"Gabe, you *ran out on me!* You left me to the *fucking* wolves!" Esther whipped her head towards him. She was certain that her eyes blazed fury.

He glared back. "Seriously? Esther, my dad is a senator! Tryin' to win the primaries! I can't get put on a damn sex registry and embarrass him, he'll *murder* me!"

"That's right, make this about you."

"*Esther.*"

Fuming, she sat upright in her seat. "So you were just going to let me get arrested? Prance off after a good *shoot* in an alley and move on with your clean record? God forbid the senator's son get any consequences!" Esther didn't feel beautiful anymore. Not while snarling. Not with the semen of an ungrateful boyfriend on her dress.

Gabe's hands trembled, and he spoke through his teeth. "I didn't ask for a public hand job."

"Unbelievable. I thought you wanted some sexual tension relieved, Gabe."

Gabe screeched the truck to a stop at a stop sign, just down the block from her house. His face twisted with distraught emotion, and it almost frightened Esther. "I want to *make love with you*, Esther! I didn't ask for a quick hand job in an alley, and I wouldn't have. I want *you*." He smashed his foot on the gas pedal, and the tires spun for a moment before the car lurched forward.

Esther braced herself, slapped her hand against the dashboard as her body jolted forward. "I *told* you I'm not ready."

"Why?" he screamed. "Because you're pining after a fucking *dead man?*"

Happy-go-lucky Gabriel Donovan looked different now.

"Get *over* it, Esther. He's *dead*." Gabe leaned towards her, glancing back and forth from her to the road. "He's *not coming back!*"

"Stop it, Gabe!"

"You're not gonna have your *dream fuck* with Mariel! You know why?" The truck fishtailed a little.

"I said, stop. *Stop! Stop the fucking car!"*

"Because he splattered his brains all over his shower! *That's* why!"

Crying, Esther pushed him from her. "Please, stop. *Please*."

Gabe caught his breath. Wiped his forehead. Let out the breath. "I'm sorry."

"Please pull over. I'll walk the rest of the way."

"No."

"Please?" Esther pleaded. "I promise, we'll talk tomorrow. I'm exhausted. I need to think. And why are you looking at me like that?"

Gabe's eyes were on her neck. "Where's your goddamn necklace?"

"What? My neck...?" Esther looked down at herself, running her hands over her skin. "I—*shit*, I don't know, I had it on me!"

"Great." He parked the car in the middle of the street and glared out of the window. "You're home."

"Gabe—"

"I'm tired, and I love you. But please get out before I say something else I'll regret. I'll call you in the morning."

Esther struggled to remain composed. Reality was always harder to deal with once she started to sober up, and she was not prepared to deal with the lonely consequences she'd feel on her own tonight.

"Good night, Gabe." With quiet sadness, Esther gathered her purse and slammed the door. As she walked towards the house in the blistering snow, she heard the truck's engine behind her, but Esther knew he was still going to wait to make sure she safely entered the house. A sob caught in her throat.

I can't drink. I can't drink anymore. It never ends well.

The keys rattled when she inserted the house key into the lock and turned the deadbolt. Esther entered the dark, heated house, and she heard the truck roar down the road. Sniffling, she listened to the sound fade into the distance and then closed the door and bolted it.

As her body sobered, Esther ate a peanut butter and jelly sandwich, showered, and then slipped into sweatpants and a t-shirt before going to bed. Needing the distraction, she turned on the television in her room and muted it so that she could fall asleep to something other than her thoughts.

Gabe didn't deserve that. Any of it.

The television flickered, and the snowstorm howled outside of her window.

Esther closed her eyes and drifted in and out of sleep. While her mind blurred, she saw the face of the beautiful police officer bent over her; saw the green eyes that looked so *familiar*. Those lonely, striking eyes that seemed to know everything about her.

And then she heard it. The randomized tapping sounds against her window.

Her eyes opened. Quickly, she sat up and looked at her alarm clock.

12:28 A.M.

Tap!

Startled, Esther jumped and stared with wide eyes towards her window. The tree branches waved in the darkness. Had she *dreamt* up the noise? It sounded like a—

Tap!

—*rock* striking the glass.

Breathing hard, she flung the sheets from her legs and fell, hands down, onto the floor as if she'd served on a military task force. Feeling ridiculous, she crawled towards the window. Most likely, it was the wind causing trouble, flinging items against the window.

Tap!

Nope. That was definitely a rock.

Esther paused just below the window, took a breath, and then realized just how dehydrated and thirsty she was. In the darkness, she raised her head until her eyes peeked just above the ledge of the window.

Within the snow flurries, just beneath the streetlight, a figure stood in jeans and a dark hoodie. Esther's eyes narrowed, and as she contemplated calling the police, she leaned closer.

Something in her gut sank.

The figure came closer and raised a hand.

Esther fell backwards onto her butt, eyes wide, hair falling wild about her face and shoulders. Crawling, she scrambled back to her bed, pulled herself up, and dove onto it. It creaked as she landed on her stomach, and, whimpering, she reached for her phone on the nightstand.

It wasn't on the nightstand.

Fuck, she'd left it in the car with Gabe.

"Alright, this is a dream. Calm down," Esther whispered with frantic intensity. "It's just a dream. Take a breath. Lucid dream. You're in control."

Then she heard a familiar, muffled voice calling her name on the lawn below her window.

"Esther! Please open the door for me."

No, no, no, don't open the door. Horror movies. Don't do what they do in the damn horror movies.

She despised this dream. This *nightmare.*

"Esther. I know this makes no sense, but I need to see you! I can explain."

Shaking with terror and shock, she sat upright on the bed and clutched her arms around her body. Realistically, if this were a dream, she would wake up at some point.

Or perhaps this was the final phase of moving on from *him* within herself.

The only other explanation was that someone was playing a *horrible* prank on her.

How would someone be able to pull it off? Mariel's clothes, hair, exact body shape and frame? *Voice?*

"Esther, *please!* I know you're awake."

"Please, God," Esther whispered.

Plus, the *real* Mariel would not risk coming here with the possibility of her family being home. Her father would kill him. Murder him. In fact, the gun—

She gasped.

The *gun.*

Lucid dream. Good. You know where he keeps the case. Get the gun and finish this madness once and for all. You'll wake up.

"*Esther!*" the poltergeist screamed.

Esther rolled from the bed. Her feet thumped to the floor. Before she could change her mind, she fled from her room and down the upstairs hallway. Wheezing, she burst into the master bedroom and stumbled straight for the bed, fell to her knees, and dug underneath the bed frame.

There it was. The safe.

Her fingers sped across the buttons to enter the code. Withdrew the gun, looked at it for a breath's pause, and then chambered a round.

It was ironic.

She held the gun that Mariel had used in his first attempt to kill himself.

Downstairs now, she crept towards the door. The gun was up, her finger outside of the trigger guard as she approached the door.

Why the fuck did she feel *pulled* to investigate? It was dumb. This was, literally, every horror movie on earth.

Outside, the man knocked.

"I know you're in there, Esther, I know you are. It's okay. I promise I won't hurt you."

Her voice shook. "Whoever you are, you need to leave. The police are on their way, and I have a gun."

"It's Mariel. Please... let me in. Look through the peephole, and you'll see it's me."

But she had *already seen* him.

He *looked* like Mariel.

He *was* Mariel.

But he *couldn't be* Mariel.

As Gabe had said, Mariel was dead. He'd splattered his brains all over the shower.

However, as Esther lowered the gun and canted it to her left, she looked through the peephole. Her entire body quaked when she met the eyes of the hooded man that stood outside of the doorway.

The man she'd never stopped loving.

Don't. Don't do it, Esther warned herself.

What if this nightmare was *real?*

That's what scared her.

Her free hand crept towards the latch on the door.

It's only a dream. Dead people in dreams can't hurt you.

She flipped the latch. With a sudden gasp, Esther turned the knob and flung the door open. As freezing wind and snow howled into the house with chaotic fury, the young woman staggered backwards and lifted the gun again.

The tall, hooded man raised his hands and took a slow step into the doorway. He slipped off the hood to reveal his face, and his long black hair caught in the wind. "Esther," he said. "I'm sorry. I'm so, so sorry."

Esther shook her head, her lips trembling. The gun shook in her hand, her eyesight blurred.

He stepped farther into the house.

And closed the door.

In the darkness, one year later, Esther Caravan and Mariel Nadier were together once more.

VERSE 3

~ ALIVE ~

Esther did not know what to do. For a moment, she stood there, gun raised, its sights aligned at the center of Mariel's forehead. Perhaps his face. Maybe his throat. She didn't know, because she was looking at *him*.

Frozen.

What *was* one supposed to do in this situation? How often *were* people in this situation?

Biblically, there were many stories of the dead rising.

In the fictional world, folks who rose from the dead were usually considered zombies.

But Mariel was neither Jesus or Lazarus, nor was he a flesh-eating zombie.

So there were three other possible options.

One, she'd lost her mind.

Two, she was dreaming.

Or three, he was a ghost.

Looking back at her family history, number one seemed feasible. Considering number two, she'd always *had* strange and vivid dreams. As for number *three*, she did believe in ghosts.

All very explainable reasons.

So, when she spoke, her voice sounded calm.

"You have thirty seconds to explain this phenomenon, or I'm shooting."

The ghost of a smile played on Mariel's lips. He gestured towards the gun. "Ironic. That's the same gun I tried to use the first time, isn't it?"

That wasn't funny. That wasn't fucking funny at all.

Esther's knees felt weak. Her finger dropped to the trigger. "You're wasting time. And personally, I don't even know who or *what* I am threatening right now, but I hope it's working."

"Esther. Look at me." Mariel stepped closer. "I'm real."

Keeping her finger on the trigger, Esther stepped backwards and turned on the hallway light. "You can't be real. It's not possible, and you know that."

Mariel stuffed his hands into the pockets of his sweatshirt and stared into the muzzle of the gun. "What can I do to prove myself to you?"

Esther's gaze did not falter. As she looked at him, her eyes searched his entire face, trying to find some identifying *difference* in his features to help her determine that he indeed was not Mariel. If he *was*, and she was not dreaming, something inside of her might break, and it would be ugly.

Very, *very* ugly.

"What was the last thing you told me before I never saw you again?" Esther whispered. Her sight blurred. More tears. She was tired of crying. She was *tired*.

Mariel's countenance fell. He lowered his eyes and then raised them to hers again. "Don't make me repeat that. Please."

"Tell me." Esther's eyes narrowed, and her breaths came quickly. The gun shook in her hand. "Tell me what you said."

Hands still in his pockets, he kept his eyes locked to hers. "I said... I said I made a bet with myself and a few of my buddies, and Victoria Jameson would look better on her knees." His voice trembled. So did his hands. Despite this, Mariel stepped closer.

Her breath wavered. "Don't come closer." The tears trickled again. As her lips quivered, she struggled to keep the gun upright. "*Fuck* you," she whispered. "If you were really here, I wouldn't forgive you."

Mariel didn't listen to her. Instead, he stepped even closer. "I am real. I am really here, and I wouldn't blame you if you didn't forgive me." His voice was soft. The look in his eyes made Esther's legs go numb.

And slowly, he reached his palm towards her.

Now, Esther felt a lump in her throat.

His nearness... it reminded her of how she'd felt about him before his suicide.

How she *still* felt about him.

"Touch my hand," he whispered, his gaze unwavering. "And then I'm yours to direct your anger towards when you realize I'm here, and I'm *real*."

With trembling fingers, Esther reached forward. Closer.

Even *closer*.

Her fingertips narrowed the distance. Stopped... and then continued to close the space between their hands. After one more breath, Esther Caravan finally touched Mariel's skin.

The tips of their fingers brushed together. The soft sensation hummed through Esther's nerves... through her fingers, her hand, her arm, down through her chest, and into her beating heart.

Her heart raced. Esther flattened her palm against Mariel's so that she could feel the warmth of his hand. She caught her breath, and she felt the pulse of his heart within his palm, touching hers, telling her that he was—

Alive.

Esther shook her head. Whimpering, she backed into the kitchen. The gun lowered. "It's not possible," she said, bending down to touch her knees. "It's *not* possible."

What was happening? The nightmare hadn't ended yet, and she *wanted* it to end. And yet she wasn't *ready* for it to end either.

What had she done to deserve such confusion in her life? Such turmoil? God, if only her mother was alive—if only she could *talk* to her mom about the insanity brewing in her mind.

This was *too* much.

Mariel's shadow came closer.

Esther could not move. Frozen in the kitchen, her head spun.

Mariel knelt before her. "I'm going to take the gun," he whispered, reached for it, and slid it from her fingers.

Esther let out a cry and staggered backwards. Then she turned and sprinted towards the counter where the knife block sat. Grasping the handle of the first knife she saw, she withdrew it.

It stuck.

Crying, Esther tugged it and yanked the entire knife block from the counter. It crashed to the kitchen floor and left her with a steak knife in her hand.

She snarled at him.

Mariel did not attack. Instead, he stood up from where he'd knelt and looked at her with pleading eyes. "Esther. I love you."

No.

No.

She pointed the knife towards him. "Stop lying to me. Whoever you are, stop *lying to me!*"

"Everything I said before was a lie, just like you told me at the bookstore. I love you, Esther, you *know* I love you." He walked towards her, his hand outstretched.

Gasping, Esther slashed the knife at his exposed skin. The blade gashed the skin between his thumb and his forefinger, and it split the padded skin beneath his thumb.

She had not expected to hurt him, because spirits *didn't bleed.*

But he did.

Mariel bled.

"*Fuck!*" Mariel gripped his wrist, let out a hoarse gasp, and fell against the wall. In a moment of shock, he clutched his wrist and watched as blood rose from the split skin and drained over his hand.

Esther froze.

"Dead people..." she whispered, "don't bleed."

She dropped the knife. It clattered to the tile floor. Breathing hard, Esther came forward, whispering his name. "Mars. Mars... I'm... *sorry.*"

How was this fucking possible?

"Mars." Esther stood close to him, and she reached out to touch the wrist he held. "Let me see it." She felt his labored breathing on her hair, and she quivered. If Mariel had wanted to hurt her, he would have by now. She'd be okay if she was near him... right?

"I guess I deserved that," he said. Blood filled his palm and drained down his arm. It shook.

"I've got bandages upstairs," Esther said, dazed, and then darted across the kitchen for a roll of paper towel. She unrolled it, came close to him again, and placed it against the wound. "Come on. Upstairs bathroom."

The floor creaked beneath their feet as they ascended the stairs in ear-splitting silence. The sound of the howling wind danced with their heavy breaths.

Mariel was *here.*

Alive in the same house. Behind her.

Her skin prickled.

When they reached the bathroom, she turned on the light, and the reality of his presence gripped her mind and body like ice.

In silence, while he waited behind her, she dug through the medical items and withdrew a roll of white bandaging and an antibiotic cleanser. Esther could feel his eyes on her back.

How could she feel cold *and* warm at the same time?

Trembling, she turned around, and their eyes met.

"Give me your hand," Esther said, and reached for him.

Mariel obliged. His eyes melted with hers as she took his wrist and pressed a cloth onto the wound.

"We'll... just hold pressure until the bleeding slows," Esther murmured, breaking her gaze from his to look at his hand.

"Are the police actually coming?" he asked, laughing a little.

"No." The blood reddened the white cloth. Her thoughts ran wild.

Esther had many questions. She was not certain she wanted to know the answers, and she was convinced that she'd spun through four stages of grief—denial, anger, bargaining, and depression. But she hadn't yet reached the fifth.

Acceptance.

Was this how hamsters felt? Trapped on a spinner?

With a sudden snap of her head, Esther looked up. "I need to know, Mariel. I need to know why you *fucking* humiliated me, and why you *killed yourself.*" Her face grew warm, and her grip on his hand tightened. "I was vulnerable to you. I told you I loved you, and you made me look like a *fool* in front of my dad!"

Mariel winced.

Esther squeezed his hand harder.

She *enjoyed* hurting him now, *enjoyed* giving him pain, and her rage rose from lukewarm to hot.

"Esther—"

"You were selfish. It was *selfish.* You should have seen your dad. He wasn't himself for months! Forget *me*, how could you do that to your own *father?*" Her voice rose, her breath quickened, and her body was no longer cold. It *burned.*

Blood oozed through the wet cloth and onto her own hand.

It rendered a sharp gasp from him, and his face paled.

Esther no longer held his hand to stop the bleeding. Now she held it so that she could give him pain, and she knew it. She wanted to stop, but her anger took control.

Fury owned her now.

"Esther," he said breathlessly, "I said those things because I needed you to be angry with me. I needed you to hate me so that it wouldn't be as hard on you if—"

"If *what?*"

"If we couldn't be together. You don't—fully know me, and you wouldn't have believed me if I had tried to tell you."

Esther removed the bloody cloth and squirted antibiotic ointment onto the wound. She'd lost sight of the steps one took for wound care.

And she didn't fucking care.

"See? No trust for me. You didn't even give me the benefit of the doubt. *Instead*—" she wrapped the wound tightly, squeezed again, and gritted her teeth, "—you humiliated me, broke my heart, and then killed yourself to make whatever *you* were going through easier on *yourself.*"

"That's not *untrue*, but not entirely *true*. Esther, please stop trying to hurt me."

"You *hurt me!*" she cried, and warm tears spilled and rolled down her jaw before plopping against his hand. She did not want Mariel to see her cry for him—not like this, not after the last humiliation. "You... hurt *me.*"

Mariel's eyes glistened. He touched her face with his other hand. "I'm sorry." His whisper seemed sincere. God, his *eyes* seemed sincere. "I love you."

"Don't say that." Esther's heart pounded quicker, harder. The rage hadn't left, but she felt *something else* too, and it frightened her more.

"I love you, Esther." Mariel came closer, brushing his fingers against her temples. He trailed them over her ears, across her tear-stained cheeks, and onto her neck.

The desire for him was hot.

But now the rage boiled.

Her palm cracked across his face. Gasping, Esther watched him with wide eyes as he stepped back, as the area on his cheek reddened.

It was quiet. Their eyes clung.

Neither moved for a brief moment.

Then Mariel let out a wavering breath.

So did Esther.

She reached out and grabbed for him.

Mariel came to her, and her fingers curled into his sweatshirt. With a violent gasp, Esther pulled Mariel towards her until their bodies met, and their lips smashed together with a force that jolted her head backwards. Their lips met again and again, with desperate fury, withdrawing to gather air.

Hungry.

Meeting again. Licking.

Biting.

Esther's head spun. She tasted her own salty tears.

Grunting, Mariel drove her against the sink. The counter dug into her back, and she knew there'd be a bruise. But as her mouth opened to accept his tongue, Esther gloried in the pain. It meant she was alive, *he* was alive, and this was not a dream.

Esther heard her own cries, her heated moans, and felt the vibrations of his throat against her hands as he groaned into her mouth. She felt him, all of him, as his hips pressed into her. It ignited a lust, a desire, inside of her that she'd never known. In her blurry thoughts, Esther knew he wanted her as much as she wanted him.

Quickly, Esther unzipped the sweatshirt, biting his lip, and then pushed the hoodie from his shoulders. She rocked her hips against his, feeling his bulge between her thighs as small bites of pleasure hummed throughout her nerves.

Shuddering, he rocked against her, and he raised the bottom of her shirt.

Esther lifted her arms.

As he pulled it over her head, it left her hair disheveled. Mariel's fingers traced over her throat, across her clavicles, finding the full cleavage that pushed from the top of her bra. The bandage on his hand tickled and scraped her skin as he explored her, touching her with curiosity and awe. It triggered a reminder.

He'd never been with anyone before.

Breaking the kiss, Esther pushed him back.

"My bedroom," she panted. "Now."

Esther's thoughts were messy, confused. As she pulled him towards her room, she even felt guilty. In the darkness, his lips met hers again, and she thought of Gabe. Esther thought of the necklace, how she'd lost it, and she felt...

Horrible. She felt horrible, because tonight, she didn't care.

As they grabbed for each other, falling against the wall, devouring each other's mouths with vehement need, she thought of the impossibility of this situation.

Hours ago, Esther had thought him dead.

But Mariel was here, and she was pushing him towards her bed. Breathing hard. Tugging at his white t-shirt to pull it from his body. Thinking about how her dad would disown her. How she hadn't set her alarm to open the store for the maintenance workers in the morning.

She didn't care.

Shirtless, Mariel fell back onto the edge of the bed, sitting upright and looking up at her with wide eyes. The familiar blue eyes beckoned her, calling her forward. Groaning, Esther stripped from her sweatpants as Mariel kicked off his shoes and socks.

Wet and eager, Esther straddled his waist. Feeling his body between her thighs, she realized how smooth Mariel's skin was. She wondered if she'd ever expected anything different.

With forceful command, the young woman pushed her tongue into his mouth. Tasted him. He tasted her back.

Esther's hands explored the smooth, rigid muscles of his chest and abdomen. Mariel's thumbs hooked into the ridge of her black panties. She thought of Gabe again, how hurt he'd been, how hurt he *would* be.

But once again, right now, Esther Caravan didn't care.

His warm skin burned into her palms. Mariel lifted his hips and pushed his groin into hers. Kissing him, she tightened her thighs. He pulsated against her with hard, frustrated jerks. Each movement drove quick, desperate breaths from Esther.

Mariel unclasped her bra.

The bra straps fell from her shoulders. Swiftly, she rid herself of it, flinging it somewhere, *anywhere*. Esther needed it gone, needed her nipples touched. It didn't matter how.

Mariel obliged that desire, brushing her with his thumbs, pinching and rolling as he buried his hot mouth against her neck. Whimpering, Esther fell against him, pushing her breasts further into his hands, and reached for the fly of his jeans. Her fingers shook.

"Off," she said. "Now."

Mariel scooted himself backwards, Esther straddled his leg, and their fingers met as they both attempted to undo his pants. One of them became frustrated, she wasn't sure who, but Mariel leaned back and let her do the work. As she tugged at his pants and boxers, he tried to help and flung his leg. He knocked her chin with his knee.

Mariel apologized, and she could sense his embarrassment, but it didn't matter.

Esther buried her fingers in his wavy hair, pulled his face to her breasts. Mariel shuddered. Fumbling, he slipped his hand between her legs and cupped the damp cloth.

Grinding against his fingers, Esther seized his hair and pulled, felt herself going mad. He teased her, playing his mouth across her breasts.

Murmuring inaudible words, he pulled her panties down.

They were both naked now, and Esther knew there would be no going back. This time she wanted it, she was not drunk, she was on birth control, and she would not regret it in the morning. And Gabriel Donovan?

She would deal with him later.

Feeling each other's skin, they kissed, rolled on the bed, grinded against each other, struggled to breathe. Mariel fell on top of her. Esther rolled on top of him. The bed creaked, moaned, and shook. Muscles flexed. Sweat glistened. There was a wild frenzy of licking and biting. The bandage came undone. Blood smeared. Neither cared.

The wind howled and rattled the window.

Esther felt him pull her hair, felt her scalp burn, realized she would be one of those girls that liked painful, rough sex. On his skin, she used her teeth, as if claiming him and telling the *fucking* universe that this man belonged to her, and how dare he be taken from her.

Mariel did the same, grasping at her, bruising her. Sucking. Nibbling. Gasping. They could not bring their bodies close enough to each other.

Esther straddled his hips, ready, hungry, frightened. She could not see him well, but she had felt him with her hands, and he felt large. As she rubbed herself over him, and dug her fingernails into his chest, her thoughts ran wild, and she remembered that she had only fucked Gabe—

—Fuck, I'll need to break up with Gabe!—

—who was, to her knowledge, average, and, suddenly, she was terrified to let Mariel—this beautiful, frightening, resurrected man—inside of her.

"Are you alright?" he panted, grasping the crevices behind her knees. "We don't need to—" He stopped speaking and let out a sharp breath.

Biting her lip, she guided him inside of her, gyrated her hips, caused Mariel to whimper. Their eyes met. Their breaths rose and quickened together. Their bodies melted together.

Exhaling soft breaths, staring at him, Esther took him slowly at first, trying to adjust to him, wondering if it would get more pleasurable. Watching Mariel's head rock back, seeing his chest heave upwards, hearing him gasp in delight as she moved her hips, was nice. *Really* nice, and it loosened her. It was getting more pleasurable.

Esther's moans grew louder as her body welcomed more of him. Ramming his hips upwards, Mariel sat up and grasped the small of her back, pushed himself deeper. She cried out, caught an unexpected sob in her throat, accepting both pain and pleasure, wondering if it had hurt this bad with Gabe, telling herself she *needed* to stop thinking about Gabe because she *promised* herself that she would end it tomorrow.

With each thrust, their heavy sighs broke the night's silence.

Mariel would not last long. It made sense. He'd never had sex before.

It was strange, because she had always known him as the quiet, shy, young man who had struggled to even look at her. Now... Mariel was animalistic. As he remained upright to hold her waist and bite her neck, he slammed into her—faster, harder, and he was *close*. It hurt her. It tore her. Ignited and confused her nerves. She experienced the pleasure *and* the pain, but she wanted it, wanted to be reminded and assured that Mariel Nadier was... *real*.

Esther pushed him back down, sat upright, and brushed her wavy hair to one side of her face. Ran her fingers along the contracting muscles of his abdomen. Even though this felt amazing, she would not come this way, not tonight. So, as he gazed at her, and she at him, Esther ran her fingers downwards, over her abdomen, and touched herself.

The wind howled again.

With threatening warning, the bed creaked. It would be a bitch trying to explain why the bed broke. It would be a bitch trying to explain *any* of this.

Each of her cries became higher in pitch. As every muscle contracted, Esther bounced her hips, quick and hard, with the furious need to gratify both of their desires. Mariel stiffened, raised his hips, and cried out. He came hard, spilling into her, squeezing his eyes shut, grasping the bedspread as she encouraged him. Then his body relaxed, and he touched her, waited for her to finish.

Esther apologized, whimpering with embarrassment that it was taking her this god-damn *long* to orgasm, but he brought his wounded hand to her throat, helped her, coaxed her, rubbed his fingertips against her clitoris until she came. As the sensations tingled from between her legs and through the rest of her body's nerves, Esther let out a loud cry. Her hips moved with critical desperation, thrusting herself into his fingers as hard as she possibly could, and she dug her nails into his chest while her body quivered from release.

Sweaty, exhausted, and still in shock, they held each other. They did not speak.

What could be said?

Cuddling and roaming about each other's skin with their fingers, they stared into the darkness. The rhythm of their hearts eventually slowed.

Esther wanted to be in his arms for the entirety of the night. But after she re-bandaged his hand, he fell asleep, and she grew uncomfortable and moved away from him.

Quietly, Esther rolled onto her side and curled into the fetal position. The guilt returned, stronger this time. Then the tears again. Part of her was certain that, when she awoke in the morning, the resurrected man would be gone, non-existent, and she would have to move on with her life once more.

Dread filled her mind and body.

The winter storm dissipated outside of her window.

And as her thoughts faded into sleep, and she could no longer control them, Esther Caravan saw hauntingly beautiful eyes once again.

But they were not blue.

They were green.

Verse 4

~ Problems ~

January 11th, 2020
Chicago, Illinois
9:15 P.M.

"I *know* you're not calling to ask how I'm doing. What did you do?" Michael chuckled on the other line.

In downtown Chicago, parked on the side of the street and sitting in her cruiser, Tira scowled and clenched the phone in her hand.

Per usual, it was a busy Saturday.

People filled the block and the restaurants; the nightclubs and bars.

Tira had made the mistake of parking next to the dance club. A purple neon sign flashed and lit up the interior of her cruiser.

SATURDAY NIGHT SWING—LADIES DANCE FREE!

Trumpets screamed in rhythm. Every time people opened the double doors, the cruiser vibrated from the drums.

"I didn't *do anything*, Michael," Tira lied, brushing a ticklish strand of hair away from her cheek.

"Okay, then what emergency do you need help with?"

Agent 4 spoke through her teeth. "There is no emergency."

But there was.

And she still hadn't figured out how to save herself from the consequences.

Some woman shrieked on the sidewalk, and Tira's hand went to her gun before she realized that the big-breasted woman with a fifties-style hat was laughing and swatting the ass of a man with a handlebar mustache.

Her hand left the gun on her belt, but she did not relax.

Anxiety—was *this* how subhumans felt when they were anxious? Sweaty palms, a thundering heart, and racing thoughts?

Tira didn't even remember getting ready for her road patrol shift. Once the surveillance program alert went off, everything after that had gone from wild chaos to numb panic. The system shutdown. Fire alarms. Burnt food.

God, it was the *second* time she'd burnt perfectly good meat this week.

But that wasn't the issue.

Tira had solved problems her entire life. She'd been given problems *and* tasked to *create* them just to ensure her growth in adaptability.

Shutting the system down to monitor Petrov's government asset?

Tira was stumped.

That Caravan microchip was Petrov's *baby.* How was one supposed to solve the homicide of Petrov's baby... without taking the consequences as its murderer?

"First of all," Tira said, "what I am about to ask you is a purely hypothetical situation. Understood?"

"Sure."

Was Michael eating chips again? Did the man ever consume healthy food, or take care of his fitness?

"If, hypothetically, the subject's microchip shutdown... well, let me rephrase." Tira cleared her throat and rubbed her forehead. "*If,* hypothetically, someone hit the system deactivation button for the microchip... how might that person reactivate it?" Her eyes slammed shut.

Dispatch blabbed on the radio, babbling about some ridiculous domestic violence call—a woman whose ex-boyfriend wouldn't leave her residence.

Tira didn't understand subhumans. A quick slice to the arteries would do the trick, and then a cover-up story if self-defense claims didn't fly within the pathetic legal justice systems.

Michael crunched into a chip—a pretzel—*something* annoying, gulped into the phone speaker, and then said—

"You shut down the microchip. Didn't you?"

Tira's eyes flew open.

Drums pounded. The cruiser vibrated. Men and women in 1950's style clothing mulled about the club with the doors open, giggling and shouting with their friends.

"I said it was *purely hypothetical, Michael!*" Agent 4 growled, and her face stung with heat. "Do you know what the word *hypothetical* means?"

"Tira—"

"And frankly," Tira shrieked, "I am offended that you would think that I am *so idiotic* that I would *shut down the system!*"

The blinking lights overwhelmed her senses. So did the laughing clubbers. Michael's chewing.

And her fucking inability to *solve the goddamn problem.*

"Tira. Take a breath."

"I am breathing."

"You're snarling. Take a deeper breath. Pretend you are hunting someone."

The jazz music slowed as Tira closed her eyes for a brief moment. She pretended her firearm was in hand, canted a little as she crept down a long corridor and hunted the two figures at the end of the hall.

Recruit Matthew Thompson.

And Esther Marie Caravan.

"Okay," Tira said, and opened her eyes again. "Now what would need to be done to reactivate the chip?"

A bag crumpled somewhere in Michael's world, and he cleared his throat before speaking the words that terrified her soul.

"Petrov would have to know, and he'd send another."

"*What?*" Tira screeched. On impulse, she switched to Russian. "What kind of microchip is this? Why can't you just insert a—a—*normal* one for tracking purposes?"

Dispatch called her unit number.

She yanked the radio to her lips. "*What.*"

"*Can you start to assist on that domestic on Ayre St?*"

"Negative," Tira said, and she slammed the radio back into place. "Michael," she said. "There's really no other way?"

Michael sighed. "Here are my *hypothetical* tips. Call me... hypothetically, of course. Request an update on the microchip due to technical issues. Meanwhile, use other means to track her as best as possible until the chip comes in."

This was fucking humiliating. She felt as stupid as a subhuman, and if she put in a request for Michael now, he'd know. But—

"Hypothetically, I should probably request an extra," Michael said. "And then you can hypothetically meet up with me soon and grab it."

"You are mocking me, aren't you? Saying that word?"

"Only hypothetically."

"I am going to kill you."

"...But hypothetically, right?"

"No," Tira sneered, and then hung up.

She'd figure it out herself. Human beings were worthless.

She was worthless—and what was *most* embarrassing about this ordeal was that she'd been complaining about how *simple* this job was.

Monitor the subject at all times. That was it. Limited violence, reasonable tech, and few problems to solve.

But she'd proven she couldn't even do that. Couldn't even cook without setting the fire alarms off. Couldn't have sex with someone without the Department of Homeland Security breathing down her neck.

Throwing the cruiser into drive, Tira completed a U-turn and squealed her tires down the road. She was pissed at herself.

Livid.

So, as she drove on, and ignored all of the messages that came to her cruiser's computer to ask what the hell she was so busy with that she couldn't assist on the domestic, Tira Arcelin plotted temporary solutions to the problem she'd created.

Agent 4 settled on one—tracking Esther's vehicle and monitoring her phone. Esther Caravan took her Jeep and her phone almost everywhere.

It'd be easy.

So why did it seem so *fucking daunting?*

Tira pulled her cruiser to the side of the road, next to an old tattoo shop, and turned off her lights. Grumbling, she looked through the messages on her MCT and rolled her eyes.

"Are you too busy to take the pending indecent exposure call that's like... right by you?" The dispatcher sent.

Growling, Tira looked at the map. Sure enough, a pin dropped in the area, almost on top of her little cruiser that was pictured on the map.

"Goddamn it," the angry cop snarled, but she responded to the dispatcher's message. *"Send the call if you must."*

Tira exited her cruiser, shut the door, and marched towards the dark alley. It was too cold for a typical mid-westerner to expose their genitals. It was likely a homeless person, someone trying to piss in peace.

The homeless community *loved* Tira when she patrolled their areas. Some of them told her that she was funny. Many idolized her, especially after she'd addressed a group of teenagers that'd been harassing Cara and Joe, the only homeless couple in the area. Tira had arrived on scene to observe the teenagers pressing cigarette butts against Cara's skin as Joe struggled to fight them off.

So Tira used the appropriate level of force.

She'd announced herself. *"Police, stop!"*

She'd turned on her bodycam.

And then she'd kicked their asses.

Several roundhouse kicks, elbow strikes, and one taser deployment later, the teenagers had fled, crawled, and sobbed their way down the alley.

She'd been written up.

"Tira, I'm not worried about your officer safety or tactical abilities," Sergeant Rick sighed. *"It's the public I fear for."*

Tira rolled her eyes, turning the corner to the alley.

"Too many use of force reports," Tira mocked. "Too much escalation. Not enough de-escalation, bla, bla—*hey!"*

As her voice bounced through the alley, her flashlight settled on a male and a female.

The woman, dressed in green, stood stationed against a man who leaned against the brick wall. Her hand lingered on the man's cock.

The man bolted.

After turning hazy eyes towards Tira, the young woman fled after him.

Tira darted to the other side of the building and sprinted down an adjacent alley. The equipment on her belt jostled as she spoke into the radio and alerted dispatch that she was involved in a foot pursuit. They responded and acknowledged that they would send backup. She didn't *need* backup, but Sergeant Rick had told her that she *needed* to call for backup to ensure the safety of the suspects due to her history of "excessive force".

Tira still hadn't figured out if he'd been joking or not.

On the other side of the wall, Tira could hear the girl's heels. The clicking sounds grew louder. How arrogant to assume she could escape Tira, much less in *heels*.

Tira laughed.

Just ahead, there was a break between buildings—another alley that intersected the others.

Tira could tell that she'd passed the heeled girl. As the alley break approached, she alerted dispatch to her location, released the mic, and then darted around the corner.

Like a cat, Tira faced the oncoming girl and crouched.

"*Gabe*, fuck you, don't *lea—!*"

Tira struck. Her arms encircled the tight waist, and her equipment clattered as Tira drove the woman against the cement pathway. Fumes of alcohol filled the agent's nostrils as they collapsed against the ice.

Face down, the woman struggled and whimpered like a captured puppy. Her disheveled bun fell loose, and it wobbled back and forth. Annoyed, Tira pressed a knee into the girl's back, and reached for the handcuffs.

"Police, *stop resisting*!" Pushing the woman's face into the ground, she alerted dispatch and then grasped the woman's arm. "Come on. Get up." Tira lifted her knee from the groaning, drunk woman and rolled her onto her back.

And Tira stopped breathing.

Her eyes widened as they met familiar blue-brown eyes. Eyes that looked even more gorgeous this close.

The eyes of Esther Caravan.

As a cop, Tira Arcelin had tackled many people. Most suspects looked at her with rage, dismissal, or didn't look at her at all.

This was different.

Because for a moment, Esther Caravan searched her face with hazy, half-lidded eyes. Drunk, but curious... flicking about Tira's face, as if she had a strange investment in understanding who Tira Arcelin was and why they'd met in this manner.

As Tira knelt over her, her face went hot, and she felt a strange sensation coil up from her stomach and vibrate her racing heart. Indigestion? She wasn't sure, but she did not like it. It made her feel weak.

Human.

Then—panic.

She'd just tackled Aleksey Petrov's project.

The one she'd accidentally *shut down*.

"Shit. *Shit!* Get up. Now. Come on."

Angry, Tira yanked the drunken woman to her feet, noticing how soft her skin was, barking out the location of her boyfriend, ordering her to find him and *go home*.

But Agent 4 was distracted.

As Esther swayed, and Tira uncuffed her public indecency suspect, she could not keep her eyes away from the soft curve of Esther Caravan's waist. It trailed like a sinewy valley to the young woman's wide hips. And when Esther turned, Tira's wide eyes fell to the swell of her large breasts that pushed from the cloth of her dress, and Tira wondered what it'd feel like to take her hands and—

"Am I not under arrest?" Esther asked, confused.

Anger replaced the lust. Now her uniform looked disheveled, and it was Esther Caravan's fault.

Tira glared at the building in front of her. "You need to go home, or you will be."

Tira meant it. She wanted to arrest Esther Caravan, stuff her in a trunk, find a way to ship her to Russia, and order Petrov to babysit her for once.

Esther scanned her... and took her time with it. A confused, but playful smile quivered on her lips. "No need to be an asshole. But thank you."

Suddenly, Tira felt helpless. Victimized. She wanted to leave, get out of there, never see Esther again.

And the young woman left, stumbling away and clutching herself from the cold. Something about the way she sheltered herself with her own arms brought a twinge of discomfort to Tira's chest.

"I mean it," Tira screamed. *"Go home!"*

Esther Caravan faded into the night.

And when Tira journeyed back to her cruiser, she saw a necklace—a silver chain with a pendant of a dancing girl. She picked it up, placed it in her pocket, and continued on.

There was no doubt in her mind—it belonged to Esther.

* * *

After one more call (she was dispatched to another public indecency call between two drunken men who claimed their names were Bert and Ernie), Tira had had enough.

She could not stop thinking about her mistake. How she'd shut down the microchip. How she would have *known* that it was Esther Caravan in that alley had the microchip been working.

So, unable to focus on anything else and needing to solve at least part of the problem, Tira called off for the rest of her shift and blamed sudden illness.

"I will shit my pants if I do not go home," Tira told a coworker in the locker room as she unsnapped her belt keepers and tossed them into the locker. "That would be unpleasant."

"Is that why you didn't go to the domestic earlier?" The young woman, Meredith, grinned.

"Why is everyone harassing me about that?" Tira snapped, and she slammed her locker shut. "I was busy."

"Yeah, on the toilet."

Tira scoffed and left the locker room. "Have fun with the drunks."

She went home, made a protein shake, took a breath, and then prepped.

"No need to be an asshole," Esther had murmured.

"Well, no need to be a nuisance," Tira snapped, shaking her protein bottle with sudden violence.

Tira changed into running gear and gathered her necessary items—her firearm, and a simple tracker that she intended to use on Esther's vehicle. After that, she waited for the clock to strike twelve, and then she left.

Esther would be home by now. From what Tira knew of the subject's behavior patterns, the young woman wouldn't spend the night with Gabe. So, Agent 4 decided she would plant the tracker, connect her phone, and then figure out the rest tomorrow.

Tira arrived in the neighborhood and parked down the road at 12:28 A.M. After adjusting her mask, the agent slipped the tracker into the pocket of her athletic jacket, exited the car, and began to jog.

The winter storm surged against her body. Her black running shoes thumped against the sidewalk's surface. The frigid air brought tears to her eyes, and she decided she'd become a wimp since living in Chicago, because Chicago's temperatures were nothing like Russia's. She'd have to find a way to reverse the damage she'd done to her body before she became like Michael—couch-obsessed with a beer gut.

As Esther's house came into sight, she slowed her jog to a walk. The Jeep was parked in the driveway, but she stopped walking. Her hand crept to her firearm.

A tall, hooded figure stood at the edge of the driveway.

Wind howled and whistled into her ears. Grinding her teeth, Tira jogged to the nearest tree to get out of the open but keep the figure in sight.

And though she couldn't see him very well, there was something *very* familiar about him. His height. His stance. His voice when he said—

"It's Mariel. Please... let me in. Look through the peephole, and you'll see it's me."

What?

The firearm came out.

Who was this?

Tira twisted the silencer onto the gun.

Had another government agent come to seize the asset? Trick Esther into opening the door?

God, this was all her fucking fault. Had she not shut down the system, maybe she'd have been able to *stop this.*

From behind the tree, Tira raised the firearm and aimed. The streetlight reflected against his face, and Agent 4 almost gasped.

The door opened.

Don't, Esther, Tira thought, and her finger fell to the trigger. If she shot him now, there'd be no going back.

"Esther," the man said, and he stepped into the house. "I'm sorry. I'm so, so sorry."

And, as Tira froze with shock and confusion, the door closed behind him. Agent 4 was left alone as the storm raged and wailed a terrifying reminder...

Her problems were far from over.

Chapter 10: Verse 1

~ Yes, I've Lost My Shit ~

Sunday, January 12th, 2020
Chicago, Illinois

Mariel opened his eyes.

The room was cold.

He lay on his stomach, his head facing the window across the room. It was still dark outside. He relaxed into the bed, his heart rate slow.

Mariel felt happy.

Very happy.

His hand throbbed. It burned, reminding him of...

"Esther."

Drawing in a breath, he rolled over. Instead of seeing Esther, he saw an indent on the other side of the bed where she'd slept. Blood covered the pillows and the sheets. The room had an odor—a combination of perfume and sex.

Rubbing his eyes, he sat up and leaned against the headboard.

What now?

He wasn't sure when Esther's family might return, and he sure as hell didn't want to exit the room to face Todd and a muzzle to his forehead.

Mariel grinned at the irony. He couldn't die anymore.

So he shouldn't be afraid of a gun.

But he wasn't in the mood to explain, especially since he still hadn't figured out how to *explain this to Esther.*

He'd taken a major risk coming here and throwing rocks at her window in the first place. But *something* had told Mariel that she was alone, and the need to see her overcame the fear.

And after their night together? Mariel no longer felt they weren't supposed to be together. If anything, he could *protect* her now. If Fr. Paul had spoken the truth, it would certainly give him more reason to be with her, protect her, *warn* her.

Yes, Mariel still intended to give *an* explanation, but he knew Esther would need time to process.

She'd lived a normal life.

He'd risen from the dead.

That wasn't normal.

But, as the silent night pressed upon the room, Mariel promised himself one thing. He wouldn't mention the kill chip. He wouldn't *frighten* her.

Sometimes ignorance was bliss.

Where *was* she?

Already, Mariel missed her. He noticed the clothes that were scattered about the floor.

He played their night through his mind—over and over again, remembering how her body felt, how she tasted, how she sounded.

Mariel smiled and closed his eyes. Finally, he'd been released from the guilt of loving her and *looking* at her.

Esther Marie Caravan was finally his, and Mariel would do *anything* to keep it that way.

Even as complicated and frightening as it was, having a purpose from God felt freeing.

And having the woman he loved seemed too good to be true.

The door creaked, the light switched on, and his eyelids fluttered open. Mariel's heart rate quickened, and he beamed when Esther entered the room. She was wrapped in a white towel. Her hair was wet, and it covered her bare shoulders. Clearing her throat, Esther closed the door with a soft click and then turned to face him.

His smile grew smaller. "Are... you alright?"

She was pale.

Her lashes hung half-lidded over red, downcast eyes. Droplets of water pearled on her eyelashes, and as she stood there in the towel, her body trembled a little.

"Esther? Tell me what's wrong?" He leaned forward, felt a twinge of pain on his hand, and winced.

Esther looked up, met his gaze, and let out a wavering breath. Then, a quick smile flickered across her lips. "You need a shower. You're all bloody." She glanced at the sheets. The smile was gone. "And I have to take care of these sheets before I go to the bookstore." Her voice was quiet, and, still not moving, she brought her eyes back to his. "How did you sleep?"

Mariel stared at her. Suddenly, he did not feel as happy. "I slept good."

Things felt different. Awkward.

Changed.

"What about you?" Now Mariel could only think of basic questions. Nothing too deep. He did not know what to say.

"I didn't sleep much, but that's okay." Esther wandered to the side of the bed. She sat across from Mariel, angled halfway towards him but… away from him as well.

Suddenly uncomfortable, Mariel looked at her. "Anything I can do to help you? Cleaning up, I guess? We left a pretty big mess." He tried to chuckle, but it came out of his throat like several forced grunts.

"Mars." Her voice, though soft, commanded his attention. "You need to explain everything to me. We can't just pretend that this isn't strange." Esther tugged at the bedspread, pulling it up and down as she stared at her working fingers. "I slept for an hour last night, and when I woke up you were still here." She raised exhausted, glistening eyes to his. "I thought this would be a dream of some sort. It's not. So… now I don't know what to think. Or do… or say. So please, Mariel, tell me how this is possible."

Fuck. Now he had no choice but to explain.

Disappointment stung his chest.

When he'd awakened, Mariel had expected Esther to be in bed with him, expected her to be curled in his arms, expected her to turn and look at him with love, happiness, and desire.

Was it wrong to experience this disappointment? It probably was, because Esther had every right to feel scared.

Indeed, rising from the dead was not normal.

Mariel looked at her, noted the areas of her neck where many bruises had formed. Blushing, he tried to redirect his focus to the problem at hand.

This was difficult, and he had hoped his first sexual experience might have had a different aftermath (cuddling in the morning, laughter, gentle caresses, breakfast), but he tried to see it through the lenses of her eyes.

"Will you sit closer to me?" he asked quietly.

"Why?"

"Because I want to hold you."

"Mariel, please. I need some time, and I need you to talk to me."

"So you regret last night?"

"No. Yes. *No*. I don't fucking *know*." Esther brought her palms to her face and rubbed them across her skin for a moment. "I'm begging you." Her voice shook. "Just tell me."

Feeling rejected, Mariel leaned against the headboard again and closed his eyes. He could not look at her, not while she seemed so distressed. It diminished what they'd had together. "You have to promise that what I say stays between us. Can you do that?"

Tracing her finger along the bedspread, Esther nodded.

Mariel told her about the times he should have died. He told her about the figures that had followed him since childhood. He told her about the humanoid, how it'd always mocked him and threatened those he loved.

Feeling her eyes on him, Mariel kept his own closed as he told her about the messenger—how it'd ordered him to stay away from Esther, how the only way he could find the strength to leave her was to hurt her as much as he could.

The room chilled more as Mariel described the day of his suicide, about the moment he pulled the trigger.

Then he stopped, remembering the gates of Heaven, remembering the Cherubim. As he heard Esther's uneasy breath in the morning silence, Mariel said—

"I remember something about the Kingdom of Heaven. I remember that whatever I saw was beautiful, indescribable, and that I was sent back to complete a mission on Earth. Next thing I knew, I awoke in Russia." His mouth was dry.

And he stopped there, because he *couldn't*. He *couldn't* tell her about the kill chip, about the order to kill Aleksey Petrov.

Mariel *knew* he should tell Esther the full story, tell her exactly who he was, how there might be limited time on Earth... but he couldn't.

Not yet. Not after such an intense, beautiful night together. Not after he'd finally received a *chance* with the woman he'd loved for years.

Surely, God would understand.

Kill Aleksey Petrov. That was God's command.

Not to stay away from Esther.

"Mars. Look at me."

He looked up.

Esther trembled. "If you were someone else, I wouldn't believe you. You know that, right? So I sincerely hope that you're telling me the absolute truth—" She was crying now. "—Because I can't take any more heartbreaks. I *can't*. What you just told me, Mars, is unbelievable. I don't know how I *can* believe it. But I have to. Unless you faked your death, I have to believe you. Do you understand why this is hard for me?"

Mariel's chest felt heavy.

Tears spilled over her cheeks. She sat at the edge of the bed, and he noticed how she held the towel tight around her trembling body.

Esther had always been fearless. Now she was using the towel as a shield, and she looked to him like a frightened puppy that'd been kicked.

Suddenly, Mariel did not feel like the rescuer.

He felt like the abuser.

"I understand," he said, his voice gloomy.

Esther stood, moved closer to him, and sat next to him. As the bed shifted, Mariel watched with a furrowed brow as she winced and placed her palm over her lower abdomen.

"Are you alright?" He wanted to touch her, but he felt like he had no right.

Esther nodded, smiled just a little. "Sorry. Embarrassing. I'm just sore from last night."

"Oh. Esther, I'm sor—"

"Don't apologize." She slid closer to him, leaned her head on his chest. Took a breath. "I don't regret it."

Finally. But—

"You haven't... *done* that before, right?"

Silence. Then feebly: "No."

Relieved, Mariel reached his arms around her and held her close. Her wet hair dampened his chest, and he leaned his cheek on the top of her head.

On the surface, he supposed it didn't matter, but he'd always felt that she was *his*, that they were meant to consummate *together* for their first time. He didn't want to think about the rage he'd experience if he found out—

"That makes me happy. I wanted to share that with you." Mariel kissed the top of her head.

Esther's body seemed stiff.

More silence. An engine roared outside as it passed.

"What else?" Esther sounded... off.

"What else, what?"

"What else do you want to know? Would that have *changed* anything about me if I'd fucked someone else? Would I not be *good enough* for you anymore? What else, Mars, are pigs flying now?" She stood up and laughed. "Did God send you back with wings?"

"Esther, you're losing your—"

"Losing my shit?" she shrieked, stepping backwards. Her face, no longer pale, reddened fast. "Damn *right*, I'm losing my shit!"

Mariel sat up. "Esther, I thought you believed me!"

"I *do*, that's the problem. I *do* believe you. I believe you when you tell me these absolutely unbelievable things, and—and—and that you rose from the dead, and God sent you back to *fucking Russia* to complete a *goddamn mission* like a *fucking* special agent from Heaven!" Esther paced, shrieking, spitting. "Hi, I'm Nadier. Mariel Nadier—I've been sent by God to arrest you, or whatever the hell God tells people to do when *they come back from the dead! So yes, Mariel!*" she screamed. "I have *lost my shit!*" Esther heaved in a breath and pulled the towel tighter around her.

The doorbell rang.

Esther's face paled again. "Who the hell is here this early in the morning?" She darted to the window.

Eyes wide, Mariel slid from the bed and searched for his pants. He found them in a pile on the floor and stepped into them, watching Esther as she peered from the window. "Who is it?"

Esther flew to the dresser and opened the drawers. Breathing fast, she pulled out a black hoodie and grey sweatpants. She dropped the towel from her body.

As Mariel reached for his t-shirt, he watched her, enjoying the brief view of her beautiful nudity before she covered herself in haste. "Esther? Who is it?"

"Stay here."

With the hood up, Esther rushed from the room. Mariel felt the breeze as the door slammed shut, and he heard her galloping down the stairs.

Curious, Mariel pulled the t-shirt over his head and wandered to the window. Peering through the misty window, he saw a familiar truck in the driveway near the garage. His eyes narrowed.

"Gabe? Why the hell are you here?" Mariel murmured through his teeth.

Frowning, he crept to the door and opened it; peeked out into the dark hallway. He heard muffled voices getting louder, and he stepped outside of the room.

"Let me in, just for a sec!" Gabe's voice.

Mariel scowled.

In a low tone, Esther spoke. "Thanks for the phone. I *really* have to get ready to go to the bookstore, can we talk later? Please?"

"The bookstore isn't open on Sundays!"

"I *told* you that I have to let maintenance in this morning!"

"Babe. It'll take like sixty seconds."

Babe?

A low growl rumbled through Mariel's throat.

Downstairs, Esther gasped. Footsteps shuffled.

"*Gabe,* seriously? *Gabe!*"

Mariel drew back into the darkness of the upstairs hall and pressed against the wall next to Hawk's bedroom. From his positioning, he could see the downstairs hallway, and he observed the blond-haired man stalk through the hall.

And Gabe held flowers in his hand.

"Esther, I'm sorry. I'm sorry I freaked out on you last night. I had no right to say all the things I said, and... Babe, why do you look like you seen a ghost? You look like shit."

"Thanks, Gabe."

Mariel's hands shook as he watched the top of Gabe's head. He had not expected to see his best friend *here*, with flowers, with *Esther*. His upper lip twitched. Jealousy circulated in the pit of his stomach like rotten food.

"Gabe, you need to go. I'm serious. I have to get ready to leave." Esther's voice was firm, but Mariel could hear the rising panic in her voice.

Gabe sighed. "You're impossible. Fine. I'll just put these in a vase, then."

"Wait, *Gabe, don't—*"

Mariel watched Esther tug Gabe's arm. The young man pulled her towards the kitchen.

Esther hadn't cleaned the mess yet—had she?

"What the fuck? Esther, why is there a *gun* just chillin' on the kitchen floor? And blood? And knives? Baby, are you *okay?*" Gabe whirled to look at Esther.

Mariel's nose flared. *Baby,* he thought, repeating Gabe's voice in his head. His anger heightened.

He thought of Gabe *with* Esther. Kissing her. Touching her.

"Gabe, I'm fine. I was drunk, remember? You need to go."

"Are you *hurt?* What's with the blood?"

"*Gabe!*" Esther screamed. "I thought there was a *fucking* intruder, okay? I cut myself by accident, *now get the fuck out of my house!*" Her feet thundered against the floor as she stormed towards the door and opened it again. "Out."

Briefly, Gabe stood there. Then he tossed the flowers into the kitchen. "Fuck you." He stormed from the house.

Esther slammed the door. Picture frames rattled. The stairwell vibrated.

Mariel retreated back into the bedroom and closed the door as quietly as he could. The stairs creaked, and the engine to Gabe's truck roared. It reversed with a mad screech and then screamed down the road.

Esther burst into the bedroom and slammed that door too. Her chest heaved up and down. The hood cast a shadow over her exhausted eyes, and it was then that Mariel noticed the off-colored, sleep-deprived bags forming beneath them.

"Really, Esther? Gabe? You're dating *Gabe?*" The words came out before he could stop them.

Did the air shift?

He wasn't sure, but suddenly Mariel Nadier felt absolute terror as Esther raised furious eyes to him.

"You," Esther said slowly, "are in no position to be jealous right now."

Mariel's body warmed. "So... have you always had it for him? Just waited for me to leave the picture before you finally admitted it?"

Esther stared at him. "You are *far* too jealous for a dead man." She opened her bedroom door. "Out. Now."

"Esther—"

Lips tight, she banged her door into the wall and gestured to the doorway. Her eyes burned holes into his body. "I'm done with both of you right now. I need time to think."

Trembling with anger, and the knowledge that he *knew* he was in the wrong, Mariel gathered his keys from the floor and walked by her. He wanted to stay.

He wanted to hear Esther call after him, to *tell him to stay.*

As he jogged down the stairs, angry rap music vibrated the walls. The bass rumbled through the floor. Gritting his teeth, he checked his surroundings to ensure that he was safe to leave, and then he slammed the house door behind him as loud as he could in hopes that she'd *know* he was fucking pissed.

Fucking *bitch*.

"I'm sorry," Mariel gasped in response to the intrusive thought, and his breath filled the air. He'd parked several blocks away, not too close to Esther's house.

Paranoid.

But he glowered during the entire drive home. He had *no* right to feel this angry—but he couldn't help it. In fact, a fast-fleeing thought crossed his mind.

The thought that leaving Chicago, killing Aleksey Petrov as God commanded, and just *ignoring* the kill chip in Esther's body would be easier.

It would be easier than seeing her with Gabe.

Shaking his head, he rubbed his forehead and apologized again. He was not sure if the apology was to God or to Esther.

When he returned home and opened the door, Fr. Jerome waited on the couch with the cat in his lap.

His soul dropped. He hadn't even *thought* about his father.

"Dad."

Fr. Jerome looked up. His eyes were red, his cheeks tear-stained. "Hi, Son."

"Dad, I'm sorry, I didn't mean to be out all night."

Fr. Jerome scratched the top of Harlow's head, who lifted her chin and closed her eyes in bliss. "It's not that. I mean, that *didn't help*—but that's not why I'm upset." His eyes fell to Mariel's hand. "Son, what happened to your hand?"

"Ignore that. Just... yeah." Mariel came forward and knelt before his father. "What is it?"

He felt nauseated. He hated all of this—seeing everyone he loved so upset.

Harlow looked at him. Opened her small mouth and hissed.

Fr. Jerome gestured towards his phone. "I received an email last night from our Bishop. They want to meet with me to discuss the possibility of removing me from the priesthood."

Mariel's eyes widened. "Dad. *Why?*"

Fr. Jerome leaned down and kissed the top of Harlow's head. She flicked her fluffy tail in response. "I don't know. I truly don't *know*." He wiped tears from his eyes.

Mariel sat back, brought his knees to his chest. "I'm sure it'll be okay. Are you still having a service today?"

"Yes, of course. I guess I'll find out my fate on Monday." Fr. Jerome's bottom lip trembled. He tried to smile. "At least my son is back. Right? Silver lining." But his shoulders shook, and sudden sobs exploded into the silence.

Mariel came close to him. He wrapped his arms around his father's legs and leaned his head against the old man. "It'll be alright. I love you so much, Dad. We'll get through all of this together."

But as he spoke, Mariel thought of Esther, of Gabe, of *God*... and he was not certain that he could even believe his own words of encouragement.

Verse 2

~ The Blindfold ~

Friday, January 10th, 2020
Chicago, Illinois

"We are proud of you, Ahdam," Haleef said.

Birds tweeted.

Ahdam loved birds. He appreciated their wings and their ability to fly away. To find freedom and look upon the Earth and its beauty.

Ahdam wished he could do that.

Haleef's large arm encircled his wife's waist, and the family stood before many bags of colorful fruits and vegetables.

Haleef bounced a pepper in his hand. He flashed a large, magnificent smile at his wife.

Ahdam smiled too. He looked at the food and put his hands on his hips, just like his father did whenever he seemed proud of a finished project.

Indeed, Ahdam was proud of himself, and he knew his ability was a gift from Allah. He was most proud of the fact that he'd been able to feed hungry families.

Ahdam looked up and squinted. Within the horizon's heat waves, many people trudged towards him.

The villagers were coming. They were coming because they were eager to partake in the food he'd helped grow with his ability to control the environment.

Here in the village, the Palestinians did not judge his gift. They did not judge him. They welcomed him, and they were always grateful for the generosity of the Kaseem family.

Gratefulness was difficult to find in the eyes of the villagers. It was hard in the West Bank as a Palestinian—with one's home under constant threat by Israeli settlers and the Israeli government. He wondered if it had always been this bad, having that threat over their heads, but he did not want to think about it.

The boy wanted to revel in the knowledge that his gift was a blessing to his fellow people. Perhaps one day, he would see all famine go away. Perhaps he could help others in different regions of the earth.

But he would never help the Israelis. They had proven that they were able to take care of themselves—by pillaging and stealing, destroying and taking the lands of the Palestinian people. When the time came, Israel would not receive his help.

His gift was not theirs to take.

"*Ahdam,*" *Haleef said, approaching his son and resting his hands on his shoulders.* "*You must run.*"

Ahdam turned and searched his father's face. His mother stood beside him, trembling. Both looked afraid.

No, something beyond fear.

Terror.

Their faces expressed terror.

"*Ahdam!*" *Haleef said, pushing the boy from him.* "*Run!*"

Terrified, he ran.

The earth shook. Dust billowed into his eyes, and he heard someone scream his name as the sky broke apart.

Allah.

"*Ahdam! You will bring famine to the ear—!*"

His eyes could not open at first because a cloth barrier kept his eyelids from fluttering open.

Blindfolded.

His head pounded. His mouth felt sticky, and his lips were dry. As he awoke, Ahdam realized that he was lying flat on his back. Multiple straps, or *something*, pinned his arms to his sides and pressed across his legs and feet.

Numb, Ahdam was stiff, as if he had been sleeping for much too long, longer than a man was supposed to sleep. Haleef, his father, had always said—

"*Rest only as much as you need, because the world needs you more.*"

Ahdam tried to free himself. He couldn't. He moved his fingers, dug them into the bedding on which he was strapped, and tried to slip his arms free of the barriers that held him down. The straps burned the skin on his forearms where he attempted to wriggle, twist, and turn his body free, but his limbs could only jolt against the materials that imprisoned his body. As his eyelids fluttered against the blindfold, the cloth scratched his eyeballs, and Ahdam began to gasp. Air felt denied to him.

Where was he?

Ahdam moaned, trying to scream. Like an earthquake, his body trembled and, as the veins stood from his neck, his mouth opened wide to push out a blood-curdling cry.

Where was his family?

The boy's head thrashed against the surface. The surface—maybe a table—creaked and moaned as he writhed beneath the barriers. He knew there were tears in his eyes, but the blindfold devoured the liquid drops before they could trickle down.

There was a crash, something that slammed against a wall, and footsteps approached him. As his head thrashed up and down and whipped back and forth, a woman's voice spoke in a language he didn't understand. Cold hands pressed to his face. The voice had an odd sound to it, unlike anything he'd ever heard, and she spoke real slow... *real* slow, as if she thought he was dumb in the head.

But the hands on his face were gentle, like his mother's touch whenever she soothed him.

Ahdam's body slowed, but his breathing remained labored. Pain jabbed a muscle in his neck, as if he'd strained it.

He heard the drawling voice rise, as if she were speaking in annoyance to someone.

Then another woman spoke in his language.

"Hello, Ahdam."

Ahdam listened.

"You are safe. I need you to trust me, okay?"

His skin crawled. People were staring at him... weren't they? And it wasn't in the same way the villagers looked at him with gratitude.

He was being *studied,* wasn't he?

The woman continued. "You are here because we would like to help you. You are not in any danger, okay? The reason you are blindfolded is because we believe your eyes might be connected with your ability to control the environment... but we don't know yet."

Ahdam wanted to go home. He wanted his parents. He wanted to fight. But the voice was Palestinian... perhaps he *was* safe?

"Can we trust you enough to let us take the blindfold off, Ahdam? That's your name, correct? I love that name. It is beautiful."

Ahdam nodded. He was not even *sure* if he could use his gift right now. Was *he* even in control of it?

He didn't feel like he had control of *anything* right now.

Gentle fingers lifted his head and then loosened a knot on the base of his skull. Squeezing his eyes shut, he waited until cool air brushed his sweaty skin where the blindfold had trapped his eyes.

"It's okay, Ahdam. You can open your eyes."

And he did.

Blurriness. Bright lights.

How long had it been since he'd seen light?

The day of the fire. He'd seen daylight on the day of the fire.

The blurriness cleared. Above him, he saw white ceiling tiles with little holes scattered about the squares. Were the holes part of the design?

He brought his eyes downwards and saw his bare brown toes. Ahdam moved them a little.

Then he noticed the bands that strapped him against a lifted cot of some sort. Why was the cot on wheels? Why did it have a railing?

A bed should not have straps.

A small plastic bag rested between his ankles, filled with yellow liquid. Urine.

Humiliation singed his nerves, and his face warmed.

Finally, Ahdam assessed the two women who stood in the small, white-walled room where he was imprisoned.

Neither of them were his mother, and the hope went away.

First, he noticed the large white woman who stood a slight distance from the wheeled cot. Medium height, big-boned, large-breasted, and middle-aged. Shoulder-length, wavy brown and grey hair. Round glasses that covered her small eyes. Large, dimpled chin. Big nose. Small lips.

Mean-looking.

She wore a white coat of some sort, and her hands fidgeted inside of her pockets.

He didn't like her.

Then he looked at the younger woman closest to him. She was not in a white coat, and she *was* Arab. Her dark hair hung in a ponytail below the collar of her burgundy polo shirt. No hijab. Small waist and wide hips. Blue jeans and patterned lace-up shoes. Her eyes looked kind.

Maybe the other woman was kind too. His father had always said—

"*Do not judge a person by their looks. Give everyone the chances they deserve.*"

But Ahdam simply felt more trust for the Arab in the room.

"My name is Adela, and I'll be translating for you," she said, smiling. With a flick of her small hand, Adela gestured to the other woman. "This is Diane. She is here to help you and make sure you are healthy."

With wide eyes, Ahdam stared at her. He wished he could speak. No one in this room would understand the questions in his eyes, all of the things he wanted to ask and say. His eyes fell to his straps, he wriggled his hands a little, and then looked back up at Adela.

"They're for your safety," she said. "I promise, we won't hurt you. We want to help, but we need to make sure you can't hurt us either. Does that make sense?"

But where was he?

Ahdam let out a moan, trying to form words, to force himself to speak even though he never had.

He looked past Adela and saw a tall, wheeled stand behind her with a screen on its platform.

"You want to know where you are?" Adela asked, and then she glanced at Diane and spoke another language.

Jostling his feet this time, Ahdam nodded too. Of course, he wanted to know where he was. He could not remember the previous events. *He wanted to go home.*

"You're in the United States of America," Adela said. Swallowing a little, a smile touched the corners of her lips, as if she did not want to smile, but she *had* to smile.

The United States of America?

Ahdam stopped breathing.

He wasn't going home—*was he?*

Ahdam thrashed again. The wheeled cot rattled and shook as he bashed his skull against the cushion and croaked out loud, desperate cries. The urine sloshed inside of the bag.

He was only eleven, and he did not know much, but he understood that the United States of America was very, *very* far from home.

Diane rushed to the computer and began to type. In that slow, drawling voice, she said something to Adela, and her small eyes looked a little bigger now. Beneath those spectacles—round, wide, and beady.

Adela bolted forward and placed the blindfold over the boy's eyes. The cloth pressed against his eyelids and forced them shut as the younger woman blinded him with it.

"Ahdam, you *must* be calm!"

The blindfold's pressure brought sparks to his sight within the darkness, and pain crept from the bottom of his neck, upwards into his skull. Grinding his teeth, Ahdam complied to the pain and stopped moving as his chest heaved up and down.

Diane spoke in that drawl, and the boy heard her fingers pounding against the keyboard.

He needed to know if his parents were alive. Ahdam felt certain that they were not. If they *were* alive, the Kaseems had most likely been imprisoned by the Israeli government.

Diane spoke, and then Adela translated.

"Ahdam, you have an incredible gift. A gift that could help people. But it's also a gift that could hurt people. Do you remember anything about your journey here?"

Swallowing hard, Ahdam shook his head. He last remembered being in the truck with the U.S. military.

And screaming.

He remembered screaming.

"On your journey here," Adela said as she massaged his forehead with gentle sincerity, "we had to keep you sedated. Even then, when you'd awaken, you would trigger *something* in the environment."

Ahdam wanted to look at her, but he couldn't. The blindfold kept him trapped, like he was staring in the mouth of a black pit.

"Three soldiers froze to death." Her voice shook a little. "And a tornado took down a helicopter."

Ahdam lay still.

How? *How* had he done such a thing?

"You triggered the start of a small earthquake once you arrived here. All of these things happened within the short timeframes you woke up," Adela continued, and her thumbs brushed against his temples. "It was necessary that we kept putting you to sleep."

Tears came again. He wondered how his father had always been so strong.

Adela lowered her voice. "It wasn't your fault, Ahdam. You were frightened. That's why you're here... so we can see how we can help you. We haven't learned much yet, but we want to. You're in a safe place now, where you can relax and let us help you. Okay?"

Ahdam did not want to know any more about himself.

He wanted to go home.

Diane spoke in that drawling voice, and Adela translated.

"Ahdam," Adela said. "You need to work with us if we are to help you. I'll be right back, alright?"

She removed the blindfold again.

Ahdam's eyes followed her. He did not want to be alone with the strange, beady-eyed woman. It seemed she did not want to be alone with him either.

Diane avoided his glance.

He avoided hers.

"You promised, Ahdam!"

Thinking of his father, he jolted.

Immediately, Diane jumped. She placed a hand over her heart, looked at him with wide eyes, and said something to him.

"You scared me!" Ahdam imagined her saying.

Good.

The door opened. He turned his head towards Diane and looked behind her. His eyes widened, and a cry caught in his throat.

His mother stood between Adela and a white security officer.

Dina's hands were handcuffed in front of her. Her hijab was still on, and she wore a white hospital gown that draped past her knees. Her eyes were red. Tearful.

But Dina smiled.

His mother, very much alive, smiled.

"Listen to what they say, Ahdam," she said, sniffling. Her lips trembled. "We will be okay. Allah will care for us, alright?"

Diane rolled her eyes a little. Impatient, she shifted on her feet and tapped her thumbs together.

Grasping Dina's arm, Adela looked at Ahdam. "You'll see her soon, but we need to keep running some tests on her. To make sure she's okay. Come on, Dina, he will be okay."

As Adela pulled her from the doorway, Dina choked back a wail.

It faded, and she was gone.

The door closed.

And Ahdam began to thrash again.

As soon as the door closed, and he could no longer see his mother, Diane stormed forward and cracked her palm across his face. It stung and brought more tears to his eyes. But he stopped thrashing, and he snarled at her.

She looked like a giant over him, and her thin lips pressed tight against each other. Looking down upon him, she smirked a little.

Ahdam looked up at her.

His breath steadied.

Sudden droplets of sweat formed on Diane's face and rolled over her reddening cheeks. She gasped, wheezed, as if hot air had trapped her within its grasp.

Ahdam smiled too.

One day soon, he would free himself, and he would rescue his mother and find his father.

Diane spluttered and managed to grasp a syringe from her pocket. Her red skin made a sizzling sound as she stumbled towards him with the syringe raised in the air.

Ahdam closed his eyes.

The needle stung his neck.

And as Diane brought the blindfold down upon his eyes, and her smug face disappeared behind the black cloth, he decided he would kill this woman. He did not care if Allah's wrath came upon him for the deed.

One day soon, he would find a way to escape this strange prison in the United States of America.

VERSE 3

~ OFFICER MYSTERIOUS ~

Sunday, January 12th, 2020
Chicago, Illinois

E sther wished she hadn't lied.

It'd just *bolted* from her mouth. And even though his possessive question had *pissed* her off and had triggered a hell-storm of emotions, she still hadn't been able to tell Mariel the truth.

She wasn't a virgin.

And Esther wished she was—but not because sex was shameful.

Gabe just hadn't been the one she'd wanted to lose it to.

But she wasn't a fucking virgin anymore, and it shouldn't goddamn matter to Mariel.

Yet somehow, Esther feared it *would* matter—and it'd be ugly.

That, however, was the least of her concerns right now.

Anger, confusion, frustration, and fright. She couldn't handle all of those emotions at once. So, after Mariel left the house, she cleaned.

Deep cleaned.

With wrathful speed, she scrubbed the kitchen, the bathroom, and vacuumed the hard floor for good measure. After hiding the bloody sheets in her closet, she got ready to leave, and she fought to survive the abundance of thoughts she could not ignore.

And while Esther wound her hair into a loose bun and exited the house, she tried to save all of the questions and doubts in her mind for later.

But when she reversed the Jeep like a madwoman out of the driveway, Esther thought of Hawk's miraculous recovery last year—how he'd just *walked* out of that hospital room.

Was it all related?

"Move!" Esther screamed, slamming on her brakes as she raced towards a box truck.

What the fuck was happening?

Shit, what if she was losing it? Going insane like her crackhead grandfather?

Regardless, Esther felt trapped in a situation she wanted *nothing* to do with.

There was no escape.

Esther was fucking exhausted. If she weren't driving, she'd drink. So, as exhausted as she was, the only option she had right now was to simply accept.

Esther whipped her car around the truck. The older man behind the wheel raised his middle finger out of the window.

"Yeah. Fuck you too," Esther spat, and drove on.

She couldn't *just accept*. Something was drastically *wrong* in the world, and Mariel was involved, which meant *she* was involved—because she loved him so much.

Too much.

She loved Mariel Nadier so much that she'd welcomed his ghost into her bed long after she'd watched his casket lowered into the grave.

Long after she'd managed to slip the photo of him and his father into the pocket of his suit jacket.

Now new questions consumed her.

Did she love the same man?

Had he told her the entire truth?

Shouldn't it be *expected* that people might *change* after resurrecting?

God, that sounded ridiculous.

Esther *wanted* to be happy he'd returned. However, until she had a logical explanation presented to her about this phenomenon, it would be hard to find any form of peace.

Maybe *this* was why her grandfather, Jacob Caravan, went mad. Maybe *he'd* seen someone rise from the dead.

As Esther drove to work, she tried to treat the day like a normal Sunday so that she could delay the onset of her insanity.

Yes. A normal day, after she had been dump tackled by a—

—*stunningly gorgeous*—

—police officer for drunkenly jerking off a boyfriend she did not love in an alleyway before returning home to cheat on said boyfriend with another man a year after he'd blown his brains out all over the shower.

"*Fuck* my life!" Esther screamed and struck the steering wheel. As she finished her tantrum, the music on her phone stopped.

"*Dad*" blinked across the screen.

Grinding her teeth, she answered it.

"Yes, Dad, I'm awake. I'm on my way."

"Oh. That's good, Honey. That's not why I'm calling though." His voice was gentle. "Gabe called me this morning and told me that you might have had an intruder last night? Are you okay, Squirt? What happened?"

Esther let out a sharp breath. "I *thought* there was an intruder, Dad. I was tired. It's fine, the house is fine, I'm fine."

"Are you sure you're okay?"

"I'm marvelous, couldn't be better."

He paused. "Okay. We'll be home a bit later. Let me know how the maintenance check goes."

"Cool. I'll see you later, Dad. I need to go."

On Sundays, the *CLOSED* sign dangled on the entrance doors of *Caravan's Books*. The day of rest. The Lord's Day, as Phil Jameson always called it.

Today, for the first time in its history, Esther flipped the sign to *OPEN*. It clattered against the glass door as she unlocked the store at 8 A.M, an hour she knew would bring *no one* on a Sunday.

But Esther didn't care.

She needed to work—to do something productive so that she didn't have to think. Thinking was painful right now.

For both brain and heart.

Esther's father might be confused, but he wouldn't argue too much against the sales. The conversation might be strange, but she'd already planned it out.

"I thought it was Monday," she'd tell him. *"Oops."*

And he'd scratch his head and move on. Because that's what Todd did. He didn't *notice* things because he lived in his own battleground of a mind.

Today, Esther was okay with that.

Maintenance came as scheduled. Half an hour later, so did the first customers. They trickled in with coffee and good spirits as Esther dusted, vacuumed, and reorganized bookshelves that'd been disordered the last couple days.

Esther worked with calm vigor until she managed to numb herself from the frenzied thoughts in her mind. Occasionally, she glanced outside, towards *Pete's Diner*, with the unrealistic hope and expectation that she would see Mariel. She *wanted* to see him here, at the bookstore, to remind her of simpler times. Less confusing times.

To tell her that maybe all of this horror had been a sequence of nightmares.

Because pining after him had almost been... easier.

As it neared mid-afternoon, the last person left the bookstore, leaving Esther to eat her lunch and continue bookshelf organization. She completed all of the aisles.

Except for one.

With distant eyes, she stood before the aisle where she and Mariel had first kissed—that sweet, yet horrible day.

"That aisle," she told herself, "looks organized enough."

It was time to dance. Let out some steam.

Esther connected her phone to the surround speakers in the store and selected a song her dance team had been practicing for the last week. It was a sleek, sexy song with strings, a hip-hop beat, and suggestive vocals.

Esther took off her shoes. She removed her sweatshirt and pulled the ponytail holder from her hair. It tumbled over her shoulders and down her back as she stood poised and ready in her yoga pants, lace-ups, and crop-top tank.

Every time she danced, she felt free. It did not matter what kind of dance.

Pride and determination filled her soul as she moved her feet with lightning speed, spun, rocked her hips, and sped up again, feeling—

—his hot mouth—

—the sweat on her skin. Esther inhaled and exhaled with clarity and determination. She heard—

—his urgent breath—

—her own breaths as she moved and locked her limbs. She attacked breakdance movements on the floor and diverted from the choreographed blueprint, freestyling as she desired. Each movement was a problem, and Esther Caravan solved each one. Esther gyrated and rotated her hips as she felt the pain of—

—his desperate, invasive pumping—

—her exhausted muscles as they worked with a vigorous intent that only a certain skill-level could accomplish. As the intensity and speed of the music increased, so did the movements of her body.

Her cheeks were flushed, her heart rate high, her skin sweaty. Wavy hair fell about her face. Esther mouthed the words, lifted her arms, and spun around to face the front of the store.

And her eyes melted into the tantalizing, powerful green eyes of a young woman standing before her.

Her shriek was short, high-pitched. It fell off-key with the music that continued to play. Startled, Esther caught her breath in gasps as she gazed at the young woman. Her response faded from fear to recognition.

Then recognition returned to embarrassment.

"Oh, *fuck*," she said breathlessly, dropping her arms. "You've changed your mind. You're here to arrest me, aren't you?"

The young woman leaned against the bookshelf closest to the couch. Her left hand rested in the side pocket of her black, double-breasted, hip-length pea coat. It was fully buttoned, but it still highlighted her slender form. So did the form-fitting black cargo pants that she kept tucked into her mid-calf, lace-up boots. Falling almost to her navel, her long blonde ponytail coiled over her right shoulder.

Esther's face was on fire.

The green-eyed officer did not avert her gaze.

And the song stopped playing.

An ad played. Something about erectile dysfunction. Ever since her brother had hacked into her phone, she'd gotten advertisements for male enhancement products and balding cures.

But for a moment, neither said a word. Despite the air of confidence, authority, and respect that this young woman clearly demanded from anyone who met her gaze, Esther realized that this mysterious officer was... shy.

Or socially awkward.

The *words* were there, in her slender throat, waiting to be spoken... but the dialogue seemed *stuck*.

But finally, the quiet words came in the form of a question, and the young woman arched her eyebrow. "*Should* I arrest you?"

Esther was hardly in the mood for games. Feeling the woman's eyes on her, she moved to the counter and disconnected her phone to stop the music. "You're off-duty. Plus," she whirled to face her again. "If *I* were arrestable, *you* would have done it by now. So why are you *really* here?"

She wasn't about to admit how embarrassed she was that this woman had just seen her display of dance.

The young woman did not flinch. Simply continued to stare. "Would it be entirely impossible that I *might* be at the bookstore for... a book?" Ever so slightly, the corner of her soft mouth twitched.

Wiping sweat from her forehead, Esther leaned against the counter. She struggled to catch her breath, her chest heaving up and down. "Alright, Officer Mysterious. What book are you looking for, then?"

Officer Mysterious hesitated. "*War and Peace.*"

"Ah, naturally a Russian novelist."

Shit.

Esther flinched a little, realized how prejudiced that had sounded, but today she did not want to spare anyone's feelings. After all, if anyone could handle her emotional outbursts, it'd be this woman. Gabe couldn't handle Esther. Mariel couldn't handle Esther with *Gabe.*

No one had the emotional stability to let Esther freak the hell out for once.

Except this walking, live-wired, kind-of-suspected-to-be-autistic beauty standing before her.

Not a *good* excuse to be a *bitch* to her, but—

"Do you have an issue with Russians?" The officer raised an eyebrow again, and it arched perfectly, as if it were used to being judgmental.

Esther could not stop firing insults. Today, her emotions were like an oncoming freight train—and this woman was her unfortunate victim. A human punching bag. It was wrong.

But Esther felt safe enough to misbehave a little.

"You..." Esther said, "... are the only Russian I have a problem with. If I remember correctly, you told me to shut up while you were with me in the alleyway." Her fingers crept up into her tousled hair and combed it over her shoulder. "Aren't you taught professionalism in policing?" She smirked a little to let the officer know she wasn't being *one hundred* percent serious with the insults, but Esther was now invested in the banter.

She wanted more.

Wanted the officer to bite back.

"You don't get very far in life being nice," Tira responded, her voice cool... and her eyes *did* bite.

"I've gotten *very* far being nice."

"Yes? Where?"

"In my boyfriend's pants, for one." Esther was not very sure why she'd felt the need to say that, but she lifted her head and committed herself to the statement.

"Oh?" Officer Mysterious' mouth twitched again. "Ah, yes. *Gabe*, if I remember correctly. The one who took off on you? Left you to hide after you served him, hmm?"

Esther's entire body went hot as an awkward silence fell. She stared at the officer.

The officer stared back. Her eyes didn't waver.

"Yes," she said, because that was all she could think to say. "Gabe."

"Mmhmm." *Finally*, the officer blinked. "Well, I'm actually here to give this back to you." She withdrew her hand from the pocket and pulled forth Gabe's necklace. It dangled over her fingers as she extended her hand.

Esther's eyes widened. Stepping forward, she investigated the necklace in the outstretched hand, almost hoping that it was *not* the necklace because she still had yet to break up with its giver.

But it was indeed the dancing girl pendant.

And something about this officer seemed very familiar—especially as she handed the necklace to Esther. As if it'd happened before...

Years ago.

"Thank you," Esther murmured, and took it from her hand. Their fingers brushed, and her thoughts frenzied until they arrived at a sudden memory.

"You have ice cream in your hair."

Esther's fingers darted to her hair. She fluffed it a little. "Oh," she laughed, and her hand shook.

"We should go." Mariel's voice sounded gruff.

The runner ignored him. Looking at Esther, she backed away. "One last thing."

Esther's attention belonged to the runner, and she disregarded Mariel's loud sigh. "Hmm?"

Faint dimples emerged again. "You're annoying... but you're not so bad looking yourself."

Esther's hand lingered on the officer's as she attempted to ground herself in the massive coincidence. "Where did you find it?"

"Where do you *think* I found it?" The woman snatched her hand away, as if she'd been burned. "Remember our little foot pursuit? After your boyfriend's public wank-job?" Mockery and annoyance oozed from the mouth of Officer Mysterious.

As her heart rate rose again with steady humiliation, Esther slipped the necklace into her pocket and stared at her.

If this was the runner from years ago at the track—that fucking *wallpaper-worthy* runner that'd run her over and then made it seem like *her fault*—then her selfish personality hadn't changed one fucking bit. "What's your name?" Esther demanded.

Tira tilted her head, and her eyes narrowed. The sunlight glinted on her hair. "*You* don't *demand* things from me. And why does it matter?"

Right now, Esther wanted to slap her. But, at the same time—not really. She wasn't sure what was going on in her head. "So I can report you to your department as a *fucking* asshole."

Returning her hands to her pockets, Officer Mysterious came forward a little. Her eyes burned but, as if caressing herself, she ran her tongue across her bottom lip. "You *really* want me to arrest you, don't you?"

Frustrated, Esther stood firm. When their angry eyes melted together with molten fire, she could almost see the red hot sparks of rage in the space between them. She spoke, and she expected something vicious to flow from her mouth, something very harsh. Instead, her voice turned low and soft. "You wish... you *wish* you could put handcuffs on me again."

Esther expected another response. Another comeback. Instead, she noticed a steady red flush start to creep into the young woman's cheeks.

Satisfaction tingled her nerves.

Because Officer Mysterious was *blushing*.

"My name is Tira," the officer snapped, and she turned on her heel to leave.

Esther went after her, as if she'd been dragged. Just a couple steps. Because this strange woman annoyed her. *Pissed* her off.

But Esther wasn't ready for her to leave.

"*Wait.* I have to see if we have your book."

"I'll find it elsewhere. This place has horrible customer service."

"Well, *yes*," Esther fired back, and inched closer. "But only when I deal with customers like *you*. Plus, *you* represent the city of Chicago so your position looks far worse than mine."

Furious, Tira turned on her heels, and her eyes flashed like a neon green warning signal. Somehow, that seemed more dangerous than a flashing red signal. "At least *I* am doing something of importance." The Russian accent thickened in her voice.

Now Esther was pissed, but she laughed. "A street cop. How cute."

Which was an ironic insult, considering her father had been a cop. She felt like a fool, but she was furious. The bitch sounded like Hawk.

"You're not doing much to contribute to society with dance, Sis."

God, she was fucking tired of people talking to her like a useless piece of ass. And maybe this officer hadn't *meant* to do that, maybe this officer was hurting too, but today was not the day. Not after last night. Not after Mariel decided to drop in without logical explanation and claim her as if she *should* have waited for him like a good girl with nothing better to do than fucking *dance.*

So, as Esther stood her ground against the snarling officer in her bookstore, she wanted to dig the dagger and twist.

Both women, flushed and hot-tempered, stared at each other.

Tira cleared her throat. Switched her ponytail to the other shoulder. "I am surprised the bookstore is open today."

Such an awkward statement, but it was a touch of normalcy, and it relieved Esther. "Wait. How did you find me? How did you know I even worked here?"

Uninterested, Tira gestured. "I patrol the area. I get coffee around here, I see you wander in and out all the time." Scowling, she tapped her foot, her face turned away from Esther. Was she procrastinating her exit?

Biting her lip, Esther rubbed her palms against her thighs. Her eyes couldn't help but follow the excellent profile of Tira's face. "Be honest. Why didn't you arrest me?"

Tira shrugged. "I knew you were the daughter of a former Chicago police officer. Your dad is still well-respected there." Her eyes met Esther's again and clung.

"He'd appreciate that."

Esther never thought it would be tumultuous to look into someone's eyes, but this woman unlayered her with her gaze. It was difficult looking into the sharp green eyes, because they seemed to know everything about her—every secret, every thought. The longer she looked, the more the eyes unlayered and searched.

Yet... it was *necessary.*

She *had* to look.

As her heartbeat pulsed within her throat, Esther broke the interrogative gaze. "I'll see if we have the book."

Quietly, Esther stepped past the officer and walked several aisles away from her. She was relieved to be away from her, relieved that her innermost thoughts might have been saved from investigation of Officer Mysterious' invasive eyes.

As Esther searched the shelf, her fingers shook. When her forefinger landed upon the thick paperback, she reached higher to tip it from the shelf.

Then Esther stopped. No logical explanation would have sufficed in helping her understand the reasoning for the next decision she made.

With calm decisiveness, she let the book snap back onto the shelf, and Esther Caravan left the aisle.

"We don't have it," Esther stated as she came down the aisle. "I can order it. If you come back Wednesday, it'll be here by then."

Leaning against the counter now, Tira played with the end strands of her ponytail. It was *such* long hair. Wavy. Almost with a hint of curl to it. "Or... I could just order it from Amazon."

Oh. Okay.

"You'd regret that," Esther said, and she adjusted her tank top.

"Oh? Why is that?"

"Because my books are better."

"Think so?"

"Mmhmm. You don't want a book that is processed and fake looking."

"What does that even mean?" Officer Mysterious said, and she tilted her head as if she'd been lost a long time ago.

"It means that *my* books look better, *smell* better, and are used just enough to be less stiff at the seams when you open them." Esther leaned her cheek into her palm and smiled.

Tira blinked. "Huh?"

Jesus Christ.

"You seem confused."

"I am only confused when human beings make no sense," Officer Mysterious protested, stressed.

This was *fun*, and Esther had no idea why. "Hmm, I think you're just confused as a person."

Tira's face was reddening again. "I am buying from Amazon."

"No, you're not."

"Yes, I *am*."

"Then do it," Esther laughed. "Order it now. In front of me."

Snarling, Tira pulled out her phone. "I will."

"Good. Do it."

"I *am*." The young woman's thumbs raced with mad intent over her phone screen.

And Esther watched. For a moment, she forgot about last night's chaos, forgot that she'd been sad, confused, and exhausted. Instead, she appreciated the sight of the flustered officer ordering a goddamn book on Amazon just to prove a *point*.

And there was something *hilarious* about the intense hyper-focus that overcame Officer Mysterious as she typed with the phone in her face.

And something captivating too.

"*There.*" Tira thrust the phone towards Esther.

"*Order placed, thanks!*" the screen said.

Esther's eyes snapped up. "Well, fine. Take your stupid *Amazon* Russian book."

"Oh, I will."

"Good. So why are you still here?"

"To make myself feel more intelligent."

Esther shook her head. "You're a dick."

"Don't you like those?" Tira tilted her head again. There was a *dash* of a smile, one of mockery and entertainment, and dimples appeared in her cheeks.

Esther looked at the dimples for a minute and then realized it was her turn to speak. "Don't you?" She wanted to backhand her, slap that smug look from her face.

Although Esther was more curious about what might happen if she *tried*.

Tira blinked. She seemed taken aback by the question, as if it had never been asked of her. "I'd rather not have this conversation with you," she snapped.

"You *don't* like them, *do* you, Officer Mysterious?"

"This is irrelevant. I'd prefer it if you would stop talking, please." Tira's nostrils flared, her cheeks red, her gaze averted.

"*Or*... you could just leave the bookstore and never have to hear me talk again..."

"Fine. I am gay," Tira snapped, as if she hadn't just told Esther that she didn't want to talk about it.

"I see, I *see*. Not surprising. You've got an angry lesbian dominance thing going on with your personality."

"What?" Officer Mysterious looked confused again.

Esther shrugged. "I'm saying it doesn't surprise me that you don't like dick."

"You're very assuming about who I am as a person. You're not really selling yourself."

Esther laughed. "The lady doth protest too much. And also, I wasn't aware I was supposed to impress you."

"There's no need to try. I was unimpressed the first time I saw you." Tira turned her head and brought her eyes back to Esther's.

Something in her tone implied that it was true. Despite everything else Tira had said, the words hurt a little more this time. The banter was no longer fun.

"Okay," Esther said, and she reached for her sweatshirt. She put it on.

Tira's demeanor shifted, as if she wasn't sure how to handle the abrupt, uncomfortable silence.

"Do you have a hardcover?" the officer croaked. "Of *War and Peace*?"

The woman confused the hell out of her, but Esther nodded.

"Order that for me, then."

It was a command.

A militant *command.*

...To order a goddamn book Officer Mysterious had *just* purchased online.

Esther opened her mouth to advise Tira that she did not take orders, especially from Russian police officers, but it didn't come out of her mouth.

Something else did.

"Anything for you, Officer Mysterious."

And at that moment, Esther wasn't sure if the statement was sarcasm, or truth. But her heart raced.

And it was very hot in the bookstore.

The police officer looked stiff. After a brief moment, Tira reached into her coat pocket, withdrew a business card and a pen, and scribbled on the card. Slapped it on the counter. "Call or text me when you have the book." She turned to leave.

"Tira?"

The officer stopped.

Esther softened her voice. "Aren't you going to ask my name?"

Officer Mysterious hesitated. "I know it already. Remember? I knew of your father?"

"So...? I'm not my dad. I'm someone else completely. And... you didn't ask for my name the day you ran into me on the track."

That was supposed to be an inside thought. Would Tira remember? Was this even the *same* woman?

As the sun glinted into the store and framed the tall officer, the dimples came back to her cheeks. A flicker of another smile.

"It's Esther," Tira said. "But I will always see you as the ice cream girl."

Her face burned now.

When the officer turned to leave again, Esther felt the need to say one more thing. "I'm not usually this rude, I promise. It's been a horrible couple days for me and..." she hesitated, realizing the actuality of her next words as they exited her mouth. "To be honest, I haven't had anyone to vent to, and I felt safe with you today. So... thank you."

Tira stood with her back to Esther. Her hands shifted in the pockets of her pea coat. "I stand by what I said... you have *horrible* customer service." She gestured towards the business card. "Let me know when it arrives."

Esther's eyes followed the police officer as she walked past the store windows and disappeared into the bustle of the windy city.

With sudden motivation, she felt prepared. For anything. *Everything*. Her mind felt clearer. Esther Caravan was ready to accept her problems for the day, and deal with them as they came.

And the first one?

Gabe Donovan.

Because he deserved to move on... just as much as she did.

Verse 4

~ Flash Drive ~

Sunday, January 12th, 2020
Chicago, Illinois

A humble knock on the door snapped Phil Jameson from his focus. He sat at his desk in the dark, blue-painted master bedroom. On the laptop, the video file took its time saving on the flash drive he'd almost bent from trying to jam it in the wrong way.

"Dad?" Hailey's muffled voice. "Are you in there?"

"*What*, Hailey?" Phil cried, frustrated that the file was taking too long to save.

"Are you still taking me to choir practice?" It sounded like a plea.

Phil growled at the computer. "*Yes.* Are you *dressed?*"

"Yes."

Phil stood up and stomped to the door. Flung it open.

Hailey stood in the doorway, head low, wearing an ankle-length denim dress and a long-sleeved white polo. Her hair was brushed. Many of the knots were out.

"Acceptable," Phil said and glanced back at his laptop. "Give me five minutes, and then we will leave."

"Yes, Sir."

Phil slammed the door.

Stomped back to the desk.

And sat.

Ah, good. It'd sped up, but he needed to leave in ten minutes to get Hailey to choir practice on time. It wouldn't do to be late—he'd never been late to church once, even for events. If he had hopes to stand out as a leader, and overshadow Jerome Nadier's disgusting leadership, he'd need to maintain punctuality and professionalism.

"Come *on*, hurry *up*." Phil raked his nails over the desk.

He wanted to vomit at the thought of Jerome. How *dare* he come into Phil's house and disrespect him in that manner?

"Godless idiot," Phil muttered, but Jerome's sins hadn't been without consequences. Oh, no.

Because Phil remembered the ammunition he'd photographed in Jerome's journal a year ago.

"*Yes,*" the journal entry said. "*I have given communion to a gay couple in the church, a couple that has been together for years without the knowledge of the other church members. Maybe I will be judged for giving them the sacrament, but I am not ashamed. They deserve to feel God's love, too.*"

"And you deserve to feel God's wrath for encouraging their lifestyle," Phil said to the computer, remembering the journal entry and his conversation with the upper clergymen on Thursday, January 9th.

"*Are you sure this is something he's been actively doing?*"

"*Sadly, yes,*" Phil said, shaking his head with sorrow. "*I don't want to be the person that gets him into trouble... but I knew it'd be wrong not to say anything about it.*"

And with that came the consequences. They'd address Jerome tomorrow... on Monday.

Phil brought his eyes back to the laptop. One percent left... and done.

He snatched the flash drive from the laptop and left the room.

"Take the keys and unlock the car and wait for me," Phil ordered when he reached the first floor. "I'll be there in a minute."

Hailey, who had been sitting on the couch with her hands folded onto her lap, nodded and stood up.

Phil watched her close the door and waited until the sliding porch door shut before he went to the walk-in pantry. He scanned the shelves, tapped his finger against his lips, and then grabbed a can of tuna.

Carolyn had been good for the last couple days. Silent. She deserved better food today.

The can lid popped off with ease.

Hailey didn't really understand what was going on in the basement, and she didn't ask. She knew it had something to do with her mother, and Phil had explained the situation in vague terms—while also demonstrating his abilities on a dead squirrel he'd gathered from the road.

"*This is what your father can do,*" Phil said, bringing his hands to the squirrel's furry body. "*Watch and believe.*"

Hailey watched with wide eyes as the squirrel's body molded itself back together and life filled its eyes. Its once crushed body sprang to life, and it sank its teeth into Phil's thumb before racing down the street.

"Hailey," Phil cried as blood spouted from his finger. "You will see your mother again!"

And Hailey screamed.

Phil spooned the tuna onto a plate. It plopped against the surface. He took a bowl from the dish rack, clattered it against the counter, and reached for a plastic bottle of—

—*Spring water's finest!*—

—water. He twisted off the cap, and it swirled as he poured it into the bowl and glanced at his watch. Time to step it up.

"My dear!" Phil called after unlatching the basement door and swinging it open. "I've brought your dinner!" His feet thumped against the basement stairs, and the steps groaned beneath his weight as he descended.

An odor of feces and urine drifted into his nostrils. It wasn't pleasant, and Carolyn needed to do a better job cleaning after herself. He'd even provided her a bucket to use, but she seemed to have forgotten *how* to use it like a toilet.

When Phil brought her to life three months ago, he hadn't expected to potty-train his wife. But he had faith that, just like a child, she would adapt and grow to become more independent.

"My honey, are you awake?" Phil came to the bottom of the stairs, and the water sloshed a little in the bowl. "Ah. There you are."

There she was indeed.

Carolyn lay curled against the wall, wrapped in the dark blanket he'd given her. She was still naked. He was fine with that, because he'd promised her clothes as an incentive to use the bucket properly.

"I need to go somewhere," Phil said, approaching his wife and placing the bowl of water and the plate of tuna on the floor. "Sit up so I can take the duct tape off. You've been very respectful the last couple of days, and you've earned time without it."

The chains rattled. Whimpering, Carolyn sat up with slow caution, her eyes cast down to the floor. He'd secured the twelve-foot chains to the wall and had purchased the items at an unbelievable price at *Menards*. This had only been because, much like the squirrel, she'd attacked him after springing up from the body bag.

Carolyn had screamed like a banshee and had attacked like a rabid cat. Biting. Scratching. Drawing blood like an animal, rather than appreciating what he'd done for her.

Phil made sure to delete all of *that* from the video.

And so, after hitting her hard enough to knock her unconscious, Phil had tied her up and marched straight to *Menard's* for the appropriate items. He'd worked too hard to gain Kaemon Spears' approval to allow him access to Carolyn's body. He would not risk losing her again by allowing her to attack him and flee like that squirrel.

"I want nothing to do with this," Kaemon Spears growled, when he'd granted Phil the resources to retrieve Carolyn's body. "I will get it for you, but whatever sick thing you're doing? It better not come back to me. I'll cook you alive on my grill. Understood?"

Fine.

If the governor wanted to disassociate from the miracles that would soon come to the United States of America, then *fine*.

"Have you soiled yourself again?" Phil demanded, standing above her and tapping his thumbs together. He gestured to the bucket several feet away from her. "The bucket is right *there*."

Carolyn blinked up at him with red, tearful eyes. She was looking very thin. He'd need to fatten her up soon. He hadn't married a skeleton, and what was the point of raising her from the dead if she *looked* deceased?

"I will leave the radio on for you," Phil said, reaching down and peeling off the duct tape. It tugged her lip a little and left behind red streaks around her mouth. "You eat, and use the bucket. I'll be back soon."

After crumpling the duct tape and tossing it into the bucket Carolyn didn't use, Phil switched on the early 90s vintage AM/FM radio that they'd used on their first dance together on their marital night.

"Enjoy the sermon," Phil said, and he left her.

* * *

When Phil arrived at St. Michael's, he noticed something different.

Fr. Jerome often came to choir practice nights to sit in his office and do whatever on earth he thought was important. Tonight was different.

He wasn't there.

That was fine for Phil, considering he'd been tempted to murder him on Wednesday, January 8th, for having the audacity to tell him that *he wasn't a creation of God.*

If only that old man knew what Phil was capable of.

And he would.

"Have a good practice, Dear," Phil told his daughter, who sped off down the hall towards the sanctuary. Clearing his throat, he straightened his tie and turned right to walk down the long hallway where the offices and Sunday School rooms were located.

"Looking for me?" A voice behind him.

Phil turned.

A dark-haired priest, who looked incredible for his proclaimed age of sixty-something, stood at the end of the hallway with the Bible in his hand. He smiled. "Hi, Phil."

"Oh," Phil said. "Father Paul. Yes. I was looking for you. Where is... um—"

"Father Jerome?" The priest smiled again. "Not feeling well. He asked me to open the church for choir practice."

As if on cue, soft, muffled voices rose in the distance and echoed through the large church building.

"Shall we talk?" Fr. Paul gestured to an office.

"I, er—need to run back home for a little bit while Hailey's practicing. I just wanted to give you the flash drive." Phil dug into his back pants' pocket to search for the item. He half expected to find a hole in his pants, especially since that green-eyed *jezebel* had managed to get away with slicing his pants and *threatening* his life the other day.

She'd go straight to Hell too. She could burn alive together with Jerome, and they could sing the homosexual version of *Kumbaya* as the flames licked their feet.

Fr. Paul smiled a little. "Are you sure, Phil? You want to do this?"

Phil stopped digging in his pocket. "Well... *yes*. Why wouldn't I?"

The priest searched his face, and the smile left. "Because once you become an extension of God's hand, there's no going back. You are *His* to serve. *His* to obey. That is no easy task."

Phil felt something stir in his chest. Pride. That's what it was.

Of *course* it wasn't an easy task. Phil had never been handed *easy*. He'd survived the bullies at school, the football players who'd pushed him into the locker, the wrestlers who'd sliced his pants and underwear from the back—

—like that jezebel—

—and the cheerleaders who'd wrinkled their noses at him. He'd survived an abusive mother at home. He'd been laughed at his entire life, and it was only until he'd met Carolyn and had made a name for himself as a lawyer (which also hadn't been easy) that the path had quieted down a *little*.

No true warrior of God had *ever* had it *easy*. Moses. King David. *Jesus*.

But that's why God chose them.

"I understand," Phil said, and his fingers struck the flash drive. With a quick gasp, he pulled it from his pocket.

Fr. Paul's eyes settled on the drive. "This is it?"

Phil nodded. He began to sweat. "This could either destroy my reputation, or elevate it." He cleared his throat. "Please don't be the one who destroys it."

Fr. Paul walked forward. A gentle smile returned to his lips, and he closed his hands over Phil's extended one. "Philip. When I met you at your wife's funeral, I knew you were special. But I also sensed you were broken." He squeezed Phil's hand. "But sometimes, it's the most broken spirits that are called to the highest missions."

Phil swallowed as the priest came even closer.

Fr. Paul's breath tickled his nose and lips. "I would never, *ever* risk breaking your spirit any more than it already is. I only want to elevate it, and put you in the position to save people's souls before the Great Tribulation."

Phil's breath shook. "Really?"

Fr. Paul stepped back. When he did, the flash drive was gone from Phil's hand. "Something big is coming, Phil. Something terrible, but Holy. That's why I asked you to film what you did—so you can prepare everyone for what's coming."

Phil straightened his shoulders. "Right. Yes. Hmm."

He wasn't sure he could trust Fr. Paul, considering the man had mentored Fr. Jerome years ago, but a part of him trusted this man more than anyone he'd ever met.

Due to Fr. Jerome's coma, Fr. Paul had been requested to facilitate the service for Carolyn's funeral. The reason he'd been chosen was unknown to Phil, but he'd liked the priest. After meeting at Carolyn's service, Fr. Paul had asked if he'd like to meet for coffee as a means of providing condolences. Since then, the two men hadn't stopped talking.

In fact, Fr. Paul had become somewhat of a mentor to Phil too.

And when Phil let his abilities *slip*—the priest had been more than just supportive. He'd been excited.

"Go see your wife," Fr. Paul whispered, and he placed the flash drive in his pocket. He patted it. "And don't worry about the future. It's yours."

Giddy, Phil left. He whistled for the first time in years. Smiled and allowed a vehicle to merge in front of him in traffic. He felt light.

Happy.

Fr. Paul had taken him seriously about Jerome's sins, and the priest had taken him seriously about the resurrection.

Things were moving in the right direction.

Until Phil Jameson saw a rental car parked in his driveway.

"Oh, no, no, no!" Phil hissed, and he almost flung himself from the sedan. The figure on the neighborhood watch sign squinted at him as he raced towards the porch.

The sliding door was open.

Someone was here.

And he had a feeling he knew who it was. Because—

"I can see the future too," he'd told Kaemon Spears.

But no. Not that. Because there was only one person who still had a key, and only one person who'd come sniffing around his household.

That *jezebel* viper... the slutty, self-proclaimed feminist brat that'd shown no appreciation for her family. His other daughter.

Victoria.

Phil entered his house and slammed the door. He didn't care if Victoria knew he was home—maybe he'd stop her from entering the basement in time.

It was a false hope.

As he strode through the house and into the kitchen, his eyes turned to the basement door. Sweat rolled into his ears and muffled the sound of his breathing.

The basement door was cracked open.

Victoria had found her. She'd found Carolyn.

And it would not look *good* for Phil Jameson's reputation.

"I want nothing to do with this," Kaemon Spears growled. *"I will get it for you, but whatever sick thing you're doing? It better not come back to me. I'll cook you alive on my grill. Understood?"*

Had Victoria called 911 already? *Had she?*

Phil needed a paper bag. He needed to poop, and he suddenly understood how Carolyn continued to soil herself. But as his eyes darted around in an attempt to help him *think*, they landed on the one thing that gave him hope.

Her phone.

Gasping, Phil grabbed it from the counter and moved towards the basement door. He slipped through the crack and began a slow, creeping descent down the stairs.

The radio sermon screamed through the basement.

Phil wasn't sure what he'd need to do, but he'd do what he *needed*.

The stairs shifted beneath his feet. The phone almost fell from his trembling hands. As he descended, Victoria's figure appeared, and his lower intestines growled with a threat.

Forgive what I may have to do, Lord, for the benefit of your people, Phil prayed, and he stopped at the center of the stairs.

Fr. Paul had been right. *"Once you become an extension of God's hand, there's no going back,"* he said. *"You are His to serve. His to obey. That is no easy task."*

Victoria whirled, and her pale face distorted in horror as she looked up at him.

Suddenly, Phil felt like a god, because his eldest daughter looked up at him with terror, rage, and awe—all things God experienced from His own children.

So, as Victoria turned to face him for judgment, Phil raised the phone and lifted his eyebrow.

"Left your phone on the counter," he said.

And Victoria screamed.

Chapter 11: Verse 1

~ Seven. Thirteen. Zero. Eight ~

Monday, January 13th, 2020
Chicago, Illinois

"Yes," Fr. Jerome said. "I've been giving communion to a gay couple in the church."

It was almost eleven in the morning. Though it was a sunny day, it was very cold.

Nervous, the priest stuffed his hands into his cardigan sweater. He wondered if Mariel was awake yet, considering he'd been up all night playing video games. The young man had still been playing when Fr. Jerome woke up at six. Seeing Mariel in a chair with the gaming remote in his hand? It was a sight he adored and was *grateful* for.

But Mariel looked tired. Sad.

And that scared Fr. Jerome, because *sad* reminded him of Mariel's suicide. His *death*.

"... Are you okay, Jerome?"

Fr. Jerome reached up and rubbed his fingers against his forehead. "Not really." He looked across the desk at the two men in front of him—Fr. Paul Rinaldi and Bishop Alexander Oliver—archbishop of the Midwest's Antiochian Eastern Orthodox Church.

Fr. Paul sat a little further behind the bishop, scratching the peppery white stubble on his jaw. His eyes clung to Fr. Jerome. "This isn't the end of the world," he said.

"And I get it," Bishop Alexander added as the edge of his chest-length beard bounced while he spoke. "I understand your intentions, because I *know* you as a person, Jerome. But what you're doing is not how it should be. You know that."

Fr. Jerome was weary. His mind felt it, and so did his body. He wanted to argue, to tell them that anyone who *truly* sought *theosis* with God deserved to take the sacrament. But when he opened his mouth, the words he wanted to speak did not come out.

"What is it you need me to do?" Fr. Jerome said and fidgeted with a piece of paper. Awaiting more words, his journal lay on his desk beside him.

"Well," Bishop Alexander said, and he tapped his fingers on his lap. His black vestments draped over his big belly, and the light glinted against the large cross that dangled from his neck all the way past his chest. "I personally don't want to see you disciplined, but these things go above my head. If you're willing, I'd like to do my expected diligence."

"And what would that be?"

"Three months monitoring. And by monitoring, I don't mean a spy over your shoulder at all times. I just mean—a helper. Another priest who can share the role with you."

Fr. Jerome closed his eyes. His heart thudded against his chest, but it was *slow*. It surprised him, because the prickly feelings on his skin suggested he was far more stressed than his heart believed.

But right now—his heart didn't know what to believe. He still wasn't certain he *hadn't* gone mad... because humans *could not catch bullets*. Humans couldn't splatter their brains in the shower and then just *come back* and—

"Okay," Fr. Jerome said, and he opened his eyes. "I am too exhausted to argue against this. Tell me the next steps."

As if processing the request, Bishop Alexander shifted his eyes upwards and then responded. "How do you feel about Father Paul helping out?"

Fr. Jerome looked at the priest across from him. Their eyes met.

What was he supposed to say? He wasn't a fan of any of this—but it seemed odd that the priest who'd been released from a mental hospital had been chosen for this role. At the same time, Fr. Jerome did not feel as though he could judge, especially since he wasn't even sure he could recognize reality right now.

But Fr. Paul smiled, and it was a reminder of his first days in seminary. A reminder that good people existed, and that Fr. Jerome didn't have to *do this alone*.

Fr. Paul was the only one who seemed to have *more* answers than not. And somehow, deeply, that gave him a sense of peace.

And that terrified him.

Because he couldn't trust *any* peace right now. It all seemed...

False.

"Will I still be allowed to do my sermons?" Fr. Jerome asked and tore his eyes away from the other priest.

"Yes. Of course. Consider Father Paul as your support. That's it." Bishop Alexander smiled and patted Fr. Paul on the shoulder.

"Alright," Fr. Jerome said, nodding in effort to keep tears from forming in his eyes. "Thank you."

Bishop Alexander stood. So did Fr. Paul.

"Call if you need anything, Jerome. We care about you... even though you didn't warn me about a cat running around." The bishop frowned, but it was an expression filled with unwanted humor.

"I'm sorry."

"You should be. Gosh darn it, the cat attacked my beard! See you, Jerome." Bishop Alexander shook his head with a slow grin and then left the room.

Fr. Paul followed.

"Paul."

The dark-haired priest stopped in the office doorway and turned in response to his name. "Yes?"

Fr. Jerome traced the binding on his journal. Dazed, he stared with idle concentration at his finger. "Please tell me what's going on."

"With what?"

"You know." Fr. Jerome looked up. "With Mariel."

Fr. Paul tapped his palm against the doorframe and then turned to face the other priest. His eyes seemed distant. "Something Holy."

"Paul, he won't talk to me. He won't tell me why he's... *here*. Why he's *back*."

"Jerome—"

Fr. Jerome rubbed his palms over his face. "Please. Can you give me something? Anything. I just need to know if I've lost my mind. You were always so great at... at helping me find peace."

Fr. Paul came closer, his face unreadable even in the overhead light. "What was it that Jesus said when he appeared to his disciples after his death?"

Peace be with you.

"Peace be with you," Fr. Jerome said, playing with the cross around his neck.

Fr. Paul didn't wear a cross. Years ago, he'd always worn one.

"Yes." Fr. Paul spoke with gentle confidence. "I don't know what's planned for Mariel's future. But I do know this—he *has a future*. Isn't that what you've always wanted for him?"

Yes. Of course. But—

"Yes," Fr. Jerome said, squeezing the cross around his neck.

"Then don't question yourself." Fr. Paul cocked his head towards the doorway. "I'm grabbing a sandwich somewhere. You want anything?"

"No, I'm fine. Thank you."

With a thumb's up, Fr. Paul left the office.

And returned a moment later. Eyebrows glued together, the priest stuck his head in the office. "You might want to go to the sanctuary. Someone's there."

Fr. Jerome closed the journal he'd opened and stood up. "Who?"

"Not sure. A woman. Your cat is in the sanctuary too, just FYI."

Chuckling, Fr. Jerome left his desk. "I was wondering where she went."

*　　*　　*

When Fr. Jerome met Harlow Nadier at the shelter, the staff had warned him that she did not bond well with strangers. In fact, she had a history of attacking them. She'd attacked her former owner's newborn—hence her arrival to the shelter.

But she'd *purred* when Fr. Jerome visited her, and he'd made the decision to take her home. She hadn't approached anyone since then.

Well... Esther Caravan had managed a few ear scratches, but no one else had earned that honor since then.

Until now.

Fr. Jerome stopped in the wide sanctuary entrance. The sun's rays beamed into the large, magnificent church, bouncing against the icons, the walls, the pews, and glowing atop the black baseball cap that sat on the head of a blonde-haired woman in the middle right pew.

In comparison to the large sanctuary, the woman looked small.

Lonely.

But she was not alone.

Harlow lay on her, and the cat opened her eyes in sleepy bliss as she rested her head upon the woman's shoulder like an infant being burped.

Fr. Jerome couldn't help but feel a little jealous. So, as he stepped into the church, he spoke.

"Hello, may I help—"

"*Ssh.*" The church walls captured the young woman's hiss.

Fr. Jerome blinked.

"She's sleeping," the woman whispered, and turned her head a little. The sunlight caught her profile, and the blonde wisps of hair that trickled from her cap. It glinted against her left eye, the only eye Fr. Jerome could see.

And it was green.

Then it happened.

That *shift*—that *pulse* that tore through his mind like a storm and yanked him from reality.

Crowds roared like thunder. A stadium shook with glee, and the green-eyed woman with a blood-smeared face clung to the top of a cage and screamed. "Seven, thirteen, zero, eigh-!"

"Priest. *Priest.*" A cold hand tapped his cheek.

Fr. Jerome opened his eyes.

He was on the floor. On his back. The green-eyed woman knelt over him, and her face shadowed him as her frame blocked out the sun.

"Are you okay?" the blonde snapped, as if inconvenienced from his collapse.

"Seven. Thirteen. Zero. Eight," Fr. Jerome whispered, reaching up to rub his head, and he wasn't sure *why* he whispered that.

He just... *did*.

Fr. Jerome whispered the numbers as if they were the final notes to the chaotic orchestration in his mind.

The most important notes.

But the young woman?

Her face *blanched*.

As Fr. Jerome rose up onto his elbows, the sharp-eyed blonde cleared her throat and stepped backwards, as if he'd just uttered nauseating news.

"You're fine," she muttered, quickly wiping her palms against her tight jeans.

"I'm sorry, I'm not quite sure what that was," Fr. Jerome said, and he sat up. He turned over onto his hands and knees, hoping the young woman would assist him but swiftly realizing she had no intention to. Harlow didn't either.

In fact, the damn cat rubbed against the woman's legs instead.

It's fine, the old man thought, grabbing for a pew to ease himself up. *'I got it.'*

But when Fr. Jerome rose to his feet and turned to face her, the look on her face was very telling.

The strange woman wasn't ignoring him on purpose.

She was *frozen*.

Trying to process *something*.

"How about you sit?" Fr. Jerome suggested. "You seem as though you are going to have a fainting spell too."

The woman shook her head and looked at him with narrowed eyes, like she didn't trust him. "Bad batch of chicken," she said, clearing her throat. "But yes. I'll sit. You sit, too."

It seemed like an order. The priest obeyed.

With a *blurp*, Harlow trotted over to the woman and hopped onto her lap.

"Would you like me to take my cat? She's kind of needy some—"

"I'd rather you didn't." Her head snapped up, and her eyes flashed in warning.

As if she'd murder him for retrieving his own cat.

But Fr. Jerome smiled a little. This young woman–the woman he'd seen *murder* him in an alleged vision last year—found comfort in Harlow. He loved that. It was pure. Genuine.

Fr. Jerome hoped the vision wouldn't come true.

"I'm Fr. Jerome Nadier. Or, if you prefer, you can call me '*priest*'." He flashed a smile.

Tira cocked her head and scratched Harlow's ears. "Why would I call you that if you already told me your original name?"

"I was joking. Nonetheless, what's your name, young lady? And how can I help you today?"

"My name is Tira." She looked down at Harlow as the cat accepted butt scratches with pure happiness. "I am looking for a church to attend. Would you suggest this one?"

Fr. Jerome almost laughed. In his entire career, he'd never heard an individual express interest in a church in this manner. But when he looked at her, Tira's eyes tore into his soul like a buzzard with its prey. She expected an answer, and a good one.

"Heh, erm." Fr. Jerome scratched his head. "My dear, it's not that simple."

"It is. I am trying to find God. Would you, or would you not, recommend this church?"

Harlow tried to sneak inside of the woman's black sweatshirt. The small cat made it halfway, leaving her butt sticking out, until she decided that it wasn't going to work and pulled her face back out of the pocket.

"There are nuances to these things. Let's start with this. Have you ever attended an Eastern Orthodox Church? Any other type of church?"

Tira looked bored, her expression as thrilled as a child forced to peel potatoes, but it was evident that she was fighting to act interested. "I am just trying to find God."

Bullshit. Perhaps that was an unforgivable assumption to make but—bullshit. This woman seemed much too self-aware and aggressive right now to simply be embarking on a journey to find God. He wasn't sure *how* he knew... but he *knew.*

Smiling a little, he leaned forward. "What really brought you here today, Tira?"

"Well, God. Presumably."

"Don't tell me a falsehood, young lady."

Her face reddened. "You are supposed to be a priest."

"I am?"

"Well, you are not doing a very good job encouraging me to find God and attend your church."

"Am I not? Aren't I encouraging you to find God by helping you un-layer each and every motive you have by being here?" Fr. Jerome placed a hand over his heart. "Our hearts speak to our minds, and our minds to our hearts. Sometimes those voices become so loud that we don't let anyone else in. It gets so noisy that we don't always *hear* God speaking to us."

Tira blinked at him. Her finger traced lazy circles around Harlow's ears.

"Self-awareness is key to finding God, because so often He makes the journey easier for us. You know why?" Fr. Jerome smiled with gentle encouragement.

"Er... no. Why?" Tira seemed transfixed now.

"Because," Fr. Jerome nodded with confidence, "God so very often finds *us.*"

Tira was silent for a moment, and she tilted her head a little into the sun as if in mad thought. Her eyebrows came together, and her green eyes darted about as she computed the words that Fr. Jerome had spoken.

"That does not make any sense," she concluded, dipping her head back down and speaking through her teeth. "No one *finds* me. I find *them.*"

Law enforcement of some sort. Guaranteed. And her limited social skills suggested something else—either trauma, lack of exposure, or... autism. He wasn't sure, but she had strangely endearing quirks.

"You're a police officer, aren't you?" Fr. Jerome asked.

"What makes you say that? Do I look like one?"

"Yes. And your mannerisms suggest as such. And," he gestured, "the *Thin Blue Line* flag on your hoodie."

Tira looked down at her hoodie as if she hadn't expected to see the flag there.

"It's okay," Fr. Jerome chuckled. "I won't tell anyone."

Tira eyed him with a mix of suspicion and an unexpected hint of playfulness. "I like this church."

He chuckled. "Do you, now?"

"Perhaps. We'll see." Still cuddling the cat, Tira rose to her feet.

"Would you like to meet with me sometime? I can leave you my card, but you've made it very clear you know where to find me."

Tira hesitated. "Why did you say those numbers? When you were having that—" she waved her hand, "—episode."

Oh, if only he knew that answer.

"Do they mean something to you?" He wasn't quite sure how else to respond.

Tira assessed him with slow concentration. It was the longest she'd looked at him without breaking eye contact. "I asked you a question first."

She had him there.

"I'm not sure, to be frank," Fr. Jerome said, and he broke his gaze from hers. He hated this—not understanding the meaning of these *dreams*. He wasn't even comfortable calling them *visions* yet. It seemed too... narcissistic. "I've been having these moments—these *déjà vu* moments—where I see things that I don't understand."

Why did he feel the need to *tell* this young woman these things? It was embarrassing, and she didn't seem like the sort of person to acknowledge something as scientifically unproven as *visions*.

But Tira's face didn't change. "I see," she said. "I hope you can find some answers. I know what it is like to not... *understand* something."

Fr. Jerome looked at her again. Warmth filled his heart. "Thank you. I needed to hear that."

She broke eye contact. Gave him a quick nod. "I need to go. Thank you again." She turned on her heel. Her boots thudded against the tile.

Fr. Jerome stood up. "Tira."

Tira stopped and turned.

"Will you give me my cat back? I rather like her."

Harlow flicked her fluffy tail across the young woman's face.

Tira stared at him. A piece of Harlow's fluff dangled from the brim of her cap, but the woman still looked intimidating. In fact, she eyed him with bewilderment, as if she were unaccustomed to returning people's property, or pets, to their rightful owners when requested.

But when she let out a small sigh and came over to him, Fr. Jerome saw something in her eyes. Sadness. Loneliness.

"You can see her again if you stop by the church," Fr. Jerome said with a smile. "I promise. Do you have a cat?"

"No." When she stopped next to the pew, Tira lowered her arms and allowed Harlow to leap from her embrace. The cat let out a raspy meow, looked up at her, and then rubbed against Fr. Jerome's thigh. "Thank you for letting me borrow her." A smile played across her lips, and she outstretched her hand.

His hand met hers. Pain sliced through his head like bolts of lightning and jolted his body.

Tira. Over him.

Gun. Over him.

Muzzle. Over him!

"I'm sorry," she said, and fired.

Fr. Jerome's eyes molded with hers, but he gripped her hand and held himself steady as last year's vision flashed through his mind.

"Are you alright?" Tira asked, with a hint of sympathy in her voice this time, and she kept her hand in his.

"Yes," Fr. Jerome said, and patted her hand with his other one. "Just a dizzy spell."

Clearing her throat, the young woman snatched her hand away. The sunlight glowed through the tall glass windows and cast shadows into the walkway. The yellow light illuminated Tira Arcelin, who stood at ease with her legs separated and her hands against the small of her back. One would think she'd look ridiculous—standing like that in the church sanctuary—but it didn't.

It looked rather appropriate, actually.

"I'll leave then," Tira said, "if you're sure you're alright."

Fr. Jerome watched her. He did not understand the feelings he experienced—of both safety and fear.

Fear begged him to flee from her.

But he wanted to help her.

After all, Tira wanted to *"find God"*. That was his job... to lead his flock.

Even though last year the wise Dr. Philip Jameson, M.D. had said—

"Leading the flock has clearly had a negative impact on your health, Father."

Fr. Jerome stooped to scratch Harlow's back. "You never answered my question." As he squinted through the sun beams, tiny specks of dust swirled in the light.

"Ask."

He straightened his shoulders. "What do those numbers—seven, thirteen, zero-eight—mean to you?"

Beneath the hat's low brim, the emerald eyes dimmed. Her upper lip curled into a snarl. When Tira spoke, her voice oozed with scorn. "Those numbers are a reminder to never fall victim to weakness again. Have a good day."

And Tira strode from the sanctuary.

Harlow leapt from the pew. As she entered the aisle, the cat glanced at him, meowed her intentions, and then trotted after the woman. Her tail flicked and stood upright as the spellbound calico followed Tira from the sanctuary.

"I never liked you anyway, you traitor," the priest said, shaking his head, but the cat only followed Tira to the hallway before returning to the sanctuary.

Fr. Jerome pulled his phone from his pocket. Mariel had texted him. He was awake. Eating breakfast. Going to the gym after breakfast.

Normal life activities.

Fr. Jerome closed his eyes.

What was normal?

There'd been *nothing* normal about today. But he realized a couple of things.

Tira liked cats.

With or without Fr. Paul, Fr. Jerome still intended to lead his flock.

One day, maybe, he would help Tira Arcelin *"find God"*.

And finally, if truth existed within his visions, the eccentric young woman would eventually take the old man's life.

VERSE 2

~ YOU'RE HURTING ME ~

Tuesday, January 14th, 2020
Chicago, Illinois

It was 5 A.M, and the morning air nipped his face. Shivering in his sweatshirt, Mariel tapped his knuckles against the alley's back door to the bookstore. Red paint flaked from the old wood.

Five years ago, he'd offered to paint that door. Todd Caravan let him. It'd been an excellent excuse to see Esther—she'd been there helping her grandmother clean the store that day.

Mariel knocked again. Louder. His lips peeled apart from dryness as he opened his mouth to take a breath. He needed water. Or something. He wasn't sure, but his stomach twirled with nerves.

It made sense. He'd fucked up. Simple as that. He hadn't treated Esther fairly at all. Now he was left to deal with the aftermath: humiliation and regret.

After his father purchased a new phone for him, Mariel had texted Esther. Begged for her forgiveness. Hours later, she responded.

"I want to see you."

They'd set a time. Esther said it'd be easier to meet before school. If questioned, she said she would tell them that she had had an early workout.

Mariel struck the door again, this time with a hammer fist. As he waited, somewhere in the city, a car accelerated. Then, from the other side, the door latch clicked.

Mariel thrust his hands into his pockets and held his breath.

The door swung inward. Esther stood in the shadowed doorway. "Hey."

Behind her, the bookstore was dark, but the restroom light gleamed in the hallway and cast a glow upon her face. Her loose ponytail fell over her right shoulder, and he couldn't help but settle his eyes on the black tank top—

—*University of Illinois Athletics*—

—that enclosed those large breasts he hadn't stopped thinking about since their last night together. They rose and fell, drawing in his gaze, and—

"Mars. Are you going to come in? Or stare at my tits all morning?"

He jumped, looked up, and stuttered. "I'm sorry. Really sorry."

Esther eyed him and stepped aside, allowing him to pass.

Grinning, Mariel glanced around the hallway. "No knives this time, right? Gun?"

Esther locked the door and came up to him. She reached for his hand. "How is it?"

"It's healing. It's a little itchy."

"Has anyone asked about it?"

"Dad tried to, but I told him not to worry about it." Mariel looked down at her, brought his eyes to hers in the soft glow of the light coming from the restroom. "Hey," he whispered and brushed his fingers against her hair. "I'm sorry, Esther."

"It's fine, Mars."

"No, really. I shouldn't have reacted the way I did. I had no right." He rested his palm against her cheek, and he shivered as Esther closed her eyes and rubbed the side of her face against his hand. "I was selfish. Is there any way I can make it up to you?"

She traced his fingers with her own and let out a soft breath. "Come cuddle me on the couch, and let's talk."

In the darkness, they sat close together. Enveloping her in his arms, Mariel leaned back and rested his legs on the coffee table.

Esther curled up on the couch, and she buried her head into his chest.

For several moments, they sat in the dark, quiet morning and listened to their own soft breathing.

"So," Mariel said. "How are you?"

"As well as you can expect. I guess I'm not accustomed to people returning from the dead, you know."

"Understandable."

Silence.

Mariel leaned closer, buried his face against the top of her head. Smelled the sweet fumes of her shampoo. It was still surreal... the fact that Esther was in his arms. As his thumbs brushed the skin of her bare arms, and he stared at the cleavage her tank top exposed, he whispered to her. "I love you so much."

Esther shivered a little. "I broke up with Gabe."

Feeling a little slighted, Mariel lifted his head from hers. "How'd that go?"

She shrugged. "Well. He was upset. Said that I strung him along which... I did. And, I feel bad for that." Her voice was low and held a tone of melancholy. "I wish..." her voice faded.

"Tell me."

Esther nestled closer. "I wish things could've been different. I wish you wouldn't have..."

"I know. And I'm sorry, Esther. I'm so sorry. I know I was selfish, and I've hurt a lot of people."

Eyes wide, Esther sat up. She rested her hand on his leg, and the soft touch sent electrical signals humming through his nerves. "Do you think it's the end times? Like, do you think the world's gonna end soon?"

His heart rate increased. "I don't know," Mariel said, and he wasn't sure what else to say. The Cherubim had implied that his role *was* to trigger the end times... but he still wasn't confident he'd been given clear instructions.

And Esther looked *worried. Scared.*

Mariel's eyes fell to her parted lips, and he wanted to kiss them. He wanted to stop talking, to stop thinking about the future and focus on *this moment.*

Was that selfish?

"I'm scared," Esther said, and she tightened her grip on his thigh. "I still don't know what any of this means. Mars... people aren't supposed to rise from the dead. *People.* They're not supposed to—"

"*Esther.* Can we just enjoy our time together? *Please?*" The blood rushed to his face.

"We have to talk about this. You need to help me work through—"

"Just *shut up!*" With a clap of his hand, Mariel pushed her away from him. Breathing hard, he stood and ran his fingers through his hair, tried to calm down.

Fuck!

Gasping, Esther stared at him with frightened, glimmering eyes.

He'd fucked up again.

Again. Like always.

"I'm sorry," he said, rubbing his face with his hands. "I shouldn't have pushed you like that. Or yelled at you."

Looking away, Esther made no move to stand. Instead, she shrugged. Spoke as if she didn't care. "I'm getting used to it. It's happened before. Last time you shot yourself."

"Please, *please*, don't be cruel about this."

Esther did not respond. She did not look at him. Her lips quivered.

Mariel sat beside her again. Back stiff, he sat upright while he rested the palms of his hands upon his knees. "It's hard for me to talk about it, because it reminds me I'm not normal. And you... *you* deserve normal. You deserve someone who doesn't keep hurting or scaring you like this. I don't *understand* what I am, and I'm so afraid you'll leave me and—"

"What do I need to *do* to help you trust me?" Her eyes were red, and her cheeks glistened with tears. "I just want to *understand* what's going on. Can you blame me? I love *you* for you. But can't you just let me be confused for a while without getting mad at me?"

Mariel nodded, reached for her hand and squeezed it. "Come here."

Sniffling, Esther leaned backwards, positioning herself into the embrace of his arms again. "Don't fucking push me like that again."

"I'm sorry, I won't."

"Or so help me, you will *never* see my body again. Ever."

"Well, in that case." Mariel grinned. He ran his fingers over her arms until goose-bumps rose on her skin. Kissing the top of her head, he traced his fingertips over her clavicles and stroked them in circles beneath her throat. "Anything else new?"

Esther shivered. "Hawk got in trouble. That was fun to experience."

"Oh yeah?" Mariel murmured, bringing his fingers a little lower, just above the center of her cleavage. "What'd he do?"

He didn't really care.

Esther's breath quickened. "Well, he was supposed to shovel yesterday. He hitched a ride to that research center he hangs out at instead."

Mariel brought his fingers against her throat. In response, the young woman's head fell back against his chest. He smiled. "What does Hawk getting in trouble look like?" He held her throat with one hand; slid the other hand down to cup her right breast.

Immediately, her body responded, and she lifted her hips a little. "Mars. You're distracting me."

"Tell me what it looks like for Hawk to get in trouble." His groin pulsed; the pressure built. As Mariel tightened his grip on her soft throat, he circled the fingers to his other hand around the nipple of her breast. It hardened. He pinched it.

Esther jolted in his arms, struggled to remain composed. "He... he gets grounded from—Mars, you're being *cruel*."

He'd slipped his hand beneath her tank top, beneath her bra, and was now teasing her without mercy. He flicked, pinched, and tugged her nipples.

Mariel Nadier could not think of anything other than *this* right now. It took priority. It was more important than talking. It was more important than listening. It was more important than helping her recover from his return.

He'd get to that later.

So, as he worked her breasts in his hands, he realized being with Esther brought an animalistic desire to surface. It always had. Now it seemed even harder to control in her presence.

"You like this?" Mariel whispered, nipped her ear with his teeth.

"Fuck you." Esther's voice was hoarse, her eyes closed.

But she did like it. He could *tell*... because Esther arched herself into his hands and wet her lips. She gripped the cloth of his sweatpants, made a fist, and pulled.

Mariel felt the young woman's pulse slam within her chest. "Finish telling me your story. What does Hawk get grounded from?"

Removing his hand from her bra, Mariel trailed it over her taut stomach. He felt a scratch on her stomach, or a scar of some sort, and he wondered if it'd been there before. Then he slid his fingers into her grey sweatpants and brushed his fingers against her panties.

Lifting her hips, Esther gasped and pushed herself against his hand. "He gets grounded from—that—that stuff he does. Oh *God*."

Outside, tires squealed. A bus hissed.

Mariel's mouth fell against her ear, nibbling, licking, biting as he stroked her with his fingers. "What stuff?" he whispered.

Again, he didn't care, and he *wanted her*. Wanted to fuck her on the couch and *fill* her again.

But Mariel enjoyed the process. He took pleasure in the control he had over her body. As he traced his tongue over her ear, he pressed his fingers against the hardened, wet spot beneath her panties and quickened his strokes in fast, light, circular motions. To his excitement, the cloth dampened.

Esther whimpered now, writhing her hips, squirming against his fingers. "That—*thing* he likes to do. Whatever you call it. *Science*. He gets grounded from—from—*Mars*, if you keep doing this I'm going to come."

"Good, I want you to." Taking her ear into his mouth, Mariel tweaked her nipple and then increased the pace of his fingertips between her legs.

His voice must have commanded her. As soon as he spoke, Esther cried out and arched her back.

In the dim light, Mariel could see that her face was flushed, her lips full with desire, her eyes closed. He brought his lips against her neck, just underneath her ear. With fluid motion, he slipped his hand beneath her panties, located the drenched warmth of her skinfolds, and then vibrated his fingertips against her clitoris.

Her breathless cries were beautiful.

Angelic.

As Esther shuddered with quick, sharp jolts against him, Mariel wondered if she'd found satisfaction. If so—

Would she still want to fuck *him?*

God, he'd be disappointed if she didn't. Probably angry, too. *Blue-balled*, as Gabe always used to say.

Mariel shifted, and his breath hitched. His groin hurt, and if she told him no—

Esther's mouth slammed against his, and she clawed at him. Her tongue filled his mouth. Her fingers darted beneath his shirt. She scraped her nails over his chest. It stung.

Hungry for her, Mariel threaded his fingers into her hair. Yanked. Their kisses grew more feverish.

While kneading the muscles of his chest with one hand, Esther pulled her mouth from his. "Did you ever have a fantasy?" she panted. "About me?"

Oh. *Many.*

But he couldn't tell her about *those* fantasies. Where blood ran, skin split, and—

No. He didn't have those fantasies anymore; not since leaving the Kingdom of Heaven.

Well. Maybe a few.

"Mars!" Esther urged, and her breath struck his lips.

Make something up. As Mariel struggled to remain composed, he nodded.

"What was it? Tell me fast."

"Remember when we kissed in the aisle? Against the bookshelf?"

"Uh, yes. The day you rejected me and then killed yourself. I remember. You're not helping yourself right now, Nadier."

"I want to fuck you against the bookshelf."

Esther's teeth nipped at his bottom lip. She grasped his face in her hands. "Come on."

In the darkness, they stumbled past the aisles, laughing, kissing, tripping once or twice. Once they found their way to a familiar aisle—where their passionate kiss had led to screams and tears on the day both hearts had been broken—Mariel Nadier and Esther Caravan tried to make new memories.

Grasping her hips, Mariel pushed her against the shelf. His entire body trembled.

Swiftly, Esther pulled down his sweatpants and stepped out of her own. The garments fell and encircled their ankles. The young lovers molded their bodies against each other.

Breathing hoarsely, Mariel lifted her, attempted to bring her legs around his waist. Doing so, he realized the pants were still surrounding her ankles. Embarrassed once more, he apologized.

"Stop apologizing during sex. This is an easy fix," Esther said, pulling her right leg from the pants and then slinging it around his waist with surprising ease and balance. "Lift me now."

Mariel hoisted her onto his hips. Moaning against her mouth, he brought his hands to Esther's buttocks, pressed her against the bookshelf, and pushed into her.

He let out a moan.

Her body stiffened.

Mariel wanted this to be pleasurable for her, but he was desperate. He could only think about the delight he experienced as he pushed through her wet—almost unwelcoming—walls.

Trying to breathe, he tore his mouth from hers, pressed his face into her hair, and pounded himself into her. It was incredible, being inside of her like this, being close to her. Every nerve in his body felt like a live wire.

But even as he heard his own whimpers, Mariel realized he heard nothing from Esther.

No expression of pleasure.

The bookshelf creaked, and her head thumped against the shelf. "Is this good for you?" Mariel whispered.

"To be honest, the encyclopedias are stabbing my ass. Maybe adjust me a little?"

Esther's voice.

It was strained.

Frustrated.

Embarrassed.

"Oh, yeah. Sure."

This was frustrating. It was supposed to be romantic. *Hot.* But—

"Ow."

"You good? What'd I do?"

"I'm sorry, but... can we start simple and keep it to the floor today?"

Mariel tried his best to hold back a sigh.

On the floor, he lost track of time, but Mariel knew he lasted less than two or three minutes. In the moment, as the floor scraped his knees, and Esther's legs tightened around his waist, it did not matter. He could only think of the electric rhythm of her body. The way she met each of his vigorous thrusts. The way her hands explored his chest and shoulders, how one hand reached up and seized his ponytail. The way she looked at him and bit her lip. But then, one thought crept forward from the back of his mind.

Had she looked at Gabe like that?

Icy jealousy merged with the fire of his lust for her. Mariel gritted his teeth. His gasps grew louder. His head buzzed. Sweat trickled.

Had she ever touched Gabe? Slipped her tongue into his mouth?

Grasping the undersides of her knees, he sat upright, letting out stiff grunts and ramming his hips as he loomed over her. He realized how small she seemed below his tall, muscular frame, and he stared down at her in the darkness with a snarl on his face that was less directed at her and more directed at—

Gabe.

And Mariel could tell that Esther was in a *little* pain—because she grimaced with each thrust.

Just a *little* though, and he was *almost* finished, so if she could handle it just a *little* bit longer—

"Mars, baby—"

He heard her strained voice, but his eyes caught a fleeting glance of something in the dark aisle, something familiar, something he thought he would never, *ever* see again—

"Sweetie, can you soften up a little?"

The humanoid.

A growl tore from his lips, and he heard Esther's voice—

"Mariel, *soften up*, you're *hurting me!*"

"I'm sorry—oh, *fuck.*"

This was shameful, wasn't it?

Stuttering an apology.

But still *coming* inside of her—even though he *tried* to slow down and lessen the violence of his hips.

But it was too late.

You're hurting me!

His eyes rolled back.

Blood ran. Skin split.

And he filled her.

Breathing hard, Mariel collapsed over her and leaned his forehead on the floor. He felt her chest rise and fall beneath his. Then he rolled from her, onto his back, and stared at the darkness of the ceiling. Emotions flooded his psyche. Anger. Fear—

—*the humanoid*—

—but mostly shame.

He'd hurt her. Now, Mariel didn't know *what* to say. In fact, he was certain that if he said anything she would tell him to leave, tell him that she could not handle his behavior anymore, and that—

"Mars." Such a soft voice.

Mariel jumped and felt her fingers thread into his. Relieved, he turned his head towards her.

Rising up onto her elbow, Esther looked down at him. The hair tie had slipped towards the end of her hair, which now fell disheveled around her face. "Are you okay? I've realized through all of this I haven't asked." Her voice was soothing, calm. Not a trace of anger or disappointment.

It made him feel worse.

"I know I keep saying I'm okay, Esther, but... in reality, I don't know." Mariel sat up, stuffed his hands into the pockets of his sweatshirt. Something he'd always done.

For comfort.

"If I didn't have you... I wouldn't be okay."

Mariel wasn't sure if that was a manipulative statement, but he meant it. He meant every word.

Leaning forward, Esther caressed his lips with hers. "I'll be right back." Grabbing her sweatpants, she balled them up and stuffed them between her legs, stood, and waddled away. "And don't look at me right now."

Minutes later, Esther returned and proceeded to spritz the aisle with a scented spray. "Did I remove the evidence?"

Smiling, Mariel stood and searched for his pants. "I don't know. It smells like orange-vanilla sex now."

"Fuck you. Does it really?"

"No." He yanked up his pants, went to her, and pulled her into his arms.

For several moments, they stood in the aisle, their bodies pressed together like it'd be the last time they'd hold each other.

Mariel searched the area with his gaze, looking for the humanoid, convincing himself it'd been a hallucination.

The humanoid wouldn't come back after being cleansed in the Kingdom of Heaven. Right?

Mariel closed his eyes. "Don't forget the couch," he murmured. "And the encyclopedias."

"I'm going to send those to Phil Jameson."

They both snickered.

After more tender kisses, they agreed that it was time to leave. Esther had dance practice. Mariel wanted to go for a run. They'd meet again soon. Perhaps go on an actual date, somewhere outside of Chicago where no one would know them.

They kissed again.

Gathered their things.

And went separate ways.

As Mariel jogged through the cold city, he thought about the last few days, how he hadn't been as productive as he wished. He'd managed to worry his father and piss off Esther—that was about the extent of his return.

He'd attempted to research ways to remove a microchip, but the only results yielded to him implied surgical methods.

He had no fucking idea what to do.

And remembering the panic on her face today—when she'd gone pale and grabbed his pants' leg while asking about the end of the world—gave him zero ambition to tell her about the kill chip.

It'd destroy her.

And it'd destroy *them*.

Verse 3

~ I'll Get That Book ~

Tuesday, January 14th, 2020
Chicago, Illinois

"You guys are all set. Esther, can I talk to you a second, please?"

Esther ran the back of her hand across her forehead. Sweat rolled from her skin. As the other members of the dance team gathered their athletic bags and shuffled from the stage, she approached her coach and smiled. "That's unsettling."

"Don't be a negative Nancy." Jackie Morgan was a lean, athletic woman in her late twenties with dark brown skin and long, straightened hair. At the back of the stage, she stood near the folding table, shuffling papers with choreographic scribbles that only she could read.

"What's up?" Esther approached her, leaned the small of her back against the table. Momentarily, she closed her eyes and envisioned herself back in bed and under her blankets. Bed was the safest place to be these days. It didn't judge, and it held her like a warm hug whenever she wanted.

But in reality, the morning tryst with Mariel had been exhausting.

Esther felt *horrible* thinking this way, but... his mere presence was *exhausting*.

Jackie tapped the papers against the table and then slipped them into a black folder. "I know this is last minute, but I wanted to ask your opinion about possibly changing the song for the competition."

"What? It's in March. I don't know that we can get everyone ready for—"

"I want to use one of your choreographs."

Esther looked at the woman, her jaw slack, eyes wide. "Wait. *Really?*"

"Girl, of course. Unless you don't want to. We've got stiff competition this year, and I think you've grown a lot in your choreographs since our last one."

Esther felt *elated*... so much so that the adrenaline surge swept away her exhaustion. For a moment, at least.

It was the first *exciting* news she'd received in a while. Mariel's return had been *good*, but *this* was normal.

Safe.

Good, safe, normal news.

"That'd be... incredible. *Amazing*. Did you have a particular one in mind?"

Jackie reached for her red and black duffel bag and slung it over her shoulder. "Send me videos of your favorites. We'll go from there. And there's time. We've got a great team and you're a great captain."

Unable to contain the grin that moved across her lips, Esther grabbed her bag from the floor. "Thanks so much. For real."

Jackie smiled. Her eyes sparkled. "I have a good feeling about this. One question though. Are you alright? You've seemed... off lately. Everything okay?"

The smile faded. "Yes. *Yes*, I'm fine. Stuff going on at home, but I'll be alright."

"Walk with me to the locker room. You sure you're okay? I might know a thing or two about family issues. Parents can suck. *Siblings* can suck. Honestly, family, in general, sucks." Jackie shot her a glance, laughed a little. "Sorry. Offloading here. Clearly, *I* need therapy."

As they left the stage and exited the large auditorium, Esther chewed her lip.

Coach Morgan's statement wasn't entirely incorrect. Esther's family *had* been a fucking nightmare as of late. Hawk's misbehavior was annoying. But nothing, however, had been more *annoying* than the intervention she'd received Sunday evening.

"Why are you breaking up with Gabe, Honey? He loves you!" Todd exclaimed, and he clutched his chest as if the news would kill him.

"We aren't a thing, Dad. We never were, and we never will be. So drop it."

Todd rubbed his cheeks. *"I don't think you know what you want. And I think you're confused. Is this because of the bisexual thing?"*

"Don't ever," Esther screamed, pointing her finger at him, *"tell me what you think I do and do not know about myself!"*

"On Sunday, I broke up with my boyfriend," Esther said, adjusting the duffel bag on her shoulder. "Didn't end well. My dad thinks it's because I'm bi."

"Ouch."

"Yeah. Needless to say, I was interrogated all evening about being bi. If I'd ever kissed a girl, if I was going to remain *'faithful to the church teachings'*. *'Maybe it's a phase, Esther'*. No, fuck you. It's not a fucking phase."

They stepped into the grey, snowy morning, and their boots crunched against the snow.

Jackie shivered and spoke quietly. "That sucks. I'm sorry you have to go through that. They'll come around, I'm sure."

"Maybe. I'm just lucky Dad only ended the conversation with a warning. '*Ya can't live under my roof if you decide to act on it, Esther*'. And now he's thinking about switching churches because our priest is gay and '*might not be the best person to confess your same-sex attraction to*'. Sorry, Jackie, I'm just mad now." Glowering, Esther stuffed her hands into the pockets of her sweatpants.

"Wait, your priest is gay? And he can serve as a priest?"

"As long as he doesn't act on it. And I don't think that sweet old man has ever kissed anyone, much less—well, I'm not going to say it. I don't want the image in my head."

They entered the gymnasium and approached the locker room. Bid their goodbyes and departed to the showers. It was steamy and warm. In one of the showers, a girl screeched a country song.

As Esther undressed, she glanced down, noticed an odd mark on her stomach.

Frowning, she ran her fingertips over it. It looked like scar tissue, shaped like upside-down L's.

Three of them.

The mark appeared *old*, as if her body had healed a wound without her knowledge of ever having one.

But Esther chalked it up to the moment she'd been dump tackled in the alley on Saturday night.

Embarrassing.

So embarrassing.

But that green-eyed officer hadn't been super horrible to look at, so she'd gotten something out of it, she supposed.

Or maybe Mariel had scratched her.

Yeah, she could see that.

The hot water coursed over her sore muscles. It removed the stench of sweat and sex. Humming, Esther turned and allowed the water to rush over her face. It drained between her legs. Cringing, she set her teeth. It burned.

He'd torn her skin. A lot.

Mariel Nadier had never *scared* her. He'd been odd at times, and he'd caused her psyche to unravel in ways she'd never experienced with anyone else. But even though he wasn't blood-related to his dad, he'd obtained Fr. Jerome's gentle personality and empathetic personality.

But not today.

That hadn't been evident *today.*

And this morning—Mariel Nadier had scared her.

The look in his eyes had changed from lust to something *else.*

At first, Esther had managed to relax her body a little, at least enough to ignore the pain. She appreciated his moans and the pleasure she experienced from sharing intimacy with him.

But Mariel's eyes... God, his *eyes.*

First, there'd been awe, pleasure, and affection. After that, they'd been harsh. Distant. *Furious.*

Mariel's thrusts became vicious, as if he'd remembered an unspoken grudge against Esther. At that moment, the man inside of her body had been unrecognizable.

It'll get more comfortable... the more we do it.

Wincing, Esther lowered the temperature of the water and finished her shower in quiet discomfort.

*   *   *

Throughout the rest of the day, while in class, Esther texted Mariel.

They didn't discuss much. Mariel mentioned Fr. Jerome's strange predicament, how his former mentor had been instructed to work alongside him.

Babysit him, really.

And God, the irony. The irony that Fr. Jerome now bore the weight of punishment for giving communion to a same-sex couple, when Esther *knew* of *many* single heterosexual individuals having sex outside of marriage.

She included herself in that list.

Regardless, it was fucking wrong, and she wanted to check in with Fr. Jerome to see how he was doing, to see what he *thought* about his son's resurrection.

But Esther had limited energy right now, especially for a conversation like *that.*

"Hi. I'm sleeping with your son. As a priest, what're your thoughts on his resurrection?"

"… Your thesis papers that are due in April." The female professor's voice cut into Esther's spiraling mind.

Her phone buzzed again.

Mariel asked how she was doing. She told him she was alright. He said that he missed her. She told him that she felt the same. He asked if she would ever consider going away with him, somewhere in a place where no one knew them.

As Esther hovered her thumbs over the screen to respond, another text vibrated the phone.

Officer Mysterious.

And her pulse went mad.

"*I will be there to get the book at seven tonight.*"

A smile flickered over her lips.

The whole thing was hilarious, really, because Officer Mysterious had *no idea* what sin Esther had committed right after the young woman left the bookstore two days ago.

"*Sue me,*" *Esther murmured, and tapped her finger against the purchase button with an illegal amount of glee.*

Esther hadn't wanted to wait a week for the manufacturer to supply the book.

So she'd ordered it from Amazon.

Same day shipping.

And when it had arrived yesterday, Esther had texted Officer Mysterious with strange urgency.

And the rude-ass woman hadn't even responded until now.

"*Took you long enough to respond,*" Esther typed, trying to control the smirk on her lips.

Officer Mysterious: "*I work. I have a life. Something you wouldn't understand.*"

Oh, hell no.

Esther's fingers sped across the keyboard screen. "*Were you beaten as a child?*"

A minute passed. And then:

"*Sometimes.*"

Esther stared at the phone.

Had Tira been *joking?* Or?

Mariel's name popped up.

"*Don't you want to be with me?*"

"Oh, for fuck's sake," Esther whispered, face hot.

Before his death, she'd pined for him. Begged for his attention. His acknowledgement. But *now*—

"*I love you, Mars. I would leave with you in a heartbeat.*" Esther sent the message and slipped her phone into her backpack.

* * *

"Why is my attacker in our store?"

It was quiet, save for the distant sounds of motors rumbling down the streets, and the bookstore television's commentary about political bullshit.

Eyes bulged, Esther stood with her fists clenched.

Todd Caravan stood behind the counter, mouth open like he'd been caught digging around in the cookie jar.

And Jacob Caravan, in his tan overcoat, leaned against the counter as if he owned the goddamn place.

"Esther—" Todd started.

"Get the fuck out, crackhead," Esther growled and pointed towards the bookstore entrance.

"*Esther.*"

"*Get the fuck out of my store!*"

"It's okay," Jacob said, and he eyed her with the quiver of a smirk at the corner of his mouth. "I was just about to leave."

Jacob looked just as shitty as last year, when he'd raced towards her, grabbed her, lifted her into the air.

"*It's gonna come out of you, like Will came outta his harlot mother!*"

"You're disgusting. If I see you again, I'm going to call the cops," Esther sneered, backing up against a bookshelf as Jacob moved to walk past her.

"Esther, *please stop.*" Todd sounded more exasperated than he did angry.

But Jacob was gone.

Esther watched him disappear into the city traffic. Maybe he'd get hit by a fucking bus.

"He's a crazy old man, Esther. What he did was unacceptable, and he served his time. But I need answers from my dad. I need to know why he left us. I need closure." His voice was low, humble.

Sad.

And *sad* was what *always* got Esther. *Sad* was what always shifted her emotions from anger to the desire to nurture.

Esther approached the counter and rested her elbows on the surface. She searched her father's face. He looked *really* pale. "Why would you want to invite someone like him back into your life? He *hurt me*. He hurt *you* and your brother. He hurt Grandma. And I *know* you want closure, but can you really get it with—"

"I just need some time, Esther. You don't have to see him."

What the absolute fuck.

Last year, on the night of Mariel's death, he'd raged about keeping Esther safe. But now? What the *actual*—

"Dad, are you okay? You don't look well."

He didn't. He really, really didn't, and it scared her.

Of course, Todd was white—like, "ya workin' hard or hardly workin' sort of *white*, but his face had this grey, off-color look to it, like he was about to be sick.

But, as if he understood her thoughts, Todd smiled at her. "Yeah. Listen, you okay here at the store? I need to get going."

"I'll be great. Because I'm going to shoot that motherfucker in the face if he comes back."

Todd shook his head. "Stop. And he won't, because he'll be at dinner with me."

"Does Grandma know? She's going to kill you, and she doesn't even *like* violence."

Todd raised his eyebrows. "Please don't tell her."

"Dad—"

"Honey, I *need* this." Tears glistened in his eyes. "I need to know what happened to my brother."

Esther turned her eyes towards the television to process.

Gaza. The commentators were talking about an attack on Gaza.

"He better not bleed back into this family," Esther said through her teeth. "He's a *you* problem. Not a me problem, or a Hawk problem, or a Grandma problem." She turned her eyes back to him. "*You.*"

Todd nodded, stepped around the corner, and kissed his daughter on the head. "I love you, Squirt. Get your backpack off the couch. We don't collect our personal items there."

"Yeah, yeah."

For the following hours, Esther cleaned, sold books, ordered books, explained to a few customers that the Caravans *had*, indeed, considered adding a coffee shop, texted Mariel, sprawled on the couch, googled *"real life resurrections"*, and watched dog videos. Time moved slowly, and she found herself eyeing the clock.

Awaiting 7 P.M.

Gabe texted her, asked her if she'd broken up with him because she liked girls.

"Don't get me wrong, it's kinda hot," he told her.

It was his way of joking, she knew that. His way of dealing with pain.

And when Esther told him that she had the necklace again, Gabe told her to keep it.

"It's for my best friend," he texted. *"She loves to dance."*

At 6:54 P.M, the pain arrived.

Harsh, dreadful pain that left her crumpled over the couch, clutching at her stomach. Like something had punctured her uterus.

"Fuck!" Esther cried, and she writhed against the couch cushion. The pain electrocuted her nerves and dimmed her eyesight. She'd had horrible menstrual cramps before, but nothing like this.

This pain brought white splotches to her sight. For several minutes, it raced through her heart and pulsed into her head. She tumbled to the floor, onto her knees. But... as Esther's fingernails dug into the fabric, a firm, yet gentle, voice touched her ears.

"Breathe. Let me get you back onto the couch. Can you move?"

Icy hands touched her arms. While the pain pulsed within her stomach, Esther allowed the firm hands to guide her to the couch until she was doubled over on the cushion.

Her eyes opened... and latched onto green.

Tira Arcelin knelt on one knee, as if she were preparing to ask for Esther's hand in marriage. Her cheeks were flushed, likely from the frigid wind, and her bound-up hair sparkled with droplets from the melted snow.

Esther let out a cry, gritted her teeth. "I'm so sorry, but *holy shit*. It hurts so bad." She shook her head. Embarrassed. Miserable.

Gentle fingers took her hands and turned them, palms upwards, and she felt the officer's thumbs press lightly between the tendons of her wrists.

"What does that do?" Esther whispered. For a moment, the woman's odd touch distracted her from the pain.

"It is acupressure. It may help subside the pain a little. Just breathe."

Goodness.

Still snippy.

Even while massaging people's palms.

Esther closed her eyes and let out slow, deep breaths. She focused on the soft pressure of Tira's thumbs as they kneaded and pressed into the tendons of her wrist. Steadily, the pain subsided, and when it had gone, she opened her eyes a little.

Officer Mysterious was not looking at her. Instead, her focus remained glued to her thumbs as they worked the tendons and nerves. She looked...

Vulnerable.

Yet, even so, Officer Mysterious still exhibited an air of confidence... a *demand* for respect.

As if aware that she was being watched, Tira spoke. "Are you still in pain?"

"Just a little. It's getting better though," Esther lied.

The pain was gone.

But the massage was nice.

"Thank you," Esther added. "I'm not sure why that happened, but it hurts like *hell*."

Thoughtfully, Tira gazed at the hands in her own. Her thumbs gently brushed against the veins outlined within Esther's wrists. "Menstrual cramps?"

"No, it's worse. Sharp."

Tira raised her eyes and, setting her jaw, released Esther's hands. She stood, slipping her own hands into the pockets of her pea coat. "Well, hopefully it doesn't happen again."

Awkward and warm as she sat beneath Tira's gaze, Esther stood up. "I'll get that book."

On a shelf just below the counter, Esther withdrew the thick book in a paper bag. She passed it over the counter, and she watched as Tira drew her black wallet from her coat pocket.

"It's on the house," Esther stated, faster than she expected.

"I do not take handouts."

"It's not a handout. Consider it a thank you for helping me tonight."

"That is a hand out. My massaging of your wrists will not result in a currency exchange that will feed back into the economy." Tira slapped her credit card onto the counter.

"Who even *thinks* about that?"

Esther's clear bewilderment did not render a smile from Tira. Instead, she pushed the card across the counter and waited. Her sharp eyes darted from the wallet to Esther's hands to the register and then back.

Moving at the speed of a sloth, Esther pushed the card back.

Both women stared at each other and said nothing for a long moment.

"I have a brother. A *little* brother. I can do this all night." Esther pushed the bag towards Tira, watching the woman's frustrated face with sincere enjoyment. "The economy," she whispered, "will live on."

Letting out an abrupt breath, Tira snatched the bag. The paper crinkled loudly. "Fine."

Esther smiled. A wide, victorious smile. The next question, however, almost startled her.

"When are you done with your shift? I'd like to buy you a coffee, or a tea, at the very least."

Esther stammered a little. "Oh. We close at eight. But, it's been slow tonight. I can venture out for a minute."

The lights went off.

The door locked.

The sign read *CLOSED.*

Alongside Officer Mysterious, Esther stepped into the freezing air and pulled the sweatshirt hood over her head. Shuddering, she folded her arms as the wind nipped at her face.

"Will you get in trouble for leaving early?" Tira asked as her boots thudded against the icy sidewalk.

"I've done it so many times without getting caught I just don't think about it anymore."

Lie.

Her father would kill her. The store had already received one bad review for its "inconsistent hours". All her fault, of course.

But he had no right to talk, dragging her crackhead grandfather back into her life. She'd claim emotional distress if she had to. So—

"I see."

The window lights of the city buildings twinkled in the darkening sky. Snowflakes flurried. People walked. Mulled about. Chatted on their phones. Held hands. Smoked. Sneezed and coughed.

Texting. Crying. Laughing. Enjoying life.

As they reached the crosswalk and stopped, Esther turned her eyes towards the woman at her side. With hands in the pockets of her cargo pants, Tira stood with her head tilted back, her eyes searching the sky, her lips parted while puffs of air coiled from her mouth. Her throat looked smooth, creamy, and color had risen into her cheeks again. Wisps of blonde hair fell across her ears. Entranced, Esther realized that she knew nothing about this beautiful creature.

And she wanted to know more.

"Did you have a question for me?" Tira gazed at the sky, her voice thick with the Russian accent she seemed to let slip.

Startled, Esther felt her cheeks warm. "No, sorry, I was just looking at that guy past you, about a block away sleeping by the building. He looks so cold."

"Oh. Interesting. He left about thirty seconds ago."

"Different guy then." Embarrassed, distracted, Esther stepped into the crosswalk as the signal changed.

Tira's hand slapped against her arm. Yanked her backwards. Her joints popped in protest. Gasping, Esther stumbled back to the sidewalk as a silver van streaked past her and accelerated through the red light.

"Now you can go," Tira said, and her voice was quiet, unlike the aggressiveness of her grasp. Releasing Esther's arm, she walked forward in leisure, as if she hadn't just snatched Esther away from oncoming death.

Breathing hard, Esther followed her. Tried to joke. "Thanks. I'm surprised you didn't push me in front of that thing. You said you didn't like me."

"I don't like you. And I *did* think about pushing you. Trust me." The corners of her mouth lifted, but only a little.

Men and women pushed past them on the crosswalk. An older car rattled at the light. The exhaust pipes drifted fumes that smelled like burnt oil.

"If you don't like me that much, why are you here with me right now?" Esther hurried to keep up with Officer Mysterious.

Tira did not respond. The muscles of her jaw twitched. She was grinding her teeth.

Esther knew she was bugging her, but she persisted. "*My* guess is that you have no friends. Is that correct?"

"I don't have time for friends." Tira stepped onto the sidewalk and approached the door to the coffee shop.

"You have to make time. Do you have hobbies?"

Sighing, Tira opened the door. She gestured to allow Esther and an older couple into the shop. "You ask too many questions."

The warmth of the building embraced Esther, and the strong smell of coffee filled her nostrils as she entered. "So, no hobbies."

"I like to shoot."

"Nerf guns?"

"What is a Nerf gun? Is it automatic? Assault?" Her face twisted in panic, confusion.

Astounded, Esther stepped in line with the other patrons, mouth open. "You—you don't know what a *Nerf* gun is? Or are you being sarcastic? I can't really tell with you." She pulled her phone from her pocket.

Three missed calls. Seven text messages.

Mariel.

Annoyed, Esther cleared the screen of the notifications.

Tira turned burning eyes towards her, leaned closer, and spoke with heated frustration. "I have been studying *every* weapons' system... *hands-on*. Since I could walk! I have *never* heard of a—"

Esther pushed her phone into Tira's face, where her brief internet search provided a photo of the toy gun.

As the anger on her face dissipated, Tira looked at the screen with a furrowed brow. "Oh. It is a toy gun."

"*Yes,* you clearly haven't seen or used one. How old are you? Forty?"

"I am twenty-three."

Dumbfounded, Esther assessed Tira's face. It was a young face, definitely, but she had not expected this woman to be *so young*. For so many reasons.

Established police officer.

More mature than the average twenty-something.

Tired—as if she'd already lived a long life, but with the energy and alertness of a young person. And her eyes... they were unreadable, but they suggested a level of wisdom unmatched within that typical age range.

"You seem surprised." Tira's voice was quiet.

"I am. You act like you're forty." Esther stepped to the counter and ordered her coffee. "When is your birthday?"

Idly tapping her card on the counter, Tira hesitated. Her eyes shifted around the coffee shop, avoiding Esther's gaze. Tira's stature seemed stiff as she handed the card to the cashier and watched her take the payment.

"What is it, top secret?" Esther studied the profile of Tira's face. The sharp, but feminine shape of her jaw. The lashes that looked longer in the light. Even though she *knew* she was annoying Officer Mysterious with her non-stop questioning, she wanted to know the answers.

It was necessary.

"No, it's just not important. What is so significant about the day of one's birth?" Tira nodded her thanks to the cashier. Tightening her jacket around her body, she stepped around the corner of the counter to wait for the drinks.

Tugging the strings to the hood of her sweatshirt, Esther leaned her elbows against the counter and watched the baristas work. Her eyelids drooped. She needed sleep, but she was having a good time despite the fatigue. Enjoying herself. It had been a while since she'd met someone *this fascinating*. "Most of us enjoy getting acknowledged and showered with gifts to recognize the day we popped from a vagina."

"I suppose." Tira gnawed the corner of her bottom lip. Sighing a little, she adjusted her stance. "July 13th. My birthday. Satisfied?"

Esther, smiling slowly, glanced outside and then looked back at Officer Mysterious. She ran a tongue over her bottom lip. "Oh look, the world isn't ending now, is it?"

After retrieving their coffee, the young women ventured into the cold once more. The snowflakes were heavier now, and the gusts of wind pulled and tugged at their clothing. For several moments, they walked in silence, side by side. Their sleeves brushed on occasion. On cue, they widened the space between each other.

It was interesting, walking in silence, because Esther didn't feel forced to share a conversation. But she wanted to.

Esther still wanted to know more.

So, she spoke, and she realized her lips were numb from the cold. "So, when I sent that text about you being beaten as a child, I'm sorry if you actually—"

The laughter that ensued interrupted Esther's apology. She watched, confused yet captivated, as Tira threw her head back and laughed. The laugh was genuine, and she wondered if this woman *ever* laughed, and if she should be offended that *she* was the object of the laughter.

But the action... it was beautiful.

Officer Mysterious' eyes sparkled and narrowed, her soft lips spread to expose a whitened row of teeth, and her cheeks revealed soft dimples that did not seem to exist without a smile.

Fascinated, but growing angry, Esther watched her. "Did I say something?"

"Yes, your apology is humorous."

"So, I take it you weren't beaten then?"

"Oh no, I *was*," Tira laughed, bringing the coffee to her lips and sipping.

"You're a confusing person. There is nothing normal about you." Esther's phone vibrated, and she reached for it as they approached the bookstore. Glancing at the screen, her heart rate increased. "Fuck, it's my grandma. One sec. I'm sorry." She looked at Tira as she answered the call. "Grandma? I'm sorry, I will get back to the—"

"*Esther!*" Inaudible words, high-pitched shrieks and cries, shot through the phone.

Esther's breathing grew ragged, and she met Tira's as she tried to speak. "*Grandma. I can't understand you, what's wrong?*"

Each word was strained. "Your dad's on the way to the hospital. They think he had a heart attack, Esther, I can't *breathe*. God, first Hawk, now your dad—"

Cold fear brought goosebumps to her skin. Or perhaps they had already been there from the air. The rate of her breathing increased. This was horribly familiar... like the phone call she'd received last year when Hawk had been struck.

And after Mariel had died.

Esther wavered on her feet. Raising her eyes, she saw Tira step close, felt the officer's hand rest lightly on her arm as she swayed.

"*Which* hospital?"

"Same one Hawk went to. The Savior Center."

"I'll call you when I get there." Esther ended the call, looking at Tira. "My dad is—"

"Tell me where you need to go, and I'll drive you." Assertive. "I'm parked very close." Turning sharply, Officer Mysterious strode down the sidewalk, her head high, her shoulders square. "Let's go."

And Esther's body moved on command, and she took a step after Tira Arcelin—as if she had no other choice but to follow.

VERSE 4

~ MAMA ~

Wednesday, January 15th, 2020
Harvard, Illinois

After years of little contact, Phil Jameson finally visited his mother.

But Phil was a little frustrated. He still needed to figure out what to do with his daughter's body.

Eyes half-lidded, Victoria Jameson's body remained propped at the corner of the stairs since Sunday. Phil was rather surprised, because he'd expected her to resurrect from his touch.

She hadn't.

He wasn't sure why, but he suspected it was due to his lack of desire to heal Victoria. Perhaps that was *wrong* as a father, but she was far too much of a risk to come back to life. She'd scream his activities from the rooftops and get him arrested for doing the Lord's work.

Matthew 15:4 had been clear.

"Honor thy Father and Mother, and anyone who curses their father and mother shall be put to death."

But the law didn't care about that.

The law would send a *diverse* group of officers, wouldn't they? Not just to investigate Victoria's death, but to *crucify* him. To push their agenda. To paint a very specific picture for the media.

"Breaking News: Conservative, rich, white male arrested for the murder of daughter, imprisonment of wife."

He'd be painted as a bigot.

Biblical times were simpler. Wives were held accountable. So were daughters. *Men* were expected to lead. To direct their families towards God. To preach His word and let no one tear them asunder.

No matter the cost.

Because families no longer put God first, nor did they walk the path of righteousness.

Due to the growing plagues within churches, the splitting of the laity, and the rise of false prophets like Fr. Jerome Nadier, Phil understood that the world had plunged into its last days. The end times.

Armageddon.

It'd be time to fulfill his purpose soon. To reveal God's light. To bring the world back to Christ before it was too late.

So, before Phil Jameson went to see his mother, he bid goodbye to his dead daughter.

Phil Jameson purchased the necessary cleaning supplies and a new axe. He felt sick.

It *seemed* wrong.

Especially because he felt Carolyn's eyes on him as he dragged Victoria's body to the center of the floor. Once in a while, he'd glance at her, and he'd find her staring at him as she lay in the fetal position. Sometimes, Phil looked at her with pity. Other times, disgust.

As she breathed, he could see her ribs. Even so, belly fat and loose skin flopped loosely to the floor. The whites of her eyes were red. Pale skin peeked from balding areas on her head.

Phil no longer found her attractive. However, the Bible had made it clear. He was not to leave or abandon his wife, regardless of blemish. The Bible demanded that he love and cherish her.

So, as he prepared to downsize his daughter's corpse, he smiled at her.

To show his appreciation.

But Carolyn Jameson did not return the smile.

"Why don't you give me a smile, darling?" he asked, tapping the axe upon the floor and turning to face the woman. "Come on. Just a little smile."

Mrs. Jameson blinked.

She looks like an animal, he thought, disgusted. "Carolyn. Smile." Phil clapped his hands. "*Smile.*"

Her mouth lifted a little.

Phil stared down at her. The axe dangled from his hand as he stood over his daughter's lifeless body. "Good," he said. "Now. Close your eyes. I'd rather you not see this."

The half-smile froze upon her face. Phil raised the axe over the body of their daughter.

Carolyn closed her eyes.

After the atrocious mess had been cleaned, and the pieces of Victoria Jameson had been bagged and secured inside of the basement freezer, Phil planned the overdue visit to his mother's.

Planning meant that he had to ensure Carolyn had enough food, water, and toiletries for the day without giving her full freedom to roam the house. Before he left that day, he provided open cans of dried tuna, a bowl of grapes, and a large bowl of water. Feeling generous, he dressed her as well.

"Don't soil your clothes," he said, pecking her on the forehead. "I'll be back, but it'll be later tonight." Phil smiled, patted her on the head, and then left.

Hailey came with him, and he advised her that she would study her Bible at a nearby coffee shop until he was finished.

Beatrice Jameson lived in Harvard, Illinois, which was approximately a ninety-minute drive from Chicago. There were a lot of historical events that took place in the small town of 9,000 people. It was the self-proclaimed Milk Capital of the world, it'd opened and closed a Motorola factory, and, long before that, Phil Jameson had been conceived in the least respectable trailer park in the town.

Or so he assumed.

Before approaching the rusty tan mobile home, Phil sat in his sedan for at least ten minutes. The lawyer clung to the roses in his hands. His skin was clammy, his heart rate felt dangerously high, and the knots within his intestines threatened to explode all over the driver's seat. Phil Jameson feared two beings.

God.

And his mother.

The sky was grey as he stepped from the vehicle. He did not slam the door. Rather, he left it cracked open to avoid alerting Beatrice to his presence.

He wasn't ready.

So, for another ten minutes, Phil Jameson stood outside of his mother's doorway, flowers held hip-level, his head bent low. It was very cold, but he perspired in his blue, long-sleeve button-down and black dress pants.

Finally, Phil knocked. Turned his eyes to the wide window.

In the window, a seated figure glanced around and then stood up. As his heart beat with wild fury, Phil listened to the floor creak inside of the trailer as his mother stomped to the door. Inhaling, he squeezed the flowers.

And Beatrice Jameson opened the door.

The smell of cigarettes, both old and fresh, drifted into his nostrils. The television in the trailer vibrated the walls.

In width, Beatrice was a large woman. Short in height. Lopsided from the hip surgery she'd had years ago. She wore grey sweatpants and a white sleeveless shirt that clung to her large, sagging breasts, and it exposed the freckles on her arms. She kept her flaming red, oily hair in a large black clip, and Beatrice eyed him with clear disdain.

"Took ya long enough," Beatrice grumbled. "How long were you gonna stand outside my door?"

Phil kept his head low, but his eyes shifted about with unease. "Hi, Mama."

"What do you want?"

"May I come in? Please?"

Rolling her eyes, Beatrice moved to allow him space.

Sniffling, Phil took the offer and stepped inside the malodorous trailer.

Beatrice slammed the door. Annoyed, she gestured towards the old couch in the small living room.

For a moment, Phil looked at it with a flared nose. It was *that* couch. He remembered it well. He'd entered the home to find her performing fellatio on an unknown gentleman.

"Well? You gonna sit or what?" Beatrice limped to the couch and reached for the pack of Marlboro's on the cluttered coffee table. She grabbed the large remote and muted the game show on television.

Phil stepped into the living room. Unlike the rest of the trailer, the kitchen was clean, organized... which meant she was on what he'd entitled "the two week cycle".

From early memories, the woman only liked to clean her kitchen every two weeks or so. An oddity of hers, he presumed. For two weeks, the kitchen would reek of rotten food. Jelly and peanut butter were left smeared and crusted on the counters. Fruit flies would hover over the trash can and breed in the sink where the dishes piled high.

But goodness, once she *did* clean? Lord have mercy on his soul if a smudge appeared.

When Phil was eight or nine, Beatrice told him to wash his cereal bowl. After forgetting, she'd ear-grabbed, skin-pinched, and face-slapped him for a hefty fifteen minutes until Beatrice had grown bored and had gone to bed.

It wasn't a fond memory.

Phil stepped around the couch and remembered seeing the *Beatrice Blowjob* take place on the old thing.

Satan dwelled inside of this place.

Perhaps Beatrice *was* Satan.

"Flowers?" he questioned, and then he handed them to her.

Beatrice took the flowers and tossed them onto the coffee table. "What do you want, Phil?" Cigarette smoke drifted from her mouth and circulated in the air.

Her mouth was the pit of Hell, and smoke billowed from the flames.

Phil sat on the floor. He could not sit on the couch, could not get the blowjob out of his memory. "Mama, how are you doing? Financially?"

"Same as usual, dumbass. Is that why you're here? To rub it in?" A hoarse, high-pitched voice.

"No, Mama."

"Then what, Phil? Here to grieve Carolyn?" Beatrice scoffed, rolled her eyes and coughed a little. "None of your church friends helpin' you deal?"

Phil dared to raise his eyes. "That's not why I'm here, Mama. But... I need your help."

Beatrice let out a laugh... no, a shriek combined with a howl from a beast that only Satan could spawn. Her freckled shoulders shook as she threw her head back in laughter, in mockery, and the cigarette hung lazily from her fingers. Finally, when she stopped, she looked at him and wiped her eyes. "You *need my help*? If I thought you took drugs, Phil, I'd think you were on 'em now. What'd you do? You runnin' from the cops? Legal trouble? Lost your job?"

Phil struck his fist against the coffee table. *"No, Mama!"* He grinded his teeth together, turned his eyes to hers as she *dragged* from that horrid death stick. "I'm here because I'd like to offer you a different place to live, more income. *A lot* more income."

Beatrice squinted at him. "I'm listening."

"You need to believe what I have to say here. Don't laugh at me or mock me, because I'm telling the tru—"

"Philip, you're boring me now."

"Stop *interrupting* me, Mama!" He slammed his fist again, and this time she looked a little startled. It gave him a sense of power. "Kaemon Spears is running for President. He is the co-CEO of *KS Industries.* Have you heard of him?"

"Nope." She inhaled again, shook her head.

"The Governor of Illinois. The black man, Mama."

"Oh, yeah! Yeah, I know him. Well-spoken for a nigger." Beatrice flicked her cigarette. The ashes fluttered to the carpet and settled there for what would be an unspecified length of time.

Phil continued. "I've been assisting him with legalities. He is requesting my assistance more heavily right now due to a potential... issue."

The *issue* involved a rumored whistle-blower who, if outspoken, would paint KS Industries in a horrible manner. It was a rumor, of course, but Phil had been assigned to quash any potential problems. Still, he needed help. Hailey wasn't mature enough to babysit Carolyn.

And, as past history revealed, Beatrice Jameson did *anything* for money.

"What're you blabbin' about, dumbass? Get to the part where I get involved."

His heart rate spiraled upward. Hissing, Phil lunged up, flipped the coffee table so that its contents smashed to the floor. *"Shut up, pig bitch! Just shut up!"*

As his mother attempted to rise, Phil pushed her back onto the blowjob couch and twisted the cigarette from her fingers. He slapped her. Again and again. Phil's ears burned, his entire body burned, and he wanted to hurt her, but not *too* bad because, as he slapped her chubby cheeks, he still felt a little fearful of Beatrice Jameson.

As she flailed, kicked, and shrieked, Phil burned the cigarette against her forearm skin and then tossed it aside as she protested against him.

"Just shut up, Mama! Stop making me hurt you. Stop *flailing* and I'll stop!"

Wheezing, and almost realizing just how badly the years of smoking had destroyed her lungs, Beatrice stopped moving and stared at him with wide, frightful eyes. Hatred too.

Sweating, Phil placed his hands over the cigarette burns and closed his eyes. *"Heal,"* he prayed, and jolted.

He removed his hands from her to reveal the healed skin. With a wavering breath, he stepped back and left her to stare at her arms.

"You see that, Mama? Did you see what I did?" Phil clasped his hands in front of his waist. A moment ago, he'd felt powerful, angry, and dangerous.

Now, he awaited his mother's approval like a disobedient puppy.

Beatrice looked at her arm, and then her son. Something in her face changed, her demeanor. She almost looked...

Proud?

"Mama?"

She did the unexpected. Something she had never done before.

And it terrified him.

Beatrice hugged him.

She lunged from the couch and threw her arms around him, pulled him close and *squeezed*. "Maybe there is a God!" she exclaimed.

Phil stood there, arms at his sides, chin on her shoulder, eyes round.

"Mama?" He mumbled again.

Beatrice pulled back, grasped his shoulders, stared up at him with pride. *Smiled* at him. "Philip. *Philip*."

"Yes, Mama."

Beatrice sighed. "I have waited and *waited* for this day."

"You have?"

"*Yes*. My boy, you've had this ability for a long, *long* time." She slapped the sides of his arms. "I always wondered if you'd be able to find it."

Phil pulled back a little. Blinked. "You've known about this? Since *when*?"

Beatrice laughed, but this time it did not mock him. "It showed here and there, when you were little. At some point, when you got closer to memories I guess, it stopped. I don't know why."

Phil stepped back again. "When did it start? What did I *do*?"

"I cut myself. You were all concerned and touched me. Healed the cut immediately. You were around three, after you came back from the—" she stopped, paled.

"Came back from the *what*, Mama?" Phil stared at her.

"Daycare."

"That's not what you were going to say."

"Yes, it was."

"*Mama!*"

"*Alright!*" In frustration, she threw her hands in the air and then returned to the blowjob couch. Lit another cigarette. "Came back from the dead."

Phil's eyes widened even more. With a gasp, he fell to his knees in front of his mother. His voice shook. "You need to tell me everything."

"Phil, it was prolly all the drugs I took. I'm sure you didn't actually come back from the—"

"*Mama!*" he screamed, raised his hand again, watched her shrink back in fear. "*Tell me!*"

Exhaling smoke, Beatrice turned her eyes up to the ceiling. "All I know is... you were dropped at my doorstep. I don't know who brought you there. But... there you were. For all I know, someone coulda lied to me about your death. I wasn't at your funeral. I never saw your goddamn body."

"Mama, please don't use the Lord's name—"

"*Shut* the *fuck* up, Philip. *Christ.* Let me finish." Beatrice coughed again, lowered the cigarette and grasped her chest as she choked for a moment. When she had recovered, she continued. "Anyway, they sent me a note a week before you showed up again. Said you were dead. Courtesy I guess, but they never said how. Just said it was an unfortunate accident."

"*Who* is *they*?"

"I don't shittin' know, boy, but I know it was creepy as hell. Prolly some excuse to stop takin' care of your dumbass and thrust you onto me."

"You never *had me from birth*?" Phil shrieked. He could not breathe, and the cigarette smoke did not help. "Was I *adopted*?"

"Yes. Kinda."

Phil sat back, rubbed his forehead. He'd known that he was an illegitimate child, but there'd never been any reason to believe he'd not lived with his mother since birth. "By *whom*?"

"It was semi-closed, I don't know. Probably whoever your father was." She chuckled. "Could've been anyone. Now, would you tell me why you're here, and what you have to offer me?"

Phil leaned forward. The pulse pounded hard in his throat. He wanted to know more, *needed* to know more, but he had to first tend to business. "Mama. I need you to help take care of Carolyn. She's alive."

Her eyes bulged.

And Phil had to explain to Beatrice why she shouldn't call the cops to arrest him for keeping his resurrected wife in the basement.

It took an hour.

But finally, after raising the wage to five thousand a month, Phil's mother agreed.

Beatrice Jameson would do it. She would babysit Carolyn Jameson while he campaigned with the well-spoken nigger. Her duties would begin as soon as Phil demanded her presence.

So, after Beatrice said that she was tired and demanded that he get the hell out of her house until he was ready for her services, Phil journeyed home with both relief, curiosity, and confusion in his mind. He intended to dig deeper... to figure out the truth about himself.

But not tonight.

The Lord had another trial awaiting him. Another test.

When Phil Jameson pulled into his driveway, two cops stood upon his porch.

They were there to complete a welfare check on a young woman by the name of Victoria Jameson.

CHAPTER 12: VERSE 1

~ GENIUS ~

Thursday, January 16th, 2020

Chicago, Illinois

Hawk Caravan had new determination now, especially after his father's heart attack. Soon, thanks to Kaemon Spears, his invention would save lives.

God, if only he'd had the capability to save his mom's life.

The hospital intended to keep his father, Todd Caravan, for a couple of days to monitor his heart. On Thursday, the day after the heart attack, his grandmother opened the bookstore due to Esther's class schedule. Once Esther took over her shift, Patricia retrieved Hawk from school and brought him to visit Todd.

Todd was in good spirits. He joked, asked Hawk about his day. While Patricia sat at the edge of the hospital bed, the boy sprawled on the cot and told Todd about the topics he'd learned, about the substitute teacher who had taught history.

"She was kind of stupid," he said, slurping on his straw from a Styrofoam cup of water. "It was like she didn't know history at all."

"Hawk, don't talk about your teacher like that." Patricia's voice was firm.

Instead, Todd laughed. "He's probably not wrong. The kid is smart, Mom. He's got a darn invention about to be released to the public. If he says the sub was stupid, she was probably stupid."

Waving the cup outwards, Hawk gestured his thanks. "Exactly. Trust the intelligent grandchild, Grandma. I'm the only smart one you'll ever have."

Patricia frowned, whipped her head backwards to look at her son. "Jason. You need to stop berating your sister."

"I didn't even *say* her name, Grandma."

Todd tapped the bed. "Stop it, Hawk."

Eyes wide, Hawk stared at his family. "I didn't do anything. Why am I in trouble all of the sudden? It's not *my* fault Grandpa wants to kill Esther for whatever reason."

"Hawk!" Todd slapped the bed.

Patricia's face whitened. She twitched. Slowly, the woman turned her head towards her son. "Todd...?" She dragged out his name in a slow drawl. "What is he talking about?"

Hawk slurped the rest of his water, realizing that he'd just announced information that he wasn't even supposed to know.

Last night, after his dinner with Patricia at the cafeteria, he'd returned to the hospital room to grab his cell phone. As he opened the door, he heard the soft murmurs of Todd and Esther.

"What do you fucking mean that fuck-head said I'm a problem that needs to be handled?" Esther squealed.

"Makes sense to me," Hawk mumbled to himself in the doorway.

"I'm sorry, Squirt. He's nuts. I lost my shit on him, and then I think that triggered the heart attack. He won't be an issue for us anymore because I told him I'd kill him if he came around us again."

"Yeah, makes me feel better, Dad. Awesome," Esther growled.

Granted, Hawk agreed that Esther *was* a waste of space on Earth, but he didn't want her hurt. Not *dead.*

Behind the hospital curtains, Esther had asked Todd for further clarification, wanting to know exactly what "a problem that needed to be handled" meant. Quoting Jacob Caravan, Todd had said something about *"giving the people on Earth a little more time to find God".*

His grandfather was crazy. But he meant well. His intentions were good. Unethical, but good. *Not* that he wanted his sister dead, but he could see how Jacob could come to the conclusion that Esther was evil. Personally, Hawk did not think she was evil. Stupid, maybe. Definitely slutty. But not *evil.*

Hawk knew his thoughts regarding Esther were harsh at times. He used to like her, but they'd grown more and more distant throughout the years. Maybe if she hadn't taken interest in mindless things (dancing, boys, and girls apparently), he'd find her worth his time.

No, Esther wasn't evil. In fact, she wasn't even significant. So why, Hawk wondered, would his grandfather believe she was momentous enough to even *be* a problem?

"Mom, it's fine," Todd said, agitated. His face was red. "Hawk." He turned cold eyes to the boy. "Why would you even say something like that?"

Hawk opened the lid to the cup. Dug his hand into its depths for an ice cube. Popped it into his mouth and shivered a little. "I overheard you last night," he said, speaking over the ice. "You said grandpa thought Esther was a problem that needed to be handled. I *heard you.*"

"*Todd,*" Patricia exclaimed, standing up. She looked a lot like an old, angry version of Esther as she stood with clenched fists and wild eyes. Her grey hair fell across her face as she glared at her son with the expectation of a response. "What is he *talking about?*"

"Mom. Dad—Jacob is crazy. Insane. He needs to be in a mental home. There is no help for him. Ever. I tried. You would know, you were married to him."

"What did he say?"

"Mom..."

"What the *hell did he say, Todd?*"

Hawk crushed the ice between his teeth, listened to it crunch, and watched the frightful look distort Todd's face as his mother glowered over him.

Todd sighed, scratched his head. "What he said about Esther was basically the same crap he rambled about Will. You know. '*Will was evil. Will could do supernatural things*'." He deepened his voice in an attempt to mimic his father's.

Patricia's face grew even paler.

Hawk popped another ice cube into his mouth.

"Todd."

"Yes, Mom."

"Will is *dead!*" Patricia screeched. "He says he *killed your brother because of those things!* Now, your baby girl is at the bookstore with—with *no one* to protect her if something happens!"

"Mom, she's fine. He's old, and I don't think he means anything he says. Okay? Plus, she has a gun locked under the desk at the bookstore."

"When did you get a *gun* for the bookstore, Todd?"

"For *God's sake*, Mom, it's Chicago, you need to get over your issue with *guns!* Esther will be *fine!*" Todd shouted, striking the bed again, and it bounced back up and struck the "*help*" button on the remote.

This brought a flustered nurse through the curtains. Smirking at the chaos, Hawk wandered from the room and dumped more ice into his mouth.

For a while, he wandered the halls until he made his way back to the cafeteria. There he sat, contemplating, thinking about the last time he'd been in this hospital. How he'd been crippled.

Until Phil Jameson's arrival.

The entire thing had been hard for his mind to grasp. There was *no* scientific logic in the ability to heal someone via touch.

But Phil? *He* said it was a God-given ability.

Hawk wasn't sure how much he believed that. He'd never even really believed all that much in God. His dad forced him to go to church. That was the extent of it.

Maybe God had healed him. Or maybe it'd been a scientific phenomenon he had yet to research and understand.

One thing he was positive about—Phil Jameson wanted credit.

"If you allow me to film this miracle," Phil whispered, raising his phone. *"I will introduce you to Kaemon Spears, and your dream will come true."*

It'd been worth it. After the February 15th Kaemon Spears rally... his dream *would* come true.

* * *

After Todd instructed him to salt the driveway and the walkway to the back of the house, Hawk said his goodbyes. He heard his grandmother protesting as he left. She told Todd that Jacob might try to kill him while he salted the icy walkways.

Rolling his eyes, he approached the elevators. He took a moment to appreciate the ass of a smiling, young nurse who stepped out of the elevators and walked past him. Her hips swayed as she ventured down the hall.

While awaiting the taxi to go home, Hawk held a conversation with an AI chat model and researched the ability to heal via touch.

It wasn't very helpful.

After a boring drive home, the dark neighborhood was quiet when the taxi stopped at the driveway. After paying the driver, Hawk slipped his backpack onto his shoulders and approached the Caravan home. Looked across the street.

And frowned.

Was that *Fr. Jerome's* vehicle parked across the street?

Curious, Hawk approached the old, white car. It definitely looked like the one the priest kept as backup after Mariel's death. 2005 Honda Accord.

But it was the black, Eastern Orthodox prayer rope that hung over the rearview mirror, one with a red stripe down the center of the knotted cross, that answered his question. It was definitely Fr. Jerome's car.

But why was Fr. Jerome here?

Ignoring his instructions to salt the driveway, Hawk bounded towards the back door. He liked drama, and he hoped that the old priest was here to convince Esther that she had, indeed, sinned due to her random bisexuality. It was unlikely, though, since Fr. Jerome was a homosexual himself.

As Hawk stepped through the back door, he glanced around in confusion. Most of the lights were on. As he shuffled into the kitchen, he frowned again.

The counter was a mess. Lemonade. A tall, half-empty bottle of vodka. A brown, empty pizza box with two leftover slices. Paper plates.

Giggling, Hawk raised his phone and took several photos. He couldn't give Esther time to clean the evidence of whatever the hell she'd been up to.

But... where was Fr. Jerome? This was odd.

Very, very *weird*.

As he moved towards the stairs, down the hallway, Hawk's eyes fell upon a black blouse on the floor. Then, on the first stairway step—a red bra.

"What the—" Hawk began and then stopped. His ears perked.

Hip-hop music. Upstairs.

And creaking. Repetitive, rhythmic *creaking*.

Was she dancing again?

It'd make sense, but then again...

Where was Fr. Jerome?

And was *that* Esther's voice?

These were not ordinary *dancing* sounds.

Brushing his fingers along the wooden railing, he crept up the stairs. As the stairs creaked, the music grew louder. So did the other weird sounds coming from his sister's room.

His heart rate increased. Hawk paused at the top of the dark stairway, suddenly praying to a God he wasn't sure even existed.

His face wrinkled in disgust, and he wanted to vomit.

Esther's bedroom door was cracked open, emitting a yellow glow into the hallway. From where he stood, Hawk could certainly not *see* what was happening, but there was *no* mistaking the sounds coming from that fucking bedroom.

Esther was having sex.

"Oh, *God,* yes! Yes, *yes...* "

Her cries were nauseating, sickening, and he wanted to burst into the room. Humiliate her for life. Shame her forever.

The bed creaked again and again. It was as if each creak of the bed brought more cries from Esther—

"Oh my God, yes, *fuck* me!"

—and for a moment, Hawk was paralyzed, unable to move, frozen in pure horror for two reasons. One, the fact that he was listening to his sister having sex was horrendous enough. It was something he had never wanted to experience and, moving forward, he was certain that he would need therapy. However, the second reason brought more thoughts and emotions to his head than he could handle.

Why was Esther sleeping with *Fr. Jerome?* Their *homosexual parish priest*? Was it some form of sick therapy? What in *God's name* was going on?

With shaking fingers, Hawk withdrew his phone. No one would believe him if he told anyone without proof. So, as the bed continued to creak, the boy crept towards the door and opened the camera on his phone.

The door was cracked just enough to see the end of the bed. As he raised the phone, Hawk angled it, filming, glimpsing Esther positioned downwards on her hands and knees, clutching the bedspread as her hair fell over her right shoulder. The camera captured everything. Her cries. Her movements. It caught the strangely *young*-looking hand that reached forward, balled her hair within the fist, and yanked her head backwards.

If God existed, everyone in this household was going to go to Hell. Esther. The priest. Hawk for filming it. This was *wicked* and—

As her hips slammed backwards, Esther let out several high-pitched cries and opened her eyes. Within a second, her gaze found Hawk.

"What *the fuck, Jason?*" Esther shrieked.

Hawk fell into the shadows. The bed creaked again, but this time it was from Esther and her lover as they scrambled over the mattress.

The boy knew he'd be caught. Not that *he* should get into any trouble, but he'd most likely be beaten and forced to bleed out in his own home if he allowed Esther to catch him.

Fuck.

She was coming.

Hawk's body reacted in a way that he did not expect.

He ran.

Scrambled down the stairway.

And fled for his life.

His body stumbled over the stairs and, as he fell into the hall, he tossed the backpack onto the floor and darted for the front door. He heard Esther's footsteps—

—damn, she was fast—

—sprinting after him and, gritting his teeth, Hawk fled into the icy, night air.

As he bolted down the driveway, towards the street, he heard Esther's angry shrieks echo in the neighborhood. Then, as he heard Fr. Jerome's car scream—

—damn, he was fast too—

—from its parking spot and jolt into the night, Hawk realized something.

Jacob Caravan was right. Esther *was* evil. She had to be. For some sick, gay-conversion therapy, his sister was fucking the family priest. The family priest was fucking his sister.

Phil Jameson was also right.

Fr. Jerome was evil too.

"Hawk!" Esther's voice was too close. It was frightful. Her bare feet slapped against the ground behind him.

In an instant, Hawk felt her upon him. His body collapsed. He struck the pavement and slid against the icy cement. The teenager's chin cracked against the ground. Harsh, excruciating pain bounced from his teeth and into his head.

"I will break all of your fucking teeth," Esther seethed, sitting on him, grasping his hair and bending close. "Were you *filming me*?"

Hawk struggled, but he'd depleted his energy fleeing from her. Gasping, the thick odor of alcohol from her breath choked his throat and nostrils. Her hair tickled his face. "Esther, you are a sick, *sick*—"

She bounced his head against the pavement again. "Where's your phone?"

"I'm not telling you. Also, you're assaulting a minor."

"Give me your *fucking* phone, or I will *murder* a minor!"

Several moments of struggling and slapping ensued. At one point, Hawk felt his arm twisted behind his back. The harsh angle tugged at the shoulder socket and forced a howl from his throat, and he stuttered into the cold cement: "Alright, alright, *alright*, it's in my right pants' *pocket!*"

Her hands invaded both pockets, giving him ample opportunity to arch his back and throw Esther from his body. As the streetlight flickered above them, he crawled forward and scrambled to his feet. He gripped the cell phone on the inside of his coat pocket. "I'll send this video to Grandma and Dad if you attack me again. I'll *do* it."

Furious, terrified, Esther stood before him in the middle of the quiet street. The wind tugged at her hair. It whipped at the white t-shirt that appeared to be inside-out, as well as the knee-length basketball shorts that looked a bit too large for her. She was barefoot, shivering, and Hawk was pretty sure she bared her teeth at him.

But she pleaded with him now.

"Hawk. Please. I'm serious. This isn't funny."

Hawk glared at her. "No, you slut, it's *not* funny. Dad's in the hospital with heart issues and you're at home *fucking our parish priest!*" His screech, as it broke the still of the night, sounded very similar to a... hawk.

For a moment, Esther stood very still, and her eyes were the widest he'd ever seen them. In streetlight's glow, her face paled. Then, in a shrill voice, she spoke.

"*What the fuck?* You sick little bastard, I'm not *screwing* Fr. Jerome, oh my *God!*" Esther covered her face, turned away from him, dry heaved a little, and then whirled back. "Seriously, what the *hell* is wrong with you?" Pulling her hair in front of her face and clenching it, she moaned into her fists, her voice muffled. "*Jesus*, Hawk, what the fucking *shit?*"

"What is wrong with *you?* Who drove Fr. Jerome's car here, then? *Huh?*" Hawk waved his arms outwards, wondering when Esther had become so mentally ill. A gust of wind shoved him, and he staggered a little.

Esther dropped her hands. "Okay, listen, Hawk. I *know* this is weird, but I promise on my *honor* that I am not fucking—sleeping with—oh *God*, I can't even *say it.*"

"Who, then?"

"Hawk. You wouldn't understand."

"Alright." He raised the phone. "Sending to Grandma and Dad in three... two..."

"*It was Gabe.* Okay, it was *Gabe!*" Esther lunged forward, reaching for Hawk, but the boy fell backwards and placed the phone behind his back.

"Gabe drives Fr. Jerome's car now?" Hawk shook his head.

Unbelievable. The lies.

She was full of them.

"Father Jerome needed his car fixed. Gabe helped him out, and—and took his car for a spin to make sure it was okay. Then I asked him to come over for pizza and... and the rest is *fucking* horrible history." Her voice was desperate, fearful, *insane.*

"Sounds fishy. You broke up with him."

Esther gritted her teeth, furiously rubbed her face. "It's called *closure,* Hawk. Please. Just give me the phone. Or let me see you delete the video."

"Would Gabe be able to confirm this?" This was enjoyable now. It was rare that he could fluster his sister to this extent.

It was awesome.

"Jason, I swear to God, if you tell Dad about this, it'll kill him. I'm serious. He's not at a good place to be stressed out. I'm begging you. *Begging you.* I'll do whatever you want, when you want. *Please.*"

Oh. Oh, *now* she cared about the family. *Now* she cared about their health. Convenient how she cared *now* when he held a phone filled with her sinful evidence.

"Since when did you care so much about our family?" Hawk yelled. Things had always been about *her* friends, *her* boyfriends.

Everyone *else* came *first.*

He never fucking came *first.*

"What do you want from me?" Esther cried. Tearful, her voice shook. "I don't understand what you *want.* Why do you hate me so much? What did I ever do to you?"

Tears stung his eyes. He didn't want to cry. Esther wasn't worth it. But the wind whipped salty droplets from his eyes, and his throat tightened. Then, with sudden passion, feelings he hadn't yet faced blurted from his mouth.

"I used to be *important* to you!" Hawk exclaimed, suddenly aware that his ears had numbed from the cold. Snot trickled from his nose. "You—you used to come home and sit with me, and I'd show you my newest projects, and—and you'd say you were *proud* of me!"

"Hawk. Sweetheart, I'm sor—"

"And then you started *dancing*, and started *dating*, and you thought you were too cool for me. I stopped mattering to you! Last year, you promised me breakfast so I could show you what I've been fucking slaving over. I got in the accident, and you *still* haven't taken me to breakfast. You haven't asked me about my current science project, Esther, because it has nothing to do with *you*." Hawk bent his head, wiped tears from his eyes. Now he was embarrassed, angry with himself for the outburst. "Everything has to be about you. Ever since Mom died... you and Dad got to steal the show. And it *sucks* when—"

Hawk felt himself yanked. For a moment, he struggled, but Esther wrapped her arms around him and forced his face against her shoulder.

Shivering, they stood together in abrupt silence. It'd been at least six months since they'd hugged. It was awkward, mainly because he could feel her large, braless breasts smashed into his chest. The alcohol on her breath had a sickening smell. A car drove past them, honking, illuminating the Caravan siblings in the middle of the street.

"I was always jealous of you, ya know," Esther said softly, shivering against him. "You were always the smart one, the one everyone talked about. Mom and Dad gloried in your successes. Even though you were like... six. What have I done? Dance. I got attention because of my body and the way it moves. I've always wanted to do something significant, just like you want to do, but I don't have the genius to pull off what you can, Hawk."

As he leaned against her, he stared at the dark pavement. Sniffled. "Really?"

"Yeah, dude. You're smart as fuck. Popularity isn't everything. Besides, you met *Kaemon Spears*. Not only that, but he's helping you with your dreams. Someone that important wouldn't waste time on someone he didn't find significant." Esther's breath was hot against his neck as she rested her chin on his shoulder. "I'm sorry, Hawk. I never wanted to hurt you. Please forgive me?"

The boy blinked. He didn't trust her, especially since she had everything to lose, and he had everything to gain. However, he realized that if he *did* share that video, it'd certainly eliminate *any* hope of a healthy relationship with his sister in the future.

And, in that moment, despite everything Jacob Caravan believed about his sister, Hawk Caravan realized something horrific.

He *missed* her.

"If you make more effort to spend time with me," Hawk said slowly, "I'll delete the video. Deal?"

As they returned to the house, Esther's fingers tapped his phone screen with desperate urgency to delete the necessary material.

Hawk bit his lip.

He wasn't sure he believed Esther's story. He *knew* she was keeping a very important piece of information from him, but he wasn't sure what it was. Maybe it'd been Gabe. God, he hoped it was Gabe... at least for his own mental sanity.

The last thing Hawk wanted to believe was that she had willingly bent over for the parish priest.

"Hawk. You're thinking something weird, why is that look on your face?"

Hawk just looked at her, bit the corner of his lip, and took back his phone. "Did you delete everything to your satisfaction?"

Cheeks flushed in shame, Esther nodded.

Hawk gave her a firm nod back. "Good."

Esther turned and faced him as he closed the door. Tilting her head a little, she swayed on her feet, and her glassy eyes still brimmed with tears. "Are you hungry?"

He was.

"Turn on the Xbox," Esther said, and she gestured to the television. "I'll make pancakes, and we can play video games. Sound good?"

He couldn't stop the big smile that spread across his face. "Sounds good."

Verse 2

~ God, Forgive Me ~

Thursday, January 15th, 2020—

Hello, journal.

It's past 10 P.M, and I've not heard from Mariel. He took his old car this evening, but (once again) didn't tell me where he was going.

I need to speak with him. Since his return, he's avoided any conversation regarding his resurrection and God's supposed 'mission' for him. I've tried to keep my distance and give him time. I know it's only been five days, but I've barely seen him. When I do, he goes to his room. He's barely acknowledged the rising issues I'm having in my church. It's a selfish thought, I suppose, wanting him to care. But he used to. Now, he's dismissive. If only I could see what was in his head...

Fr. Jerome placed the pen on the dining room table and rubbed his jaw. Harlow plopped onto the floor and licked her fluff before glancing up at him and letting out a slow, soft meow.

"Oh, do you have advice for me?" Fr. Jerome peered down at her. "Would you like to tell me what to do with Mariel?"

Harlow stared at him and then returned to her ritualistic cleanse.

But what *could* he do? If Mariel didn't want to speak, he wouldn't.

As Fr. Jerome leaned back in his chair, he considered their relationship, how they'd always *felt* close. However, he wondered if that's all that it'd ever been.

A feeling.

He'd always wanted to be the dad and the priest that offered a listening ear, even if he could not always provide a solution.

But Mariel had a side that he'd always kept closed off, as if he were afraid that Fr. Jerome wouldn't be able to accept and love him *despite* his weaknesses.

Mariel had a pattern. If he kept secrets, it was normally undesirable information. Now, as Fr. Jerome watched Harlow spin in an effort to catch her tail, the old man could not help but wonder what he was hiding now.

Was it Godly?

Or sinister?

Fr. Jerome had given Mariel space his entire life, almost to the point of neglecting his duties as a parent.

His son was an adult now.

But it was time to invade Mariel's space.

He was barely holding on to his job as a priest... he wanted to hold on to his son.

The phone vibrated on the wooden table. "Finally," Fr. Jerome muttered, and he reached for the phone.

It wasn't Mariel.

It was a text from Esther Caravan and, despite his disappointment, Fr. Jerome was curious to see what she had to say. He opened the text. Frowned with confusion.

"Hi, Father Jerome. I know this is random but... if you hear any extremely strange or horrible rumors about us in the future, please, please forgive me and understand that it isn't entirely my fault."

"Huh?" The priest blinked at the screen and scratched his head. As he stood from his chair, he returned the message, murmuring the words as he typed. *"Would you like to tell me what this potential rumor might be?"*

As he awaited Esther's return text, Fr. Jerome shuffled past Harlow and approached the hallway. The cat sped past him, winding through his feet and almost tripping the old man.

Despite everything, Fr. Jerome still felt guilty for what he was about to do. He rarely invaded someone's privacy, including his son's. The priest thought of Phil Jameson, and, for a moment, wondered if his behavior were as deplorable.

"I'm the parent," he muttered. "I just want to make sure he's safe."

Sighing, Fr. Jerome entered Mariel's bedroom.

The room was tidy, something that had always been a disciplined habit of Mariel's. During his time without Mariel, Fr. Jerome had left the room as it'd been before his death. He hadn't even touched the white paper plate Mariel had forgotten on his nightstand.

Fr. Jerome switched on the light and scanned the room. The phone buzzed in his pocket, and the queen-sized bed creaked a little as the priest sat down and looked at Esther's text message.

"You don't want to know. Just... try to carry on and pretend I never texted you."

Fr. Jerome was very confused. Whatever potential rumor she might have in mind couldn't have come at a worse time in his life.

Another message from Esther. *"That sounded really rude. I'm so sorry, Father Jerome. We need to talk soon though. I am slowly losing my mind."*

"You and me both, kid," he grumbled, scratching his head again. His suspicions of Mariel's involvement were rising very fast.

And that certainly wasn't a good thing.

Sighing, the priest responded. *"Let me look at my schedule and we will talk soon. Be well, Esther."*

He turned his attention to the laptop on the small desk that sat across from the bed. It was open, its screen black. Swallowing hard, Fr. Jerome approached the desk and seated himself in the wheeled desk chair that always creaked when used.

"Do you have a password, my boy?" Fr. Jerome whispered and tapped the keyboard.

Indeed, it was password protected.

Harlow sprinted into the room. Stopped. Glanced around wide-eyed. And continued running in circles.

Fr. Jerome stared at the laptop.

What exactly did he expect to *find?* This was annoying.

He wanted to trust his son.

But he *couldn't*, and it made him sick.

Harlow spun around, swatting something under the desk and meowing in frustration before she sprinted towards the bed, galloped over the surface, and then pounced back at the desk again.

Fr. Jerome was tired—from Mariel's return. The visions. Fr. Paul. He wanted time to himself. He needed time to think, to process, to let his mind go blank. To relax.

"Is that selfish, Lord?" Fr. Jerome murmured.

Harlow swatted the object again, causing it to fly across the carpeted floor and strike the wall. It clattered against the surface, and the entertained cat darted after it.

"What are you *playing* with, Harlow?" Fr. Jerome sighed, standing up. The chair creaked beneath his movement.

Squinting a little, he approached the wall and lifted Harlow into his arms. He peered down at the object.

A black flash drive.

His knees crackled as he stooped to pick it up. It looked new, and he hadn't remembered seeing it before. Granted, he was old, and he'd also never done a scavenger hunt in his son's room.

"I guess we'll see what's on here, then," Fr. Jerome said, and he let Harlow drop to the floor. She darted from the room, as if terrified of what might be on the flash drive.

After returning to his room, guilt tore his insides as he inserted the flash drive into his own laptop. The screen light glowed in the darkness. He clicked the file folders under Mariel's name. His heart pounded fast, his ears felt hot.

Was he nervous because he was doing something wrong?

Or nervous by what he might find?

"Just college stuff," Fr. Jerome assured himself as he double-clicked the file folder entitled "*Mariel*".

Multiple pictures flooded the screen. Father and son photos. Facebook screenshots of memes that he didn't understand. Esther, Mariel, and Gabe together as high schoolers. Mariel and Esther.

Fr. Jerome smiled. Minutes passed as he scrolled through the pictures, and he lost track of time.

But another folder caught his eye.

A recent folder. Today's date, to be precise. Entitled: "*More*".

The priest clicked it.

And wished he hadn't.

"*Good God.*"

Pornographic images and videos flooded the screen. Abuse towards women. Violent sexual encounters. Materials from what could only come from the depraved, violent corners of the dark web.

Like sexualized murder. A woman bleeding out from a slit throat while a man used her and—oh God, he'd *known* this evil existed, but he hadn't had to *see it!*

The priest sat wide-eyed on his bed as he scrolled downwards, wanting to stop, wanting to close his eyes. His stomach churned. Inhaling sharply, the priest lunged for the trash can next to the bed and vomited.

"Lord," he gagged. "Please forgive him."

These images *had* to have been from prior to Mariel's death. God, he hoped, and he *prayed* because, if they weren't, he wasn't sure how the *hell* he'd deal with the fact that Mariel was...

... was *sick!*

What madness would drive him to look at such imagery when his soul had been allegedly perfected for a mission *ordered by God?*

A mission Mariel still wouldn't *speak about?*

The front door creaked and then slammed.

Mariel was home.

Fr. Jerome slapped the laptop shut and rose to his feet as he heard footsteps in the living room.

Yawning, Harlow rose up and arched her back.

"Dad?" Mariel's voice. Tired. A little out of breath.

Fr. Jerome prayed. Tried to breathe.

He wasn't pissed.

He was *fucking furious.*

But he needed to remain calm.

The floor squeaked in the living room.

Fr. Jerome exited his bedroom and trudged down the hallway.

Mariel leaned into the refrigerator. The light glowed on his jet-black ponytail.

"I think I've seen a ghost," Fr. Jerome said, trying to sound cheery as he stepped into the dining room. He rested his hand on the chair. It shook.

Mariel straightened up, standing taller than the refrigerator, and put the milk carton to his lips. "Did I wake you?"

"No." Fr. Jerome assessed him. Shoes untied. T-shirt inside out. As Mariel threw his head backwards to drink the rest of the milk, the priest noticed a medium-sized, red mark on the side of the young man's neck. "Where were you?"

Mariel tossed the empty carton into the trash and wiped his mouth. "Out."

"I gathered that. Out where? It's almost eleven."

"I'm an adult, Dad. I think I'm old enough to be out at night."

Fr. Jerome tried to push the pornographic images from his mind. He couldn't. "We need to talk." He grasped the top of the chair and pulled it from the table. It scraped across the floor. "Sit down."

"Dad—"

"Sit... *down*." Fr. Jerome's hands trembled as he stared up at Mariel. Sweat moistened his skin.

Mariel shuffled to the chair and sat. His blue eyes shifted and then rested on Fr. Jerome with annoyance. "What's wrong?"

"We need to discuss a couple things." Fr. Jerome seated himself across from Mariel and placed his hands on the table. "First, we need to establish a very important rule. You need to be honest with me during our discussion."

"*Dad.* What is this? What did I do, and why am I under interrogation?" Mariel glanced up and around, as if expecting a spotlight to appear from above.

Fr. Jerome didn't blink. "I'll be honest, Mariel... when I adopted you, I wasn't sure if I could ever be a good parent to you. I certainly wasn't expecting a baby who could not only defy death, but who'd be granted the opportunity to speak with the Holy Ones in *Heaven*. Now, I wasn't there, but I'm assuming that that's what happened."

"*Yes,* Dad, I'm not ly—"

"Let me finish." Fr. Jerome's voice was curt. "I thought I raised you with adequate amounts of discipline and leniency, especially since you were never one of those kids who would go out of your way to disrespect me. However, it seems that I might have raised you with too much leniency. That was my fault. *My* failure."

"Dad, what are you *talking* about?"

"Mariel, where were you tonight?"

"I was just—"

"While you were *out* today, was it a reason related to your resurrection or—"

"Slow down, Dad, can we just back up a sec—"

"—*or* were you with Esther Caravan?" Fr. Jerome spoke with sharp finality, and his eyes did not flinch.

Mariel sunk into his chair. "Dad. I told you not to worry about anything. Everything is under control. Esther had nothing to do with this."

"It's a yes or no question. Were you, or were you not, with Esther Caravan tonight?"

Mariel's jaw hardened. "No."

"What were you doing then?"

"I can't tell you."

Fr. Jerome breathed slow, raging fire and stared at the table. "So, you were instructed not to tell me anything regarding your mission here, correct?"

"...Yes."

"Perfect." He looked up and met Mariel's eyes. "Then I suppose they probably wouldn't want you to tell me about the rape pornography on *this*, would they?" He held up the flash drive.

Mariel's face went white, his eyes widening. His Adam's apple bobbed up and down as he struggled to speak.

"This *is* part of your mission on Earth, isn't it, Mariel? Watching women get beaten into submission before their rape? Finding dark web videos of women getting murdered in sick ways for entertainment? When I went to seminary, I was taught that these things were vile. We must have been *wrong*, seeing as the Kingdom of Heaven approves of these things now."

Mariel spoke with an eerie calm to his voice. "You wouldn't understand. You never have."

Fr. Jerome smacked the flash drive onto the table. "That's what you said the last time I found that vile *shit* on your computer."

"Dad, I'm not going to *rape* anyone." Mariel spoke through clenched teeth. "I—don't know how to explain it, but—*fuck!* Why am I talking about this with my *gay* father?"

Harlow hissed at Fr. Jerome's feet.

The priest studied his son's face, nauseated from the hurtful words. "Has that always been how you viewed me? Just the *gay* father? The faggot?"

"It's not untrue, Dad! It's not your fault you never figured out how to talk about sex with me, especially since you've never even done it yourself."

Fr. Jerome's voice was hoarse, and he pointed at the flash drive. "That's not *sex*, that's *violence! It's murder!*"

"Calm down, Dad. I'm not as evil as you'd like to think," Mariel snorted.

"Mariel, I'm not *saying* you're evil. We all have our struggles, but—"

"—But you can control yours?" Mariel's eyes narrowed. "Is that what you're saying?"

"We're not talking about me, we're talking about you." Fr. Jerome shifted in his seat. "You need to tell me what's going on. Now. You need to tell me where you're going, what this so called Heavenly mission is, and when you need to get it done. And *then* I'm going to watch you destroy this disgusting flash drive." He glared at Mariel. "Start talking."

"I'm not telling you anything, Dad."

Fr. Jerome caught his breath. "Mariel, I'm warning you."

"And I'm an adult. I don't need your threats." Mariel stood, towering over the table and his father. "I *was* going to talk to you eventually, but now I don't want to. Sorry."

"Alright, that's it." Fr. Jerome lunged from his chair. Stomped down the hall, entered Mariel's room, and snatched the laptop. As his breathing came ragged, he returned to the kitchen, approached the sink, and turned on the water.

"Dad, what the *hell*?"

"I've been through enough hell, Mariel Nadier, I am not allowing *hell* into my house!" Fr. Jerome held the laptop over the sink.

"Give it back. I swear to God, you've lost your shit."

"Tell me where you were tonight."

"I was out of town!"

He dipped the laptop lower. "Do you want to tell me why Esther texted me and suggested that a *potential rumor* between us might form?"

Mariel's face reddened. "*Jesus,* Dad, what is *wrong* with you? Maybe if you spent less time getting involved in *my* business, you wouldn't be a fucking *failure* as a *goddamn priest!*" He caught his breath. "Dad... *wait, no!*"

As tears brimmed, Fr. Jerome raised his arm and smashed the laptop into the sink. The water splashed over its cracked encasing. He stood there, shaking, realizing that he might have gone too far, frightened that he had just ruined his relationship with his son.

Mariel's nose flared. His fists opened and closed. "Well," he sneered. "If we're throwing away trash—" Leaning over the table, he snatched Fr. Jerome's journal and stormed towards him.

The furniture rattled.

Mariel knocked him aside, thrust the journal into the sink, and ripped pages from the book.

"If that's the game we're playing," Mariel hissed, slamming the rest into the sink and stepping back, "then your crazy ramblings get to go too." His chest heaved up and down as he struggled for air. Tears slipped from his eyes. "I don't know where I'm going to go, but I'm not staying here tonight."

Fr. Jerome felt a sob form within his chest as Mariel headed for the door. "Mariel, *please.*"

"Don't worry, I'm not taking the car." The door slammed, and the picture frames clattered against the wall.

"God, forgive me," Fr. Jerome whispered. The tears came, and he leaned his forehead against the counter. Harlow snaked her tail around his leg, and the old priest's tears combined with the water in the sink.

VERSE 3

~ WRONG ~

When he'd left in a rage, Mariel hadn't brought his coat. He regretted it. By the time he stepped onto the bus, his bare arms had numbed. His breathing came ragged from emotion.

Anger. Hurt. Regret. Shame.

What he'd saved to that flash drive was something that he'd *never* wanted his father to find.

Mariel hadn't intended to succumb to the temptation again. But after experiencing sex with Esther for the first time, the desire returned.

The *need*.

He'd tried to ignore its beckoning. He didn't *want* to find pleasure in watching women suffer but... the more he'd been unoccupied at home, the higher the temptation had grown.

Since Wednesday, he'd eased himself into it. Soft porn. Just a taste. One video. Two videos. Harder porn. Then... extreme. Still consensual, but extreme.

And then—he'd tapped into a new universe. The dark web. A web of darkness—black sin and vile things that made him flinch a little as he stroked himself.

Fuck, he hadn't meant to fall back into this, because it certainly wasn't God's will. However, God had been clear.

Commit the First Death. Kill Aleksey Petrov. Receive the Kingdom of Heaven.

He'd repent later.

But the videos bled into his mind. His own thoughts had worsened.

And Esther Caravan was at its center.

"*You're hurting me!*" Esther cried in his thoughts, and his hand always moved faster.

He felt guilty. Sick. He didn't want to think of Esther in that way, because his father was right. It wasn't just *rough sex*, it was *murder*.

But the pornography gave him the outlet, fulfilled a fantasy that he wanted but knew he could never have. It brought his thoughts away from the task God had given him, the oh-so-confusing task of murdering a political figure.

A task that could *kill* the woman he loved.

But right now, he was angry, his body desperate for release. Mariel had been so close to finishing before Esther's brother had interrupted. Now he was uptight. Enraged.

Desperate.

Earlier that night, he'd planned to eat dinner with Fr. Jerome, watch a movie, and go to bed. However, as his father prepared a cashew chicken recipe, Mariel had received a message from Esther that he couldn't ignore.

"*The house is empty tonight. I'm alone. ;)*"

"*Is that a hint?*" he'd responded.

Esther: "*Mmhmm. I'm a little tipsy, and I really, really need you to come take care of me.*"

Then, Esther had texted a photo. Facing the mirror. Leaning over the bathroom counter. Hair spilling over one shoulder. Biting her lip. Clad in a pushup bra that did not shield her cleavage.

So he told her he'd be there soon. And fast. And he'd called her beautiful.

He'd kissed his dad on the head, and then, apologizing, bounded from the house.

Esther met him at the door, pulling him in, closing the door and pushing him against the wall. She teased him with her hands, with her kisses, with her tongue, murmuring that she'd missed him, that she *needed* him, and Mariel would have taken her at the doorway. But she pulled back.

Told him that she wanted one more drink.

"Why are you drinking?" he'd asked, puzzled, staring at her flushed cheeks and hazy eyes.

"Just to loosen up a bit, baby, that's all."

And their night together had begun.

He'd really enjoyed sex with her tonight. She *was* loosened from the alcohol. More experimental. More giving. Louder. Dirtier. *Rougher.* She enjoyed it more. She offered her mouth. He threatened to take her ass, but she'd shrunk back a little, telling him he was too big, telling him it'd hurt her.

Telling him it'd tear her apart.

And he loved that image.

But not wanting to destroy the mood, he settled for her cunt.

He'd convince her later.

And then Hawk... that little fucker. He'd ruined it all.

The bus screeched to a halt downtown. Digging his hands into his pockets, Mariel stepped from the transit and strode down the sidewalk.

His phone buzzed. Two messages. One from Fr. Jerome. The other from Esther.

Ignoring the message from the priest, he opened Esther's text.

"What the fuck, Mars? Why did you park in a place where your car could be recognized?? Sooooo many other places you could've parked but you CHOSE TO PARK ACROSS THE STREET FROM MY HOUSE."

"Oh, don't start," Mariel muttered. He typed.

"I parked near the back, I did my best. Calm down."

Esther: *"CALM DOWN????"*

His thumbs flew. *"Yeah. I believe in you. And btw, why the fuck did you text my dad? Don't ever communicate with him about ANYTHING regarding us. Got it?"*

As he stalked the cold sidewalk, passing bundled individuals sleeping in the alleyways, Mariel waited for her response. Minutes passed. He grew nervous.

Finally, Esther responded again.

"Don't you ever talk to me again like I'm your bitch, Mariel."

His bitch. Spicy. *"Want some angry make-up sex?"*

She did not respond.

It pissed him off.

As he continued forward, he glimpsed the multi-colored sign that illuminated the sidewalk in purple, blue, and white. Loud music thumped from the walls.

Mariel had never been to a strip club. He'd always been curious, and he *knew* Gabe had been.

He wanted the distraction. He wanted to try the things that he hadn't had the opportunity to experience before his death.

"Fuck it," Mariel whispered, and he approached the doors.

The music vibrated his ears as he presented his identification to the large bouncer at the doorway. Once he moved past the bouncer, guilt formed in the midst of his thoughts.

Would this be considered... *cheating*?

Could he *cheat* even if he and Esther hadn't actually *defined* their relationship?

Everything about tonight felt... *wrong*.

But the guilt melted into his thoughts. He didn't care.

He'd repent later.

As the hip-hop music pounded the building's walls, he analyzed the unfamiliar atmosphere. In the darkened room, multi-colored lights flashed and cut across the large stage where a nude, large-breasted blonde performed on the pole.

Mariel's face went hot, and, as his eyes scanned her body, he thought of Esther. How *well* she danced. She'd look good up there. Especially with a little bit of a bruised up face and a bloody—

Shit, stop thinking like this.

Diverse groups of men, young and old, mulled around tables. Drinking. Laughing. Flirting with half-naked servers. Clapping. Whistling.

"Hey, Cutie. Any way I can be of service to you?"

Mariel jumped and looked down at a petite, black-haired young woman that stood before him. Tan. Toned. Small breasts. Clad in a sparkling two-piece bikini, her hair sat bound in a high ponytail. Her lip gloss sparkled. Her perfume had a fruity smell, and Mariel inhaled it as he struggled to speak.

"Um... sorry, I've never been here. New to this." Mariel smiled and dug his hands into his pockets. "Looking to celebrate my twenty-second birthday solo, I guess." He cleared his throat.

Shit, he wanted Esther. He envisioned the look on her face, the one that'd be devastated that he'd crawled back from death to seek solace *here*.

"Oooh, congrats, Sexy!" Her dimples deepened. She flashed him a wide smile. "Did you want to start with a drink? We have discounts on lap dances tonight."

"I'll start with that drink first."

"Find yourself a table, Sweetie, and one of the servers will be with you soon, alright?" She winked. "Hope to see you after that drink." She strutted away, and Mariel's entire body burned.

Fuck. Dad raised you better than this. The porn. All of this.

But he shuffled to the nearest round table where a broad-shouldered, light-haired man sat facing the stage.

Mariel pulled out a chair and sat. Tapped his fingertips against the table.

The blonde finished her routine with a slight grinding motion of her hips and then left the stage.

"Ever wonder how they walk so damn *smooth* in those heels?" the young man next to him asked as his eyes followed the blonde dancer. He swirled the ice in his glass and sipped the dark beverage.

Mariel glanced at him. "Yeah."

In the following moments that he sat in dazed guilt, a server came to him and took his order. He didn't know what he wanted, or what he might like, and the brown-haired server waited patiently as he sorted through the drink options.

"You never drink, or something?" The man finished the rest of his drink.

Mariel blushed. "I have."

The man slammed the glass down and turned to face Mariel. He had a square-jaw, handsome features. "I'll help you out. How are you feeling tonight?"

"Uh..."

"Pissed? Happy? Heart-broken?" The man narrowed his eyes, and his speech slurred. "Jealous?"

Mariel shrugged. "Pissed."

Jealous too.

Earlier, while Esther prepared another drink for herself, he'd had the opportunity to look through a few text messages and some of the pictures on her phone. For the most part, she'd saved images of herself, videos of dance, etc. However, when he'd stumbled upon a saved photo of a shirtless Gabe Donovan, he'd almost smashed her phone.

Also, who the *hell* was Officer Mysterious?

"Jealous too," he mumbled.

"Oh, you need shots," the other man said, chuckling. "We both do. Get us a round, Babe?" He snapped his fingers at the server. "My tab."

Mariel looked at him as another song began, and a rather flat-chested redhead walked onto the stage. "So what are you? Pissed, heart-broken, or jealous?"

The young man let out a breath. His eyes were glazed. "All three. Ever had your girl cheat on you?"

Mariel raised an eyebrow. "No."

"Well. It sucks. Especially when it's with your female boss."

"Oh?"

"*Yeah.*" Intoxicated, he drawled. Swaying in his chair, he frowned. "I thought she'd get in trouble. The boss. But.... *naaaah.* Bitch got away with fucking my girl. She'll get her karma, I guess. One day."

"That sucks."

The server placed the shot glasses on the table, brushed Mariel's shoulder, and then left them to drink.

Mariel's new friend lifted a glass. "Cheers, I guess," he said. "Drink up. Get smashed. Watch tits." He gulped it down.

Mariel threw his glass back and shuddered at the alcohol's intensity. The booze burned through his body like hot fury. "It's kind of gross," he said. "But I see why people do it."

The man raised another glass. "Happy birthday." Downed the drink and slammed the glass down. Held out his hand. "Thompson. Call me Matt, I guess."

"My name's Mariel."

Thompson squinted and grinned a little. "Why you got a girl's name, brother?"

"Please don't."

They continued to drink.

"So are you still with your girl?" Mariel asked. His vision blurred. His head spun. The ass in front of him looked great.

"Nope. I got better things to do."

"Like?" Mariel wanted to smack the ass.

Matt leaned over the table, grabbed Mariel's shoulder, and leaned close. "Like find my father's fucking killer."

Mariel's ears perked.

"I know what you need." Thompson leaned back.

"What?"

"A lap dance. You need some pussy on your lap."

The idea sounded appealing. He wouldn't touch. Just watch. After all, Esther had half-naked pictures of Gabe on her phone.

"Who killed your dad?" Mariel caught the eyes of the black-haired girl.

Her dimples deepened again, and she bit her lip.

Matt shrugged. "I hope to find out soon. There are rumbles within the political world that may help a poor, forgotten fucker like me."

Mariel looked at him. "Political world?"

Matt giggled and wiped his mouth. "Sorry. Spoke too much." He slumped into his chair.

And the black-haired girl beckoned him.

Desire coursed through his nerves.

Fuck it.

"Good luck, man. I'm gonna get that lap dance."

As Mariel stood, his legs threatened to give out. Was he more drunk? It seemed like it, because he wasn't sure how long it took for him to approach the girl.

Shame, desire, and curiosity combusted, and his voice was a distant muffle as he asked for a dance. He told her he was innocent and had never had one before.

"My favorite," the girl said, gesturing for him to follow her. "I love the innocent ones. They appreciate the dance more."

Mariel staggered after her

Think of Esther. Fuck, man, think of—

Soon, the girl grinded on him, presented herself to him as he clung to the chair in a daze of awe, confusion, and guilt. Thinking of Esther. His dad. Of that *poor forgotten fucker* out there slumped at the table.

He was a *poor forgotten fucker*, and it made *sense* because he was supposed to be dead.

The girl's hips gyrated.

He didn't want this anymore.

Feeling sick, Mariel nudged the girl from his lap. "I'm sorry," he mumbled. "Got a girlfriend."

He almost fled. Purple lights flashed. Music vibrated his ears. It was warm. He pushed past women.

"*Excuse* me, Sweetie," they said.

And then it was cold. He was outside. The world spun, and the city lights blurred. Horns blared. A few angry voices shouted at him.

"Watch where you're going," they said.

But Mariel didn't know where he was going.

He never had.

Mariel puked. It sprayed. Disoriented, he leaned against the wall in an alley.

His phone buzzed. Someone was calling him.

Breathing hard, Mariel answered the phone. "Captain Loser talking," he slurred. "How may I be of assistance?"

"*Mariel.* It's Dad. Where *are you*?"

"I don't wanna tell you. I feel sick."

"*Tell me* where you are."

Mariel slumped to the ground. He mumbled in broken fragments. "Did I ever tell you how much I *hate* how... *perfect* you are, Pops? Like—I feel like I should be the perfect one since I'm immortal and shit. You know?"

"Mariel. Tell me where you are before I call the police. Son. Talk to me, please, *I love you!*"

Despite his desire to keep his location unknown, the words spilled from Mariel's mouth. He described his surroundings, described the strip club, *begged* his father not to say anything to Esther. Vomited again.

And then he curled into the fetal position further down the alley until his father arrived.

Mariel fell into the car, gasping for air, shivering. "Feel so sick, Dad. I'm sorry."

The world moved in fragments.

Fr. Jerome was crying.

"Please just talk to me, Son," he sobbed, slamming on his brakes at a red light.

"When I came back, the figures were gone," Mariel murmured. His eyes rolled to the back of his head, and he jerked awake. "No weird messenger. No humanoid. Just myself."

That whisper, that horrible whisper, tickled his ear.

For a moment, he thought he was going to vomit again. "It came back. In the last couple days, it *came back*." Tears spilled over his cheeks.

"What did?"

Mariel's voice broke into a wail. "The *humanoid*, Dad."

Fr. Jerome didn't say anything. Mariel didn't expect him to.

"I need to fight it," he mumbled, and leaned his head back into his seat. "Need to kill..."

"Kill whom, Mariel?" Fr. Jerome's voice faded.

"First Death, Dad..."

And Mariel fell into a deep slumber.

Chapter 13: Verse 1

~ Inhale. Exhale. Breathe. ~

Sunday, September 30th, 2012

Chicago, Illinois

"You have one last task to do tonight, Four. It will be quick. Easy. Understood?" Trainer Boris had a strange edge to his voice, like he was so close to discovering something that would change his life.

Sixteen-year-old Tira Petrov glowered out of the back passenger window of the SUV.

The city blurred; she glared at it.

And the sun glared back.

"What task?" Tira turned her eyes to the front.

Boris smirked at Trainer Artyom, who sat in the front with him. The smirk was ugly, crooked, and it passed between the two men like a slithering viper. "It'll be easy," he repeated, and focused his attention back on the road.

She didn't like the sound of that. For multiple reasons.

One—no task was ever *easy* if the trainers said it was. It often came with almost impossible expectations.

Almost.

Not impossible.

Two, she didn't like it because she'd completed all of her assigned tasks for the day. The morning itinerary started with fitness. First, weight training, followed by offensive tactics and defensive tactics. After her shower, she'd been tasked to scout the city of Chicago. Find its trains, its hiding spots, its *people*. She didn't know *why*, but she determined it was because Petrov intended for her to memorize every fucking city on the globe before she graduated.

Even if it didn't matter in the future. Not if she succeeded and gained top status as *Agent 4*—not Project 4.

But Tira wouldn't be here in Chicago much longer. She and her trainers were scheduled to fly back tomorrow. She'd return to Russia and continue her training there.

Even though she'd only journeyed over the Atlantic a few times to train surveillance and study U.S. culture during the summers, she hated America.

Hated it.

But Tira enjoyed the break from Petrov. His minty breath over her shoulder. The wigs and facial masks he'd make her wear in order to offer a disguise as his daughter if public scrutiny came too close. The random tasks he'd have her do, such as bring him food to his room even though he was most often in a bathrobe with a bitch worshipping his fucking feet.

Yes, Tira hated America.

But she hated her papa more.

"Go to the room and shower," Boris ordered, pulling into the quiet lot near the motel.

"I'd planned on it," Tira snapped, grabbing her athletic bag. Her clothes still clung to her body from the sweat she'd produced at the track.

The track where the brown-haired, wide-eyed ice cream girl had ruined her fucking run.

"Eat something," Artyom said in English, and cocked his head as if something to eat were standing outside of his window. "We will be up after dark for the final task."

After dark.

"What is this *task?*" Tira demanded, standing outside of the vehicle with her bag over her shoulder. "There is nothing else listed on the itinerary."

"Speak *English*," Boris growled, and his eyes snapped to a lower-level hotel room where a large man waddled out from the doorway to light a cigarette.

"What is this *task?*" Tira hissed in English, and the wind tickled her ears.

Boris leaned closer, his massive hand tight around the top of the steering wheel. "*Go upstairs. Now.*"

Shaking, Tira stormed towards the stairway that led to the upper level. The motel, though private, had its share of activity. Drug deals. Prostitution. Affairs.

For the last month, they'd stayed at different locations throughout the city. Trainer Boris had taken cover as her father, and Trainer Artyom? The lucky uncle.

"Fucking idiots," Tira raged in Russian, keying into the motel room. For a moment, she considered calling Petrov to ask about this *after dark* task, but she'd have to deal with far worse consequences if she did *that*.

"Do not call me," Papa said. *"Your trainers are your lifeline now. Whatever they say, you do."*

Grumbling, Tira turned on the shower, stripped from her clothes, and placed her bruised, scarred body beneath the sputtering water.

And after dark, as promised, her trainers returned.

But Boris and Artyom were not alone.

* * *

January 15th, 2020
Chicago, Illinois

On Wednesday, January 15th, Tira Arcelin wondered what would happen if Esther Caravan died.

Granted, it was Tira's *duty* to protect the subject.

It filled her bank account.

But Tira *had* considered pushing Esther Caravan in front of the oncoming van. It would solve a lot of problems.

One, she wouldn't have to listen to her persistent questions anymore.

Two, she would no longer need to obtain a new microchip from Petrov.

And three, it'd eliminate the odd, fluttering sensation in her stomach whenever Esther Caravan texted her.

Agent 4 wasn't sure *what* it was, and she'd been exposed to many different sensations of pain in torture simulation. She'd never felt the fluttery feeling before, and she hated it the most.

When Tira returned home from driving Esther to the hospital, she tried to settle in. After showering, wrapping a towel around her hair, and tying her robe, Tira folded her legs on the bed and leaned against the headboard. Her new book, *War and Peace,* lay on the bed.

Guns surrounded her. Assembled. Unassembled.

Her phone lay next to her leg.

And it buzzed.

"Fuck," Tira snapped and reached for it.

One text message. Esther Caravan.

"Thanks again for the ride. I'm sorry our banter was cut short. I know you don't give a fuck, but I was having a good time. Lol. Anyway, my dad's stable, but he definitely had a heart attack."

Tira did not want to respond, told herself *not* to respond, because there was no productive *reason* to return the message. Regardless, she typed.

"Good. I am glad he is stable."

To Tira's annoyance, Esther messaged again.

"Thank you. And thanks for the coffee. And telling me your birthday. I know that was extremely painful for you. How are you handling the trauma?"

A smile flickered across her lips. But it went away fast.

"You think you are funny."

As Tira leaned her head back and closed her eyes, she thought about the other day, when she'd met Fr. Jerome Nadier at St. Michael's.

More importantly, the day she'd met his cat.

And even more alarming, the day he'd rattled off *those numbers.*

Seven. Thirteen. Zero-eight.

Tira swallowed hard, reaching down to rub her shins, trying to rid herself of Hamster's memorable screech.

"Enough," she snarled, digging her nails along the scars on her shins.

Coincidences didn't exist. At least, not in her line of work. So, as Tira rubbed her shins, she turned her mind to the coincidence of those numbers spilling from Fr. Jerome's mouth, and the coincidence that *brought* her to visit St. Michael's in the first place.

Mariel Nadier.

Why the *hell* was he alive?

Had he faked his death? Was *he* also an agent? Perhaps within KS Industries?

"What do you know about him?" Tira demanded of Michael. "Is someone taking on his identity to get to the subject?"

"No clue," Michael responded. "Maybe? Did you see his body?"

"No."

"Well then," Michael said. "I'd keep an eye on it. Talk to his dad—Fr. Jerome Nadier."

"Why would I talk to the priest? What would I even say?" Tira cried, unsure how the hell she was supposed to socialize with a man who represented a faith she cared nothing about.

"I don't know, Tira," Michael said, and he sighed. *"Tell him you're trying to find God."*

Her eyes snapped open as her phone vibrated again. The agent picked it up and then rolled her eyes.

Esther: *"You need laughter in your boring life. If you spent some time with me, I bet you'd laugh more."*

Tira stared at the message, felt steady heat creep from her neck, into her cheeks, and into her ears. Her heart pulsed against her chest.

Hard.

"No. I'd rather not."

Snarling, Tira turned off the phone. Tossed it across the room.

She hated useless conversations. She hated Chicago. She hated America.

And she *really* hated Esther Caravan.

Tira hated the smell of alcohol on her breath when she'd tackled her last weekend. She hated the extra steps she'd had to take when she bugged Esther's car; when she had to figure out if the Mariel Nadier *ghost* was a threat to the subject. She hated that she'd had to climb to the goddamn window, only to see Esther's naked silhouette bouncing like a fucking rag doll on top of *Agent Zombie*—

—and about *time* that loser fucked her—

—to which she'd almost screamed in disgusted horror before losing her grip and falling into the bushes.

And *then* Tira Arcelin had been forced to bring the stupid dancing pendant necklace to the bookstore as an excuse to plant more temporary bugs until Michael brought her the new microchip tomorrow.

The microchip situation was stressful enough on its own.

Not because Petrov had contacted her.

It was stressful because he hadn't.

"Did he say anything when you requested a new one? For the hypothetical situation?" Tira asked Michael, eyeing her pan-fried chicken to ensure nothing burnt again.

"No," Michael chuckled.

"What did he say?"

And Michael's response chilled her.

"He told me that systems fail. And you replace them when they do."

And Tira hadn't been able to figure out if Petrov had been referencing the microchip. Or her.

Tira crawled through her guns, left her bed, and stomped to her phone.

All fears aside, she decided it'd make sense to maintain some form of contact with the subject in order to insert the chip.

Letting out a slow breath, Tira opened the conversation and began to type. Her lips trembled, and she snarled as she composed the message.

"I realize that my words came across badly... but I was joking. I do need a friend. That being said, when you are ready, I'd like it very much if you would take me to do something fun. I suppose."

Done. Message sent.

Grumbling profanities in Russian, Tira turned off the phone screen, cleared the bed, set the alarm, and pulled the covers over her head.

Bzzz.

"Shut up!" Tira screamed, and her hand thumped around the nightstand to find her phone again. It lit up the blanket fort she'd created, and she frowned at the message she'd received from Esther.

"I knew you didn't hate me. ;) What about this weekend? We could go bowling. Indoor mini golfing? Or something? You've probably never done any of those things, have you?"

Bowling?

What was the purpose of bowling?

Or—even worse—mini-golf?

Tira's thumbs sped across the screen. *"I will pick you up. You can tell me where to go. 2000 hours on Friday if that works for you."*

Esther: *"Aye-aye, Captain Mysterious ;)."*

"Waste of my time," Tira grumbled, and went to sleep.

* * *

Friday, January 17th, 2020

That Friday, Tira Arcelin received a message from Esther Caravan that concerned her.

Jacob Caravan was back, and that was a problem.

Tira paced on the range, clad in her tactical training gear. Ear protection and goggles on. Apple in hand. Recruits stood on the line, hands above their holsters. Gun smoke fogged the air as she paced behind them. It was 10:30 A.M. when her phone buzzed with Esther's text.

"May I vent?"

"No," Tira said, biting into her apple.

"I'm going to vent."

"Great," Tira hissed.

"What?" A recruit turned.

"Eyes on your enemies!" Tira roared.

Her phone vibrated again.

"So, my dad was having dinner with my crazy grandpa before the heart attack, and he (my grandpa) suggested something about needing to take care of a problem to 'give the world more time'. Apparently... that problem is me?"

Technically, Esther *was* a problem.

A headache for Agent 4. But—

"Any advice on how I can speed up a PPO process?" Esther continued.

But, as Tira screamed at the recruits to fire, she processed the message.

He was insane. Batshit crazy, in fact. But Tira didn't understand *why* he, too, carried such an obsessive interest in Esther.

She wanted to find out. Maybe it'd provide more insight to *why* Esther Caravan was such an important asset to the Russian government.

To Aleksey Petrov.

And, for the purposes of accomplishing her duties as assigned, she wondered—if Jacob Caravan disappeared, would anyone miss him?

"Fire!" Tira screamed again and planned her next steps.

She needed to retrieve the subject at 2000 hours tonight. If she planned her evening properly, it'd give her time to speak with Jacob Caravan and gather information from him. After all, the last time she'd checked his GPS location, he hovered near his old apartment.

How the man wasn't homeless, she wasn't sure, but he'd managed to keep the same place.

Tira would pay him a visit after work.

"Don't worry about the PPO process," Tira texted Esther. *"I will help you."*

At 6:00 P.M, Tira Arcelin contacted Esther's grandfather. Water droplets dripped from her long, blonde hair as she stood in the misty bathroom.

"Hello?" An old, ragged voice.

Thank God, his phone was still in service.

"Is this Jacob Caravan?"

A breath's pause. "Yes... who's talking?"

"Call me a..." Jesus. What was it those people from the Bible were called? Prophets? Angels?

"Call me a messenger," Tira said hoarsely. "I've got some concerns about your granddaughter and—"

Blyat. This was *ridiculous*.

"And the apocalypse," the agent finished, and covered her eyes with her palm.

"What?" Jacob said, and he sounded surprised.

"If you'd like, I'm free to meet you this evening. Would that work for you?" Tira reached her pinky into the corner of her mouth and removed the remains of the chicken she'd eaten earlier. She needed to brush her teeth.

"Um... I think so. I'm not home yet. I'm in an apartment complex just outside of the city. Would you be able to meet in the next hour?"

"Certainly. Please send me your address." Tira ran her tongue over her teeth. She knew where he lived.

"Okay but... why are you doing this? No one else has *ever* wanted to listen to me." The man was so confused, she almost felt sorry for him.

Almost.

Tira withdrew her toothbrush from the holder and turned on the faucet. "Because," she said, wetting the brush. "I am trying to find God."

After she brushed her teeth, Agent 4 prepped. She laid out her gear: baggy black sweats, a zip-up hoodie, and a snapback hat for the meeting with Jacob Caravan. It fit the neighborhood.

Then came the outfit for bowling. Jeans, combat boots, a white tee, black winter jacket. The kind of thing society deemed *outing* appropriate.

She dressed, packed, and prepped weapons.

Two switchblades. Two pistols.

Then the not-so-random extras: a body bag, gloves, cleaning supplies. Carpet cleaner. Air freshener.

Just in case he pissed himself.

Or worse.

But Tira hoped he'd cooperate. She was too tired for body disposal, followed by dealing with his "*dangerous*" granddaughter. For God's sake, she just wanted to sleep.

At 5:50 P.M, Tira arrived at Jacob's home. The rundown apartment complex stood three stories high with red brick walls. Keeping her head high and her eyes active, Tira pressed the buzzer.

Jacob's apartment was on the second floor. Tobacco and weed odors filled the air as she ascended the stairs and approached Apartment #201.

She knocked.

And the floor creaked.

The door opened. A cigarette dangled between his lips. He held a beer bottle in his hand. Barefoot in the doorway, he stood dressed in dark, thin pajama pants and a large t-shirt. Bloodshot whites. Blue-brown pupils.

Like Esther's.

"Didn't know my messenger was a rap artist," Jacob grunted as he scanned her outfit. "What's with the gym bag?"

Tira flashed a very quick smile. "I was at the gym, and I took the bus. Clearly."

"Come in." The man opened the door wider. He ran his fingers through his white hair, and his lips moved as if he was speaking to himself.

The apartment was very small, open-spaced, and well-kept despite the random gashes and dark-colored stains on the tan walls. It contained a small living room with a flower-printed recliner, a television that looked like it'd been plucked from the eighties, and a coffee table. The kitchen was tiny, and Jacob had lined four white plates in the dish rack. A small dining table, not far from the apartment entrance, contained a black Bible that lay centered on the wooden surface. And right beside it—a lone pill bottle.

"Anything to drink?" Jacob asked, gesturing towards a chair. He glanced up at the ceiling.

She followed his gaze. "No, thank you." Tira tossed her bag to the floor and looked at her wristwatch. 6:11 P.M. It would take at least twenty minutes to reach Esther's house, and she could meet Michael on the way to get the microchip. She had plenty of time to talk. "Thank you for meeting with me."

Jacob sat across from her with a fresh bottle of *Jack Daniel's* and withdrew the cigarette from his mouth. His lips moved again, and his eyes shifted from her to the Bible and back to her again. He swayed in his chair. "What did you want to know?"

Tira eyed the alcohol. Tried to process the fact that she'd mowed this man down with her motorcycle last year. "Can you tell me a little about your family history?"

"Not much to say. And what's it to *you?*"

Tira tilted her head. "Because I trust you. I've seen the signs. The evil. And I want to give people more time to find God too."

Jacob leered at her.

"Can't do that if your granddaughter's gonna be an issue, now can I?" Like a bird, Tira cocked her head the other direction.

Jacob's lips trembled. "So how do you know her? How do you know my family?"

"I know everything about your family, Mr. Caravan." Tira leaned forward. "I know what you did to your son."

Perhaps she was grasping at theatrics a bit too much, but it appeared to be working. He *was* a Caravan, after all.

And the Caravans *loved* theatrics.

Jacob shook his head. "I just wanted them to know I'm not crazy. Especially Todd. I did what I did to save people, not hurt them."

"Save them from what?"

"Will could do things. Evil things. Unnatural. The Bible warns us about them... do you read it?"

"Sure," Tira said.

"Then listen to me," Jacob whispered. "He ain't *dead.*"

Good grief. This family was too messed up to contain a microchip of government secrets. But maybe that was the *point.*

Maybe no one would *suspect* this parade of clowns to carry anything of importance.

"Who's not dead, Jacob?"

"My son. Will. I was stupid to think something satanic could die. It's still alive."

"What is?"

"The evil. The *demons* in my bloodline. Someone in my family," he growled, exposing yellow teeth, "is gonna start Armageddon."

"Well, that's unfortunate."

"You don't take me seriously."

"I'm sorry, am I coming off that way?" Tira raised an eyebrow, and it was only when Jacob's demeanor changed that she realized she'd allowed her true self to bleed into the conversation.

Fine. She'd play along.

"Tell me about Will," she said, holding back a sigh.

Jacob shivered. "False prophets will arise, perform signs and wonders to deceive the elect. The Lord gave me that scripture the night Will died. The same night he healed Todd's elbow with a touch."

Tira's watch vibrated with a message from Esther.

"I'm looking forward to beating your ass in bowling tonight ;-P."

Oh God, *that*.

Tira had almost forgotten about it.

"I always hoped I could break the cycle," Jacob muttered, raising the bottle to his lips. "I doomed us all when I slept with that whore."

Tira lifted her head. "What whore?"

"The whore of Illinois," Jacob spat. "I knocked her up with Will. God punished me."

Jacob Caravan—a man unhinged. Time ticked on. Jacob rambled. Scripture. The whore. An antichrist.

When Tira spoke, Jacob drank. When Jacob spoke, Tira assessed.

He belched, lit another cigarette, and then reached for the Bible. He knocked over the bottle of pills. It rocked to and fro. Licking his lips, he thumbed through the Bible. "Let me... let me just—" he mumbled and glanced towards the ceiling once more.

Tira did not follow his gaze this time. She'd already determined nothing was up there. "What are the pills for, Mr. Caravan?"

Peering into the Bible, Jacob stopped flipping the pages, raised his eyes, and frowned. Grunting, he grasped the bottle and flung it across the room. It struck the wall with a sharp patter before hitting the floor.

Tira's fingers snuck to her waistband. Narrowing her eyes, she watched him.

"They medicate us to—to hide *Biblical truths*!" Jacob yelled, pointing downwards at the Bible. He dragged on the cigarette and then fell into a coughing fit. Wheezing, he sipped the *Jack Daniel's* and stumbled. "They kept trying to tell me I was sick in the mind. That I was bipolar, or schizo, or whatever diseases they come up with to mask the *truth in our minds*." He jabbed the side of his head with his forefinger.

"Why, Mr. Caravan?" Tira was growing impatient.

"Because," he coughed, "I can see things other people can't. I can see demons." He finished the whiskey and then slammed the bottle onto the table. "I'm well-practiced, ya know. Seeing demons." He leaned forward. "After talking to Todd, I'm convinced that they—they all need to go." The old man slumped back in his chair.

Alright.

It was time to be more direct.

As Tira opened her mouth to speak, Jacob lunged from his chair and stared at the ceiling.

"*No!*" His palm came down hard against the table. His grey-stubbled chin quivered a little. "*Jesus* heals. Not you, not *me*, not my *son*." He ran fingers through his hair. Tears streamed from his eyes, the eyes that reminded her so much of Esther.

Calmly, Tira stood and glanced at her watch. 7:27 P.M.

"I need you to be clear with me, Mr. Caravan. Are you going to kill Esther Caravan?"

With a gasp, Jacob flung the bottle. It ricocheted off the surface, and whiskey splattered all over the wall.

Suddenly, Tira understood the stains and cuts on the walls. Her eyes fell to the bag on the floor and then returned to Jacob, who was now pacing back and forth in the kitchen and muttering '*Adso*' repeatedly like a madman.

He *was* a madman.

"*Jacob.*" Agent 4 spoke his name with tart annoyance. "*Jacob*, do you intend to *kill your granddaughter?*"

He stopped pacing, looked up at the ceiling again, and then spoke in a clipped tone. "Phil Jameson." Swaying, he fell against the refrigerator and put out the cigarette on his arm. "Phil... Will. Phil. Will."

What the *hell*?

Phil Jameson?

The Phil Jameson whose underwear *she'd sliced* at the research center?

Tira watched him in stunned silence. She wanted to ask how he *knew* Phil Jameson, but she wasn't getting anywhere with him. When he reached to open another bottle of whiskey, the agent realized she never would.

"Phil. Will," Jacob muttered, twisting the cap from the bottle and drinking again. He turned towards the knife block and stared at it. "God said my family is a fucking breeding ground for Satan."

Sighing, Tira bent down and unzipped her bag.

She'd heard enough.

Jacob paced again. "Phil. Will. *Phil. Will!*" His veins stood out on his neck.

Rolling her eyes, Tira straightened up and pulled tight, black gloves onto her hands. She took off her hat and placed it on the table. Her vision narrowed to the pulse in his neck.

Jacob let out a breath, glanced towards her, and inched towards the knives on the counter. "You shouldn't be here," he slurred. His legs wobbled, and he looked at the knife block again.

Tightening her jaw, Tira approached him. "Please don't struggle, and it will be much quicker."

"Oh, *hell!*" Jacob flung his arm towards the knife block.

Tira landed on his back. Covered his mouth before he could scream. The larger man thrashed in her arms, letting out muffled cries, tried to bite her hand. His fingers snaked towards the knives as he bucked his hips and tried to regain control.

He couldn't.

"Nuh-uh," Tira hissed, and drove his body into the edge of the counter.

Jacob reached for a glass in the sink. Clanked it against the counter to make noise. *Any* noise. His arm flailed up. He tossed the glass into the air.

Smart.

It flipped. Came rushing down.

Tira drove her knee into his groin.

Reached out.

And caught the glass before it could shatter against the sink.

She returned it to the counter.

Minimum mess. Minimum noise.

Inhale. Exhale. Breathe.

Jacob was large. For an old man he was strong.

Tira was stronger. Agile.

She swept his leg, and letting out a breath, pushed him face down into the carpet. The way she did it... it was almost gentle.

Broken, muffled screams. Face down, he rocked back and forth like a wobbling canoe.

Tira kept her hand hard over his mouth as he rolled to face her.

Their eyes met.

She crushed his floundering legs between hers.

Panic rose into his eyes.

He tried to bear hug her.

It gave her leverage. Tira met his eyes. Listened to the desperate hissing sounds his breath made through her fingers. Smelled the tobacco in his spurts of air.

Snaking her other arm into his grasp, she placed the bony portion of her forearm across his throat, just above his Adam's apple, and pressed down.

His eyes widened. Time passed. Tira's mind ran blank.

And his face lost color.

Tira's muscles quivered as she crushed the air from his body—

Inhale. Exhale. Breathe.

—and their eyes met one last time. As she sank into his dying gaze, Tira caught her breath at the familiarity of his eyes. Grimacing, she crushed his windpipe, thinking of Esther's eyes and how they sparkled with mischief. How *prominent* those odd, blue-brown eyes seemed to be in this family.

No matter how evil, or murderous, or insane this family could be, the beauty in their eyes never changed.

Tira looked away.

An unfamiliar feeling tugged at her gut. She focused on the yellow kitchen tile as Esther Caravan's grandfather died beneath her arm.

When his body stilled, she released her grip. Sniffing mucus back into her nose, Tira brushed his eyelids down to cover his eyes. "You should have given me a straight answer."

She checked her watch.

Fuck.

Bowling might need to be postponed.

"Er..." Tira bit her lip and pulled out her phone.

"What's up, Tira?"

"Michael. New plan. I need you now, at Jacob Caravan's apartment. I'm messaging you the address now. Bring the microchip."

"Damn it, Tira, I'm trying to get foo-"

She ended the call.

Tira pushed up her sleeves and got to work. After rolling the dead man into the body bag, she zipped it, straightened up, and then scowled at the tile where his body had been.

Stains. Fresh urine and feces.

Cursing in Russian, Tira stormed towards the cleaning supplies.

"I'm going to be late," the agent texted Esther.

And Tira scrubbed the floor, discarded the trash, repositioned the items as they'd been.

Esther would have to wait.

When Michael arrived and stepped into the apartment with a black case in his hand and a *McDonald's* bag in the other, he stared at the body bag. "Jesus."

Impatient, Tira gestured to the body bag. "Can you take care of this?"

Michael leaned his head to the side. "Really? Again?"

"I'm sorry. I lost track of time and—" Tira stopped. "What do you mean *again?*"

"Nothing. I got it. Where are you headed?"

"I have a business meeting."

"In *that?*" Michael waved his McDonald's bag towards her outfit. "What the hell are you wearing, Ice Cube?"

"You are not making any sense. I am not wearing an ice cube. Is that the chip?"

Michael handed her the case. "Yes. Quick distraction—shove it in. Just like I was conceived. Anyway, what *business* meeting is happening at dinner time? My food is cold now, you know." It was his turn to gesture at the body bag.

"I don't have time for this. I'll repay you. Favorite hooker?"

"I've got two."

"Threesome on me." Tira flung the athletic bag over her shoulder and started towards the door. "If you need me, I will be bowling."

"*Bowling?*"

"Yes. It is the thing where you throw the ball at the—"

"Please just leave," Michael said.

And she did.

Agent 4 sauntered down the hallway.

Then, once she reached the parking lot, she ran.

In the SUV, clothing flew. Deodorant smeared. In the backseat, she tugged up her jeans, jerking her hips up in repetitive frustration as the vehicle shook.

Once changed, she crawled to the front, smashed her boot against the gas, and screeched from the parking space.

The drive to Esther's home was a wild one. She was certain the city cameras would send her another ticket.

"Be there soon," Tira typed, clearing the intersection and then blowing through a stop sign.

She *despised* being late.

Even for dumb things like bowling.

Tossing the phone onto the passenger seat, Tira re-bundled her hair into a sloppy bun and swerved with one hand to avoid a jaywalker.

As she sped towards the suburb, her mood felt strangely elevated. Tonight hadn't been her ideal night, and she still wanted to go to bed, but she supposed after a successful evening she could allow herself a little fun. Relaxation.

Whatever the subhumans called it.

"Remember to insert the microchip," she said under her breath, glancing to make sure the road was clear before continuing past another stop sign.

For the first time today, her heart *raced*. Higher than it'd spiked while killing Jacob Caravan.

She didn't like it.

So, as Tira whipped around the corner and flew onto Esther's street, she snarled a little.

"I've arrived," Tira messaged.

The tires screamed as she screeched to a halt against the icy driveway.

Inhale. Exhale. Breathe.

Tira eyed the front door and let out a slow, drawn-out breath. The front door swung inwards, and Agent 4's breath caught as the brown-haired girl stepped outside and strolled towards the car.

The house light glowed against her hair, bound in a loose bun at the back of her neck.

Tira scanned.

Noticed the way her hips swayed in her tight jeans.

Acknowledged the hint of cleavage beneath the long-sleeved black V-neck shirt.

Then Esther smiled, biting the corner of her bottom lip as she approached the car.

"Fuck," Tira whispered.

Cold air broke into the heated car as Esther Caravan opened the door. "Hello, Officer Mysterious," Esther purred, and her eyes sparkled.

"I apologize for my tardy behavior," Tira said, flashing a brief smile, and realizing that the torturous, fluttery feeling in her stomach had returned. "I needed to take care of an issue at work."

VERSE 2

~ WALK. DON'T RUN. ~

Friday, January 17th, 2020
Chicago, Illinois

Esther had cried twice today.

Once in the shower. Once on the way to dance practice. But she wasn't sad.

She was fucking mad.

It was humiliating, what'd happened last night. And she was hurt that Mariel didn't seem to give a shit.

Not one fucking shit about her feelings.

No, she wasn't sad.

She was *fucking* livid.

Mariel texted his first apology at 10 A.M. She didn't respond. He texted again. Still, she didn't respond.

Because fuck him.

But by the third apology, Esther decided she'd cooled off enough to reply.

"It's fine," Esther texted, and stuffed the phone back into her pocket.

But he persisted throughout the day, throughout her classes, throughout her time at the bookstore.

"You're still mad at me, aren't you?"

"Please talk to me."

"I miss you."

"I want to hold you again. And not sexually, I promise I won't expect sex for a while."

"Esther, can I see you tonight? Let's meet somewhere."

Finally, after she finished scanning the last customer's purchase, Esther responded to him again. *"I have plans tonight."* When she sent the text, she felt a ripple of excitement, and then it was overshadowed with a small sense of guilt.

"Where?"

Sighing, Esther slammed the register drawer, typing with one hand. "*Friend of mine.*"

"*Who? What friend?*"

"Mariel, just shut the fuck up," she snapped, turning off her phone. As she stood behind the counter, Esther wanted to cry again. The emotions overwhelmed her.

Anger. Embarrassment. Fear that Hawk would *say* something. Excitement. Guilt. Excitement that she had an evening with Officer Mysterious. Guilt because she felt excited about it.

But why *should* she feel guilty? Because she hadn't appreciated a second chance with Mariel? She wanted him.

Now she had him.

And yet she was *choosing* to spend time with someone else tonight.

But still, he didn't seem to understand that she deserved space to process and figure out what the hell was going on—not only in the world, but within herself.

But as for the strangeness of Mariel's return, she began to create logical scenarios to explain away his supposed resurrection.

Perhaps he had never been dead. Maybe he worked for the government. Maybe *she* was insane.

And this is why she drank.

And how Mariel ended up at her place again last night.

The thing was—Esther had settled in to enjoy a night on her own. Pizza, and mixed drinks that had *burned* down through her system and right between her legs. That was normal when she was drunk. She didn't mind it, because she'd most often just take care of it her damn self.

Well, Esther tried.

Sprawled across the couch. Closed her eyes. Slipped her fingers into her panties and rubbed herself a little, humming in self-pleasure as her face burned, and her thoughts dissolved into fantasies like normal. Her fantasies varied. People were normally shadows. Males. Females. Depended on what she craved that day.

Today she craved ownership. Not *owning*.

Being owned.

Someone confident. Skilled. Expert in denial and skillful in release. Someone who let her *bite* just a little before gripping her by the throat and saying—

"*Enough.*"

And that shadowy person slammed into her from behind, pulled her hair, and whispered commands and dirty things in her ear while making her squeal in all the right ways until those whispers became loud and familiar and—

Russian.

And as Esther's body nearly seized with impending orgasm, she jolted up and pulled her hand from her pants. Wide-eyed and confused, Esther then grabbed her phone and begged for Mariel to meet her at home.

She needed Mariel, wanted him, needed to fill her mind and body with *him*.

But for fuck's sake, Esther hadn't expected the night to end with a pornographic video. It'd sobered her very fast, enough to chase down Hawk and consider snapping his neck.

While the evening ended in a heartwarming manner, Esther still didn't trust him.

Oh well.

So, with all of these things in mind, including the health of her father and his random decision to break bread with Jacob Caravan, Esther's mind was a mess. Only one thing grounded her and gave her warm anticipation.

Bowling with Officer Mysterious.

As Esther counted money in the register, the door swung open. She looked up and then froze. "Gabe. What're you doing here?"

The young man grinned and came towards her. His hands fidgeted in the pockets of his athletic winter jacket. The tight baseball pants he wore squeezed his muscular legs as he leaned onto one leg. "Just got out of practice. You're wearing the dancing pendant." His smile grew warm.

Esther nodded. "Mmhmm." This was awkward. "Need a book or something?"

"No." Gabe came up to the counter and leaned into it. He looked down at her. "I've got a question. Any reason why I had to lie for you this morning?"

Esther blinked. "Huh?"

A grin flickered across his lips. "A little birdy messaged me on Facebook this morning, asking me if I was... " he snapped his fingers. "How did he word it? Oh. *Fucking* you last night."

Now she was cold.

Fuck Hawk.

"What are you talking about?"

"Don't freak out, Esther, I told him yes." Gabe's jaw twitched, and he tried to smile again. "I told him we were together. Had Hawk been *smart*, he would've asked where I was last night instead of asking a direct question like—"

Catching her breath, Esther rushed around the counter and snatched him into a hug. She squeezed her eyes shut. "Thank you so much," she whispered. As she tightened her arms around his neck, she felt him rest his chin on her shoulder. "I'm sorry. You deserve so much better, Gabe. I mean it."

He slipped his arms around her waist. "So... who was it? Was it a girl?"

Esther kept her eyes closed and enjoyed the embrace. "Yes."

She *wanted* to tell him that his best friend had come back. But she couldn't.

Chuckling, Gabe released her and stepped back. "Esther. My dick will always be ready for you. And feel free to add your girlfri—"

"Gabe." Lightly, she backhanded his cheek. "Keep your small penis in your pants."

He laughed and swaggered towards the door. "You're missing out." Stopping at the door, he glanced at her, and there was a sense of longing in his eyes. "Don't feel guilty, Esther. You're my best friend and you always will be." Winking, he opened the door. "See ya. Have fun eating pussy."

Gabe's laughter faded as a paperback streaked through the air. The door slammed before it could strike his head. It bounced off of the glass and dropped to the ground.

* * *

The rest of the day crawled.

Esther tried to ignore Hawk's incessant questioning as she dug through her closet to find an outfit. Yoga pants and a t-shirt didn't seem... good enough. "Go away, Hawk, I'm trying to change," she snapped, sifting through the hangers on the rack.

"Well, where ya going?"

"Hawk, *please.*"

Finally, he became bored and left her alone.

By the time she'd showered, perfumed, and dressed, Tira had messaged to tell her she was running late.

And that was just fine, because Patricia would be home from the hospital in a few minutes, and her arrival would distract Hawk. A blessing.

Because Esther had no desire to expose Tira Arcelin to her annoying little brother.

As she threw her hair into a bun at the back of her neck and rubbed the lip gloss into her lips, her phone buzzed. Her heart rate peaked.

Tira: *"I've arrived."*

So damn *formal*. Officer Mysterious needed to relax. A massage. She looked fit—did she let people touch her the way she'd massaged Esther's wrists?

Did anyone else *care* for her? Spoil her?

Hell, did she ever get *drunk?*

That image was hilarious to think about.

But after the emotional rollercoaster Esther had managed to survive that morning and afternoon, Tira Arcelin was the most *refreshing* thing she'd placed her eyes on today.

How could someone look so arresting by simply leaning back in the driver's seat of a big, black Yukon with blackened rims?

As she rested her hand upon the steering wheel, Tira's body reclined a little, and the angle accentuated the length of her body. The t-shirt emphasized the muscles of her arms, the swell of her breasts, her rigid abdomen, and the curve of her hips in those tight jeans. Blonde strands of hair fell over her green eyes, as if she'd been in a rush to get her hair up. It suited her—the chaotic, militant look.

It suited her real nice.

So did the arched eyebrow.

"Hello, Officer Mysterious." Esther stepped into the car, unable to restrain the grin playing across her lips.

"I apologize for my tardy behavior," Tira said. "I needed to take care of an issue at work."

"You work too much." Esther buckled her seatbelt. "This is why we're doing this."

Tira put the car in drive. "Where are we going?"

"*Bowling JoJo's.* It's just outside the city. It's a cool place. It has a game room, food, karaoke. I'll get you there." Esther rested her arm on the door and smiled.

Tira did not respond. Her eyes glued to the road, as if the city had committed a crime against her.

Silence.

Esther spoke again. "So... when you're with someone you usually talk to them."

Tira's jaw twitched. A few seconds later, she responded quietly. "How are you?"

Suddenly, Esther wasn't sure how to respond. "I'm... I've been good. How about you?"

Small talk.

The air in the car held so much more than *small talk* but—

"I am tired." Tira brought her other hand to the steering wheel and leaned back a little.

"*And* moody." Esther darted a glance towards Tira, looking at the position of her body again, sliding her eyes over the outline of the young woman's profile. Her soft lips. Her jaw. Her throat.

How could driving a car be *sexy*?

"Did you have a question?" Tira asked, meeting Esther's eyes with a slight smile on the corner of her lips. "Or did you see another person sleeping on the side of the road?"

Esther's body went hot. "I was *appreciating* the view. Outside."

"Hmm. I see." Tira turned her eyes back to the road.

It didn't take long to get to *Bowling JoJo's*. The parking lot was busy, bustling with teenagers and young adults, loud music and loud cars. The building spread across the parking lot with one main entrance. Several groups smoked outside. A young couple made out near the doorway as Tira and Esther approached.

Tira led the way, her hands in her back pockets, and she cleared her throat as she approached the doors ahead of Esther.

Immediately, the couple broke apart and shot towards the parking lot in a fit of giggles.

Tira opened the door and stepped aside for Esther. "They're probably going to do *illegal things* in the car," she said, watching them.

Esther stepped by her, eyeing her. "And you've never done illegal things in a car before?"

The blush crept into Tira's skin. She followed her and huffed a little. "No."

"Well, aren't you boring."

"But I have done illegal things on the countertop of a public kitchen." Tira's voice was nonchalant, a soft whisper.

Like the whisper in her ear during her short-lived fantasy.

And Esther could feel the warmth of Tira's body behind her; the heat of her breath near her ear.

Her legs lost stability.

"Maybe not so boring then," she said, breathless. "Shall we?" Esther approached the end of the long line of people that awaited the help desk.

Young people laughed, shouted, and mocked each other as the lights flashed in the dim alley. A nervous, off-key, red-headed girl sang *Hit Me Baby One More Time* on the karaoke stage. Her voice shook.

After waiting in line for fifteen minutes, Esther and Tira took the alley near the wall, farthest away from the karaoke stage and its audience. As Esther tightened the strings on her bowling shoes, she looked up at Tira, whose eyes fixated on the screen above them.

"So, you've never bowled," Esther said, laughing. "Why am I not surprised?"

Tira stood. Looked around. Her eyes darted quickly, as if she couldn't stop observing, couldn't stop reacting to every stimulus around her. It looked exhausting. "I am a fast learner," she said, finally looking at Esther.

"*Mmhmm.* Let's make a bet."

Tira frowned. "What bet?"

"Well, let's see." Esther smirked, moving towards the alley screen to begin the round. The karaoke girl was getting annoying. "You seem confident. We'll play three rounds." Her fingers tapped the screen. It froze, and she pounded it furiously until it responded again. "If you win two out of three, you can make me do anything you want. And if *I* win two out of three..." Esther turned and faced Tira. "You have to do anything *I* want."

Tira placed her foot on one of the chairs. Placed her elbow onto her knee. She tilted her head and then descended her cheek into the palm of her hand. A smile played across her lips. It twinkled into her eyes. "Alright," she said, her voice cool. "Let's bowl."

Esther went first and struck nine out of ten. When it was Tira's turn, she laughed as the woman tried to mimic her movements. She swung too hard, and she flung the ball into a different lane just as a young man prepared to bowl his round.

He glared at Tira.

Tira scowled back.

Esther just laughed.

Esther threw two strikes in row. Tira's movements grew more natural, more comfortable, but she missed the pins two more times.

"Loser," Esther said gently, bumping Tira aside with her hip as she retrieved her ball. "Sorry, Officer Mysterious. This round is mine."

Quickly, she moved. Esther brought her arm back but, before she released it, Tira's ball slammed into the alley and sped downwards. Esther's pins exploded apart, all ten of them, and she watched with wide eyes.

Behind her, Tira's breath warmed her skin as she murmured into her ear. "Who's the loser again?"

Furious, Esther whirled to face her, and the neon lights flashed against Tira's composed expression and increased the intensity of her eyes. For a moment, she became lost in them, and then her breath came fast when she remembered she was angry. "That's *cheating.*"

Tira tilted her head and smiled a little. "I'm sorry. Remember, I don't know how to bowl. I misunderstood the rules, I suppose."

Esther whipped her arm behind her, towards the alley. "That one counts as mine."

"*Hmm.* Alright." Tira stepped backwards. "I'll still win though."

Esther won the first round and mocked Tira before the second round began. However, her mockery faded fast as Tira threw continuous strikes.

Pissed, Esther watched as the young woman's slender form moved with grace across the alley, noticing the way her hips swayed in the dim lights, how tight those jeans hugged her *extremely* well-proportioned ass and—

"Wake up," Tira brushed off her hands and snapped her fingers in Esther's face. She approached the table to take a sip of water. Sweat glistened on her face and neck, and a few strands of hair clung to her skin. "You've got one more round. Make it count."

Esther narrowed her eyes. "Have you ever heard of the mercy rule?" She stomped towards the alley, and her shoes clunked against the floor. "You suck."

"Ah, but I don't," Tira called. "Clearly. It seems I will have won after you throw this round."

"Fuck you," Esther threw the ball without care. By some miracle, she managed a strike. Shaking her head, she turned to face Tira and frowned. "Well, at least I ended with some dignity."

Tira finished the last of her water and rested her foot on the chair again. "I'd apologize, but I am not sorry."

Cautious, Esther approached her. Her heart thundered against her chest, and she fought to ignore it.

Bowling was a workout.

Stopping in front of Tira, she locked into the eyes of Officer Mysterious. "So... what is it?"

"What is what?" Tira raised an eyebrow.

"You won. We made a bet." Esther cleared her throat. "What are you—going to make me do?"

"Ah." Tira straightened up, removing her foot from the chair and stepping a little closer. Once again, she tilted her head, and her eyes scanned Esther's face like a fucking laser. As the lights flickered across her face, the blush deepened within her cheeks. "*Hmmm.*"

They were very close. Tira smelled of perfume and fresh shampoo, and Esther could see the soft pulse beneath the officer's creamy throat. She followed Tira's eyes with hers and flushed when they fell to her lips.

Panic crept to her heart. It went wild. Pounded in her ears as Esther found herself running her tongue along her lips. Tira's lips looked very soft, very alluring.

And Officer Mysterious leaned in, just a little closer. "I want..." she spoke in a soft, low voice, hesitating for a moment.

Esther wanted to step back. Push her back. Something. But she *couldn't.*

"I want..." Tira whispered again, "...to give you my win."

Catching her breath, Esther looked at her with confusion and relief. "*What?*"

Tira stepped back and shrugged. "I am curious. I am giving you my win. You tell me what to do."

"You're not serious, are you?"

"I am. What could you do to me?" Tira raised her eyebrows.

A deep, mischievous laugh bubbled from Esther's throat.

Minutes later, Tira stood on the karaoke stage, stiff beneath the spotlight. Squeezing the microphone, her fingers went white. Her eyes were wide, her face red, and her nose flared with rage.

Esther nearly tumbled from her chair with laughter. The onlookers whistled, hooted, and yelled at her to sing as the music for *It's Raining Men* blasted through the speakers.

"Cheer her on, guys, she's nervous!" Esther shrieked with glee, holding her stomach as the muscles burned from her laughter.

The *Weather Girls* began to sing about the rise in humidity. As her upper lip curled in a snarl, Tira's eyes turned towards the lyrics' screen.

"Come on, Tira, you promised!" Esther put her forehead against the table and then rocked back into her chair. She hadn't laughed this hard in...

Well, she couldn't even remember.

"Tonight, for the last—no, first, time. Half past twelve. No. 2200." Tira's voice was flat and furious, growling the wrong lyrics into the microphone. Her face grew redder.

Esther screamed and stood up, clapping, calling attention to the stage from the rest of the bowlers. "You're supposed to *sing* the lyrics, not *speak* them!"

Lips moving, Tira shot Esther a scowl that almost frightened her.

"You look better than you sing!" a drunk man called out, waving his hand towards her in blatant disregard.

Tira's head whipped to find the bearded drunk.

Something about the way her eyes *hunted* for him gave Esther the chills. Not because she was frightening.

But because she was *beautiful* up there—a woman filled with rage, loneliness, and social ineptitude. A woman who masked so well but *felt* so much she'd probably combust if triggered at the wrong moment.

But combustion wasn't always *bad*.

And, for an inexplicable reason, Esther wanted to be that trigger.

But first, Esther needed to shut down the impending homicide.

On stage, Tira's body shook, and her eyes were murderous.

"The deal's over," she spat, and she twisted the top of the microphone and pulled its contents out of it. A shrill tone shrieked from the speakers.

Several women gasped.

"Oh dear," Esther said, and stood up.

"And for the record," Tira shouted, pointing her finger at the man and storming towards the edge of the stage. "I'm going to—"

The lights went off.

Black.

Everything went black.

The power died with an exhausted groan.

And the earth began to rumble.

First a tremor. And then, as the lights glitched and began to strobe, the building began to sway.

"Um," Esther gasped.

People began to shout.

"It's a bomb!" A man roared in the darkness.

And then—panic.

People shouted for each other. Scrambled. Tables tipped. Glass shattered. The earth kept shaking.

And Esther realized it wasn't a bomb.

It was an earthquake.

And it was getting worse.

"Tira?" Esther cried, dropping to her knees to find cover, any cover, in the darkness.

"Tyler! Baby! *Where's my son?"* A woman screamed across the chaos.

Esther scrambled to get under a table, but patrons flipped them, fought for them, knocked them down. Ice water spilled across the floor as Esther tried to crawl away from the animalistic terror. And with horror, she realized something that should have calmed her, but it didn't.

The earthquake wasn't even that bad.

The people, the crowd, the *panic*—now *that* was *bad.*

"Tira!" Esther cried out and searched for her in the strobing lights.

Had she fled? Was she hiding? It'd be *smart*, and Tira was *smart.*

A girl wailed, sobbing next to her. A brief flash of light captured the girl's red hair as she sobbed on the floor with her butt in the air. The karaoke ginger.

A hand grabbed her arm.

"Tira?" Esther gasped, but the lights cut across a young man's face. Blood smeared over his lips.

She shrieked.

"You're not my wife," he cried, but his grip tightened, and she realized it was buffalo sauce on his mouth. Not blood.

"Let go of me then, please," Esther hissed, pulling away, falling backwards until her hand landed in something slimy, mushy, *wet.*

She didn't know what it was.

"She looks like you," the man laughed, but it wasn't a real laugh. It was too desperate. "Have you seen—"

"Get *off* of her."

Tira.

Sharp. Cold. Commanding.

But still murderous.

Esther felt herself yanked to her feet.

"Walk, don't run," Tira ordered, and the lights flickered over her face.

Focused. Calm. Collected.

"Okay," Esther breathed, and latched onto her arm.

And they walked forward.

As people scrambled, screamed, and sobbed, and as the building shook and swayed, Esther followed Tira through the chaos.

A bowling ball rolled across the walkway.

"Where are we going?" Esther asked, but she didn't need to ask. She knew wherever Tira took her, she'd be safe.

"To the office down the hall. To find cover," Tira said through her teeth, and angled her way through the scattering crowd with lithe concentration. "We'll survive the earthquake. The *people* are making it worse."

Their pace quickened. Down the hall. Past the restrooms. Past the people covering their heads next to the walls. People still screamed of bombs, of terrorism, of missing friends, and missing family.

Wobbling, swaying, Esther clung to Tira in the darkness as they approached the private office door. "Can you kick it down?"

A pause. Was the woman *laughing?*

"No," Tira said, and she turned the handle as if she hadn't a care in the world. "It is unlocked."

The darkness swallowed them. As the lights flickered and lamps wobbled, Esther felt herself pushed towards a wooden office desk with limited space beneath it.

One person. Two, if you squeezed.

"Get under the desk until this stops," Tira ordered, pushing her.

Sweat trickled over her face. Mascara stung her eyes, and Esther fell to her knees and crawled beneath the desk. She curled up her knees and embraced herself. Would it stop? What if it didn't?

What if this was the first sign of the Great Tribulation mentioned in Revelations?

The signs and wonders. The earthquakes. The wars.

The *resurrections.*

But as she peered out from under the rattling desk, and the lights dashed on and off, her gaze found Tira. Suddenly, she felt no fear.

Tira knelt outside of the desk, blocking her in, scanning the little office as if she could capture the ceiling by herself if it collapsed. And if the earthquake grew worse, and the ceiling cracked apart, it *would* collapse. It would split and cave in, and it'd fall upon Tira's head while her body guarded the desk to ensure Esther's safety beneath it.

And Esther would never forgive herself.

So, with a small whimper, Esther Caravan touched the officer's arm. "Tira?"

Her head tilted a little. The lights flickered over her face. "Are you okay?"

"Yes. But you aren't. Come protect yourself, too. Please?"

And Esther reached for her, grasped her arm, and Tira's body felt stiff. Taut. Unyielding. But Esther persisted, tugging with gentle persuasion, until the officer relaxed and gave in to Esther's pleas.

Esther readjusted. Pressed against the wooden surface, her head became stuck on the exterior until Tira's hands grasped her face and pulled her in.

Close against her chest.

It was very tight. Tira's elbow dug into her shoulder. Their arms and legs locked together. Their breathing, loud and warm, shook like the building. And yet, their bodies molded as if survival offered them no choice.

And Esther listened to the beat of Tira's heart. It thumped into her ear until the shaking reduced to tremors, and the tremors rumbled to a gentle end.

The lights buzzed again. On. Off. Flashed.

And then clicked on.

The voices outside of the office were muffled. Sobs. Shouts. Even laughter.

Thump-thump. Thump-thump.

Tira's heart almost lulled her to sleep. She didn't want to move. She *couldn't* move... because they'd tangled their limbs beneath the desk.

"Are you okay?" Tira murmured. She didn't move either.

"Yes," Esther whispered, eyes still shut. "Are you?"

"No." Curt.

Esther's eyes opened.

Tira made no effort to release her, but her tone suggested annoyance.

"Why not?" Esther asked, and she made the decision to move first. Her head came up, away from Tira's chest, and when she raised her eyes—she couldn't breathe.

Because Esther's lips were a breath away from Tira's jaw. And, as she created distance, she found herself face to face with the officer, breathing hard, the space so tight that if either of them moved they'd...

... kiss.

And she'd betray the man she'd desperately wanted back.

Mariel Nadier.

"I'm not okay," Tira whispered, and something flickered in her green eyes, the eyes that looked like the northern lights up close. "Because you made me go bowling. And made me sing *It's Raining Men*. And look at what happened."

Esther wasn't sure if she was supposed to laugh or punch her. She could only detangle herself from Tira, eye her with a relieved smirk, and shimmy out from under the desk.

"Well, next time," Esther said, "you can cuddle your rifle as the ceiling collapses."

*   *   *

"I'll be home soon. I'm glad you guys are okay. I love you," Esther said, and ended the call.

"Are they okay?" Tira kept both hands on the steering wheel and scanned the dark, suburban streets.

There'd been minimal damage, primarily from the mass panic the earthquake had caused. Mostly littering. A few abandoned cars.

"Yes. They're fine. Apparently, this was a mid-level earthquake. It knocked over some lamps and dishes. Maybe my dad's grill. That's it. Midwesterners caused more damage than the earthquake."

"Mmhmm." Tira didn't look at her. Just kept driving.

Esther didn't look at her either. For some reason, she couldn't.

Her phone began to vibrate, and Mariel's name flashed against the screen. Instead of excitement, she felt a sickening sense of guilt burn through her stomach like acid.

Was *he* okay? Fr. Jerome?

She should have been with him.

Not Tira.

But she didn't regret it. How could it be that she could feel both guilt and lack of regret at the same time?

"You can answer that if you want," Tira said, flitting her eyes to the lit-up screen.

Esther turned it over. "It's okay. Not right now."

The SUV rolled to a stop in front of the Caravan driveway.

"You're home," Tira said, as if Esther couldn't see where she was.

Shouldn't they discuss what happened? Discuss the reason an earthquake *that strong* shook Chicago? Wasn't that what two people *did* after they'd been tangled in each other's arms beneath a private office desk at *Bowling JoJo's?*

"Would you have kicked the door in if it hadn't been unlocked?" Esther asked and smiled a little. Her hair, having fallen loose from the bowling alley, tickled her face.

Mariel was calling again.

"I would have destroyed it using any method I could." Tira finally looked at her. There was a softness to her voice, the same one she'd had when she massaged Esther's palm.

"I had fun," Esther whispered, slowly opening the door. "Thank you for keeping me safe."

Tira didn't respond. "Good night."

It felt like good-bye.

God.

It *should* be—

"Good-bye," Esther murmured, and she stepped out of the car.

"Good-bye," Tira said, behind her, emphasizing the word as if she *meant it.*

And when Esther shot one last glance at Officer Mysterious, the glance came too late, because the tires squealed against the ice.

Tira Arcelin was gone.

Moments later, after hugs, chatter, and good-nights, Esther climbed the stairs to her room.

"Hey, Mariel," Esther said, closing the door to her room and locking it.

"Baby! Are you okay? I'm so sorry—"

As Esther lay in the fetal position in her bed, Mariel talked, filling her ears with apologies and love. He'd figure it out. Figure out what came next. Talk to her more. Give her space when she needed it.

Thump-thump. Thump-thump.

Her heartbeat had been so comforting.

"I'll figure out how to keep you safe," he was saying.

Esther closed her eyes. Imagined the heartbeat. Wondered if anyone kept Tira safe.

Or if she took on that responsibility by herself.

Mariel kept talking. His voice faded.

"Get off of her," Tira commanded.

Esther tried to stay awake.

"You there, Esther?" Mariel asked.

"Yes," she said.

"Walk, don't run," Tira ordered, and pushed her beneath the desk.

Crawled next to her for safety.

And pulled her into her arms.

"Fuck," Esther whispered, and she opened her eyes.

"What?" Mariel said, his voice loud over the phone.

Esther sat up. Cleared her throat.

She wasn't sure what was happening in the world, but one thing held true. God granted second chances in many different ways. The Caravan family rarely received second chances.

Karma, that's what they got, according to Todd and Jacob Caravan.

So, as Esther formulated the right words to say, she took a deep breath. Paused. And then—

"Mariel," she said, her voice no louder than a whisper. "I love you. So much. But I'm very confused... and I'm at my breaking point."

"Are you breaking up with me?" Mariel's voice rose to a shriek.

"No," Esther said, eyes watering. For a moment, she wished she *could*. "But I need to see you this weekend. We need to talk. No sex."

A pause.

"Just to talk," she added, and closed her eyes once more.

Verse 3

~ He Would Move the Earth ~

Friday, January 17th, 2020
Chicago, Illinois

Poked. Prodded. Manipulated.

Physically and emotionally.

It'd been Ahdam's life for the last several days, and yet the White Coats were still disappointed. Still hadn't found his *trigger*. Or whatever it was they were looking for.

He wasn't sure. Ahdam did *nothing*, and it seemed that doing *nothing* upset them more. He didn't care. He wanted to see his mother, and he was desperate to know if his father was still alive. But the White Coats kept punishing him.

"Until you pass one of our tests," Adela translated for Diane, *"you won't be able to see your mom."*

So he tried to pass the tests.

Tried to cry. To rage. To *feel*. To trigger the environment as he'd done in the West Bank.

But nothing happened... because since arriving he'd only been exposed to poking and pinching—and clicking noises in his ears as he smelled the hot, rancid breaths of White Coats who didn't brush their teeth but shined small flashlights into his pupils and bigger lights over his body.

What did they want from him? Vegetables? Wasn't this the *United States of America*? Didn't *they* have *everything*?

Each day was the same, yet different. In the morning, he'd wake up to more prodding. Eyelids pulled up. Flashlights in eyes. Spoken words he didn't understand. Gum chewing and smiles. Cartoons in the white-walled room.

Same room. Same White Coats. Same process.

The Palestinian woman, Adela, was the only light in the environment. There were a couple of White Coats who weren't all that bad, but Adela was the only one who looked at him with gentleness and care in her eyes. Sometimes she'd hold his hand.

But Diane? Oh, he still *hated* her—and she, him. Diane hadn't forgiven him for the incident last week, when he'd managed to warm the atmosphere enough to burn her skin so much that she'd been a tomato for days. The White Coats wanted vegetables? They got one. And that, too, was why they were frustrated—they'd *seen* what he'd done to that evil woman, and he hadn't been able to since. He was tired, confused, defeated. Off the routine he'd kept at home.

It'd taken him a while to figure out day versus night, because it was always dark beneath the water. He wasn't sure if he was in an ocean or a lake.

But he'd figured out a routine. At night, the White Coats went away.

And the security guards came.

In the morning, the White Coats came back.

And they'd prod again.

But because he hadn't changed the environment like he'd done to burn Diane, they weren't happy with him. That's why he hadn't been allowed to see his mother, and why they told him no news of his father.

Because he was bad. And bad kids didn't get rewards.

That's what Diane told him on a translation app.

But tonight was Friday, according to the calendar. Diane didn't work Fridays, and from the little bit of English he'd picked up, it sounded like she was doing something in Florida. Something about Disney. He'd heard of Disney before.

It sounded fun.

Still, he was happier tonight because he hadn't had to see Diane... and for another reason.

Cartoons weren't on.

Basketball was.

He *loved* basketball.

He'd been given a windowless room with a hospital bed next to the bathroom, an armchair, and a flat-screen television. As Ahdam ate his dinner—chicken nuggets, cold fries, and an apple sauce—he lounged in the armchair. His eyes darted back and forth, narrowing in on the players while they bounded back and forth and jumped.

Maybe one day he could play.

Ahdam dozed.

He awoke to a whirring sound outside of the door behind him. Then a click.

And the door opened.

The basketball game was over. Commentators filled the screen, shiny-haired white men in suits. Ahdam caught his breath and whirled in his chair to see who'd entered the room.

A security guard. A tan-skinned young man with dark, curly hair and a smug grin. His lanky body barely filled the tactical uniform he wore, which hung baggy around his hips.

The night shift guards were messier than the day shift guards. Their uniforms weren't as neat, and they were often louder outside of his room.

But they didn't come in. They *never* came in.

A fry dropped from the corner of his pocket. Ahdam didn't flinch as he looked at the guard, but his heart rate shot up.

The guard glanced around, as if he was checking to make sure no one else was in the room, and then he walked towards Ahdam. Grabbed his shoulders.

And nudged him towards the exit.

Wide-eyed, Ahdam obeyed. What choice did he have?

But this was all very abnormal, and he was very confused. How long had he been sleeping? Had he been bad again? What would they do to punish him?

Sleepy, Ahdam stumbled into the hallway. Another security guard, a bearded white man who filled his uniform *too* much, waited in the dark with a nervous grimace on his face.

They led him down the hallway. Red exit signs cast a dim glow and broke the darkness just enough to allow Ahdam a glimpse of the other steel doors that lined the walls.

The other prison cells.

Was his mother in one of them? His father?

Maybe they were taking him to see his family.

Quietly, the men spoke, guiding him with little pokes, reminding him of their control. So Ahdam kept walking until they stopped outside a steel door at the end of the hallway, scanned a card, and pushed him inside the room.

* * *

The lights clicked on.

It was a lab—windowed walls with a view of the night-blackened water. Hospital bed. Computers. Nothing he hadn't seen before.

Except for one thing.

In the center of the room stood an upright, tubular enclosure with a latched door and three metal steps leading to it. Ahdam wasn't sure if it was glass or plastic, but one thing was clear—whatever was meant to go inside was meant to be *watched*.

The curly-haired guard opened the latch to the door and gestured for Ahdam to go in.

Ahdam shook his head.

The guard gave him a look, one that reminded him of the Israeli construction worker before he'd bulldozed the villager's home.

He didn't have a *choice*, did he?

Swallowing hard, Ahdam mounted the steps. Entered the tube. And turned.

The door slammed shut.

And locked.

Wide-eyed, Ahdam rested his palms on the surface and leaned his forehead against it.

The guards looked at each other, spoke again, and then left.

Ahdam's heart thumped faster.

What were they *doing* to him? Was it another test?

Moments passed.

The lights clicked off, leaving nothing but the minimal glow of the computers.

Ahdam's breath fogged the tube.

And then the door latch whirred. It opened. The room lit up again. The guards came back in. And with them?

His mother.

Ahdam gasped and smiled. The smile faded.

Handcuffed in the front, Dina stumbled into the room, wearing a uniform like he'd seen the nurses wear—but orange. Her eyes were red, her cheeks wet. The hijab loosened a little as the guards gripped her by the arms and turned her to face Ahdam.

"Be brave, Ahdam," she whispered, and she smiled through her tears.

The curly-haired guard—Curly—laughed a little and pushed her down to sit on a stool with wheels.

Ahdam scowled and slapped his hands against the surface. He growled. He wanted to tell them to stop touching his mother.

Curly typed something into his phone and held it in front of Dina's face.

She shook her head.

The guard shouted at her. His skinny face looked bigger when he did that. His mouth opened like a snake.

Dina jumped, let out a sob.

Ahdam pounded the surface. It was glass. Thick glass. The impact of his strike rippled through his muscles.

Curly drew his firearm and pointed it towards Ahdam.

Dina lunged up. They pushed her back down. Told her something else.

Ahdam let out a wail.

Slowly, Dina looked up to meet his eyes. With a shuddering breath, she spoke to him. "Ahdam, he wants me to tell you if nothing else will work, maybe this will. I don't know what that means, but be brave and—"

The bearded guard clamped a hand over her mouth and cocked his head towards his coworker.

Curly holstered his gun. Reached for Dina.

And yanked off her hijab.

The light glistened against her dark bun, casting a beautiful sheen that he'd always loved to see.

But it was not for *them* to see. They had no right, and Allah would make them suffer for it.

Curly reached into his pocket and produced a pocketknife. With a grunt, he gripped Dina's ponytail and sliced into her hair.

Dina sobbed.

Ahdam opened his mouth to *say* something, but he couldn't.

He *never* could.

Thick bunches of hair darkened the floor.

Ahdam could never defend his people. He could never stand up to evil like his father could. How could he? He didn't have a voice. He couldn't shout or warn these men that Allah's wrath would come, because it always did, and he couldn't curse them as he'd heard the villagers curse the construction workers.

Ahdam could only watch. Like a caged animal, he could only *watch*.

Her hair fell in clumps. The ponytail was gone.

The guards were laughing.

But they weren't done.

One of them produced a razor. He wasn't sure which one, because the pressure in his skull mounted like a machine in his mind.

Beard. It was the bearded guard, because his huge thumb flipped the razor's switch and brought it to life. It vibrated. In a way, it reminded Ahdam of the bulldozers in the West Bank... because those monsters vibrated too.

And as the razor hummed through the rest of Dina's hair, and sheared the remainder of her dignity, Ahdam let out an animalistic scream.

And the earth vibrated too.

With abrupt force, the building rocked.

It flung the guards against the counter. Dina tumbled to the floor.

But Ahdam stood strong. Tears spilled from his eyes as the building vibrated and shook. Outside the window, bubbles rose and water churned. Rocks slammed against the building. The lake, the ocean—*whatever* it was—*gargled* and rushed with sudden force against the walls.

With widened eyes, the guards floundered and laughed in awe as the building shook. High-fived as they tumbled against the counter, almost trampling his mother as she crawled towards her trapped son.

The scream released the pressure in his chest. The building groaned. And the lights went off. Monitors flickered, a white light flashed, and an ear-splitting alarm screamed into rhythm,

"*Ahdam!*" Dina screamed and reached for the stairs.

The guards weren't laughing anymore. The emergency light illuminated their twisted faces, and their mouths opened as they grabbed for any stable surface.

The world swayed. Ahdam felt nothing. Yet he felt everything. It ripped through his soul. The tubular door opened, and his mother, still handcuffed, had him by the arms. Pulling him. Sobbing. Begging him to calm.

But he couldn't.

The guards scrambled for them, snatched Dina by the ankle as a computer monitor crashed and shattered against the floor.

Ahdam roared.

Hinges blew from the door.

Glass splintered.

And water sprayed.

Dina grabbed him by the arm and yanked. They tumbled from down the stairs, landed on their knees, and then fled towards the open doorway.

Ahdam looked back.

Water jetted through a long thin crack in the window. The guards crawled to their feet, splashing in ankle-deep water as it filled the room. Wires hissed and sparked.

"Ahdam, run!"

Ahdam obeyed his mother, sloshing through rising water as the alarms screamed their rhythmic rage. Behind him, water splashed, items crashed, the guards shouted, and a robotic voice cut through the sound system.

"Worr-ning," it said. *"Breech. Worr-ning. Breech."*

The water flooded through the door.

Ahdam and his mother ran.

He didn't know where they'd go, but he followed his mother as she sprinted down the hall. The water came to their knees now.

Ahdam shot another glance back.

The guards weren't far behind them, and their angry screams shredded through the blaring alarm and robotic voice.

"Worr-ning. Breech. Worr-ning. Breech."

The earth shook.

Water rose.

Further down the hall, a steel door groaned and descended from the ceiling.

Ahdam looked at his mother, and she looked at him. In silent acknowledgment, they both understood the stakes. If they didn't reach the exit, it'd trap them.

"Go!" Dina urged, her cuffed hands at shoulder level as she splashed through the rising water.

The door groaned, beeping its warning as it rushed downwards.

Ahdam ran. Tripped. Sank into the water. Splashed in it. Choked. It surged through his nostrils. Blotted his sight. He gasped. Spluttered water. Heard muffled cries—his mother's. Hands dragged him through the water towards the oncoming steel door. Through it all he could still hear his mother's labored breathing, the screaming security guards, the roar of the plummeting door.

There were seconds left.

Dina pulled him through the neck-level water.

Ahdam wheezed and looked up at his mother.

Water droplets glistened on her head, where her hair had been, and Ahdam realized that the security guards could never take away her beauty.

And then, as Dina Kaseem shoved her son forward with every ounce of strength she could muster, she smiled one more time at him before the door descended between them with a roar.

Ahdam pounded the door, beat his head upon it. Behind it, trapped in the rising water, the guards screamed. They *sobbed*. Their cries muted beneath the water's wrath.

But for one last time, before the water silenced her forever, Dina's voice held strong.

"I love you, Ahdam! Be *brave!*"

The child screamed.

Something stung his neck as the building shook from his pain. His senses dulled; his muscles relaxed.

Hands grabbed him.

He stared up at the ceiling.

Closed his eyes.

Guards lifted him and pulled him from the water.

"Be brave, Ahdam!"

Voices muffled. His body went limp.

But Ahdam still saw his mother. He saw his father. He saw their shack in the West Bank, and the meals they shared as a family. He glimpsed his mother's smile; his father's laugh broke into the sunlit day.

"I would move the earth for you, my love," Haleef whispered in his mother's ear, as if Ahdam could not hear.

But his father wanted him to hear.

Wanted him to know *just how much* he loved Ahdam's mother. Wanted him to know just how far he'd go to *show* her that love.

Ahdam wanted the same.

He didn't *want* war. He didn't *want* to use his abilities to destroy families and wreak havoc upon the earth.

But if that's what it took to be brave? To protect his people and find peace in his heart?

So be it.

He would move the earth.

VERSE 4

~ HE'LL BE FINE ~

Friday, January 17th, 2020
Chicago, Illinois

P hil Jameson decided that his daughter, Hailey, deserved a *GoPro*. Unlike what other folks seemed to think, he *did* love his children. Both of them.

Victoria as well.

Because God *still* loved His children, even while they burned in Hell.

That being said, Hailey had always been an obedient child. Phil hadn't expected to trust the girl, but once she'd finally stopped screaming at the sight of her mother in the basement, she'd straightened up.

So, acknowledging her love for photography and videography—which could come in handy while he developed as an end times reverend—Phil purchased a *GoPro* with superb recording capabilities.

A BETTER NIGHT CAPTURE EXPERIENCE!

But something else had changed in the Jameson household. Something far more wonderful than a brand-new camera.

Carolyn was now free of the basement and slept beside him as she once did.

On Friday, January 17th, two days after the cops came to check on Victoria Jameson, Phil opened his eyes in the darkness and reached out to make sure his wife was still there.

The cops hadn't stayed long. They explained that the UCLA department had requested a welfare check on behalf of her professors and her roommate. They'd asked basic questions. Had he seen Victoria? When? Where? Mental health conditions? To which he'd responded—

"Many. Many mental health problems. I've worried about her for a while, but she hasn't reached out to me lately. Please find my baby."

"We'll follow up," the officer said. *"Let us know if you hear anything."*

After wiping his face of sweat, Phil had returned to the house, shut the door, and made a decision.

It was time for Carolyn to come up from the basement. Time for Hailey to see her mother. Time to be a united family again.

And Phil was far more concerned that Carolyn's chain rattling was a higher risk than her ability to... what was it the ghetto people said?

Snitch?

Phil rubbed his eyes. Bright spots clouded his vision. He squinted at the alarm clock. Almost ten.

The entire family had gone to bed early tonight.

It was strange being in bed with his wife again. He'd missed it. The basement had always been too cold, too smelly, too *creepy* to join her there for the night. Ever since he'd banished her to the basement, he'd had trouble falling asleep. She'd always done so well soothing him before sleep, whether it was with a cup of tea or a gentle back massage.

"Thank you, Lord," he whispered, brushing the bony structure of his wife's shoulder. Phil pulled her into him. He was content.

But something irked him.

In the last couple of days, since her release from the basement, Carolyn had gained an odd sense of lucidity, even in the midst of her insanity. Many reasons could cause this. Better nutrition. Sunlight. His loving touch.

But it happened very fast.

For obvious reasons, he couldn't just *take* her to the doctor yet to determine the actual status of her health, but he did wonder if his own healing hands had triggered the sudden mental improvement.

It shouldn't concern him.

But it did.

Frowning, Phil peered down at Carolyn for a few extra moments before rolling over to check the baby monitor on his nightstand.

Phil hadn't felt an ounce of guilt connecting the video monitor inside of Hailey's room. It was necessary, as it'd be unwise to *fully* trust his daughter not to decide she'd lost her mind and flee.

And talk to the cops.

"This is a miracle of God!" Phil told Hailey, catching her arm before she could run through the front door. Carolyn stood at the end of the basement stairs, peering up at them

*in her flower-print dress. "Look at your mother! The Lord saved her. He put me in charge
of saving her, Hailey! She is alive. If this wasn't God's plan, He wouldn't have allowed it to
happen."*

She hadn't questioned him. In fact, after that, she hadn't said much at all.

And that bothered Phil. He'd expected *some* form of thanks for bringing her only
mother back from the dead.

But it could be worse. She didn't ask questions. Hailey accepted the situation as it
was.

Unless... she was trying to trick him.

Phil gasped.

He whipped his head back to the video feed, reached for the baby monitor, and
peered into the screen.

Still sleeping.

Stop worrying so much, Phil thought, and laid back down. He stared at the ceiling.

Because something felt *wrong.* Off.

Sighing, he left the bed and put on his slippers. The door creaked as he opened it. He
stepped into the hallway and tiptoed towards Hailey's room. Turned the handle.

And opened the door.

Hailey shifted in her bed and then sat up onto her elbow. "Dad?" she said, sleepy.

"It's okay, Sweetheart, just put your pretty face back to sleep, alright?" Phil glanced
around the room, found nothing, and then stepped back into the hall.

"*Aghh!*"

Carolyn stood in the hallway.

"Goodness, Darling, you scared me." He covered his heart with his palm.

"Tea," she said.

"Hmm, what's that, you'd like tea?"

The dark outline of her head shook. "For you. Come downstairs." Abruptly, Carolyn
turned and started down the stairs. She made no sound as the soft pads of her feet struck
the stairway.

Like a ghost.

Confused, Phil followed her.

In the kitchen, Carolyn slipped on her apron, the one she'd worn the day before she
died. She placed the silver kettle on the stove and started the gas flame. In the dim light,

she looked like a pale skeleton, but she moved around the kitchen with a grace she'd never had before.

Cautiously, Phil turned on the dining room light and sat at the head of the table, eyeing her. "I appreciate this gesture, Carolyn. Why don't you make yourself some as well and come sit next to me?"

Facing away from him, Carolyn wiped her hands on her apron and then halted. Cocked her head a little. Then, she turned with wide eyes and smiled. "Good demon."

He slapped the table. "Stop *calling* me that! You're not in *Hell*."

Solemn, Carolyn lowered her head. Whispering, she turned to gather two cups from the cupboards above her head. Occasionally, she paused, as if to remember what she'd been doing in the first place.

Phil cleared his throat.

Carolyn placed the tea before him. The large *World's Greatest Dad* mug clunked against the table. She sat next to him and smiled a little.

The steam warmed his face and moistened his skin. Comforting.

Like the olden days.

"Thank you, Darling," he said, and sipped the tea. "My favorite. Chamomile Peach. Mmm."

Carolyn nodded and sipped hers. "When does she start?"

"When does who—what?"

"Your mother. Beatrice. When does she start?"

"Ah." Phil nodded once. "Her. Well, my sweet, you've had an unexpected turn-around." He eyed her again. "Clearly. So perhaps we won't need her. I'd rather *not* need her, for what it's worth. I hate that woman." He slurped his tea.

Carolyn did not respond. Rather, she took a drink of her tea, and her eyes became dull again. Then life returned with an abrupt surge to her eyes once more. "I am very excited," she responded, and finished her tea.

"To see my *mother?*" Phil gasped. "She's horrible. Satan's personal—personal, eh—"

"Side-kick?"

"Er, sure."

"Demon."

"*Yes.*"

"Hmm," Carolyn said, and raised the mug to her lips. "I see."

The bumblebee clock ticked.

"You'd be proud of me, you know," Phil said, becoming sleepy once more. "I healed Hawk Caravan. You know... the boy you struck driving drunk. I made him walk again."

Carolyn's eyes closed briefly, her eyelids fluttering as she kept the mug to her lips. She opened them again, revealing eyes Phil realized were actually quite striking. He wasn't sure *why* they looked so beautiful, but he couldn't help but lean forward to investigate a little further.

"I was proud of you for all of your ideas," Carolyn murmured, returning the cup to the table. "You were always able to captivate me with your ability to play Devil's Advocate and talk big ideas, no matter how controversial or shocking they were to people."

"Don't call it Devil's Advocacy, my sweet, that is not a *good* thing. I never played advocate. I always meant what I said." Phil gave a firm nod. "Sometimes the Lord demands uncomfortable things from us."

Carolyn nodded.

"Next," Phil said, rubbing his eyes. "St. Michael's will need to make an uncomfortable decision. Jerome Nadier won't be there long... his blasphemous, homosexual teachings won't dilute our young ones anymore." He yawned. "Maybe Hawk's sister will be replaced as a Sunday School assistant. We don't need another homosexual, or *bisexual*, teaching our children."

Carolyn blinked.

It was time for bed. He was about to fall asleep at the dining room table. So... Phil stood from his chair. His legs wobbled, and the room spun. He struggled to keep his eyes open. His heart rate shot up, and his skin was slimy and hot.

"Hmm," he said, confused, frowning towards Carolyn as she sat with the mug secure in her hands. "I feel like I might pass—"

The room turned upside down.

And his head slammed against the dining room table before stars burst into his eyes and—

* * *

Phil snapped his eyes open.

Black sky. City lights.

There were no stars—only grey, puffy clouds against the night, city-lit sky.

His head *pounded*. Like a jackhammer.

Why was he *outside?* He couldn't remember the last time he'd been out for a joy walk at night, and normally he wore a sweatband and ankle weights for those.

Not pajamas.

Phil tried to move.

But there was a very concerning problem.

His arms, outstretched against the cold earth, were bound at the wrists. So were his ankles. He was still in pajama pants and a t-shirt. His feet were bare. Snow melted into his back.

"You're awake."

Phil cranked his head to the right.

Carolyn and Hailey Jameson towered over his body.

Panic sent his heart into a state of erratic pounding. He couldn't breathe. Whipping his head back and forth, up and down, he tried to make sense of where he was, but he couldn't *see* very well.

"What, in God's Holy *name*, are you *two doing?*" Phil shrieked.

Hailey's face was white.

Carolyn looked as though she'd never left the tea table.

His eyes widened.

The tea.

They would pay for this. Whatever they were doing, *they would pay for it.*

"Carolyn?" Phil screeched, hopeful that someone would hear him. "*Hailey?* Someone speak to me right *now.*"

"Mom *told me to*," Hailey exclaimed, and a sob tore from her throat. She looked forlorn and pathetic as she stood in her oversized winter coat, Winnie the Pooh pajama pants, and Ugg boots.

"*Huh?* For gosh sakes, untie me. This is ridiculous," Phil huffed. When they didn't move, he lifted his heels and impatiently slammed them against the ground. "Well, come on. Untie me. Don't just *stand* there!"

"I think God is telling me to do it this way," Carolyn said quietly. "I didn't want to do it. I really didn't, and I hope you forgive me if you come back—"

"Wait a minute, what do you mean *if I come back?*" Phil's breath caught, and he struggled to sit up.

He couldn't.

Instead, he strained a muscle in his back as he flopped like a fish.

"I think the Lord is at work here," Carolyn deadpanned. "But I need to know for myself."

"*Huh?* Hailey, Sweetheart," the red-headed lawyer turned desperate eyes to his daughter. "Your mother came back, but she isn't the same woman. Untie me. Let's figure out how to get her help before you both do something stupid. Come on, now."

Hailey sobbed and shook her head. "I don't know what's happening anymore," she cried, burying her face in her hands. Her shoulders shook.

"Hailey, *Hailey,* Sweetheart, look at me. Tell me what's going on." Phil tried to breathe and found that it was becoming increasingly more difficult. "Talk to your daddy, little girl, tell me—"

A train screamed in the distance.

Phil froze.

His eyes widened, and he looked at Carolyn, who stood over him with that dull look in her eyes. Her skinny silhouette loomed over his body. The wind tugged her long-sleeved pajamas, and the apron flapped against her in the breeze. Slowly, she reached back and untied the apron strap.

"You... *wouldn't,*" he whispered. He wanted to scream, but the shock was still too new.

"We're lucky we didn't get here much later, or we might have missed this one," Carolyn said thoughtfully, as if she'd almost missed a sale on a rotisserie chicken.

"*Carolyn!*" Phil cried.

"Come here, Hailey." Carolyn gestured for her daughter.

Carolyn and Hailey came behind him and hooked their arms through his. Grunting, they lifted his torso and dragged him backwards.

"*No, no, God, no, just st-mmph!*" His screams muffled as Carolyn plunged her apron into his mouth.

"Don't use the Lord's name in vain, Dear," Carolyn said, her voice a little strained from dragging her husband.

Phil thrashed, twisted, and turned. The binds cut his skin. Muffled protests broke through his mouth and into the apron, which smelled of rotten eggs and tasted like spoilt milk.

Phil dry heaved. Prayed. Tried to reason with the crazy women pulling him towards what he could only presume were *railroad tracks!*

"Hailey will make sure this gets on film," Carolyn said in a distant, soothing tone.

The train whistle blew again.

And the earth rumbled.

Not from the train... but from something else.

"If you come back," Carolyn cooed, "you'll thank me later."

Vomit caught in his throat.

And the ground began to shake.

At first, Phil thought the train was upon him already, but it was still a distance away.

"Mom," Hailey warned, stumbling and nearly falling. "There's an—"

"Earthquake," Carolyn hummed. "I know."

As Phil tried to scream upwards towards the night sky, urine trickled down his leg. He thought of the green-eyed jezebel, how she'd threatened him and forced him to piss himself. His thoughts spiraled. While flailing his body in useless desperation, Phil Jameson realized that he, right now, had far less faith in God than he'd ever had in his life.

Pebbles tapped against the ground. The earthquake grew stronger, and the two women struggled to stay on their feet as the vibrations thundered through the ground.

His back struck the tracks.

"Mom, *please*, maybe we can try something less drastic," Hailey pleaded, turning to her mother. She'd been crying. Her voice had always been raspy when she cried.

Hope burst through his mind as he lay perpendicular to the tracks. Every sound became louder. The loose screws that rattled on the track; the metal that hummed beneath his back; the train's screams. The earth's screams. *His* screams.

"Get your *GoPro* out, Hailey," Carolyn said, calm.

"Mom, *please,* this is horrible! I—"

"Your father will be fine."

"*Mom,* what if God doesn't bring him ba—"

"He'll be *fine*." Her voice sounded stiff, but certain. "Right, Phil?"

Choking, Phil turned his head and bit down onto the apron. He squinted as the oncoming train light expanded and brightened. He tried rocking his body, back and forth, but the earthquake tossed him back.

Phil was stuck, and the train fast approached.

It screamed. The shrill sound echoed into the winter night.

"Carolyn, please!" Phil begged, but the apron trapped his cries.

In the darkness, Mrs. Carolyn Jameson stood oddly still with her hands folded in front of her. Sobbing, Hailey lifted her *GoPro*—

—A BETTER NIGHT CAPTURE EXPERIENCE!—

—and wobbled as the earthquake shook the city.

They were crazy. Both women were *insane*. Possessed by Satan. They *had* to be, because God wouldn't let something like this happen to him.

As the lights exploded in blinding white, Phil shot one last pleading glance to Carolyn.

"If I came back with *your* help, Phil," Carolyn called, "you'll come back with God's."

The tracks rattled louder.

"*Mmmurph! Ahhgmurph!*" Phil choked over the apron.

Like a trumpet from Heaven, the train screamed its warning. The lawyer's body thrashed and squirmed over the vibrating tracks as the lights pierced his eyes. Tears streamed over his cheeks, urine over his legs. Philip Jameson bawled and tried to roll away from the oncoming train.

The wheels screeched. Lights exploded. Oil and smoke fumes burst through his nostrils. The whistle shrieked. It would be upon him in five, four—

I'll come back! Phil's final thoughts roared. His blood-curdling screams melted within the train's deafening roar. *God is on my side and I will fucking come ba—!*

CHAPTER 14: VERSE 1
~ THE PRAYER CORNER ~

Sunday, September 30th, 2012
Chicago, Illinois

"Your dad's gonna kill us if he finds out," Mariel said, glancing down at the pretty girl beside him. The sun illuminated her brown hair. There were a few strands that were darker than others.

She was so pretty.

No.

Beautiful.

Especially as she raised the ice cream cone to her lips, smirked at him with twinkling eyes, and said—

"Not *us*. Just you."

"Ha," Gabriel Donovan said as he shuffled ahead. "Let's go to the track so I can piss."

Mariel brushed hair out of his eyes and responded to Esther, because Gabe was never worth a response. "Yeah," he said. "Me."

It was warm, but he shivered.

And he walked a little faster now.

Not because Esther was right, but because she was *wrong*.

There was no question that Todd Caravan *would* try to kill him. But he wouldn't succeed. He wouldn't succeed at all.

Because Mariel Nadier couldn't fucking die.

He'd *tried*.

"He just doesn't get it," Esther said, pausing the cone licking to stare at it. "He doesn't get you were just joking."

"Right." Mariel pushed his fists into his pockets. It wasn't cold, but something chilled him. He knew what *it* was. *It* wasn't far from him. Like normal, *it* lurked in the corner of his eye.

The humanoid.

As they approached the gated soccer field and track, Esther's voice captured his attention again.

"You... you *were* joking, right?"

He hadn't been joking at all. But Mariel couldn't bring himself to tell her that he'd always wished for death. Or the concept, at least. How could he explain that he wasn't sure if he wanted mortality, or if he yearned for the ability to wake up each day with the realization that, like everyone else, his days were numbered?

He couldn't. So—

Mariel laughed. The feeling had started as a sob in his chest but exploded in laughter. He tossed his head back. The breeze tickled his cheeks and throat. "Why would I want to die? I'd miss seeing your face. A lot." He stopped at the gate and turned to her.

"Yeah?" Esther gazed up at him.

Mariel stepped closer. His eyes fell over her throat and down to the cleavage in the tight tank top she wore. His breath caught. Was it wrong to want her body?

His dad had always told him to think of things that gave glory to God.

Lust did not.

But it was a *normal* part of the human condition. He didn't want to feel guilty anymore.

He wanted to *kiss* her.

Would she let him?

Gabe had always said that girls fluffed and played with their hair when they liked someone. She'd done it multiple times today. Maybe—

"Esther—" he started.

"Hurry the fuck up, you goons, I gotta pee," Gabe yelled.

Mariel swallowed a snarl. He loved Gabe, but he was *always there*. Always *interrupting.*

"Do you need help peeing or something, Gabe?" Esther called.

"No, I'm talking more to Mariel. I wanna tell him a guy thing."

Mariel sighed. "That's never good, and it's normally always gross."

"Don't hide your guy things from me," Esther whined. "I can appreciate guy humor."

"Nah. You wouldn't get it."

Mariel's gaze caught the three subjects at the other side of the track. Two large men and a female runner.

And *damn* she was fucking fast for a girl.

Well, fast for anybody, really.

And, from what he could see, she was hot.

"I'm going to guess you're just looking for moral support."

"For what?" Gabe scratched his jaw.

"To hit on that girl who's running."

Gabe laughed and then stopped. "Well..."

"Go piss," Mariel said. "I'm gonna walk with Esther. We'll meet you over there."

"He's so predictable," Esther said.

Mariel snorted. "Yeah."

They walked across the track. Mariel wanted to hold her hand. "How's your Mom doing?"

"She's struggling," Esther murmured.

A whistle sounded. The blonde-haired runner took off.

"Is Jason still being a brat about everything?" Mariel asked. He wanted her to talk more. To let him in. To acknowledge *him* as the strength she needed for this horrible time in her life.

Losing her mother.

He wondered what it'd be like to have a mother.

Esther's voice faded in. "...about what's being served for dinner, he's obsessively reading health book shit. Or about hawks."

"Hawks?"

"Yeah, mom started calling him Hawk."

"Ah. I didn't know eight-year-olds could read advanced stuff like that."

"He can. All he does is read and talk about how he's going to heal mom one day. It gets annoying. Like, you're eight. You barely poop on the potty, shut the fuck up."

"I feel like he's toilet trained now."

"Yes, well, he smells like a poopy brat, so I forget he's eight. How's your dad?"

"Good. Boring."

"Stop. Fr. Jerome is amazing. He's like a bonus dad."

"More like a bonus grandpa," Mariel snickered. It was true. His dad wasn't all that young.

"Be nice. He has to deal with you. He *chooses* to deal with you."

"Yeah, yeah."

That was true too. The poor man dealt with Mariel's chaotic mood swings on a daily basis. He deserved better.

"I think Gabe got lost in the toilet."

The conversation wasn't going anywhere. It was boring, and Esther seemed distracted. So—

"I'll check," Mariel said. "I need to pee now, anyway."

As he jogged towards the bathroom, a dark SUV parked in a space outside of the gate. Trying to get his mind off of Esther, he raised his hand to wave. He wasn't sure if the person waved back.

It didn't matter.

"What the hell are you doing in here, Gabe?" Mariel called as he entered the men's restroom and slapped a spiderweb in his face.

Gabe called from the stall, muffled. "Taking a shit!"

"What guy stuff did you want to talk to me about?" Mariel entered a stall and positioned himself over the toilet.

Gabe chuckled in the other stall. "I just wanted to get you away from Esther."

Mariel scowled and stared at the graffiti on the wall.

"FCK WHITE NIGGAS."

"Why are you trying to get me away from Esther?" He sneered, holding in the piss for a moment to make sure he heard Gabe's response.

"Because I want a chance with her, dude. You're always stealin' the show." Gabe let out a fart.

"Bro, that's gross," Mariel snarled, and he released his bladder. He wasn't sure if he'd responded to Gabe's fart or to Gabe's comment. "Stop chasing her, she's not interested. If anything, she's interested in me."

The toilet flushed. "Yeah, but you don't have money," Gabe chuckled.

Mariel's face went hot. He fucking *hated* when Gabe *made jokes*. Because they weren't *fucking* funny.

Did Gabe think Mariel didn't *know* he had the life of a spoiled brat? Did he think Mariel hadn't *thought* about the fact that his politician daddy lined his pockets with cash and the ability to buy Esther more things than Mariel could ever afford?

"You're not fucking funny." Mariel stormed out of the stall and pointed a finger in Gabe's face.

The humanoid pointed too.

"Chill, bro," Gabe said, holding up his hands. "Relax."

Mariel let out another snarl, turned on his heel, and strode for the door. As he opened it, he collided against the burly chest of a dark-haired man with sunglasses.

"Sorry," Mariel said, clearing his throat and stepping aside.

"All good, brother." The man tilted his head a little, as if analyzing Mariel's tall lanky frame through his sunglasses.

"Have a good day," Mariel stammered, slipping past him as the sunlight burst into his eyes again.

He wanted to get back to Esther. Wanted to make sure Gabe knew that he could fight for her gaze and win.

Gabe had money.

Mariel had respect.

But what *the hell* was Esther doing on the ground? And why were those people standing over her?

Gabe was right behind him, panting like a dehydrated dog for some reason. "Why's Esther on the ground and what are those people doing?"

"I don't know." Mariel began to run.

Esther rose to her feet and wobbled.

Mariel caught a glimpse of the pretty runner, and he realized she was looking at Esther a bit longer than he liked. As he approached, the runner turned her back and walked away.

"What was that about?" Mariel demanded.

"Oh man, you got to talk to *her*? Look at the ass in that spandex."

Gabe needed to shut up.

"That girl just ran me over."

Mariel shot his gaze to her. There'd been an edge to her voice... something he couldn't pinpoint. Confusion? Fascination?

No.

Attraction.

Because, when Mariel looked at the girl he'd always wanted, he noticed rapid, erratic breathing. Flushed cheeks. Parted lips. Distant, amorous gaze.

The gaze he'd always wanted.

Fury bubbles from his chest. "I'll kick her ass," Mariel hissed.

"I don't think you could," Esther said.

And that? It *crushed* him.

Made him want to choke her to death like he'd seen in those porn videos.

But lust was normal.

That wasn't.

Abruptly, Esther walked away, and Mariel's attention snapped up to see where she was going.

"Where are you going?" Mariel cried, following her.

"I think she wants to talk to me."

"But you said she's rude," he protested, suddenly feeling desperate.

"Maybe she wants to apologize."

Mariel looked at the blonde runner, and his chest tightened as she approached them with calm, collected confidence. She paid no attention to him. Instead, her gaze locked upon Esther as if she, too, was...

Hooked.

"Is this yours?" the runner asked, lifting a necklace into the air.

Mariel watched them. He wasn't sure what the two girls were saying. It was all a muffled, claustrophobic mess in his head. He felt forgotten as he stood there, watching Esther's eyes as they lit up, noting the way her smirk widened as she reached out and accepted the necklace.

And now they stood face to face.

Watching each other.

The runner turned cold green eyes to him.

It frightened him.

"I should go," she said, and then looked back at Esther. "You have ice cream in your hair."

Esther's fingers darted to her hair. She fluffed it a little. "Oh," she laughed.

Mariel felt sick.

She'd played with her hair for this fucking bitch.

"We should go," Mariel snapped.

But the runner ignored him as she backed away. "One last thing."

Mariel sighed. Loud.

"You're annoying..." the blonde said, and dimples appeared in her cheeks, "...but you're not so bad looking yourself."

She left.

And Mariel wanted to bash her fucking face in.

"What the fuck is she on?" he snapped. "Why'd she say that?"

Why did he feel as though he'd been denied the privilege of knowing an inside joke? That he'd walked in on a private moment between the two of them?

"She's beautiful... isn't she?" Esther purred.

His thoughts went mad.

What a fucking bitch. Leading him on like this, and then—

"She's not *that* pretty." Mariel kicked a pebble across the track. He pretended the pebble was the goddamn runner.

"Esther!" Gabe's footsteps approached. "Your dad's on the phone. You forgot yours at home. He needs to talk to you."

"What's wrong?" Esther cried.

Mariel tore his eyes from the distant runner. He needed to focus on Esther. He needed to fight the negative thoughts and *be* there for her. He'd studied her for years, and he could tell that she was drawn to people with strength, confidence, and the ability to lead.

If *he* was the *strong* one, then—

"He says you need to come home now," Gabe said. "Your mom's not doing well."

And her face went white. Her body swayed.

Matiel reached for her.

"Okay," Esther whispered.

He touched her, placed his palm on her back. Now was his chance.

His time.

His moment to prove that no one... *no one* would love her or protect her like he could.

And if they tried?

He'd laugh in their faces.

"Let's go," Mariel said, and smiled a little. "You'll be okay."

*   *   *

Saturday, January 18th, 2020
Chicago, Illinois

When the knock came, Mariel's heart went wild.

Esther stood outside of his door.

It was time to get her back.

He wasn't sure how it had all fallen apart so fast, so soon after she'd returned to his life just a week ago.

But it had—like he was black mold forming in her mind since coming back.

And he *hated* that.

He *would* prove he could change. That he could offer her joy, stability, reassurance.

He would get her back.

Because Esther Caravan was his. Always had been. Even when her eyes wandered, she always turned them back to him.

As his sock-covered feet thumped against the hardwood floor, Mariel looked at the time on the oven. 5:36 P.M. Ten minutes ago, his dad had left to lead the Saturday evening Vespers service.

"You should come, Son," Fr. Jerome pleaded, standing at the door.

"You're forgetting something, Dad," Mariel said. "I'm not supposed to be alive."

Fr. Jerome smiled, but tears brimmed in his eyes. "Please... please don't be gone when I come back. I can't lose you again."

Mariel made no promises, considering life had been unpredictable as of late. An irony, really... because he would have believed it would have gotten easier after receiving direct instructions from the Kingdom of Heaven.

Maybe that'd been his fault. He wasn't sure, and guilt ate at his soul like a rotten apple because, at the moment, he didn't give a flying fuck about the fact that he hadn't followed orders yet.

He just wanted Esther.

Biting his lip, Mariel opened the door.

The look on Esther's face twisted his stomach—because it was an unreadable expression.

That terrified him.

"Hi," he said, and he stepped aside.

The wind caught her hair. Her eyes glistened... sleep-deprived and red. She didn't reach for him like he'd hoped she would. Instead, she kept her hands in the pockets of her grey joggers as she stepped inside.

"A little cold, or something?" Mariel chuckled, eyeing her outfit.

Baggy white hoodie. Joggers. Winter boots. There was leftover mascara around her eyes, and his chest tightened when he realized that she'd worn it last night.

For that *friend* she wouldn't tell him about.

"Is my outfit not good enough?" Esther snapped, shuffling to the couch and sitting. He'd started off wrong.

"No, I'm just joking." Mariel stood in his own living room with sudden awkwardness. "Need me to get you anything?"

"No." Esther looked up at him. "I always liked your V-neck shirts. They look good on you."

Mariel blushed and smoothed out his shirt. He'd picked it with intention—it fit his muscles in all the right places. "Thanks." He moved towards her and sat next to her on the couch. "So..."

"I won't waste your time, Mars," Esther said, sniffling. "I'll jump right to it."

"Okay..."

"I'm very confused. I love you so fucking much, but my brain cannot comprehend *any* of this. Maybe if I could talk to your dad, or get some sort of spiritual insight, I could get past this chaos in my mind whenever I'm with you." Tears rolled. Her face was flushed.

"I... don't know what more I can tell you," Mariel said, and he wondered if maybe he should change his story. Maybe if he told her that he'd lied, that he'd never really died, and that it'd been a fucked up conspiracy of some sort... maybe she'd be better off.

Esther lowered her head. Her eyes shifted and then closed. "Mariel—"

"Esther, I love you. I don't have all of the answers. You don't think it's been hard for me? Living with this has been *fucked!*" His roar bounced against the walls.

Esther flinched.

He'd made her *flinch*.

But he couldn't hold back the emotion.

Everyone was so goddamn selfish... trying to make sense of things for themselves rather than letting him *fucking* breathe.

"I killed myself because of this shit," Mariel cried. "I shot myself because I couldn't look at you every day and wonder if you were going to reject me, or hate me, or *fear me!*"

"I *am* afraid, Mariel! This isn't *normal!*"

"*Exactly!*" Mariel screamed and stood up; backed away, pulled his hair. "*Gabe is fucking normal! You* are fucking normal! Every person you've put eyes on, or could *have* you, is *fucking normal, Esther! I am not!*"

Tears came. Sobs. Desperation. He couldn't see her through the wetness of his eyes. "I just want you to look at me the way you looked at that girl on the track—like something to be worshipped, adored, and... and *followed.*"

Would that word scare her away? It'd slipped out, and he wasn't certain she would appreciate his desire to command her, make her completely *his.*

Esther's face was pale. Eyes wide. So wide, as if she'd been caught in a lie.

Mariel thought she'd slap him. Maybe laugh at him.

But she didn't.

Esther stood up, glanced towards the doorway, and looked back at him.

Mariel wiped his eyes, watched her. "I want you, Esther, more than I want death itself. I want you." He inched closer, afraid she'd move.

But she didn't.

And soon Mariel was very close, hovering over her, smelling the remnants of the perfume she wore.

He'd get her back.

"When I went to the Kingdom, they asked me what my greatest desire was," Mariel whispered, brushing his fingers against her cheek.

Esther shuddered.

"Esther," he murmured, and bent his head until his lips were a whisper away from hers. "I told them I wanted to obtain the Kingdom of Heaven."

Esther brought her eyes up to his. Her lips trembled.

"I lied to them," Mariel purred, and he planted a small kiss on her lips. "My greatest desire is having you."

She kissed him. Hard.

So hard that he *knew* he'd gotten her back.

Victory bled through his nerves.

Mariel grabbed her throat, squeezed, drove his tongue into her mouth.

She whimpered, choked.

He thought she'd pull away.

But she didn't.

He wanted her, so he kept going. Grabbed her hips, owned her mouth, and rocked his groin against her as his dick hardened.

She'd always come back. Until the end of time—Esther Caravan would always come back.

Mariel clawed at her sweatshirt. He got it off, and he wasn't sure if he'd forced it off—or if she'd helped him. Her t-shirt and bra came next, and he squeezed her heavy breasts in his hands, heard her whimper as he pulled her nipples and twisted them.

Mariel ignored the guilt. He was tired of feeling guilty. Tired of losing out on everything he wanted because he was Mariel Nadier—the priest's son, the boy who knew scripture, the boy who helped out around the church.

So Mariel grabbed her throat again. Pushed her down. Felt the necklace around her neck.

Gabe's necklace.

Was *he* the mysterious *friend* she'd gone out with last night?

Esther's knees thumped against the floor.

Mariel pulled down his sweatpants and grabbed his cock. "Suck it," he growled, pulling her head, his eyes flicking from her breasts, her mouth, and the necklace.

That would need to come off.

But Esther put him in her mouth, tried to fit him, and her hair shielded her eyes as she sucked him into her soul.

"Fuck!" Mariel grabbed her hair.

He'd found it—the confidence that'd always attracted her to people.

But Mariel looked down again, and he saw the necklace swinging from her neck, and a growl rumbled from his chest. His hips snapped forward, driving himself deeper into her mouth.

Esther pulled back, tears spilling, gasped for air and coughed. "You're being *rough*. You're too big, *please* slow down."

Oh God, it was hot when she begged for mercy on her knees. He was so fucking hard, so ready to fuck her and—

"Take off the necklace," Mariel said, "and I will slow down."

Esther's eyes narrowed. "Mars... no. It's a gift, it doesn't *mean* anything. I—"

"Take it off. Take it off and put your mouth back on my cock."

Esther slid back. Shook her head.

And something inside of him ruptured.

Mariel grabbed the necklace.

Tore it from her neck.

It made a sickening popping sound as it broke.

"You wear this again," he sneered, "and I'll make you choke on my cum."

He expected her to stay, to obey, because she was loyal to him.

But she didn't.

"Fuck you," she said, scrambling to her feet and snatching the necklace from his hand. "You're a fucking pig. And we're done."

No.

Esther yanked her shirt over her head.

No.

Fuck *her*. Fuck her for failing as a girlfriend, for failing to support him when all he'd ever done was try to protect her—from himself, from God's orders...

And from the—

"...kill chip," he sneered, and he cocked his head like the humanoid in the shadows of his vision. "Maybe you deserve the kill chip."

Esther's face paled, like she'd puke.

Mariel held his breath. He hadn't meant to say that. Why the *fuck* had he said that?

Esther turned.

"Esther," he cried, pulling up his pants as she grabbed the rest of her clothes. "I was joking about everything. It was a fantasy of mine. I thought you'd like that. Esther—"

Sobbing, she ran for the door.

"Esther, *please! I'm sorry!*" he screamed, reaching for her, grasping air.

The door slammed shut. It rattled the windowpanes.

He was alone again.

Mariel hadn't gotten her back... he'd scared her away.

"*God!*" he screamed, and he tore at his hair. Slammed his head against the door. Again. Again.

And again.

He didn't feel the pain. There was too much of it inside of him as he smashed his skull against the surface and screamed.

Tears flowed. Sobs tore from his throat.

He had hurt Esther.

He'd ignored God, and now he'd hurt the woman he'd do anything for.

Mariel slowed his movements and wiped the mucus from his nose. He straightened up and looked at the ceiling, as if he'd find God's answers written on the tile.

"I need to make this right," he said, and he shook his head as shame crawled through his body.

The humanoid shook his head too.

Ignoring it, Mariel stumbled to his room and fell to his knees before his prayer corner. His father hadn't even forced him to get such a thing—he'd *wanted* it. He'd requested it as a young boy.

"It keeps the bad things away," Mariel said, pouring cereal into his bowl. "It makes me feel safe."

His dad smiled and stole a Cheerio from the bowl. Threw it at him. "Then we'll make you a prayer corner."

Mariel closed his eyes and reached for his phone.

There was only one other person who could help him find his way back to God. Only one person who had been there since his return—who'd guided him, had given him blunt honesty.

Vespers would begin soon, and he might not pick up, but Mariel felt the urge to try.

He needed to make this right.

And he needed to get Esther back.

As Mariel knelt in the prayer corner, the phone rang against his ear.

Perched on the desk, the humanoid watched him.

"Hi, Mariel, Vespers is about to start. Are you okay, Son?"

"Not really. I messed up. I *keep* messing up." Mariel closed his eyes. "Can I see you later? For confession?"

A pause.

"Of course. Your dad is about to start the service. How about you swing out in a couple hours and meet me at the church?"

Mariel opened his eyes and cocked his head towards the humanoid.

It was still there. Watching.

"Thank you, Father Paul," he said softly, and turned his eyes back to the icon of Christ. "I'll see you soon."

And soon, in the final hours of the night, Mariel Christian Nadier kissed his father good night.

He went to St. Michael's, the beloved church that had always symbolized both hope and despair for him, and he knelt before Christ's icon to pray in the darkened sanctuary.

Fr. Paul stood beside him and placed a gentle hand on his head. "Tell me what's on your mind."

Mariel spoke of his sins—his weaknesses of the past, and his fears of the future. He spilled his soul, and the darkest secrets of his mind, things of which he'd never once spoken.

And as Fr. Paul draped his vestment robe over Mariel's head, and as the secrets of the Horseman spilled beneath the priest's shelter—the humanoid watched and listened.

Like it always did.

VERSE 2

~ LANTERN ~

Sunday, January 19th, 2020
Chicago, Illinois

Fr. Jerome Nadier spat the toothpaste out of his mouth and rinsed the sink.

It was seven in the morning on Sunday—two days after the mysterious earthquake, and about three hours before the collapse of St. Michael's: Fr. Jerome Nadier's beloved church.

It'd been an odd couple of days.

Friday morning, long after Fr. Jerome had found Mariel in his drunken state, the priest had awakened to something very strange.

His journal—the one that Mariel had destroyed—looked as though it hadn't been touched. He'd found it at the center of the dining room table, as if Mariel had not torn its pages and thrown it into the sink.

But *why?*

"*I am a madman,*" he'd whispered, thumbing through the pages in awe. "*A madman.*"

He didn't question it. There were enough strange occurrences to deal with. He couldn't process one more.

Fr. Jerome wiped his hands, sighed, and then left the bathroom.

He stopped outside of Mariel's room.

Sobs.

His boy was crying.

And it broke his heart.

Fr. Jerome knocked on the door and leaned his forehead against it. "Mariel? You okay, buddy?"

The sobs slowed and turned to sniffles. "I'm good."

"I don't believe that," Fr. Jerome said. "Can I open the door?"

Silence. Then—

"Yes."

The priest opened the door and peered into the room.

Mariel lay curled in the fetal position, wrapped in his blankets like a burrito. His shoulders shook, and Fr. Jerome could only see the top of his head.

"Whatever you're struggling with," Fr. Jerome said, and inched forward, "I'm sorry. I'm so sorry, Mariel. I hope you know how much I love you."

His sobs tore from his throat and shook the bed.

Fr. Jerome wiped tears from his eyes and sat next to his son. He rubbed Mariel's shoulder, closing his eyes and praying for the words. He wasn't sure what to say anymore. He wasn't sure what to *do*.

It took him back to his first night with Mariel... when the infant had cried, and cried, and cried until Fr. Jerome had made the decision to go to Marty's.

The night Mariel should have died in the backseat of his 1995 Buick.

And for a fleeting moment, Fr. Jerome wondered if that might have been more merciful for his son.

It was a *terrible* thought, one that brought him much shame. But the priest had always wondered why God would place such a burden on someone so young—someone so naive.

"Please, Lord," he whispered, "let me take his burden. Give him a chance to find peace."

And as the clock ticked on, closer to the first morning service, Fr. Jerome wrapped his arms around his son—just as he'd done on the night Mariel should have died—and he rested his head on his shoulder and held him before his departure to St. Michael's.

*   *   *

When Liturgy began, the church pews were fuller than normal. Packed—like the Paschal (called Easter in the Western church) service every year.

But it was not joyous as the service for Christ's resurrection so often was. It was dim. Quiet, as if the congregation had lost hope.

As Fr. Jerome approached the podium, he scanned the congregation.

Todd Caravan and his family, including Esther, sat in their normal spot—the fifth row from the front.

As if in pain, Esther's hands rested on her stomach. She looked pale. Dazed. Heart-broken.

Mariel, Fr. Jerome thought and chewed his lip. It had to be.

He needed to speak with her soon.

Esther deserved peace, and it seemed she'd begun to heal before Mariel came back.

He didn't like to think that his son's return might have caused her pain, and he hoped he was wrong. But all signs pointed otherwise.

As the congregation awaited his sermon, and Fr. Paul stood off to the side, his eyes found the empty spot in the front pew where Mariel used to sit.

It devastated him, seeing it empty like that. After Mariel's death, it'd been horrible looking at that empty space.

It hurt more now.

He missed his son. He missed Mariel as he was before the suicide. He missed seeing him at church, hearing his voice as he sang Byzantine chant in the quiet, morning services. He missed seeing his excitement to complete his goals, missed seeing the happiness in his eyes when he was with his best friends.

Mariel had returned, but he was still... gone.

Fr. Jerome cleared his throat, adjusted the microphone.

Someone else was missing. Phil Jameson and his daughter. *That* was far more concerning than his presence. His presence was *normal*.

His absence was not.

One other thing was odd too—the wheeled projector screen that was set up in the corner at the front of the church. It was a large screen, used for church council meetings, classes, and more.

But why was it in the sanctuary *today*?

Unsettled, Fr. Jerome put those thoughts from his mind, rested his hands on the podium, and began to speak.

"Friday night," he said, "the earth shook. Some called it a rumble. Others called it an earthquake." He paused. "There was no explanation for it. It was an event that happened, and then the world moved on. But whether you called it a rumble, or you called it an earthquake, one thing stands true. We all experienced it. All of us. Across Chicago, and even into state lines, we experienced this event together."

The congregation stirred a little. It was always a good sign when they did that. It meant something had *resonated*.

It encouraged him... which was a nice change from feeling obsolete. And Lord, did he feel obsolete lately.

Fr. Jerome found Esther's gaze on him, and he smiled a little.

Though it was small, she returned the smile.

"I was at my favorite coffee shop when the earthquake struck," Fr. Jerome continued. "I saw ripples in my coffee. Then the cup began to clatter. At that time, I started to understand what was happening, and so did my favorite baristas. We looked at each other, nodded, and found cover."

His voice echoed. The congregation watched him with focused gazes.

"When the tremors increased, and dishware clattered to the ground, I heard screams outside; honking horns; fleeing footsteps. Certainly, I was scared because the furniture rattled above me, and it swayed me around a bit—but I realized something crucial. Whatever was happening outside was much worse than what was happening inside. Outside, people fled, panicked, abandoned their vehicles because something was happening that they did not understand, and it was frightening." Fr. Jerome placed a hand on his heart, and his lips trembled. "Sometimes life happens that way. Things happen that we may not understand. But how we respond? That's key. It's okay to be frightened. It's okay to be anxious. I'm an example of that—long history of anxiety. But even though my father sometimes said things that made me feel as though I wasn't allowed to *feel* things deeply, he always told me one thing that stuck with me. *Give your anxieties to God.* That's what he told me. And that might not always look pretty. It's not always smooth... because life's going to throw you earthquakes and rumbles and floods, and it'll all *shake* you to your core, and rattle us inside and out."

Fr. Jerome took in a breath. Scanned. Let out the breath.

"But sometimes we're not meant to carry everything alone." His eyes fell to Esther again. "Laying aside the cares of the world won't make our problems disappear. Giving our anxieties to God doesn't mean we won't *feel* anxious. The chaos of the outside world will strike, but if we allow space in our hearts for peace... maybe then can we find more clarity in the earthquake around us, and acceptance of the storms within us."

Fr. Jerome glimpsed movement outside of the sanctuary.

A familiar face. A familiar stance. Militant. Blonde.

Green-eyes.

The woman who was *trying to find God.*

She stood just outside of the sanctuary's threshold, dressed in grey slacks, a white V-neck, and a black pea coat. Eyes wide, lips parted, she caught his gaze, and she took a step backwards.

Like she hadn't wanted him to know she'd come.

Fr. Jerome smiled again, trying to welcome her without calling everyone else's attention to her presence.

"If I may..." Fr. Paul's voice rumbled behind him. "...I have something to add."

Confused, Fr. Jerome turned to look at the priest standing behind him.

Fr. Paul walked forward, and his vestments rustled as he approached. He came up to the podium and stood side by side with his colleague.

Something shifted—the air, perhaps? Maybe it was his nerves, but Fr. Jerome felt a sudden need to create distance from Fr. Paul.

"It's okay," Fr. Paul whispered, resting a hand on the podium. "When I was in Russia, priests shared homilies all of the time."

Cheeks warm, Fr. Jerome looked across the sanctuary.

Tira was gone.

He turned his head a little.

Moving fast, Tira strode across the parking lot in her heeled boots—as if she couldn't get away from the church fast enough. She entered her black Yukon, slammed the door, and squealed away from the parking lot.

Fr. Jerome rather wished he were escaping with her, because something was wrong. So, so *wrong,* and he couldn't pinpoint what it was.

"My colleague here is speaking on something we all struggle with—faith, fear, and understanding. I'd like to add to his homily with a reminder of what we are taught in the story of the myrrh-bearing women." Fr. Paul placed his black smartphone onto the podium.

Fr. Jerome eyed it and then looked at his former mentor.

"Strange things have happened, are happening, and *will* happen. Fr. Jerome brings up a phenomenal point in saying that trying to understand things that don't make sense to us is *frightening.*"

Esther shifted in her seat, glanced around the church.

Fr. Paul ran his finger along the edge of his phone. "When the myrrh-bearing women saw *His* empty tomb, don't you think they were shocked? Concerned? Afraid? And when they turned and saw *Him,* don't you think they struggled to believe? How could a *man* rise from the dead? What *evil* could have caused this resurrection?" Fr. Paul paused and tilted his head. "That would have crossed *my* mind, at least. The idea that evil, witchcraft, or sorcery could have done such a thing. Tell me, if you saw Satan raise a man from the dead, how would you react? Think about it."

The congregation was silent.

Fr. Jerome cleared his throat. This had taken a strange turn, and he wasn't quite sure he understood the goal.

"You *wouldn't* react," Fr. Paul continued. "Because you *wouldn't* see such a thing. Satan does not *have* this power. That power comes directly from *Him.*" Fr. Paul pointed, jerking his arm upwards.

The congregation looked up, following his finger.

Fr. Jerome watched Paul's finger and stepped back from the podium. Just a little bit.

"The power it takes to heal and to resurrect is *only* given by *Him*. To *His* chosen. To those found worthy of such a magnificent, *Holy* gift. So, before you scoff at what is about to take place, remember these words. *He... is... risen!*"

Heat rushed into Fr. Jerome's face. His eyes snapped up to the sanctuary entrance, and he expected to see Mariel walk through the doors.

He didn't.

"Hawk," Fr. Paul called. "Can you cast the videos to the projector screen, please?"

Hawk Caravan stood up and pulled his phone from his pocket as his perplexed family frowned up at him.

"What *is* this?" Fr. Jerome hissed, covering his mouth to avoid the microphone.

"Jerome," Fr. Paul whispered, and placed a hand on his colleague's arm. "Give your anxieties to God."

The screen turned on.

Dressed in a suit with impeccably combed hair, Philip Jameson filled the screen as a video began to play.

"*I am downtown Chicago right now,*" Phil said, aiming the camera towards his face as if to take a selfie. "*I'm in a hospital. Joining me...*" The camera shifted to Hawk Caravan, who was lying in a hospital bed with bruises, bandaging, and casts. "*... is Hawk Caravan.*"

"What the *fuck!*" Esther cried, standing up, and Todd yanked her back down.

"That was me a year ago!" Hawk called to the congregation, ignoring his sister as she trembled in her seat. "Now watch!"

Fr. Jerome moved up. "*Paul. Stop this.*"

Fr. Paul did not budge. He just smiled.

In the video, Phil approached Hawk and placed hands on him. The camera shook, Phil gasped, and within seconds—Hawk slipped from the bed with widened eyes and pale shock.

"Phil Jameson is a fucking *scamming piece of shit!*" Esther screamed, lunging up again. She looked at her brother and implored him with her eyes. "What is this, buddy, *please just be honest* and *tell me* what happened that night! How much did he pay you?"

"*Look!*" Todd roared, standing up, and his eyes burned with a combination of awe and rage. "Look at him *running!* He had *spinal injuries!*"

The congregation murmured, growing louder by the second.

Fr. Jerome covered his mouth with his hands. "I'm not a part of this," he whispered, but no one could hear him.

"Where's Phil?" Todd shouted over the congregation. "I want to thank him! Praise God!"

"*Dad, no!*" Esther cried.

Patricia Caravan sat still in the pew, her hands over her mouth, and Hawk beamed towards the screen.

"Wait until you see what comes next." Fr. Paul leaned into the microphone as he spoke. "And remember the myrrh-bearing women as you do."

Sharp pain churned in Fr. Jerome's stomach. He was going to puke on the stage of his own church, and that's what it was right now.

A stage.

The video changed—but it was Phil again. He was standing in a blue suit and tie before the camera, as if prepared to do the commentary introduction of a true crime documentary.

"*My brothers and sisters in Christ, what you are about to see will shock and, perhaps, concern you.*" His voice boomed through the choir-loft speakers.

The congregation hushed again.

Esther jutted up her middle finger.

Todd slapped it down.

Fr. Jerome held his breath.

And Phil kept going.

"*A year ago, my beautiful wife met a tragic end. She took her own life. She drove drunk, struck a dear friend of mine—the boy you saw walk—and then stepped in front of a train.*"

"Pray with me!" Fr. Paul called, raising his arms. His vestments spread like wings.

"The Bible says—for as in Adam all die, so also in Christ shall all be made alive." Phil stepped aside.

A black body bag lay on the basement floor behind him.

"Oh my God," Fr. Jerome whispered.

Congregation members covered their mouths and clung to their family members. The air buzzed with silence.

"Behold." Phil strode to the body bag, knelt, unzipped the bag, and outstretched his hands.

"This is *fucking* sick!" Esther.

Phil's body jolted. His head dropped back, and his pointy Adam's apple protruded from his throat. It bobbed with wild abandon as he grunted.

A moment passed, a moment so long that Fr. Jerome began to hope that nothing would come from it. Was that wrong? Hoping a woman couldn't rise from the dead by the hands of her own—

The body bag moved.

The congregation gasped.

And two white hands clawed out from the bag and grasped Phil's suit. A pale face exploded from the bag with a gasp, eyes bugging out in horror as if the woman had awakened to Satan himself.

Carolyn.

He didn't want to believe it. But it was an undeniable resemblance despite the fact that she'd just clawed her way back from death.

Esther screamed.

And the congregation erupted.

"She's alive!" Phil cried, his voice booming from the speakers throughout the sanctuary, grasping Carolyn's face between his hands. *"My sweet, sweet wife has returned!"*

"I'm calling the cops!" an older man cried, shooting up from his seat. His wife pulled him back down.

But others were on their feet.

Someone collapsed. Men and women shouted. Cried. Covered their mouths. Raised their hands in the air with praise.

Children sobbed. A young couple lifted their kids into their arms and stumbled out of the pews, marched out of the sanctuary with screaming little girls on their hips.

"Think of the myrrh-bearing women!" Fr. Paul cried. "Only *God* can give such power!"

Esther turned glistening eyes to Fr. Jerome.

He couldn't do anything.

There was *nothing he could do.*

Ever since he'd fought that carjacker in the front seat, Fr. Jerome hadn't been able to do a *damn thing.* He hadn't been able to stop the bullet. Even though Mariel hadn't died, Fr. Jerome hadn't actually *saved* his son. He'd tried.

But he'd failed.

Sharks fed upon his thoughts, and his brain became a bloodied mess of rage, terror, and hopelessness.

"Stop this." Fr. Jerome came forward, reached for his former mentor. "Stop this *now.*"

Fr. Paul caught his wrist and squeezed. He turned cold blue eyes to Fr. Jerome.

Fr. Jerome gasped. Those eyes—they looked so familiar now, so intimate, so *close* to someone he knew but couldn't place because his mind was a frenzied mess.

Mariel. That was it.

Their eyes were identical—especially now as Fr. Paul looked at him with cold distance.

"I'm not a part of this," Fr. Jerome said again, louder, as if convincing the congregation would *change* something.

"Oh, but you are, my friend," Fr. Paul said, squeezing his wrist and pulling the old man into his arms for an embrace. He murmured in his ear. "You've been a part of this since you called me years ago to beg for an explanation. You've been a part of this since you looked Philip Jameson in the eyes and told him his ideas weren't good enough, and when you told him *he* wasn't good enough for the priesthood. You've *molded* some of this, and now you're losing your church because you were too swept up in helping a group of minorities that will *never* find God."

"*Hey!*" Esther's voice.

She stormed towards the two men and slapped Fr. Paul's hand away from the old man's wrist. "Don't you *fucking* touch him, you psycho."

Fr. Paul turned his eyes to the angry young woman. They flickered to her stomach and then back up to her face. "Soon." He cocked his head.

Bewildered, Fr. Jerome glanced towards Esther.

Esther's face was white. Ignoring him, she grasped Fr. Jerome's arm and pulled him down the steps and towards the sanctuary entrance where Tira had stood not long ago. "Father," she said, *"look at me."*

Fr. Jerome inhaled, trying to control his oncoming tears, but droplets tumbled over his cheeks. "I'm sorry," he muttered.

"No. *No, Father Jerome!*" Esther grabbed his chin and turned his face towards hers. "You have *nothing* to be sorry about... unless you *don't* put your foot down and help these helpless *idiots!*" She jerked her arm towards the groveling congregation. "*Please.*" Her lips trembled. "You were always there for us. For the kids. For everyone in this congregation who needed emotional and spiritual healing. This is my second home. With *you*. It's everything I remember in my childhood that was *good.*"

Fr. Jerome bent his head.

"Praise God!" someone wailed.

"Father," Esther said, squeezing his hand. "My friendships here are broken now. Sunday School and this sanctuary are the only good, *healthy* memories that I have of Mariel and Gabe. *Please.* Say something." Mucus dribbled from her nose. Her eyes were wild. "*Do* something! Because I'm getting the feeling that things are about to get much, *much* darker, and *you* are the only lantern I know."

Fr. Jerome sniffled and looked up. The tears tickled his cheekbones. "I don't have that sort of persuasion anymore," he whispered.

"Father, take *back* that control and—"

"I am not in control over *any* of the chaos on this planet," Fr. Jerome wailed. "Mariel is." He squeezed Esther's shoulder, pursed his lips, and then stepped past her. "I'll be with my cat."

The voices of the congregation rose in excitement. Cell phones clicked as snapshots flashed throughout the sanctuary. Kids shrieked and ran about. A joyful woman laughed.

"*Father Jerome!*" Esther cried.

He kept going, leaving the church as Tira had, passing through the narthex, walking past the candles that were always lit for someone in need of prayer or intercession.

"*Give your anxieties to God,*" *Charles Nadier said, scratching his jaw.* "*All you can do.*"

He stripped his vestments from his body, sobbing as the coverings crumpled to the floor. But he continued on until the cold breeze tickled his face, and the church doors slammed shut behind him.

And when the priest returned home and saw his son still buried beneath the sheets of sorrow, guilt, and shame, Fr. Jerome Nadier did one thing. It was the only thing that had ever helped him calm his mind and find peace within himself during the chaos of the outside world.

He picked up his journal, and he began to write.

VERSE 3

~ BALLOONS ~

Sunday, September 30th, 2012
Chicago, Illinois

Trainers Artyom and Boris had a key to her room because, as Papa had ordered, they were not to let her roam free on her own accord.

Tira was used to the men entering her hotel room when they pleased. She knew to always wear some sort of attire. But that wasn't the issue tonight.

Tonight... someone else followed them in.

As the dim lamp flickered, Tira stood near her bed, scowling as a tall, large man in a peacoat and dress slacks entered the room behind her trainers. His shadow loomed and shape-shifted against the wall, and a large smile spread across his middle-aged face when his eyes found hers.

"What is this?" Tira snapped. "Who are you?"

The light flickered over his grey and blond hair. His blue eyes scanned her face for much too long, and then dropped to the rest of her body.

She'd seen that look many times. She wasn't ignorant. But the look wasn't what scared her.

It was the *task*.

The one not listed on the itinerary.

"Answer me!" Tira demanded.

Boris put a finger to his lips. "Settle down. You are not being polite to your guest."

Her guest?

"I do not have a—"

"My name is Levi," the older man interrupted, and reached into his coat pocket. "Do you like chocolate?" He produced a dark chocolate bar from his coat. It glinted in the lamplight.

"No," Tira snapped. She wasn't an idiot.

"You know what, that makes sense," Levi chuckled and set the chocolate bar on the desk beneath the light. "I've got something you might actually like."

"I am not interested."

"Well, hold on there, tiger," Levi grinned and cocked his head towards the trainers. "Give me a chance here."

Boris and Artyom moved towards the doorway.

They were leaving her.

They were leaving her *alone with this man.*

"We will be back in forty-five minutes," Artyom said.

"I paid for an hour," Levi hissed, and his smirk went away as he glowered at the trainers.

"One hour is forty-five minutes in Russian time," Boris chuckled, and he opened the door. He looked at Tira. "Do not make us punish you for misbehaving, understood?"

Tira opened her mouth to protest, but they were gone.

She was alone with Levi.

He locked the door.

"Now," he said, taking off his jacket. "Can I show you something you'll *actually* like?" He reached into his pocket.

Standing by the bed in her t-shirt and sweatpants, Tira glanced at the backpack at the side of the bed—the backpack where she kept *everything.* Knife. Pistol. Silencer.

Levi pulled a black switchblade from his belt. He tossed it to her feet. "I was going to give it to my son Matthew for his birthday—but he hasn't done so good with his grades. It's yours."

Tira tried not to look at it. Her fingers tingled with the urge to grab it.

She loved knives that she could manipulate, especially the ones that glinted in the light when flipped open.

"Come on, just flip it open once and see it," Levi urged.

Tira shook her head.

Levi sighed. "Okay." He smiled a little. "Tell you what, I'm going to use your restroom, give you some time to relax. I'm not going to hurt you, but I, and your trainers, would like it very much if you'd do as I say."

Yes... Tira understood quite well, and, even though he smiled, he meant every word he said.

She had no choice but to comply.

She *never* had a choice—not in Petrov's world.

Levi's tall frame blotted out the lamp for a moment. He left the common area and entered the bathroom.

Tira looked down at the knife, chewed her lip, and then picked it up. She ran her thumb against the shiny black surface before flicking open the blade.

God, it was beautiful. It glinted, and she could see her reflection; the healing bruises on her face, the long, wavy hair that fell across her cheeks as it dried from her shower.

In the bathroom, the man cleared his throat. Pills clattered.

The door opened.

Quickly, Tira placed the knife on the nightstand next to the bed and backed away. Waited.

Levi came around the corner. The pea coat was gone. Dress slacks and a white button-down remained.

"Get on the bed, please," he said, coming towards her.

Tira backed away, and her hips struck the dresser. Her mind grew frantic, her palms moistened, and her breathing became ragged. "I thought you'd want to take your time," she said, her voice quiet, trembling.

Levi snapped his head towards the bed as a reminder. "I only have forty-five minutes."

Tira swallowed hard.

"Here, I'll even turn the light off for you since you're so shy." Levi switched off the lamp. He became a looming shadow, and the shadow moved forward. "Get... on... *the bed.*"

What would happen if she didn't obey?

Would Petrov end her future?

Kill her?

He couldn't do what he'd done on July 13th, 2008, because she hadn't been *fond* of anything since Hamster's death.

And she *refused* to be *fond* of anything ever again.

But transitioning from *Project* 4 to *Agent* 4 was all she'd ever wanted. She'd endured much pain—mental and physical—to get to this point. In six short years, she'd graduate, get the tether removed, and find freedom as the top agent in Petrov's kingdom.

Levi crawled onto the bed.

It'd only be forty-five minutes.

Forty-five minutes... and she could leave Chicago in the morning, continue on, and put the sacrifice behind her.

She'd do anything to become Agent 4.

So, with a shudder and sickening tug in her stomach, Tira Petrov crawled into the bed with the man called Levi.

He snatched her, pulling her close to him as his minty breath tickled her nostrils. "You're such a beautiful woman," Levi murmured, and slipped his hands beneath her shirt.

She screamed, but it didn't come out of her mouth. It stayed hidden in her mind, a blood-curdling cry that only she could hear. As his hands crawled over her skin, and his mouth and tongue kissed and licked like a creature from hell, Tira wondered if this is what a first kiss was like for subhumans. Messy. Filthy. *Shameful.*

"Come here, pretty little lady," he grunted.

Would she feel different if Levi was a female?

Maybe if she imagined away the stubble on his face, and the rod in his pants that he kept dragging her hand against, she could pretend he was a female and deal with the forty-five minutes.

The belt buckle clinked. Levi's pants slipped down. The bed shifted, and he pushed her down, grunting, reaching for the waistband of her sweatpants. "This will feel really good, okay? Just relax and it'll feel good."

But it didn't feel good. He wasn't even inside of her yet, and it already felt *horrible.* His body trapped her against the bed, pressed on her chest, stomach, and hips, deprived her of oxygen.

Ever since her walk below the pool water as a four-year-old girl, her body responded to training in a predictable manner.

"Your lungs will feel like they are exploding balloons, do you understand?" Trainer Sergei yelled as Project 4 stood looking down at the murky pool water.

Balloons had burst in her mind then.

Beneath Levi, balloons burst in her mind now.

And when the balloons burst?

It was time to fight.

Tira gasped.

Reached for the switchblade and flicked it open.

It clicked.

And she drove it into his neck.

The first time didn't break the skin very much. He squealed like a pig, tried to crawl backwards.

She got it further into his neck this time.

Blood trickled over her knuckles.

He grunted, whimpered, wheezed.

"Fuck you," Tira hissed, pulling out the knife and driving it into his belly. She was angry now. Wanted to destroy his body. Wanted him to feel the pressure of losing oxygen, of losing his life, of losing blood.

"It feels like bursting balloons, doesn't it, when your body loses oxygen?" Tira growled, stabbing him again, and again, and again, realizing that it *did* feel good. It felt good to kill a monster, and she had no shame.

Levi spluttered.

Tira drove the knife into his right eye. Her arm burned. Her hair was wet again—from sweat.

Liquid splattered her face.

Levi collapsed and gargled. His agonal breathing sounded like an alarm that would alert anyone walking past the hotel room.

Her adrenaline shot up.

She scrambled to get out from underneath him.

The darkness squeezed her.

Footsteps were coming.

Would they be back so soon?

Balloons burst in her mind again.

Wheezing, she thumped to the floor, landed like a cat next to her bag.

The footsteps grew louder. The motel room seemed to quake from the impending approach, and she *knew* it was them because they walked like elephants. It'd always made her laugh because they *walked* like *elephants*, and they were supposed to be *tactical*.

Tira unzipped the bag. Her hands shook.

Don't do this! she thought, but found herself twisting the silencer onto her pistol. Rage moved her limbs.

So did fear.

They'd beat her.

Probably fuck her just to punish her.

She knew they wanted to—especially when they were drunk. It'd been evident in the way their eyes followed her, the way the men always found reasons to use the restroom while she was in the shower.

Yeah, they'd definitely fuck her to punish her.

And they'd be far worse than the dead man on the bed.

Tira slapped the magazine into the pistol. It snapped.

That's probably why her trainers were coming back—to *catch* her in the act of misbehaving so they'd have have an excuse to—

The lock whirred.

Tira's pistol came up.

Artyom and Boris entered the room.

They opened their mouths—like startled bears exiting their dens.

Balloons burst.

And Project 4 fired twice.

* * *

Sunday, January 19th, 2020
Chicago, Illinois

The sooner Tira inserted the new microchip, the sooner she could continue on with her life and go back to avoiding Esther Caravan.

It'd been a madhouse in that place—*Bowling Jane's*, or whatever it was called.

Bowling JoJo's. Yes.

On Friday night, the chaos had distracted her from her primary goal—

Inserting the microchip.

But something else had distracted her too.

Something she didn't care to think about because it confused the hell out of her—that *small* temptation to brush Esther's hair away from her eyes as she lay against Tira's chest.

It didn't make logical sense. She'd done little things like that to Olivia. Hair stroking. Gentle massage.

Tira was well aware that she'd done those things to Olivia because she contained a small level of fondness towards her... but there was absolutely no fondness for Esther Marie Caravan.

There was *no* reason to be fond of that disastrous human being.

But—

"Protect yourself too," Esther murmured, and reached for her.

Tira hadn't been able to forget that moment. She wasn't sure why. Of course, it'd been a *nice* thing for Esther to say to her, but the words had struck her faster than the fucking speeding tickets the city of Chicago liked to hand out.

Those words had been a blow to her psyche. It was quite unsettling. It was even *more* unsettling that she couldn't figure out *why*.

So rather than trying to figure out a *reason* for something so abstract that there'd be no viable way to solve its equation, Tira Arcelin decided it'd be easier to just not think about it anymore.

Still, Agent 4 *needed* to find an excuse to see the subject. She still had unfinished business.

And Tira didn't like that.

Papa wouldn't like that.

Because duty should always come first.

It was Sunday, January 19th—10:30 P.M.

Tira Arcelin had taken a midday shift to ensure she'd get adequate sleep before training the recruits in the morning. It'd be time to go home soon.

ABBA played softly through the cruiser's speakers as it sat with dimmed lights in a *NO PARKING* zone near the Ogden Slip River.

Tira played with the old switchblade she always kept close. Opened it. Closed it.

Click. Click. Click.

Outside, distant noises echoed against the silence of where she sat. The river was very close to the parking garage where the boats came to transport staff to the research center. She'd heard word of flooding in the lower level during the earthquake. There'd been three deaths.

She thought about the boy.

The one in the wheelchair.

The boy who'd awakened with a cry—just as the building began to vibrate beneath her feet outside of Kaemon Spears' conference room.

Tira hoped he wasn't one of the three.

Sipping her coffee, Tira's eyes darted over the streets, and she listened to anything that might capture her interest.

Cars screeched. Drunks yelled. People laughed. The air was warm tonight, warmer than usual, and more people bustled about the city.

Leaning her head back against the seat, Tira finished the rest of her coffee and thought about the day.

She'd gone to the church to scan—to make sure the subject was okay, and to see if Mariel Nadier happened to be there. She still hadn't been able to figure out who he was or *what* he was, and it drove her mad.

Why had he faked his death? How was Esther Caravan involved? Or was he just a lovesick puppy who wouldn't give her up?

Whoever he was, Mariel Nadier was pathetic.

But he hadn't been at the church... and Tira hadn't expected to arrive at the same time Fr. Jerome was giving his speech. Or sermon—whatever those people called it.

Fr. Jerome had found her eyes so easily that it'd almost startled her.

So Tira left.

She'd completed the priority task—making sure Esther Caravan was safe. There'd been no reason to stick around and listen to an old man blab about a sky ghost.

An engine revved. Tires squealed.

Adjusting in her seat, Tira buckled her seatbelt. She was excited to go home. Perhaps she'd read for a little bit in the hot tub.

Her phone buzzed. Tira looked at the caller identification and sighed.

"Hello," she answered cautiously.

"Hello, my sweet. How are you?"

Tira scowled. She hadn't expected the pleasantries from Petrov. It stressed her. "I am... doing well. How are..." she trailed off. What was she supposed to do? *Ask* how *he* was?

What the hell did he want?

"I am great, thank you for asking," Petrov chuckled. "Calm your pretty mind, Tira, I just wanted to call and congratulate you on a job well done."

"Er..."

"You know—protecting the subject."

Tira blinked, remembering the warmth of Esther's body against hers, feeling the sensation of the heartbeat she'd been monitoring for a year. The heartbeat she could no longer *hear* because she hadn't inserted the new—

"Thank you," Tira said. "I suppose, as horrible as it was, it is a good thing I went bowling."

Silence.

"Bowling?"

Tira's eyes shifted. "Er..."

"What are you talking about?"

"I went... for the... you know the subject wanted to... what are *you* talking about, Papa?"

"I am talking about the *threat* you crossed off on your file. Ring a bell?"

Oh.

JACOB CARAVAN: SUBJECT ELIMINATED.

Not bowling.

"Yes, correct. I did that." Tira cleared her throat.

"... Now I am curious. Tell me about this bowling."

For fuck's sake.

"It was nothing. I went bowling with the subject because I needed a reason to make sure she was safe." Tira's eyes followed a man stumbling down the walkway.

"And?"

"And what?"

"Did you insert what you were supposed to insert?"

Tira's face burned—she imagined her fingers in places she shouldn't imagine about a government asset, and thought about how certain parts of her would jiggle just right if she inserted—

"There was an earthquake," Tira said quietly. "I didn't get the opportunity."

"Little girl..." Petrov warned.

"I *will* see her again, Papa, she is a needy brat. I will make sure it happens." Tira tightened her jaw, watched the drunk man wobble and stumble to his knees about twenty feet from her cruiser. "I promise."

Another pause.

"Are you listening to *ABBA* again?" Petrov asked.

Tira slammed her hand against the volume knob and turned it off. Her face was on fire now. "The American stations are pathetic," she spat.

Had he called just to chit-chat? To embarrass her?

"Mmhmm. Well. I will let you go. I am still handling the riots here."

"Have they calmed at all?"

"Some. They don't dare protest near our home, at least."

Our home.

Nothing felt like home anymore. Chicago would never be home, and the Kremlin seemed like such a distant memory. The only attachment she had to it was—

Olivia.

How *was* she?

Tira didn't dare ask. Petrov might mistake her intentions for something much worse than fondness.

Love.

And the last time she'd *loved* something (if that's what it was) he'd murdered it.

So Tira decided she'd find contentment in not knowing how Olivia was, and she forced her mind to determine that Olivia was fine.

Safe.

Happy.

"Remember your duty," Petrov said. "It is what will get your name chanted one day. Understood?"

Tira nodded and rubbed her palm against her thigh. "Understood."

Petrov ended the call.

It was time to return to the station.

As she put the cruiser in drive, Tira saw the shadow of the drunk man swaying back and forth.

She flipped on the spotlight. It illuminated him, showcasing his hands on his dick as he sprayed the sidewalk with his urine. The spotlight did not deter him.

In fact, he ignored it.

Very slowly, Agent 4 rolled the cruiser next to him and lowered the window. She eyed him.

The bearded man kept pissing, kept rocking back and forth.

"Hey," Tira said slowly. "Put your dick in your pants. Or I will tase it." She tapped her yellow taser.

Nodding, he obliged, still pissing, and staggered away. He tripped over a lone brick on the ground, howled as he fought with his zipper.

Snorting, Tira slammed her foot against the gas and screeched the cruiser away.

Thunder rumbled in the distance.

Her phone buzzed again.

Tira ignored it.

Once again, it vibrated. Another incoming phone call.

Grumbling, Tira snatched the phone from behind the sun visor and looked at the screen.

Esther Caravan.

Goddamn it.

Growling, Tira swiped the screen. "Arcelin speak—" she stopped and pursed her lips.

Loud techno bass burst through the phone speaker.

Stopped at a red light, Tira frowned in utter confusion as she heard excited screaming and inaudible words.

Was Esther at a *nightclub?*

It was *Sunday,* for God's sake.

"Hello?" Tira demanded over the phone. *"Miss Caravan?"*

"Hi! Can you—can you *hear me?* Ashley, *stop!"* An obnoxious giggle.

The light turned green, and Tira pressed on the gas. *"Esther?"*

"Can you come pick us up? *Please?* We're *s-smashed!"* Esther screamed over the phone, and then she laughed again. "Ashley, *no...* you don't get to talk to her."

"Good *night,* Miss Caravan." Tira ended the call and slammed it onto the dashboard.

It buzzed several seconds later.

A text message.

"Please?! We're sooooo smashed. And I'm not doing well :(. Please? Element Club."

Furious, Tira's heart slammed against her chest. Cursing, she switched on her overhead lights, waited for the oncoming vehicles to stop, and then completed a U-turn. Of course the club was the opposite direction of the station, which meant she would have to backtrack away from her own car and her own fucking bed.

But Tira couldn't leave the subject drunk and vulnerable in downtown Chicago.

God, she hated Esther Caravan.

"On my way." Tira sent the message and then gripped the steering wheel with clenched teeth. There was never a moment of goddamn peace—especially with that entitled little bitch.

She couldn't wait to insert that microchip and disappear from her life.

The phone buzzed again.

"Thx sooooo much. And Tira... I'm really, really excited to see you ;)."

Tira felt something turn in the pit of her stomach. She set her teeth, tried to ignore the feeling. Grimacing, she continued down the street, driving further and further into the city.

The nightclub was on the left of the street, requiring Tira to whip the cruiser around, turn the overhead lights back on, and park in the center of the road.

Headlights flashed in her eyes as Agent 4 slammed the driver's door with her boot and stormed into the roadway.

Bass vibrations. Screaming girls. Drunken boys.

Frustrated drivers sped around her cruiser. Tires screeched and horns blared.

After a moment of imagining the pleasure she'd experience planting sticky bombs on every vehicle that passed, Tira raised her hand and crossed the street.

Lightning flickered in the sky. The warm breeze tugged loose strands of hair into her eyes.

"I'm outside of the building," Tira texted. Then waited.

No response.

Agent 4 tried calling Esther's phone.

No response.

Now she was mad.

Chewing her lip, Tira glanced around and searched for white, drunken brunettes.

The doors burst open.

Music pounded the air. Colored lights flashed.

A large group of young women stumbled from the building, clinging to each other, shrieking and giggling. Clad in tight dresses and high-heels, they staggered over the sidewalk.

"Damn it," Tira hissed, and she checked her phone again. Nothing. "This *fucking* idiot."

Esther Caravan was going to force her to enter the nightclub—wasn't she?

First: karaoke.

And now this.

Russian expletives flew from her mouth. Tira flung open the doors and stomped into the building. She squinted. Her eardrums felt as though they'd burst.

Like fucking balloons.

The bright lights flickered and pulsed, splitting the darkness with multi-colored lightning. The bass-boosted, fast-paced, high-energy techno punched through the speakers.

On an elevated stage, the DJ banged his head up and down as he worked the turntable.

The dance floor was congested. Hordes of people jumped up and down with raised fists. Head-banged. Grinded. Made out. Dry humped.

It was a fucking nightmare.

Tira's mind was frenzied. Her mind and body hurt. She fought the rising overstimulation in an effort to assess the situation, but it was hard to process everything at once. Foot stomping. Lights. Shrieks. Dancing shadows. *Drunken* shadows. The placement of people's hands.

Buzzing from the chaos, Tira withdrew her flashlight. Her skin tingled and burned.

Someone tapped her shoulder.

Tira whirled, hand on her gun, and she aimed her flashlight.

It glowed against a tall black man's face. He recoiled, held up his hands.

Six-foot-five. Large muscles. Bald. Black shirt and black pants. A bouncer.

The music vibrated her body.

Tira lowered the flashlight and gestured for him to come closer. He complied, and she stood on her tiptoes to approach his ear. "*Esther? Esther Caravan?*" she screamed.

He straightened up, shrugged, and gestured to the crowd to remind her that there were multitudes of women.

Shaking her head again, Tira marched towards the dance floor.

Sweat. Alcohol. Marijuana. Arousal. It all infected her nostrils as she approached the writhing crowd. Pausing, she darted the flashlight over several inebriated, sweaty faces.

Esther Caravan was an attention whore. She loved music. She loved dancing, obviously, and she loved it even more when people *watched* her dance. She'd either be in the center of the floor, or closer to the stage.

Agent 4 would start there.

Like an angry storm, Tira moved amidst the flashing lights and parted the red sea as she blinded as many dancers as she could with her flashlight. She pushed, bumped, pulled, yanked, and threw individuals from her path. Eyes squinted at her; mouths cussed at her.

The bass vibrated into her feet and upwards into her chest as she neared the stage. Keeping her hand on her gun, she elbowed dancers off of her, pushing them aside as she searched for Esther Caravan. A man fell against her, and she swept his leg out from beneath him.

Finally, in the drunken chaos, Tira found her.

The agent stopped walking.

It was strange—feeling *paralyzed* for no reason. Her legs lost their ability to move as Tira watched the scene before her.

As suspected, Esther Caravan and her friend were in front of the stage. Unaware of Tira's stunned presence, the two women pressed into each other and danced. The colored lights flickered. The bass exploded.

Smooth and sensual, Esther moved her body against Ashley. The young woman gyrated her hips, grinded her ass. Threw her head backwards. Bit her lip. Buried her fingers into her wavy, disheveled hair. As she brought her arms up, the bottom of her long-sleeve, mesh-panel blouse lifted just above the button of her jeans and exposed the smooth, taut skin of her abdomen.

Tira's muscles tensed. Her body warmed with unwelcome arousal.

Letting out a sigh, and holding her head high, she strode forward. Swiftly, Tira reached forward, hooked her forefinger into the belt loop of Esther's jeans, and tugged her very hard.

The young woman's eyes flew open. Confused, Esther glanced around, her hands still buried in her hair.

Turning a little, her eyes finally melted into Tira's.

That familiar, mischievous smile flickered over her lips, exposing the minuscule dimples at the corner of her mouth. Swaying in her high heels, Esther Caravan stumbled forward.

Tira rolled her eyes and outstretched her hand. "*Let's go!*" she screamed, but her voice became lost in the music.

Esther tripped and fell into Tira's arms. She placed her palms flat against the agent's upper chest, and her eyes hesitated on Tira's lips. Then... she raised them to meet the officer's, and the lights flickered across her flushed face and pulsed against her odd blue-brown eyes.

"*Hi,*" Esther mouthed, and her legs gave out a little. She smelled like shampoo, perfume, and marijuana, and her breath reeked of alcohol and peppermint.

The fumes merged and confused Tira's senses.

Behind her, Ashley kept dancing, wobbling her head, too drunk to notice that Esther had stopped.

"Let's go." Tira snatched her hand.

Esther retracted her hand and stumbled back to Ashley. Staggering, she grabbed her friend's arm and pulled her towards Tira, pointing, biting her lower lip and giggling.

Ashley nodded her head and laughed as she followed Esther towards the murderous cop.

Snarling, Tira grabbed both women by the elbows and pulled them through the energetic crowd. As she thundered through the dancing horde, she imagined shooting her way through the crowd, clearing a bloody pathway with her gun. It calmed her, but only for a moment until she realized that she now had *two* drunk women to dispose of before the end of her shift.

She wanted to throttle Esther Caravan. All of the Caravans, really. Todd for creating her. Hawk for existing. Her mom, too, but she was already dead.

Dragging the stumbling, giggling women behind her, Tira kicked the front door open with her foot and pulled them outside—out of the suffocating environment. Fresh air filled her nostrils, and she let out a breath. "Let's go," Tira spat again, yanking them once more. She was not gentle in any manner.

"You were *right,* Esther," Ashley drawled happily. "She *is* s-stunning, *and* cute, *and* angry! At the *same* time... like, how is that *possible?*"

Tira's face grew even warmer. She hated that she was flattered. "I'm going to arrest you both," she fumed, as if she had something to arrest them for, whipping her head back and forth to watch for traffic before crossing the street.

Esther bumped her hip against Tira, moving close and looking towards her with pleading eyes. "Don't be *rude,* Ossifer Mistress," she slurred. "Maybe..." Esther reached up and played with Tira's uniform collar. "... maybe we can make another—*deal* or something."

Tira ignored her and continued to watch the traffic.

Esther leaned closer, putting her lips to Agent 4's ear. "Only this time... *you* make *me* do something *you* want," she whispered, breath hot, grabbing hold of Tira's arm as she swayed in her heels.

Her heart rate skyrocketed. Growling, Tira jerked them forward, hearing a series of—

"*Ow!*"

"*You're hurting me!*"

"Police brutality!"

Tira opened the back door to the cruiser and threw Ashley inside of it, pushing her head down as she shoved the confused woman inside. "Get in and shut up."

After discarding Ashley, she gripped Esther's arms and shoved her against the cruiser. "And what exactly do you think I should do with you?" Tira raged.

Esther slumped a little, and her eyes flickered to Tira's lips. "Anything you *want*, Ossifer Mistress," she whispered. Her eyes grew hazier as she returned them to Tira's.

"This is the second time I've caught you floundering around like a stupid, abandoned fish! I will *find* a reason to take you to jail. So, what is it? Jail? Or your dad's?"

Terror crossed Esther's face, and her eyes widened. "Please, Tira. Neither. *Please.*"

"Hmm, should I leave you on the streets then? Because the idea is looking more and more appealing. You like the attention. You'd do well."

Ashley pounded against the window. "I'm hungry!" she whined.

Esther chewed her lip and turned pleading eyes to Tira. "Please. Take me to your place... let me s-s-sober up. I've had a *really* bad couple of days. Like... *bad. Please?*"

Tira's nose flared. She swept her mind, trying to remember if she'd left any revealing evidence in her apartment.

She hadn't.

But the idea of the subject in her home was unsettling. The *entire situation* was unsettling. But—

"Fine. Get in. And be quiet or you're both going to jail. Where does your friend live?"

Moments later, Tira found herself listening to Esther and Ashley's drunken singing as they swayed in the back seat, bumping into each other, cuddling, shrieking, whispering.

Occasionally, Tira glanced in the rearview mirror. She caught Esther's eyes each time, and the brown-haired woman granted her a slow, inviting smile. Sometimes, Esther chewed her lip. She'd run her fingers through her disheveled hair, clearly drawing pleasure from the evident frustration and discomfort that Tira felt.

When the singing switched from hip-hop to country, Tira decided she'd had enough. Squeezing the steering wheel, Tira whipped the cruiser into the *NO PARKING* zone by the river. The tires screamed as she slammed the brake pedal.

Scowling, she threw the SUV in park and stormed out of the vehicle. Whipped open the back door.

The singing stopped. Two pairs of hazy eyes blinked at her.

"If you two don't *shut up*, I will tase you, and then I will put my handcuffs on you both and bring you to jail. I will. I'm too tired for this. Do you *understand me?*" Tira slammed her palm against the top of the SUV.

They stared at her, and then Esther whispered, "Ossifer Mistress says to *ssshhh*. So we have to *shish*." She brought a finger to her lips and winked.

"*Sssshhh*," Ashley whispered and followed Esther's lead, but Tira wasn't paying attention anymore.

From the alley, someone was coming towards her—a large man walking fast, hooded with his hands thrust into his pockets. He was muttering to himself. No. Maybe he was on the phone. Speaking Arabic.

Tira caught a brief sentence, his voice broken and distraught.

"... *Fucking* destroy them for taking my wife."

The man was sobbing.

He looked up.

Their eyes met.

And the rain came.

As it poured, Tira rested her hand on her gun.

The man turned and went the opposite direction before disappearing into the dark alley once more.

Strange.

"Ossifer Mistress," Esther cooed.

"Shut up," Tira hissed.

Thunder clapped. It was time to rid herself of the drunken girls.

And insert the microchip.

Drenched, Tira entered the cruiser and slammed the door.

"We missed you, Ossifer," Esther sang, leaning her head against the barrier window between them. Something clunked to the floor.

Tira whirled in her seat.

"Have you been drinking from a flask while I've been gone?" Tira roared, and she slid open the barrier window.

"*Noooo.*"

"Give it to me."

"*Fine.*" Esther slapped it into Tira's offered palm and fell backwards against the seat. "You're so *boring*."

Tira was silent as she drove to Ashley's residence. She'd been driving for at least ten minutes, listening to the women snore against each other as dispatch spoke over the radio.

Dispatch spoke with sharp authority—a caller reported finding a white male with blunt force trauma to his head near the Ogden Slip River. CPR was in progress.

It was a typical night. Drunks. Assaults. Homicides. If she were not so exhausted, and her duty to ensure Esther's safety did not come first, Tira might have responded. But her eyelids were heavy, her body ached, and her mind spun.

Was this how subhumans felt when they were exhausted?

After parking outside of Ashley's apartment, Agent 4 helped the young woman out of the cruiser before threatening her with a year in prison if the situation happened again.

"I *mean* it," Tira barked.

Sleepily, Ashley nodded. Stumbled forward a little and glanced at the cruiser where Esther lay slumped in the back seat. "She can't stop talking about you," she whispered, smirking.

And she left Tira alone in confused silence.

VERSE 4

~ DUTY ~

T ira looked into the rearview mirror and saw Esther slouched against the window.

Idiot.

Shaking her head, she began her journey home. The windshield wipers brushed puddles of rain from the window as she approached the gated parking lot to her apartment building. As she entered the code, the rain soaked her uniform sleeve.

Esther stirred and moaned a little. "Are we home?"

"We are at *my* home," Tira emphasized, and drove forward.

"I'm so drunk, Ossifer."

"I know." Tira stepped from the cruiser and opened the back door.

Esther fell out sideways. With quick hands, Tira caught her and sighed.

Esther leaned her head onto Tira's chest. "Your uniform is un-comfy," she whined.

"Then don't lean on me."

"I can't walk. The world is spinning. Carry me."

Rolling her eyes, Tira lifted Esther Caravan into her arms as if she were her bride. The rain spattered and drenched them both, and she hastened to the building entrance.

Howling, the wind blustered, blowing rain against their bodies, and Tira felt Esther's body trembling, almost vibrating in her arms.

Blinking away raindrops, Tira entered the building and slammed the door against the howling wind and rain.

Esther's arms encircled her neck and tightened.

"You smell good," she whispered.

Tira did not respond.

"You're *soft*," Esther murmured, and nuzzled her face into Tira's neck.

Tira's heart raced as she ascended the stairs. Despite her attempts to ignore the woman in her arms, she couldn't help but notice every curve of her body. How soft her skin felt beneath the cloth of her dampened shirt. The sexy curve of her hips. The voluptuous cleavage beneath the see-through mesh of her shirt.

"Ossifer—"

"Please be quiet, Esther." Huffing, Tira adjusted Esther in her arms so that she could enter the security code to her apartment.

The lock whirred.

She entered the doorway sideways, clunking Esther's heels against the door before turning on the light. "It's time for bed. I am going to get you some clothes, and then I still have to clock out at work. No thanks to you."

God, if this triggered another ridiculous Internal Affairs investigation, she'd be fu—

"Hmph. Stay with me." Esther pushed her body closer, rubbing her nose against the skin of Tira's neck. "Please?"

Tira stiffened, shrunk away from her touch, ignored her plea. Sneering, she strode into the guest room, switched on the light, and then tossed Esther face down onto the bed.

The young woman bounced against the mattress. The bed creaked.

Groaning, Esther flopped onto her back and sat up a little, squinting at the bedroom light. Her damp hair fell over her shoulders and back. "*Tira*," she whined. "Where are you going?"

"To get you a change of clothes."

"*Ohh*. Hurry back, Ossifer Mistress," Esther slurred, sitting up a little. She swayed once more, and her eyes rolled to the back of her head. Then she jerked upright as if she were trying to avoid looking drunk.

Tira almost fled the guest room. She darted to her room. As soon as the door closed, she relaxed a little.

God, she hadn't realized how tense her muscles had been, how fast her heart had been beating.

How *unsafe* she felt around Esther Caravan.

Cursing, Tira retrieved the black box that Michael had given her. It contained the new implant, as well as the pistol-grip implant remover chip in Esther's neck.

The chip she'd—

—*hypothetically*—

—*shut down* because she was a fucking idiot.

Muttering, Tira opened the box and gathered the tiny plastic encasing that protected the chip.

Tira stared at it.

"Do it this time," she whispered. "No excuses. Your job comes first. Your country comes first."

"*Tira!*" Esther's muffled voice called in the next room.

Wetting her lips, Tira slipped her necessary items into her pockets. She gathered shorts and a white t-shirt, ensured everything in her room had been returned to its proper location, and then marched back to the guest bedroom.

Esther sat upright on the edge of the bed, her legs outstretched, her heels digging into the carpet. Wobbling back and forth, she gazed at the floor. Despite her flushed face, exhausted eyes, and messy hair, Esther still looked... gorgeous.

Pathetic.

But gorgeous.

Straightening her shoulders, Tira approached the bed with the clothes. "Here. Get changed and go to sleep. Make sure you tell your family whatever you need to tell them so they don't worry about you."

Esther didn't respond, just rocked back and forth in her drunken daze.

"Esther."

No response.

Sighing with loud annoyance, Tira came closer, stooped a little, and grasped the bottom of Esther's shirt. "I am going to change you. I won't look. Alright?"

After waiting a moment for consent and receiving no reply, Tira lifted the blouse and grimaced as she averted her eyes.

"*Gotcha.*" Rapid hands seized her collar.

Tira gasped.

Laughing, Esther's eyes sparkled as she assessed Tira's shocked countenance. Her fingers worked quickly to loosen the top buttons of Agent 4's shirt. "I'll help you undress, too," she whispered shakily, and she pulled the magnetic bodycam from the center of Tira's uniform. She tossed it without care to the floor where it thumped against the carpet.

Realization snatched Tira from the moment of shock. She twisted the drunk woman's hands from her shirt. "*Stop* it, Esther!" Her heart thundered in her chest, her body lit aflame. She couldn't breathe.

Balloons burst in her mind.

Esther's hands shot out again, colliding against Tira's body and pulling at the white t-shirt she'd exposed from unbuttoning the uniform. "I'm *just* trying to help!"

Tira grasped her wrists, fought her.

With a movement so fluid it was shocking, Esther fell backwards and yanked Agent 4 on top of her, clenching the rumpled shirts in her fists. "Undress me," she panted, speaking through her teeth. "Now."

"Miss Caravan!"

Esther's hands found the buckle to Tira's gun belt. "I'm usually *so much* quicker at this but... I'm *so smashed*," she reminded, tugging with frantic desperation at the belt. "And you cops wear too much... *fucking... shit!*"

Agent 4 could not control the mounting pulse between her legs. It crashed through her body like waves as Esther tugged at her clothing, stared up at her with mischievous intent, squirmed her *fucking* hips beneath Tira's body.

"Get on the bed," Levi ordered.

Tira shook her head.

This had to stop. Now.

Hissing, the agent popped her on the cheek, twisted out of the drunk woman's arms. She staggered backwards, brushing disheveled blonde hair from her eyes, breathing hard.

The pulse between her legs—it was unnerving. Maddening. Confusion, hatred, and desire combined.

Exploded.

"Don't ever go near my firearm again!" Tira screamed, gasping. Shaking, she snapped the belt again and grabbed the bodycam from the floor. "*Sober* up, Esther Caravan, you're embarrassing yourself. Badly."

Esther stood, almost lost her footing. Her eyes were wide, lips parted. Her breasts rose and fell as she struggled to gather air. "*Please* don't be mad," she drawled. "I just... I—" she stopped talking and came forward.

"Leave me alone." Tira darted for the door.

Esther slipped in front of her and slammed it shut, pressing her back against the door and slipping downwards a little as she lost her balance. Her glistening eyes reminded Tira of a puppy's—yearning for attention while knowing full well that it was misbehaving.

And *God*, they were standing close.

Tira found herself lost in those misbehaving eyes, and the sound of their hard breathing was all she could hear.

Esther's warmth radiated from her body in heat waves. As her invasive eyes fell to Tira's lips, Agent 4 fought for oxygen.

"Why are you afraid of me?" Esther whispered, wobbling again. She pressed her palms against the door in an attempt to remain balanced.

The question startled Tira, confused her, and then angered her. Like a trapped dog baring its teeth, Tira lowered her voice. "I am not afraid of *anything*."

"*Yes*," Esther moaned in drunken frustration. "You *are*. You're so... *skittish* around me, and you try to avoid me. Why?"

"You're getting more drunk. You're going to be very embarrassed tomorrow. And I won't leave out a single detail about anything you are doing." Tira's voice was harsh, even though she *knew* she had the ability to move Esther from the door.

Agent 4 *knew* that she could twist the weaker woman's arm a certain way, or push her, or *throw her* out of the way.

Then she could leave.

In fact, she could even leave the apartment and go back to Russia if she *really* wanted to escape but... Esther's nearness brought her sudden paralysis.

"Then let's make the details interesting," Esther murmured, arching her eyebrow, and then she tipped forward and nipped Tira's earlobe with her teeth.

The pulse intensified between her legs. She was losing control. Terror shot through her body.

"*Move*, Esther." The tremors in her body intensified, and she found herself holding her breath.

"*Mmmm*, but you liked that. You're blushing."

Grinding her teeth, Tira grasped Esther's wrists and slammed them hard against the door. With a loud thud, the movement pushed Esther's back flat against the wooden surface. The walls vibrated from the force.

Shaking, Tira whispered, "What do you *want* from me?"

She was *angrier* with herself for allowing this to carry on.

Esther's breathing came fast. Her tongue touched her lower lip, and her eyes turned serious. "Help me... forget." Her voice was quiet, pitiful. As if ashamed, her eyes darted to the floor.

"*Forget what?*"

"Kiss me," she whispered, looking at Tira's lips again.

"No. Absolutely not."

"Fuck me. *Hard*. Take me against the door," Esther moaned, biting her lip. Her eyes brimmed with tears. "Make me forget about loving... *him*."

Something sank inside of Tira. The words stung. *Tore* through her chest.

And she didn't understand why. This was just another unimportant, drunken woman begging for casual sex to forget about a man... most likely Mariel.

Had they *broken up*?

Had he *hurt* her?

It didn't matter. Esther had destroyed her mind and conscience with alcohol and marijuana. Now, like a typical subhuman, she wanted a physical distraction to ease her pain. Nothing more, nothing less. A wasted, depressed, horny, white girl who would never forget her first love.

If Agent 4 obliged her request and casually fucked her against her bedroom door, Esther Caravan would moan in ecstasy—imagining it to be the "resurrected" man in this room.

Not Tira.

No. Tira was convenient. *Available*. The "highly desired" Esther Caravan's *chosen* sex toy. In fact, anyone on the nightclub dance floor could have been the "lucky" one tonight. But, for some reason, Tira Arcelin had received the beckoning.

Fuck. Why the hell was she hesitant about this?

A beautiful woman stood before her, offering her body. But it seemed *wrong*. If any other woman had asked her to fuck away the memory of a boyfriend, Tira wouldn't have questioned it.

But the request from Esther? It *cut* her in a way she couldn't explain. And, for the first time, Agent 4 understood what it must feel like to experience... *hurt*.

And Esther?

She would pay for that.

With a soft breath, Tira tilted her head, bringing her lips close to Esther's, watching as the young woman closed her eyes in anticipation. Her pulse pounded in her head. As she parted her lips, Tira could almost taste the minty alcohol as Esther's sigh blew gently into her mouth. Their noses brushed, and a low moan vibrated from the brown-haired woman's throat.

"I'd help you forget," Tira whispered, pressing harder against Esther's wrists. "I'll tell you how." She brought her lips close to the other woman's ear. "I'd lift your blouse." Gently, she brushed her thumbs over Esther's wrists.

Esther shuddered hard.

Tira continued her assault. "I'd remove your bra... and then I'd lick, twist, flick and *pull* those perfect, little nipples I can see hardening through your blouse."

Gasping, Esther turned her face to Tira's, searching for her lips.

The agent didn't allow her access.

Instead, with cruel and angry intent, Tira murmured into Esther's ear. "I'd mold, squeeze, and tug until you begged for more, Esther, and then—" she trailed her fingers to the button of Esther's jeans, tugging a little. "I'd slip my fingers inside of your jeans..." Moaning, Tira freed the button with her fingers. "... and I'd *play*."

"God, *please*, Tira—"

"Just lightly brushing my fingers against your panties until you are hungry, wet, and *aching* for me to *fuck* you against this door until you *scream*."

"*Tira!*" Esther was begging, arching her back against the door, grasping at Tira's shirt with her free hand.

"Which I won't do because I don't *fuck* children," Tira spat, releasing Esther and pushing her away from the door. "You are inebriated beyond *all* cognitive ability. Go to bed, Esther. Maybe when you are a self-sufficient adult, we will speak like adults and discuss the possibility of friendship. Good night."

Without hesitating to see Esther's reaction, Agent 4 stormed from the room and slammed the door, desperate to leave, trying to calm herself. Something about that woman in her room fucked with her mind, and she needed clarity. Time to think. Time to understand why she was so upset. Time to free herself of strange, unnecessary emotions and do her *job*.

Tira was almost to the front door, buttoning her uniform, when she heard a light sob from the other room.

Don't you fucking stop walking, she thought, clenching her jaw and reaching for the doorknob.

Another sob. *Pitiful* cries.

And she stopped walking.

"It's your own fault that you're upset, Esther," Tira whispered, her hand still outstretched towards the doorknob.

But she retracted her hand.

Pursed her lips.

Closed her eyes.

And then turned away from the front door.

"Fuck." Grimacing, she stomped back towards the guest bedroom and opened the door.

Esther lay curled in the fetal position on the floor. Her shoulders shook with sobs.

As Tira approached, she noticed a pool of vomit on the carpet where she lay.

Her features softened, and, with quiet caution, she knelt beside the sobbing young woman. "What can I do?" she asked.

"Leave me alone. You're an asshat," Esther whimpered.

"I know, but I will not apologize for who I am. Tell me what happened."

"No."

"Esther. I'm not leaving you like this."

The young woman lay silent for a moment, and then she spoke in a soft voice. "You think you know someone. I thought I did. Then... he came back. *Different.*" She sniffled. "I met him yesterday to talk and figure out how I *felt.*"

Tira lowered herself onto the floor behind Esther.

"I just wanted to talk. I needed to work things out with him and understand everything that was *happening.* Nothing makes *sense* right now, and I just wanted to fucking *know.*" Another sob broke through her voice. "*Fuck.*"

"It's okay just... try to keep going. What happened?" Tira's voice was smooth, soothing.

She pitied Esther.

Esther didn't *deserve* the pity, but it was there.

"He's charming. S-so fucking charming. He has a way of-of manipulating me into doing what he wants. So instead of talking, we... we... he..."

Tira closed her eyes. "Did he hurt you, Esther?"

"He doesn't understand that he's *big.* It *hurts* me. He shoved himself into my mouth. I asked him to slow down and... and he said he would if I took off that *stupid fucking* necklace."

Tira's body warmed again—this time with rage. She kept her eyes closed and bit her tongue.

"I told him no." Esther coughed, dry heaving. Sitting up, she clutched at her stomach. "Sorry."

Tira placed her palm on Esther's back. Rubbed it a little. Yanked it back and cleared her throat.

"He ripped the necklace from my throat."

"Did he *rape* you, Esther?" Tira's body shook.

Esther shook her head. "No. But he said that if—" her voice faded, and she slumped back towards the floor. "I'm gonna pass out."

"What did he say? Esther." Tira tapped her shoulder, shook her a little.

Jerking awake, Esther spoke in a whisper. "He said he'd make me choke on his cum if he saw me wear it again. He *said* he was being funny but his—his eyes *weren't*." She dry-heaved again, convulsed for a moment.

"I don't know the subject you are referencing," Tira lied, "but I will murder him." Her voice was low, dangerous.

"It wasn't *him*," Esther cried, struggling to sit up before falling again. "God, I feel so *sick*. And... he's nuts, or maybe he isn't. I don't *know*, because when I broke up with him, he said that I—God, it doesn't even make any s-sense."

"Tell me. Esther, just *tell* me."

Esther rolled onto her back, and her eyes fluttered to the back of her head. Her chest heaved up and down. Tears stained her reddened cheeks. "Kill chip... something about a kill chip. He lost his shit and s-s-said I deserved the *kill chip*. I don't even know what that *means*, Ossifer Mistress, what does that...?" Esther's voice faded. Her eyes closed. Drool trickled from her mouth.

"Esther?"

A soft snore.

The room was cold. Then hot.

Now Tira felt dizzy. Drunk. *Off balance.*

Her pulse beat down her ears.

A *kill chip*?

She rubbed her face with her palms.

Everything was a mess. The world. The mission. *Her mind.*

She needed to get away and *think.*

Tira lunged to her feet and left the room. Paced inside of the hall. Her palms were clammy. Her chest was heavy, as if Senator Levi Thompson had collapsed on top of her again.

A *kill chip*?

That didn't sound right. Aleksey Petrov *emphasized* that her duty was to *protect* Esther Caravan—not to ensure her *death!*

How was *Mariel Nadier* involved, and how did he *know*?

She *presumed* he wouldn't lie about it, considering that he did indeed have an attachment to Esther that was possessive in nature.

"Think, Arcelin, *think*," she whispered. Her chapped lips peeled apart.

She walked up and down the hall, thinking of the other microchips that she'd used *against* people. Against potential *threats*.

Was Esther Caravan a *threat* to the Russian government? If so, how? How could this idiotic, drunken woman possibly be a *threat* to Aleksey Petrov?

Was there *something* about Esther that did not meet the eye? Something she'd been too blind to see?

The floor creaked again and again as she paced the apartment, growing more and more confused.

The minutes passed. Time fled.

She found herself sitting on the floor, scribbling ideas on pieces of paper in an effort to narrow down what the *fuck* was going on.

Nothing made sense.

Petrov knew the truth.

And Mariel Nadier *might* know the truth.

But Tira Arcelin, top agent and daughter to the world's richest, most powerful leader, knew *nothing*.

Breathing slow, Tira leaned against the wall just outside of the guest room. She heard Esther's heavy breathing.

It was late. Esther slumbered, and Tira hadn't yet clocked out of work.

She needed to make a decision.

This was her *job*.

Her *duty*.

Devotion to her *country*.

Her country and duty came first. Nothing could, nor would, ever interfere.

She'd *killed* people because of this job, this duty. So, as Tira leaned her head against the wall, she made a decision.

Agent 4 entered the guest room and knelt beside Esther.

"Esther," she said somewhat loudly. "Are you awake?"

No response.

"Esther. I am naked."

Nothing.

"Esther." Tira clapped her hands next to Esther's ear.

Nothing.

Agent 4 checked the young woman's pulse. It was steady. She opened her eyelids and observed her pupils.

Out.

Moving fast, Tira withdrew the new chip from her pocket along with the implant remover. Her fingers shook, and her heart pulsed in her throat. She stared at both, second-guessing herself, wondering if she was making the right decision.

You were given specific instructions, she thought, trembling. *Overthinking kills. Don't overthink. Just do.*

Biting her lip, Tira leaned over the sleeping girl and positioned the implant remover against her neck. She pulled the trigger. A soft, air-sucking sound pierced the silence.

Esther jolted.

Tira emptied the cartridge and lifted the old, bloody chip into the air.

It looked no different from the new one.

Softly, Tira touched Esther's arm to ensure that she was still sleeping. Next, she retrieved the new chip and eyed it, as if staring it down would force it to confess an unknown truth.

It didn't.

It just glinted in the bedroom light.

Tira positioned the point against Esther's skin on the back of her neck. The young woman stirred, curled into a tighter ball on the floor.

Overthinking kills.

Agent 4 pursed her lips.

Tried to move her fingers. They wouldn't budge.

Don't overthink.

"Come *on*," Tira whispered, urging herself to complete the task. Her voice shook.

Just –

Tira jerked her hand away.

In a motion so automatic that it surprised even herself, she snapped the chip in two.

Sweat droplets rolled down her forehead. With sudden terror, she realized what she'd just done.

And Tira Arcelin didn't *want* to understand.

She had no *clue* as to why she'd just *destroyed* a piece of equipment issued by the president of Russia himself.

She had no desire to dig deeper into her frenzied, panicked mind to determine why she'd just committed an act of treason.

So—as lightning flashed, and thunder roared, and Tira Arcelin changed the subject's clothing and tucked her into bed, she simplified it for herself.

Before leaving her country, Agent 4 had been given specific instructions in regards to her duty on asylum in the United States of America.

Aleksey Petrov had been very clear.

Agent 4's duty was not to kill Esther Marie Caravan.

Her duty was to protect her.

EPILOGUE

"But because of your stubbornness and your unrepentant heart, you are storing up wrath against yourself for the day of God's wrath, when His righteous judgment will be revealed."

Romans 2:5

Moscow, Russia

January 1st, 1998

Fr. Paul hadn't realized how difficult it actually was to smother someone beneath a pillow. The movies had always made it seem easy. A one-minute job. Maybe two, tops. As curious about death as he'd always been, he'd never stopped to research the length of time it might take to complete such a task.

As sweat poured down his face, he struggled to contain his gasps, glancing desperately towards the doorway to ensure no one would enter. Beneath the pillow, her cries vibrated his hands.

This wasn't working. Natasha was thrashing too much.

So, crawling atop her body, Fr. Paul kept the pillow over her face and added pressure with his arm.

"Kill the bitch, kill, kill, kill!" The humanoid jumped up and down with glee.

Nurses laughed loudly outside the room, the sound fading as they passed the door.

The muffled cries turned to gurgles. The gurgles transitioned to agonal breathing. Next, the breathing stopped.

His torso felt like it was closing in on his lungs. Wheezing, Fr. Paul raised the pillow. Natasha's eyes were nearly closed, and wicked marks across her throat formed—as if in judgment of his actions.

A male voice laughed outside of the room. Beneath the crack of the door, foot shadows stopped, hesitated, and then moved on.

The infant let out a raspy cry.

Fr. Paul's eyes shifted.

Gasping, he covered the infant's face with his shaking hand. His entire palm covered the child's face. Gritting his teeth, he closed his eyes.

Tears trickled from beneath his eyelids.

He was killing a baby. His own son. And *for what*? His own pride? Once the baby was dead, where the hell would he go? He had no plan. He'd never *planned* for this.

"He cannot die," the humanoid hissed.

Strangely, Fr. Paul believed him. Or perhaps he had a conscience left, and was looking for a reason to stop the act of murdering a child. He didn't know.

But he needed to figure out a plan.

Keeping his palm over the boy's mouth, Fr. Paul glanced around. There was a window, but he was on the upper floor. There was no viable way to get down without falling to his death. There was no way to *leave the room* without being noticed.

He'd fucked himself.

"Take him to the Kremlin," the humanoid cackled.

"You want to guide me there without getting caught?" Fr. Paul growled, keeping his voice as low as he could. He could feel the baby's breath on his palm. A part of him just wanted to kill the boy and run.

The floor vibrated. The bed began to creak.

Eyes wide, Fr. Paul looked around.

The vibrations became stronger. The visitor chair rattled against the hard floor, and the vibrations jostled Natasha's head.

"The gate is open! Boss is coming!" The humanoid bounced and clapped.

Footsteps ran past the door. Someone sounded frantic. People yelled.

Grabbing the infant, Fr. Paul dove from the bed. As he struck the floor, he was almost shaken from his feet.

The electricity flickered. The hospital equipment buzzed on and off. The infant began to cry again.

Fr. Paul lost balance. He landed onto his hip, and the baby struck the floor. The infant screamed louder. So did the people outside of the room.

But, cutting through the panicked cries, Fr. Paul heard a voice he'd never heard before. It called his name, sending a level of terror through his body that was unmatched to anything he'd ever experienced.

"Paul..." It was guttural, and it echoed in the chambers of his mind.

Instinctively, Fr. Paul looked towards the window, as if the voice had called him from outside the building. As the earth shook, his eyes widened.

The sky was red. Contrasted against the blood sky, black clouds approached with fury.

Violently, the building rocked and moaned.

Fr. Paul reached for the baby and crawled towards the doorway. Ceiling tile crashed to the floor. Hospital equipment slid across the room and smashed into the walls.

"Paul..."

The chilling, demonic timbre overwhelmed his senses.

The infant's screams converged with the chaos.

Reaching for the doorknob, Fr. Paul twisted it and flung it open. He crawled out of the room. Lights flashed on and off. Medical staff crawled on their hands and knees. Many screamed.

Behind him, something crashed and shattered in Natasha's room.

Gripping the infant, Fr. Paul scurried to his feet, desperately trying to move forward. He fell to his knees multiple times, crawled, and then continued forward again, evading medical staff, sliding equipment, and collapsing tile. The crashing ceiling tiles exploded into dusty particles, filling the environment with haze.

Someone grabbed his leg. Roaring, he kicked, tripped, and fell again. A female nurse reached for him. Blood trickled from her eye. With a sudden snarl, she spoke scripture. Otherworldly voices mingled with hers.

"But because of your stubbornness and your unrepentant heart, you are storing up wrath against yourself for the day of God's wrath, when His righteous judgment will be revealed!"

"No!" Fr. Paul screamed, scurrying to his feet and running again.

A woman crawled from another room, clutching her pregnant belly, screaming. Blood dribbled down her legs. Her dark eyes met his, and she spoke.

"But it shall come about, if you do not obey the Lord your God—"

Fr. Paul lost balance again, slamming against the wall. Tears poured from his eyes.

"—to observe to do all His commandments and statutes with which I charge you today—"

He scrambled forward, but the woman's voice grew louder.

"—that all of these curses will come upon you and overtake you!"

"Leave me alone!" he screamed. He saw the flickering exit sign and, with renewed determination, sprinted for the stairway.

"Paul..."

There it was again—that other voice, that unknown guttural voice from a pit that pierced his consciousness. The sound made his head want to explode. His pulse roared.

Fr. Paul slammed against the door to the staircase. It flew open and banged against the wall.

He fled.

The earthquake dissipated as he tumbled down the stairs. The humanoid fled with him, bounding, giggling.

"Take him to the Kremlin!" the shadowy figure screeched. *"Boss is here!"*

Fr. Paul ignored him, tried to hush the screaming child. Still, he had no plan, but he knew his body acted on behalf of the humanoid's guidance. He couldn't stop it.

"Paul... find rest in me." As the voice spoke, with it was also a shrill sound, like wind screaming in his ears.

He saw the emergency exit. His legs buckled on the last few steps, and he collapsed again. His knees smashed against the cement, sending rippling pain into his hips.

The infant's scream rose in pitch.

Fr. Paul wobbled to his feet and darted for the exit door. He hadn't a clue where he was in relation to his vehicle's location.

Cold air stung Fr. Paul's face as he fled through the doorway and into an alley. Catching his breath, he stopped, glancing back and forth. His breath coiled through the bitter air. The earth had stopped shaking. Ambulance sirens pierced the night.

Fr. Paul looked up. The sky wasn't red anymore, just black.

The baby kept screaming.

"Shut up," he spat, covering the child's mouth again. Would it be so horrible if he left the child here in the alley and ran?

"Paul." The voice was that of a man. Deep. Powerful.

He whirled.

In the shadows, a young man with light brown hair stood about twenty feet away. He was dressed in a security uniform with a symbol on the coat that suggested he worked for the hospital.

Shaking his head, Fr. Paul turned on his heel and fled towards the end of the alley.

He heard footsteps behind him.

"Paul, give him to me! At least give him the chance for a good life and redemption too!"

The air pierced his lungs. He'd never run so fast in his life. He turned left, and darted down another alley. His car keys rattled in his pocket, reminding him that the car was *somewhere* close.

"Paul..." said that unknown voice again, that deep, breathy voice that surrounded him; that had come from the red and black skies; that brought pain to his head.

"Take him to the Kremlin!" the humanoid cackled.

Red flashing lights lit up the snowflakes that swirled in the air. An ambulance screamed by the alley on the main road.

"Paul! Give Mariel a chance to trust God's plan!" The security guard's roar held both frustration and desperation. The sound of his boots pounded against the snowy pavement.

"Mariel?" Fr. Paul sobbed, and his cries echoed into the night alongside the sirens. He nearly slipped on the ice, but he continued forward. There were so many voices. The security guard's voice, the humanoid's voice, and that unearthly voice that kept saying his name, calling him to the pit of Hell.

"Paul..."

"Take him to the Kremlin, and his destiny shall be fulfilled!" the humanoid squealed, mimicking his movements, slipping on the ice next to him, cackling with a voice of many pitches.

Fr. Paul entered the dark streets of the city. He clutched the screaming infant.

The security guard's voice sounded more distant, but just as strong. *"Mariel is what the man you mentored will name him. You remember Jerome Nadier? You loved him! Please... do what is right and save what soul you have left!"*

Fr. Paul couldn't breathe. He thought of Fr. Jerome Nadier—the bright-eyed, hopeful seminarian. He remembered how jealous he'd been of the man's level of faith; his ability to wholly love; his passion for his flock.

"Take him to the Kremlin!"

Fr. Paul couldn't contain the sobs. He cried together with his son.

"Lucifer is coming for you, Paul!" the security guard roared.

"No!" he screamed. A horn blared, and a car sped past him. The tires shrieked. *"God is coming for me!"*

The sky flickered red and turned black again.

There was a pressure in his head, growing, as if someone were slipping into his skull and coiling around his brain like a snake. Squeezing him. Crushing him.

It was unbearable now.

Fr. Paul screamed in pain and despair.

The guttural voice whispered to him, filling his head, speaking in a language he'd never heard before. Yet, he understood the words as if he'd always known it.

"The pain will subside soon, Paul."

Fr. Paul's own thoughts were fading in and out. The invisible serpent not only crushed his mind, but its fangs were now latched, inserting its venom and destroying Fr. Paul's last remainder of self.

A train whistle screamed distantly in the city. So did the infant.

Clutching the baby, he glanced behind him. The security guard was gone. *Where?* Paranoia seized him.

Through blurred eyesight, he saw his car across the street. He first recognized a familiar dark sedan parked behind his car. It had been parked there when he'd arrived earlier in the day.

"Take him to the Kremlin!" the humanoid giggled, but he was no longer visible to the fleeing priest.

Fr. Paul knew the Kremlin was his destination. He did not know why, because his body now acted on behalf of something else—or for *someone* else. And he was convinced it was not *God*, because he couldn't even *think* of that deity's name without wanting to let out a bloodcurdling scream.

The train whistle blew once more.

Fr. Paul slipped, falling to his knees, nearly dropping the baby. For a moment, he remained on the icy ground, his car a short distance away. The baby shrieked.

The pressure in his head was gone. He felt sudden peace. As the cries pierced the abrupt and strange silence of the city, Fr. Paul turned his eyes to the baby. A slow smile quivered across his lips. In a quiet whisper, he sat in the middle of the roadway and spoke to the child.

"I... am your Father God.*"*

The train whistle screamed. The city came alive again.

"Do not mock the Lord your God!"

The voice broke above the baby's screams. Fr. Paul's head flew up, searching for the security guard, seeing no one.

Something rumbled. An engine.

Panicked, his eyes shot towards the vehicle parked behind his car. Fr. Paul saw movement in the driver's seat, and with rising terror, he staggered to his feet.

Headlights snapped on.

An engine roared.

Tires screeched.

As Fr. Paul jolted into a sprint, he realized two things.

The Messenger would not stop pursuing him, and it was about to be a race to the Kremlin.

Seconds blurred.

Fr. Paul flung himself into his car. He was certain he had thrown the child into the passenger seat, because something *thumped* and the screams got *worse*.

As the sedan behind him lurched forward and rammed into his car, Fr. Paul slammed on the gas.

Snowflakes swirled. Headlights bounced. His sedan skidded, fishtailed, and spun. But he kept his foot on the gas, because no matter how frightened he was, he *knew* it would end the way it was supposed to end.

He drove on.

Down the streets he'd often walked.

Past the church where he'd prayed, ministered, and cried.

Past the billboards of Aleksey Petrov. Past the billboards of *Project Savior* and its inspiring photos of militant, smiling soldiers.

WARRIORS OF THE FUTURE! the signs said.

Behind him, the headlights brightened.

Fr. Paul pressed on the gas.

Mariel shrieked, as if his own soul had been clawed, ripped, and forced out of his gut.

"You need to get to the Kremlin!" Fr. Paul roared, his vehicle swerving back and forth, back and forth, as if in some effort to rock the child to sleep through violent means.

But Mariel did not stop screaming, and Fr. Paul wondered if the boy's soul ever would.

How could the child ever find peace serving God—if the *all-powerful* never had any intention of saving him?

How could he ever find peace if he'd always been destined to catalyze the end?

The other vehicle rear-ended Fr. Paul, jolted him forward, made his body snap.

The priest drove on, his eyes set forward.

On his right, another light broke through the snowy night.

Gasping, Fr. Paul slammed on the brakes. The tires squealed.

As his sight settled, he realized he was racing towards a railroad.

There was an oncoming train.

And a young woman stood in its path.

MARIEL: THE CATALYST
A Novel by A.J. Frazier

Death has returned. Love never left. And war is no longer waiting.

After falling away from Mariel Nadier, Esther stumbles toward sobriety, faith, and something unexpected: her growing bond with Tira—a human weapon she still knows almost nothing about. But when attraction turns to connection—and connection threatens control—Mariel strikes.

As Tira falls, Mariel rises.

Meanwhile, Fr. Jerome is cast out, a zealot plots, Ahdam is exploited, and the world inches closer to a disaster no prophecy could fully name.

In Book Two, the lines between savior and weapon, love and loyalty, prophecy and madness begin to collapse.

Because when the Horseman of Death takes his first life...

the end stops waiting.

BOOK 2 COMING SOON